MODE

Vera Brittain

Vera Brittain (1893–1970) grew up in provincial comfort in the north of England. In 1914 she won an exhibition to Somerville College, Oxford, but a year later abandoned her studies to enlist as a VAD nurse. She served throughout the war, working in London, Malta and the Front in France.

At the end of the war, with all those closest to her dead, Vera Brittain returned to Oxford. There she met Winifred Holtby – author of *South Riding* – and this friendship which was to last until Winifred Holtby's untimely death in 1935 sustained her in those difficult postwar years.

Vera Brittain was a convinced pacifist, a prolific speaker, lecturer, journalist and writer; she devoted much of her energy to the causes of peace and feminism. She wrote 29 books in all, novels, poetry, biography and autobiography and other non-fiction, but it was *Testament of Youth* that established her reputation and made her one of the best-loved writers of her time. The authorised biography, *Vera Brittain: A Life* (1995) by Paul Berry and Mark Bostridge, is published by Chatto & Windus.

Vera Brittain married in 1925 and had two children.

Also by Vera Brittain

Testament of Friendship
Testament of Youth
The Dark Tide

HONOURABLE ESTATE

A Novel of Transition

Vera Brittain

With an Introduction by
Mark Bostridge

A *Virago* Book

Published by Virago Press 2000

First published in Great Britain by Victor Gollancz 1936

Copyright © Mark Bostridge and Rebecca Williams,
Literary Executors of Vera Brittain 1970
Introduction Copyright © Mark Bostridge 2000

The moral right of the author has been asserted.

A CIP catalogue record for this book is available
from the British Library

ISBN 1 86049 782 9

Typeset by Palimpsest Book Production Limited,
Polmont, Stirlingshire

Printed and bound in Great Britain by
Mackays of Chatham plc, Chatham, Kent

Virago
A Division of
Little, Brown and Company (UK)
Brettenham House
Lancaster Place
London WC2E 7EN

To G.

WITH LOVE

and in memory of
E. K. C.
who worked for a day that
she never saw

AUTHOR'S ACKNOWLEDGMENTS

I AM DEEPLY and gratefully indebted to the following:

Mr G. T. Bagguley, Mr B. J. Bell and Mr Alfred Haigh for books, maps, visits and advice relating to Staffordshire; Major G. P. Brett for valuable first-hand information about the organisation and campaigns of the American Army in France; Mr Arthur Hollins, M.P., for a useful interview on the politics and economics of the Potteries; the late Miss Winifred Holtby for her helpful criticism and discussion of the plan of this book in its earlier stages; Mr J. F. Horrabin for the gift of his *Workers' History of the Great Strike*; the Labour Party Research Department for courteous replies to several inquiries; Mr A. G. Macdonell for most generously placing at my disposal his personal records of the Russian famine; also Miss Ruth Fry and Miss Evelyn Sharp for the chapters on the same subject in their books *A Quaker Adventure* and *Unfinished Adventure*; Miss Marie Scott-James for putting me in touch with the National Society of Pottery Workers; the Suffragette Fellowship, and especially their Secretary, Mrs Elsa Gye, for allowing me the use of their Record Room; Dr John Thomas for his constructive comments and criticisms on the Staffordshire sections of the story; Mrs Greta Tweeddale for information about Glasgow and a tour of the Lanarkshire colliery district; the Right Hon. Colonel Josiah Wedgwood, P.C., D.S.O., M.P., for general information and much encouragement. I have also to thank Miss A. C. Boyd and the Editor of the *London Mercury* for permission to quote 'Maritime Invocation,' and the Editor of the *Windsor Magazine* for allowing the reproduction of '*Ave atque Vale.*'

The friends who have kindly supplied me with information are not responsible for the use made of it or the views expressed.

V. B.

CONTENTS

Introduction   xiii

Foreword   1

PART I
(1894–1919)

Chapter I.	Husband	7
Chapter II.	Wife	37
Chapter III.	Son	142

PART II
(1906–1919)

Chapter IV.	Husband	205
Chapter V.	Wife	233
Chapter VI.	Daughter	285

PART III
(1921–1930)

| *Chapter* VII. | Son and Daughter | 407 |
| *Chapter* VIII. | Husband and Wife | 491 |

'Our quickened apprehension of continuing change, our broader and fuller vision of the history of life, disabuse our minds of many limitations set to the imaginations of our predecessors. Much that they saw as fixed and determinate, we see as transitory and controllable. They saw life fixed in its species and subjected to irrevocable laws. We see life struggling insecurely but with a gathering successfulness for freedom and power against restriction and death.'

H. G. WELLS: *The Open Conspiracy*

INTRODUCTION

W HEN *TESTAMENT OF YOUTH*, the book that made Vera Brittain famous, was published in 1933, one American reviewer went so far as to describe this memoir of Brittain's First World War experiences as 'a novel masquerading as an autobiography'. Brittain herself probably took the remark as a backhanded compliment, for she had set out to make her 'Autobiographical Study of the Years 1900–1925' as 'truthful as history, but as readable as fiction'.

Indeed, it was only after several failed attempts to tell her story as fiction that Vera Brittain had recognised that an autobiography was the most satisfactory way of presenting her experience of the war. As early as 1918, a few months before the Armistice, she had completed her first war novel, based partly on her time as a Voluntary Aid Detachment nurse at the 24 General Hospital at Étaples, not far from the Western Front. But this, like several other novels either planned, or written but not completed, from the immediate postwar period through to the mid-twenties, foundered because she was still too close to the events she described for them to be made the subject matter for imaginative reconstruction. By late 1929, Brittain had resolved 'to tell my own fairly typical story as truthfully as I could against the larger background . . .'.

While her works of autobiography and biography were consistently to employ novelistic devices, each one of Brittain's five published novels contains strongly autobiographical elements. In varying degrees they are all *romans à clef* in which identifiable persons from real life are presented as thinly disguised fictional characters. But Brittain's autobiographical impulse was even stronger than this term suggests. For, in all her writing she was intent on promoting the values associated with her own social and political activism. In 1925 she wrote that her literary and political work were closely interrelated, and that 'The first . . . is simply a popular interpretation of the second; a means of presenting my theories before people who would not understand or be interested in them if they were explained seriously.'

This approach would be at its strongest in the novels she wrote from the thirties onwards, after *Testament of Youth*, where her feminist and pacifist ideals would be disseminated within the framework of the novel of traditional forms and allusions, and in which the influence of the moral tone of the favourite novelists of her youth, George Eliot and Olive Schreiner, is sometimes discernible. She remained a steadfast believer in the 'power of ideas to change the shape of the world and even help to eliminate its evils', and argued that writers, whether of fiction or non-fiction, 'have the important task of interpreting for their readers this present revolutionary and complex age which has no parallel in history'.

Certainly, none of Brittain's subsequent novels ever quite equalled the impact of her first, *The Dark Tide*, which appeared in 1923. The book caused a minor sensation through its portrayal of an Oxford women's college (a thinly veiled Somerville College, where Brittain had been an undergraduate in 1914–15 and 1919–21), and because it came dangerously close to libelling a number of Oxford dons, and to causing offence to Winifred Holtby, Brittain's most intimate friend, who was caricatured as Daphne Lethbridge (in the event, Holtby accepted the characterisation with good humour). *The Dark Tide* received a total of seventy-three reviews, and established Brittain as a young writer of promise. In her next novel, *Not Without Honour* (1924), published the following year, Brittain turned to a treatment of the provincial society of her upbringing. The main action of the novel is set in the years just before the outbreak of the First World War, and the fictional market town of Torborough, with its narrow-mindedness and social snobbery, is recognisably the Buxton of her own 'provincial young ladyhood'. Christine Merivale is a self-portrait of the author, and the plot, which centres on the heroine's infatuation with a charismatic Anglican curate of unorthodox views, the Reverend Albert Clark, carries clear echoes of Brittain's own preoccupation with Buxton's Reverend Joseph Ward which she had described in her 1913–14 diary. Although *Not Without Honour* is in some ways a more coherent novel than *The Dark Tide*, it overall lacks the vitality of its predecessor.

Following the success of *Testament of Youth*, Vera Brittain planned a work of fiction which in its themes and expression might match the range and power of her autobiography. *Honourable Estate*, published in 1936, was the result, and today the novel is generally recognised as Brittain's most ambitious and sustained piece of fiction. In her foreword to the book, she explained that *Honourable Estate* 'purports to show how the women's revolution – one of the greatest in all history – united with the struggle for other democratic ideals and the cataclysm of the War to alter the private destinies of individuals'. The novel covers the period from the late-Victorian era through to 1930, and its narrative thread is composed of the stories of three marriages in which Brittain explores developing attitudes to women in the decades before and after the attainment of the vote.

Honourable Estate sold well, but its contemporary reception, especially when compared with the acclaim that had greeted *Testament of Youth*, was muted. In the immediate aftermath of its appearance, Vera Brittain worked on an idea for at least one other novel, based on the life of Mary Wollstonecraft, but her time was now increasingly taken up with her campaigning work, as a Sponsor of the Peace Pledge Union, to prevent another world war, and with the research and writing of *Testament of Friendship*, her biography of Winifred Holtby.

When Brittain did return to writing novels, in the midst of the Second World War, it was perhaps inevitable that a pacifist theme would predominate. In *Account Rendered* (1945) and *Born 1925* (1948), she dealt with the effects of another war on two individuals, both of whose lives have already been irretrievably altered by their experiences in the 1914–18 war. In *Account Rendered* (inspired by the real-life case of Leonard Lockhart), the protagonist, Francis Halkin, who was shell-shocked in France in 1918, still suffers from periodic loss of memory, and is sent to trial when his wife dies suddenly, and he is suspected either of having murdered her, or of having been part of a suicide pact. *Born 1925* (which Brittain actually started writing at the end of 1944) is based on the conjunction of two plot elements: the story of Robert Carbury, the pacifist vicar of a West End church, clearly recognisable as a portrait of Dick Sheppard, the founder of the Peace Pledge Union, and of his son Adrian, whose conflict with his father represents in some ways Brittain's own generational clashes with her son John.

Vera Brittain considered *Born 1925* to be the most important of her five novels, but although the book enjoyed strong sales in Britain it was not the triumph that she had hoped for. Like *Account Rendered*, *Born 1925* is too dominated by Brittain's pacifist convictions, and it is tempting to go some way towards agreeing with a reviewer of *Account Rendered* who commented that the novel marked 'the final collapse of the artist and the emergence from the novelist's ashes of the unapologetic propagandist'.

But to subscribe too heavily to this point of view would be to overlook the other pleasures which, at her best, Vera Brittain offers as a novelist. *Honourable Estate* is undoubtedly a major achievement of a conventional, non-modernist type of fiction, while *The Dark Tide* is a thoroughly diverting novel of strong biographical and historical interest. Both deserve to be read and revalued by a new generation of readers.

Honourable Estate has had a chequered publishing history. A cheap reprint was destroyed by the Luftwaffe in December 1940, and it has never been reprinted until now, largely because Vera Brittain's husband, George Catlin, intensely disliked it. He considered that it a gave 'a grossly libellous' portrait of his father, the Reverend Catlin, as the irascible parson, Thomas Rutherston. Furthermore, the representation of the disintegration of his parents' marriage in the early sections of the novel was another factor hardly likely to endear the book to him.

Honourable Estate originated in plans Brittain made in the early twenties for two books about the Alleyndenes, based on the fortunes of her father's prosperous Staffordshire family through three generations, beginning in the late nineteenth century. 'I shall take Father's generation just as they are,' she had told Winifred Holtby, 'shrewd, lazy, stupid, quarrelsome, unloving.' Only in the third generation would she depart dramatically from fact with the story of Ruth Alleyndene, another idealised self-portrait, who goes to Westminster as Member of Parliament for her old home town 'to make up to it for the selfishness of past Alleyndenes'. Following the publication of *Testament of Youth*, Brittain had the idea of amalgamating this family saga (known as 'Kindred and Affinity') with another projected novel (called 'The Springing Thorn') based on the life of the mother-in-law she had never known, Edith Catlin. Mrs Catlin, as Brittain later wrote in *Testament of Experience*, had been 'a turbulent, thwarted, politically-conscious woman who died prematurely in 1917'. She had been desperately unhappy in her marriage to the Reverend Catlin, a dogmatic, domineering Congregational minister, and in 1915 had deserted him, and abandoned her son, in order to work for women's suffrage and care for the poor in the East End of London.

Edith Catlin's refusal to compromise her feminist sympathies in deference to her husband's wishes had marked her out as something of a heroine in Vera Brittain's eyes. George Catlin lent Brittain his mother's diaries, and Edith Catlin's struggle (as Janet Rutherston) would provide a central narrative component for *Honourable Estate*, in which the story of the changing institution of marriage is set against the history of the Women's Movement. The family histories of the Alleyndenes and the Rutherstons would intersect throughout the novel. 'Why not marry "Kindred and Affinity" to "The Springing Thorn",' Brittain wrote, revealing the novel's inspiration, 'make the book a story of two contrasting provincial families calamitously thrown together by chance, and then, in the next generation, join the son of one household with the daughter of the other?'

Several other autobiographical elements played their part in the novel's evolution. For the first time in her published fiction Brittain drew heavily on her memories of the First World

War for the chapters in which Ruth Alleyndene nurses as a VAD in a hospital in France. She also tried to resolve the effects, through fiction, of three recent traumatic experiences from her own life. The first of these was Brittain's abortive friendship with the novelist Phyllis Bentley; and in the character of the playwright Gertrude Ellison Campbell, and her brief, intense relationship with Janet Rutherston, Brittain is able both to portray an unmarried woman and 'arch-opponent of the women's movement' to set against her feminist characters, and to suggest the fleeting possibilities of the friendship between the two women.

The two other experiences that Brittain wished to fictionalise in *Honourable Estate* were even more disturbing. One was the discovery that her brother Edward had been homosexual, and that he had possibly been responsible for his own death in battle in 1918 in order to avoid the disgrace of a court-martial. The second was Brittain's infatuation, while she was writing *Honourable Estate*, with her American publisher, George Brett, the head of the Macmillan Company in New York. The two situations are worked out in the fate of Ruth Alleyndene's brother Richard, and in Ruth's affair with the American officer Eugene Meury, who becomes a kind of composite of Brett and Brittain's dead fiancé, Roland Leighton.

Vera Brittain believed that *Honourable Estate* was a 'fated' book. Begun in a spirit of optimism after *Testament of Youth*, the novel was overshadowed, halfway through its writing, by the deaths in quick succession of Brittain's father, who committed suicide in August 1935, and of Winifred Holtby, Brittain's great friend, who died of Bright's disease at the end of September. 'Never, never, if I'd known when I began it a year ago, what last year was to be, would I have started a book of such dimensions,' Brittain wrote to Storm Jameson in January 1936. 'To try to get the whole of the women's movement in all its aspects – political, professional, social, moral, economic – within the covers of one novel is to court defeat.'

However, she was being unduly pessimistic. The finished novel, published by Victor Gollancz in November 1936, is perhaps held back sometimes by the very scale of its own ambition, and by the need to convey complex social and political ideas through characters who occasionally become little more than mouthpieces for the novelist's personal philosophies. Nevertheless, Brittain succeeds to a very great extent in dramatising the different stages of the Women's Movement. The novel's title, as Brittain explains in her Foreword, does not refer simply to the marriage service: 'it also stands for that position and respect for which the world's women and the world's workers have striven', and for 'that maturity of spirit which comes through suffering and experience'. *Honourable Estate* ends on a note of reconciliation and enlightenment as Ruth Alleyndene becomes one of the first women to enter Parliament after the passing of the 1928 Equal Franchise Act; but on the horizon there are the gathering dark forces of Fascism and anti-feminist reaction which, as Brittain has acknowledged, 'makes it the more important to contemplate that which was gained during the four decades which ended in 1930'.

Mark Bostridge
London, March 1999

SELECT BIBLIOGRAPHY

Paul Berry and Mark Bostridge, *Vera Brittain: A Life* (London: Chatto & Windus, 1995)

Deborah Gorham, *Vera Brittain: A Feminist Life* (Oxford: Blackwell Publishers, 1996)

Jean E. Kennard, *Vera Brittain and Winifred Holtby. A Working Partnership* (New Hampshire: University Press of New England, 1989)

Susan J. Leonardi, *Dangerous by Degrees. Women at Oxford and the Somerville College Novelists* (New Brunswick: Rutgers University Press, 1989)

Muriel Mellown, 'Reflections on Feminism and Pacifism in the

Novels of Vera Brittain', *Tulsa Studies in Women's Literature*, 2, 1983

Britta Zangen, *A Life of Her Own. Feminism in Vera Brittain's Theory, Fiction and Biography* (Frankfurt: Peter Lang, 1996)

FOREWORD

'Overproduction is due largely to the fact that so many authors have never asked themselves the all-important question: "Why do I write?" But if all authors had a creative philosophy as well as a creative faculty, critics would be interested in their apologies and explanations, for who can know half so much about a book as its author? ... So let us encourage authors to tell us something about their aims and ambitions.'

GEOFFREY DEARMER in *The Author*, Spring 1935.

THIS NOVEL is not autobiographical. It makes no attempt at any self-portrait, and nowhere is the story, as related here, that of my own life. Although, with one exception, there is no country or region described in the book with which I have not been at some time familiar, the incidents themselves are fictitious except in so far as they involve the actual details of historic events.

But though I have abandoned chronicle for invention, I have tried to leave a truthful impression of certain changes and movements – and especially of the social revolution that has so deeply affected the position of women and their status in marriage and other human relationships – which began before my own time but have largely coincided with it. I have not sought to draw conclusions so much as to give imaginative life to the struggles, doubts, fears, misgivings and experiments of men and women passing through a period of rapid and momentous transition in manners and morals.

Just as *Testament of Youth* attempted to describe and assess the fate of a young generation ignorantly and involuntarily caught up into the greatest catastrophe with which diplomats and politicians have thus far favoured us, so *Honourable Estate* purports to show how the women's revolution – one of the greatest in all history – united with the struggle for other democratic ideals and the cataclysm of the War to alter the private destinies of individuals. It continues the endeavour made by my autobiography to tell the recent story of social and political change, and to interpret some of the larger tendencies of mankind through their effect upon personal lives.

Of the difficulties and failures implicit in this endeavour I am only too sadly aware. In the same way that, when writing *Testament of Youth*, I was still too close to the War to give a complete picture of all that it has meant and will mean, not only to my generation but to the twentieth century as a whole, so I realise that I am still too deeply involved in the movements and changes which I have attempted to describe here to see them in their final perspective.

Some day a writer of Olympian stature will present the Great War in a fashion equal to that of Tolstoy's *War and Peace*, which did not begin to appear until fifty years after the epoch of which he wrote had ended. Some day a titanic novelist will show how the social changes of the past half century have altered the structure and meaning of human relationships. But we, who have lived through all or part of this age of transition, we who are still deafened by the catastrophic explosions that we have heard and blinded by the lightning revolutions that we have seen, cannot wait for that time. One or two of our generation of writers, the loveliest and the best, have already departed. Life has its limits and fate its monstrous uncertainties; neither omnipotent deity nor inventive humanity has yet made us to know the measure of our days. We are obliged, as Ruskin exhorted the women of his era, to 'work while we have light,' trusting that our efforts will at least provide raw material for the creative artist of to-morrow. Truth, I suppose, is at last achieved through the intermingling of contemporary impressions and judgments with the long-distance view of those who can look back upon the panorama of the past from the citadel of time. I can only hope that this novel, together with *Testament of Youth*, may at least contribute its modicum to that ultimate assessment.

In order to give my story shape and unity, I have purposely ended it in the year when the women's movement for equality and the workers' contest for freedom and power had come nearer to the realisation of their ideals in England and elsewhere than at any time since their beginnings in the French Revolution. The subsequent setback to their achievements, the repudiation of democracy in many countries, the growth of Fascist dictatorships, and the return of pacts, alliances, competitive armaments and militaristic manifestoes after a short era of comparative sanity, belong to another volume which will deal – perhaps as a sequel to *Testament of Youth* – with the tale of these later and crazier years. But the fact that we are now living in a period of reaction makes it the more important to contemplate that which was gained during the four decades which ended in 1930.

I make no apology for dealing in a novel with social theories and political beliefs, nor for the extent to which these are discussed by some of the characters. I cannot share the outlook of that school of literary criticism which seeks to limit the novelist's 'legitimate' topics to personal relationships. Personal relationships have no more significance than the instinctive associations of the sub-human world when those who conduct them are devoid of ideas. If large areas of human experience – political, economic, social, religious – are to be labelled inadmissible as subjects for fiction, then fiction is doomed as an organic art.

Throughout this book I have made considerable use of historic events and real persons both past and present, but such persons are always introduced, usually as incidental characters, under their own familiar names. I have also tried, with the same purpose of verisimilitude, to select Christian and family names which are typical of the various countries and districts covered by the story, but in using these local designations I have had no particular individuals in mind, and if by chance I have selected a combination of names belonging to a living person, the coincidence is accidental. Whenever I have used a name which I believe to be fictitious, a purely fictitious character is intended. This is as true of the characters who achieve distinction in the course of the story as of those who remain obscure. *Ellison Campbell* is not the portrait of any writer living or dead, nor does *Ruth Alleyndene* represent any living politician.

In order to fit my imaginary borough of Witnall into the map of North Staffordshire, I have taken certain geographical and political liberties with the area north-east of Stoke-on-Trent. I have not in every instance been able to verify the purely fictitious nature of the names that I have given to houses, churches, and other institutions in the numerous towns and cities described in the book, but in no case do I intend any reference to an actual institution.

The title of this story has not merely the obvious application derived from its origin in the Church of England Marriage Service. It stands also for that position of dignity and respect for which the world's women and the world's workers have striven since the end of the eighteenth century, and which, within my own lifetime, they have partly achieved.

Finally, it represents that maturity of the spirit which comes through suffering and experience. It suggests that the dignity which attaches to honoured and acknowledged sorrows may also be achieved by those men and women whose pain must be concealed because it arises from emotions or situations to which society is only now beginning to accord recognition and pity. Thanks partly to the developing science of psychology, and partly to some of the changes in moral values indicated by this story, we are becoming more merciful to one another than we used to be; and experts in the subtle yet overwhelming dramas of the human mind are seeking to understand and eradicate those complexes which so often tormented the misunderstood and repressed men and women of an age now passing into history.

VERA BRITTAIN.

April, 1934–August, 1936.

PART I

(1894–1919)

CHAPTER I

HUSBAND

'For him life was a conflict between an absolute right
and an absolute wrong, and never that more deeply
tragic thing, a struggle between right and right.'
> *The Times'* Washington Correspondent on
> the death of William Jennings Bryan, July
> 28th, 1925.

I

AT EVENING PRAYER on Wednesday before Easter, the Reverend Thomas Rutherston, Vicar of Christ Church, Upper Sterndale, went up to the lectern to read the Second Lesson.

Easter was early in that year 1894, and a short spell of sudden gales had interrupted the fine, warm spring. The vigorous wind, galloping across the dry Derbyshire moorlands, relentlessly buffeted the grey stone walls of the church.

Unimpeded by the noisy gusts, Thomas's sonorous voice boomed across the half-empty pews in the creeping spring twilight.

'Verily, verily, I say unto you, That ye shall weep and lament, but the world shall rejoice! and ye shall be sorrowful, but your sorrow shall be turned into joy. A woman when she is in travail hath sorrow, because her hour is come: but as soon as she is delivered of the child, she remembereth no more the anguish, for joy that a man is born into the world.'

One or two members of the scattered congregation surreptitiously nudged each other, intrigued by the appropriate coincidence. For some time now, everyone in the parish had known that young Mrs Rutherston was 'expecting,' and earlier in the afternoon Mrs Maconachie, the sexton's wife, had seen Dr

Bannister's gig outside the Vicarage gate. An hour or two later, by that mysterious process which gives rumour its authority in every small community, the whole of Upper Sterndale knew that Mother Whiston, the Quarry Street midwife, had been sent for in a hurry to go to Mrs Rutherston. The knowledge had more than doubled Thomas's week-day Lenten congregation.

Anxious not to miss any sign of interesting emotion that their vicar might display, that congregation watched, with a curiosity little tempered by sympathy, the clerical figure which four years' association had rendered habitual to them. They saw, without consciously observing in detail, a man of thirty-seven, rather below medium height and still creating the impression of a slender build, though already a slight thickening about the waist-line gave an undeniable forewarning of portliness to come. The sleek brown hair was beginning to recede a little from the high, bumpy forehead with the wide, indeterminate brows; above the short, straight nose, dreamy eyes of a watery blue-grey looked out upon the world with a hint of defiant apprehensiveness in their shallow depths. A long drooping moustache concealed the full lips and disguised the incipient pathos of a weak, narrow chin. The hands which held the massive Bible were pale and podgy, with broad wrists and short, thick fingers.

As he read the familiar verses from the sixteenth chapter of the Gospel according to St John, Thomas's thoughts gathered round the imminence of his domestic crisis, and he endeavoured to stifle his inward misgivings with the comfort of those reassuring words. Throughout his clerical life the faculty for finding comfortable texts in uncomfortable situations had never deserted him. His only trouble was that a situation which fitted the text quite admirably at the beginning so seldom succeeded in fitting it at the end; it somehow lost its consistency, and failed to develop in the direction warranted by the Gospels. In spite of this recalcitrance on the part of events, Thomas's capacity for expectation remained unimpaired, and he felt reluctant to admit even to himself how deeply he had been shocked by the vehement resentment with which Janet had acknowledged the coming of her pains. However unwilling an insufficiently disciplined young matron might be to submit herself to the will of God and the processes of nature, she should surely, even in her suffering, have displayed some sort of reverence before the supreme miracle of birth, some realisation of the sacredness of her divine function. He could but hope that, as St John had predicted, more suitable sentiments would come with the termination of her ordeal.

Profoundly he wished that Janet's mother, vain and irresponsible though she used to be in the daily conduct of practical affairs, might still have been alive to modify her daughter's unnatural attitude towards maternity. In her gentler moments he knew that Janet still grieved for both her parents, and especially for her father, James Harding, the retired Putney jeweller, who had taught her to read Herbert Spencer and to share his philosophical speculations about God, Man and the Universe. No doubt of it, James Harding had been an out-and-out agnostic; Thomas often regretted his influence, which had proved anything but beneficial when exercised too early upon a precocious girl destined to become the wife of a minister of God. It was obviously his contempt for religious ceremonies which had been responsible for that deplorable scepticism on the subject of confirmation once revealed to Thomas by an entry in Janet's childish diary:

'At 10.45 went to St Anne's to be confirmed, but did not feel any better for it.'

Even Harding's death a year before that of his hero and model Charles Bradlaugh, in the influenza epidemic of 1890 when his daughter was only fifteen, had not occurred soon enough to free Janet from his domination over her mental processes. It was still her father, he often lamented, rather than her husband and rightful protector, who directed the development of her immature and questioning mind.

He closed the huge Bible with the gold-embroidered marker which Janet's mother had worked for him during some of her less frivolous hours, and dragged himself out of his domestic meditations to lead the congregation in the Nunc Dimittis.

'Lord, now lettest thou thy servant depart in peace; according to thy word . . .'

What real peace, he might justly have asked, had there been for him since his marriage? Surely no young woman ever had a more difficult, inconsistent nature than his orphan wife; for all her soft prettiness of complexion and the radiant spontaneity of charm which she could exercise when she chose, she seemed incapable of realising the respect due to a husband more than seventeen years her senior. This, at least, was not the fault of her mother. Although at first she had seemed a little reluctant to consent to their engagement on the ground that Janet, especially in view of their disparity in age, was unsuited to be his wife in either tastes or character, it had been, he knew, a real consolation to Mrs Harding during her fatal attack of bronchitis a year ago to feel that Janet was engaged to a God-fearing man who could be trusted to understand her best interests, and to put them before her obstinate determination to sacrifice her duty to worldly pleasures.

From the first he had made it clear to Mrs Harding that he was not in the least blind to Janet's shortcomings, but was prepared to devote time, trouble and the prestige associated with his office to helping her to overcome her faults. After the initial hesitation natural enough in a mother who was faced with the prospect of losing her only child and companion, Mrs Harding had always deferred to his judgment. She fully appreciated his position as the holder of a good living in the famous moorland health-resort of Sterndale Spa, and a preacher with a growing reputation throughout the Midlands which had been founded during his curacy at Cheet.

As a loyal follower of Mr Gladstone, that Liberal statesman and Tory churchman, Thomas felt impelled to propagate Radical doctrines whenever opportunity offered, and the semi-political character of his sermons brought quite a number of eminent visitors to Christ Church. Had not Lord Rosebery himself, the new Prime Minister, come to hear him preach when he visited Sterndale to take the waters only a short time before forming his Cabinet? Already, then, there had been rumours of Mr Gladstone's resignation, and Thomas had preached on the text, '*Rest in the Lord*,' as a suitable injunction to a future premier. That sermon, like his famous address on '*Let the dead bury their dead*,' after the death of Parnell, was one of his proudest memories. Nobody had ever spoiled it by inquiring why his sermons, for all their political bias, so often emphasised the duty of passivity rather than that of action or challenge. Not even his critical wife had scandalised him by suggesting that to thrust the moral responsibility of choice on the Lord was one method of avoiding it for oneself.

'O God,' he intoned expansively, '*make clean our hearts within us!*'

'*And take not thy holy Spirit from us,*' dutifully echoed the congregation.

He turned to the Collect.

'*O God, from whom all holy desires, all good counsels and all just works do proceed . . .*'

The restless, unsettled life which Janet had led since her father's death had been a great handicap to her, he reflected. She should never have been taken away from Eastbourne Academy when barely sixteen, in order to accompany her mother on a series of never-ending visits to drawing-room apartments in expensive quest of health at half the spas in England.

'You once said you would like to see me cross,' she had written to him during the early days of their acquaintance. 'You ought to go apartment-hunting with me, your wish would be gratified then.'

Brighton – Bath – Droitwich – Malvern – Tunbridge Wells – Harrogate – Matlock – finally Sterndale; he really couldn't remember all the places to which they had been during the fruitless peregrinations of those extravagant years. Mrs Harding's best friends could not have called her a provident woman, even if her inordinate love of fine clothes for herself and her daughter were the only item to be considered. Janet had once allowed him to read the first volume of her childish journal. She had been an inveterate diarist from the age of thirteen and he had certainly found its round-handed *naïveté* amusing, but he could not help feeling perturbed by its evidence of extravagance on the part of a mother and daughter living on a moderate income, and by the unexpected preoccupation with her clothes displayed by a girl who was nearly always top in every school subject and had passed the College of Preceptors' examination in the First Division while still under fourteen. Even when he first saw the diary, long before he and Janet had become engaged, he had shaken his head over the sartorial details in some of the entries.

'Went to have new blue stuff dress fitted.'

'Went into town to order black velvet hat.'

'Went to concert at Public Hall given by Nigger Minstrels – wore new brown merino dress and pink shawl.'

'After tea had a warm bath, and in evening made myself a black lace boar' (that strange object, he presumed, which young ladies who knew how to spell usually described as a 'boa.')

The eventful day which marked her recovery from chicken-pox had also been celebrated with the customary attentions to finery.

'At 10.30 dressed and came downstairs for the first time since illness. In morning painted in water-colours; in afternoon lengthened pink cotton dress. My new flannelette under-petticoat (pink and blue stripes) came home from dressmaker.'

The money wasted on fallals had all been part of Mrs Harding's inability to distinguish between capital and income – a deplorable trait which was only to be expected from ladies, who had no head for business and never would have, for all the wild talk now prevalent about their 'rights.' Rights to spend their resources, he presumed, until debt and starvation landed them in the workhouse! Even before she died, Mrs Harding had made a considerable hole in the modest fortune left her by her jeweller husband. If Thomas hadn't obtained control of it through the marriage settlement during his wife's minority, Janet would soon have had nothing at all. When it came to spending money, she and her mother were two for a pair; their immediate whims and fancies blotted out ulterior considerations. Not wisely but too well, you'd say was their motto.

'*The grace of our Lord Jesus Christ,*' he pronounced, '*and the love of God, and the fellowship of the Holy Ghost, be with us all, evah-mo-ore, Ah-men.*'

2

A small stir rustled through the church as the elect of Upper Sterndale got up to depart.

How glad Thomas was, that evening, to see the last of his congregation! Their nudges, their nods, their inquisitive interest in his anxiety, had not been lost upon him whatever they might think. One or two would-be inquirers stayed behind to hang about the church door – hoping, no doubt, to satisfy their curiosity with their insincere solicitude. Ignoring them, he went into the vestry.

It had been in that vestry, on a bright June day of 1892, that he first met Janet.

His church had been filled, that fine morning, with the visitors who had come to Sterndale for the beautiful early season which followed the cold winds of the bracing Derbyshire spring, and one or two of the more distinguished residents had congratulated him on the originality of his sermon (on the text from Isaiah xl.: '*They who wait on the Lord shall renew their strength*'). He had just removed his surplice and was preparing to go home, when the verger came in with the message that a young lady wanted to speak to him. A little annoyed because he was very hungry after his sermon and had begun to picture with satisfaction the roast beef and brown potatoes prepared for him by his housekeeper, he was nevertheless mildly curious because his visitors were not usually young ladies. He told the verger to show her in.

The next moment he was seeing her for the first time – a slender, immature girl not yet eighteen, with brilliant light blue eyes, wide open and ardent beneath heavy lids and brown lashes tipped with gold. Her nose, broadly bridged, and blunt at the tip, struck him as over-large for the small, delicately-rounded face, and the deep cleft between the sensitive nostrils and the full, curving upper lip gave an odd impression of adult determination to a countenance otherwise quite undeveloped in its serious, sensitive eagerness. Her clothes, he had noticed even then, were tasteful and expensive though somewhat carelessly worn. The high-necked frock of dark maroon silk, with tiny white frills caught lightly together at the throat by a bird brooch made of seed pearls, fitted closely and elegantly to her round girlish figure, but the small hat was perched insecurely on the loosely piled, fluffy golden-brown hair curled into a short fringe above the fair, lightly-marked brows. One shoe, he observed with his unremitting eye for detail, was down at the heel, and a button was missing from the long row curving from her neck to her waist beneath the white frill.

'Good morning! And what can I do for *you*?' he had inquired, in the benevolent, semi-jocular tone which he judged appropriate for young ladies who called uninvited upon stranger clergymen.

She flushed a little, but spoke in a clear, direct voice, without hesitation or shyness.

'I liked your sermon,' she said. 'You do seem to know a lot of ecclesiastical history.'

Thomas, who was aware that he had a reputation for scholarship even among the more scholarly members of his profession, smiled indulgently.

'Well,' he replied, 'it's a field in which I'm not considered altogether uninstructed. But I didn't know it was a subject especially interesting to charming young ladies!'

'Oh, but I *am* interested in it!' she exclaimed. 'What I really came for, if you don't mind, was to ask you if you could help me about some books. You see, I'm working for an examination – the Senior Cambridge – and there don't seem to be many history books at the Free Library here, either ecclesiastical or otherwise. Our landlady told us you had a wonderful library, and I thought, – if you could just *possibly* lend me one or two books, on the subjects I'm working on . . . I'd take the utmost care of them, I promise . . .'

The conversation had ended, of course, in the suggestion that she and her mother should take tea with him the next afternoon, and then she could choose whatever volumes she liked. He had not, in spite of the interruption, been very late for his dinner, but though his appetite was usually keen, he has found his interest in roast beef and brown potatoes strangely diminished.

When the books had been selected over a friendly cup of tea, it seemed natural that he should offer to show her and her mother – strangers to Sterndale, who had only just arrived there from Matlock – some of the sights of the district. Expeditions had followed to Topley Woods, to the Blue Spar Cave, to Pirate's Leap, and once, in a hired pony-cart, to the Dog and Harp, that highest of English inns with its incomparable view of the moors between Sterndale and Cheddlefield. They had planned, that afternoon, a train excursion to Cheddlefield itself, the little country cathedral city where the Bishop of Thomas's diocese lived in a real moated grange with the black and white frontage so characteristic, Thomas had explained, of historic Cheshire; but when the day came Mrs Harding had found herself too poorly to attempt so long an expedition. Inactive and a little corpulent, though still bearing traces of former beauty and possessing the same bright blue eyes as Janet, she had seemed to him somewhat elderly for so young a daughter until Janet explained that her mother had married her father late in life, and was already forty-three when her only child was born.

After the failure of the Cheddlefield excursion, Mrs Harding herself had suggested that 'the young people,' as she called them, should go off alone on the long walks which they both enjoyed. A clergyman, as she had realised, was quite different from an ordinary man, and she had been astonished and even, at first, perturbed, when he began to display some of the emotions of ordinary men.

He and Janet had become engaged on a fine October afternoon during a long walk to Fisher's Dale. Though he was seldom disposed to waste time in day-dreaming, he could still see, if he closed his eyes, the spreading purple of the moors in the mellow autumn sunshine, still hear the narrow stream of the River Thrush babbling between the brown rushes in the sheltered valley. Above all he could still feel the overwhelming tenderness and gratitude which had flooded his heart when Janet's soft fingers trembled in his as she spoke so humbly of their life together.

'I look forward,' she said, 'to helping you in your work as my greatest happiness.'

If only that sentiment, so appropriate for a young girl towards

her future husband, had really been true! At first, after she and
her mother, who feared the effect of the biting Derbyshire cold
upon her chronic bronchitis, had left to spend the winter in
Brighton, he had found no reason for doubts or misgivings.
Janet's prattling letters, ingenuously describing her singing lessons, or her latest expedition to the photographer, or her visits
to school friends who had been children with her only a year
or two before, were natural enough to an eighteen-year-old girl
with nothing of any real importance to occupy her time after
she had passed, so triumphantly, her Senior Cambridge.

'I feel it a grave responsibility to have to order the dinner,' he
had read, with an amusement which her naïve admissions had
not yet transformed into apprehension. 'I am also going twice a
week to the School of Cookery (I know you will laugh about
this). I tell Mama that at my first lesson they will have to show
me which is a saucepan and which an oven, for I am not at all
sure which is which, and I don't even know when a kettle is
boiling until it boils over! And then I have undertaken to do
all the mending this winter and sewing always has a bad effect
on my temper, which I shall work off every day by an hour or
two of piano and singing practice, which will probably have a
bad effect on everyone else's temper. However, I am going to
keep the long evenings for reading and study and writing – no
sewing or housekeeping then! I have been taking large doses
of philosophy (*The Mystery of Matter*) sweetened with a little
poetry (Rosetti and Mrs Browning), so now I am going to try
politics for a change. I have already got a few literary curiosities
in the way of essays of my own. Once, when I was fifteen, I sent
one of these to the Editor of the *Girls' Own Paper*, and asked for
his opinion of my writing; I took the *nom de plume* of 'Excelsior,'
but he didn't reply! I never look at my things after I have written
them – am afraid to – but I daresay if any of them are found
among my papers after my diseace they will be considered very
valuable and a subscription will be raised to publish them for
the public benefit!'

'N.B.,' he had written in the note-book he always carried, 'tell
J. in next letter how to spell "decease."' Pity, he thought, that for
such an intelligent girl her spelling is so poor. She must have been

very badly taught in Eastbourne at that young ladies' so-called school.

It was only after they had been engaged for about three months that his complete ignorance of the inner workings of her mind began to dawn upon him. He had always urged her to write him not less than three sheets in her weekly letters; self-expression, he told himself, was good for her, and he never failed to reproach her – kindly, of course, and with appropriate little touches of badinage – when the quantity fell short. But one Sunday evening, going over her correspondence after the day's work, he had realised with dismay that though her letters gave him unlimited information about her cookery classes, and her attendance at church services, and her mother's disputes with landladies, and the titles and themes of books she had read, and the theatres – far too many – to which she had been, they told him next to nothing about the young woman with whom he proposed to spend the rest of his life. Late though it was, he had seized his pen in a panic and written her an imploring exhortation.

'Your silence about your inner life and lack of spoken sympathy with me is the one thing that comes between us and perfect happiness. Sympathy can no more be silent than sunlight be cold. If my life is not to be one of isolation and loneliness, I claim that you give me your *whole* heart. Our sympathies must be one and for the same things; I want you to show that you are really with me. Our souls must not live apart, housed in two different abodes; that is but to establish an eternal menace of loss. We must give ourselves more unreservedly to each other and to God. Then we shall be happy not only for time but for eternity.'

Her reply, though not altogether satisfactory, had been modest and affectionate; at least it reassured him for the time being that she meant to do her best.

'You want me to tell you more about myself – my inner life. Darling, I don't know what to tell you or where to begin. My inner life is still in the chrysalis stage! The "analytic mind," as you call it, is very young yet; you must give it time and not expect too much from it. I *cannot* tell you all I think and feel when I seem to have no grasp on a single thing. I cannot cheer you up when I am only too ready to give up myself. I have a horror of severity and sarcasm – especially the latter, as you know. I am afraid that "blowings-up" have very little effect on me. I always feel like saying "I'll do it again!"

'I long to tell you everything that is in my heart sometimes; I have always felt that I could not give all my love unless I could give confidence and sympathy as well. I do feel that our love brings out all that is best in me – and yet when I sit down to write to you, I cannot get beyond mere commonplaces. I know it is my own fault, but it is a fault I seem powerless to get rid of. It is just this unfortunate habit I have got into of shutting myself up within myself. I began it when I lost my father and in him the only confidant I ever had. For two years I tried all I could to get reserved and hard, and I succeeded only too well, until it has become almost second nature.

'I suppose I do seem indifferent, but darling, I really am with you heart and soul in your work. I am sorry that you felt so miserable in settling down to ordinary routine after the Christmas festival. Sterndale sounds very difficult at times; it *is* hard work, with that unsympathetic set of people. I only hope, when I eventually arrive there as your "help-meet," that I shan't make things worse! The thought that I shall be a hindrance rather than a help – and it comes sometimes – is just *agony*, and I know I must be one or the other.'

Queer, he reflected as he hung up his cassock and closed the cupboard, that she should have written that! She never meant, of course, to defy him openly about anything; it was just her childishness, her undisciplined youth, that made her *appear* to do so. All the same, the parishioners had a diabolical habit of seizing upon their differences of temperament and emphasising those differences by taking sides. Some day, when this business of the baby was over, he must have a long talk with her on the subject, and point out that even divergencies of opinion which were not real but only apparent were best kept for home display. No doubt most of their difficulties had been due to her condition. It was a pity, perhaps, for some reasons, that she'd got into the family way so soon – but these things were in God's hands, and doubtless all would work out for the best.

He felt certain he could handle her whenever he remembered how passionately she had clung to him after her mother's death just a year ago. A series of mild March days had brought them back, at Janet's earnest entreaty, from Brighton to Sterndale; but it had proved too early for Mrs Harding's carefully guarded chest and lungs. Janet, he knew, still secretly reproached herself for having been the indirect cause of her mother's last illness. Mrs Harding had kept her bed only nine days, and even the specialist summoned by Thomas from Manchester had been unable to pull her through the crisis of acute bronchitis and pneumonia. With the aid of a night-nurse, Janet looked after her mother herself, and had proved for once that she was capable of devoted if inexperienced ministrations.

'Mother told me I was a splendid nurse!' she sobbed after the night-nurse had laid out Mrs Harding's body and left Janet and Thomas alone together in the furniture-crowded sitting-room of the Ashwood Walk apartments on that snowy March morning. 'She said she'd never have dreamed I could show so much thought! Except about her illness it was almost the last thing she said, and I shall remember it with thankfulness to the end of my life . . . Oh, my darling, don't leave me! You're all I've got now and I want you dreadfully. I want to make you very happy, and never, never cause you any worry – only I'm often afraid I shall find it hard to succeed in that!'

She wasn't so far wrong either, he thought, for she had begun to cause him worry immediately after Canon Maybury, the Vicar of St Mary's and Thomas's rural dean, had married them quietly one early morning in Christ Church at the beginning of June. Never had she given him any satisfactory explanation of the long, moody silence which she had inflicted on him almost the whole way from Fisher's Dale Junction to St Pancras. There was nothing in reason to account for it; he had made the most elaborate arrangements to take her for a really enjoyable honeymoon in London and Switzerland, and they had not then had that evening's argument about the seats he had reserved for Tennyson's *Becket* at the Lyceum after Janet had insisted that she'd rather see *The Second Mrs Tanqueray* – a most unsuitable performance for an innocent young girl. It had been a perfect summer's day, too, the beginning of the settled fine weather which persisted throughout their honeymoon, and the country was looking beautiful in the freshness of its early green. As young and sweet, he thought, as Janet herself, sitting there so silently in her black cloth dress with the white lace collar and the row of filigree buttons down the centre of her bodice. What possible cause for discontent could be provoking those uncomfortable speculations which furrowed the smooth forehead of his newly-married wife?

'Tell me what you're thinking!' he had urged her; for silence, which gave perturbing problems too much opportunity to thrust themselves importunately upon the mind, was an enemy which he had always done his best to defeat by bouts of learned loquacity. But she only replied in her usual obstinate fashion that she could not express herself through conversation.

'It's no use your always asking me that!' she protested. 'I've told you I can put my thoughts down on paper, but they just won't go into words. I can't talk, and sometimes it makes me miserable to try.'

'Not even to-day, of all days?' he implored her. 'You're very unfeeling, Janet! Your mother told me once she didn't think you could care much for anyone – at least you'd never shown you could to her. I'm your husband now, my dear, and I have the right to know all your thoughts. I will pray for you, to-day and always, that marriage may soften your heart.'

He had tried then to take her hands, but she only clasped them in her lap and turned her head to gaze out of the window. So he had never seen the tears which welled up into her eyes, or looked through them to the thought at the back of her mind: 'He doesn't know the nights I still spend crying for Mama – and for dear Papa, that beloved companion with whom I could talk about anything, and who was never shocked at my difficulties and doubts.'

In spite of its inauspicious beginning, the honeymoon had been a success. Although Janet and her mother had travelled so much in England, Mrs Harding had never ventured abroad, and Janet became almost communicative in her delight at the Lake of Geneva, and the Castle of Chillon, and the ranges of mountains ascending, on clear days, to the rose-tinted peak of distant Mont Blanc. When they watched, on their way home, the marriage procession of the Duke and Duchess of York, her high spirits had almost shocked him in their near approach to *lèse-majesté*.

'Oh, Thomas, what enormous crowds! Don't they thrill you? I always feel in my element in a crowded street – that's the result of being born a Cockney! Didn't you think the "happy couple" both looked intensely miserable? And the Queen, too – didn't she look cross! But then, of course, she always does. It must be terribly tiresome to be perpetually on show when you're getting so old!'

The next day they returned home in a thunderstorm, and another had flooded the back yard of the Vicarage just when they were due at the At Home for 'the presentation of the parishioners' wedding-present. Janet had not waited to take off her wet stockings, but, thrusting a clean pair into her pocket, had hurried with him to the parish room to receive the silver salver from Mrs Earle and Mr Collier. But no sooner had Mr Collier, the people's elderly church-warden, concluded his carefully-prepared little speech of welcome, than she had to scandalise the whole critical crowd of them by changing her stockings in that very vestry without even closing the door!

3

Before leaving the church for the night, Thomas looked round with his usual meticulous care to make sure that everything was in order. It was a modern church, put up to accommodate the extension of Sterndale Spa from the basin-like valley to the slopes of the nearest hills, and Thomas was only its second incumbent. Built of the blue-grey stone from the local quarries, its slaty imperviousness, streaked with hard white lines of mortar, had not yet succumbed to the mellowing influence of rain and snow. Inside, the church was light and bare, with its pitch-pine gallery still smelling of unseasoned wood, and its plain leaded windows. The only stained glass window was above the altar, before which Thomas was able to persuade so few of his practical middle-class parishioners to receive the Sacrament. It depicted, somewhat inappropriately, the Feeding of the Five Thousand.

Thomas locked the door and went out into the fresh spring evening. A sudden gust of wind flapped his thin black overcoat round his solid legs, and he shivered a little as he pulled the rough collar up to his chin. Above the western ridges the faint vermilion of sunset still stained the sky, but towards the east, beyond Grin Tor, tiny pin-points of stars had begun to twinkle coldly. From the steep slope on which his church was built he could see the twilight gathering in the hollows of the hills and the lights appearing one by one in the shadowed basin which held the small town. Mechanically, preoccupied with his anxious thoughts, he watched the sprinkling of visitors, already assembled for Easter, leaving the Pump Room immediately below to go back to their hotels.

'I could easily throw a stone on the roof,' he thought for the hundredth time, rousing himself with a start from his meditations. Gazing across the valley, he noticed how the clear curve of Ploughman's Ridge cut into the evening sky like the upper segment of a gigantic circle, and his mind leaped with satisfaction upon the obvious text.

'*I will lift up mine eyes unto the hills: from whence cometh my help.*

'*My help cometh even from the Lord: who hath made heaven and earth.*'

However contrary things might appear for the time being, in the long run, Thomas knew, the Lord always cared for his own. He would comfort and protect the child who was about to be born in its path through the pomps and vanities of this wicked world. Not that, in his secret heart, Thomas really thought the world – apart from some of his parishioners in Upper Sterndale – so wicked or so vain; in fact, he identified morality with the persistence of familiar customs and values, and the continuation of life as he had always known it.

There were certain disquieting elements, of course, as there must be in the history of even the happiest eras. He doubted, for instance, whether all this free education was really good for the people, who never valued what they hadn't to pay for. The more they got, the more they wanted, and the result was discontent, such as the present agitation for an eight-hour-day, which would mean an interference with natural economic laws which he, as a good Gladstonian Liberal, could only deplore. Everyone, on the other hand, must wish for better relations between capital and labour, and a more humane treatment of workers by their employers. There was moderation in all things, and British working men, thank God, would never descend to the use of those infernal machines which had lately become a terror on the Continent. Only last Christmas, a London crowd had broken up the meeting which the Anarchists tried to hold in Trafalgar Square.

Political anarchy was not, of course, the only kind with which an upholder of order and morality had to contend. He felt concerned sometimes about the insolent attempts now being made by the writers of merely popular literature to discredit the inspirational character of the canonical scriptures, while this new Parish Councils Act was an indirect blow to the prestige of the Church, however the President of the Local Government Board might attempt to explain it. He personally would have something to say if it made his lay managers imagine that they could interfere with his administration of the Christ Church School! Not that he really thought they would; they were a slack lot, and it was difficult to get even half of them to attend the monthly meetings. On the whole, the world that awaited his son wasn't so bad. Queen Victoria – God bless her – could not be expected to go on reigning for ever, but he didn't doubt that the long era of peace and prosperity which her reign had established would see him through his own lifetime and probably last out the boy's as well.

Turning his back on the church and the terrace of tall houses of which the last was his Vicarage, Thomas walked through a network of narrow streets towards the Golden Dragon. Mrs Pedler, the pious bed-ridden wife of the too-jovial publican, had asked him for the loan of *Great Souls At Prayer* from his library, and though her phlebitis was not serious nor any change in her condition imminent, he felt that he ought not to delay in fulfilling an invalid's request. As he had always made quite clear to Janet, the business of the parish must come before family affairs, however urgent. Not for a second would he have admitted to himself his deliberate postponement of the moment when he must return home and face the atmosphere of tension and hostility which awaited him in the Vicarage. His would-be optimistic philosophy, his conviction that the righteous man ought to meet with no opposition in a well-ordered universe, found expression in the comfortable belief that 'things' would 'get on' satisfactorily if only they were left alone. Most people, he was accustomed to reflect, worried and interfered far too much with the course of events.

Mrs Pedler, who like the rest of Upper Sterndale had for some hours been aware of Janet's predicament, was agreeably surprised to see him.

'Ay, but it's good of you, sir, to look in to-night. You must be fair wild to get back to the young lady.'

'Thank you; Mrs Rutherston is doing very well,' Thomas responded in his most pompous tones, which countered any slight remorse that he might have felt from the fact that it was at least an hour since he knew how she was doing.

'And when do you expect the little one to come, sir?'

'Oh, not before midnight – certainly not before midnight. Dr Bannister told me this afternoon it might well be tomorrow morning,' replied Thomas, thus disposing in a sentence of that pain-stabbed eternity which opens before every woman labouring of child. He felt a little restless beneath this direct questioning, though he supposed that Mrs Pedler, whose maternal history, as she was never tired of telling him, consisted of nine births and three miscarriages, had a certain right to indulge her curiosity.

'Well, don't you fret, sir,' Mrs Pedler commented comfortably. 'There won't be near so much waitin' wi' the next one, and by the time your young lady's had three or four, it'll all be over before you can say "knife." Now, the night I was expectin' my sixth . . .'

Thomas regarded it as his duty to remain for another twenty minutes beside the stalwart four-poster with the patchwork quilt, listening to gruesome reminiscences of Mrs Pedler's confinements. During the recital he found his eyes drawn again and again, with irresistible if inexplicable fascination, to the wooden-framed photogravure above her head. It represented a Grecian lady of ample proportions and complacent countenance standing in a shrubbery of arum lilies, her conspicuous bosom modestly if suggestively concealed by white draperies. The inevitable quotation from Longfellow added the finishing touch to this work of art:

> *Bear a lily in thy hand,*
> *Gates of brass shall not withstand*
> *One touch of that mighty wand.*

Still uncertain of the relevance of this legend to an experienced matron who had borne nine children, Thomas escaped with relief from the small stuffy bedroom. It was now almost dark, and a tiny crescent of moon like a silver nail-paring floated in an indigo sea above Grin Tor and the dark moorlands spreading south-westward towards Cheet on the borders of Staffordshire. Returning to the Vicarage, where in spite of domestic upheaval the remains of his high tea had been satisfactorily cleared away, he lit a pipe and settled firmly into his arm-chair in the hope of adding a few paragraphs to his Easter sermon.

4

Before finally shutting himself into his study, Thomas crept half-way up the stairs to listen whether any significant sounds were emerging from the upper floor.

The Vicarage was a tall, narrow house, built like the church of local grey stone. In front a short asphalt path divided a pocket-handkerchief of lawn, and then plunged steeply downhill through a tangle of bushes to a neglected plot of stubbly grass at the back. Immediately beyond the fence enclosing this plot, the ground, intersected by the bleak back gardens of houses on the road to the town, sloped downward towards Lower Sterndale. The interior of the house looked untidy, and periodically harboured a good deal of the town's habitual white dust owing to Janet's spasmodic attentions to domestic order. The only really comfortable room was Thomas's study, in which a careful selection of historical and theological publications was varied by the complete works of Sir Walter Scott, Charles Dickens, George Eliot, Charles Kingsley and George Macdonald. Parish magazines and copies of the *Guardian* littered the chairs and tables, half covering a number of the more substantial weeklies and monthlies – mostly on loan from parishioners or the local library – such as the *Nineteenth Century*, the *Contemporary Review*, *Blackwood's Magazine* and the *Quiver*.

Janet had chosen to be confined in a large bare room at the top of the house, in which she was accustomed to do what she called 'my political work,' and occasionally to sleep when her 'moodiness' led her into the iniquity of spending a night apart from Thomas. Thomas had protested that their bedroom was far more comfortable, and since she was so eccentric as to prefer a period of solitude, he could easily move for a few nights into the spare room. But she had so persistently asserted her dislike of turning him out and her obstinate preference for 'her' room, that he had decided, in the circumstances, that it was best not to thwart her. Neither then nor later could she have explained to him her mortal dread lest in her agony she should prove unable to restrain her cries, which from the lower floor might be audible to the cook and the housemaid in the basement. Never again, she thought, would she be able to exercise over them even the poor modicum of authority which Thomas allowed her, if she had once so given herself away.

The apparently complete silence which prevailed upstairs convinced Thomas that another visit to his wife was at present unnecessary. In any case, if she was still in the same mood as she had been before the evening service, seeing him again would only upset her. Better leave her alone with Mrs Whiston as long as possible, and when everything was over she would certainly come round.

He pulled the small table which held the scattered sheets of his Easter sermon across his knees in front of the fire, but his thoughts on the text: '*Likewise reckon ye also yourselves to be dead indeed unto sin: but alive unto God through Jesus Christ our Lord,*' refused to be organised. He might as well face the fact that what was really troubling him was not Janet's danger, nor the domestic discomforts which childbirth involved for the neglected father, nor even the persistent inability of their joint incomes to keep pace with the constant expenditure to which his son's arrival was adding, but his realisation, from the accidental discovery of Janet's most recent diary, of her bitter and sinful rebellion against motherhood.

He had persuaded her to go to the special service at the parish church after Dr Bannister had called that Thursday evening five weeks ago, in the hope that the atmosphere of St Mary's would put her into a frame of mind better suited to an expectant mother than the one she had just revealed. No doubt about it, Bannister's visit had upset her, though he had only called in the kindness of his heart to make the arrangements for the confinement in plenty of time. She had been waiting to tell Thomas all about it the moment he returned from his afternoon class with the Church Lads' Brigade, pacing up and down his study with a disturbing vehemence most unbecoming in one so heavy with child.

'The doctor's just been here to settle about this wretched business,' she burst out indignantly. 'He thinks it'll be about the middle of March, but he wasn't exactly cheering. He said being my first he couldn't tell how it would be with me, but I should want a lot of patience and he supposed I should get through it as well as most people. I think my stock of patience will soon run short!'

The trouble with women nowadays, thought Thomas, after she had reluctantly agreed to go to St Mary's and pray for more patience and endurance, was that they were all too pampered; they made such scenes about these natural processes that you'd think having a baby was a major operation. Janet, for instance, had a most exaggerated notion of the care that ought to be given to women in childbirth, and her insistence that a properly quali-fied midwife ought to be in attendance on every case was nothing less than morbid. His own mother, the hard-working wife of a Nottingham estate agent, had never dreamed of spending more than a guinea on any of her numerous confinements.

'Ten shillings for the doctor,' she'd reckoned, 'and five for the nurse, and the rest for a few little comforts for myself!'

Women weren't afraid of doing their duty in those days – and made no fuss about it either. After all, if the Lord in His wisdom did occasionally choose to take a mother or a baby to Himself, it was a loss which a large household could sustain much better than the small, spoilt families of to-day. Nowadays child-bearing had become such a performance that the death of a small infant was treated as though it were a first-class tragedy.

He couldn't exactly remember now why it was that he had gone up to the room on the top floor that evening, and found the diary which Janet, who was usually so secretive, had evidently forgotten to put away in her anger and alarm. At the head of the open page, in a calligraphy still childish, but straighter and more pointed than the round schoolgirl hand in which she had recorded the arrival of her striped under-petticoat, she had copied a sentence from *John Inglesant*: 'Nothing but the Infinite pity is sufficient for the infinite pathos of human life.'

It struck him as an odd quotation for a nineteen-year-old girl to choose, and he looked back through the preceding pages to find whether they offered any explanation. Never once did it occur to him that in thus reading through her diary, he was violating any confidence or perpetrating any deceit. What was hers was his; a wife had no right to shut her private thoughts away from her husband. His acute misgivings arose, not from any doubts as to the propriety of his conduct, but from the pages of introspective, free-thinking stuff which he had discovered on faith, repentance, the value of prayer, the will of God, the divinity of Christ and the practical effectiveness of Christianity.

Thomas failed to perceive in these confused questionings the craving need, the pathetic bewilderment, of their immature writer. What did disturb him was the distance that they revealed from 'a right state of mind' – which in his view involved the unquestioning acceptance of 'truths' that actually repre-sented, as nearly all 'truths' do, some of the most controversial uncertainties of the universe. But the perturbations caused him by her philosophic doubts were nothing to the horror aroused in him by the revelation of her attitude towards her coming child. No wonder he had been puzzled by her unaccountable silences, her inexplicably sullen moods! Never had he imagined that Janet – his wife whom, for all her temperamental vagaries, he believed that he knew and understood – could have written such terrible things. Not even yet had he felt able to speak to her about them.

'It is already evident to me,' he had read under August 5th, 1893, 'that unless I am mistaken, the thing which I most dreaded has happened. I have hoped against hope since early last month, but am afraid my fears have a good ground. The thought of the duties before me has raised in me a rebellious spirit which frightens me. When I think about my life in the future, with its occupation of looking after a home and church work which I detest, and now the additional burden of a child for whom I believe myself incapable of feeling much affection, the whole outlook seems infinitely weary and uninspiring. No time for reading or theatres or politics – nothing but a deadly monotony of house-keeping, cooking, bearing children and nursing them, always in the midst of the same dull people and surroundings. Of course I know that this is intensely selfish of me, that such a life would be the height of many a woman's ambition, that there is a beautiful, tender side to it, but is it my fault that that side does not appeal to me? I cannot help shedding bitter, if unworthy, tears of disappointment at the thought of all the best years of my life being spent in hum-drum. Of course it is the lot of most women – but it is a hard lot.'

He turned on to the entry which even more than this had distressed him. Obviously he had allowed Janet too much time for these unnatural speculations; he ought to have insisted upon her running the Christmas bazaar and giving more attention to the Sunday School classes, however much she professed to feel unable to tackle them just then.

'I remember Thomas saying once, when I remarked that I did not care about having a child,' she had written – on Christmas Day, too, of all days in the year for such sentiments! – 'that did

I not think *he* ought to have a say in that matter? Surely he
has had *all* the say! It seems grossly unfair, while it is I alone
who am to spend my health and imperil my life in childbearing.
What "say" have I had in it? I suppose it is one of the sacrifices
distinctly understood in entering into marriage – but why should
the woman be called upon to make an unwilling sacrifice any
more than the man? A motherhood which cannot be voluntarily
accepted as a sacred joy as well as a duty *must* be wrong
somewhere. I would not shrink from the peril of life and the
ordeal of the physical pain – though I suppose that is awful –
if I believed there were in store for me the joys of maternity of
which one hears so much, but I see nothing before me but the
sacrifice and the pain and the added lasting cares and the cruelty
of it all. I suppose it sounds inhuman, but my great hope now is
that the child may not be born alive.'

Could anything, he thought, be more dreadful for a woman to
write than that last sentence! Surely she must have known that –
failing those measures of interference with nature which a few
misguided people nowadays were wicked enough to attempt –
children were the natural consequence of ordinary married life?
He certainly wasn't to blame if, not knowing these things, she
had chosen not to consult him! From an entry in January he
gathered that she had been reading *Ecce Homo* and trying
to work herself into a better frame of mind – 'After all,'
she had written, 'it *is* a solemn and wonderful period of my
life; I am brought face to face with the great mysteries of
our existence, the universal tale of sacrifice repeating itself in
me' – but unfortunately these protests against the prospect of
child-bearing had not been the only evidence of rebellion that
he had found in her diary.

All that rubbish about women's rights, for instance – whoever
could have put it into her head? It resembled the pernicious
nonsense talked by that preposterous organisation which called
itself the Women's Emancipation Union, and had caused so
much amusement when a speaker at one of its recent conferences
suggested the use of dynamite to enforce the rights of her
sex! But Janet, he felt certain, had never been to any of its
meetings. Could it be, as usual, from her father that she had

derived the inspiration for those strange notes and queries in her journal?

'Should women only have influence – not power?'

'If women enter political life, can their home influence be the same?'

'Purity – prudery – vast difference!'

'Why should strength be considered the prerogative of man and weakness – I mean particularly moral – that of women? I refuse to swallow the dogma of "womanly weakness."'

The final reflection had seemed to him most wrong-headed of all.

'The woman question is the result of girls' education and the mistaken conception of marriage which they are taught. Girls should have perfect freedom to exercise their wills in the disposal of their lives, to use their brains and bestow their affections. They should possess or make for themselves independent positions, so that love and loyalty to each other and each other's interests may be the keynote of marriage. With educated women possessing this independence, they would marry only men who themselves could rise tô the higher conception of marriage.'

The smudged, untidy pages presented themselves to Thomas's mind as clearly as if he had seen them only a moment before.

'It's not right!' he burst out explosively in the silence of his study, thereby enunciating that blind principle of social propriety which has always been one of the main impediments to feminine freedom. A good and decent woman ought not to worry about such things; no wonder Janet hadn't the proper attitude towards motherhood! The last word on the subject of women's rights, so called, had been said by Mr Gladstone in that letter he wrote a year or two ago and afterwards issued as a pamphlet. Thomas had bought a copy at the time in order to confute the nonsense talked by one or two ladies at the Liberal Summer School in the Ashwood Park Pavilion – where was it? Rummaging in a drawer marked: 'Notes for Sermons – Political,' he soon found Mr Gladstone's Letter to Mr S. Smith, M.P., dated August 21st, 1892, explaining his objections to Sir Albert Rollit's Bill to extend the Parliamentary franchise to women.

'As this is not a party question, or a class question, so neither is it a sex question,' read Thomas with satisfaction. 'I have no fear lest the woman should encroach upon the power of the man. The fear I have is lest we should invite her unwittingly to trespass upon the delicacy, the purity, the refinement, the elevation of her own nature, which are the present sources of its power ... Such great progress has been made in most things that in regard to what may still remain, the necessity for violent remedies has not yet been shown. I admit that in the Universities, in the professions, in the secondary circles of public action, we have already gone so far as to give a shadow of plausibility to the present proposals to go farther; but it is a shadow only, for we have done nothing that plunges the woman as such into the turmoil of masculine life. My disposition is to do all for her which is free from that danger and reproach, but to take no step in advance until I am convinced of its safety.'

He started violently as a sudden agitated knock sounded on his door, and Harriet, the cook, appeared with a nervous absence of ceremony even more conspicuous than usual.

'Mrs Whiston wants you at once, sir! She says the baby's all but here and she must 'ave some help.'

She added desperately as Thomas, for once too startled to protest against this unexpected demand for his services, threw down his pen and hurried to the door: 'I'd a gone meself, sir, honest I would, but I'd be no use at all there, honest I wouldn't. I can't abear the sight of blood – never could, sir! It makes me come all over queer!'

5

Her frightened, apologetic voice pursued him up the narrow staircase. Hastening into Janet's room he found the midwife, her heavy face flushed and damp with perspiration, frantically contending with the convulsed, screaming form which he barely recognised as that of his wife. The hearty words of encouragement and exhortation which he had intended to use died upon Thomas's lips, and he flinched as he approached the bed and saw the sanguinary spectacle which every poorly-conducted birth relentlessly offers to those who behold it.

For the first time since he knew that the child was coming, he wondered whether he had been justified in condemning Janet to this ruthless anguish of humiliation without consulting her or making certain that she really understood how motherhood occurred and what it would involve. As he endeavoured, in accordance with the midwife's instructions, to hold on to his wife's struggling limbs, he asked himself what his congregation would think if they could see him involved in this undignified contest.

It was disgraceful, really disgraceful, of Bannister to let him in for it! According to every decent tradition of life and literature, the anxious father waited downstairs in difficult but heroic composure until nurse or doctor came to announce to him that all was safely over. Was it due to the distasteful conviction that his parishioners would derive a malign satisfaction from his predicament, or did he really see, as Janet's cries ceased for a second, a look of angry malevolence darken the stricken terror in her eyes? In spite of his determination to regard the whole business as natural and normal, a faint misgiving about Dr Bannister's breezy indifference to anæsthetics arose within him when her screams redoubled in violence, and as though by telepathy the midwife's words echoed his thought.

''Twasn't right, sir, to leave her to it like this! He ought to have put her straight under chloroform – she bein' so young and the baby coming too quickly as 'tis. I knew 'twas all rubbish, his talk about midnight. I could have told him at the start she was the sort to miss out the second stage altogether – but it's as much as my job's worth to teach him his business . . . Look out, sir, quick – the baby's coming!'

A shriek such as he had never before heard in his life preceded, only by a second, one terrific, grotesque convulsion, and then the sudden catapulting from her body of a damp, downy head was succeeded almost at once by a second convulsion and the complete emergence of the child. The silence which followed the immediate cessation of her crying seemed almost audible to Thomas; he found it as oppressive as the previous clamour until it was broken by the thin wailing of the child and the midwife's comment: 'It's a boy, sir!' But there was no time for satisfaction that Nature had justified his calculations and provided him with the son for whom he had prayed. The gruesome aftermath of birth, about which he had known next to nothing, required as much of his attention as the process itself, and Mrs Whiston's obvious terror lest Janet, whose lips were now blue and whose teeth were chattering wildly, should collapse altogether from shock, sent him scurrying in search of hot-water bottles and extra blankets with temporary indifference to his dignity.

At last, when comparative peace was restored and he had time to wash his hands and mop his streaming forehead, the midwife, picking up the now vociferous baby from the foot of the bed where it had lain wrapt in an old flannel blanket, again spoke with feeling.

'He's come out of it better than she, sir – a fine boy if a bit on the thin side – but all the same he'd no right to be born in a rush like that. Doctor ought to have been here to slow things down; the Lord knows – beggin' your pardon – how many stitches he'll have to put in her, poor child. If men had the babies, they'd get a bit more of a move on when one arrived, I'm thinking. Now, sir,' she added, 'I can manage if you'll get someone to go for Dr Bannister; he ought to come as soon as may be to fix her up. She'll be needin' a good rest after a shock like that, and the sooner she gets to it, the better!'

Thomas hurried thankfully downstairs to find an excited housemaid only too eager to perform his errand. Not until he was once again safely in his study did he remember that he had neither spoken to Janet nor kissed her. Had anyone asked him why he had forgotten her in what he had been accustomed to regard as a supreme moment in the life of husbands and wives, he would only have replied that he thought it better to avoid disturbing her as she lay speechless, with closed eyes, exhausted and indifferent to him as to her child. He could not have put into words his strange impression that the tormented body through which he had watched Nature's purpose being so ruthlessly accomplished was hardly that of a familiar individual with a human personality.

Later that evening, while Dr Bannister – who seemed far more affronted by Janet's confutation of his reckoning than disturbed by any consequences which his miscalculations might have had for herself – was occupied in repairing the damage entailed by his absence, Thomas took charge of his infant son.

It was now past ten o'clock; in the windy sky the winking eyes of a thousand stars closed and re-opened as the restless indigo clouds scudded between them and the silent earth. The thin crescent moon, already high in the heavens, swung above the black outline of Ploughman's Ridge like a phosphorescent boat in a stormy sea. Thomas pulled back the curtains from his study window, and lifted up the baby as though its half-closed, indifferent eyes, blue with the slaty opaqueness of the newly born, could see the dimly lighted town in the shrouded valley.

'Well, what do you think of the world, old chap?' he inquired tenderly, as deeply moved as though the backward stretching and spreading of the minute rose-pink fingers had indeed been a gesture of gratitude and affirmation. His strong paternal instinct sprang into active life when the child suddenly whimpered; the protective love that he felt for it renewed and intensified his genuine desire to help and serve his kind, provided only that the service were of a type which he himself thought right and proper, rather than that desired or needed by the individual served. The boy, he hoped, would represent not only an extension of his own personality, but a willing recipient of the benevolent affection which Janet appeared unable to accept and his sturdy parishioners seemed never to require. Please God, this little son would be the first of many children, who would warm and cheer his unappreciated isolation and make him the loved and respected centre of a happy Christian home.

Already, by the use of that convenient psychological shutter which now responded automatically to the prolonged demand made upon it for the exclusion of unwelcome facts, he had banished from his mind both the spectacle of mismanaged suffering that he had just witnessed and the memory of Janet's resentment against motherhood. Her hour was over, and now, like the mother in the Gospel, she would remember no more the anguish for joy that a man was born into the world.

It did not occur to him as even possible that the woman who had carried and given birth to this blind, helpless scrap of humanity – so pathetically dependent upon her for all its needs – could fail to be stirred by it to the same passion of tender solicitude as he had just experienced. Not having paid the price himself, he never dreamed that the person who had could possibly regard it as too high. Nor did he ever discover that the subsequent record, in Janet's diary, of March 21st, 1894, contained no mention of her son or his birth, but merely the terse, unembroidered entry:

'Women doctors? YES!!'

CHAPTER II

WIFE

'*Socrates*. And will not the better and abler soul when it does wrong, do wrong voluntarily, and the bad soul involuntarily?
Hippias. Clearly.
Socrates. And the good man is he who has the good soul, and the bad man is he who has the bad?
Hippias. Yes.
Socrates. Then the good man will voluntarily do wrong, and the bad man involuntarily, if the good man is he who has the good soul?
Hippias. Which he certainly has.
Socrates. Then, Hippias, he who voluntarily does wrong and disgraceful things, if there be such a man, will be the good man?
Hippias. There I cannot agree with you.
Socrates. Nor can I agree with myself, Hippias; and yet that seems to be the conclusion which, as far as we can see at present, must follow from our argument.'

PLATO, *Hippias Minor*.

I

THE LIBERAL PARTY offices in Sterndale Spa occupied the top of an ancient and ramshackle house at the unfashionable end of the town's chief thoroughfare, Spring Parade. On the ground floor front, the least opulent of the three local fishmongers displayed his kippers and haddock and herrings, which during the summer months wafted their pungent and persistent odours through the open political windows above. Liberalism did not flourish in Sterndale, which was the centre of a Derbyshire division that for years had returned a Conservative Member to

Parliament, but the spa had become a favourite meeting-place for party conferences, and the local group, though far from affluent, was obliged to maintain spacious offices on account of the organisation periodically involved.

On a July evening of 1899, Janet Rutherston sat alone in the front office waiting for young Gerald Cosway, the part-time party agent to the division, to talk over with her the preparations for the special meeting of the Northern and Midland branches of the Women's National Liberal Association which was to be held at Sterndale in August to discuss the situation in South Africa. After assiduously attending for five years the meetings of the Sterndale Association, she had recently been elected its honorary secretary, and the local arrangements for the Conference and the correspondence with the speakers had been turned over to her by the Central Office.

Those years had changed her from a bewildered, defiant, ambitious child into a young woman with a passion for politics and a zest for sitting on every committee to which she could get herself elected. One of these, the Women's Suffrage Society, even took her as far as Manchester, where she sat as the representative for Sterndale, which had not yet its own branch of the National Union of Women's Suffrage Societies.

'Can't think, Mrs Rutherston, why you don't start a suffrage group in this place,' Gerald Cosway had suggested one day. 'It mayn't be exactly go-ahead, but you've almost got a nucleus in your own parish, with Miss Garston and Mrs Flinders and one or two others.'

'I only wish I could!' she had replied, voicing a secret ambition of which the birth of her son Denis had first made her aware. 'But you know what a parish is, Mr Cosway. The Vicar's always telling me I neglect the church work as it is.'

'Oh, I'm sure you don't, Mrs Rutherston! You've got energy enough for twenty parishes.'

Inevitably she compared his admiring suavity with Thomas's perpetual and explosive complaints that she was constantly rushing off to committee meetings, or running up to Manchester in pursuit of 'suff.,' when she ought to be leading sewing bees, or playing the organ – which she did well – or preparing her Girls'

Friendly Society and Sunday School classes. His unceasing passion for improving the characters of his associates had prevented him from recognising that she was unlikely ever to wrestle with certain qualities which he still called her 'faults,' for the simple reason that she did not want to change them. To her father, long dead but still her accepted mentor, political preoccupations had been no more reprehensible than religious doubts. The periodic remorseful misgivings which, at twenty-four, she was too young to have outgrown related solely to her marriage with Thomas, but though they were reserved for the pages of her diary, they had perhaps helped to deepen the emphatic cleft between her upper lip and her nostrils, and to paint the shadows beneath her limpid eyes. Despite the melancholy which often clouded their clear blue and hardened the soft corners of her full, curving mouth, she still appeared a trim and very youthful figure in the stiff white cotton blouse with its workmanlike tie, and the long cloth skirt finished neatly at the waist by an elastic belt fastening with a large steel buckle.

Though summer was usually cool and pleasant in Sterndale, the first week of the new month had brought a sudden mild heat-wave, and vigorous intimations of the fish shop below assailed Janet's nostrils as she watched the less pretentious summer visitors walking arm-in-arm on the opposite pavement. Unconscious of it as she had long become, the homely smell of herrings and kippers was to be associated for her until the end of her life with these early experiments in political self-education. Years afterwards, the fried-fish shops in the East End of London incongruously revived with unbearable persistence the recollection of her young and hopeful efforts to reform a world which had not yet demonstrated to her its periodic capacity for defiant repudiation of human endeavour.

It was of her political obligations and their increasing demands upon her time that she was thinking as she waited for Gerald Cosway. If only she were not so much tied to Thomas and to Denis! – who had not had a successor for reasons into which Thomas, though he was always trying to raise the subject, had never been permitted to inquire too closely. Why should the interests of a husband whose work did not attract her, and

the requirements of a son whose unpremeditated conception
and mismanaged birth had destroyed such limited capacity for
maternal affection as she possessed, be thought sufficient to fill
her eager, vigorous life, when what really interested her was
political work and the suffrage movement and all the larger
aspects of social reform? These were the subjects which she
discussed with Gerald Cosway, her now constant companion,
on late evenings in the Liberal office, while he was going through
his party books and she was finishing her secretarial work for the
Association after putting Denis to bed. The extent, for instance,
to which the prestige of the United States had really benefited
from the Spanish-American War, or whether it was possible for
a woman to be both a good Liberal and a good suffragist.

'I can't see why not,' Cosway assured her. 'It's an appropriate
reform for a progressive party.'

'But the party leaders are always so non-committal about the
women's vote – and then look at Mr Gladstone! If they were all
like he was I should turn Conservative, though I'd hate to do it.
Suffrage means even more to me than a party programme.'

How had the legend grown up that a woman's husband and
children should take precedence of and indeed exclude these
far more absorbing interests? Did all men of Thomas's age
and calling share his apparent conviction that affection and
service on the part of a wife not only could but ought to
be commandeered? Whence, above all, came the illusion that
children were a uniting element in marriage? It might, perhaps,
have been different if Denis had turned out a normal healthy
baby, but a serious fit of convulsions a few weeks after his
birth had made him extremely difficult to rear. Even when he
had outgrown babyhood he caught cold after cold, providing
Thomas with an excuse for constant interference, and giving
substance to his complaints that the child was never properly fed,
clothed or washed. Why, it was that very attack of convulsions
which had led to their first serious quarrel! If only, she sometimes
caught herself thinking, Denis had died at that time, instead of
being still here to impel Thomas to perpetual expressions of his
belief that maternal instinct and domestic predilections could
be inculcated by compulsion! Mrs Whiston, called in to assist

their desperate efforts to drag a sick baby from the edge of the grave, had shaken her head and murmured her conviction that Dr Bannister's indifference and the shock of a too rapid birth were the real sources of Denis's illness. But Thomas, frantic with anxiety and indignation, had accused Janet of 'shocking neglect' and 'leaving the child to the servants,' till she finally turned on him in an uncontrollable passion of rage.

'I hate my child and all the work he gives me! I hate my home, and housework, and everlasting devotion to "duty"! I hate you and the way you're always accusing me of every sin and wickedness under the sun!'

And she had rushed upstairs to sob bitterly over her diary and put down in it her forlorn, rudderless sense of being without a mature guide or companion. Had the period been thirty years later she might have recorded her growing conviction that Thomas was a non-adult type, more infantile than her nineteen-year-old self and incapable of further mental or spiritual development, but in 1894 her words reflected the simpler psychological reactions of her day.

'We are not in sympathy on a single point – religion, aims in life, interests, pleasures, all are different. Henceforth I shall do as little as I can, and occupy my time with my own pursuits, regardless of what pleases him as he is regardless of what pleases me. We were happy enough together until that wretched child began to come, but he has been a veritable source of discord. Thomas has been a changed man – so fault-finding, irritable and excited that he almost wears the life out of me. How is all this to end? If only I had someone, something to help me, whom I could really respect and worship! But I cannot pray, I do not know God; I have no faith that he will listen to me. The words of prayer rise from my heart, but the thought always meets them, there is no one to pray to. My father was taking a great responsibility when he openly talked agnosticism before me, a child. He has left me a terrible legacy of doubts and unsatisfied wants.'

What a distance, she thought, she had already travelled since those days when she was the precious only child of affectionate elderly parents, a child in whose secure life her first dance, at the age of fourteen, had ranked as a tremendous occurrence! How far away seemed even the recent period of her engagement to Thomas! Could she ever really have recorded – as the evidence of her eyes told her that she had, in October, 1892: 'Engaged to Thomas. I cannot write about it yet; it is all too wonderful?' Was it with thoughts of him that she had soon afterwards formulated her philosophy of love: 'It is a maxim of mine that true love must include reverence; that we must believe the object of our love to be better than ourselves?'

Doubts of her wisdom in promising to marry him had of course come later, combined with unhappy misgivings about her vague knowledge of 'the facts of life.' Realising that she would learn nothing definite from her mother and too shy to consult Thomas himself, she had wrestled perpetually with her questionings and fears.

'Ignorance is *not* innocence. Is it wrong of me to try to get at the root of these matters? How much *ought* girls to know on these subjects? Can the innocence which is only ignorance make a woman good and pure and strong?'

She had believed herself, she knew, to be in love with Thomas, but might not this assumption have been due to the flattering admiration of a man so much older than herself? Had she not, perhaps, merely been attracted by the intellectual stimulus of his conversation after the vacuousness of her pretty but vain and self-indulgent mother, whose sole preoccupations had been her health, her clothes, her shopping, and the shortcomings of apartment landladies? Even before her mother's death had given immediate precision to the unspecified date of her marriage, she had confided to her diary the alarm with which the prospect of clerical life sometimes inspired her.

'I often feel terribly depressed. My life as Thomas's wife fills me with dread. It will be an unceasing fight against all my tastes and interests. There is nothing that is agreeable to me in it – parish work, talking to people, influencing them, giving in to them, when with my nervousness all merely social intercourse is absolute pain. Religious work is irksome, too, when religion to me is an unsolved problem, and I am destitute of all religious feeling. On the other hand I should never be happy without his love. Rather all this with him, than a life more suited to me without him – yet at times the future looks very hard.'

And it *is* hard, she reflected. How was it I never foresaw the added misery of having a child before I was prepared for it? Motherhood seemed so alien to my nature that a baby never occurred to me as even possible for a very long time. I wonder if I should ever really have married Thomas, and had Denis, if Mama's death just then had not left me so utterly alone? How well I remember trying to put into words my feeling of desolation just after she died; 'I am lonely – absolutely alone; no mother and father, no God, no faith, and Thomas said he could not marry me if I had no religion. Last night I prayed to God to let me die and then stopped in the middle of my prayer, remembering that I had no God.'

It had indeed been during that period of bleak solitude that Thomas had accused her of despising Christianity, and had persuaded her – an unhappy eighteen-year-old girl, troubled by doubts, who had just lost her mother – to spend a few quiet days in studying the New Testament. It had never dawned upon anyone – least of all, perhaps, upon herself – that what she really needed was a holiday and a change of scene. Instead she had earnestly resolved to turn the weeks before her marriage into 'a period of very serious thought and self-examination.' She had honestly intended to make that hazardous experiment succeed, and even to-day, six years afterwards, she could repeat almost by heart the ardent, idealistic prayer which she had composed and uttered on her wedding eve:

'O Lord Christ, give me Thy grace that I may live my new life as Thy disciple! Strengthen me that I may be able to do Thy will and so come to feel Thy love. I know that of myself I cannot keep the vows I make to-morrow, or maintain our lives on the high level which I have marked out for myself. Christ, I trust wholly in Thee; be with us always and bless us. May we see in our love for each other a token of Thy divine love. Bless our union, may it be a very real and sacred one, and may we use our happiness to Thy glory and do more to further Thy kingdom working together than we could do separately. Make me more worthy of my husband and above all grant that I may never stand in the way of his work for Thee. O Lord Christ, keep us both always loyal to Thee and then we shall be loyal to one another!'

What wordy vapouring that childish petition seemed to-day! It had, of course, been utterly useless. Even if the God whom her father had repudiated somewhere existed, He was too remote for the strivings and woes of puzzled humanity to reach Him in His portentous isolation. Far from her prayer being answered, the quarrels and disputes between herself and Thomas had not even been limited to the household and the parish.

One of the worst causes of dissension was always her annual visit to London to stay in rooms near her old Putney home. The house had been left her by her parents, but was now let to a builder and his family. A yearly fortnight in which to visit familiar scenes and satisfy her passion for theatre-going did not seem, she thought, an excessive allowance, but even before their marriage Thomas had begun objecting to what he always called her 'worldly pleasures.' Once, during their engagement, she had actually offered to forgo her visits to plays in order to please him.

'I would, of course, willingly give up my amusements simply *because* you disliked them. But I should not be quite satisfied in doing so if I did not feel that I heartily agreed with you,' she had written.

Five years of marriage had made her less acquiescent to demands which she considered unreasonable. She could not understand why Thomas should object even to such plays as *The Sign of the Cross*, which Wilson Barrett had made so famous, or to Beerbohm Tree's recent production of *Julius Cæsar*.

'If only,' she thought, 'he'd tried to guide me, instead of always scolding! If only, instead of insisting and ordering, he'd sometimes try to *understand*! If only he wouldn't talk about "suff." when he means the suffrage movement! If only . . .'

2

A board creaked suddenly, and she started from her perturbing meditations to find Gerald Cosway standing beside her desk.

'Well,' he announced heartily, 'here we are! Sorry to be so late – I was kept at the Club trying to convert one of the doubtfuls!'

She blushed a little as his bold glance rested with approval upon her neat shirt blouse and the soft fair fringe which she had re-curled for his benefit. Because he always treated her as an equal and agreed with her that the present political position of women was quite intolerable, she hardly noticed his tousled dark hair, his slightly prominent teeth, his faintly insolent attitude of familiarity. What she did see was the athletic grace of his lean young body – which she instinctively contrasted with Thomas's growing portliness – and the seductive brown eyes which always regarded her with a soft caress in their gaze. Again unlike Thomas, he was ready at any moment to discuss with her those political topics which fascinated her even more than plays and the theatre. Thomas, she had to admit, was in his own limited fashion a sound Liberal who had never believed that politics ought to be kept out of the pulpit, but he had recently been so much preoccupied with the zealous Mr Kensit and the wearisome subject of ritualism, that it was impossible to divert his conversation to those events which were rendering somewhat incongruous the big Peace Conference now sitting at the Hague and summoned by – of all people! – the Czar of Russia.

'I see you've picked out some possible speakers from head-quarters' list,' said Cosway, looking over her shoulder.

'Yes,' she replied, and read the names aloud: 'Sir William Harcourt, Mr John Morley, Mrs Fawcett, Mr W. T. Stead, Lady Aberdeen, Mr Leonard Courtney, Mr Keir Hardie. But there's so little time,' she added. 'I'm afraid we can't hope to get them all. I rather thought of trying that talkative member for Carnarvon Boroughs – Mr Lloyd George. He seems so much alive and he's got such strong ideas about South Africa. Would he come, do you think?'

'I'd certainly ask him. Some people say he's only at the beginning of a remarkable career, and it's youth we want at these conferences. They're too apt to drop into the hands of the elderly and the cautious. We're young ourselves, aren't we, Mrs

Rutherston? Let's see if we can't get one or two people who'll express our point of view.'

Wondering whether she ought to allow the gentle but apparently unconscious pressure of his hand on hers as it lay on the table, she became conspicuously busy over the discovery of another sheet of jottings.

'Central office hasn't suggested any subjects for the speakers yet, so I've drawn up a few which I thought we might submit to them. Oh, here it is!'

Cosway, leaning across her chair, looked at the scribbled list of topics.

'Attitude of women's organisations to present crisis.'
'Hague Conference and Czar's message.'
'War-like speeches of German Emperor.'
'Dreyfus case and trials of M. Zola.'
'Spanish-American War and Philippine Insurrection.'
'?Armenian Massacres. Anarchists.'

'I think the Armenians are getting a bit stale, don't you?' he said.

'Well, it *is* rather a long time since some of them were massacred,' she responded.

They smiled at one another foolishly, like two children.

'Of course,' Cosway went on, 'those subjects all *ought* to be discussed if the Conference is going to get a proper review of the situation during the past five years or so, but I expect, you know, that South Africa'll eclipse the lot. Now the Bloemfontein Conference has failed, war really does seem to be inevitable.'

'Yes,' she commented, 'it's terrible, isn't it?' But in spite of this automatic response to his speculations, the South African situation no more appealed to her as truly terrible than the plight of the races subject to Turkey in Eastern Europe.

Three or four years earlier, public meetings had been held all over the country to discuss the problem raised by the insatiable brutality of the Turks and the ineradicable masochism of the Armenians. There had been one in Sterndale and Janet had gone, to find it thronged with respectable elderly ladies who felt no real interest in the maltreated though troublesome victims of oriental sadism, but found release from the repressions to which the age condemned them by listening to stories of Turkish atrocities. Though too young to have acquired their passion for blood-thirsty details, Janet shared with them that feeling of detachment from political catastrophe which Victoria's long and prosperous reign had given to her subjects. Belonging to the younger generation born after Sedan, she thought of war as a distant phenomenon which could never come near her or anyone dear to her, although as a good Liberal she went faithfully to peace meetings and conscientiously voted for resolutions supporting the proposals of the Hague Conference.

At that moment the lengthening of the shadows over the Transvaal interested her chiefly as a reason for a political gathering which obliged her to spend evening after evening in the company of Gerald Cosway. Side by side they settled down at her desk, and in prolonged consideration of speeches and agenda, the troublesome claims of Thomas and Denis temporarily disappeared into oblivion.

3

On the afternoon of her twenty-fifth birthday at the end of August, Janet sat beside Denis's bed in a new mood of black despair.

Denis was slowly recovering from the effects of a feverish cold which had brought him nearer to pneumonia than any of his similar previous illnesses, but the danger to which he had been so close was not the source of her melancholy. Looking down at the child's thin, flushed cheeks, his soft fair hair and closed blue eyes which were the exact replica of her own, she saw in him only the unwelcome image of his father.

'This afternoon,' she scribbled as he slept, 'I am alone with the poor little boy who has no mother's love,' but she went on immediately to other topics which absorbed her more than the contemplation of her son.

'It is my twenty-fifth birthday. O God, help me – at twenty-five years of age my life is an utter failure! How miserable and restless I feel! I am getting older – my youth is passing and I have achieved nothing. Almost before it had begun, my brief period of contact with the centre of things is over. No more delight of organisation; no more correspondence for Central Office or receiving letters with famous names as their signatures; no more evenings with Gerald or discussion together of our political ideals!'

The Women's Liberal Association Conference in Ashwood Park Pavilion had been over for a fortnight, but Janet's despair was not due to its failure. On the contrary, it had been an outstanding success, with flying visits from Sir William Harcourt and Mr John Morley, and Mrs Fawcett, as President of the National Union of Women's Suffrage Societies, appropriately driving home the lesson that if the political rights of the Uitlanders in the Transvaal were important enough to be regarded as a subject for war, the denial of votes to English women was harder than ever to defend. The Marchioness of Aberdeen, representing the view of the International Council of Women, had made one of the final speeches, emphasising the importance of peace to women Liberals; and unanimous resolutions had been passed condemning the Government's policy in South Africa, which, if they were unlikely to have much effect on the subsequent fate of the Transvaal, at least provided a satisfactory outlet for political indignation on the part of those who drew them up. Young Mr Lloyd George, who was said to be thirty-six but seemed so much less, had even stayed for the final Saturday's picnic on the moors between Sterndale and Cheddlefield, and had presided by request over the festal feminine tea at the Dog and Harp which ended the Conference.

Most of the delegates had driven up from Sterndale in wagonettes, but a few of the younger ones, such as herself and Gerald Cosway, had ridden the seven miles on their bicycles, caring nothing for the steep hills and the long intervals spent in pushing their machines up the dusty chalk-white roads. She would never be able to explain the mood of rash abandonment in which she, a clergyman's wife who was supposed – as Thomas so frequently reminded her – to set an example to the young womanhood of the parish, had allowed Gerald Cosway to lead her away from the rest of the party, and then take her in his arms and deliriously kiss her lips as they sat beside a brown peaty stream under a concealing clump of bilberry and heather. She still went hot whenever she recalled the ardour with which she had responded to that kiss, and the tingling sensation of excited enjoyment that ran through her body instead of the feeling of outrage and humiliation which, by every accepted canon of conduct, ought to have possessed her.

'Of course,' she had told herself many times since, 'I shouldn't have allowed him to go so far.'

She had realised that already as they rode home, a little self-conscious and almost silent, with the sun setting exuberantly behind them and the moors turning to a deeper purple until their contours were lost in twilight. She ought to have seen what was coming when he picked her that heart's-ease pansy by the roadside and began to quote those lines from Shelley:

> *'One word is too often profaned*
> *For me to profane it . . .'*

But it had been impossible to remain unaffected by the enchantment of the day, or to forget that one was sometimes an individual and not merely the unsatisfactory helpmeet of the Vicar of Upper Sterndale. After all, she was still so young, and the bees had been humming so deliciously in the warm heather, and the rolling hills had spread so richly downwards to the green Cheshire plain stretching away to the horizon, where a faint etching of deeper blue outlined the distant mountains of North Wales.

She had reached the Vicarage after dark, to find Thomas pacing up and down the little oilcloth-covered hall inside the front door.

'I thought you were never coming home!' he burst out the moment she opened it. 'Denis is ill! I came back from the choir practice to find him crying in the nursery and not a soul anywhere near him! I made the girl put him to bed at once, and instead of getting on with my sermon I've been waiting about the whole evening for you to come in and take his temperature!'

Janet had long ceased questioning Thomas's complete inability to take temperatures or measure out doses of medicine or make beds or help to clear tables.

'I'll go up and take it at once,' she said, wrestling with the flat sense of anticlimax so familiar to every mother who returns home after a joyous day to find a sick child and an agitated household.

Denis was lying wide awake in his small bed in the back bedroom, hot and uncomfortable beyond even his very considerable powers of endurance, under a pile of blankets beneath which he had been vainly endeavouring to sleep since six o'clock. In accordance with Thomas's reiterated instructions to both Janet and the maids, Denis's bed, like his fragile body, was always heavily overclothed, and his bedroom window was tightly shut except for a narrow crack at the top during the midsummer months. To-night every breath of air was excluded and the thick curtains were drawn across the panes.

Janet lit the gas and looked down at him as he lay there, flushed and glassy-eyed.

'Oh Denis!' she exclaimed, 'why *did* you have to go and get ill to-day, when I was so busy! How you manage to catch cold in this warm weather I really can't think!'

His ear, quick with the sensitiveness of an intelligent five-year-old child, at once caught the note of irritation in her voice. It was one that he heard frequently, and would have given everything he most treasured – his wooden horse with the broken nose and the scarlet tail, his flowerpot full of ripe seeds collected from the nasturtiums in the garden, his knobbly stone with the vein of blue spar which he had found at the foot of the Ashwood Quarries, and even his new reading-book with the coloured pictures of Baby Jesus – to avoid having to provoke. Knowing himself, for some strange reason which he could not fathom, to be a burden and an obstacle to his mother, he nevertheless adored her with all the strength of his affectionate, devotional nature. To spare her annoyance, he had schooled himself to obey without demur the often-repeated injunction of the maids in the kitchen: 'Now run away and play, Master Denis, do!' For her sake, passionately desiring her constant presence, he had taught himself to play alone.

'I'm not really *ill*, Mummy,' he protested in a tone as propitiatory as his sore throat could command. 'It's only my head's rather hot and my throat hurts a little.'

She took his temperature and found it to be 102 degrees. Downstairs, while they waited for Dr Bannister – who was still, in spite of Janet's objections, the family doctor; you couldn't, alleged Thomas, give a man the go-by when he'd attended you free ever since you came to the parish – the storm which she had already sensed in the atmosphere burst over her head.

'The way you've conducted yourself would be bad enough even if your poor uncared-for child hadn't been as ill as he is!' thundered Thomas, allowing himself to explode into the full fury of righteous indignation.

'What do you mean?' she asked, in the dull, emotionless tone to which his rages always reduced her.

'You know perfectly well what I mean! You were seen to-day at the picnic behaving disgracefully – absolutely disgracefully – with that brazen young scoundrel Gerald Cosway!'

With a stupendous effort she checked the furious defence of Cosway that rushed to her lips.

'Who says they saw me?'

'Never you mind. That's my business. I don't make a habit of betraying confidences to irresponsible people who don't know how to conduct themselves in public.'

'Except when they're *my* confidences!' she burst out, remembering how often she had heard a garbled version of her domestic difficulties from some obscure quarter of the parish.

'The whole thing's scandalous,' proceeded Thomas, ignoring her interruption. 'Before we were married, you promised you'd make the promotion of my work your chief interest in life – and what do you do? You neglect your house; you completely disregard my parish – it mightn't exist for all the notice you take of it; you spend your time running about after things that are absolutely incompatible with your duties as a wife and mother – and now you crown everything by making a fool of yourself with that insolent, half-educated youth the Liberal agent! At this rate you'll turn me into a nervous wreck within half a year!'

It had ended, of course, in her agreeing to resign the secretary-ship of the Women's Liberal Association just when she had discovered from it her capacity for making large-scale arrange-ments and her efficiency in carrying them through. At first the bitterness of abandoning this cherished occupation had been eclipsed by the anxiety of Denis's illness and the careful nursing which he had required, but as soon as he started to recover, the realisation of her lost joys returned, and for the first time the idea of leaving Thomas for good began to take definite shape in her mind.

'I could live quite comfortably on the income Mama left me,' she thought optimistically. 'I know it isn't much, but it ought to be enough for one.'

Theatres, she reflected, were her only extravagance. Apart from these, she would like to spend her whole time upon study and political work, which cost very little although it was a field where hardly any paid positions as yet existed for women. But could Thomas and Denis manage without her contribution to their joint expenses? Ever since they married, she and Thomas had been perpetually in debt. The stipend at Christ Church was as limited as that of most new, unendowed livings, and though his semi-political, semi-theological sermons – now widely celebrated – diverted the summer visitors in large numbers from Canon Maybury's conventional dissertations at the parish church, he was not the beloved type of vicar whose congregation hurries enthusiastically to his support. The Easter offertory and other perquisites of ecclesiastical office were mod-erately respectable, but had never yet provided any pleasant surprises.

Thomas attributed this misfortune entirely to Janet's lack of interest in his parishioners; had it not been for her disgraceful neglect of the work which every vicar's wife undertook as a matter of course, his congregation would have done their duty. But Janet, though she said nothing, recollected that even during their engagement his letters had complained bitterly of the lack of support received from the parish, and she faced the fact that

Thomas was unlikely ever to solve their financial difficulties by his popularity. After all, his congregation probably enjoyed no better than herself being treated as though they were all black sheep. A passion for righteousness might be admirable, but it was not necessarily an endearing quality.

Hence their debts, though not excessive, were never entirely disposed of; no sooner had one series been met than others arose, providing Thomas with a constant excuse for his protests against the 'extravagance' of her annual visits to London. Although she had now ceased to regard her marriage as a matter for anything more hopeful than resignation, Janet felt reluctant to leave her husband and son in financial difficulties. She could not love Denis, but his delicacy aroused in her an intermittent compunction which, while it added to her dislike, increased that sense of responsibility for him which she so much resented.

'Now if he had been Gerald's son . . .' she caught herself reflecting one evening – and hastily banished the immodest, outrageous thought from her mind. Bitter as the picnic episode had made her feel towards Thomas, the authority over her imagination by means of which his age and prestige had originally captured her had not yet vanished so completely as to leave her with the active desire to hurt or ruin him. Only the previous evening, his birthday gesture of affection and reconciliation had caught her in a vulnerable mood and had overcome, for the time being, her will to depart.

'If we go on as we are,' he pleaded with tears in his eyes, 'we must inevitably drift away until we're eternally lost to each other! That means perhaps twenty or thirty years of increasing estrangement, and then everlasting separation in another existence. The joy most men have of a deep and eternal bond with the woman they've married seems to be entirely out of my reach – and yet my wife ought to be, and could be, the crown of my life. Without you and Denis, my work, my career, means nothing. Won't you be kinder to me, and help me to start afresh?'

'I'll try, Thomas,' she answered earnestly. 'If I can't be tactful and sociable in the parish – and I don't seem able to – at least I'll do my best not to hinder you. If only you'll be patient with

me and try not to lose your temper! When people shout I just
go deaf and feel I don't care.'

But privately she thought how much easier it would have been
to subdue her pride if only he had said: 'Let us try to be kinder
to each other.'

4

During that winter Janet's personal preoccupations at first made
her blind and indifferent to the disastrous beginnings of the war
in South Africa.

She never learnt by what undisclosed machinations Gerald
Cosway was transferred to the Liberal office in Derby, but
she suspected a secret alliance between Thomas and one of
his leading parishioners, Matthew Langdale, family grocer and
ex-treasurer to the Sterndale Liberal Party. The new part-time
agent, she heard, was a bald-headed individual of more years
and discretion than initiative, but she did not meet him for
several months.

From Gerald Cosway came a brief, formal note asking her to
forgive him for any inconvenience that she might have suffered
as the result of the 'liberties' which he had ventured to take
at the picnic. Her reply, though guarded, was friendly; but
complete silence followed. For a time she fretted and shed a
good many secret tears; their association that year had stirred
a spring fever in her warm young blood, and Cosway's youthful
vitality had disconcertingly revealed to her the extent to which
her relationship with Thomas had left her sexually unawakened.
But it had been their joint interests, the subjects of their mutual
conversations, which had fascinated her rather than his energetic but commonplace personality, and though for a time she
missed the sweet anticipation of their meetings, the ever-growing
conflict between her convictions and her marriage gradually
diminished his hold upon her mind.

She was awakened to the tragedy being enacted in the
Transvaal by hearing W. T. Stead speak at a Peace Demonstration held in the Pavilion soon after the defeat of Lord

Methuen at Magersfontein. Three weeks later, her diary heralded the coming of the new century with an unusual outburst of good resolutions, which by identifying domesticity with virtue reflected the measure of her unconscious subservience to the standards of her time. Because she was able to record that she had spent several evenings in sewing, had re-potted the drawing-room ferns and helped 'the girl' to turn out the bedrooms as well as assisting Thomas with his Greek, she felt for the moment less of an outcast from the small but critical world of which she was obliged to be part.

One historic night she roused Denis to show him the beacons blazing from Ploughman's Ridge and Grin Tor to distant Rough Edge between Sterndale and Cheet.

'Look!' she told the excited child. 'They're for the Relief of Mafeking!'

The war with its sieges and reliefs was more real to her now than it had been when she first discussed it with Gerald Cosway, and as she tucked Denis back into bed, she reflected how little their earnest Women's Conference had really counted with its fervent resolutions against the Transvaal tragedy, and how futile such protests were likely to remain unless women obtained the vote.

Two Sundays afterwards, a sermon preached on a text from Ephesians v. – *'As the church is subject unto Christ, so let the wives be to their own husbands in everything'* – by a visiting Archdeacon who took the opportunity to expatiate on the natural subordination of women, led her to spend an afternoon indignantly reflecting on the complete powerlessness of her sex within the Church.

'There is no place for woman's independent work in the Church of England,' she wrote in her diary. 'She may be a district visitor or a Sunday School teacher, in which case she takes her orders from the clergyman. She may arrange the church flowers and see to it that the cleaner does her work and she may give in money or kind to any amount. In return for this, the clergy will be careful not to offend her. They will be polite and, if inclined to vulgarity, they will be obsequious, but if a matter involving the conduct of church affairs comes up, a *man* must be found, even if he be an ignorant boy of eighteen.

'Years ago Charles Kingsley said: "There will never be a good world for women till the Canon Law is civilised off the earth." I strongly resent women being publicly insulted before a mixed congregation as Archdeacon Braithwaite insulted them to-day. I refuse to serve a body which turns the wives of its clergy into unpaid curates, but offers them no prestige in exchange. My task is rather to work for a world in which such exploitation will no longer be possible.'

Thus the idea of forming a Sterndale Women's Suffrage Society – born with the birth of Denis, supported by Gerald Cosway, and encouraged by the monster petition for Mr Faithfull Begg's Woman's Suffrage Bill, which she had signed in company with two hundred and fifty thousand other women in 1897 – was further reinforced by the war and the Archdeacon. It seemed more than a coincidence when she discovered, in turning out Thomas's desk during the spring-cleaning, the pamphlet by Mr Gladstone which Thomas had re-read and underlined on the evening of her confinement. Well, the old statesman's death two years ago had at least removed one of the most implacable enemies of the women's cause, and though so little progress had recently been made, the dawn of a new century seemed an appropriate moment for further effort.

The more Janet thought over the proposition, the more it appealed to her, and good-tempered Miss Garston, the plump, intelligent head mistress of the girls' section at Christ Church elementary school, seemed equally enthusiastic. Janet's promise to Thomas to drop her political work had only involved her secretaryship of the Sterndale Women's Liberal Association; her dislike of domesticity and parish work led him to suppose her equally incompetent in all practical matters, and the idea that she might endeavour to start an organisation on her own simply had not occurred to him. Quietly, using the top room in which Denis had been born as an office, she set to work to form a committee. This task, among the female inhabitants of Sterndale Spa, whom their staunchest apologists could not have described as politically minded, occupied the greater part of that spring and summer. The Second Reading, in May, of the Women's Disabilities Removal Bill turned one or two timid Laodiceans into active supporters, and for the time being the secret stimulus helped to obliterate her sense of grievance against husband and home.

But her reconciliation with her circumstances for the next four years owed even more to the presence in Sterndale that autumn of a new celebrity whose star was just beginning its ascent to the zenith of national recognition.

5

'*October 25th, 1900*. Lecture and Conversazione given by the Sterndale Shakespeare Society at the Free Library. Took the chair at the lecture – my first attempt at public speaking. Ellison Campbell, the Scottish woman dramatist whose play, *The Unconquered*, has just had such a success in London, read a paper on "British Drama To-day and To-morrow." She is staying here for a fortnight with her invalid brother.'

Thus Janet's diary recorded the opening of a phase which was to prove as significant, as absorbing and as deeply tragic as anything that her life had to offer.

In 1900, Gertrude Ellison Campbell was only at the beginning of her extraordinary career. After several years of minor theatrical experiments in the small colliery towns surrounding Glasgow, her first really ambitious drama had been accepted for the London stage. In spite of the fine quality of the play, its producers at the Rendezvous Theatre felt that they were taking a grave risk of complete failure, for the theme, which was based upon a terrible incident that had occurred in Lanarkshire in 1891, was grim and not immediately attractive to a London audience.

'A serious riot took place at Motherwell, near Glasgow,' ran the description on the programme which Janet had saved from her August visit to London, 'in consequence of the attempt of the manager of the Caledonian Railway to evict from their houses tenants who refused to return to work. Only two out of sixty consented, and on the Sheriff-Substitute attempting to carry out the order, the men, reinforced by large numbers of miners from Hamilton, resisted. A squadron of Hussars was sent for to assist the police and to disperse the crowd, which had reached the station-master's house and destroyed the signal boxes. The Riot Act was read and the street cleared, but the evictions were not carried out.'

After a few weeks of uncertainty the theatre-going public, suddenly released from its acute anxiety about South Africa, sought diversion in a variety of other topics, and *The Unconquered*, which described a tragedy of quite another type but exhibited the popular invincibility of the British character, became the play of the hour. At the age of thirty-one Ellison Campbell, the gaunt, reserved, sandy-haired Scotswoman whose life had been darkened by grief and responsibility, found herself besieged for autographs and pursued by reporters from London to Glasgow. Like all who suddenly 'arrive' after years of obscure endeavour, she discovered that success, if more rewarding than failure, is at least as exhausting, and welcomed with relief the decision of her paralysed and embittered brother to visit Sterndale and take the waters for his chronic neuritis. Provincial health resorts, as she knew from the many to which she had conducted Charles in his vain search for release from suffering, were not places whose inhabitants made a practice of reading plays or studying dramatic criticism.

She reckoned too soon upon a complete respite from interruption. It had, in fact, been Janet who had come to the rescue of the Shakespeare Society by discovering Ellison Campbell's name in the list of visitors published weekly by the *Sterndale Chronicle*.

In support of the well-established fact that the few members of a small community who do anything at all outside their homes usually do everything available, Thomas and Janet both belonged to the Shakespeare Society. In Thomas's view a literary organisation was not in the same category as theatres or politics; a smattering of Shakespeare might even be regarded as part of the duty of a good wife and mother.

'I tell you, I saw *The Unconquered* and it was magnificent,'

insisted Janet, who found the harassed secretary very ready to
listen to suggestions after three unsuccessful attempts to get
their annual outside speaker from Manchester. 'If only we can
persuade Miss Campbell to give us a talk, it ought to be worth
hearing.'

Reluctant to accept the invitation, but too new to fame to be
willing to offend, Miss Campbell replied that she was not used
to public speaking, but did not mind reading a paper, and the
Shakespeare Society rewarded Janet's initiative by asking her to
take the chair. For at least an hour after putting Denis to bed
the previous evening, she rehearsed the 'improvised' speech of
introduction and welcome which she was to make before the
celebrity, but when the time came her nervousness vanished.
As she listened to the slow deep voice with the strong Scottish
accent defining the trends of British drama, she realised that the
large loose-limbed woman whose bony hand shook as it held the
paper was at least as much alarmed by the audience as herself. It
was perhaps this sense of an emotion shared, perhaps the friendly
atmosphere of the Reference Library books which surrounded
them, that made her turn so impulsively to Miss Campbell after
she had declared the meeting closed.

'Must you go back to your hotel at once, or would you care
to come home with me and have a cup of coffee? The Vicarage
is only at the top of the hill.'

What a merciful intervention it was on the part of Providence
that Thomas should have been away for the night attending
the Diocesan Conference in Cheddlefield! Had he been present
she could never have plunged so swiftly into that intimate talk
with Ellison Campbell which led to the amazing, unbelievable friendship that within a week had changed the world for
both of them. He would have been quite unimpressed by Miss
Campbell's reputation – if, indeed, he had ever become aware
that she possessed one – and would as usual have dominated the
conversation with his informative dissertations on the Synoptic
Gospels or the Homeric scholarship of Mr Gladstone.

At first she could hardly credit her good fortune in persuading
Ellison Campbell to come to the Vicarage. Except for her secretarial relation to the distinguished Liberals who had spoken

at the Sterndale Conference, and her perfunctory rôle of hostess
to visiting clerics of moderate eminence who inspired her with
neither awe nor interest, it was her first intimate contact with the
owner of a 'name.' But Miss Campbell, who seemed nervously
exhausted after reading her paper, betrayed no consciousness of
conferring any favour by her visit.

'Do take off your hat and be comfortable,' urged Janet. 'I
won't be long getting the coffee.'

Ellison Campbell obeyed, pushing back the limp strands of
sandy hair from a high, round forehead that throbbed a little.
For some reason inexplicable to herself, she felt more honoured
in this bare untidy room with its shabby furniture than in the
wealthy houses now beginning to welcome her in London and
Glasgow, more appreciated by this young wife of a provincial
clergyman than by the celebrated actors, managers, and playwrights amongst whom she had lately moved. This seemed the
more extraordinary because, in spite of her English mother's
south-country tradition, respect for the Established Church was
not characteristic of her family. Her father, Kenneth Campbell,
had been a pioneer of the Rationalist movement in Scotland,
and an early supporter of the agitation which resulted in the
establishment of the Rationalist Press.

The leaping fire had already begun to warm and soothe her
when Janet returned, carrying a tray of coffee and sandwiches
prepared and flung together with an untidy enthusiasm which
Ellison Campbell found human and endearing.

'You know,' exclaimed Janet, her eyes very blue and her
cheeks flushed. 'This is a real red-letter day for me! I've never
had anyone famous in my house before!'

'I'm afraid I'm not exactly famous,' protested Miss Campbell.
'I mean to be one day, but I haven't arrived there yet. One
successful London play doesn't make fame.'

'Do tell me how you first began!' cried Janet eagerly. 'Did you
always mean to write plays?'

Her hands trembled with unwonted excitement as she poured
out the coffee.

'No. Oddly enough I nearly became a lecturer at Oxford. But
it's a long story – and rather a sad one, I'm afraid.'

'Is it too sad to tell me about?' asked Janet. She leaned forward, her brilliant eyes alight, her glowing face cupped in her slim hands. 'Miss Campbell, you don't know how much I want to hear! You can't think what it means to me to have you in this house! You see, I'm no good at all as a clergyman's wife. I hate the parish work and domestic things, and I'm afraid I don't even care for my little boy as I should. I was very young and terribly ignorant when I was married, and he came before I'd even thought whether I wanted children . . .'

She paused, a little breathless, surprised at her own outburst, but Ellison Campbell's look of interested attention encouraged her to go on.

'What I really love are politics and books and plays. But I had to give up the best bit of political work I ever had because of Denis, my son, being so delicate, and I never get a chance to see any plays except for one fortnight in the year when I go up to London, and my husband doesn't even approve of that. Having you here is like a breath from the world I've always wanted to belong to. How did you first get into it – do tell me! Have you always lived in Glasgow?'

'No, not in Glasgow itself,' replied Ellison Campbell, more moved than she could have explained by this ardour of confidence, this interest in a personality which she often felt that her life's tragedy had rendered harsh and repellent. 'We live in Motherwell, a district near by, right in the midst of the Lanarkshire collieries. My father was a mining engineer from the Highlands; he and my brother were attached to the Keir Company's Coal Pits. It's a grey and barren part of Scotland, and I don't think my mother, Mary Ellison, ever really got used to it. She came from a family of Dorsetshire landowners and always hoped we'd go south when my father retired. But as things turned out he never did . . . We still live in the same house, my brother and I, but we're alone now. I'd like to leave – it has too many memories for me – but all Charles's friends are in the district, and I have to stay for his sake.'

It was a square, isolated house, she told Janet, with a four-sided slate roof and a yellow-grey stone front. Behind it an unproductive half-acre of smoke-blackened garden sloped uphill to a thin copse of grimy birch-trees, standing above a deep, narrow glen. Through the glen ran a muddy stream which ended in a small mill dam, though the mill itself had been swept away by nineteenth-century progress.

Janet's mind, as she listened, formed a clear picture of the atrocities perpetrated by 'progress' upon the Scottish landscape which to her London-born experience seemed almost a foreign country. She could see the cluster of small industrial towns – Bailleston, Coatbridge, Motherwell, Hamilton, Blantyre, Cambuslang, Rutherglen – verging upon Glasgow but separated from it and from each other by blighted fields of coarsened, tufty grass. Pit-head gear, chimneys, and the huge banks of refuse known as coal bings, towered starkly against a dun rainy sky. In the little bleak towns – at a distance almost invisible owing to the smoke from collieries and iron works – the squalid miners' rows, oblong and low with each roof a few inches higher than its neighbour, stood back to back against a melancholy stretch of dirty unpaved street.

Ellison Campbell's deep, musical voice vibrated with pity as she described the inhabitants of these wretched hovels. To the end of her life, though their problems and conflicts figured so largely in her plays, she never regarded the miners for whom her family had suffered so deeply as other than objects of profound commiseration. Her very pity for them divided her from close contact with their personal lives, for she could not imagine them as emerging for a moment from an acute consciousness of their poverty and discomfort in the grim surroundings about which her earliest recollections centred.

'The first thing I remember,' she said, 'is seeing chimneys against the horizon and the Keir Pits' winding engines across two sloping fields. Almost the next is sitting on an old iron bridge with stone arches, trying to compose a dialogue between my dolls. It's quite near our house, over the upper reaches of the Clyde on the way to Hamilton. Sometimes I still sit on that bridge when I'm working out my plays.'

'When did you actually begin to write them?' asked Janet, as she dropped on her knees and stirred the sinking fire. Neither of them noticed the onward racing of the clock, for Thomas would not return until the morning, and Ellison Campbell had helped her brother to bed as usual before starting out for the Conversazione.

'I wrote quite a number when I was still going to the Park School in Glasgow,' she replied. 'The girls used to act them on Saturday evenings, but no one took them seriously in those days. What they did take seriously was my class work, and my father decided to send me to a university. We've never been frightened of Higher Education in Scotland,' she added, seeing Janet's look of envious surprise, 'and I suppose he calculated my brains were likely to be more of an asset than my looks!'

Her grey-green eyes, light and curiously penetrating, smiled ruefully at Janet, and a sigh followed the recollection of adolescent gawkiness. ('Why am I talking to her like this, when I've never told anyone my story for nearly ten years? Even the reporters didn't get more than the barest outline. Why do I want her to know all about me? She's interested, but even if she weren't I should have to go on telling her. Now I've begun, I can't stop myself . . .')

'As I'd been to a Scottish school,' she continued, 'my mother wanted me to go to an English university, so my father sent me to Oxford. He'd always taken an interest in the new women's colleges at Oxford and Cambridge. I went up in 1888, when my college, Drayton, was only ten years old. A real nineteenth century bluestocking, you see! I read English and loved it, because they let me specialise on the Elizabethan dramatists. I've never felt so happy as when they told me I was sure to get a First, and offered me an English lectureship at Drayton. But then, after all, I never finished.'

'You never finished!' echoed Janet. 'Oh, but why?'

Ellison Campbell turned a little away from her, staring into the fire. But it only showed her ashes . . . the wreck of a home . . . the crumbling away of young, confident hopes.

'It was about half-way through my last term – there was a dreadful accident in the mine. One evening my father was sitting smoking with Charles – he's two years older than I am, and he'd just been taken on as assistant engineer – when word came they were wanted at the pit. They hurried down there, and the foreman said he didn't like the look of South 17. South 17 was a roadway leading to the coal face, where the men were working on the seam; it was about four feet high and propped all the way for some thirty yards. My father and Charles went along the roadway and found the props beginning to bend, so they hurried through to the coal face and told the men to get out . . .'

Her voice failed for a moment. Janet, her hands clasped tightly in her lap, sat motionless as a statue until she went on.

'The men crawled out in single file, and as they went the props were cracking and bending inwards – like melting candles, Charles told me afterwards. He and my father were the last to leave; they were responsible, you see, for the safety of the men and the mine. Just before they got out, the roof crashed down. My father was completely buried and they didn't recover his body for days, but Charles and one of the men in front of him were trapped face foremost. The man died, but they managed to get Charles out after about ten hours. A prop with all its weight of coal and earth had fallen on his legs and the lower half of his spine, and he's been partly paralysed ever since.'

There was silence for a moment as the fire blazed up suddenly. Its flickering shadows danced across their faces while Ellison Campbell concluded.

'I shall never forget that journey home from Oxford and the next few weeks . . . Just when I should have been doing my Finals, my mother was dying from the shock of the accident. Before she died she asked me to promise that I'd always look after Charles, and of course I said I would. It hasn't been easy . . . he was very energetic and ambitious and being an invalid drove him nearly mad. At first, with my parents gone and all hope of the Drayton lectureship given up, I felt as though my life had ended . . . especially when one of my Oxford tutors was appointed to a professorship in South Africa, and asked me to go out there as his wife. I couldn't, of course. It would have meant leaving Charles, and he was too ill to be taken abroad even if he'd been willing to leave Glasgow. I often used to wish we'd been poor, so that I'd *had* to take the Oxford post or – marry, but my parents left us enough to live on.'

Janet's feelings suddenly boiled up into irrepressible speech.

'But to give up all that – your work at Oxford, your chance of marriage – even for a brother so tragically injured – surely it wasn't *right*, Miss Campbell? I mean, nobody would have expected it of you if you'd been a man, and your brother would have been cared for in some other way.'

Ellison Campbell looked keenly at her, puzzled and astonished. Never before had anyone, least of all herself, questioned that it was her obvious duty to abandon everything she valued and dedicate her life to Charles.

'But then I *wasn't* a man,' she said. 'I'd promised my mother to look after him. There was no alternative.'

'Oh, but there must be alternatives for women!' cried Janet passionately. 'There must and shall be! It was fine and noble of you to sacrifice yourself like that, but all the same I don't think someone who's dying ought to bind up other people's futures by promises – especially such a future as yours. It's such a waste of ability when there's so little of that in the world as it is.'

Ellison Campbell was silent for a moment, endeavouring to find some point of contact between Janet's interpretation of duty and her own. But the effort of adjustment was too great.

'I suppose,' she commented at last, 'you're what they call the New Woman – like one or two of my friends at Oxford. I'm afraid I'm not "new" at all. I believe in education, as we all do in Scotland, but I did think my family ought to come before anything else. Of course, if ever I were *really* to succeed as a dramatist . . .' She paused, unable for the moment to contend with the implications of that looming possibility. It seemed simpler to describe the beginnings of her recent ascent to fame.

'For a long time,' she said, 'the shock of that summer took away all my ambition. In any case it was weeks before Charles was out of danger. But gradually, as I came back to life, I found I couldn't give up my work on the drama altogether. Since there was no possibility of lecturing on it, I started to write. I began by doing studies of Kyd and Ben Jonson for the Oxford University Press – their "Famous Playwrights" Series – and then I tried my hand at plays of my own. The miners' organisations acted

some of them on Saturday evenings, and the Glasgow Literary
Society did one or two. But nothing really happened till Bunty
Tolmie came to Glasgow on tour about two years ago in *The
Little Minister*. She's a native of Forfar and knows Barrie quite
well. If you've seen *The Unconquered* you'll remember her.'

Janet nodded. 'I did see it, last summer. I thought she was just
right for the part of Jeannie Maclean.'

'Well, she thought so herself as soon as I'd taken my courage
in both hands and persuaded her to read the play. Everything
seemed to happen very quickly after that. I had to get a nurse
for Charles and come to London for several weeks – and very
strange I felt among the theatre people, with their stage talk and
fine clothes. I found they'd all imagined I was a man, because
I'd taken my second name – my mother's – instead of just
calling myself Gertrude Campbell. It doesn't matter now I'm
beginning to get on, but it's hard to get a start in the theatre
world if you're known to be a woman. It's bad enough being
a playwright, but I doubt if there'll ever be women managers in
the West End theatres.'

She looked at the clock and stood up suddenly.

'Why, it's nearly midnight! I've kept you out of bed all this
time and I'm sure you have to get up early.'

As Janet, too, rose from her chair, she turned to her anxiously,
a little diffident, but impelled by an irresistible desire to have
more of this unwonted companionship, this genuine, whole-
hearted admiration.

'Now that we've met like this, we'll see each other again, won't
we? You'll come and have dinner with me at my hotel?'

'Oh, may I really go on knowing you!' cried Janet, clasping her
hands eagerly and gazing at Ellison Campbell with an ingenuous
ardour which brought a strange warmth into the heart of that
dour, reticent woman.

Something trembled in the air between them, as though an
unspecified yearning in the heart of each had met and kindled
into flame. Ellison Campbell, for whom Janet's spontaneous
interest was a new fountain of life, perceived, not the clergyman's
neglectful young wife, discussed and criticised by the parish for
her strong unorthodox views and her inattention to household

duties, but an ambitious, intelligent girl full of sensitive vitality and generous appreciation. Janet, in her turn, did not see the tall green-eyed Scotchwoman with the big bony frame and lank hair the colour of wet sand, whose unfashionable attire had discredited, for the more elegant members of the Shakespeare Society, her estimate of Mr James Barrie as superior to Mr Arthur Pinero, but a genius who went to the theatre, not as a mere enthusiastic playgoer, but as mistress of its arts and controller of its destinies.

If anyone had told her that for Ellison Campbell rehearsals were unmitigated purgatory and that she was terrified to rigidity of stage-managers, Janet would simply have refused to believe it. She had no idea that her visitor was only induced by spartan courage and frustrated ambition to face the actors and actresses whose confident elegance filled her with an annihilating sense of awkward ungainliness, and made her even more conscious than usual of her large feet and big nervous hands. For her Miss Campbell, who was actually arranging to meet her again the day after tomorrow, had already become superb, incomparable, the heaven-ordained embodiment of British drama. And, as it happened, her vehement admiration was better justified than many such youthful extravagances, for the ultimate verdict of English literature on Gertrude Ellison Campbell was not to be so very dissimilar from Janet's estimate of her that October evening.

6

When Janet told Thomas about her visitor, he was frankly incredulous.

'What!' he exclaimed, 'That raw-boned Scotswoman who goes about with the chap in the bath-chair – written a play! Fine sort of play it must be!'

All the same, his disapproval of Janet's passion for theatre-going was modified, in the course of time, by Ellison Campbell's very disadvantages. In spite of his complaints about 'worldly escapades,' it was impossible to regard anyone so plainly, sensibly Scottish as the gateway to frivolity or the road to an

immoral life. He found it, indeed, so difficult to credit Miss
Campbell's attraction for Janet, that more than once he suspected his wife of using her friend in order to conceal less
innocent reasons for her increasingly frequent visits to London.

'I returned home last Monday,' Janet's diary recorded, 'to find
Thomas ill in bed and most unhappy about *me* – he imagined
he knew not what! He declared that before our marriage I had
taken two most solemn vows, of loyalty to Christ and loyalty
to himself; and since through my irresponsible actions, I had
repeatedly committed adultery and blasphemy against Christ,
how could he believe, in view of my desire to leave home so
often, that I had not been equally false to him? The greater
part of that night he tried to impress on me that *he* was a
most loyal servant of Christ, but I was going the way to ruin
him and myself.

'I acknowledge that there is some truth in what he says. I
ought perhaps not to have gone up to London with our finances
as they are and Denis only just recovering from influenza, but
his suspicions of my disloyalty are beneath contempt. Gertrude's
friendship, her brilliant intellect, the world of literature and the
theatre which knowing her has opened before me, are all I want
to make me happy, and far, far more than I deserve. Thomas
has never realised what Gertrude means to me. He has NO
real friends of his own, and does not understand what a great
friendship can be.'

From the first it had been surprisingly easy to tell Gertrude
– as almost at once Janet began to call her – those doubts and
difficulties which she was never able to explain to Thomas in
spite of his reiterated injunctions to let him know what she
was thinking. She could talk, for instance, about her feeling
of mingled antipathy and remorse towards Denis, and her
disappointment that he had been a boy. They spoke of it on
the day that she had dinner with Gertrude at the Pavilion Hotel
and met her brother, the crippled fair-haired man with the sallow
face and restless eyes, who appeared – quite excusably, of course
– to resent her presence. Because of him, Gertrude explained as
they walked beneath the falling autumn leaves in Ashwood Park
while he rested until tea-time, she could never have friends to

stay with her in Scotland. But she would try to persuade him to come to Sterndale again next year – or perhaps she and Janet could meet in London.

'It would have been easier for you if you'd had an invalid sister, instead of a brother,' commented Janet. 'Sometimes it seems as if men were put into the world simply to get in women's way and prevent them from doing what they want. If only Denis had been a girl, I should have felt quite different about him. I'd love to have had a daughter to do the work I never get the chance of, and perhaps become a great power in politics. Just think of being the mother of a Florence Nightingale or a Josephine Butler! I know exactly what kind of a daughter I'd want – educated and intelligent, with a disciplined, logical mind like yours, and the courage to put her ideals into practice in public life. Free womanhood ought to be such a *grand* thing – especially if we do get some of the chances we're asking for.'

She paused, forgetting even Gertrude in her absorbing speculations on woman's future position. The gusty October wind whirled the dry yellow leaves round their feet.

'Thomas is always dropping hints about increasing our family,' Janet continued, 'but the fear of having another boy is just too terrible. I simply can't face it. Denis has never really seemed mine. He's always been Thomas's child – in appearance and everything else.'

How strange, thought Ellison Campbell, that she can't see that Denis is growing up in her own image? What makes her think that he's like his self-important little father when the two of them haven't a feature in common? Shy as children usually made her, she had already taken a liking to the pale, fair-haired boy with the long thin legs who smiled at her so confidently out of Janet's wide blue eyes.

'The real trouble is,' pursued Janet more vehemently, 'I'm the wrong sort of person to be Thomas's wife or Denis's mother. I'm all wrong for the life I have to lead, and it's too late to change. I can't take anything for granted. I go about my daily work puzzling my brain over something or other, and then when Thomas or Denis make some demand on me I get irritable. Over and over again I'm accused of being in a bad temper when really

I'm worried to death over some question of religion or politics.
Thomas says: "Have Faith! Pray!" but he might as well tell me
to fly. I just *can't* believe in anything that my reason won't
accept.'

'I don't see why you should try,' said Gertrude. 'Surely
the greatest triumph of the nineteenth century has been its
establishment of the ascendency of reason over blind faith and
superstition?'

How I love her! thought Janet. She's everything I've always
wanted to find in a person!

'I know,' she answered aloud. 'That's just what my dear father
used to say. But if I accept that view, my work in the parish
becomes impossible. It's difficult enough as it is. On the one
hand I see all the coarseness of thought and indifference to
religion of these people here; on the other I'm almost daily at
a religious service where they call themselves miserable sinners
but wouldn't dream of changing their lives in the smallest degree.
What *is* the relation between the two, Gertrude – between human
sin and ignorance, and the teaching of Christ which the Church
professes but never follows?'

Ellison Campbell stood still for a moment, gazing blankly at
the ornamental beds of pink and purple asters in front of the
Pavilion.

'I don't know any better than you do,' she said at last. 'In
a way it's the problem I'm trying to solve in my own work.
My plays always seem to be about conflicts between groups
of people who each have good intentions, only the intentions
are somehow incompatible.'

It had been a splendid talk – the best, Janet thought afterwards,
that she'd had with anyone since her father died. Even Gerald
Cosway, with his quick intelligence and political knowledge,
couldn't be put into the same category as Gertrude.

'It is strange,' her diary recorded that evening, 'to be talking
to someone on the deepest subjects of life. I have never done it
with anyone but Papa before. I have a curious feeling of a long
fight and a final victory over myself in having allowed another
person to know something of my inner life and beliefs.'

For the next four years, her friendship with Ellison Campbell occupied a great deal of Janet's time and dominated her waking thoughts. Although Gertrude only came once more to Sterndale – Charles had decided, she said regretfully, that he preferred Pitlochry – she invited Janet to join her once or twice a year at Tindall's in Piccadilly. Promoting herself from the modest obscurity of a Bayswater boarding-house, Gertrude now stayed there whenever she was interviewing managers or supervising rehearsals. Janet soon came to share her affection for the old-fashioned but comfortable little hotel, so much patronised by writers and artists because of the view from its great bow-windows looking south-west over St James's Park. During the period of mourning for the Queen and the postponement of the sick King's coronation just after peace had been signed with South Africa, Janet's beloved London had seemed a staid and quiet city. But once the new reign began in earnest, a sense of release from elderly formalities entered into the world of diners, dancers and playgoers, and the theatre itself scintillated with life.

Soon it became impossible even for Gertrude to deny her growing reputation, for during that period she had three new plays on the London stage. She had struck, said the critics, a new and very modern note in basing her dramas upon the conflicts and problems of Scottish national life. It was surprising – and even, some of them suggested, a little disquieting – to find such themes selected by a lady.

The third play, *Highland Saturday*, did so well after its opening at the Connoisseurs' Theatre in December, 1903, that the following spring Drayton College gave a dinner at Oxford in Gertrude's honour. When she returned to London, she told Janet that she had put aside part of her remarkable earnings to found an annual prize at Drayton for the best work done by a Second-Year student in English or History taken alternately. She would have liked, she said, to limit her gift to the English School in which she had learnt so much from Elizabethan drama, but the Principal persuaded her to include History because the subject was poorly endowed.

To Janet, too, Gertrude gave a present, of a gold chain bangle studded with turquoises and fastening with a padlock shaped as a heart. She also took her to see many of the important plays put on, besides her own, during those vivid and prosperous years – Mr Stephen Phillip's *Paolo and Francesca*, in which George Alexander and Henry Ainley were acting with Evelyn Millard and Elizabeth Robins at the St James's Theatre; Mr J. M. Barrie's *Admirable Crichton*; and the famous *Marriage of Kitty*, that French farce which provided such an appropriate part for the celebrated comedienne, Miss Marie Tempest.

'I do wish we could see something by that extraordinary writer, Mr George Bernard Shaw,' Janet said to Gertrude in the autumn of 1902, but Gertrude assured her that the spectacular red-bearded Irishman, though impressive and original as a critic, was the kind of dramatist whose plays, unfortunately, were read but not seen. She even showed her a recent notice by an official critic which endorsed this opinion: 'Among playwrights who scarcely expect to see their works produced on the stage, Mr Bernard Shaw occupies a foremost place.'

Janet noticed with satisfaction how quickly Gertrude's Scottish dourness was melting in the warm sunshine of public appreciation. She no longer assumed that all theatre people regarded her as a clumsy female monstrosity whose wishes need not be considered. She became more courageous with dictatorial stage-managers, those little-great men who still intimidated her with their tendency to thwart her dramatic intentions. It gave Janet a good deal of secret pleasure to reflect – as Gertrude, indeed, so constantly affirmed – that her friendship was partly responsible for the change. No wonder Gertrude had become so self-contained and dispirited after ten years with only the saturnine Charles for an intimate companion! One couldn't blame Charles, of course; it was very sad for him to look on at Gertrude's success when he was incapable of doing the only work in which he excelled. All the same, he needn't have been quite so bitterly anxious to humiliate her in other ways. He might have refrained from making acid comparisons between herself and the wives of his Glasgow acquaintances when he was himself responsible, whether he realised it or not, for Gertrude's self-sacrificing spinsterhood. Not that, in spite of his comments, she regretted it now, Gertrude told Janet. Marriage and children would have been incompatible with her art, and if ever they were offered her again she would forgo them.

How much Janet wished that she had had the strength of mind to do the same! But then she was such a child when she married Thomas; she had not known as she knew now what she wanted to do with her life. Her new preoccupations, however, caused even Thomas and Denis to exasperate her less. Never had she dreamed that one friend, one confidant, could make all the difference between joy and misery. But Gertrude, of course, was not just an ordinary friend, but a genius who took her into that theatrical world which had always spelt romance and enchantment. She would have found it intolerable to return to Sterndale from the atmosphere of rehearsals, the revelation of back-stage mysteries, the introductions to famous players in whose presence she and Gertrude were rivals for awkwardness, had it not been for their correspondence and the slowly growing Suffrage Society.

She did not often write of this to Gertrude, who took little interest in women's politics and thought the achievements of individual women more likely to further their cause than the vote. But there was no lack of topics for letters when she had finished her housekeeping, and distributed the parish magazine, and given Denis his lessons in Reading and French and History. In spite of his aptness and docility – he was absorbed in Dickens and Charles Kingsley before he was nine – she found these lessons tedious, but to Denis she seemed more patient than Thomas, who took him for Latin and Arithmetic and Scripture.

'Thanks to you,' she wrote to Gertrude, 'I believe I'm actually beginning to acquire a sense of proportion and to get some true idea of my place in the scheme of things! The text the first decade of the Twentieth Century seems to have taken for itself is "Behold, I make all things new" – the New Woman, New Realism, New Theology, New Politics; even these new non-stop trains and this new science of wireless telegraphy! With a new God and a new Woman we ought to be able to do something striking. Perhaps after a few years of what Sarah Grand calls "the spanking process," we may even be able to produce a "New Man." It is good to be still quite young – still on the threshold of life so wonderful, so inspiring, so full of possibilities lying before me!'

And it was just then, in the midst of this newly-found happiness, that she discovered herself to be again pregnant, condemned once more to Sterndale and domesticity by the coming of another child.

7

Early in October, 1904, Ellison Campbell received from Janet a letter which considerably embarrassed her.

'For the last week,' it ran, 'I have had reason to believe that I am again confronted with the prospect of motherhood. I am terribly upset about it. For several days I resisted the temptation to take medicines to stop it but at last I gave in, and for the past two days have been doing everything I could think of to prevent it going further. I have done this deliberately, knowing it to be a sin. I am acting on the assumption that I have a child, and I am doing my best to destroy its life.

'Again and again, before Communion, I have tried to please Thomas by promising to surrender myself to Christ. Must I perhaps say that God has taken me at my word, that He is proving me by giving me work to do for Him which demands the greatest sacrifice of all my desires? Is He calling me away from the things which, He sees, absorb me, to quietness with Him and the mysteries of life and death?

'I suppose it would be good for me – would it? – but I rebel. I *cannot* say yet, "Not my will but Thine." I want my active life, my suffrage work, my lovely times in London with you, my solitary cycle-rides of thinking and planning. So I am dosing myself recklessly and will not speak to Thomas.'

Three weeks later, she added a note to the similar record in her diary.

'I am all right again so far as I can tell, but whether it is because of the means I have taken I do not know. However, my deliberate purpose from the time I gave way to the temptation was to destroy pregnancy, and only God knows whether I committed that crime in act as well as intention. I *cannot* obey God by having another child. My whole inclination revolts against the idea.'

It was immediately after this entry, on All Saints' Eve, that Thomas again discovered and read her diary. For some time now he had known of the Suffrage Society, and considered himself entirely justified in periodically going through the papers on her desk in order to discover how far it was diverting her attention from the parish. Believing it to be somehow responsible for the now exceptional 'moodiness' of the past few weeks, he went up to the top room to investigate. The diary lay open beneath a pile of papers and the word 'pregnancy' inevitably caught his eye.

Ten minutes later, as she was laboriously cutting out a blouse on the dining-room table, the full fury of his rage and horror surged over her like a volcanic eruption. Laying down her scissors, she walked to the window and stood with her back to him. She stared at Lower Sterndale drowsing in the afternoon sunshine while the phrases 'mortal sin,' 'scandalous hypocrisy,' 'the wrath of God,' exploded like bombs in the waiting silence of the room.

'You dare, you actually dare,' he concluded, 'to refuse, in the face of God's obvious intention for you, to give a brother or sister to poor Denis, who's been alone for ten years through your wicked selfishness!'

'I never wanted Denis,' she answered stonily. 'You know that. He was your doing, not mine. You took advantage of my ignorance. I wasn't ready for children, and I didn't understand properly how they came. I'd never have had him if I'd known.'

But Thomas, absorbed in the new sin to the exclusion of the old, had not been listening.

'I challenge you,' he said, 'to tell me truthfully, before God, whether you have or have not taken means to prevent the birth of another child?'

'It's unnecessary for me to tell you. Next time there's something I want you to read, I'll write it here in my *private* diary.'

'Upon my word!' shouted Thomas, 'this diary was left lying open on your desk, right under the nose of anyone who happened to be up there! The servants might have seen it, for all you cared

– and since I unqualifiedly condemned what you'd been doing,
I read it to find out how long this sort of thing had been going
on. Whenever you don't want me to see things, you know you
always *lock them up*!'

Slowly she turned at last and faced him, with his swollen,
angry face and the veins standing out like knotted cords on his
damp forehead.

'I suppose,' she said, through stiff, half-closed lips, 'you'll
never understand how much *you're* responsible for my wrong-
doing! Not once, to myself or anyone else, have I excused my
sins by blaming you. But I do say now it's your bad temper, your
excitability, the disgraceful shouting and scenes you make, that
have turned me into the unhappy irritable woman I sometimes
am! Not that anything in the world'll convince you of that. Your
self-righteousness is far too satisfactory and complete!'

'*I* suppose,' he commented furiously, 'it's my *self-righteousness*
that objects to your taking the Sacrament with a lie on your
lips and your sin still unrenounced! Very well. I propose to be
self-righteous again for the sake of your false and unhappy soul.
I forbid you to go to Holy Communion until you have amended
your ways before God.'

'And that means . . . what?'

'I shall give my consent only after you have repented of this
terrible sin of extinguishing the nascent life, and have proved it
by bringing a child into the world.'

'I see,' she said, shuddering, for the memory of the past three
weeks was still intolerably vivid. 'It doesn't seem wrong to you
for a woman to bear a child she neither wants before it comes
nor cares for when she has it?'

'It's a married woman's first duty to God and her husband
to bear him children,' reiterated Thomas. 'Only an immoral,
unnatural woman would shirk this sacred duty! How you dare
sing the Magnificat as you do, Sunday after Sunday, with the
burden of this mighty wrong on your soul, I simply don't
know!'

He pressed his hands to his aching brow, then dropped his
head into them with a sense of utter defeat. Never, never
had he dreamed that such scandalising wickedness could occur

in his own household! Janet, suddenly afraid of him with a dim foreboding that she had never experienced even in their tempestuous relationship, slipped quietly through the door and escaped upstairs.

'Can it be possible that Thomas is right?' she meditated desperately, pacing up and down her room. 'Does God really approve of our having children when we don't want them? Am I to blame, or is God, for bringing me into the world with so little maternal instinct? Has He no work for me to do besides this work of bearing and rearing children for which I'm so unfitted? Oh, God, if you do exist, I ask you to help me and give me an answer! Would it really be for my soul's health to have another child? I want to do what is right for *me* – but honestly, my God, and truthfully, I don't know how!'

Late that night, Thomas came upstairs to their bedroom long after Janet had retired. The window stood wide open with the curtains drawn back – a habit to which he always objected – and he closed it abruptly without seeing the black silhouette of the sleeping town or the red half-circle of the waning moon, set like a sinister jewel in the velvet blue of the sky above Ploughman's Ridge. Janet did not move but he was conscious of her eyes, wide open and miserable, fixed upon him as he drew the curtains and turned towards the large double bed.

'For two hours,' he began ponderously, 'I have prayed that God may forgive my unhappy wife the terrible sin of which she has been guilty. God is merciful; I have interceded with Him on your behalf, and I believe that He will pardon your offences if you give Him assurance of your true repentance and desire to make amends. I will consent to your going to Communion again only if you make, here and now, a confession of your wrong-doing with me before Almighty God.'

Janet, trembling, sat up in bed and covered her face with her hands.

'You leave me no choice,' she whispered brokenly. 'You make religion impossible for me unless I convict myself of sin. Very well, I'll try to feel as you feel. I'll obey you blindly and make my confession, hoping it'll help me in ways I don't understand.'

'Then kneel down beside your bed,' commanded Thomas, 'and
repeat these words after me.'

He looked with virtuous satisfaction at Janet's bowed head,
at the soft curves of her figure which shuddered with cold
and emotion beneath the decorous folds of her white flannel nightgown with its high buttoned neck and long frilled
sleeves. Nothing would have aroused his righteous indignation
more fiercely than the suggestion that his histrionic temperament enjoyed the drama of that moment as keenly as his
senses appreciated the dejected but seductive outline of his
wife's body.

'I confess before God the Father, God the Son, and God the
Holy Ghost, and before the whole company of Heaven, that I
have sinned exceedingly in thought and deed by my fault, by
my own most grievous fault. I have knowingly and deliberately
committed a sin which was not only a crime but an act of
rebellion against God. I frustrated God's purpose for me, I
murdered my unborn child, I refused my duty to my husband,
I polluted my own body – and this after promising loyalty to
Christ and solemnly surrendering my life to His will at His Holy
Table. I wanted to serve Him in my own selfish way and not in
the way of His righteousness, and when He gave me the noble
work for which I had no inclination and which meant giving
up my worldly pleasures, I rebelled and committed this evil,
knowing full well what I did. For this and the many other sins
of which I have been guilty I am heartily sorry, I earnestly repent
and promise to make amends, and I ask God to pity and pardon
me. Amen.'

As she uttered the concluding words after him, the church
clock began to strike twelve. When its last echo had died away,
Thomas continued.

'You will now repeat after me two verses of Hymn Number
265 – "Not as I will, but as Thou wilt"—

> *"Thy way not mine, O Lord,*
> *However dark it be,*
> *Lead me by Thine own hand,*
> *Choose out the path for me.*

> *"Not mine, not mine, the choice*
> *In things or great or small.*
> *Be Thou my Guide, my Strength,*
> *My Wisdom and my All."'*

For a few moments there was dead silence, and then Thomas spoke again.

'Now you shall prove to me that you meant what you said in your confession. Get back into bed . . . Now make the sign of the cross upon your body and say: "Behold the handmaid of the Lord. Be it unto me according to Thy will."'

A sob of rebellious misery half choked her as she obeyed him. But when she had fulfilled his instructions she lay still and passive, shivering a little as he came towards her.

8

Janet recovered very slowly from the late miscarriage which turned the spring of 1905 into a nightmare memory. She had already suspected that she was again pregnant when, six weeks after the hideous scene with Thomas, Canon Maybury preached at her with such forcible indirectness during his annual sermon to the Mothers' Union.

'I know there are women in this church,' he announced, 'who refuse to have children or will have only one, who look upon children as a trial and a burden. Such women are defying God; they are turning married love into evil lust.'

After the service, when the Sterndale mothers had dispersed and the Canon was leaving the church, Janet went up to him.

'I think, Canon Maybury, you were referring to me just now. If so, you must regard my attending church as hypocrisy and profanity.'

The Canon looked hastily up and down the steep hill, but the road was empty. It seemed easier to fulfil in a sermon Rutherston's repeated requests to him to remonstrate with his erring wife, than in a public street face to face with the offender.

'I did mean what I said, Mrs Rutherston – for you and for

others,' he replied. 'I know how terribly prevalent this sin of refusing motherhood is to-day. You must remember that, as a married woman, motherhood is your vocation and a very high one. It is your Christian duty to your husband and your God. You make your husband's life very hard, when it might be so happy. Just simply and quietly give yourself up to him.'

'I know you and my husband both think me a wicked woman,' said Janet. 'But then I, too, have my ideas about what wickedness is, and I can't believe motherhood right for anybody who doesn't want it. Having a child forced on one without one's consent – *that* seems to me as much lust as anything else.'

Canon Maybury's colourless, emaciated face hardened with displeasure.

'You are speaking very improperly, Mrs Rutherston. I cannot discuss the matter further with you while you are in this unhappy frame of mind.'

Well, it had been evident that men had no mercy on women, and the holier they professed to be, the less mercy they had. Like St Paul, and some of the Early Fathers, with their closed, cruel minds. All the more reason for women to get the vote and fight for themselves . . .

At least she could be thankful that Thomas had been with her that February afternoon when the garden steps gave way, and knew as well as she did that her fall was accidental. Never would she have heard the end of a second attempt to terminate pregnancy . . . if, indeed, she was ever to hear the end of the first. At any rate, that spring's experience had been final. No more children for her – and no more miscarriages or abortions either. There were better ways than that of avoiding the obligations one detested, and if one was careful they need not fail.

During those months of physical distress, those alternating moods of resignation and rebellion, the idea of leaving Thomas had continually returned. To the periodic hatred and contempt which his rages had always inspired in her was added a new fear of his increasing violence. Did the wrathful and intolerant God with whose alleged wishes Thomas identified his own moral principles really exist? If so, was the worship of Him worth what it cost in anguish and self-abandonment?

'Am I ever going to be mentally at rest?' she wrote from her bed to Ellison Campbell after listening with scant attention to Thomas reading aloud from the *Life of Bishop Westcott*. 'I am still as far from finding out what God is as I was ten years ago. Why don't I give it up! It is no mere sentiment when I say that my heart aches with thinking. I think perpetually of my own shortcomings, my utter failure as a woman, a daughter, a wife, a mother. If it were not for our friendship and the fact that you care for me, I should conclude that I was not fitted for personal relationships at all. And yet I once loved Thomas and would willingly have helped him with his work, little though I cared about it, if he had not expected my entire personality to be always at his disposal. Why isn't there some sphere other than the domestic in which a woman who is not a genius like yourself can excel? I long to work hard all the time – but at what? If only we could go in for politics properly as men do and have careers in Parliament! But how inconsiderate it is of me to complain like this about my misfortunes, when you, who matter so much more than I do, have such a heavy burden of your own to bear!'

Ellison Campbell certainly had her troubles that year. It was largely their mutual commiseration which helped Janet to readjust herself to Sterndale after this new upheaval. There would in any case have been no joint summer visit to London, since Charles Campbell had been seriously ill for weeks with a return of the kidney trouble which periodically afflicted him. Owing to the care and attention which he demanded, Gertrude's new play, *Danger Signal*, had been laid aside, and the managers of the Soho Theatre, who had already advertised its appearance in the autumn, were obliged to abandon the project.

'I could bear the disappointment better,' ran Gertrude's letter to Janet, 'if only Charles did not vent all his bitterness on me, and indeed seem almost pleased because I have been unable to finish my play. Of course I know that it is not his fault and that I ought to be more patient, but to be treated, year after year, as though I were the cause of his wretchedness is hard to endure.'

'I don't suppose,' thought Janet, 'that Thomas is any more difficult than Charles. Both Gertrude and I are prevented from fulfilling our own true natures by the selfishness of a man. If she, a famous woman whose work really counts, has learnt to put up with it, I must try harder to do the same. After all, I'm thirty now, and Thomas is nearly forty-eight. We're both getting too old to begin family life all over again, and anyhow it wouldn't be fair to Denis. Thomas may be devoted to him in a way I never have been, but he'd get on his nerves and upset him continually if it weren't for me.'

There were times now when she thought of Denis, if not with affection, at least with gratitude. The prospect of another baby, helpless and dependent, had made him seem very old and responsible, and she recognised at last that though he had been unable to inspire her love, he had always done his best to win her approval. Absorbed, at eleven years old, in the social and industrial aspects of *Alton Locke*, and endeavouring to apply such elementary economic principles as he perceived to the planning of a Utopia for quadrupeds, he was less troublesome to his preoccupied parents than many a boy three or four years older. He had recently begun to attend the junior classes at Sterndale College, the big secondary school on the road to Grin Tor, and if it had not been for the vigilance which his indifferent health still required, Janet could have ignored him altogether.

9

Deprived for the time of both London and Gertrude, Janet again gave her mind to politics as soon as she recovered from her illness.

Her Suffrage Society had now risen to monthly meetings with an occasional outside speaker; like every other political organisation that autumn, it was galvanised into activity by the prospect of a General Election. The old Parliament, dominated for nearly twenty years by the Conservative party, was at last coming to an end, and everyone anticipated the return of the Liberals to power with a large majority.

When Janet learnt, from the *Manchester Guardian*, that Sir Edward Grey was advertised to speak in Manchester at the Free

Trade Hall on October 13th, she resolved to take the twenty-mile train journey in order to report to her fellow-suffragists the probable intentions of the new Government as outlined by a future Cabinet Minister.

'Won't you come with me?' she asked Miss Garston, the Society's treasurer, whose long friendship with Bill Fishwick, the owner of the bicycle shop in Upper Sterndale and a pensioned veteran of South Africa, was slowly ripening towards matrimonial reciprocity. Unknown to most of the parents whose children attended the school, their popular, comfortable teacher had been turned into a suffragist by learning how little influence the mothers of her girl scholars were able to exercise in their modest homes.

In Manchester that evening Janet was immediately reminded of Ellison Campbell, for outside the Free Trade Hall large newspaper placards announced the sudden death, in Bradford, of Sir Henry Irving, whom she and Gertrude had seen two or three years ago in *Coriolanus*. As she sat in the crowded hall waiting for the speaker and thinking of Gertrude rather than the meeting, she noticed in front of her two young girls half concealing a small white banner inscribed with black letters. One of them, thin, haggard, golden-haired, had the Lancashire cotton operative's shabby clothes and knotted, restless hands, but the other – about twenty-five, thought Janet, as the girl turned for a moment to observe the audience steadily massing behind her – looked quite a different type. From her round, chubby face with its dark brows and full pouting lips, clever humourless eyes of an indeterminate shade gazed intently at the occupants of the chairs in her neighbourhood.

Janet, her interest aroused by their conspiratorial air, pointed out the girls to Miss Garston.

'I'm sure they've come to ask a question or something. Can you see what's written on their banner?'

'You're right!' commented Miss Garston, looking over the shoulder in front of her. 'It's got "Votes For Women" on it. Seems to me they're out for trouble!'

'What fun!' Janet exclaimed. 'Thank goodness this isn't Sterndale! If anything happens here, we can join in.'

A loud burst of clapping and cheering interrupted her speculations as Sir Edward Grey, tall, close-lipped, immaculately
correct, came on to the platform followed by Lord Durham,
Mr Winston Churchill and Sir William Holland. The speeches
began, and she listened eagerly for any reference to the franchise.
Sir Edward Grey, like every seasoned campaigner, was censuring
the Government.

'They know they can no longer live with credit, yet the time
has gone by when they might have died with honour!'

Now he was talking of unemployment in the big cities;
now of the Anglo-Japanese alliance and the Anglo-French
understanding. But of women, that inconsiderable undergrowth
of politics, there was no mention at all.

The two girls sat quietly through the meeting, and even
listened to several questions being put by male members of the
audience and courteously answered from the platform. Then
Janet gripped her chair, for the rosy-cheeked young woman
was holding aloft the little white banner and the golden-haired
one was on her feet, asking in a clear Lancashire voice which
carried all over the big hall: 'If the Liberal party is returned to
power, will they take steps to give votes to women?'

The question elicited no reply. To Janet's indignation several
men sitting near the girl forced her back into her seat, while
a steward pressed his hat over her face. Shouts and catcalls
arose sporadically, but as soon as they had died down, the
dark-browed young woman stood up and asked: 'Will the
Liberal Government, if returned, give votes to women?'

This time a tumultuous babel of shouts and cries burst up from
the floor – 'Be quiet!' 'Sit down!' – but Janet, to her own surprise,
found herself on her feet shouting at the top of her voice with
a minority which was crying: 'Let her speak! Let her speak!'

She saw a man from the platform – it was the Chief Constable
of Manchester, she learnt later – come down and say a word to
the girls. The dark one wrote something on a slip of paper and
gave it to him to take to the speaker. When Sir Edward Grey read
the question he smiled broadly, and passed it round the platform.
In a moment the same amused grin was reflected on every face,
but still no answer came to the inquiry. So eager was Janet to

go up to the young women and tell them that she, too, was a worker for suffrage, that she could hardly wait until the end of the meeting. But as soon as Sir Edward Grey had replied to the vote of thanks, the fair-haired girl stood on her chair and again shouted: 'Will the Liberal Government give votes to women?'

The audience, now goaded to furious hostility, surged round the girls like a stormy sea lashed by a hurricane. From all sides indignant male spectators, annoyed at the interruption of their meeting, rushed at the young women with the banner, striking and scratching them as they defended one another and continued to shout: 'The question! Answer the question!' Janet, instinctively hastening to their aid, found herself warding off the hammering fists of a grey-haired man whose bloodshot eyes gleamed with sadistic excitement. Only when she was back in the train with Miss Garston did she discover that her shoulder was bruised and her silk sleeve torn at the elbow. She emerged from her own contest to see half a dozen stewards seize each girl and hurl her out of the hall into the murky Manchester night.

Janet would rather have died than refrain from following them. A strange emotion had entered into her, a sense that something new and vivid, which would not end here, had begun. Followed by the loyal Miss Garston, now panting and perspiring from alarm and excitement, she went into the street to find the two young women, battered and dishevelled as they were, making speeches of protest to the crowds which had followed them. As she left the hall she heard Sir Edward Grey, who had sat silent and unmoved during the hubbub, explaining to the audience that as Women's Suffrage was unlikely to become a party question, it was not 'a fitting subject' for that meeting.

For some time after the two girls had been arrested for 'obstruction' and escorted off to the police station, Janet and Miss Garston endeavoured to find out who they were. At first nobody seemed to know, but they finally discovered a woman with a badge who appeared to sympathise with the questioners. Their names, she said, were Christabel Pankhurst and Annie Kenney, and they belonged to a little organisation called the Women's Social and Political Union. Oh, it was quite small and unimportant – just a family affair. It had been started about two years ago at her house in Manchester by a certain Mrs Pankhurst, the mother of one of the two girls and a member of the Independent Labour Party.

Janet's enthusiastic letter next day describing the incident to Ellison Campbell met with a disappointing response, for Gertrude was entirely preoccupied with the arrangements for Sir Henry Irving's funeral in Westminster Abbey. She hoped, she wrote, to rush up to town and attend it. But long before she received her reply, Janet had decided to find out more about the Women's Social and Political Union, and if possible to get her infant Suffrage Society attached to it. And even in this superhuman effort she might ultimately have succeeded, had not Thomas's dispute with the Christ Church School managers the following spring divided the parish into two hostile camps.

10

Janet often thought afterwards how strange it was that the cause of their leaving Sterndale should have been a quite unintentional but definite victory for the principle now being put forward by a few daring suffragists – the right of a professional woman to continue her work after marriage.

It was, perhaps, stranger still that this would never have happened if the Christ Church School managers' meeting – usually a mere formality – had not been 'swung' by Joe Pond, the Hill Street fishmonger, an habitual absentee who came just because he was the bosom friend of Miss Garston's intended.

For two hours, on the night after the controversy in the headmaster's room at the school, Thomas strode up and down his study excitedly justifying his point of view to Janet.

' "When a woman gets married," I said to them, "her first duty is to her husband and children. There can be no question of that; no question whatever." '

'Mightn't it be better,' inquired Janet, trying hard to be patient, 'to wait and see whether Miss Garston has any children? She's no longer young, and Mr Fishwick was seriously wounded in the war.'

'The children are neither here nor there. It's the principle of the thing. "I couldn't," I said, "conceive of any of you gentlemen taking a different view, and when I told Miss Garston I expected her resignation to be placed in my hands within a month, it seemed to me I was simply performing an obvious duty in which all the managers were bound to concur."'

Only by degrees did Janet learn how far from concurrence the managers, led by the determined Mr Pond, had actually been.

'Just a word on that, Mr Rutherston, before you go on,' Pond had interrupted. 'Now, as you gentlemen know, Bill Fishwick got pretty badly smashed up when he was with me at Kimberley. That boy had nigh on a dozen operations before they took his leg off, and though 'e potters about a bit in his father's old bicycle shop, he's never likely to have much to live on but 'is pension. Now seein' Miss Garston's salary would make, as you might say, all the difference to their comfort, I think there's some call to regard this as a special case.'

He cleared his throat but continued before Thomas, shocked by this unexpected departure from orthodoxy, could produce a reply.

''Owever, let's assume the Vicar's right and it's the managers' duty to relieve the lady of her job in the usual way in these marriage cases. Does that entitle 'im to forestall the managers and order her to resign, without consultin' them and gettin' their agreement to 'is course of action? Does it, gentlemen, I ask you?'

'It does not,' affirmed Mr Philip Sawdon, head cashier at the local branch of the Midland Counties Bank.

'That's right!' echoed Mr Julius Buckley, the Upper Sterndale auctioneer.

Mr William Sutcliffe, proprietor of the Royal Spa Hotel, rose to his feet to pursue the argument towards its logical conclusion.

'Gentlemen, I think Mr Pond has put in a nutshell what's been in the mind of us all for some little time. Agreed that the Vicar, as our Chairman, has the right to persuade the meetings to his way of thinking and even to take preliminary steps between committees, it's *not* the Chairman's job to make final decisions without the ratification of the managers. It's not constitutional, and I for one don't care to serve on a committee where I'm only called in to be told what the Chairman's decided for me.'

'Nor I, Mr Sutcliffe!'

'Nor I, neither.'

'I, too, prefer to tender my resignation, sir, in the hope that you'll find a more compliant committee.'

Three minutes later Thomas was left alone, a solitary Chairman without a committee of managers. In the unexpected fashion by which a controversy suddenly arouses the pugilistic instincts of everyone within range, the question of Miss Garston's resignation became a *casus belli* in the parish. Opinions on the merits and demerits of her case were bandied about over shop counters and domestic tea-tables. While most of the Upper Sterndale matrons agreed that it was, of course, Miss Garston's duty to devote her entire time to her husband and home after marriage, their menfolk maintained that the Vicar had exceeded his rights in forestalling the managers, who were there to be consulted on such matters. The Sterndale Women's Suffrage Society – a tiny group, but unfortunately for the Vicar so closely connected with both his wife and Miss Garston – took the astonishing view that no woman ought to be dismissed from her post on marriage unless the care of her household made her inefficient. It was no part of an employing body, they said, to inquire into personal relationships. This attitude aroused so much antagonism amongst the less fanatical residents that a number of the neutrals now rallied to Thomas's support, maintaining that in such an obvious matter of duty the managers should have taken the whole thing for granted, instead of creating a storm in a tea-cup over a mere point of constitutional order.

When the battle between these divergent groups was at its height, Thomas went down one evening to St Mary's Vicarage to consult Canon Maybury. He felt weary and harassed, for Janet now refused to discuss Miss Garston's preposterous claims at all, but quietly left the room whenever he raised the subject. It never occurred to him that this refusal to return argument for argument was any evidence of self-control, or that Janet was, as usual, strung between the dilemma of Thomas's interests and her own convictions. Since the beginning of the controversy his church had been crowded, but even the most optimistic interpretation of this phenomenon could not present it as a sudden universal impulse towards worship and prayer.

The rural dean listened gravely to Thomas's request for advice. Hitherto he had been discreetly deaf to the numerous criticisms of Thomas's autocratic methods with school managers and other committees which had recently assailed his ears, but he would have been more than human if he had not realised that an opportunity for which he had long hoped in secret was being offered him in a simple and recognisable form. Undoubtedly his task in Sterndale would be lighter if the incumbent of the second largest parish were someone less – well, temperamental – than Thomas Rutherston. There was his troublesome wife too, whom he seemed quite unable to control, with her unsuitable interest in political questions and her indifference to the parishioners. It would certainly be a relief to have an even-tempered man with a hard-working unobtrusive woman as his helpmate at Upper Sterndale – and there were plenty of both to be found.

'Let me see, Rutherston – when was it you came to the parish?'

'In July of 1890,' answered Thomas. 'Before that I was senior curate at St James's, Cheet.'

'Ah, yes – that was in Bishop Dodge's day, two years before my own appointment here ... You know, Rutherston, sixteen years is a long time. Has it ever occurred to you it might be an advantage to seek a new field of work?'

'A new field ... Are you suggesting I should ask for a transfer?'

'Well, the idea was in my mind. Occasionally, you know, a change of that nature is beneficial all round. Only the other day the Bishop was discussing a vacancy which is just about to occur at the Staffordshire end of the diocese – an elderly rector retiring through ill-health. I forget the name at the moment, but it's a good living, well endowed. I could easily mention your desire for a transfer to the Bishop.'

'But surely,' said Thomas, to whom the idea of any personal

upheaval was always extremely repugnant, 'I ought to stay and see the right thing done at Christ Church School?'

Canon Maybury puffed slowly at his cigar.

'Sometimes, my dear Rutherston, a dispute of that kind settles itself better when the chief protagonists have departed. But don't let me hurry you, man. Think it over and give me your decision by the end of the week.'

After nearly a month of argument and perturbation, Janet wrote a long letter to Ellison Campbell.

'I should be thankful that we were leaving Sterndale if my Suffrage Society – the only thing I have to show for my thirty-one years of struggle and study – were not just getting into full swing after much hard work. I seem to be very unlucky; the same thing happened five years ago when I had to give up the secretaryship of the Women's Liberal Association just after I had organised a conference that went off splendidly. But it really is better for us to go, especially as Thomas has now had a petition from some of the parents asking for Miss Garston to be kept in her post. He can hardly refuse after the trouble that has already arisen, but he says his position in the parish would be impossible if he climbed down over a matter of principle like that. The whole thing has been very difficult for me. Thomas as usual was much too dictatorial, but I could have pretended to agree with his actions if only the women's rights issue had not been involved. However, we avoided having a serious dispute over it ourselves, which I assure you is quite an achievement on my part!

'The other day we went to look at Witnall, the new parish to which the Bishop is appointing Thomas. It is at the other end of the diocese, on the edge of the Staffordshire Potteries, and a *very* different place from Sterndale. There is a population of nearly 11,000, with many well-to-do people and a number of smaller middle-class households who look up to the family at the big house (Dene Hall) as if they were gods. But beyond the country part of the parish where the church is, there are streets and streets of small cottages about 4s. and 5s. a week. We were told that the number of these is growing every year. The people who live in them seem nearly all to be employed at pot-factories, collieries or breweries.

'When the Bishop asked Thomas to come over to Cheddlefield and discuss the work he suggested that he should bring me with him, but I made the excuse that I was too busy packing up, so did not go. I did not like the idea at all. The Bishop is not appointing *me*, nor do I intend it to be regarded as a matter of course that I do so much of Thomas's work. I am quite willing to take a district, teach in the Sunday School and help in various small ways, but I am not going to be an unpaid curate or be told by the Bishop what I must or must not do.'

But her desire that this new venture should succeed better than Sterndale was more profound than her words to Gertrude suggested. In spite of her convictions and regrets, Thomas's unhappiness after the school episode and his genuine bewilderment when principles of conduct which he believed to be absolute were challenged by familiar acquaintances, had moved her to pity and an uncomfortable sense of remorse. The night before they left Sterndale, her prayer to the elusive Deity Whom for so long she had been vainly seeking was more sincere than any that she had uttered for years.

'O God, for my husband's sake, help me to be obedient to Thy will in this new life to which I am going! For the sake of the work which Thou art giving him to do for Thee, help me in all temptation, give me strength to curb my temper, to restrain all cynicism and thoughtless speech. Give me grace to be sympathetic and helpful to others that I may not by *my* life give the lie to what he is preaching and acting. O God, strengthen my will that I may surrender it wholly to Thine!'

Thomas Rutherston read himself in at St Peter's church, Witnall, North Staffordshire, on the first Sunday after Easter in 1906.

11

What they would have done and where they would have gone if the builder's family had not moved to Windsor and left her old home on Putney Hill vacant, Janet could not imagine. They took refuge there in that miserable summer of 1907, when Thomas's brief incumbency of Witnall came to its sudden and humiliating end.

In spite of his certainty that he wasn't to blame, it was never possible for the rest of his life to mention the Witnall episode to Thomas without rousing him to fury. He had done his best – he *knew* what was right – but a man really couldn't be responsible for the troubles brought upon him by other people's obsolete prejudices.

'It's no use your mother denying it was partly her fault,' Janet heard him explaining to Denis. 'If only she'd had the sense to keep her obsession with "suff." to herself, the whole thing might never have happened!'

But the people really responsible, as he told the boy, were those ignorant snobs the Alleyndenes. It was sheer wickedness for a half-educated family like that, with too much money and too little brains, to have any say in the affairs of a parish.

'Oh!' cried Janet, in sudden exasperation. 'Can't you stop for ever going on about the Alleyndenes! If you hadn't quarrelled with Mr Alleyndene, it would have been somebody else!'

Their predicament was not improved by the Bishop's letter, which came when they were having breakfast next morning in the old-fashioned dining-room. Its French windows looked out on the neglected but spacious garden, where the rainy summer had washed the vivid sapphire and orange from the wet tangle of cornflowers and marigolds.

Thomas, his hands shaking with agitation, read the letter aloud:

'MY DEAR RECTOR,

I have already expressed to your rural dean my regret at your somewhat hasty decision to resign from Witnall. I still feel that with due consideration some less drastic means could have been found of terminating the disagreement between yourself and your churchwarden, Mr Stephen Alleyndene.

'As you know, the patronage available to me in this diocese is not extensive, and I regret that at present I have nothing in mind which seems suitable to offer you. Under the circumstances, and having regard also to the situation which developed before you left Sterndale, I cannot help feeling that for the time being it would be wise for you to seek some field of work where the burden and anxiety would be less heavy than that of a parish of this kind with its difficult personal problems. I shall of course be ready at any time to give you my licence to officiate.

Believe me,
Yours sincerely,
WILBERFORCE CHEDDLEFIELD.'

The same evening Janet's weekly letter to Ellison Campbell – an escape and a consolation which now periodically replaced her diary as a record of events – described the aftermath of the Bishop's conclusive communication.

'Thomas and I have had another serious disagreement. At breakfast this morning he heard from the Bishop that he was not prepared at present to consider him for another living. My husband at once turned this into an accusation of *me*, and started to say the most scathing things about my conduct as a wife and mother. There was hardly a crime or a despicable action he did not accuse me of. As he said, "There has never been anyone except me who has cared for you in the least." You, who have been my dear friend for seven years, know how true that is!

'It is no use our trying again, I am sure. I shall not attempt to hide the unhappiness of our married life any longer. My husband may be a good man, but I simply cannot live with him; he just wears me out with his temper and excitability. I know I am not an amiable patient woman, but the greatest saint on earth would find it hard not to quarrel with Thomas. He loves Denis dearly – at least he says he does, and is always pointing out how much time he gives to him while I lack all maternal feeling – but in spite of this he worries and nags the child whenever he is feeling upset until Denis is pale and ill and nervous. He shouted at him this morning as well as at me, and made him cry.

'I have now told Thomas that I do not think we can go on living together. I refuse, after what he has accused me of, to touch one penny of his money or do any household shopping for him. I will not go on indefinitely paying rates and taxes, and waiting on him and doing his necessary cooking, after the way he has behaved. I have given him back his wedding and engagement rings; I refuse to use his bedroom, and avoid him as far as possible during the day. Last night after I was in bed he came up and ordered me down to his room to sleep. I told him I would not go, and he then said, 'You understand this is the last time I shall ask you.' I nearly gave way and began to cry, but I am very glad now that I did absolutely and finally refuse. Every time I think of him, the remembrance of what he said causes a revulsion of feeling against him. The Witnall business was most humiliating and I suppose it has ended his prospects of ever getting anything good, but to say that I was wholly or even partly responsible is an unjust and cruel lie.'

Ellison Campbell's response was a large box of pink roses and white carnations, sent from the most expensive florist in Bond Street with a letter enclosed.

'Janet, my darling, I know you have had a hard time lately and my heart just aches for you, but don't, for poor Denis's sake, do anything irrevocable. I realise that Thomas is quite intolerable, but the world has no pity for a woman who leaves her husband and child. Where would you live and what could you do, all alone? If only I were free, dearest, it would be different; we could join each other and have great happiness. But you know that as long as Charles lives I am tied to him, although he often hurts me as much with his cold, acid tongue as Thomas does you with his tempers. Some day I think I shall write a play about the hell made on earth for women by men who are utterly unworthy of them, but to whom society insists that they have to be chained. I shall call it "The Parasite" – but the parasitical character will not be the one that the audience expects.

'Try to bear it for another three months, my own Janet, and then I hope to be up in town for some early autumn rehearsals of *Danger Signal*, which the Soho is putting on at last. We'll have a good time together and do all the theatres. I want to see *The Mollusc*, don't you? – and Mrs Patrick Campbell in *Hedda Gabler*. Could you not meanwhile get one of the political organisations in London to give you work of the kind you used to do in Sterndale, which would keep you out of the house most of the day? You have not nearly enough scope for your brains and your energies; that has always been the trouble, hasn't it? You belong to *my* world, not to the narrow, petty little world of clerical duties and conventions.'

Two days afterwards, Janet replied.

'I lay awake till three o'clock this morning thinking about your letter. I suppose you are right that for Denis's sake I ought not to leave Thomas – and perhaps a little for his own. The Bishop refuses him a living; the Vicar here already knows about our domestic difficulties and even the tradespeople (so Thomas says) realise that something is wrong. If this is so, I suppose it is partly true that I am ruining the work to which he has dedicated his life. *I* care nothing about a living – life in a vicarage has always been a nightmare to me, and I don't love Thomas enough now to make any sacrifices for him. But if, as it seems, my right attitude is so essential to his work, then I dare not take a course which would prevent it. So I shall try to do as you say – find something which takes me outside the house, and live for September when you come to London.'

Never, she felt, would she be able to escape from Thomas now. She had made up her mind to leave him so often, and on every occasion found herself forced back into the clutches of domestic circumstance by lack of training and experience, by the difficulty of finding any niche that would hold her, by the overmastering stranglehold of habit. Each year, too, brought her nearer to the time when she would be too old to reorganise her life. Thirty-three now – but sometimes she felt that she looked forty, and the difference in years between herself and Gertrude, who would soon reach that age, was no longer so apparent as when they first met. Success and fame, she thought, would never completely remove Gertrude's endearing awkwardness, but she had periods of intermittent self-assurance which, while they increased her control over the production of her plays, seemed in some curious fashion to reduce rather than add to her age.

Fifteen months of poverty and disappointment followed this fresh attempt at readjustment. Immediately after receiving the Bishop's letter, Thomas retired to bed with a prolonged chill; he was now beginning, whenever difficulties developed, to adopt the expedient which psychologists were later to describe as 'escape into illness.' Even, Janet recalled, during their engagement, every small epistolary disagreement had left him with a bad cold or a nervous headache.

'Thomas comparatively well now but getting no engagements,' ran a typical letter from Janet to Gertrude early in this period. 'We have come down to our last pound or two. He has an engagement for Christmas, but nothing before that. How we are going to get through financially I do not know – there is anxiety wherever I turn.'

A series of appeals to the Bishop only brought further polite but decisive replies, and Thomas was reduced to occasional sermons and relief work for the local clergy. For a long time his search for a locum-tenency through the advertisement columns of *The Church Times* and *The Guardian* proved unavailing, owing to the limitations which he imposed upon his own choice of work.

He would never consider a slum parish, for slum parishes presented problems, and problems were phenomena which he spent his life in trying to avoid. Not even his experiences at Sterndale and at Witnall had taught him that the very troubles from which men fly have a habit of running after them and catching them up; that dangers, like nettles, hurt least when grasped with firmness and resolution. His untiring loquacity led him to prefer health resorts or seaside towns where the leisurely parishioners had plenty of time for conversation. Though he would never have admitted it, his ideal of clerical life was a perpetual tea-party with elderly ladies of sufficient intelligence to appreciate his scholarly qualities, and to listen respectfully while he discoursed upon such undisturbing topics as Old Testament history or Liberal ideology.

'Out of the question! The wrong sort of place altogether!' he would comment scornfully whenever advertisements appeared which related to mining areas, agricultural communities or industrial towns, where homes were poor, time scarce and manners abrupt. The Witnall appointment had been a mistake which he did not propose to repeat. In these places, he told himself, the people were not sufficiently educated to value a scholar as they should. When most of the clergy were such ignoramuses, it was sheer waste for a man like himself to go to a place where the years he'd put in on Greek and Hebrew simply meant nothing. 'Thou shalt not cast thy pearls before swine' was a phrase that frequently came into his mind and too often, for Janet's impatience, reproduced itself on his lips.

The one fortunate aspect of their retreat to Putney was the better chance of education which it offered to Denis, who at thirteen began to attend the famous but inexpensive public school of St David's, Hammersmith. Here, at last, he found teaching worthy of his mental equipment, and was thus the only person who benefited in any way from the Witnall catastrophe.

12

One afternoon in the autumn of 1907, Janet spent a few moments at the Earl's Court Exhibition on her way home from the West End. There she saw an unfamiliar Women's Suffrage stall, which conspicuously displayed the first number of a new magazine entitled *Votes for Women*.

Unable to resist the extravagance of buying a copy, she found her mind carried back to the Manchester meeting at which two young women had interrupted Sir Edward Grey, for the paper described itself as the mouthpiece of the Women's Social and Political Union, 'the advance guard who, throwing aside all other party ties, are determined to press forward their claim to victory.' It was edited by a husband and wife, Frederick and Emmeline Pethick-Lawrence, a fact which suggested that – incredible as it seemed – there must be a few men in the world who preferred free women with interests of their own, and a marriage based upon mutual respect and equal companionship.

From the magazine Janet learned that the Women's Social and Political Union had now grown into a national organisation with

Mrs Pankhurst as Chairman and an office at Clement's Inn. She studied, fascinated, the portrait of Mrs Pankhurst included as a supplement within the magazine. It depicted the tired but still lovely face of a woman nearing fifty, with sad eyes, firmly closed mouth, and hair piled loosely into a knot on the top of her head. The strange excitement which had seized Janet in the Free Trade Hall came surging back as she read the introductory lines of dedication below the cartoon on the outer cover:

'To the brave women who to-day are fighting for freedom; to the noble women who all down the ages kept the flag flying and looked forward to this day without seeing it; to all women, of whatever race, or creed, or calling, whether they be with us or against us in this fight, we dedicate this paper.'

Throughout that summer Janet had intended to fulfil Ellison Campbell's advice to renew her political work, but Thomas's illness, and the amount of cooking and cleaning which their poverty forced upon her, had hitherto prevented her from taking definite action. Now, quite suddenly, she resolved to go to Clement's Inn and ask if she could help the new organisation. An active and determined women's suffrage society was not, she suspected, quite what Gertrude, who was still tentative and evasive regarding the vote, had really meant to suggest. But the enthusiasm generated by the magazine took precedence even of Ellison Campbell.

A few days later, surprised at her own temerity, she went to the Strand and called at the recently established office between Aldwych and the Law Courts. Here she asked for an interview, and after waiting for a few minutes was shown by a girl wearing a purple and white ribbon into a small room where a youngish, dark-haired woman was sitting at a desk. Janet's nervousness disappeared as she looked at the open, candid face, the blunt nose, the resolute but generous mouth, the brown eyes which smiled benevolently upon her. She explained that she had read *Votes for Women* and wanted to work for the Union, but the claims of Thomas, whom she had not consulted, reluctantly compelled her to qualify her audacity.

'I'm afraid I can't offer to do anything very daring like interrupting meetings or going to prison. You see, my husband's a clergyman, and I don't want to cause him trouble or prevent him getting work.'

'I take it, then,' said the brown-eyed woman, 'he's not a supporter?'

'Well, no – not exactly. He thinks women should stop at home and look after their husbands without troubling themselves about the vote.'

Her sympathetic questioner smiled reassuringly.

'Well, don't worry too much about that. We have others like you and our Union's expanding fast. There'll be plenty of organising work to do which won't get you into prison.'

Outside the door, Janet asked the young girl with the purple and white ribbon who it was that had interviewed her, and received the information in hushed, respectful tones.

'That's Mrs Pethick-Lawrence, our treasurer. She and Mr Lawrence are putting no end of money into the Union.'

During the next few months the work of acting as steward at meetings or helping with the organisation of speeches absorbed much of her time, and produced several complaints from Thomas about the number of cold meals that he was expected to eat. Whenever she could spare a few consecutive hours she went to help with the overflow of correspondence at Clement's Inn, but these early routine tasks were soon obscured by the part which she played, as a marcher and banner-bearer, in the great Hyde Park demonstration of June 21st, 1908.

That summer Mr Asquith had just become Prime Minister in succession to Sir Henry Campbell-Bannerman, who had died in April. During the recent Woman Suffrage debate, Mr Herbert Gladstone had emphasised the holding of mass meetings as a legitimate and effective means of inducing the Government to give votes to women; it had been, he said, one of the chief methods used by men before the various extensions of the franchise. In answer to that challenge, the group already popularly known as 'militants' had organised the Hyde Park demonstration. Its purpose was to demand the immediate extension of the Parliamentary franchise to women.

'This great gathering will show,' wrote Christabel Pankhurst, 'whether agitation by way of great public meetings is an adequate means of bringing pressure to bear on the Government. If the Government refuses to obey the will of the people, as expressed in public meetings, then it will be evident that by militant methods alone can the vote be won.'

On June 21st – to be known for long afterwards as 'Women's Sunday' – Janet Rutherston marched from the Thames Embankment with the Chelsea procession. In the brilliant midday sunshine, as the four sections assembled, a silver-gold pathway shimmered up the centre of the river between the Chelsea and Battersea bridges. Above the scarlet geraniums in the Embankment Gardens, the radiant air quivered as though about to dissolve into flame. Walking, in her capacity of unrepresented taxpayer, just behind the Fulham Prize Band, Janet marched along the King's Road and up Sloane Street to the animated blasts of cornets and trombones.

For an hour and a half from noon onwards, the peaceful Sunday streets of the West End resounded to the beat of drums, the call of bugles and the tramp of marching feet. Soon after two o'clock, the thousands waiting to watch the demonstration heard the distant strains of the approaching bands. Suddenly, the Park became a moving pageant of lifted banners and waving colours, purple, white and green. Like most of the women, Janet wore a white dress against which her bright ribbons showed up bravely. The procession to which she belonged entered Hyde Park by the Albert Gate and massed itself, with the six other processions converging upon the Park from Kensington, Paddington, Marylebone, Trafalgar Square, the Euston Road and the Victoria Embankment, round the twenty raised platforms with their eighty women speakers.

Janet never forgot that Sunday. Its benevolent sunshine turned the multitude of men and women with their straw 'boaters,' coloured parasols and large hats trimmed with flowers and feathers into one immense kaleidoscope moving against the vivid green of the summer trees. Surely, she thought, so many people can never before have been gathered on one spot in the history of the world? Afterwards she read in *The Times* that the crowd had probably amounted to half a million; 'like the distances and numbers of the stars, the facts were beyond the threshold of perception.' An organiser who directed the programme from the central conning-tower – a furniture van equipped with bugle and megaphone – told her that from the vantage point of its roof the Park appeared as though some gigantic flood of multi-coloured atoms had been let loose. From the midst of this flood with its slow, steady currents, the platforms, each with its cluster of white-clad suffragists, emerged like pale islands in a brilliant sea.

Standing stiffly to attention with her banner, Janet felt deliriously dizzy as her senses absorbed the compelling animation of that vital stream. Looking at the throng surging back and forth to the boundaries of the Park, she shared the exhilarating consciousness of the individual lost in the mass, the glory of anonymous effort and sacrifice.

'This,' she reflected excitedly, 'is the invincible force which is going to count! The contemptuous smiles that greeted us from windows and balconies represented a traditional, unreasoning antagonism which cannot stand for ever against this united determination! Whoever would have thought that in less than three years the little "family organisation" in Manchester would have achieved anything like this!'

For a moment another banner-bearer – a tall angular woman with dark hair and green fanatical eyes – stood beside her to listen to the speeches; Janet recognised her later as Emily Wilding Davison. On the platform just above them Mrs Pethick-Lawrence was already putting their thoughts into words.

'We went out to win the vote, the symbol of freedom! And now we are becoming aware that this winning the vote is only a small part of what we are destined to accomplish. We are effecting a complete revolution in the whole conception and attitude of men to women and of women to their own womanhood!'

The attitude of men to women! Yes, thought Janet, it *will* be harder to change that than to get the vote. Will it ever really alter widely, and if so, how soon? I wonder whether Denis, if he marries, will treat his wife as Thomas has treated me? Will he order her about and disapprove of her interests? Will he try to control her actions and keep her at home? I expect he will. In ten years' time he'll be ready to marry, and that's too soon for husbands to change. What shall I feel about his wife, I wonder? Shall I be sorry for her and take her part?

'Why!' exclaimed a half-forgotten voice beside her, 'if it isn't Mrs Rutherston! Just fancy meeting you here – with a banner, too!'

She turned to confront Gerald Cosway. Eight years, she observed, had changed him for the better. His figure looked as lean and athletic as in 1900, but his youthful familiarity of manner had matured into a balanced self-confidence.

'Why, Mr Cosway!' she exclaimed, a little astonished by her own freedom from embarrassment. 'What are you doing here yourself? Are you working in London?'

'No. I came down to see the demonstration with some ladies from Leicester – all suffragists, though they're Liberals too. This suffrage question is a bit of a poser for our party, isn't it! Seems to me it's going to take more than demonstrations to get old Asquith to move.'

'Then you're still working for the Liberals, Mr Cosway?'

'Yes, rather!' he answered, as he gazed at her white dress and coloured ribbons with the old caressing glance. 'I've got a very good job now – organiser to a group of Midland counties. I didn't stay long at the Derby office.'

The reference to Derby struck him as unfortunate, and he went on hastily.

'And you, Mrs Rutherston? Are you still in Sterndale?'

'No. We left there to go to Staffordshire, but my husband . . . didn't like the place, so at present he's doing temporary work and we're living in Putney.'

'Good for you – you always wanted to come to London, didn't you?'

Privately he wondered that they were still together, if some of the reports were true that Upper Sterndale acquaintances had given him two or three years ago about the change for the worse in the Vicar's temper. No doubt it was the strain of her unfortunate marriage rather than the passing of the years which had worn away the soft contours of her face, and drawn those emphatic lines across her forehead and beside her mouth.

'Well, I'll be moving on, Mrs Rutherston,' he said, taking her hand and gently pressing it before he dropped it. 'I mustn't interrupt the speeches – or your own part in this first-class show. We'll meet again soon, I daresay. Bye-bye!'

'Good-bye, Mr Cosway,' she answered, still surprised because the incident had not agitated her more. Should I have forgotten him so quickly if Gertrude hadn't come into my life, and brought me into contact with a world so much more brilliant and fascinating than the one I used to share with him? I wonder if I *shall* see or hear of him again?

With a curious feeling of finality, she watched him disappear into the crowd.

13

In the autumn of 1908, Thomas Rutherston's fortunes took a turn for the better. A series of locum-tenencies, of the kind that he considered eminently suitable, happened to fall vacant in succession. He divided a year between the agreeable and unexacting parishes of St Symphorian's, Sidmouth; St Nathaniel's, Cheltenham; and St Cadoc's at Trefally, the pleasant seaside village a mile beyond Tenby in the county of Pembroke, South Wales.

Janet and Denis had less reason for satisfaction. She was obliged to abandon her work at Clement's Inn just as militancy began in earnest with the October disturbances in the Ladies' Gallery of the House of Commons, while he spent two terms in different schools and worked at home for a third. But each of them accepted the release from acute financial tension almost as thankfully as they welcomed the occupation of Thomas's time and the intermittent improvement in his temper.

At Sidmouth, too, Janet experienced three weeks of unusual happiness. They had just moved to their furnished house on the Esplanade, when a letter came from Ellison Campbell asking Janet to find her some comfortable apartments where she could finish writing her play *The Parasite*. She would have to conclude her holiday, she said, with two days in town; she must visit the Haymarket Theatre to see Bernard Shaw's *Getting Married*, which dealt with a similar theme to her own. But at present she was in search of such peace and companionship as London could not give.

'Charles,' she wrote, 'has been quite impossible lately. As I cannot write or think when I am lashed so continuously by his bitter tongue, I have decided to send him to Pitlochry with a nurse for three weeks and get a holiday myself. No doubt these constant verbal wounds are good material for the dialogue in my play, but for the moment I simply must get away from him or I shall never see the position in perspective.'

On the mild October afternoon of Ellison Campbell's arrival, Janet walked up the tree-shaded hill to the station to meet her. They had not seen one another since the rehearsals of *Danger Signal*, which was still running, in the autumn of 1907, and Janet was again impressed by the fact that Gertrude, though now turned forty and nervously exhausted by Charles, looked younger and less gaunt every time that they met. She still did not realise – for fifteen years of a disapproving husband had given her, in spite of her resistance to his criticisms, a humble estimate of her own attractions – that the prospect of her company seemed always to lift from Gertrude's shoulders her own prolonged burden of patience and isolation.

Ellison Campbell was familiar, now, with the chief theatrical and literary figures of Edwardian London. Like most persons of distinction in literature or politics, she moved from reception to reception to meet always the same group, and hear the same brand of conversation. London, she sometimes thought, held no more surprises than Glasgow or even a small provincial town like Sterndale; it might have been a village for all the social variety it provided. The fact that the well-known faces were those of celebrities no longer added exhilaration to these constant encounters, for she herself was rapidly outstripping in fame the famous people whom she had once regarded with envy and awe. In spite of her own reputation, too, she still found their society exacting and embarrassing; there was not one who came within miles of meaning for her what Janet meant. As she got out of the train her heart seemed to turn over, as it did whenever she met Janet after a long separation. She never saw the familiar figure as the slowly fading ghost of the girl whom she had known, but always as the vital young woman with warm fair hair and eager brilliant eyes, who had taken the chair for her at the Sterndale Conversazione.

When tea was over they sat on the wide verandah of Gertrude's sitting-room and looked across the narrow esplanade to the red-tinged waters of the bay rolling gently against the shingle between the encircling terra-cotta cliffs. After they had talked briefly of Thomas's congenial duties at St Symphorian's, Gertrude began to tell Janet about Charles, and the way in which his resentful invalidism blighted the atmosphere of their home until she had no spirit left for writing.

'He doesn't seem to realise, even now, what a celebrated woman you've become!' Janet said.

'He doesn't *want* to realise it, Janet. So long as he can think of me as his disappointed spinster sister, he can feel superior. If once he allowed himself to recognise my success as a playwright, he'd have to face his own failure to find compensation. As it is, he never tires of telling me all the things he'd have been and done if the accident hadn't happened.'

'Gertrude,' Janet suddenly inquired, 'if Charles were to die, ever, would you come to London?'

'I'm not sure, though I've often thought about it. It would be convenient, of course, but London sometimes strikes me as a place where you're perpetually interrupted by a crowd of acquaintances, all of similar types. They take up your time, but teach you no more about human nature than you'd learn from a small group in an unimportant place. Do you know, Janet, what I'd really like to do if I were free?'

'No. Do tell me!'

'I'd want to come wherever you were – Sterndale or London or Sidmouth or anywhere else. There's no one whose companionship satisfies me and helps me with my work in the way yours does.'

'Oh, but Gertrude—' Janet stopped, a little startled by the expression in the penetrating grey-green eyes which observed her so keenly. Her own eyeballs pricked, so unaccustomed was she to warm appreciation.

'But I'm so obscure, so unqualified, such an utter failure in everything I do,' she finished brokenly.

'I don't care, Janet – and anyway it's not true. It isn't what you *do* that matters, it's some quality of understanding in you, something that you *are*. You make me realise what Ruth meant when she said to Naomi: "*The Lord do so to me, and more also, if aught but death part thee and me.*"'

She picked up Janet's hand – slim and shapely still, but recently roughened by the housework that she hated – and kissed her worn fingers.

'I too will be faithful to you till death,' whispered Janet, turning away to hide from Gertrude the tears that sprang to her eyes. Long after Ellison Campbell had gone back to Scotland she re-lived that episode, which gave a fleeting joy and glamour to her recollection of the small Devonshire town.

Thomas, also, found Sidmouth agreeable – he continually compared his leisurely, good-tempered congregation with the parishioners at Witnall to the wearisome disadvantage of the latter – but he liked Tenby even better. Although the political atmosphere of 'Little England beyond Wales' was not comparable to that of Merioneth or Carnarvon, there was a large enough group of Welsh Liberals to make him feel thoroughly at home. Sometimes they invited him to their houses to argue, pleasantly but inconclusively, about the recent ambitious manœuvres of the Young Turks or the international implications of the Czar's forthcoming visit to England and France, and quite a number of them acquired the satisfactory habit of walking across the sandhills on Sunday mornings to hear him preach at Trefally. At last, he reflected, he had a congregation, however humble, who understood and appreciated what eloquence meant.

The village church at Trefally, with its tall narrow tower, stood on the side of a steep hill overlooking the sea. When they first came to the parish the churchyard of rough unmown grass was starred with spring flowers – blue and white hyacinths, brown and yellow wallflowers, scarlet and magenta tulips which bloomed vividly against the crooked grey stones. Now, in August, red roses and tangled honey-suckle had supplanted the tulips, and the sweet scent of mown hay filled the soft warm air.

Janet, who found this neglected, unorthodox graveyard a place of healing for her unquiet spirit, sat beneath a bent yew tree writing her diary.

'My 35th birthday,' she recorded. 'All my life I have wanted to work hard and achieve something, but except for Gertrude I have nothing to show for 35 years. My girlhood is far behind me now. If ever I am to enter into the strong and gracious womanhood of which I have so often dreamed, it must be soon – soon – soon! Yet what opportunity of any kind will Gorseford provide?'

Only that morning, a letter had come from the Bishop of Cheddlefield offering Thomas a living at the village of Gorseford, in Cheshire. It had provoked one of their customary breakfast-table scenes, for Janet had refused to be permanently buried in a country parish where political work was unobtainable.

'Now that the Bishop has done his duty at last, I can't possibly reject his offer,' maintained Thomas heavily. 'If my wife refuses to support me, I can only inform him that, thanks to her, my career is at an end.'

After an hour's wrestling with herself in the churchyard, Janet told Thomas that she withdrew her objection. But she watched him post his letter of acceptance with a feeling of self-immolation and despair.

The sequel, however, was quite unexpected.

'On the 29th,' wrote Janet to Gertrude, 'another letter came from the Bishop suggesting that we go instead to St Michael and All Angels at Carrisvale Gardens in West Kensington. It appears that the incumbent there has a weak heart and wants a country living. We are now waiting to hear whether the Bishop of Hammersmith will consent to the exchange. If not, of course, we go to Gorseford. I feel ill with the suspense. I said I would go to Gorseford, and I will, but I would rather commit suicide than do it.'

A fortnight later she wrote that the exchange had been accepted by both Bishops.

'The more I think of this Kensington parish, the more wonderful it seems! It is a chance for both of us to redeem the past. Again and again during the last three years I have prayed that, in spite of the Witnall catastrophe, Thomas might still get something congenial. Perhaps, after all, God has been preparing us, through set-backs and misfortunes, for this responsible position. And now, my dear, dear Gertrude, I shall be in London whenever you are, and we can meet without the difficulties of the past! Real happiness – the happiness of working hard and being *valuable* – seems at last to be in store for me! My heart is filled with thankfulness for this great opportunity!'

On the Sunday that Thomas was instituted at his new church by the Bishop of Hammersmith, Janet attended the Communion service at Trefally for the first time since leaving Witnall. She and Denis were following Thomas to Kensington next morning, and she felt moved to pray that the years to come might indeed atone for the conflict and failure of their life together. Kneeling in the front pew of the small dark church, she listened to the curate who had come from Tenby to take the service uttering the familiar prayers in his clipped Welsh voice.

'*We do not presume to come to this Thy table, O merciful Lord, trusting in our own righteousness, but in Thy manifold and great mercies. We are not worthy so much as to gather up the crumbs under Thy table. But Thou art the same Lord, whose property is always to have mercy . . .*'

Suddenly, as she knelt, a feeling of annihilating sickness invaded her senses, and her body went taut in the fierce grip of internal pain. Pressing her hand to her right side she called upon all her powers of endurance – when almost immediately the agony was gone, leaving her weak, shaken, astonished.

'Could it possibly have been my imagination?' she wondered.

Still sick and trembling, she forced herself to go up to the altar and receive the Sacrament, but she felt too ill to remain for the final blessing. Lying down on her bed in the Vicarage she opened, instead, her copy of the Ordination Service. It reminded her that a priest's duties aspired to '*the perfecting of the saints, the edifying of the Body of Christ till we all come unto a perfect man – the measure of the stature of the fullness of Christ . . . How great a treasure is committed to your charge: for they are the sheep of Christ which He bought with His death and for whom He shed His blood.*'

'*How great a treasure is committed to your charge.*' Was

Thomas, as she alone knew him, really able to undertake the responsibility of a large London parish? Were he and she, after all that had been and still remained unreconciled between them, fitted to guide and strengthen the souls of other men and women? Panic seized her as she lay beneath the window on that grey October morning, staring anxiously into the uncertain future but seeing no light.

14

Yet, after all, the next three years, though more exacting than any she had experienced, showed no immediate signs of fulfilling her apprehensions. Although she became tired more easily than in the past, no further threat of serious illness followed the strange manifestation at Tenby, and only once, after the failure and fatigue of the suffrage demonstration on Black Friday, did the perpetual tension between herself and Thomas burst into a really serious quarrel.

Thomas, it was true, opposed her suffrage allegiance more explosively than ever now that his church was close to the storm-centre of the movement, but he was usually too deeply absorbed in carrying his responsibilities with the help of only one curate to pay much attention to Janet's activities outside the parish. The organisation involved, as he frequently complained, kept him continually on the run, and left him no time to prepare his sermons. How could a man maintain a reputation for eloquence when he was always visiting, or taking meetings, or answering correspondence? Now at Tenby . . .

At first, in her endeavour to atone for the past, Janet flung herself into parish and household work with a new determination. For a few weeks her diary recorded a series of Sundays which were typical, she told Gertrude, of the uncongenial rôle of 'good woman' that she had adopted.

'7.0, Holy Communion; 8.0, home and helped cook to get breakfast; 11.0, Matins; 12.0, Choral Celebration; 2.30, Sunday School; 4.0–6.0, G.F.S. girls to tea; 6.30, Evening Service; 7.30, prepared supper; 8.30, cleared it away and washed up.'

But gradually her lack of real interest in home and church and the growing drama of the militant campaign drew her back to Clement's Inn. She prepared propaganda during the two General Elections of 1910; she joined in the evasion of the 1911 Census; she organised processions and window-smashing expeditions. They could just afford now to keep two maids at the low wages paid in pre-war England, and the old-fashioned red-brick Vicarage received a bare minimum of Janet's attention. Only the most inveterate battle against dirt and ugliness could have wrested beauty from its ten sparsely furnished rooms, its heavy stone-decorated exterior, and its few yards of surrounding gravel enclosed by railings and a dusty privet hedge.

'I prefer,' thought Janet, 'a house unornamented to a life unlived.'

In order to save herself from further announcements that 'suff.' could not be countenanced in a London parish, she began her expeditions to the City by walking in the opposite direction towards the parish room, so that Thomas might suppose her destination to be St Michael's Mission or the Mother's Union. She had now started to do quiet propaganda for women's enfranchisement amongst such younger parochial groups as the Girls' Friendly Society, but Thomas's discovery of these ventures was satisfactorily slow. So completely did the militant movement absorb her, that except during Ellison Campbell's visits to London the milestones of her life were chiefly political. The death of Edward VII, for instance, seemed almost a personal episode because it revealed how rapidly Denis was becoming interested in those public events which had always mattered more to her than family preoccupations.

On the evening of May 6th, 1910, he came home as usual at five o'clock from St David's School, to which, fortunately for himself, he had returned at half-term the previous Michaelmas. Although he was only just sixteen he had already been moved to the Lower Sixth, and was beginning that new term to work for the 1911 scholarship examination at St Giles's College, Oxford.

'They're saying at school the King's illness is pretty serious,' he remarked as he hung up his cap in the narrow hall.

Janet put down a letter from Ellison Campbell describing Rostand's *Chantecler*, which, like the King himself, she had recently seen in Paris.

'We might as well take the 'bus after supper and see if there's any news at the Palace,' she said, less interested in the King's health than in the possible effect of his death upon the Liberal Government which it was now the policy of the dissatisfied militants to oppose.

For a long time afterwards she remembered the dark stir of the crowds before Buckingham Palace. As night came down, the formal, massive building seemed to withdraw into a gloom relieved only by a few lighted windows. Neither the sharp descent of a shower nor the announcement that no further bulletin would be issued that evening diminished the steady surge of men and women against the Palace railings. She felt neither surprise nor emotion when just before midnight a member of the Royal Household came up to the tall gates and announced, in a low, impressive tone: 'The King is dead!' but Denis, she saw, was moved by the hush that fell upon the waiting multitude and the grave silence in which it dispersed.

'I wonder what'll happen now,' he said, as they walked slowly towards Hyde Park Corner. 'It's a bad time for him to die, isn't it, Mother? – I mean with the Veto Bill still unsettled and all these scares about Germany. At History to-day, Carter was saying that if the King didn't recover we should be at war within the next five years.'

'I can't imagine England fighting Germany,' observed Janet, and then remembered that little more than a decade ago it had seemed impossible that she should fight South Africa. How far was it true that Edward VII had restrained that menace of war which had lately begun to stalk Europe like a threatening ghost? Had she and Denis just witnessed not merely the death of a King but the end of an epoch? Above their heads as they walked up Constitution Hill, the rain-clouds massing in the midnight heaven might well have been those of the deluge which was so soon to undermine the rigid structures of Victorian morality, and with them to sweep ruthlessly away the best and bravest of a generation.

Next morning Thomas, reading aloud *The Times* with even greater impressiveness than usual, reported at the end of the King's long obituaries that the august newspaper had decided to postpone the issue of a special 'Women's Supplement' which was to have appeared for the first time that Saturday.

'"We cannot doubt,"' he intoned with approval, '"that our readers will agree with us in thinking that in such an hour of national mourning the first appearance of a supplement which necessarily deals with some of the lighter sides of life would be untimely."'

'"Necessarily" is good,' thought Janet. Glancing across the breakfast table, she caught a gleam of amused understanding in Denis's eyes. Again, as on the previous night, she found herself reflecting with astonishment: 'Why, he's almost grown up!'

Six months later, on the November afternoon which witnessed the most daring demonstration so far made by his mother on behalf of woman suffrage, he became, for the first time, her defender.

Just before the second General Election of 1910, Janet went up to Westminster for a Conference organised by the Women's Social and Political Union to discuss the coming campaign. The Conference was still sitting at the Caxton Hall when the militant leaders learned that the Prime Minister had decided to shelve the Conciliation Bill, a measure sponsored by all the suffrage societies which promised votes to women property owners. They immediately organised a Parliamentary deputation of three hundred women, divided into detachments of twelve. Janet volunteered to walk with a Victoria Street group. Her confidence in her ability to impress the recalcitrant members of a hostile Government was reinforced by a new coat and skirt, recently acquired after months of saving. With it she wore a white ermine stole and toque trimmed with ostrich feather tips, made out of an old evening cloak inherited from her mother.

'At last,' she thought, 'I can do something more active than secretarial work, and in my new things I don't look at all like a "typical suffragette." Thomas can't possibly object to my joining a perfectly peaceful deputation!'

Unfortunately for her, the occasion afterwards known as

'Black Friday' turned out to be anything but 'perfectly peaceful.' As the detachments of women pushed their way towards the House through a jeering, jostling crowd, they met with rougher treatment from the police than any legal demonstration had so far received. A group of men sympathisers forced a path for Mrs Pankhurst and Mrs Garrett Anderson, the leaders of the deputation, through the double line of police constables outside St Stephen's, and even from the hostile spectators a cheer went up when the two women reached the steps of the Strangers' Entrance.

The suffragists who followed were not so fortunate. For six hours, from midday onwards, members of the detachments arriving in Parliament Square were beaten back, knocked down by policemen, and pulled half-conscious along the ground. At every guarded approach to the House – Tothill Street, Victoria Street and Whitehall – a new battle raged each time a fresh group of women reached the area of war. Gradually the ground became littered with fragments of feminine clothing and torn scraps of purple bunting from the lettered bannerettes – 'Asquith Has Vetoed Our Bill' – 'Where There's a Bill There's a Way' – 'Women's Will Beats Asquith's Won't.' One by one, individual women, bruised and dishevelled but still struggling, were arrested and led away to the comparative security of the police station.

As Janet's detachment fought its way down Victoria Street to Parliament Square towards the close of that long afternoon, a woman who appeared, she thought, to be German, was pushed against her by the crowd.

'I beg your pardon,' apologised a voice with a foreign accent, 'but I do not understand what is happening. I thought it was going to be a procession of women to the House of Commons! Why will not Mr Asquith come out and speak to them? Why do the policemen push the women back? What have they done?'

Before Janet could reply, a sudden blow on the side of her head obliterated her questioner and the surrounding tumult in the pitch blackness of instantaneous night. A second afterwards the darkness lifted, and she found herself lying in the muddy street with her ermine stole immersed in a puddle and the feather-trimmed toque torn from her hair. Vainly struggling to rescue it from the trampling feet around her, she realised that some unseen assailant was dragging her by her shoulders along the road. With a violent effort she shook herself free and stood up, but the tall office buildings surrounding her began to oscillate as though in an earthquake. She would have fallen again had not the German woman, who was still beside her, seized her firmly by the elbow and held her up.

'It is shameful!' the woman exclaimed. 'I had not realised that those who do merely desire to vote are so treated in your country!'

As the rest of the detachment moved painfully past them she looked anxiously at Janet, who swayed uncertainly as she stood there with ashen face and hatless dishevelled hair, still tightly clutching her mud-stained, bedraggled ermine stole.

'What will you do?' inquired the German anxiously. 'Where will you go?'

'I think I'd better go home,' replied Janet, forcing herself back into full consciousness with an agonising effort. 'If I try to go on I shall probably only faint, or get arrested – and that would be fatal, because my husband's a clergyman. Perhaps . . . if you wouldn't mind helping me to find a cab . . .'

As they struggled across Parliament Square to the cab-rank in Whitehall, she turned to see the red fury of the western sun setting over the river towards Chelsea. For a moment its glow caught the upturned faces of the rebel women still standing against the door that remained closed to them; then a brilliant shaft of sunshine suddenly broke through the heavy violet clouds and flooded the Victoria Tower Gardens with a glory of golden light.

Those leafless Gardens were empty now; not even a shadow marked the place where the statue of Emmeline Pankhurst was one day to stand, her sculptured hands held out in appeal to her successors to remember how hardly political freedom had been won. No vision of that remarkable canonisation was vouchsafed to the women who took part in the battle of Black Friday; its achievement would have seemed too fantastic to have any relevance for that riotous scene of frustrated endeavour.

The light had not yet faded when Janet's cab deposited her, slightly recovered in equilibrium but still wildly disordered in appearance, before the Vicarage gate. At that instant she saw, to her dismay, a group of fashionably attired women emerging from the front door. She remembered too late that the Christmas Present Bazaar Committee, of which Thomas was Chairman, had arranged to meet in their drawing-room at three o'clock.

It was impossible now to escape or return to the cab, and the next moment she was surrounded by solicitous, inquisitive female parishioners. They assailed her with questions while carefully avoiding contact with the damp mud conspicuously adhering to her clothes and hair.

'Why – it's Mrs Rutherston! I should never have recognised her!'

'What *has* happened?'

'Look, she's lost her hat – and her *poor* clothes!'

'Has there been an accident? . . .'

'Are you ill?'

Their voices smote upon Janet's tired senses like the battering of breakers on a distant shore.

'I'm quite all right,' she answered wearily. 'I only . . . got involved in a disorderly crowd in the West End . . . a riot . . . I was knocked down accidentally . . . Please forgive me if I go in now and put on some clean things.'

As she stumbled up the steps a whispered comment, vibrant with malicious satisfaction, followed her into the house.

'I shouldn't be surprised if it's something to do with those militant suffragettes . . .'

Thomas, who heard the comment and had witnessed the unpropitious encounter with horror, greeted her indignantly in the doorway.

'What in Heaven's name have you been doing now? You've been mixed up in one of these disgraceful suff. raids after my express prohibition to the contrary – is that it? I *insist* on your telling me at once!'

She walked uncertainly past him into the morning-room where Denis was preparing his homework.

'I did take part in a deputation to Parliament,' she answered briefly, 'but none of us expected the treatment we got from the police.'

'I thought as much! I suppose it's nothing to you that you're likely to destroy all my work here by turning up in that appalling state just when the Bazaar Committee was due to leave the Vicarage! How can I be expected to retain a vestige of authority in this parish when my wife comes home at all hours looking like a common dirty slut! Just look at your clothes – you squander money on them we can't afford, and then get them ruined in these monstrous breaches of order and decency! Upon my word, I don't know what we're coming to next!'

'I didn't know there was going to be a riot when I put them on,' protested Janet. She sat down abruptly in the worn arm-chair and, to her own astonishment, burst into tears.

Denis, pale but determined, hurried across the room to her side. A sudden blaze of indignation lit his meditative blue eyes to brilliance as he turned upon Thomas.

'Why *don't* you let her alone, Father! Can't you see she's absolutely done up! At least give her a chance to recover before you go on asking questions!'

'It's a fine thing,' roared Thomas, 'when my own son turns against me! If you're going to uphold your mother in these disgraceful affairs, I've no more to say! The parish can go hang for all the two of you care!'

As the reverberating slam of the door thundered through the house, Denis knelt down beside Janet and gently caressed her hair.

'Can I get you anything, Mother?'

She asked him for a glass of water, and while he fetched it her angry tumultuous heart slowly recovered from its violent beating. For all his school prowess which gathered prizes and scholarships without apparent effort, she still took no pride in Denis; thanks to his prolonged ill-health and Thomas's persistent cosseting, he was not, she realised regretfully, a virile and athletic specimen of modern youth. Though he had grown a head taller than Thomas and by no stretch of prejudiced imagination could be said to resemble his father, his sensitive face was pallid and immature, and his thin undeveloped figure stooped at the shoulders. But her gratitude to him now was constant and profound; her indifference changing to remorseful devotion. Though he was not yet seventeen his thoughtfulness and consideration were those, she admitted, of a fully-grown adult. Was it really possible that, after all these years, the life which she had produced so unwillingly could become a bulwark and a source of consolation?

Looking back afterwards upon the results of Black Friday, she realised that it was Denis who subsequently helped her, by diverting his father's attention into political controversy or philosophic argument, to withstand Thomas's demand for a specific undertaking that she would abandon 'suff.' altogether. It was Denis, too, whose surprising but apparently genuine sympathy with her aims had compensated for the outburst of opposition to militancy which came from Ellison Campbell in reply to her description of the march on Westminster.

'I cannot feel anything but strong disapproval for this wanton destruction of property, this breaking of the laws made for people's protection. I detest violence of any kind. Surely persons who desire to be citizens should respect everything that is for the benefit of society! This "direct action," as you call it, can hardly fail, in my view, to alienate public sympathy and suggest that women are unfit to exercise authority.'

After all, thought Janet, as she endeavoured, a little dismayed, to console herself for this first open expression of Gertrude's hostility to a movement in which she was now so deeply involved, even the greatest friends can't be expected to agree about everything. Whatever Gertrude may say and feel, her fame as a dramatist is helping the women's cause whether she cares about it or not.

It never even occurred to her that Ellison Campbell, whose gifts had thriven and flowered in the long sunshine of devoted admiration, was capable of feeling resentment and bitterness against any interest which might rival her unchallenged ascendency in Janet's personal life.

15

After the domestic whirlwind surrounding Black Friday and the temporary parochial flutter caused by her disorderly home-coming, Janet passed into a period of unusual serenity.

The steady expansion of Thomas's work and her own enabled her to avoid all but the most perfunctory daily association with him, and she began to hope that the comparative ease with which she now evaded his once persistent nocturnal assertion of his conjugal 'rights' might be due to the waning appetites of his increasing years. With her time divided between the spectacular drama of the suffrage movement and Gertrude's now frequent visits to town – when they avoided political issues and instead enjoyed the brilliant pre-war atmosphere of the London theatre – Janet began to wonder whether after all the storms of the past she had really sailed into quieter waters.

'He told me,' she wrote to Gertrude of the Vicar of St Etheldreda's, Bethnal Green, who had spent a week-end with them in order to preach two special sermons for Thomas, 'to thank God for my high ideal of human service. "Don't be despondent," he said to me; "your sins and temptations are those of our common Christian warfare."'

Sometimes, all the same, she felt a return of the fear that had seized her just before they took over the West Kensington living. After so long an experience of tempest, it seemed impossible that her life could have quietly and permanently changed. She was right. For her, as for the rest of the world, those three years were only the hush before the hurricane, but her own crisis preceded the Great War by over twelve months. In spite of her deep-rooted rationality, it seemed to her afterwards that an insignificant episode to which only the superstitious could attach importance had marked the beginning of the end.

In the disturbed summer of 1912, when the preliminaries of the first Balkan war were rivalling Home Rule and Welsh Dis-establishment as serious newspaper topics, and the Conspiracy Trial of Mrs Pankhurst and the Pethick-Lawrences at the Central Criminal Court had replaced the stories of the lost *Titanic* in the popular Press, the Rutherstons went to Tenby for their annual fortnight's holiday.

The choice was one upon which Thomas had insisted ever since his locum-tenency there; it was the only place, he said, that had really appreciated him. Here, for a time, he could forget the problems of his exacting parish and his vain but unceasing quest for a well-regulated world based upon the accepted morality of his Victorian boyhood. He was probably never nearer to contentment than on those mornings when he wandered up and down the short promenade, clad in grey flannel trousers, college blazer, clerical collar, white canvas shoes and panama hat surrounded by a sober black band.

To Janet the short, stout figure in its strange assortment of garments appeared ludicrous and undignified. She preferred to walk alone over the sandhills, or along the cliff-top towards Manorbier with Denis, who was going up to Oxford with a scholarship at St Giles's College the following October. In addition to this success he had been awarded a London County Council scholarship and a school-leaving exhibition, though the old threat of pneumonia had brought his last term at St David's to a premature end.

One afternoon, returning alone to their lodgings through the walled town, Janet stopped to examine an 'antique' shop of which one window was dedicated to old china and glass wish-balls, and another to cameos and second-hand jewellery. Her eye, trained long ago by her father to recognise value when she saw it, was caught by a small opal of a deep blue-green, surrounded by seed-pearls and made up as a brooch in a large gold filigree setting.

Never, she thought, had she seen a stone so likely to please Gertrude, whose still sandy hair gave her a strong if sometimes rash preference for vivid blues and greens. If only she could afford the brooch, it would enable her for once to send Gertrude a Christmas present which would not be utterly eclipsed by the munificence of a celebrity whose plays were beginning to appear in collected editions. Sometimes Janet felt quite embarrassed by these gifts, which increased in extravagance with the expansion of Gertrude's royalties. She might even have protested that they

were too splendid for a clergyman's wife, had she not inherited
so strong a taste for jewellery that she could always cheer herself
in fatigue or depression by inspecting the growing collection of
rings and bracelets, brooches and chains.

She went into the shop. A moment later the old brooch was
in her hands. Tentatively she inquired the price.

'Two guineas, madam,' the shop assistant replied.

Janet's heart sank. Comparing the brooch with others in the
window, she had hoped for fifteen shillings or a guinea at the
most. With the perpetual demands upon their joint income and
the debts which they seemed unable to avoid, she never felt
justified in spending more than a pound or two on Christmas
presents. How was she to give a larger sum for Gertrude alone?
How could she prevent Denis and still more Thomas, with his
faculty for shrewd, inquisitive catechising, from discovering that
the meanness of their gifts had been due to her unwarranted
extravagance over a 'mere' friend?

'It's much higher than the other brooches in the window,' she
said unhappily. 'Couldn't you possibly take a little less?'

'I'm afraid not, madam. You see, this brooch is a very
superior quality to the others; the stone is a genuwine black
opal, comparatively rare in this country. You wouldn't find
better value for the money in the whole of Wales.'

Compelled by an inward vision of the brooch fastening the
high lace collar of Gertrude's latest afternoon satin, Janet made
a rapid calculation. That winter dressing-gown which she had
intended to renew – surely she could make it last another season?
Thomas, who disliked its colour, would certainly protest, but
what did she care for Thomas's fancies? Nothing could be more
absurd than the convention which assessed him as important,
when Gertrude for so long had mattered more than any other
person in her life. There were those strong walking shoes, too;
another soleing and heeling might make them rather clumsy, but
it would be foolish to get a new pair when they had so much
wear left in them still.

'I'll take the brooch,' she said aloud. 'Would you put it in a
good box, please – I want it for a special present.'

A year afterwards, listlessly going to bed weighed down by the burden of her unavailing grief, she asked herself despondently: 'I wonder – could it possibly be because I gave her that opal brooch that everything went so wrong? I know opals are supposed to be unlucky, but I didn't think it mattered when we both despised superstition . . . Perhaps it would have been better if I'd bought myself a new dressing-gown after all!'

She looked down with weary distaste at the faded mauve flannel as she brushed, with the mechanical conscientiousness of habit, the long strands of her still abundant hair. It seemed, she noticed indifferently, to have gone almost colourless, and the soft waves had disappeared which once curved so gracefully over her forehead and ears.

16

In the early spring of 1913, a serious breakdown in Janet's health gave occasion for an exchange of letters between herself and Thomas. This correspondence revealed that, in spite of an external appearance of practical co-operation, their fundamental incompatibility was as deep and irreconcilable as it had ever been.

'Thoroughly done up,' Janet's diary recorded on a Sunday in February. 'Fainted in church, heart bad, losing weight, a good deal of gastric trouble. Ordered by Dr Twinkle to give up everything and take three months' holiday. St Michael's and suffrage together have apparently been too much for me; the constant rush of classes, meetings, services and office work has left no time to read or rest.'

Janet had little confidence in Dr Twinkle, a fashionable Kensington physician whom she was obliged to use because, like Dr Bannister at Sterndale, he lived in the parish and attended the household free. His treatment of the complaint which he diagnosed as gastric indigestion seemed to bring her no relief, and she still regretted bitterly that none of Thomas's parishes had provided her with the woman doctor for whom she had longed since Denis's birth. But she thankfully accepted Dr Twinkle's insistence upon a change of surroundings, and decided to take her holiday on the Devonshire coast in a convalescent home where she had become friendly with the Sister-in-charge during Thomas's locum-tenency at Sidmouth. Only when she had spent a month there and was beginning to feel better, did she realise that her enjoyment of her solitude was anathema to Thomas, who used his sense of grievance as an excuse for the wholesale disinterment of their half-buried differences.

'This morning,' she wrote to Gertrude, after thanking her for the box of books and the basket of flowers which had arrived at the home the previous day, 'I had a letter from Thomas complaining because I have decided to stay here for the whole three months. He says I could perfectly well have rested at home, but that all I care about is to act against his wishes. After breakfast I wrote him a long and careful reply, speaking plainly about my need to be alone, and also about our disagreement over suffrage – which began again as soon as I ceased to be strong enough to do everything he wanted in the parish. I told him clearly what a strain on my nerves and my patience these arguments are, since I cannot abandon my convictions merely to please him. I now pray God to grant that Thomas may receive my letter well and at least spare me further disagreements until I have recovered my strength.'

The sequel gave no encouragement to any lingering beliefs that she might have cherished regarding the efficacy of prayer. Two days later, she recorded Thomas's reply – 'bringing up the point that I was living in sin and my "explanations" were merely hypocrisy. I felt very miserable and got no sleep all night.'

His letter began by castigating her for her part in the suffrage movement, and continued with a series of accusations which showed how ill-founded had been any hope of permanent reconciliation.

'What I object to is not only your views, but the way you have gone to work in the matter. From the first there has been *concealment* and *deceit*. You promised not to attend meetings without my consent – and ever since then you have been going to them and hiding the fact as far as possible.

'Again, as you know perfectly well, there is general agreement among the priests of our church that for a married woman, out of sheer wicked selfishness, to refuse to bear children or to play the part of a wife through reluctance to have them, is *mortal sin*. Only the other day a priest declared to me that he considered it deadly sin, and would never consciously give absolution to such a person. Yet you know, and I know, that if you imagined you were likely to have a child, you would once more do what you did in the past. You are far too much obsessed with politics to have any regard for your normal duties as a woman.

'You say that if I write of these things they only get on your nerves, yet it does not seem to get on your nerves to discuss them with the Campbell woman. The whole thing arises from your attitude to me. Your real heart and life are *elsewhere*, in your friendship with Gertrude Campbell or in militant suffrage which you know I deplore. I can only hope and pray that before you come home you will see that it is not right to burden my life by carrying on these political practices and attempting to promote them in my parish. With so much work and worry sleep leaves me, and I am all the time on the verge of a breakdown. I cannot write my sermons or think seriously about my work in such an atmosphere.'

With an aching head, and a sense that all rational argument was worse than useless, Janet was nevertheless unable to restrain herself from attempting a reply.

'At the expense,' she pointed out, 'of feeling a coward and a shirker while others are endangering their lives and their careers, I have steadily refused knowingly to do anything in the suffrage movement that might compromise you. You write of deceit, but when we first settled in West Kensington I told you I should work for the militants, only that because of the way you upset me and the whole house I should not speak of them, or say when and where I went. The concealment was not of my choosing. I should much prefer that you knew about everything, but I cannot face the terrible scenes you make when the matter comes up.'

It was even more hopeless, she supposed, to answer the other argument, since Thomas had so long identified his sexual desires with traditional morality. But a sense that she was speaking for a growing number of women who were refusing to accept the physical subjection which had crippled the lives of their predecessors impelled her to try.

'As to what you call "mortal sin," it seems that because once, years ago, I put an end to pregnancy, you feel you have always a card you can play against me. But I have no confession to make on that matter now. If I have kept my own room lately, it is because, quite honestly, the least thing has made me feel ill. At the same time, I think it would be absolute madness for us to attempt another child. We cannot meet our expenses as it is, and there would be no end of new ones. It is much too late to begin that kind of thing all over again, with Denis already at Oxford. It would certainly be very hard on him – and on me, since I still cannot feel that my lack of a strong maternal instinct is a matter for blame.'

Three days later, the reply that she had all too clearly foreseen came from Thomas.

'Your letter is one more proof that you have no intention to play the part of a wife. Right in the face of church, prayer book and marriage vows you determine to act. You know that I have never shared your dislike of children nor ceased to protest against your conduct. Your letter makes clear that you are as blind as ever to the sin of telling falsehoods. I am very, very sorry. Had you tried in an honest way to admit your wrong and amend your behaviour, I would have done anything to help you, but while you act as you do I can only pray, as I have done for years, that you may be led to the light. Let anyone look carefully at my life and judge whether I have done my duty by you. Any other woman would have given her whole heart to me – but not so you. It seems *terrible* that you should value my love and good opinion so lightly.'

Her final answer reflected the despair which now seemed unconquerable.

'I cannot value a love, however faithful, which has neither trust nor respect in it, and if you mean all that you have said, yours has neither. Let us drop the subject. It is quite hopeless and it is upsetting me again. I shall only come home at the end of my holiday as ill as when I left.'

Two days before Janet returned to London, she went to a

musical evening at the local concert-hall and listened to a fine amateur rendering of Schubert's *Unfinished Symphony* and Wagner's Overture to *Tannhäuser*. The programme finished early, and before going back to the home she walked meditatively up and down the empty Esplanade. It was a gentle May evening, but the summer season had not yet begun. She seemed alone with the waves serenely lapping the shingle in the deepening twilight, the soft caressing breezes which carried the scent of wallflowers and lilac from the richly stocked hotel gardens across the road.

In spite of the unhappy correspondence between herself and Thomas, she had planned, just before leaving, to write him one last appeal.

'Let us, with my coming home, make a fresh start together. There has never been such a break in our lives before, and all being well there probably never will be again. Let us endeavour to be more to one another, more loving, more in sympathy. I *will* try to be open and candid about everything, and you must help me.'

But that very morning a letter had come from him, commenting, with characteristic sarcasm, on their prospective reunion.

'You don't say whether you are wearying to return to your home and family! I suppose you regard it as a "duty" but a deplorable one – not so good as certain *other* delectable things!'

After that, she knew she could not send him the plea she had intended, and spent some hours of bitter meditation on his capacity for frustrating every generous impulse that she had ever felt towards him. But to-night, with the stars coming out and the moon rising luminously over the quiet sea, her mood changed again to one of acceptance and resolution.

'At least,' she told herself, 'although Thomas won't try to understand, I can do everything possible on my side to avoid quarrelling with him and yet follow my own convictions. I have Gertrude; I have my work for the suffrage movement; I have even, during these peaceful weeks, achieved a measure of reconciliation with my doubts and misgivings. Why should I seek to possess more – to have no obstacles to conquer nor problems to face?'

Through her mind, mingling with the triumphant notes of the Pilgrims' Chorus, ran the words of the familiar text from St Matthew's Gospel which she had often repeated to herself in those final days of uninterrupted solitude.

'*Think not that I am come to send peace on earth; I came not to send peace, but a sword.*
'*For I am come to set a man at variance against his father, and the daughter against her mother, and the daughter-in-law against her mother-in-law.*
'*And a man's foes shall be they of his own household.*'

'After all,' she thought, 'the trouble I've had at home ever since I married is the price which has to be paid by nearly all who are rebels for the sake of an ideal. Even Christ Himself, who died that the spirit might be free, was unable to avoid it. I can't believe that we who are struggling to gain freedom for half humanity are not following in His footsteps. I will use these last hours here as a time of preparation for continuing that work. I will search myself, I will pray for strength to endure opposition and for courage to face whatever God has in store for me.'

But what God – or His cynical lieutenant Fate – had in store for her was the one loss on which she had not calculated, the one repudiation that she would never have believed possible. In June 1913, owing to the spectacular sacrifice of Emily Wilding Davison, who threw herself in front of the King's horse at the Derby as a protest against the treatment of the suffragettes in prison, Janet Rutherston's turbulent history entered upon its final phase.

17

Towards the end of May, Janet returned to a London preoccupied with political problems. In those specialised households where current events formed a topic of conversation, the personality of the new American President, Woodrow Wilson, vied for

consideration with suffragette incendiarism and the operations
of the recent Cat and Mouse Act. At St James's Palace preparations were well advanced for the Peace Conference between
Turkey and her Near Eastern opponents which concluded the
first Balkan war. But these absorbing events, like the mingled
facetiousness and disapproval of Thomas's greeting which Janet
had dreaded, were eclipsed by a waiting letter from Ellison
Campbell. It told her that the first night of Gertrude's latest
drama, *Hour of Destiny*, at the Charing Cross Theatre had been
advanced to June 14th, owing to the unexpected failure of the
comedy that preceded it.

'It is a Saturday night,' wrote Gertrude, 'which means long
notices in the Sunday papers. Janet, darling, I am more excited
about *Hour of Destiny* than any play I have ever written, for
honestly I think it is the best thing I have done so far. I count
on your coming with me, of course. I want just you this time
and nobody else. You *are* well enough again for late nights,
aren't you? – at any rate for this late night! Oh, Janet, when
I think of all this play may mean to me, of the triumph I dream
of but scarcely dare hope for, I can hardly restrain my feelings
of anticipation! If I *do* get it, you of all others must be there to
share it with me. We'll dine quietly together at Tindall's first –
just the two of us. I shall be far too much wrought up this time
to endure the usual festivities beforehand.'

Janet, whose illness had been enlivened by long reports on the
progress of *Hour of Destiny* since the beginning of the year, sent
back an eager reply.

'Of *course* I shall go. I'd share what I know will be your
greatest success with you if I had to get off my death-bed to
do it. I'm even going to buy a new evening dress – black and
white lace – to wear for the occasion! I tried it on in Oxford
Street this afternoon after reading your letter.'

As chance would have it, these joyous and sanguine calculations were upset by the determination of Emily Davison, that
most resolute and fanatical of militant suffragists, to put to the
proof her overruling conviction that only by the sacrifice of a
life would woman suffrage be won. On the 9th of June the
daily papers published the story of her death in the Cottage

Hospital at Epsom. Five days earlier she had sprung on to the Derby racecourse crying 'Votes for Women!' and tried to stop the King's horse, Anmer. She had spoken to nobody of her intention, but the suffragette colours carefully sewn inside her coat suggested that she had calculated on receiving the terrible injuries from which she died.

A telephone call from Clement's Inn told Janet the news on Sunday evening, June 8th. The Women's Social and Political Union had not encouraged Emily Davison's rashest actions – she had already made three attempts to commit suicide by throwing herself over the corridor railings at Holloway Prison – but her death provided them with a first-class opportunity for the dramatic propaganda in which they excelled.

'Yes – a great funeral procession,' the secretarial voice over the telephone explained to Janet. 'We hope you'll be able to take part and carry flowers or a banner. Next Saturday, June 14th, we think it'll be. The coffin has to go to her home in Northumberland, so we shall be able to march all the way from Victoria to King's Cross, with a burial service somewhere on the route – probably at St George's, Bloomsbury.'

'Certainly I'll take part,' agreed Janet. 'I'll come up to-morrow and get the particulars.'

Thomas, she knew, would object as usual, but even he – forcibly as he had already expressed himself on the subject of 'women lunatics' and 'suicidal mania' – could hardly forbid her to march in a dignified funeral cortège, with solemn hymns and sacred music. Then, as she hung up the receiver, something familiar about the date struck her with a shock of acute discomfort. June 14th? Why, that was the evening of Gertrude's first night and the dinner to which she had invited her beforehand! The procession – arranged to end at King's Cross about six o'clock – would give her time to get home and change for the play, but not to keep her dinner engagement with Ellison Campbell.

It was useless to pretend that Gertrude – now a national celebrity from whom invitations were received by her juniors with awe and gratitude – would not be intensely disappointed and even offended, particularly as she felt so far from enthusiastic about the suffrage cause. Yet Janet knew that, without disloyalty to her own convictions and her colleagues in the militant movement, she could not refuse to take part in the public honours to be paid to the first martyr to women's enfranchisement. How unfortunate it was that her life's two chief allegiances, the personal and the impersonal, should thus be claiming her simultaneously!

As she went reflectively upstairs, another misgiving seized her. Could she, only just recovered from a long period of convalescence, manage a late evening at the theatre after an exhausting procession through the heart of London on a hot summer afternoon? Obstinately she thrust the disconcerting thought away from her. Never yet had she allowed her health to interfere with her enthusiasms, and she would not permit it to do so now.

On the afternoon of June 14th, dressed in black and carrying a sheaf of purple irises, Janet joined the great funeral procession at its beginning in Buckingham Palace Road. To Ellison Campbell, who was able to arrive in London only that afternoon owing to a series of engagements in the North, she had written a long apologetic letter explaining why she could not meet her at the station or join her for dinner before the theatre. Gertrude's acknowledgment of these excuses betrayed the very sense of injury that Janet had feared, but she persuaded herself that as soon as they met and she could explain the meaning of Emily Davison's sacrifice, Gertrude's power of rational understanding even where she did not share a point of view would obliterate her annoyance. It never occurred to Janet that she might prove unable to communicate her own deep emotion to another person, however intimate and intelligent, who had not been captured by the religious passion for political freedom. She could neither imagine nor comprehend Gertrude's growing hostility towards a revolution which, to the followers of Mrs Pankhurst as once to the soldiers of Washington and the disciples of Mazzini, made life and fortune of value only in so far as they could be laid down.

Headed by the golden-haired cross-bearer, the procession moved slowly through Grosvenor Gardens to the beat of drums and the muffled chords of Chopin's *Funeral March*. It passed

between thousands of silent spectators whose faces wore a
look of questioning bewilderment, as though some unfamiliar
thought-process had been started in their minds. In front of the
women who, like Janet, wore black and carried purple irises,
marched a long line of young girls dressed in white. Behind
the black contingent came another group, wearing purple and
carrying crimson peonies. These in their turn were followed by
more white-clad members, who bore their Madonna lilies before
the low open bier drawn by four black horses. Upon the coffin,
covered by a purple silver-edged pall, lay three laurel wreaths
inscribed: 'She died for women.' Fifty hunger-strikers on bail
followed the hearse, bearing in front of them an embroidered
bannerette:

'THOUGHTS HAVE GONE FORTH WHOSE POWER CAN SLEEP
NO MORE. VICTORY! VICTORY!'

A group of university women in full academic dress gave a
note of exuberant colour to the long trail of mourners, but they
had less significance for the motionless crowds than the empty
carriage which silently indicated that the leader of the movement
had been taken back to prison under the Cat and Mouse Act just
before the funeral ceremony began.

'RE-ARREST OF MRS PANKHURST!'

shrieked the newspaper posters along the route. Above them in
quiet protest floated the suffragette banners:

'GIVE ME LIBERTY OR GIVE ME DEATH!'

Beneath the beating afternoon sun, Janet marched towards
Piccadilly up the wide curve of Grosvenor Place. As her contingent passed the large houses which faced the garden wall of
Buckingham Palace, she noticed a white lace curtain being drawn
surreptitiously aside and the grinning face of the butler appear at

the window. Afterwards she learnt that the house belonged to Mrs Humphry Ward, who for some time had constituted herself the portentous leader of the anti-suffrage forces. Long before the procession reached Bloomsbury and Chopin's funeral dirge had given way to Beethoven's *Marcia Funebre sulla Morte d'un Eroe*, Janet was walking dizzily on leaden feet. She felt thankful for the brief interruption of the burial service at St George's Church.

'At least *some* members of Thomas's calling are with us!' she reflected, as a group of clergy in canonicals came to the top of the steps to receive the coffin. 'At least a few realise what we're fighting for and why!'

The very hymns they had selected, emphasising the triumph of sacrifice rather than its grief, brought home to her the startling realisation that even the Church of England had its advocates of justice as well as its disciples of the embittered Apostle Paul.

> *'Fight the good fight with all thy might,*
> *Christ is thy strength and Christ thy right,'*

sang the packed congregation of rebel women. From the back of the church their masculine supporters – members of such male suffrage organisations as the Men's League and the Men's Political Union – responded with a deeper undertone of sound:

> *'Lay hold on life and it shall be*
> *Thy joy and crown eternally!'*

The last verse of the hymn echoed back through the open door from the waiting thousands of working women and bare-headed men in the street outside:

> *'Faint not nor fear, His arms are near,*
> *He changeth not, and thou art dear;*
> *Only believe and thou shalt see*
> *That Christ is all in all to thee!'*

18

When Emily Davison's body had been left on the train at King's Cross for the final journey to Northumberland, Janet found it oddly incongruous to hurry back to West Kensington and change into full evening dress for a theatrical first night. Though she had eaten nothing since a hurried early luncheon there was no time for a proper meal, and she struggled reluctantly to swallow a cup of tea and eat a tepid boiled egg as she adjusted her new lace frock.

Whether by accident or design, Thomas, who had described the funeral procession as 'an hysterical profanity,' was out of the Vicarage on parochial work. Denis had not yet come down from his first summer term at St Giles's College, so there was no one to whom Janet could communicate the intense religious experience through which she felt that she had passed. Her head throbbed violently, and faint feelings of nausea came over her as she finished dressing.

'Almost as if I *were* pregnant,' she thought. 'Pregnant again at thirty-eight, with Denis already finishing his first year at Oxford! How triumphant Thomas would feel if it were true – but thank God, whatever is the matter with me, it can't be that!'

She peered into the glass to fasten a coral necklace which Gertrude had given her to celebrate the success of *The Parasite*.

'Really, I look more like a grandmother than a mother since my illness! My cheeks are all hollows now, and how deep those lines are getting! I wonder if my appearance will ever recover?'

The journey to Charing Cross on the Metropolitan Railway was dilatory and hot, and she arrived at the theatre – where she had arranged to go straight to Ellison Campbell's box – only a few minutes before the play was due to begin. Gertrude received her coldly, and there was no time left to change her mood by intimate conversation.

'So you've managed,' she began stiffly, 'to spare me an hour or two from your suffrage excitements?'

Janet found herself launched on a series of unfamiliar apologies, which sounded the less sincere the more ardent she endeavoured to make them.

'I'm ever so sorry, Gertrude! You must know I'd been looking forward to our dinner, and I wouldn't have missed it for anything trivial. But this procession was to celebrate one of the greatest sacrifices a woman has ever made for a cause. It was nothing less than a matter of life and death . . .'

A matter of life and death! Never had she dreamed that Gertrude's brightly lit and enviable world could arouse in her feelings of exasperation; yet as she looked over the edge of the box at the brilliantly dressed, bejewelled first-night audience crowding the stalls, their uncomprehending remoteness from the scene of exultant re-dedication in the church that afternoon struck her with the force of a blow between the eyes. Those well-fed dramatic critics in the two front rows, with their complacent affectation of long hair and flowing opera capes – what understanding had they of the truly religious life, the life in which men and women devoted themselves, body and soul, to a cause that offered its followers no reward save the privilege of dying for an ideal?

Gertrude herself, in anticipation of the triumph which every critic of standing had predicted for *Hour of Destiny*, was splendidly if injudiciously attired in draped peacock ninon, with a wide sash of turquoise velvet and a costly lace fichu discreetly fastened at the neck by Janet's opal brooch. Now and again her tall figure trembled a little and her large features grew pale and set, but her light grey-green eyes acknowledged imperturbably the greetings which came from the distinguished audience, and as yet no silver threads interrupted the burnished smoothness of her sand-coloured hair. For once, her rigid self-command entirely failed to reveal to Janet that though she might be indifferent to political freedom, she cared with a passionate intensity for the future of British drama.

The lights went down and the play began. It had not proceeded far when Janet realised, from an acute return of the discomfort which she had felt while dressing, that only by an unusual effort of endurance would she be able to remain to the end and witness the triumphant reception that Gertrude had brought her to see. A sense of extreme dismay, lest, having already failed Gertrude to an extent obviously hard to forgive, she might have to conclude by abandoning her to undignified isolation, forced her to a violent endeavour to conquer the threat of illness that assailed her. She tried to forget herself by concentrating her attention on the pleasant opening scene, a picnic on the shores of Loch Lomond organised by a group of young people whose lives were to be fundamentally changed by their 'hour of destiny,' the tragic colliery disaster in the second act. All at once, the overwhelming pain that had seized her four years ago in the village church at Trefally smote through her right side like a sword, and she had to press her face against the plush-covered ledge of the box to prevent herself from crying aloud. Again the sharp agony vanished in an instant, but it was followed, as before, by a feeling of sickness so intense that she knew it would be impossible for her to remain in the theatre until the end of the play.

'Gertrude,' she whispered as soon as she could speak, 'I'm afraid I shall have to go home. I feel so terribly ill, I don't think I can stay.'

At first Ellison Campbell, whose attention was riveted on the concluding passages of her first act, did not grasp Janet's meaning, but as soon as she realised that her only companion proposed to depart, an exclamation of perturbed disappointment escaped her. Withdrawing her eyes with an effort from the stage, she saw in the half-light that Janet's features looked sharp and corpse-like in their yellowish pallor. As she took the damp trembling hand in her own, she endeavoured to control her rising sense of grievance by making her voice sound gentle and encouraging.

'Janet, darling, you *can't* go away and leave me all alone! The act's nearly finished, and in a minute I'll get you some brandy. You *must* try to stay till the end! I'll take you home in a taxi as soon as it's over.'

'I'll have to go now!' cried Janet abruptly. In the cloakroom at the back of the box she passed through an ordeal so painful and humiliating that all sense of time was lost. She never heard the outburst of resounding applause which greeted the fall of the curtain, and when at last she returned unsteadily to Ellison Campbell, who was pacing the passage distraught by the situation, the interval was almost over and the crucial second act about to begin.

'Here's your brandy! I'm sure it'll make you feel better,' urged Gertrude, but though Janet drank it obediently, the strong stimulus seemed only to increase the persistent oscillation of the lights and the floor.

'It's no use, Gertrude,' she gasped, almost speechless with exhaustion. 'I'd give anything not to go, but I'm afraid I must. I shall only make things worse for you if I stay. I suppose it's the after-effects of that wretched illness . . .'

Bitterly Ellison Campbell resigned herself to the disconcerting inevitable. Invalidism had so long been identified in her mind with Charles and his needs and moods, that the sudden claim on her care, at a critical moment for herself, of someone who had hitherto made no demands upon her, aroused a surprise which came uncomfortably near to resentment.

'Very well . . . if you're really ill I mustn't try to keep you. You must go home and take care of yourself. I'll come down and get you a taxi,' she added with a superhuman effort as the bell rang for the rise of the curtain. Why had she never explained to Janet that the opening of the second act was the intensest, most poignant moment of the drama? How *could* she go to the entrance with her and miss seeing it on the stage for the first time, and observing its effect on the critics? Then she realised with relief that Janet, sensing her reluctance with an intuition born of thirteen years' devotion, was urging her to remain in her seat.

'No – don't come! I shall be quite all right alone – I'm not as ill as all that. I'd never forgive myself if I made you miss a moment of your play.'

'You're *sure* you can manage?' Gertrude spoke with an intensity of thankfulness that astonished even herself.

'Of course I can. Good-bye – and good luck with the critics!'

Outside the theatre, after what seemed an eternity of effort, Janet rested against the wall and gazed blankly up and down the Strand. She did not venture to move until the bobbing lights resumed their normal stillness, and the soft fresh air of the summer night had helped her to overcome the faintness that still possessed her.

'Now that I don't feel sick any more, I really can manage the train,' she told herself, tottering weakly down Villiers Street to Charing Cross Station. 'A taxi would cost at least five shillings, and we can't afford it. What a fool I was to try to do so much in a day! I ought to have told Gertrude at the beginning that I couldn't go with her.'

Then, as the stuffy train swayed on its dilatory journey to West Kensignton, another thought, unbidden but insidious, began to creep into her exhausted mind.

'She *might* just have taken me home . . . she'd have got back long before the play ended . . . or at least she could have gone down with me and put me into a taxi. She knows I can't easily pay for one myself. If *she'd* been the one who was ill I'd never have left her in the lurch like that just to hear myself clapped!'

Throughout the following day, which she spent in bed recovering from the strange attack, the same tormenting reflection recurred to her with increasing force. She said nothing of her inexplicable pain to Thomas, whose faculty for flying into a panic at every threat of serious illness had received more than sufficient opportunities for display during the past six months, but told him only that she had done too much and wanted to rest undisturbed. Lying in the small bedroom which she had at last claimed the perpetual right to occupy alone, she read and re-read the enthusiastic criticisms of *Hour of Destiny* in the Sunday papers.

'A first-rate climax to an excellent play.'

'This time Miss Ellison Campbell has surpassed even her surprising self. We cannot think of a masculine playwright who would have made a better job of the tragic scene at the pit-head.'

'One of the most tense and moving dramas put on the stage within recent years. The plot is finely conceived and worked out in convincing detail.'

Throughout the tedious day Janet waited eagerly for a telephone call of inquiry or a visit from Gertrude. When, by the evening, no word had come, she took up her pen and wrote a cold little note, which did not attempt to disguise her bitter feeling of neglect.

'My dear Gertrude,

'Although apparently my state of body or mind has ceased to interest you, I cannot refrain from sending this line of congratulation on the splendid notices in the Sunday papers. I quite realise that their united excellence has naturally put someone so insignificant as myself out of your head, and only regret that my inconvenient attack of illness should have disturbed you at the moment of your triumph.

'Yours ever,

'Janet Rutherston.'

Janet addressed her letter to Tindall's Hotel, where she knew that Gertrude was staying for the week-end before going up to Oxford for her annual presentation of the Ellison Campbell prize, but when the reply came it was dated three days afterwards and written from Glasgow.

'I am sorry,' it stated tersely, 'that I did not visit you before leaving London, and I sincerely hope that you have now recovered from your distressing attack of sickness. The truth is that I could not trust myself to come and see you after the way you deliberately failed me on the most critical occasion of my life so far. No doubt it was unreasonable of me to count on your support as completely as I did, but I cannot help feeling that a long-established friendship ought to weigh more heavily with you than just another of these innumerable suffrage demonstrations which you can join whenever you choose. Common sense must surely have told you that after your long illness a public exhibition of yourself followed by a night at the theatre would prove too much for your strength. I cannot disguise from myself that you preferred to take part in that foolish procession rather than give me your full co-operation at a time when I needed it more than I have ever done.'

'A public exhibition of yourself . . . that foolish procession . . .' The rankling phrases goaded Janet's tumultuous emotions to fury. So this was how Gertrude, the successful dramatist whose growing influence might have meant so much to the women's cause, chose to regard that solemn tribute paid by religious devotees to an impersonal end that was dearer to them than life! This was her interpretation of that love for freedom which had already proved itself stronger than death! Outraged beyond measure by an attitude which seemed to her to be one of wilful misunderstanding, Janet, whose week-end rest had restored her now low level of normal health, wrote Gertrude five passionate sheets alternately defending and extolling the suffragette movement.

'Quite obviously,' it concluded hotly, 'you have never understood what the struggle for the vote means to me and the thousands of other women who are sacrificing their lives and fortunes on its behalf. You are far too much absorbed in your own work to share my ideals for women as a whole – or indeed to care what happens to any woman except yourself. Although you understand superbly how to engineer noble situations in your plays, the heroism of such a woman as Emily Davison is quite beyond you. I cannot help feeling that if it were otherwise, anyone with your influence and prestige would be ashamed to oppose a great constructive revolution instead of doing everything possible to help it forward.'

This time Gertrude's answer came by return of post.

'Your letter seems to me so wildly hysterical that it is useless for me to attempt to reply to it in detail. Not one of your emotional statements about freedom and sacrifice shakes my belief that the only sane way for women to improve their position is by worth-while achievement on the part of individuals. You know that my regard for your husband has never been great, but in his opposition to your work for the militants I think he has been entirely justified, owing to the deplorable effect that it has had upon both your health and character. The whole movement seems to me to be violent, anti-social and utterly unworthy of the allegiance of any rational person. Since, however, it now appears to dominate your mind completely, it is, I fear, impossible for me to continue our friendship. I do not feel inclined to share your affection with a cause of which I disapprove so profoundly, and therefore it seems to me better for both of us henceforth to go our separate ways.'

Janet read this conclusive letter with a sense of unmitigated dismay bordering on panic. After her furious defence of woman suffrage, her own anger had entirely evaporated; she was incapable of feeling resentment against anyone but Thomas for longer than two or three days. Though the quarrel with Gertrude had puzzled her a little, she had never regarded it as anything but a temporary rift which mutual warmth and generosity would ultimately mend. To go on without Gertrude's friendship – why, the very thought was inconceivable! Ever since their long-ago encounter in 1900 when Ellison Campbell was only beginning to emerge from obscurity, their letters, their meetings and the steady development of Gertrude's career had meant more to Janet than anything in life. The claims of Thomas and Denis had not only paled before that intimacy but had been rendered tolerable by it, and though Janet's loyalty to the suffrage movement had occasionally led to moments of strain, the past few years had taught her the disconcerting truth that when a passionate attachment springs up between two persons, incompatible values tend to increase rather than to diminish the attraction.

Ignoring Thomas's sarcastic breakfast-table comments upon lengthy private correspondences and their adverse effect on the colour and the appetite, Janet hurried into the morning-room to pour out, in an eager letter of apology, the love and the need which Ellison Campbell's unexpected threat of withdrawal had redoubled in intensity.

'Gertrude, dearest, forgive me – I should never have written as I did. Just because I've known you for so long, I'm afraid I sometimes forget what a famous woman you've become, and how far, far above me. But you have more than punished me by the bare suggestion that our friendship should end. You can't really mean that, I know. You are much too fine a person to let one evening's disappointment – important as that evening was to you – and an angry letter defending my convictions (which after all do mean a good deal to me) count more than the thirteen long years of joy and adversity we have shared together. After the many letters we have written each other, and the conversations we have had on subjects so dear and sacred to us both, it wouldn't be possible for everything to end.

'You *must* know that during all these years, you have been the one person who made life worth living to me; that because of you I have been able to endure Thomas's explosive temper and Denis's constant ill-health. In most ways my life has been one long disappointment. As a girl I had so many ambitions, and none of them have been fulfilled. My suffrage work which you so disapprove of has been the only outlet for my love of politics, the one contact – modest as it is – with public life in which I always longed to play some part. Except for this, it has only been in the world I shared with you that I had the experience I desired, and met some of the people I wanted to know. And above all things I had you. Your love, your confidence in me, the help you said I gave you in your work, made me feel I was not the complete failure that Thomas has always called me. If you give me up I shall indeed have nothing left – no love, no friendship, no hope, no reason to go on living.'

But Gertrude was adamant. Her reply came, ironically enough, at the end of a long afternoon of suffrage correspondence which Janet had just completed at Clement's Inn.

'I am very sorry to have to say it, but I no longer desire your friendship on the terms which alone, now, are possible. By your headstrong impulsiveness you have yourself destroyed the affection of years, and in any case you have ceased, since you began to take part in militancy, to be the person for whom I cared. The Janet I loved would never have failed me at a critical moment of my creative life. This suffragette lunacy has turned you into someone who has nothing to give me and in whom I can feel no interest. Under the circumstances it is better for us to part company and pursue our respective paths. I must ask you to regard this as my final word on the subject.'

The next day, after a hot morning's shopping which followed a sleepless night of incredulous despair, Janet walked slowly back towards West Kensington down the Earl's Court Road. Her feet seemed twice their normal weight as she dragged them along the burning pavement, and though the June sun was shining vividly, the solid Victorian houses looked grey and cheerless. Upon her spirit lay that dull heaviness, that choking inertia, which descends on the soul when someone beloved has died. She recognised its crushing finality for the feeling that she had known when first her father and then her mother passed irrevocably out of her experience, but in those days she had been young, strong in her unimpaired vitality, inspired to courage and resilience by the knowledge that the future with its immeasurable possibilities still lay before her. Now she was growing middle-aged and tired, weighed down by the consciousness that none of her bright aspirations would ever be realised; and though not a person but a relationship was dead, its ending meant for her the departure of all that was lovely and desirable in life.

Driven to desperation by the certainty that she could neither accept nor endure her loss, she found herself gazing blankly into a florist's window where the rich cobalt and saffron of delphiniums and tea-roses displayed themselves in the royal exuberance of summer glory. Suddenly resolute, she walked into the shop, and spent the last few shillings left over from her savings after the purchase of the lace evening frock upon a big box of deep red roses. Against their dewy, fragrant heads she laid a little card – 'Dear, dear Gertrude, send me your love and forgiveness. Your friend Janet.' Then, taking the Underground train from Earl's Court station, she carried the box herself to Euston, and saw it vanish northwards by the midday express to Scotland.

For more than a week afterwards, sick and trembling, she rushed downstairs to the letter box at the first sound of the postman's knock. But Ellison Campbell never wrote again.

CHAPTER III

SON

'Do men gather grapes of thorns, or figs of thistles?'
ST MATTHEW VII, 16.

I

As long as Denis could remember, his parents had quarrelled. Sometimes the subject of the dispute had been money, but bitter discussions throughout his childhood had also eddied round a mysterious and embarrassing topic comprehensively summed up by his father in the phrase 'Your duty as a wife.'

More recently the cause of controversy had been the militant suffrage movement, a question to which Denis himself had given a good deal of thought since the November afternoon more than three years ago, when his mother came home, battered and mud-stained from a riot at Westminster, to encounter the torrent of his father's indignation. An instinctive minoritarian by nature, Denis at Oxford found his sympathies gradually ranging themselves with the small and much-ridiculed group of undergraduates who wanted to see women students admitted to the University on the same terms as men. Only last summer, he and Todd Slater of Balliol, who was at St David's with him, had nearly been ducked for going down the river in front of the fashionable crowd thronging the barges during Eight's Week with a pennon inscribed 'Votes For Women' fixed to the back of their punt.

Even Janet, obsessed by some secret grief as she appeared to be throughout that summer vacation, had warmed to a semblance of animation when he related the episode. Whatever would his father have said about it? they both speculated. If Todd had not been so popular and a prospective Cricket Blue, the consequences for Denis might have been even more serious.

Why, he wondered, as he walked briskly through Christ Church Meadows in the bitter spring wind that Sunday afternoon, should his thoughts have deserted the enchanting present for the stormy and comfortless past? Perhaps it was because, on the 21st of the month, he would reach his twentieth birthday; perhaps because, this very week of March, 1914, he was to sit for Honour Moderations, Oxford's first public examination held at the end of their fifth term for undergraduates taking the four-year School of *Literae Humaniores*. Sometimes he wished that his father had encouraged him to specialise in history and economics rather than classics, but he suspected that the classical tradition spelt safety to Thomas, who was never willing to acknowledge the extent to which Denis had inherited his tastes from Janet. Denis often thought that it must have been Mr Gladstone's Homeric studies which gave respectability to the Radical doctrines surprisingly professed by his father.

'At least,' he thought, 'I can be grateful to them both for the way they taught me when I was a child. As far as their intellects go, I couldn't have been luckier. It's the appalling clash between their temperaments that always makes everything go wrong.'

Denis couldn't decide which, as a small boy, had terrified him most – his father's unrestrained explosions or his mother's frigid silences, sometimes followed by her abrupt departure to London for weeks at a time. In early childhood he had always identified his father with the volcanic Jehovah of the Psalms and the Lessons, the God who was perpetually being summoned to arise and let His enemies be scattered as though this were not already His chief occupation. Even to-day, the phrase 'God the Father' still brought before him a vision of Thomas's face, swollen and crimson after one of the periodic disputes with his mother.

Denis's most vivid memory of humiliating controversy went back to a quarrel which must, he thought, have happened at Sterndale when he was between eight and nine years old. He remembered it especially because his mother's attention at that period had been chiefly occupied by her visits to London with her friend Miss Campbell, and quarrels had been less constant than usual. This particular one arose from a suggestion on his father's part that Janet had been dishonest in keeping the family accounts. Thomas's words had speedily acquired their usual hectoring insistence.

'Well, what are you complaining about? What do you want me to pay you?'

'I don't complain about money. You know perfectly well I always pay for my board and lodging as well as all my private expenses! What I do complain of is your incessant grumbling. Not only do I pay twenty-five shillings a week when you only pay ten, but I'm doing all the work of the house and getting nothing but ill-temper in return!'

'I suppose what you want is to clear off to the Campbell woman as usual and leave Denis and me to get on alone!'

'If you can't stop grumbling I should think that's the best thing I *can* do!'

'Very well, I shall be thankful to see the back of you. For nearly ten years you've made my life a hell on earth. You're utterly contemptible, and I made the greatest possible mistake when I married you. The best thing *you* can do is to go and drown yourself!'

The raised, angry voices, finally rising into unrestrained shouting, had frightened him so much that he had crept, unnoticed, under the table in order to avoid witnessing the alarming scene. He was wearing, he remembered, a white blouse with a big muslin collar, and the stiff frills had pricked his ears as he crouched on the floor. During his boyhood, as he now realised, his clothes had always been too juvenile for his age, and in winter they had tormented him with their weight and bulk. Ever since pneumonia threatened him at the age of five, his father's paternal instinct, which was sufficient for a family of twenty, had wrapped him round in a feather-bed of solicitous warmth that came near to rendering him a chronic semi-invalid. Throughout his school-days he was never allowed to play games for fear he should 'catch cold,' while the slightest breeze was the signal for his fragile body to be immediately encased in a heavy overcoat. At St David's he had only been allowed to join the school Officers' Training Corps in his last year after a fortnight's discussion. Denis had adored the Officers' Training Corps, which had hardly any military significance in his mind.

It was simply his first experience of the fresh air, the vigorous exercise and the freedom from nervous middle-aged vigilance which was the normal lot of boys of his age.

On the afternoon of the quarrel he had shut himself into the schoolroom at the back of the Vicarage, where he tried to forget his sense of misery and insecurity by continuing the 'History of the Rain of Qeen Elizzabeth' which he had begun to write several weeks earlier.

'The Qeen who all England now professes (so our brother historrians term) crule, treacherouse, uncrupulouse and regardles of truth, yet she won the war.'

He licked his pencil meditatively and went on.

'But we must give the names of all ther Knights and erls, so the Erl of Sussex, Tomas Ratcliffe and Lorrd Dundely Erl of Lester will I think be enough in the erl line but now for the Knights and for Admiralls.'

At that moment the process of historical record was interrupted by the sudden opening of the door and the impressive entry of his father. Coming over to the table, Thomas struck an attitude which was already familiar to Denis, Sunday by Sunday, in Christ Church pulpit.

'I have come, my dear son, to ask your forgiveness for inflicting such an evil mother upon your youthful innocence . . . She's gone off to London again, and I suppose it'll be weeks, as usual, before she even condescends to let me know where she is!'

After a few such indictments, his father had made him feel that the mother whom he worshipped was indeed in league with the devil, but when Janet returned a fortnight later, he heard her own point of view and readily despised Thomas. For years, as he was now aware, they had played battledore and shuttlecock with his immature emotions. Never had he known, until he went up to Oxford, the real meaning of peace and happiness.

With a sense of repose which still seemed incredible, he looked across the Meadows to the pale, clouded sky, its dull grey faintly warmed by the wintry orange of sunset. What a cold March it had been that year! Pulling up his coat collar, he turned back towards Merton gate as the college bells, echoing loudly upon the wind across the wide stretch of grass and water, began to ring for evening chapel. On one of the half-frozen reaches a swan flapped helplessly, unable to struggle through the broken ice. He crossed the marshy ground and helped it to reach the bank by making a pathway with his stick between the drifting floes.

As he walked back to St Giles's in reminiscent mood, his memory repictured the various churches in which his father had officiated. Usually, he found, each recollection attached itself to some special ceremony in the long sequence of Matins, Children's Services and Evensongs in which his youthful Sundays were spent. Sterndale church, light, chilly, and draughty, had always turned his impatient feet stiff with cold in their best leather shoes. He associated it particularly with one festival of All Saints when he must have been about ten years old, for on that occasion his mother, who never before had wept in his presence, sat rigid in their pew with the tears streaming unheeded down her cheeks.

He had fewer, but clearer, recollections of St Peter's, Witnall, that briefly-occupied parish which could never be mentioned at home because it still provoked his father to insensate explosions of fury in which the words 'insult' and 'snobbery' occurred with repetitive vehemence. If he closed his eyes he could see plainly a memorial tablet on the pillar in front of their pew. He had noticed and read it the first time he went into the church for morning service on Easter Day, before his father had actually taken over the parish. He still remembered, almost by heart, the words inscribed on the tablet:

'In Memory of
MARGARET, aged 3 months,
ROBERT, aged 5 years,
WILLIAM, aged 2 years,
the beloved and lovely offspring of
Enoch and Elizabeth Alleyndene,
whose spirits returned unto God
in the months of November and
December, 1835, but whose mortal
remains repoſe within the churchyard of St Barnabas, Hanley, in

sure and certain hope of
a glorious immortality.
This tablet is erected by
their affectionate parents,
sorrowful yet always rejoicing
that of such is the Kingdom of Heaven.'

This inscription, with its disquieting intimation of the nineteenth century rate of infant mortality, had aroused his first
conscious speculations regarding the possibility of a life after
death. Into the vague distress which the tablet caused him,
the words of the Easter service had penetrated with a timely
persistence.

'*Christ is risen from the dead; and become the first-fruits of
them that slept.*

'*For since by man came death; by man came also the resurrection of the dead.*

'*For as in Adam all die; even so in Christ shall all be made
alive.*'

Had those children risen from the dead? he wondered, his
unseeing eyes fixed upon the vase of tall Madonna lilies on the
altar. Had the sure and certain hope of a glorious immortality
really been fulfilled on their behalf? If so, what form had their
resurrection taken? Were they still children or had they grown
up? In that case did they get older and older, like men and women
on earth, or had their development stopped at some definite
point? He was no more conscious of the gay vases of daffodils
and scarlet anemones round the foot of the lectern in front of him
than he had been of the lilies, yet afterwards he could never see
the massed loveliness of spring flowers without recalling those
disturbing problems of his twelve-year-old brain.

But Witnall had meant more to him than a tablet on a
pillar. At the back of St Peter's Vicarage had spread a square,
walled garden, where he read Kingsley and Dickens and George
Meredith on hot summer afternoons with giant poppies swaying
above his head as he lay stretched on the short, dry grass.
Some time towards the end of that summer there had been
a garden party at the large gabled house whose name eluded

him, and a little girl of about his own age had been sent to show him round and reluctantly entertain him. Though his parents had suffered such bitter humiliation from the family whose ancestors had built that house and put up the memorial tablet in Witnall church, he recalled with amusement rather than shame the smouldering eyes of his youthful hostess and her bored, sulky face. She had thick dark hair, he remembered, tied up at the top of her head with a big white bow, and long thin legs encased in black stockings beneath her muslin dress.

His mind raced on to the temporary parishes which had succeeded Witnall. He recalled Sidmouth, with its incessant sound of waves beating so close to the narrow esplanade which separated the shore from the houses along the front; he remembered Cheltenham, where the somnolence of post-Regency invalidism pervaded the atmosphere even of the excellent school at which, for one term, he had continued his much-interrupted education. When they moved on to Tenby the low hills surrounding the shore had been spangled with primroses and violets. There, throughout the summer holiday which succeeded his last serious illness two years ago, he had walked barefoot across the wide stretch of clean pale sand, stopping to look seawards between the rocky islands as though, if he gazed long enough westward, he would perceive the mysterious immensity of America across the uninterrupted Atlantic.

At St Michael's, Carrisvale Gardens, the large London parish where his father still battled resentfully with recalcitrant curates and work which was never completed, his reconstruction of the past was obliged to stop short, for he had reached St Giles's College to discover that he was late for chapel. As he slipped unobtrusively into the carved pew nearest the door, the choir were singing the Lenten hymn which seemed, in the years immediately ahead, to have held a strange significance of foreboding.

> 'Lord, in this Thy mercy's day,
> Ere it pass for aye away,
> On our knees we fall and pray.

'*Holy Jesu, grant us tears,*
Fill us with heart-searching fears,
Ere that awful doom appears.

'*Lord, on us Thy spirit pour*
Kneeling lowly at the door
Ere it close for evermore.'

As the music reverberated from the vaulted roof, the famous window with its William Morris figures above the altar became blurred and shining. Even now, though his most poignant experiences were still to come, he could never attend a church service without the price of inconvenient tears at the back of his eyes, so fraught with childhood memories of passion and pain, eagerness and frustration, the ache for love and its bewildering repudiation, was every line of every psalm and every verse of every hymn.

2

As Denis travelled back from Oxford to London at the end of the Hilary term, his speculations gradually transferred themselves from the probable results of his recent examination to the atmosphere which was likely to confront him at the Vicarage.

Would home, he meditated, always spell for him the now familiar feeling of reluctance and apprehension, the sense that his lovely life of contemplative peace was about to be interrupted by the jolts and jars of practical problems and psychological complexities? He wondered especially in what condition of mind and body he would find his mother. Pre-occupied though he always was with his own absorbing ideas, his secret devotion to Janet had increased with time, and he had noticed with growing anxiety how markedly she had altered during the past twelve months.

As Denis first remembered her, Janet possessed a large selection of clothes – more, he now thought, than she could ever have been justified in affording. With the poverty and cares of later years the size of her wardrobe had diminished, but until recently she had retained an intermittent pride in her appearance. He often saw her dressed up, ready to go out, in new garments and a gay mood which she never wore for him or his father. These expeditions were associated in his mind with the visits to London of Ellison Campbell, the famous dramatist whose plays were read by the Sixth Form at St David's as keenly as if she had been a man. His mother, he realised, was intensely proud of this friendship. Though she never took him with her to the theatres and rehearsals which he knew she attended, he too felt a secret satisfaction over his indirect connection with a national celebrity, and Thomas's grunting disapproval of Janet's theatre-going only increased his private sympathy.

And then, quite suddenly, about a year ago, the expeditions and the gay moods and the grunting disapproval had all ceased together. His mother talked no more to him of Ellison Campbell and her plays; she grew pale and uncommunicative and shabby. She even knelt at the altar to receive Holy Communion with holes in her stockings and worn-down heels which, as Thomas never ceased to protest, were visible to the whole congregation. She became, too, almost as careless with her private papers as about her personal appearance.

Only last vacation, after one of those humiliating breakfast-table scenes in which his father lost all control of himself and lashed out at everything and everybody like an undisciplined child, he had found her diary on the morning-room writing-table. She had left it open at a passage which not only recorded the customary matrimonial situation, but revealed the fact that her silence and shabbiness had a definite and disturbing origin. Without conscious curiosity, his eyes had absorbed the first paragraph before he realised that he was reading a private document.

'We are quarrelling again worse than ever. This morning at breakfast Thomas struck me, Denis being present, because I refused to give him every penny of my quarter's rent from the Putney house after paying other bills. He said I should bring us all to the workhouse by giving to "suff." money that it was my duty to spend on the household. Since then I have been reading over the letters which passed between us when I was in Devonshire. History always repeats itself. It really is quite hopeless for us to try to agree or work together, but now that Gertrude has given me up I do not care. Nothing matters to me any more at home since she refused to mend the breach between us, or forgive me for what I wrote in anger, not meaning it.'

He closed the book hastily and put it into the drawer with a determination that his father should not find it and a guilty sense that he had been prying, uninvited, into the secret preoccupations of his mother's heart. But only a few more years were to pass before he read the rest of her entry:

'My work for the vote is all I have left. It has cost me the friendship that was the most precious thing in the world, as well as any chance of home happiness through Thomas being so unsympathetic to all my ideas and hopes about women's position. I may as well give to it all of my life and energy that remains. I shall not worry now whether what I do helps Thomas or hinders him. His constant rudeness relieves me of that obligation.'

When Denis arrived at Paddington, Janet was on the station. Owing to Thomas's early insistence upon being seen off and met whenever he went to preach in a neighbouring town, meeting trains was one of the few domestic rituals that she always observed. He recognised her grey coat and skirt as one that she had purchased nearly four years ago, and she looked, as he had feared, listless and lifeless.

'Only forty in August – it really isn't so very old,' he reflected perturbedly. 'In that crumpled hat, with her hair dragged back, she might be more than fifty.'

On their journey home in the Underground, she asked him a few perfunctory questions about Oxford.

'How did you get on in your examination?'

'Well, I don't want to say so to Father or he'll get too excited, but I've an idea I didn't do so badly. I liked all the papers except one.'

'I'm so glad. It'll be splendid if you get a First,' she commented, but he realised with crestfallen disappointment that her mind had again retreated to the remote region which it now constantly inhabited. In spite of the information unintentionally gathered from her diary, he was neither old enough nor sufficiently intimate with her to realise how completely ill-health and the fathomless, unillumined despair which followed Ellison Campbell's departure had caused one overshadowing obsession to dominate her thoughts.

As she had vainly endeavoured to explain to Thomas during their spring correspondence in 1913, she had long been oppressed by her own security and immunity while her fellow-workers in the militant suffrage movement broke windows, struggled with policemen, went to prison, endured forcible feeding, bore the prolonged tortures and humiliations authorised by Parliament, and even, like Emily Davison, gave their lives. In response to official sadism and the provocations of the Cat and Mouse Act, the suffragettes were now waging the most furious campaign so far attempted. The destruction of property alone, in the first seven months of 1914, exceeded the total of the previous year. Almost it seemed as though the militant leaders were making a last frantic attempt to get the vote before the England built by centuries of travail went up in universal flame. Perhaps behind the Irish threat of civil war which increased the tension of social unrest during that menacing spring, they had subconsciously sensed the looming spectre of a grimmer Juggernaut which was so soon to batter its relentless path through the lives and fortunes of a victim generation.

One revolutionary measure, at any rate, followed another; the damage to pictures in public galleries preceded riots, church burnings, bomb explosions, and window smashings at Buckingham Palace itself. Was there to be no prominent part in this vast sacrificial pageant for Janet Rutherston, who because of it had lost all that made life endurable?

A week later she asked Denis to come with her to a five o'clock meeting of the Girls' Friendly Society and give her his opinion of the paper which she was to read to her group of seniors. This paper represented one of her surreptitious attempts to do propaganda among the younger women, for she knew that Thomas, who was leaving next morning to take a series of missionary sermons for the Vicar of St Symphorian's at Sidmouth, had a confirmation class booked for the same hour. She learnt too late that owing to a brief appointment with a neighbouring cleric, Thomas had postponed his class until the evening.

As Denis sat at the back of the parish room and listened to his mother reading her paper aloud in her clear inexorable voice, he felt disturbed by its acid inappropriateness to the audience of raw, uneducated girls, who listened to the bewildering sentences with puzzled eyes and half-open mouths. Janet had obviously composed this essay on 'The British Elector; A Psychological Study,' with less intention of instructing her listeners than of relieving her own pent-up emotions.

'It fell,' she read, 'to the lot of the writer during the last General Election to have an unusually favourable opportunity of observing the voter exercising his function. A humble petition from the other half of humanity, begging that it also might exercise this function, was presented for signature to each voter as he emerged from the sacred precincts of the polling booth. For purposes of classification it was found – from the point of view of the humble petitioner standing in the gutter – that the voters might be divided into the four following classes.

'First, the Domestic Voter who wouldn't sign the petition. The voter in this class generally had strong opinions on most subjects. He always knew whether Tariff Reform or Free Trade would be best for his wife's housekeeping purse, he had strong views on the importance of his daughter's cookery classes, and he was quite, quite sure that we did not want any more petticoat government, we had enough of *that* already. One specimen said it would never do for women to have any power, because there were so many questions brought up before Parliament which concerned women – White Slave Traffic, affiliation orders, age of consent and so forth – and, of course, women's opinions could not be taken on such matters. Another old specimen, in neatly-darned black kid gloves and linen of which the blueness and collapsibleness bore evidence of amateur washing, said that *his* wife and daughters did not want votes, *they* stayed at home. One wondered how many daughters were wasted on those gloves and collars and how much pocket-money they were allowed.

'Other domestic voters were quite willing for all women to have votes except their own wives. Their solicitude that the conjugal peace should not be broken by political – or other – discussions was touching, and was indeed a tribute to that unbroken peace and concord which exists in the home of every Domestic Voter.'

As she paused for a moment, Denis saw the door behind the small raised platform noiselessly open and his father come in. Thomas remained standing with his back against the door and an ominous glint in his eye which had recently troubled Denis a good deal, for he asked himself whether such an expression betokened a sanity that was quite unquestionable ... Desperately he tried to attract his mother's attention, to warn her of the impending explosion, but she was now absorbed in her subject, and went on reading with renewed vehemence.

'Then, secondly, we come to the Untamed Voter who wouldn't sign. These specimens were often very unpleasant to handle, they were violent and always unreasonable. Many specimens expressed a desire to shoot the other half of humanity; others, less violent, said they wouldn't give women votes but they would like to give every woman a good husband. This was an expression of primitive sentiment which, while doing credit to their kindness of heart and giving a just tribute to their own great value as prospective husbands, was slightly insulting to humble petitioners who did not want and were not asking for husbands – in some cases because they already possessed them and found them inadequate.'

A sudden furious clatter sounded at the back of the platform and Thomas strode to the front of the table.

'I command you to stop reading this instant!'

Denis saw his mother start and turn white. She faced Thomas with angry, darkening eyes as his outraged sentences boomed through the little hall.

'I forbid you to teach this class again. You understand? You are to give up the class because *I* dismiss you! Your preposterous ideas and insane behaviour make you utterly unsuitable to teach at all!'

As he stood, fuming, beside her, Janet moved to the front of the platform and addressed the rows of gaping, frightened girls in cool contemptuous tones.

'I imagine you all heard what the Vicar said? It's not by *my* wish I can no longer teach you.'

Denis, his cheeks hot with embarrassment, hurried up to the platform and took Janet's arm.

'Better come away, Mother! You can't do any good by staying here.'

Ignoring Thomas, she accompanied Denis quietly from the parish room, but no comment escaped her on the short walk home. As soon as they reached the Vicarage she went quickly upstairs, and he did not see her for the rest of the day. Again he realised, as he had done for years, how much more alarming were her prolonged silences than his father's noisy loquacity. To know what Thomas thought and felt was all too easy, but nothing could have concealed his mother's emotions more completely than these speechless withdrawals into herself.

At breakfast next day she still did not appear, though Thomas's vehement and persistent indignation still boiled up at intervals as he hurried over his bacon and eggs in order to catch the early train to Sidmouth. On the whole it did not seem to Denis a favourable moment for communicating to either of his parents the contents of his letter from Oxford, which told him that he had been awarded a First in Honour Moderations.

3

Denis went to bed early that evening, exhausted both by the ugly tension of the atmosphere and the bitter irony of his unappreciated triumph. Throughout the day his mother, moving noiselessly about the house like a silent ghost, had never come within speaking distance of him; she seemed unaware of his presence and his earnest desire to offer comfort in her angry humiliation. Where and how she had taken her meals in the past twenty-four hours, he did not know. Perhaps even, he mediated uncomfortably, she had not eaten at all . . .

He woke at midnight with a sudden start and an intense

feeling of dread. Whatever could have awakened him? he asked himself, his forehead damp in the darkness. What sinister sound, what inexplicable movement, had penetrated his sleep? In a moment his disintegrated thoughts gathered themselves round his parents' latest quarrel, and at once the conviction that something was wrong with his mother began to assail his mind. He sprang out of bed and hurried across the passage to her room. When no reply came to his knock he opened the door and found, as his apprehensions had expected, that her bed was empty and had not been slept in.

With his fear growing until it almost choked him, he called her loudly, two or three times.

'Mother, where are you? Mother! Mother!'

His voice echoed back to him unanswered, and he began feverishly to search for her through room after room. Downstairs, in his father's study, he lit the gas in order to find whether she had left any letter to explain her disappearance. Immediately he noticed that the large key of the church door, which usually hung on a nail above the mantelpiece, had been removed. His attention was then arrested by a magazine propped against a pile of books on Thomas's desk and heavily marked with a cross above the illustration on the outside page. It was a copy of *The Suffragette* for January 16th, 1914. Across the cover ran the headlines: 'How Men Fought for Liberty,' and the picture below of ruined, smoking buildings represented the burning of the City of Bristol during the Reform Bill agitation in 1831. A quotation from Cassell's *History of England* described the occasion:

'The Bishop's palace was pillaged and burnt to the ground . . . The mansion house, the custom-house, the excise office and other public buildings were wrapt in flames . . . The loss of property was estimated at half a million sterling. The work of destruction commenced on Sunday and was carried on during the night.'

His mother's absence – the missing key of the church – 'the burning of the City of Bristol'? Suddenly the truth flashed upon

Denis's horror-stricken consciousness. How long had she been gone? Was there still time to stop her? He had not a moment to lose – and yet he did lose several moments, standing unhappily in the study impeded by his long-implanted hatred of emotional scenes and the characteristic hesitation in acting decisively which he had perhaps inherited from Thomas. Throughout his life, immediate quickly-considered action was to prove difficult to his subtle and tortuous mind – a mind 'perpetually tacking up and down in search of things half seen,' as he was to describe it long afterwards to the person he loved best.

Violently conquering his reluctance, he flung a coat over his pyjamas and hurried across the road to the church. To his intense relief no sinister light, no ominous flicker of destroying fire, showed through the tall stained-glass windows. Pushing open the heavy unlocked door, he could see nothing but the shrouding darkness pierced by dim shafts of ghostly moonshine, and the pulpit and lectern emerging like black spectres from the surrounding gloom. The thick oppressive silence weighed down upon him like a tangible burden until, as he stood taut and motionless, his highly-keyed senses felt rather than heard a barely audible sound behind the closed vestry door. He went in quietly, with pounding heart, and immediately smelt the pungent odour of paraffin. Now accustomed to the half-light, he could see Janet, fully dressed in her outdoor clothes, kneeling in front of the wall cupboard at the other end of the room.

'Mother!' he cried in a shaking voice, 'what are you doing here?'

The reply came in a tone so flat and frustrated that he barely recognised it as hers.

'No matches!' it said. 'No matches! No matches!'

Producing a box from his overcoat pocket, Denis lit the vestry gas and pulled the curtain across the window. He then saw that the floor was half-covered with paraffin-soaked rags and cotton wool, which were also piled up against the old dry woodwork that skirted the wall. Behind the door stood a paraffin-bottle, and on the table lay a matchbox which Janet had seized from her bedroom mantelpiece without noticing, in her haste and agitation, that it was empty. She had been looking for another box in the vestry cupboard when Denis discovered her.

As he lit the gas jet, she stood up and faced him. Her cheeks were quite colourless, her sunken eyes strained and staring, and she advanced towards him with the jerky, mechanical move-ments of a sleep-walker. It was not, he realised immediately, a moment for accusation or argument, and he was about to urge her to return with him to the Vicarage when a series of sharp knocks descended on the window, and the raucous voice of Samuel Evans, the verger, boomed through the night.

''Oo's there? 'Oo's in the vestry?'

Almost before the words were uttered, Denis had gathered into one heap the soaked rags and the paraffin-bottle. He barely had time to push them into the bottom of the cupboard and lock the door on them when the verger, a short, grizzled man with rubicund cheeks heightened in colour, appeared in the vestry. Denis intercepted him on the threshold.

'It's all right, Evans, it's quite all right! There's no one here but my mother and myself.'

'I beg your pardon, Mr Denis. I was comin' home late by the church from the Men's Social, and seein' the gas on I thought maybe there was somethin' up.'

Denis, unable to screen his mother any longer from the verger's inquiring gaze, drew desperately upon his powers of invention.

'There's nothing wrong, nothing at all. My mother was sitting up reading and thought she saw a light in the church, so she got me to come over with her to investigate. But everything's as usual. It must have been a reflection from something passing.'

He turned to Janet and took her arm.

'Come home to bed now, Mother. You see there's absolutely nothing to worry about.'

Evans moved ostentatiously aside to let them pass.

'That's right, Mr Denis! You take Mrs Rutherston back to the Vicarage and I'll just 'ave a last look round and then lock up.'

Realising how thoroughly the man's curiosity was aroused, Denis felt reluctant to leave him in the vestry with its missing cupboard key and strong odour of paraffin, but it seemed to him even more important to get his mother home before she betrayed herself. She had not uttered a word during his conversation with the verger and, still walking with the automatic rigidity of a somnambulist, she allowed him quite passively to lead her out of the church and into the house. In the dining-room he poured out a stiff dose of brandy and made her drink it. She sat down heavily at the table, and in a few moments he was relieved to see the faint return of colour to her cheeks and animation to her eyes.

He seated himself beside her, still miserably uncertain what comment or inquiry it was wise to make. Hitherto, her allegiance to the suffrage movement had seemed to him legitimate and right. He had long realised that her bitterness towards Thomas and her early indifference to himself arose from his father's automatic, uncomprehending opposition to her political aspirations, which had caused her to identify frustration with masculine prejudice. Until women had more control over their own lives, unhappy marriages such as that of his parents were bound to occur; but surely this wild attempt to burn down her husband's church transgressed the bounds of rationality and even of sanity? Some years were to pass before he understood the self-evident fact – ignored by mankind for centuries and never perceived by Thomas for all his assiduous if indiscriminate reading of history – that the energetic, gifted woman to whom society offers no outlet for her energy and no scope for her talents, invariably turns anti-social and may become anything from an Olympias to a Lucrezia Borgia.

'Oh, Mother – why? . . .' he began unhappily. His lips felt stiff, and his face looked drawn and pallid from the strain of the past half hour.

'It was my tribute – my tribute to the cause,' she answered mechanically. 'It's cost me everything I care for and yet I've made no real sacrifice – no sacrifice at all, compared with the others.'

He realised then, from her repetitive tone, that she was only echoing phrases long dominant in her mind. The plan which he had just intercepted represented no sudden impulse of revenge, but had obviously possessed her for many weeks.

'But, Mother, just think what it would have meant!' he urged, quite unable to share or understand her complete indifference to consequences. 'You'd have been tried for incendiarism – sent to prison – and Father's life would have been utterly ruined. Things have been bad enough in the past, I know – but whatever kind of relationship between you would have been possible again?'

'That wouldn't have mattered,' she said. 'I'm leaving your father anyhow. I can't possibly stay with him after being publicly insulted like that. I meant to go to Putney as soon as I'd got the vestry alight.'

'To Putney – after midnight!'

'Oh yes; I'd have got there somehow. I could have gone to the house; you know it's been empty since December.'

The conviction grew upon him that this time her intention to leave his father would endure no opposition. To his still tradition-ridden youth, the prospect of her final departure seemed even more catastrophic than her attempt to set fire to the church. Deeply as he sympathised with her political ideals for women, his views on matrimonial obligations had not yet emerged from the uncompromising orthodoxy of Thomas's teaching. If he could not save his beloved mother from taking this decisive step, could he not at least try to postpone it, and thus give time for the growth of that improbable tolerance, that untried mutual charity, which his young devotional optimism had never ceased to hope would develop in his parents? One possible argument occurred to him, and for the first time since his babyhood he urged his own claims on Janet's consideration.

'Won't you think it over again, Mother – just once more? I'll talk to Father, I promise. I'll make him understand it isn't right to criticise you publicly, however much he disagrees with your views. If you won't stay for your own sake, won't you please do it for mine? At least remain with Father till I've finished at Oxford. It's not much more than two years, and then we can reconsider the whole situation.'

His victory, to his own astonishment, was instantaneous.

'Oh, very well!' she said wearily. 'I'm too tired to talk any more. I don't propose to see or speak to your father except at meal-times, but if you really want me to stay, I suppose I must.'

She pushed back her chair and dragged herself slowly to the door.

'I've always been defeated – again and again by Thomas, and then by Gertrude, and now, of all people, by you. Goodnight, Denis. Some day, perhaps, you'll understand what you've asked me to do.'

Long after the door had closed he still sat gazing after her, pale and perplexed. By this time the inquisitive verger's presence in the vestry had vanished completely from his mind.

As soon as Janet and Denis had gone, Samuel Evans walked up and down meditatively sniffing the air. He then endeavoured to open the cupboard, discovered that it was locked and keyless, and pressed his prying nose against the cracks. Just as he was about to rise, baffled, to his feet, his attention was arrested by a limp white object – a rag, perhaps, or a handkerchief – lying under the table. He picked it up, examined it, smelt it, and examined it again. Gradually a look of sly comprehension dawned upon his face.

4

Once more it was Sunday at Oxford, but this time a clear, brilliant evening in a lovely June; the last Sunday of the summer term. Again Denis was hurrying back to St Giles's, late for chapel, after a long solitary walk through Port Meadow and Godstow to the country beyond.

Though he and Todd Slater were as good friends as ever and often tramped together through the gracious Oxfordshire lanes, he sometimes preferred these lonely meditations on themes which would have puzzled the stalwart, audacious cricketer. This evening, however, he had temporarily abandoned the fascinating preoccupation with philosophic doubt and the nature of the Absolute which his grandfather, the speculative jeweller, had bequeathed to him through his mother. The near approach of the Long Vacation brought back disturbing memories of his previous period at home, and he wondered apprehensively whether the flimsy semblance of reconciliation which he had patched up between his parents before returning to college had survived his absence. Neither Janet's brief, uncommunicative notes nor Thomas's verbose, querulous epistles had really told him any thing at all.

As he hastened, weary and a little footsore, down Walton Street on his long thin legs, Denis noticed that the heavy entrance door of Drayton, the most arrogantly intellectual of the Oxford women's colleges, stood invitingly open. The glimpse of a green lawn shaded by dignified old trees and a garden path gallantly bordered with tall blue irises tempted him to pause. Peering through the doorway, he saw that the path ran straight across the college grounds in the direction of St Giles's – a tempting expedient for a tired man anxious to save time.

For a moment he hesitated. Like other undergraduates with no sisters or friends among the women students, he had never been inside a women's college and felt a little frightened of its cloistered seclusion. Then he heard a hymn being sung which suggested that all the dons and students must be indoors for the evening service. The air was so still and the great windows of the college hall were opened so wide that the words of the hymn marched vigorously towards him across the stretch of grass:

> 'Hobgoblin nor foul fiend
> Can daunt his spirit;
> He knows he at the end
> Shall life inherit.
> Then fancies fly away;
> He'll fear not what men say;
> He'll labour night and day
> To be a pilgrim.'

He recognised the final verse of Bunyan's 'Pilgrim Song' and smiled to himself, struck by the appropriateness of the lines.

'Well, hobgoblin nor foul fiend shall daunt *my* spirit! I'll dare even the hallowed exclusiveness of a woman's college – especially as all the hobgoblins are at prayers!'

Summoning up his courage he started to walk boldly along the path, but as he turned the corner where it skirted the college buildings before cutting across the wide lawn, a tall slender girl in a blue linen dress came down the library steps with a pile of books under her arm. Her face was pale but her exquisitely-shaped lips were deep red, and her crisp, unparted hair, of so dark a brown as to appear almost black, was drawn loosely backwards leaving her beautiful forehead bare.

Sauntering carelessly in Denis's direction, she met him in the middle of the path. As she lifted her head and looked him full in the face, the gold slanting light of the evening sun was reflected in her deep-set, reticent eyes – eyes of an indescribable colour, like a moorland brook running over dark peaty earth. To his intense annoyance, Denis found himself blushing violently.

'I beg your pardon,' he stammered, 'but can I get through this way to the Woodstock Road?'

Her expression as she passed on was contemptuous, and her lip curled a little.

'Certainly – if you don't object to using us as a short cut.'

In spite of himself, Denis turned round, but the slim upright figure, almost as tall as his own, was walking on without a backward glance.

'Well, really,' he reflected, 'she looked at me as if I'd come to pay a surreptitious visit to one of the college scouts! And if I *am* an outsider, *she* ought to be at prayers.' He smiled again, a little ruefully. 'Hobgoblins after all – but what a lovely one, in spite of her haughty eyes and her sulky face! Somehow, too, that face is familiar to me . . . Now where can I have seen it before?'

His captive thought struggled slowly backward through the years – and stopped short at a memory of white frocks and green sloping lawns . . . a large grey house with fantastic turrets and pinnacles decorating its gabled roof . . . the smoke-cloud of the Potteries in the distance . . .

'Why,' he recalled, 'she's exactly like the bored little girl at the garden-party in Witnall, at the big house . . . that must have been in 1906. Yes, she'd be nineteen or twenty now, the same as I am. I wonder if it *could* be she! What did they call her . . . ? Ruth – wasn't it Ruth? Ruth!' he repeated, 'Ruth Alleyndene!'

Although it was anathema at home, the unusual name pleased him and remained in his mind. For two or three days he could not get the disturbing encounter out of his head, but as soon as he went down from Oxford her image vanished, with all the other memories of his Second Year, on Paddington Station.

When he got out of the railway carriage he saw that not only his mother but his father had come to the platform, but in a moment he realised that they were equally oblivious of his own presence and the train's arrival. Already, by the time that he reached them, their voices were raised in anger, and a few bystanders, arrested by the harsh accusing tones, had stopped curiously to listen.

'What do you mean by coming here? You know *I* arranged to meet Denis!'

'You've no right to meet Denis or call him your son! You're a wicked, insane woman – a fiend in human shape! Penal servitude for life's the only fit punishment for you!'

'Will you kindly explain what you think you're talking about?'

'Explain! Explain! Fine lot of explanation *you* need! Haven't I just been speaking to Sam Evans? The man's had something on his mind for weeks past, and at last I've got out of him what it is. That's what comes of associating with mad women and criminals against my express orders, as you've done for years! All my life you've tried to ruin me, and it's no thanks to you that you didn't succeed in your sacrilegious attempt to burn down my church!'

'It's no more than you deserved after the abominable way you behaved to me at the G.F.S.!'

'Very well, this is the end. You can take yourself off for good now, as you've always threatened. Never so long as I live shall you darken my doors again!'

'Heaven knows *I* don't want to stay! I've only stopped the last few weeks because Denis asked me to – I was going anyhow as soon as he'd finished at Oxford. You needn't imagine I meant to put up with your behaviour for the rest of my life!'

In an agony of shame, Denis pushed himself into the midst of their loud recriminations.

'Father – Mother – please, please stop! Can't you see that everyone's listening, that you're collecting a crowd? Let's all go home and talk it over quietly.'

Janet turned to him resolutely.

'No, Denis! This time I refuse. I've done with talking; I don't intend to talk things over any more. I'm going to Putney straight away, and I'll send for my things in the next few days.'

She moved away, but Thomas seized her violently by the arm.

'Denis!' he shouted excitedly, 'you're not to lose sight of your mother! You're not to lose sight of her – do you hear? She ought to be given in charge!'

Denis laid hold of Thomas's hand and forcibly removed it from Janet's sleeve.

'Don't be absurd, Father!' he said wearily. 'You wouldn't help anybody by putting her in prison . . . I expect you'd better go for the present, Mother – I'll come and see you as soon as I can.'

'I'm going for always,' she repeated, a little subdued by the pain and humiliation in his face. 'I'm sorry, Denis – but as your father says, this is the end.'

He watched her moving through the crowd, and then turned to Thomas.

'Come, Father – we'd better go home.'

Throughout the journey to Carrisvale Gardens, Thomas never ceased to rave against Janet for her unspeakable wickedness, her disgraceful conduct, her terrible crime. His voice raged and swelled against the roaring of the Underground train until it lapsed through sheer exhaustion into fretfulness and lamentation. He was still lamenting when they entered the bare, echoing Vicarage, which seemed to Denis so large and desolate now that it was finally emptied of her presence.

'And the worst of it is she takes all her money! She's not fit to have the control of it, but I can't stop her. It's terrible for you, poor old boy, to have such a mother! Your scholarships don't pay for everything – how on earth we're going to keep you at Oxford I simply don't know!'

But six weeks later came August 1914.

5

On a Saturday afternoon in the first May of the Great War, Denis walked up the Bethnal Green Road carrying a small bunch of lilies-of-the-valley wrapped in blue tissue-paper.

It was just a week after the sinking of the *Lusitania* had provoked rage and riot in some of England's greater cities. Although the wide, noisy thoroughfare which runs through the heart of London's East End was massed with the usual week-end crowd of buyers and sellers, several shops were boarded up and deserted.

As Denis passed he read the alien names above the smashed, raided windows – Halbrecht, Schwalb, Rosen, Greenberg – and reflected for the hundredth time upon the cruel stupidity of a war which for him had only intensified the humiliation of his bitter, disappointed youth. Janet alone had reason to bless the national predicament, for it had supplied her, in the innumerable war-time activities that centred round St Etheldreda's Settlement, Bethnal Green, with a more than personal reason for refusing to return to his father. This fact had led him to suppress the heart-broken plea that he had written her just before Christmas:

'MY DARLING MOTHER,
    'It's been Hell since you left. How I wish you'd come back, Mother. I can't tell you how hateful everything has been since you went away. I do love you so, and I miss you terribly . . .'

In the end, after twenty-four hours of hesitation, he had folded up the letter and pushed it away among a bundle of papers. He could not bring himself to tear up this first written expression of his adoration, but he thought: 'I shan't send it. I've no business to interfere with her life. It's *hers*, and she's got the right to do what she likes with it. That's what Father has never understood.'

Instead, he ordered her a bunch of red and white roses from a Kensington florist, and went without his lunch twice in order to pay for them.

Above his head as he moved slowly round the sweeping curve of the great road, the feathery spring clouds floated in pure, delicate contrast to the dingy brick houses with their upper windows of discoloured stone. Beneath these windows, rows of small shops flanked the bustling, paper-strewn pavements on either side, displaying cheap jewellery, second-hand shoes, dusty grain and packets of bird-seed, shiny linoleum and bright-patterned haircord carpets, stained deal cabinets at rock-bottom prices, corsets of a greyish blue or a dubious pink, and flowers which were invariably white because the population bought them only for funerals. Next door to a pawnbroker with his three grimy golden balls, the cracked purple glass window above a basement shaving-saloon advertised 'Artistic Hairdressing.'

Down the right-hand side of the street the open coster-barrows extended as far as the high railway bridge, which gave conspicuous publicity in white letters to 'The Oldest Inn in the District – Ye Olde Port-Wine and Brandy Tavern.' The loaded barrows, now mostly in charge of women, exhibited fruit and vegetables, kettles and mats, men's second-hand clothing, sturdy ferns and aspidistras, cheap toilet accessories, live eels, and children's toys decorated with miniature Allied flags. At one corner the raucous Cockney voices of two or three unenlisted male costers shouted 'Nothing over 2d.!' 'Finest toothbrushes – only 1d.!' Above them shrilled a vibrato feminine rendering of 'Keep the Home Fires Burning':

> 'There's a silver lah-ning
> Through the dark clahds shah-ning,
> Turn the dark clahds insahde aht
> Till the bo-oys coom hahm!'

Every second woman that Denis saw seemed to be pregnant, or to have been in that situation so often that her distended contours had now become permanent. With most of them it was impossible to tell whether or not they were still of child-bearing age. They wore woollen jerseys, fastened across their bosoms by one stretched buttonhole, or shapeless overcoats dyed in peculiar shades of green, brown or navy-blue. The majority carried heavy shopping baskets and bags, or pushed perambulators with purchases from the coster barrows piled on the top of small grubby-faced children.

'At least I shan't be offered white feathers here,' thought Denis with relief, as he pushed his way through the trampled sawdust littered with fragments of string and straw. Not that he wasn't quite accustomed, by now, to the allegations of physical and moral cowardice brought against him by the shrill unknown females who constantly interrupted his progress through public thoroughfares. To none would his aching contempt for both himself and them have permitted him to relate the forlorn tale of his successive rejections, on grounds of health, by the Honourable Artillery Company, the Inns of Court Officers' Training Corps, the Royal Army Medical Corps, and even the Royal Garrison Artillery for Home Service.

These attempts to enlist had been made, painfully enough, in the teeth of Thomas's panic-stricken assertions that he couldn't possibly manage without him now that Janet had gone, and in poignant disregard of his mother's pale consternation lest all her endeavours to rear him in spite of ill health and her own disinclination should have preserved him for nothing but the mud of No Man's Land. But even when the General Recruiting Office at Great Scotland Yard presented him with a medical certificate stating that he was 'below standard' for the Army, he decided that the financial situation at home, and the War's demands apart from active service, alike made impossible his return to Oxford. He foresaw, too, in spite of his father's obstinate refusal to accept the embarrassed Bishop's persistent hints at resignation, the alarming possibility that Thomas's growing strangeness and hysteria would soon make him completely dependent upon his son's earnings.

So Denis sought, and quickly found, one of the many semi-official posts created by the war-time extension of the Civil Service. It was in the Censorship office, for which his linguistic gifts especially qualified him, and was rewarded by one of those nominal salaries which every genuine patriot was expected to accept without protest in the early months of the War.

Denied the Army life in which he had hoped to forget the shame and sorrow of his ruined home, Denis often envied Janet the vigorous activities of the Settlement.

'A desk's the wrong place in war-time,' he told her. 'Your work's so much more vital than mine, so much more human!'

All the same, as he confessed to the Vicar of St Etheldreda's, he felt alarmed by her increasing thinness, by the pallor of her tired, lined face, and most of all by her obdurate refusal to spare herself strain or fatigue.

His mother, he knew, had been friendly with the Vicar, Frederick Mansfield, since he spent a week-end at Carrisvale Gardens in 1911. He was a member, she told Denis, of the Church League for Woman Suffrage, and the only cleric who had ever recognised the existence of what he called her 'ideal of service.' It was natural that Janet, who found her energies insufficiently absorbed by the discursive amateur activities of Putney Red Cross Supply depôts, should have offered him her services as a lay worker in his East End parish a few weeks after war broke out.

'I'm too old for volunteer nursing,' she said, 'and my mind's grown too rusty for office routine. But if you can use the parish experience I've had to acquire whether I liked it or not, I shall be only too glad to come and work for you.'

So, early in October, she closed the Putney house once more, and moved with her few belongings to a bed-sitting-room at St Etheldreda's Settlement in Inkerman Terrace off the Bethnal Green Road. Neither she nor the sympathetic, unconventional Vicar was moved by Thomas's protests at this new course of action, nor even by his attempt to see her at the Settlement and his subsequent letters demanding an 'explanation' from Frederick Mansfield. Later he had written threatening to report the Vicar to the Bishop of Whitechapel for encouraging Janet to 'break her marriage vows,' but Mansfield only responded by writing to the Bishop of Hammersmith, pointing out that in his view Mrs Rutherston had never received even ordinary consideration from her husband, and the first offer of amends ought to come from him.

Just after the final quarrel, Thomas sent to the episcopal palace at Hammersmith a lengthy description of Janet's insane threat to his church, but even this did not evoke from the Bishop that uncompromising condemnation of her behaviour which Thomas had confidently expected.

'MY DEAR VICAR,' the Bishop had written in July, 1914,

'I am greatly distressed to learn of the sad circumstances which have culminated in your wife leaving you and her home. Deplorable as her extreme views and her rash political actions undoubtedly are, your opposition to them has perhaps not been entirely free from provocation, and I cannot attempt at this stage to pass judgment on her or on you. I only know that for a Vicar's household to present such an example to his parish cannot be consistent with the plain meaning and intention of the Ordinance vow.

'I am also concerned to think of the very serious risk there is of a division in the parish between those who support your wife and think her badly treated, and those who may side with you. Nothing could be more lamentable or indeed more scandalous. I trust most earnestly that steps are being taken on your part with a real sense of your responsibility for effecting a reconciliation.

                              'Yours very truly,
                                      'DAVID HAMMERSMITH.'

When Denis first read the letter aloud, Thomas, who had professed himself too ill since Janet's departure to deal with his correspondence, refused to believe that it had been rendered correctly. The second reading was followed, as Denis had anticipated, by a fury of protest.

'Division! Division! Upon my soul! What does he mean by division? There's no division in the parish at all. It's solid – solid behind me! Everybody knows that without my help, your mother would have become a *moral wreck*!'

Calling upon his limitless reserves of patience, Denis had conscientiously tried to compel his speculative and rational mind to the understanding of his father's irrational, emotion-dominated psychology – a psychology which feared responsibility and criticism and unfamiliar standards as a child fears the goblins with which it peoples the dark. To escape from this fear, as Denis was beginning to realise, Thomas had created for himself a neat, orderly world in which the righteous were rewarded and the wicked punished – and now, all of a sudden, the world had become hideous, persecuting the righteous man, reviling him and trying to turn him out when it ought to have been offering him its commiseration. He'd always lived decently, setting a moral example to his neighbours; he'd done what he knew to be right, and yet here he was, being blamed and punished for something that was entirely another person's fault. Life began to seem inexplicable when his strictly correct conduct, instead of being admired and praised, was disparaged and condemned. The implied reproach of the Bishop of Hammersmith – who must surely be looked upon as the representative of righteousness if man ever was – fairly knocked the bottom out of his fairy-tale universe, and the Bishop's second letter, which came a week ago in response to a long expostulation about the injustices that he had to suffer from the now restive parish, had all but annihilated it.

'In reply,' wrote Dr Reddaway, 'to your request for advice with regard to the conduct of your parish in the present unhappy circumstances, I think you would do well to look about you with a view to making a move from Carrisvale Gardens. I would suggest this both for the sake of your work and the possibility that a fresh start in a new place might give some chance of your wife's return. Reports from your parishioners indicate that the curate's stipend is greatly in arrears, and the position with regard to St Michael's mission is very serious. At one time the Mission was of real strength to the district, but now it is rapidly becoming a source of weakness and discredit. I am confirmed more and more in the conclusion that you would best consult your own interests and those of the parish if you could take practical measures to be relieved of the charge of St Michael's. So many circumstances have been against you, and there is really nothing for it but to get a fresh opportunity under new conditions. I am sorry that I feel constrained to write this.'

Broken and hysterical, confronted with the prospect of professional disgrace and financial ruin, Thomas began wildly threatening to give himself up to the police.

'Since the Bishop chooses to regard me as a criminal, I may as well become one! It's all a plot – a plot to ruin me! The Bishop's been got hold of by your mother and that immoral scoundrel at Bethnal Green!'

Denis, as he endeavoured to quieten him, faced squarely the fact that unless their speedy descent towards chaos could be checked, he would be obliged to support both his father and himself on a salary hopelessly inadequate for one at a time when rents and prices were rising rapidly. Already they were in debt to the Bank for Thomas's income tax and the upkeep of the Vicarage since Janet had refused after her departure to contribute a penny to Thomas's expenses, and the scandal in the parish had virtually obliterated the voluntary contributions made to the Vicar's stipend at Sunday collections.

Driven to despair by the strain of his financial dilemma combined with persistent overtime at the Censorship Office, Denis resolved to beg Janet to return to his father. Before doing so he consulted in turn the Bishops of Hammersmith, Putney and Cheddlefield, each of whom made it clear to him that, in their view, morality was attainable only by persuading two individuals who detested one another to resume their destructive association. Although neither Thomas nor Janet was interested in a third party, the fact that they continued to live apart was not, in the eyes of the Church, a rational arrangement dictated by fundamental incompatibility, but a situation immoral in itself. The endeavour to end it had brought Denis, without much confidence in the result, to visit Janet in Bethnal Green.

As he reached St Etheldreda's the church clock struck three. Realising that he had arrived, in his agitation, a quarter of an hour too early, he stopped beside a curtained window to watch the Saturday crowds. The window, he noticed, was that of a surgery bearing the name, 'Dr Sarah Ross.'

'Well!' he thought, 'Mother's got her woman doctor on her doorstep at last! Odd that she should have to come to the East End to find her.'

A few minutes later, Janet joined him at the doorway of the Settlement, and he gave her the lilies, which she fastened to the lapel of her worn grey coat. He had not seen her for three months, and though she looked neater and more animated than she had been during his Second Year at Oxford, he was again impressed by her indifference to her clothes and her appearance of being ten years older than her age. Almost in silence they walked under the railway bridge and over the wide cross-roads branching off to Old Ford, Mile End and Hackney. Opposite the long, square-towered church of St John-on-Bethnal Green, they turned into the pleasant enclosure known as Bethnal Green Gardens. War-time economy had already curtailed the flowers in this East End oasis, but a belt of clipped ivy encircled the smoothly-mown lawn, and a few scarlet tulips bloomed bravely in the central bed. Although a number of soldiers and one or two wounded men in hospital blue occupied the green-painted benches, the gravelled paths were almost deserted.

Janet and Denis sat down on a wooden seat against the railings beneath the plane-trees and sycamores while he read her the Bishop's letter and explained the position at home. She listened gravely, without speaking, but Denis knew that the expression in her eyes reflected the thoughts passing through her mind.

'I can't go back. I'm terribly sorry for Denis, but not even for him can I leave this place where I'm useful and at peace, and become once more the person I always turn into when Thomas is about. It was only Gertrude's friendship that made the horrors of my life with him endurable. Now I've lost that, I can't and won't face them all over again.'

When he had finished, she told him quietly but quite definitely that she would never return to Carrisvale Gardens.

'He seems to be in a state bordering on nervous breakdown,' she said. 'I'm afraid he's giving you a lot of anxiety and I don't like the strain on you, but I can't live with him ever again. Nothing will persuade me to leave my useful work here for the old purgatory of insult and humiliation. How often I've thanked God your grandmother died before she knew what my married life was to be! She had doubts and apprehensions from the first; she was never keen on my engagement to your father. If only I'd allowed myself to be influenced by her fears – though if I had you'd never have been born!'

'Would that have mattered?' asked Denis. It was his only comment on the defeat which he had foreseen.

Fearful of being influenced by the trouble in his face and the dejected stoop of his shoulders, Janet hastened to explain how absorbing she found the work at St Etheldreda's.

'This poor parish provides what I've always thought of as ideal conditions – the union of the contemplative and the practical. There's scope for all my energies in the district, and in between times there's my lonely life day and night in my room. I don't say I've no regrets. I sometimes long for an intimate friend, though I know it's no use. But it's infinite peace to be free from your father at last.'

'What exactly do you do, Mother?'

'It would be easier to tell you what I don't do. Most of the day's taken up by secretarial work, and visiting for the Soldiers' and Sailors' Families Association. Then I have to supervise the children's dinners, and the girl workers' meals in various small factories. I've a Girls' Friendly Society class, too, and a class for the factory employees. And of course anyone who can play the piano is wanted for all sorts of meetings.'

'And political work? Is there any chance of that down here?'

'Well, the War's rather knocked political work on the head, hasn't it? – but whenever I get time I lend a hand at Sylvia Pankhurst's East End Suffrage Federation. Its headquarters are quite near here, at a place called the Women's Hall in the Old Ford Road.'

She described to Denis how the militant suffrage movement – forceful, spectacular, dramatic with sacrificial endeavour, heroic in its undefeated initiative – had virtually come to an end in the last week of August 1914. In the middle of that month *The Suffragette* – the successor to *Votes for Women* – had ceased to appear, and Mrs Pankhurst issued through the Press a statement that, as militancy would be rendered 'less effective' by contrast with the greater violence of the War, the Women's Social and Political Union would suspend its activities. Instead, she and Christabel began fervently to address recruiting meetings – a sufficient reason, in the eyes of the younger and more revolutionary Sylvia, for her East End Federation to sever its connection with the W.S.P.U. It had acted as family solicitor and adviser during the confusion which followed the outbreak of war in a district largely inhabited by foreigners.

'Sometimes,' said Janet, 'I manage to get to their demonstrations in Hyde Park or Trafalgar Square. They're usually about civil liberties or an early peace, so they're nearly always broken up before they're half-way through. I've even helped with the cost-price restaurants and the clinics at the Women's Hall. Your father might suffer from an illusion that I was a reformed character if he could see me weighing the Jewish babies.'

'I take it there are still plenty about here – and some Germans too? At least, I got that impression from the boarded-up shops as I came along.'

'The sinking of the *Lusitania* did that,' she said, and described to him how the furniture had been thrown into the street from the upper windows of the alien shops and destroyed by the crowd. 'One baker's shop was looted by a furious mob of women. They seized the sacks of flour and emptied them into the road – and in the midst of it all the Rogation procession from St Etheldreda's ended with a Litany outside the church. What a mixture!'

A clock near by chimed a quarter past four and she got up from the wooden seat.

'I must go. I've promised to play some war-songs at the factory girls' tea in half an hour. About money – you'll need some, I suppose, when your father gives up the parish. I shall have to think about that. You'll let me know if he does retire, won't you?'

'I don't see how he can help it,' said Denis. 'But he probably won't decide in a hurry, even now.'

'That's always been your father's trouble,' she commented. 'Even when I first married him, he thought it unreasonable of the Deity to expect him to make an uncongenial decision!'

In spite of his despondency Denis found himself smiling, but immediately he felt an inconvenient pricking at the back of his eyes. ('O Mother – darling, beloved – why is it Father I have to live with – to comfort, to endure, to try to understand – instead of you? Why must you always put yourself in the wrong so that I can never completely take your part? . . .')

Long after she had disappeared into the Settlement he stood looking hopelessly at the blurred buildings and the misty sky, endeavouring to face the intolerable future and to prevent the escape of unseemly tears from his swimming eyes.

6

Nearly four months elapsed before Denis returned to Bethnal Green to tell Janet that Thomas had at last resigned his living at St Michael's. Even then, as he was about to relate to her, the end had not been achieved with that dignity and determination which alone could have mitigated its humiliating sordidness.

It was a chill October evening, sharp with the first hint of approaching winter, and Denis, contrary to custom, had gone to Bethnal Green immediately after finishing his work at the Censorship. For the first time since Janet's departure his father would not be pacing the study floor awaiting his return, for only that morning Thomas, a 'nerve case' accompanied by a nurse, had been despatched by Dr Twinkle to a hydropathic home at Tunbridge Wells.

'You'll have to manage it somehow,' he told Denis. 'If your father doesn't get a few weeks of rest and treatment away from here before you decide where to move him, I won't answer for the consequences.'

Two days earlier, Denis had returned home late after over-time at the office to find a police constable waiting for him at the Vicarage.

'We thought it best not to leave him till you came back, sir, he's that strange,' the policeman explained civilly enough. 'This evening he called at the police station and said he wanted to give himself up – asked us to arrest him for disorderly conduct, he did. We couldn't get on to you as he didn't seem rightly to know where you was working. So one of my mates brought him home and I've just taken over.'

After the hurried summons to Dr Twinkle and his prescription of an immediate change, one or two humane parishioners took it in turns to relieve Denis of the charge of his father during office hours. Whatever slight sympathy his neglected parish once felt for Thomas had long been exhausted, but everyone was sorry for Denis, who could never take a rest or go away for a holiday though his work at the Censorship was now so heavy. However he managed to carry on under the double strain when he'd always been so delicate, the parish could not imagine. If only Thomas could be induced to resign – as any self-respecting man would have done a year ago, instead of staying on in a place where he'd never been liked and whining to the Bishop about his 'wrongs' – perhaps Denis would be able to get someone else to look after him. The letter of resignation, at any rate, had gone in at last. Written by Denis, and signed in a shaky, indecipherable scrawl by Thomas, it had reached the relieved Bishop of Hammersmith by the first post that morning.

Denis found his mother sitting under a dim lamp beside a low gas-fire, her feet crossed on the faded woollen mat in front of the hearth. She looked, he thought, even paler than in the spring, but she did not tell him that she had lately suffered from a return of the gastritis which had caused her breakdown in 1913, or that Dr Ross had vainly implored her to knock off work for three or four weeks.

On her knee lay *The Times*, open at the long casualty list which was the aftermath of Loos. As Denis came in she looked up vaguely, a little dazed, as though her mind had suddenly returned from some place very far away. Immersed in the crushing preoccupations of the past few days, he felt startled and almost rebuffed when she seemed to have forgotten the postcard he had sent warning her that his visit was urgent and important.

Without speaking she held out the newspaper and pointed

to a name on the list under the heading 'Missing, Believed Killed.'

'Second-Lieut. Gerald Cosway, 5th Leicester Light Infantry,' read Denis. 'I'm afraid the name conveys nothing to me. Is it someone you know, Mother?'

'Yes. It's a man I was once in love with – or thought I was. About five years after I married your father. He was the Liberal agent at Sterndale.'

She propped her chin on her hands and looked with haunted eyes into the restless, pulsating gas-fire as she continued.

'He must have been well over forty – he was about twenty-eight when I knew him, just before the South African War. It seemed so big and important in those days, that little campaign. We used to talk about it in the office on summer evenings ... Your father could never find words bad enough for him, but at least he hasn't been afraid to die for his country ... How long ago it seems! One forgets things ... Thank God there are a few things one *can* forget!'

Imagining her to be completely engrossed by her memories of Cosway, Denis had no idea of the subject that occupied her mind to the exclusion even of the casualty list. Only that afternoon she had been walking up Shaftesbury Avenue after visiting a Government office for one of her soldiers' families, when she saw three adjacent 'House Full' notices outside the Connoisseurs' Theatre. Next to them stood a big placard which caused her to turn as suddenly cold as if she had seen an apparition.

GREAT POSSESSIONS
By
Ellison Campbell
ANOTHER SPECTACULAR SUCCESS
BY THE FAMOUS DRAMATIST
200TH PERFORMANCE TO-NIGHT

So Gertrude, in spite of the War, was still prospering, still adding to her abundant stores of money and fame!

'It has made no difference to her, our quarrel,' thought Janet as she stared into the fire. 'It ended my life, but it made no difference to her.'

Denis, reluctant to interrupt her thoughts, stood patiently by the table turning over the azure-coloured pages of St Etheldreda's Parish Magazine for October 1915. In spite of his personal problems, his attention was arrested by the Vicar's monthly letter to his parishioners. The sentiments expressed were not unusual. They were, indeed, becoming universal amongst the professional disciples of the Prince of Peace; yet from that particular quarter, they surprised him.

'MY DEAR PEOPLE,

'This year, like the last, we are called upon to dedicate ourselves, body and soul, to the cause of our country in its hour of need. We are still far from the end, and from all sides the call comes for more men to do battle for our honour, more effort from those at home who cannot fight.

'Amongst us are still many who are not playing their part. Many young men have not yet joined up, and there are others who could pray more often and more earnestly for strength to be given to those upon whose courage and self-sacrifice our cause depends. We cannot all, like Joshua, be leaders in battle, but we can follow the example of Moses, whose prayers gave Joshua the victory. It is not enough to pray in private. All patriots should attend the weekly War Masses, for our Lord has told us that His spirit is present wherever men and women are gathered together in His name.

'We know that our cause is a righteous cause, in which we are fighting on the side of God against the forces of militarism and the powers of darkness. Never before has the call been so clear for the lifting up of our hearts, the quickening of our souls. God needs the help of our prayers as well as our arms in this great struggle, upon the success of which depends the triumph of righteousness and the future peace and happiness of mankind.

'Ever yours in our Blessed Lord,

FREDERICK MANSFIELD.'

Denis put down the magazine with a small gesture of despair.

'And he's such an intelligent, progressive man!' he reflected ruefully. 'But who am I to judge him? What's gone wrong with us all? Why do I spend my days trying to detect the betrayal of official secrets by inoffensive strangers – and so much of my spare time striving to get admitted to that colossal uproar of which not one ostensible object convinces me? The whole thing's getting out of hand, and the effort to retain a measure of sanity isolates one unendurably – is that the explanation?'

Through his mind ran a bewildering sequence of familiar phrases from the Gospels – incongruous phrases which had lost their meaning for a world at war. *'Blessed are the peacemakers, for they shall be called the children of God.'* ... *'But I say unto you, Love your enemies, do good to them that hate you and pray for them that despitefully use you.'* ... *'I came that they might have life, and have it more abundantly.'*

Absently he picked up from the table another leaflet – *A Message from the Bishop of London to the People of London.*

'Have we,' he read, 'been true to our manhood or womanhood in this Great Day of God on which is being dedicated the future of the world? Is the message of Christ from the Cross to be the standard of mankind, or the modern German teaching that might is right? Nothing less than that is the issue before the world to-day.

'The lads at the front are doing their bit. What is my bit? Am I doing it?

'I must do more than *serve*, I must save. The nation has to save £1,000,000 a year to pay for the War, the Prime Minister tells us; then I must see there is no waste in my household. However small a sum it may be, I must save what I can and invest it in the War Loan to help my country.'

'It's an expensive business, blowing up civilisation,' thought Denis. His eye fell upon 'A Prayer For The Nation' at the conclusion of the leaflet.

'Stir up, O Lord, a spirit of service throughout the country;

may the soul of the nation respond to the call to sacrifice and help me to play a worthy part in this Great Day; through Jesus Christ Our Lord.'

He looked up as his mother at last put *The Times* behind her and spoke.

'Well, dear, what have you come to tell me? Has your father actually decided to retire?'

Her expression grew graver as he described his experiences during the past few days. He concluded, as he had determined after much hesitation, with a final appeal to her to make a home for his father.

'You see, Mother, his mind is threatened, and I don't know whether he'll ever be able to work again. I don't want you to have the entire burden of him. I'm willing to help you look after him as long as I can, but the Army standard's being lowered already, and sooner or later a medical board may pass me as fit.'

He certainly doesn't look fit now, she thought, half troubled and half relieved by his fragile appearance as once again the perennial problem, like a sinister Nemesis perpetually rising from its grave, confronted her indecision.

'Don't ask me to make up my mind at once, Denis. I'll think it over and write to you in a day or two. There's more to be considered than you realise. It's exactly six years this month,' she continued, 'since your father was initiated at St Michael's. We were still at Trefally that Sunday, you and I. I was taken ill in the morning at the Early Service, and afterwards, as I lay on my bed, I had a sudden panic about the new parish. I felt sure he could never make a success of it, and I was right. This is how it has ended.'

Three days afterwards, Denis received from her a long letter which fulfilled the worst of his desolate apprehensions.

'MY DARLING BOY,

'You are never out of my thoughts and I pray for you daily, but I cannot, even for you, make the great sacrifice of returning to your father at this time of national crisis. I am very weak. One day I think I can make it, but the next

I know it is too hard for me and I think it is better that you should understand why.

'You already know that throughout the earlier years of our marriage your father did everything in his power to forbid me the work which expressed my convictions, and endeavoured to confine me to parish and domestic occupations for which I had neither taste nor talent. But he did more – and worse – than this; he robbed the marriage relationship itself of all its beauty and dignity. He regarded what he always called his 'rights' as a matter to be regulated solely by his own desires, irrespective of my wish or ability to respond. By forcing motherhood upon me when I was ignorant and unready, he turned what should have been a sacred experience into a hideous nightmare. Not once, but three times, did I become pregnant against my will, and because, on the second occasion, I deliberately terminated this condition, he never ceased right up to the War to taunt and upbraid me. As you yourself must have realised from his recent obsessions, he was constantly suspicious of my behaviour, and used even my visits to Gertrude Ellison Campbell in London as reasons for accusing me of infidelity.

'If I returned I should become once more the perpetual target of these degrading accusations. I should have to listen to insulting innuendoes about all my friends, especially these in the East End who have enabled me, since the War came, to reconstruct at least in part my disappointing life. He has always had a genius for making derogatory criticisms which it seems disloyalty to the persons and causes I care for to let pass without a reply.

'Not even for you can I go through this misery of humiliation again. I have talked the matter over with Mr Mansfield, and he said that though it might be noble to go back, he would not consider it a sin if I refused to do so after the prolonged failure of our married lives. Perhaps if I were a better woman I could do it, but I am not big enough to rise above the daily worry and strain. It turns me irritable and mean, and makes me despise myself.

'I am writing all this because I cannot think clearly when you are with me. I always want to do what you ask and it is only later when I am alone that I discover I have promised you more than I am strong enough to perform. I quite realise the difficulties of the financial situation, and though I am anxious to reserve all I can spare for the needs of this poor parish, I am willing to help you to the best of my ability. I propose to allow you £5 a month towards your father's expenses, and enclose the first cheque with this letter.

'Please forgive me and try to understand.

'Your loving
'MOTHER.'

Overwhelmed by the responsibilities thus prematurely thrust upon him, yet urged by his very love and longing for her to play the part of devil's advocate, Denis sent a critical and unresponsive reply.

'I do not wish,' he wrote, with the pride of one who had not yet attempted to budget for two people upon a salary of £120 a year, 'to handicap you in fulfilling your obligations to the work that you have chosen. As soon as Father's expenses at Tunbridge Wells are paid, I do not intend to take any more money from you unless some breakdown in my own health obliges me to do so. I realise that Father did all that you say and I have witnessed, as you know, many of the disputes between you, yet I cannot believe that he was ever so malevolent and cruel as your letter makes him appear. I do not think you have ever been quite fair to him, Mother. He is a child who wanted to live in a safe world where everything went right of its own accord. You expected him to behave as an adult who accepts responsibility and he was never able to live up to it. The less things fulfilled his expectations, the more he lost his head, until it ended in his becoming explosive and hitting out at everything around him. He has obviously caused you to suffer to an extent that fills me with horror, but I still think that you, as the stronger one, should have been more patient with his failings.'

Except for her brief letters sent with the monthly cheques, of which Denis accepted only two more, Janet's bitter response to this conscientious endeavour to be just and impartial put a temporary end to their correspondence.

'I will not again discuss your attitude towards me. Even if I had committed all the crimes your father so freely charges me with, it would still be a wrong attitude for you to adopt towards your mother. As it is, you are tacitly supporting your father's accusations. I will only add that if as the months pass by we lose touch with each other because I have been pushed out of your life, the fault will not be mine. I have pleaded for your understanding for the last time.'

7

In the late spring of 1916, when the hostile armies were looking apprehensively at one another across the Somme, Denis discovered that even the dreary Hammersmith boarding-house to which he had brought his still ailing father was too extravagant for their bankrupt resources. Eventually, after a prolonged search conducted when he had finished his work at the office, he found rooms for them over a dairy in a mean street of small shops off the Fulham Road.

The two little bed-sitting-rooms were going very cheap because previous lodgers had proved unable to endure the early morning roll and clatter of milk-cans. From the first Thomas complained bitterly, but Denis, who had to support himself and a neurotic invalid on his ludicrous salary, could not afford the luxury of nocturnal silence. For months after the two years that he spent in his cramped room over the dairy, he wakened automatically at 4 a.m.

The owners of the small shop provided a meagre breakfast, but no service and no other meal were available. Every morning before he started on the three-mile walk to Whitehall in order to save the 'bus fare, Denis left his father's midday meal prepared on a tray. Every evening, exhausted by his six-mile tramp and half-starved after a heavy day's work performed on a nominal lunch and no tea, he returned to tidy the rooms and get the supper. The mere suggestion that Thomas should dust a mantelpiece or put on a kettle immediately threw him into a fit of 'nerves.'

Perforce left to himself all day with no companionship and no occupation, Thomas meditated ferociously upon his grievances until they were ready to serve up afresh to Denis when he arrived back from the office.

'Your mother has sold herself body and soul to that hypocrite Mansfield for £40 a year! That's what he paid her to run away from me and live with him! What do you suppose she meant by all that stuff in your letters last year about having to stay at the Vicarage because the Settlement windows were smashed in an air-raid? Sheer lying bunk! No need to tell *me* what she went there for!'

'But, Father, I know Mr Mansfield, and he's not—'

'It's no use your arguing – I know what I'm talking about! A fine thing when the clergy become procurers and entice the wives of decent men away from them! I suppose that's what comes of working in the East End among a lot of immoral aliens. Why doesn't the Bishop sack the lot – that's what I want to know? If you ask me, he's in league himself with the whole rotten crowd!'

'Here are the sausages, Father. Would you mind putting them on the table?'

'Your mother was always a wicked woman, my boy. From the time you were born she committed mortal sin. She refused the noblest task a woman can perform – the task of motherhood. Over and over again she refused it!' he would cry, his voice rising excitedly. 'Why, I remember that night when . . .'

On one occasion, wearied by repetition and a prolonged rush of foreign correspondence at the office, Denis expostulated at some length.

'But, Father, wasn't it a good thing she did! Just think what it would mean, as things have turned out, if I'd had a brother or sister. Supposing that child you say she prevented were alive to-day, how could we keep it? It wouldn't be grown up and able to earn; it would only be twelve years old, having to go to school and be looked after and fed. In view of the financial situation even then, it seems to me Mother was entirely justified . . .'

He knew better henceforward than to provoke the torrent of insane wrath that now burst over him.

'You're every bit as bad as your mother, saying such terrible things! In God's eyes, for a woman to refuse her natural duty is *mortal sin*! . . . I don't know what you young people are coming to nowadays! A dreadful wave of immorality is passing over the country because of this war!'

He sprang from the basket-chair, waving his arms.

'How many of the girls who flaunt themselves as "nurses" and "canteen-workers" are virgins – tell me that? They're using the country's emergency as an excuse to indulge their sinful lusts! They're unashamed and unabashed in their wickedness! And for you, Denis, you, my son, of all people, to join them! You'll be telling me war babies are justified next!'

Denis did not reply that he could imagine circumstances in which they were. He bent over the gas-ring to fry the eggs with a new resolution that under no circumstances must he argue with his father again.

When the bitter winter of 1916–1917 was slowly relaxing into the cheerless April that witnessed the battles of Arras and the Scarpe, a fellow parish worker with a friend in the Censorship office told Janet that, by all accounts, Denis was looking very ill and had admitted to someone that he was obliged to do a good deal of cooking and nursing besides his daily work. He had just appeared, she said, before another medical board, but had been totally rejected. In alarm Janet broke the silence which had fallen since his return of her last cheque to ask if this were true.

'At least,' she implored, 'do see an ordinary doctor and find out what is the matter. There must be something seriously wrong with your health if they do not even put you into a category. And please, my dearest boy, do let me send you the £5 a month again. I can make it more if you need it.'

But Denis only replied with a postcard, telling her that any communication between them was always discovered and had the worst possible effect upon his father.

'Do not worry about my health; I am quite well. I am going to send you a rose every Saturday, but I think it is best for us not to meet or write.'

Only a few months afterwards, he found in her diary the record of this carefully-considered withdrawal.

'Postcard from Denis saying that he is not ill and will send me a rose every Saturday – as an indication, presumably, that he is still alive. Otherwise things are at an end between us; that is what it amounts to. I wonder if I shall ever see him again? Do I go through life henceforth with husband and son dead to me and I to them, just as the dearest friend I ever had has been dead to me for the past four years? So be it; perhaps it is best for them and best for me. In future I am alone, friendless, and must live without love or companionship. I will try to make myself useful in a quiet way so long as life lasts. Pray God it may not be too long.'

8

For the first and only time in her life, Janet's prayer was answered.

The Russians had violently made their Revolution and the Americans had exuberantly entered the War; the Representation of the People Bill giving votes to women over thirty had passed, almost unnoticed, through its critical Committee stage in the House of Commons; the disastrous autumn campaigns of Passchendaele, Caporetto and Cambrai had ended ignominiously in mud, flight and mustard gas, when one December morning shortly before Christmas an urgent summons came to Denis from Bethnal Green. Immediately after he reached his office the telephone bell rang, and instead of the message that he had been expecting from the Ministry of Munitions, he heard the grave voice of the Vicar of St Etheldreda's.

'Is that Denis Rutherston? I'm afraid I've got bad news for you, Denis. It's your mother – she was taken seriously ill in the early hours of this morning . . . Yes, the Warden summoned Dr Ross at once and they got her away to the Mary Magdalene Hospital . . . acute peritonitis, I understand, and they were obliged to operate immediately . . . Unfortunately there was no way of reaching you at your lodgings during the night . . . No, I'm afraid the reports aren't very reassuring; you'd better go along to the hospital at once, my boy. Don't delay; make your superiors understand it's urgent.'

Half an hour later Denis sat in the bare, official waiting-room of the Mary Magdalene Hospital, the great North London institution where the medical staff was composed entirely of women, while a young probationer went to find Dr Sarah Ross. He had never met his mother's doctor in Bethnal Green, but he knew that she now gave her mornings to working in the military wards of her parent hospital, appearing at her surgery only in the afternoons and evenings.

He was gazing hopelessly at the rows of correspondence files when the door opened briskly and Dr Ross came in. A small, spruce woman in a white linen coat, her brusque manner helped her to endure the tenderness of a pitiful heart, which now ached grievously for the pale, stooping young man with the anxious blue-grey eyes. He looked, she thought, as if he suffered perpetually from overwork and malnutrition. Briefly she described Janet's sudden attack of grave illness, and explained the necessity for an immediate operation without delay for consultation with himself and his father.

'I'm so very sorry I can't honestly give you much hope,' she concluded. 'Your mother ought to have been operated on long ago. From her description she's evidently suffered from chronic appendicitis over a period of years, with an acute attack twelve months before the War and another about 1909. She told me of them for the first time this morning, and apparently she didn't see a doctor on either occasion. There's also a history of nervous breakdown in the interval, with a diagnosis of gastric indigestion.'

'My mother wasn't fond of doctors – at any rate of men doctors,' Denis explained unhappily. 'She always said she wanted a woman, and if she couldn't get one she usually managed without.'

'Well, she's among women now, and one of the finest surgeons in London performed the operation. I'm afraid, though, she's got her wish too late for us to do much to help her. I'm so terribly sorry. If only she'd told me of those two attacks when she first complained of gastric trouble, we'd have had her X-rayed at once. As it was, she refused to be examined, and the symptoms she described were entirely consistent with nervous dyspepsia due to over-fatigue.'

'I suppose she did work much too hard at the Settlement?'

'Incurably so. Fatally for a person suffering from chronic illness, especially in conjunction with the many sleepless nights caused by the air-raids in the East End this year. Forgive me for saying it, but I can't resist the conclusion that Mrs Rutherston's desire to live was not overwhelming.'

'You're probably right about that!' he cried bitterly. 'Nobody made it worth her while!'

Throughout that day Denis left the hospital only for the hurried hour in which he went down to Fulham to break the news to his father. He dared not stay for more than a few moments, and departed leaving the helpless and agitated Thomas in the care of the middle-aged dairy keeper and his wife. Through his tired brain as he hastened down the littered pavement rang the tearful phrases of Thomas's lament.

'It's a judgment on her, my son, a judgment – your unhappy mother! . . . No, don't ask me to go to the hospital; I'm not equal to it, it would make me ill. Besides, I should only upset her; she wouldn't thank me for coming. You'll have to go back alone, old boy; the hospital people will know what's right . . .'

By the time that he returned to Islington Janet had come round from the anæsthetic and was semi-conscious, but they didn't think, said the Sister in the Women's Surgical Ward, that she could last the night. Denis followed the Sister between the long rows of beds cheerfully covered with scarlet blankets to one at the far end enclosed by screens. His heart seemed to stop as he sat down on the chair within them, for the deathly face on the pillow was barely recognisable as that of the tired middle-aged woman whom he had last seen – whom he had cruelly deserted, he told himself remorsefully – in her room at the Settlement more than two years before. It was too late now to hold a rational conversation with her about the past, or to discuss the future in which her wishes, could she but have expressed them, might still operate even though she herself would play no part.

Throughout the uncounted hours that he waited beside her, she spoke only twice.

'We did get the vote – didn't we?' she murmured, without consciousness of his identity, but relapsed into coma before he could reply. The next time that her eyes opened a smile of recognition came over her face – parchment-coloured now, with the worn features taut and sharpened.

'Denis – you here! I didn't know you were coming.'

'Yes, darling. They told me you were ill, so I came at once.'

Though her voice was almost inaudible a faint note of agitation crept into it.

'They only told you, didn't they – not your father? I don't want your father.'

'No, no, Mother, he hasn't come. I'm here alone.'

Once more her blue lips smiled faintly – and then tightened again.

'I wonder if they've told Gertrude. Do you think she'll come too?'

Pity and dismay half stifled him as he tried to reassure her.

'I don't know, darling – I expect she's in Scotland, isn't she? – but we'll try to find her and tell her to come.'

'That's right – I do want her so. But don't you go – ask one of the nurses. I want you to stay with me. You will stay this time, won't you?'

'Yes, dearest, I'll stay,' he answered, his own voice turned to a whisper by the impending finality of that hour. Almost before he ceased to feel the weak pressure of her hand in reply, she had again drifted into unconsciousness. As her breathing gradually became shallower, a young nurse with brown hair and a fresh complexion sat down on the other side of the bed, her experienced fingers on Janet's pulse, her usually animated countenance solemn with official concern as the feeble life flickered slowly away beneath the warm vitality of her touch. For the first time Denis witnessed the pathetic defencelessness of the dying, their helpless dependence upon the conscientious but indifferent ministrations of strangers.

A series of light, slow breaths with growing intervals between them ended at last in a long rattling sigh. Denis looked at the nurse.

'Gone?' he breathed.

She nodded gravely, and he stood up.

'Good-bye, Mother,' he said, and bending over her he kissed the lined forehead and the closed sightless eyes. Pushing aside the screen, he went quickly on tip-toe between the rows of patients, now sleeping, in the darkened ward. Above the empty street outside the hospital, the Christmas stars twinkled blandly and the night was very still.

9

Two days afterwards, Denis went down to Bethnal Green to remove Janet's few possessions from her room at the Settlement. Only that morning, he had seen the coffin closed over her at the mortuary chapel. Never having looked upon the dead before, his shocked consciousness dwelt with anguish upon the rapidity with which the face of a corpse shrinks and changes, so that even a short time after death it seems never to have belonged to the individual whose personality once illumined it, but to be merely a waxen image made in the faithful yet subtly grotesque likeness of the living.

As he collected her belongings, fulfilling the bitterest of all the tasks that mankind performs for its beloved dead, each forlorn article of discarded clothing brought back to him days that he had spent with Janet; every scrap of her handwriting recalled occasions when he might have shown more interest in her interests, more kindness for her problems, more consideration for her moments of fatigue and pain. If only, he thought, as millions had thought before him, we could apply to the living those same standards of poignant compunction which torment us for our dead; only remember that the parent or child or friend or lover whose needs we overlook in our busy preoccupation will one day vanish beyond our power to serve! Oh, Mother, my beloved, my dearest, come back and let me tell you, as I have never actually told you, how passionately as a child I adored you, how deeply as an adult I have always loved you, how dark an emptiness my life has held since you left Father and me!

He was long past tears, but the rising nausea of bereavement choked him continually as he packed her letters and folded her shabby garments. By the time that he discovered her diary in the bottom drawer of her writing-table beneath a pile of National War Aims Committee pamphlets, his powers of endurance were almost at an end. He laid the pamphlets, compiled by the organisation which was then waging violent propaganda against a negotiated peace, in a heap on the floor, and in spite of his desolate indifference, his eyes absorbed mechanically the inflamed phrases of the leaflets on the top.

'We want a Peace that will end War.

'We want a Peace that will for ever destroy Prussian Militarism.

'We are fighting to assert that Right is Might.

'PEACE-AT-GERMANY'S PRICE AS DEFINED BY THE GERMAN CHANCELLOR WOULD MEAN VICTORY ALL ALONG THE LINE FOR THE GERMAN WAR-LORD AND THE MODERN HUNS. They set out to rob every nation and they want a Peace that will sanction and condone all their unspeakable crimes.

'SUCH A PEACE would compel every nation to arm itself to the teeth, to burden itself with a crushing weight of armies and armaments, to devote its best energies and the most fruitful period of every man's life to the dreadful task of preparing for another world-war.

'SUCH A PEACE would dishonour the memory of all who have died for us in the Great War.

'SUCH A PEACE would be a heritage of shame for our children, and our children's children.

'SUCH A PEACE we cannot and will not have.

'What is the alternative?

'WE MUST FIGHT ON UNTIL THE GERMAN MILITARY MACHINE, ALREADY CREAKING AND CROCKING, IS FINALLY SMASHED. Then, and not till then, we shall be able to dictate a Peace which will be a World's Peace – not (as the German Peace would be) a mere breathing space to prepare for a NEXT TIME.'

How did she reconcile those belligerent sentiments with the pacifist demonstrations of the East End Federation? he wondered – and then remembered, with sick realisation, that now he could never ask her.

He opened her diary, and immediately a small packet of pressed lilies-of-the-valley wrapped in blue tissue paper recalled to him an afternoon when he had walked beneath drifting clouds past the boarded-up shops in the Bethnal Green Road. Pinned to the package, a pencil-scrawled fragment of paper recorded the day. 'Brought to me by Denis from Kensington, May 15th, 1915.'

Clenching his hands in impotent remorse, he turned to her diary, and came at last, after an hour's bitter reading, upon the entries for 1917. They were few and brief, with long intervals, and the hand-writing was weak. Only under one date had it recaptured its old quality of pointed firmness.

'Tuesday, June 19th. Managed to get into Ladies' Gallery at H. of Commons. Suffrage clause in Reform Bill passed by majority of 330. Only 55 against. *Sursum corda.*'

The Third Reading of the Bill had been taken so completely for granted when it passed the House of Commons on December 7th that the last entries in her diary failed even to record it. Her final memorandum ran to one line only:

'December 9th. Victory of General Allenby in Palestine. Jerusalem captured.'

Denis sat gazing at the words until they seemed to lift themselves from the page and penetrate his brain. At last he picked up a pencil in his stiff, cold fingers and wrote deliberately beneath them:

'A week before Christmas mother died. "Jerusalem captured"? I wonder. Dear God, the pity of it – the folly of myself blinded by so many good intentions, so little intelligence! How many more years to light? So irresoluble a problem of incompatible obligations – and yet, too late, how much better I understand Mother than I have understood anybody else. How much she is myself! This perpetual conflict of reason and traditional duty – how precisely it is my own conflict and always will be if I survive. *If* I survive! *Must* I survive – to fight the same battles all over again, perhaps to ruin some woman's life as she and my father ruined one another's? Never, never may I descend, unrealising and ignorantly cruel, to that! Surely this war, irrational though it is, can provide a way of escape from the vain, useless turmoil?'

10

Janet was buried close to her parents at Putney Vale Cemetery on a bitter morning of sleet and wind.

Her grave had been dug in front of the railing which divided the burial ground from the wood beyond. Above it five tall narrow elms, like closed feather fans in summer but now stark and bare, swayed and moaned as if they were rendering a dirge. On the sleet-laden wind the slow tolling of the bell sounded now near, now far, and the leaden sky was stained on the horizon with a dull rust-red, as though heavy with coming snow.

Standing in front of the small group of mourners from the Settlement, Denis listened to the Vicar of St Etheldreda's reading the lesson from Isaiah for which he had asked.

'*Comfort ye, comfort ye my people, saith your God.*

'*Speak ye comfortably to Jerusalem, and cry unto her, that her warfare is accomplished, that her iniquity is pardoned, for she hath received of the Lord's hand double for all her sins.*

'*The voice of him that crieth in the wilderness, Prepare ye the way of the Lord, make straight in the desert a highway for our God.*'

When the coffin was lowered into the frozen ground, Denis raised his heavy eyes to the long sweep of Kingston Vale and the tree-crowned heights of Richmond Park away to the right above the cemetery.

'Oh God, if you exist,' he prayed, 'let me remember this moment for ever! I vow to you, here and now, that I will die rather than marry any woman to bring her sorrow. If I survive this war, as I hope I shall not, and some day take a wife, I swear I will always subordinate my own desires rather than cause her powers to be frustrated, or the life she wants for herself denied her. Oh Lord, give me knowledge and understanding; don't let me become self-centred and forget!'

With bowed head he heard Mr Mansfield recite the burial prayer – a prayer being echoed at that moment the world over by millions of young soldiers whose flesh and spirit shrank from the ordeal to which they had been condemned by the breakdown of human reason in high places.

'Thou knowest, Lord, the secrets of our hearts; shut not Thy merciful ears to our prayer; but spare us, Lord most holy, O God most mighty, O holy and merciful Saviour, Thou most worthy Judge eternal, suffer us not, at our last hour, for any pains of death, to fall from Thee.'

The mourners scattered the dry earth lightly into the grave, and Denis knew that the final stage of Janet's warfare was accomplished.

As he walked slowly down the path to the gate between the leafless December chestnuts, the Vicar overtook him.

'I hope you're going to get a rest, Denis, and a few days of change, perhaps – now this is over?'

'I don't know, sir. I'm not sure it's a good idea to have too much time to think. They've been very decent to me at the office this week, but I don't like to ask for further concessions. And then, of course, it's very difficult to get my father to go away nowadays, and I can't possibly leave him at present. The suddenness of all this has upset him terribly. In fact once or twice I've been quite afraid of another collapse.'

'You've been a good son, my boy; I don't know what he'd have done without you. Let me see – when are you due for another medical board?'

'Not until March – but I've pretty well given up hope of getting passed through the ordinary channels. I've never been much of a physical specimen, and I haven't exactly improved in the last two or three years.'

A pity, thought the Vicar, that the lad couldn't have joined up and gone to the front with his contemporaries, instead of having to shoulder the burden of these tragic but unnecessary middle-aged disasters! The war had its terrible aspects for the young, no doubt, but he wasn't sure that, at twenty-three, semi-starvation and nerve-racking anxiety might not be worse.

'Well,' he said, 'it isn't surprising, I'm afraid, that your health should be a handicap. You've had a sad time, a trying time, through this problem of your parents. I take it the – er – financial situation will be a bit easier for you in future.'

He held out his hand.

'I don't want to say good-bye, Denis. I hope you'll keep in touch with me, though I shan't be at Bethnal Green much longer. I was about to tell your mother when she was taken ill that I've got my wish at last. The Bishop's agreed to release me, and I'm off to France as an army chaplain in the New Year.'

Denis, his junior by a quarter of a century, looked enviously at the tall impressive man with the still unsilvered black hair.

'I congratulate you, sir. I only wish I could be equally fortunate.'

'Well, don't forget that if ever they do pass you and you want any help, I shall be only too glad to say a word for you. May God give you strength and courage in this dark time.'

'Good-bye, sir – and thank you. As soon as I've found somewhere more convenient for my father to live, I'm going to try my luck again.'

But when Denis arrived back at the dairy, he realised that his father's condition was no longer remediable by the simple mitigations of comfort and convenience. The dairy-keeper, looking anxiously for him out of the shop window, warned him that the prolonged hysteria of the past few days had suddenly ended in loss of memory and complete derangement.

'He's gone all queer, and he doesn't seem to know me. He won't come out of his room, but I didn't dare leave the place till you got back from the funeral.'

Feeling that he had passed so far beyond emotion that no further catastrophe had the power to shake him, Denis dragged his leaden feet up the narrow stairs. When he opened the door his father, sitting heavily at the table, called to him in an irritable voice:

'That you, Fred? What a time you've been! I can't make out what you do with yourself when you go down town! I've been waiting and waiting for you to tell Dr Mackintosh I can't help him with his books to-day. I don't feel up to it.'

Looking steadily but with cold inward horror at Thomas's puckered brow, his thin greying hair and vacant watery eyes, Denis realised that his father was addressing, not himself, but the long-forgotten brother who had emigrated to Nova Scotia forty years before.

A few days later, all Denis's meagre savings and the small capital left him by Janet had to be mobilised in order that Thomas might spend the remainder of his life in the dim security accorded by civilisation to those whose clouded minds have rendered them unfit for the fret and torment of human responsibility. Here, for three more years, he was to meditate upon his wrongs and his virtues in self-righteous serenity varied by occasional gusts of Jehovah-like wrath, and sometimes to babble to a tolerant nurse of his far-off childhood with its mythical green fields.

It was long after Christmas before Denis, deeply occupied with Thomas's final breakdown and the provisions of Janet's Will, was able to return to Putney Vale Cemetery and visit his mother's grave. By that time the gusty wind had scattered the last withered petals of the flowers laid upon it, and the winter rains had saturated to anonymous illegibility the written messages of affection and farewell. So he never knew that, a few hours after he left the cemetery, a tall angular woman with fading hair and pale, reddened eyes had brought there a cross of rosemary and lilies with a card attached: 'For my darling Janet. In penitent love and remembrance. G.E.C.'

II

Now that Janet was, so incredibly, dead and buried, Denis found himself incapable of feeling surprised or moved by the fact that Thomas had gone permanently out of his mind.

'Ought I to have foreseen it earlier? Should I have consulted a nerve specialist when I first began to have doubts of his sanity just before the War?' he asked himself. He recalled the violent explosions which had made his childhood periodically hideous, the histrionic demonstrations of a temperament which had found insufficient expression in preaching yet sought no other useful means of relief, the unbalanced defensiveness of a character which had never been able to impose upon itself the discipline of responsibility or blame. In unemotional response to the promptings of his conscience, he also reconstructed his long purgatory of overburdened poverty and the dreary evenings in their mean lodging during which he had endeavoured to lighten with some spark of reason and charity the darkness of his father's censorious, sex-obsessed mind. Was there anything more, he wondered dully, that he could have done to prevent this catastrophe of insanity or that other crueller tragedy of untimely death?

He supposed not. A nobler, more vital character than himself might have found some solution; but he, it seemed, was without resource, able only to persevere conscientiously, to reason vainly, and to suffer long – though not indefinitely. What else could be expected from the undesired product of warring passions and incompatible ambitions, the unwelcome child of a hopeless union to whom only one course was left? Did men gather grapes of thorns, or figs of thistles?

Fortunately, he reflected, at this insane crisis of the world's history, there was an easy method of taking the course that he contemplated. He no longer viewed the Army as the muti-lated instrument of human stupidity, but rather as the blessed means by which a man could seek death without incurring the stigma of suicide. Judging by the fate of his school and college friends, it seemed to offer a sure exit which was likely to prove the more certain to a willing victim. Not one of his intimate contemporaries whom France and Flanders had absorbed survived there to greet him; they had all shared a destiny similar to that of Todd Slater, whose aeroplane had been brought down in flames over the German lines at Cambrai.

'Somehow, now,' he told himself, 'I'll get to the War. I'll make them take me if I have to turn every Government department upside down to do it!'

But this drastic expedient proved, after all, to be quite

unnecessary. By the time that he had settled his family problems it was already the 21st of March, 1918 – his twenty-fourth birthday and an ominous moment at which to become due for a medical board. A fortnight later the Germans had broken through the Allied defences to the suburbs of Amiens, and the great nations of the world, having by now slaughtered one another's finest young men and sentenced the future to a C3 heredity, began to decide that even the C3s must be filched from posterity in sufficient numbers to complete the ruin of Europe. England, upon whom the brunt of the blow fell in that overwhelming spring, began desperately to send to the front the last remnants of her manhood. Eager, ingenuous children from school, debilitated young men who for years had suffered from physical defects or chronic ailments, middle-aged fathers whose limbs time had already stiffened and weighted, were pushed with frantic haste into the constantly breaking line in order to save a depleted country from which the best and bravest of both sexes had already departed.

In this last panic-stricken enlistment of all available manpower to hold back the enemy while the rescuing divisions of virile young Americans hurried across the Atlantic to Château Thierry, to St Mihiel, to the impregnable Argonne, Denis the exhausted product of a disastrous marriage, Denis the despised and rejected of a dozen medical boards, found the life in his fragile body at last acceptable to his country in its hour of need. On April 5th, when the four-year-old strongholds on the Western Front were falling one after another and the Channel ports seemed likely to be the immediate destination of Germany's overpowering and triumphant armies, Denis the clerk, philosopher and scholar, became a private soldier in the Middlesex Rangers.

Here at last he found the peace that his short life had consistently denied him. The War which to the young civilian soldiers and their waiting, apprehensive womanhood in a dozen countries meant danger, agony and premature annihilation, to Denis Rutherston represented security, tranquillity and a divine release from insoluble problems. Deeply immersed in philosophical and religious speculations, he hardly knew whether he was cleaning latrines or polishing buttons; an object of benevolent curiosity to his fellow privates, he responded automatically to discipline and was indifferent to discomfort. Sometimes, sitting in the sunshine on Salisbury Plain at the end of a 'fatigue,' he took from his jacket the thin volume of Plato that he always kept there, and read, as he was never tired of reading, the final paragraphs from the *Apology* in which Socrates, condemned to death, confronts his own destiny.

'Let us reflect in another way, and we shall see that there is great reason to hope that death is a good ... For if a person were to select the night in which his sleep was undisturbed even by dreams, and were to compare with this the other days and nights of his life, and then were to tell us how many days and nights he had passed in the course of his life more pleasantly than this one, I think that any man, I will not say a private man but even the great king, will not find many such days or nights, when compared with the others. Now if death be of such a nature, I say that to die is gain; for eternity is then only a single night. But if death is the journey to another place, and there, as men say, all the dead abide, what good, O my friends and judges, can be greater than this? If indeed when the pilgrim arrives in the world below, he is delivered from the professors of justice in this world, and finds the true judges who are said to give judgment there, Minos and Rhadamanthus and Aeacus and Triptolemus, and other sons of God who were righteous in their own life, that pilgrimage will be worth making. What would not a man give if he might converse with Orpheus and Musalus and Hesiod and Homer? Nay, if this be true, let me die again and again ...

'Wherefore, O judges, be of good cheer about death, and know of a certainty that no evil can happen to a good man, either in life or after death. He and his are not neglected by the gods; nor has my own approaching end happened by mere chance. But I see clearly that the time has arrived when it was better for me to die and be released from trouble; wherefore the oracle gave no sign ...

'The hour of departure has arrived, and we go our ways – I to die and you to live. Which is better God only knows.'

Thus as the weeks passed away and the tramp of armies

advancing and retreating sounded from the Amiens–St Quentin road through Italian mountains and Balkan valleys to the desert cities of Palestine, that significant summer became for Denis a period of quiet preparation for the early death which he so deeply desired and for which he believed himself to be ordained.

'I am of the night,' he would meditate, 'the result of ignorance and hatred, of mutual injury and frustrated aspiration. I ought never to have been born, and it is best that I disappear as honourably as I may into the darkness from which I came.'

But even in this final determination he was destined to be defeated, for the Armistice was signed on the morning that he landed at Boulogne.

PART II

(1906–1919)

CHAPTER IV

HUSBAND

'During the years, 1817–18–19, when the epidemic of Political Reforms was extremely rife throughout the nation, several Radical gatherings took place in different parts of this Borough. ... Attempts were also made to form Political Clubs to carry the views of the Reformers into effect, but most of the Manufacturers and respectable inhabitants stood aloof from these associations ... and at most of the towns very strong Resolutions disavowing the proceedings of these itinerant politicians and denouncing their mischievous tendency were entered into, and very generally circulated ... We do not expect to be contradicted in asserting that from the excitement of that period may be dated whatever political fervour the operative classes in this District have since manifested, as well as the combinations or Trade Unions by which they have since greatly injured themselves and inconvenienced their employers.'

The History of the City of Stoke-on-Trent and the Borough of Newcastle-under-Lyme.
(Compiled by ROBERT NICHOLLS from the History published by John Ward in 1843.)

I

THE BEAUTIFUL SEPTEMBER MORNING brightened benevolently over the wide Staffordshire landscape. One by one, the distant summoning church bells died away upon the clear autumn air. By noon the sun rode high in the serene blue above the turrets and pinnacles of Dene Hall, turning to an opaque brownish-grey the smoke-cloud over the Potteries in the distance.

In front of the house, leaning against the stone fountain filled with goldfish which marked the centre of the red-gravelled sweep of carriage drive, stood a big burly man fastidiously dressed in the frock-coat and silk hat of orthodox Sunday observance. Though he was well over six feet tall his broad, powerful shoulders gave an impression of width rather than height, and his fresh-complexioned countenance, dark curling hair and crisp, exuberant moustache bore the same unmistakable imprint of suave prosperity as his faultlessly-cut clothes.

Immersed in his private meditations, Stephen Alleyndene looked with automatic approval at the estate which would be his home after his mother's death. At the moment, however, he was not thinking of her, nor of his father who had died just before the turn of the century, but of his more immediate problems as churchwarden of St Peter's, Witnall.

'Can't have the chap preaching sermons of that sort!' he reflected indignantly, fresh from listening to the Reverend Thomas Rutherston's eloquent discourse on the apparently innocent text from Psalm 16: '*The lines are fallen unto me in pleasant places; yea, I have a goodly heritage.*' For all its deceptive quality of discursive optimism, the address had simply bristled with political allusions to the new Liberal Government and the decisions reached by the recent Conference at Algeciras. As if half the folks in the congregation had the slightest idea where Algeciras was – or cared a rap either! What did the Bishop of Cheddlefield mean by sending a Radical parson to a good-class district like Witnall? Did he imagine it was one of those revolutionary areas which were all too numerous in some parts of the Potteries?

Gazing across the iron balustrade which bordered the circular carriage drive, Stephen's eyes rested upon the smooth terraced lawns, interrupted by isolated beeches or groups of elm and ash, which sloped down to the wooden fence where the Dene Hall estate ended at the first cluster of Witnall cottages. Beyond the three miles of agricultural fields about which these groups of cottages lay scattered haphazard like the uncollected litter from some celestial paper-chase, smoke-darkened red brick rows of workmen's houses merged imperceptibly into the industrial area beyond. But though, officially, he knew it, Stephen's mind refused to register the fact that these congested working-class habitations clustering beneath the rim of the horizon came also within the parish boundary. Nor did he recall so disturbing a portent as the recent astonishing successes of the Radical movement in the Potteries. His recollections closed obstinately over the appalling fact that at the General Election in February of that year 1906, not only Hanley but Stoke itself had returned to Parliament men who belonged to the sinister political party which called itself Labour. Fortunately Witnall, strong in the tradition that emanated no less from the Alleyndene Pottery Company than from Dene Hall itself, had so far kept clear of the poisonous propaganda.

Every Sunday morning on his return from church, it was Stephen's habit to stroll round the family estate before taking midday dinner with his mother. He left Jessie and the children to drive back in the victoria to their own home, Dene Lodge, a square, solid building of red sandstone half a mile further along the road from Witnall to Cheet.

'It's a bit dull for the missus now the guv'nor's gone, with only Emily and the two youngsters to keep her company,' he would reply in the genial tone that yet permitted no argument whenever Jessie, at intervals during the past six years, had protested that he never presided at their own Sunday dinner.

Every Sunday afternoon, when the solemn family meal was over, he sat dutifully with old Mrs Alleyndene in the big Victorian drawing-room, reading Saturday's *Times* while she took her customary nap. Stephen did not really enjoy the academic discussions of economic and political problems which *The Times* served up to him, and still less did he appreciate its learned centenary articles on great men of whom he had never heard. The columns of local news in the *Staffordshire Sentinel* interested him far more, but his father and grandfather, like all country gentlemen of the period, had taken *The Times* even when it cost fourpence, and he was not one to discontinue a long-established family custom.

'What was good enough for the guv'nor is good enough for me,' he remarked with finality to Jessie when she suggested that they should adopt as a substitute the youthful and lively *Daily Mail*. Nevertheless, he continued to read *The Times* only on Sunday afternoons. Nobody, least of all himself, had ever criticised his imperviousness to the influence of national events. It was characteristic of his class and even more of his district, an isolated industrial area which had always kept itself to itself.

As the stable clock struck the half-hour three startled magpies, Dominican birds cutting across Stephen's line of vision with their stiff geometrical flight, recalled his mind from its uncomfortable preoccupation with the new Rector's sermon to the satisfactory and agreeable scene which lay spread before him.

Dene Hall had been erected on the summit of steep rising ground over quarter of a mile from the main road between Hanley and Cheet. The tall mullioned windows in the front of the house, divided by their stone facings into narrow vertical groups of small rectangular panes, looked down over wide lawns to the distant roofs of Witnall, that semi-rural, semi-industrial sister to the Five Towns which extended from the scattered cottages hugging the green valley into the elongated borough enclosing the outskirts of Hanley and Stoke. From the clear heights on which the Hall stood, Stephen gazed across mellowing autumn fields to the horizon encircled by the long undulating sweep of the Potteries Ridge, rising skywards from Witnall in the valley. A pall of smoky mist perpetually dimmed this vast industrial slope, with its pithead and pot-bank chimneys consuming coal. At the edge of the urban area a horizontal stretch of newly-mown hayfield caught his eye with its startling yellow-green vividness against the dark misty ridge. On late summer evenings the setting sun, a huge empyreal reflection of the pot-bank furnaces, loomed through the smoke-cloud like an angry ball of flame descending upon a smouldering world.

Built by Stephen's grandfather Enoch in the year of Queen Victoria's accession, Dene Hall was designed in the Tudor style, its gabled façade elaborately ornamented with stone pinnacles and miniature turrets. The main block had been constructed of local red sandstone, but the smoke and grime of nineteenth-century industry, blown for seventy years across the intervening miles of verdant fields, had so deepened its colour that from a distance its complex, dominating outline appeared grey and dark against its background of birch and ash. Above the main entrance to the house, facing the carriage drive and the fountain where Stephen stood, twin lanterns of ornamented iron hung beneath a heavily carved balustrade which carried the family crest on a large central plaque. The drive itself gradually narrowed into the quarter-mile of private road, shaded by enormous spreading beeches, which ended at elaborate black and gold gates with huge gate-posts each flanked by a tall monkey-puzzle tree. The bright geranium beds on either side of the drive glowed from the enclosing shadows of cedars, hollies, laurels and rhododendrons, which blossomed into pink and white splendour in early June.

In Enoch's day the interior of Dene Hall had been decorated with the same lavish individualism as its imposing exterior.

'Eh, you should see new pleace,' a mould-maker who had been sent to Dene Hall with a message from the Pottery had reported to his envious fellows: 'There's cresses on the dernubs an' barristers on the stairs!'

Joseph Alleyndene, Enoch's son and Stephen's father, had modernised and simplified the Hall's internal equipment during the few years of his too brief dominion, but in the crested door-handles, the double-banistered staircase and the ornamented ceilings with their gilt bosses and pseudo-Elizabethan rafters, the evidences of Enoch's exhibitionist exuberance remained unsubdued. The house was still overstocked with double beds, marble-topped washstands and round-backed sofas, but the younger generation of Alleyndenes had prevailed upon their reluctant mother to part with some of the embroidered settees and heavily antimacassared easy chairs.

Stephen felt sustained and encouraged by the warm satisfaction which pervaded his senses whenever he contemplated the well-ordered acres that would one day be his. Beyond the black industrial strip of the Potteries – ten miles long and two or three wide – lay the smooth agricultural regions of North Staffordshire, that middle country where the North meets the South, and the bleak stone walls of Yorkshire and Derbyshire mingle with the green hedgerows of a gentler climate. But Stephen was prepared to wager anyone that in all those productive miles there wasn't an estate which commanded its surroundings as Dene Hall commanded Witnall.

'It's a real gentleman's place – one of the finest bits of property in the Midlands,' he was accustomed to tell his business acquaintances from other parts of the country. Not, mind you, that his own home, Dene Lodge, wasn't eminently suited for the time being to himself and family; but you couldn't class it in the same street as Dene Hall, which was a proposition that the Duke himself might have envied. When Stephen came into his own he would lose no time in putting his large and turbulent family of younger brothers and sisters into their proper – and subordinate – place; he'd soon show them he meant to be master.

Robert, the Manchester solicitor, two and a half years his junior, had long departed, and so had Henry the architect, a thick-set, fair-haired and quarrelsome man who resembled the Alleyndenes only in the last-named quality, and was quite the most enterprising of them all. Good-natured, plump Elizabeth had married her German doctor in 1902 and was seldom able to leave London, while the lethargic Daniel, his thirty-three-year-old third brother who unenthusiastically acted as assistant land-agent to the Duke of Nottingham, only appeared occasionally at week-ends.

The toughest problem would be his eldest sister Emily, now just forty, black-haired, dark-browed, and as embittered a dried-up spinster as you could find anywhere in the county. She'd lived at Dene Hall for almost the whole of her uneventful and disappointing life, but he didn't see Emily and Jessie hitting it off together, and Jessie, as he fully realised though he never admitted it to her, had already had enough to put up with from his numerous and overwhelming family. As soon as the time came for Jessie and himself to move from Dene Lodge to Dene Hall – and it wouldn't be long now, he suspected; his mother was nearing seventy and beginning to fail – Emily would have to clear out whether she liked it or not.

He didn't anticipate much trouble from the youngsters – twenty-seven-year-old Philip, his mother's darling, who 'helped' Stephen at the Pottery, and poor feeble-minded Hetty, now aged twenty-five, the fag-end of a family which had once numbered thirteen. She alone, of the eight survivors, would submit to dictation without protest, and Emily must be persuaded to take her over. The prospect was satisfactory, but offered nothing comparable to the pleasure which he anticipated in ridding his business of the riotous, irresponsible Philip.

'Canada's the place for him when the missis kicks the bucket, and a job of work for a change,' Stephen told himself. 'If necessary I'll find the brass myself – and cheap at the price!'

2

When Enoch Alleyndene moved out of the Potteries into Dene Hall, he had rebuilt and enlarged at the same time the old family pottery on Witnall Ridge, which formed the boundary-line between the strongly contrasted Parliamentary constituencies of Witnall and Hanley.

Hanley, as Daniel frequently remarked, was 'stinking with Socialism,' but Witnall, which included most of the rural district between the Potteries and Cheet, was a highly respectable area with a sound Conservative tradition. At the urban end of the constituency, it was true, the smoking chimneys, slag-heaps and pot-banks of one of England's blackest regions lent their indus-trial quality to the district, but at the other the magpie-haunted meadows, smelling sweetly of mown hay at harvest-time, had successfully resisted the threatening encroachments of the Indus-trial Revolution. Though the Alleyndene Pottery was actually in Hanley almost the entire body of its employees lived in Witnall, and at a time when organisation in the pottery trade was at its lowest ebb, the family business remained impervious to Trade Union influence.

Strolling idly through the cool plantation, Stephen was reminded by a tall tapering fir with an engraved plate at its base of the fact that his father, the first of Enoch's six sons and daughters to survive childhood, had been born at Dene Hall the year after the house was built.

'This white Norway spruce,' he read, 'was planted by me,

Enoch Alleyndene, on April 5th, 1838, to commemorate the birth of my son Joseph. "Now thank we all our God."'

In gratitude for that welcome event the father had also erected a pious tablet, worded with the Rector's assistance, in Witnall church to commemorate his son's three less fortunate predecessors. Notwithstanding the engraved plate on the fir and the inscribed tablet in St Peter's, Enoch Alleyndene, by that time the owner of a considerable fortune and the employer of nearly a thousand men, was no sentimentalist. During the last twenty years of the grandguv'nor's life, he had shown Stephen that he still remembered the training in ruthlessness given him half a century earlier by his own father, old William Alleyndene, the inventor of their celebrated 'Blue Under-Glaze Ware.' This typical product of the Potteries, with its exquisite shades of cobalt and turquoise, had laid the foundations of the family prosperity and caused the fame of Alleyndene pottery to extend from Staffordshire throughout the world.

William had displayed no mercy towards Radical rebels during the political troubles that disturbed the borough between 1817 and 1820, and just before his death he took a leading part in the Association of Manufacturers which defeated a formidable combination of workmen in 1836. All the male members of the Alleyndene family, as Stephen had often heard in his younger days from his grandfather, assisted six years later in the measures taken to suppress Chartist outbreaks in the Potteries. He still recalled the similar lack of compunction shown by Enoch and Joseph towards those employees who joined the malcontents during the earthenware workers' strike of 1881. As a youth just beginning to go to the Pottery, he had shared their jubiliation when the hollow-ware pressers' scheme for opening a co-operative factory failed in the same year.

A formidable individualist even in a district where strong individualism was the rule amongst the pottery manufacturers, Enoch Alleyndene lived to be ninety; he died only in 1892 after becoming, for the previous twenty-five years, a terror to his family and a legend in the neighbourhood. Old Job Massey, the owner of the little barber's shop in Witnall where three generations of male Alleyndenes had gone for shaves and haircuts, never wearied of describing to Stephen one ludicrous predicament in which his grandfather, who objected to the ravages of time upon his jet-black head, had found himself owing to his obstinate amateur experiments with hair-dyes.

'It was day before Mr Robert's christenin' and there was to be big party at th' Hall, when up drives old Mr Alleyndene's groom and comes into shop. Fair meythered, he was, and he says to me, "The guv'nor wants you up at Dene Hall, Mr Massey, and I've orders to take you back in dog-cart." "Never sweat," says I, "I'll come when I'm through with next customer." "Eh, Mr Massey," says he, "if you don't come at onct I'm frittened I'll get the sack! Don't know what 'a been doin', but there's a pretty commotion up there." So since he seems proper skeered I drops sithers an' off I goes with him there an' then, and when we gets to th' Hall, half the folks in place are standin' on stairs waitin' for me to go into th' old gentleman's bedroom. So I knocks at door and he says, "Come in!" and in I goes and finds him sittin' in arm-chair in front of fire in his long black coat and trousers with red bandana handkerchief over his knees. "Damn you, Massey," says he, "what the hell have you been doing? Just look at my head!" And I looks close, Mr Stephen, and 'twas all I could do not to skrike with laughin', for one side of his head is yellow and t'other's bright green. "Eh, Mr Alleyndene," says I, "you've not obeyed instructions! You didn't wash all th' grease out of yed before applyin' the dye. Now you sit quiet and we'll soon put you right, sir." So down I sends for hot watter and washes his hair and puts on dye again, and I says, "It's all but proper colour now, Mr Alleyndene, if you'd take look in glass." So up he gets and looks at himself, and then he shakes both my hands and he says to me, "You've done it, Massey, you've done it, man! Praise God from whom all blessings flow!"'

With increasing years old Enoch's eccentricity had been marked at intervals by a strain of senseless cruelty which produced more than one family disaster and led to several violent scenes with his young, undisciplined grandchildren. The cancer that killed his wife after years of painful illness was rumoured to have been due to a quarrel that occurred during a drive home from a tea-party in Witnall one winter's evening, when he had put a conclusive end to the argument by pitching her out of the dog-cart on to the frozen highroad. Not long after her death he had shot a favourite retriever, belonging to ten-year-old Henry, because it had trespassed on his game preserves. When the boy, broken-hearted and furious, laid waste in revenge his grandfather's cherished beds of prize rose-trees, Enoch had retaliated yet further by hanging the dog's body in the plantation side by side with the decomposing corpses of a stoat and a weasel.

'It's the French blood gone bad in him,' Joseph Alleyndene once told Stephen. But in spite of the hatred and resentment to which his father habitually moved him, he spoke with a certain pride, for the Alleyndenes cherished, not without justification, the Huguenot strain in their heredity. According to ancestral records, the enterprising founder of the Alleyndene Pottery had married, at the beginning of the eighteenth century, a French woman, Veronique Fourdrinier, the daughter of a Huguenot silk-worker, whose successors of the same name had founded the paper manufactory at Hanley in 1827. Veronique's father had fled from France after the Revocation of the Edict of Nantes and had settled, with others of his skilled trade, in the neighbourhood of Cheet. From that time onwards, through much inter-marrying among the Alleyndenes, the dominant Huguenot qualities had persisted, so that a family which would otherwise have perpetuated nothing more remarkable than medium-brown British colouring, round pudding faces and insignificant features, acquired paler skins and darker hair, and passed on a sequence of aquiline noses and straight black eyebrows over sulky, deep-set brown eyes.

3

As Stephen emerged from the shadowy plantation into brilliant sunlight where the lowest of the three lawns sloped down to the wooden fence at the Witnall end of the estate, a ruddy streak flashed past his head and buried itself in a tall clump of magenta willow-herb at the junction of the rough grass with the mown.

'That was a redstart,' said Stephen to himself, instantly recognising the vivid tail and bright bay breast. Like his next brother and their father before them, he was a keen lover of birds and other small country creatures. Often, as boys, he and Robert had waited for hours beside the narrow stream two fields away for a kingfisher which had made its tunnelled nest in the soft earthy bank. Sometimes, on Saturday afternoons, as they watched the emerald dragonflies dipping their opalescent wings into the shallow water, Joseph would join them until all three were rewarded by the sight of the bird's blue-green feathers and long questing beak.

Stephen had been very fond of Joseph, a genial popular companion and a kindly employer when he was not quarrelling with his tyrannical old father. It was a shame, he often thought, that the guv'nor had survived Enoch and ruled the roost at the Pottery for barely eight years, the last of those undermined and spoiled by illness. He might at least have been spared to see the new century – which would soon, please God, become as prosperous and remunerative for the Potteries as the years of expansion in the third quarter of the eighteen-hundreds.

Carefully folded in his morocco-leather pocket-book, Stephen still kept the newspaper paragraph which he had cut out at the time of his father's death in November 1899. It showed, he thought, a proper appreciation, not only of Joseph, but of the esteem in which the whole family was held throughout the district.

DEATH OF MR JOSEPH ALLEYNDENE

'Our obituary columns last week contained an announcement of the decease of Mr Joseph Alleyndene, the well-known master of the famous pottery and owner of Dene Hall, at the age of sixty-one. Mr Alleyndene, though he had recently abstained, owing to ill-health, from participation in public affairs, had made his influence felt in the commercial and social life of North Staffordshire, and his uprightness and courteous demeanour endeared him to a large circle of friends and acquaintants.

'Mr Alleyndene came of old Staffordshire stock, one of his

ancestors having founded the celebrated pottery on the boundaries of Hanley and Witnall in the first half of the eighteenth
century. The deceased gentleman was himself a native of Witnall,
having been born at Dene Hall in 1838, and at an early age
become managing partner with his father in the family business.
A Churchman and Conservative of the old type, Mr Alleyndene
took no active part in local politics, but except for the ten-year
period during which relations between the Hall and the Rectory
were somewhat strained, he was throughout his life a warm and
generous supporter of Witnall parish church and schools, as well
as of many charitable institutions.

'Mr Alleyndene married, in 1864, Marian Caroline, the
daughter of Jonathan Deakin, Esq., who with their eight children
survives him. His eldest son, Mr Stephen Alleyndene, of Dene
Lodge, now succeeds him as Chairman of Directors at the
Pottery. The family vault is at Witnall, where the funeral
took place on Thursday last. The service was conducted by the
Rector of the parish, assisted by the Vicar of St Barnabas, Hanley.
The chief mourners were: Mrs Alleyndene, Snr. (widow), Mr and
Mrs Stephen Alleyndene (son and daughter-in-law), Mr and Mrs
Robert Alleyndene (son and daughter-in-law), Mr and Mrs Henry
Alleyndene (son and daughter-in-law), Mr Daniel Alleyndene,
Mr Philip Alleyndene (sons), Miss Emily Alleyndene, Miss
Elizabeth Alleyndene, Miss Hetty Alleyndene (daughters), Mr
Walter Alleyndene (brother), Miss Agatha Alleyndene (sister),
Mr Jeremiah Deakin (brother-in-law), Mrs Alfred Wellington
Brough (sister-in-law). Many other relatives and friends, as well
as the numerous employees of the Alleyndene Pottery Company,
also attended the funeral.'

The decade of antagonism between Dene Hall and St Peter's
Rectory to which the local newspaper referred had of course been
due not to Joseph but his father. Enoch had claimed the pew
habitually occupied by the family as his private property, and
refused to sacrifice it in the interests of reconstruction demanded
by the installation of a new organ. On finding one Sunday that
the pew had already been dismantled and the organ pipes
deposited there, Enoch turned in a paroxysm of rage upon the
determined Rector who was opposing his autocratic claims.

'I'll have the law on you!' he thundered, and was equal to his word. But though he spent nine hundred pounds upon the case and carried it up to the High Court of Justice, the Church and not the Alleyndene family was decreed to be the owner of the pew.

Irritated by the resonant but inappropriate eloquence of the Reverend Thomas Rutherston, Stephen had reflected upon that incident during the sermon for the first time after many years of indifference. He was even moved to re-read the brass tablet, once conspicuously displayed beneath the east window but now discreetly banished to a dark corner behind a pillar, which recorded the democratic victory of the Church after that prolonged and acrimonious litigation.

'The pew which occupies the space sixteen feet by twelve feet in the South Chancel aisle was for many years claimed as private property by the family of Mr Enoch Alleyndene of Dene Hall, but by the decision of Mr Justice Blackmore in the Queen's Bench Division on the 20th November, 1879, this claim was proved to be without foundation, and with the timely assistance of the Incorporated Free and Open Church Association the Common Law right of the parishioners to the free use of the aisle as a part of the common floor of the Parish Church was then asserted and confirmed.'

For ten years the defeated Alleyndenes, proud and resentful, refused to enter St Peter's church or to pay for the upkeep of the imposing ancestral vault, which gradually accumulated an insidious growth of green moss and a fine collection of large, dusty cobwebs. During this period Stephen's great-aunt Charlotte, who had looked after the grandguv'nor in the interval between his wife's death and the removal to Dene Hall of Joseph and Marian with their noisy offspring, died and was buried in the churchyard of St Andrew's, Fordham. Although that village church was five miles from Dene Hall on the road to Cheet, the Alleyndenes then attended it every Sunday at considerable inconvenience to themselves. To compensate for Charlotte's isolation the old man, whose passion for leaving permanent records of his family's progress through time did not diminish with the years, put up an impressive tablet which he insisted upon phrasing for himself:

'In Memory of
Charlotte Augusta Alleyndene
of Dene Hall
in the County of Staffordshire
who departed this mortal life
with faith and hope
in the merits of her Redeemer
on the 19th day of February 1883.
Her distinguishing characteristic was
A singular combination of manly
sense and energy
With feminine modesty and softness.
Beneficence was her business and delight.
She afforded an unostentatious example
Of the Benign Influence of Divine Grace
On the Heart and Practice of a genuine Believer.
Reader,
seek from the same hallowed source
Guidance and strength, and go and
Do Thou Likewise.'

In spite of the manifest discomforts of driving to church over several miles of country road which were practically impassable in winter time, the family maintained their haughty ostracism of St Peter's, Witnall, during the lifetime of the vigorous Rector who had thwarted them. But when he died and his place was taken by a gentle elderly scholar of the old-fashioned deferential type, propinquity and the claims of a family vault successfully reasserted their influence. Joseph, whose predilection for feuds was always less marked than that of his parents or his children, resumed his attendances at the parish church, and old Enoch, who had now lost his memory and kept entirely to his room, lived just long enough to be interred with his wife and his father in the newly restored ancestral tomb.

Nevertheless, the quarrel had left a tradition of conflict between Rector and Squire which time did not completely erase. The owner of Dene Hall, though habitually elected as the People's Warden, consistently refused to stand as the Rector's, and behind the diplomatic concealing pillar inside the church, the dull gleam of brass remained to suggest to thoughtful parishioners that the historic local antagonism between dictatorship and democracy was still capable of resurrection.

4

It was not in that church, the scene of his parents' wedding, that Stephen had married Jessie Penryder, for Jessie had been no carefully chosen and welcomed bride, but only the young and humble governess to Philip and Hetty.

As he walked towards the beech-wood at the back of the house through the nearest field where the flowering grasses, purple-brown and heavy with pollen, sprang from a luxurious undergrowth of white yarrow, yellow cat's ear and brick-red sorrel, Stephen chuckled to recall that it had actually been Emily – always, since his marriage, so jealous and critical of Jessie – who had introduced his wife to the Alleyndene household.

Emily, at twenty-two, dabbled resentfully in water-colours, and in the hope of achieving by technique what she could never expect to accomplish through artistic ebullience, drove twice a week to Cheet Technical School for lessons with Mr Penryder, the Cornish art-master. She had never, Stephen knew, forgiven herself for bringing back to Dene Hall the information that Mr Penryder's eighteen-year-old daughter Jessie, the eldest of six pretty but unendowed young sisters, was looking for a post as governess.

'This girl might do for Philip and Hetty,' dubiously suggested Emily, who knew as well as her mother that Philip and Hetty had exhausted seven governesses in four years, thereby virtually demolishing the limited possibilities of the neighbourhood.

So in 1888 little Jessie Penryder, with her dark blue Cornish eyes and her rich copper-brown hair, was installed at Dene Hall as governess to the calamitous tail-end of the family, aged nine and seven. Submissive but surprisingly capable, she accepted with a resignation maturer than her years the blatant humiliations to which the younger Alleyndenes were accustomed to subject their governesses, and swallowed her bitter resentment at the raw obviousness with which the family mentally relegated her to the servants' quarters. Unlike her predecessors, who had all departed in tears or tempers, she put up uncomplainingly with everything – Philip's rages, his sulks, his outbursts of turbulent spirits which took the form of crude practical jokes upon herself or the maids; poor Hetty's deficient understanding and slurred, unintelligible speech. It was not long before Stephen, englamoured beyond calculation as only twenty-three can be, began jubilantly to realise for whose sake she exercised her much-enduring patience.

He would never forget the June morning when he saw her for the first time, walking up the drive with Philip and Hetty between the lighted lanterns of the pink rhododendrons. He still remembered the simple neatness of her unobtrusive home-made garments, the close-fitting grey alpaca dress with its tiny black bow at the neck, the little black jacket of Italian cloth. By contrast with the dark-browed plainness of his three sisters and the tall striding stature of his family, her small dainty figure seemed as lovely and delicate as a miniature angel's. Stephen stood entranced – so deeply entranced that although he was neither meditative nor introspective by nature, he recalled even now the commonplace words with which he had addressed her.

'Good morning, Miss Penryder. It *is* Miss Penryder, isn't it? It's a warm day for the time of year, don't you think? Wouldn't you – would you care to have me show you the rose-garden?'

She had answered him so meekly, yet the upward glance of her black-lashed blue eyes was subtler, less meek, than her docile words.

'That's very kind of you, Mr Stephen. I should like to see the roses exceedingly if it isn't trespassing upon your time.'

Eighteen years ago now, that first meeting in the golden freshness of a summer morning. It didn't seem as much as two years afterwards that they had planned and carried out their run-away marriage – a marriage to which neither the autocratic old grandguv'nor, nor the guv'nor for all his genial tolerance, nor the missis with her strong sense of social propriety, would ever have dreamed of giving their consent. He and Jessie had arranged it together one September evening at the delicious close of just such a day as this, in the very wood with its roof of intertwined beech branches and its carpet of fox-gloves and convolvulus where he now stood remembering.

'Are you sure you can trust me to take care of you, Jess?'

'Anywhere, Stephen. Anywhere in the world. I only wish I wasn't so poor. I wish I had something to bring you.'

'That's all right; don't you worry, little girl. I've enough for two and there's plenty of brass in the family,' he had answered, never dreaming in his generous, arrogant simplicity that it was chiefly for the sake of the 'brass,' but also to revenge herself upon the overbearing, self-satisfied family which had despised and humiliated her, that she was persuading herself to marry a man whom she did not love. Domineering and obstinate like his grandfather before him, Stephen was yet incapable of duplicity. Even after his marriage he never suspected the carefully laid plan of campaign by which, in true story-book fashion, the humble governess had captured the heir of the household in the interests of her struggling parents and her tribe of growing sisters. He was only conscious, and always had been conscious, of a baffling sense of disappointment, a feeling that he had sought, with a great deal of perturbation and defiance, something which was not only unattained but unattainable.

It had begun, that feeling of disappointment, on the very night of their secret wedding at Llandudno; in fact disappointment was a mild word with which to describe the mortification that had overwhelmed him. He'd always prided himself upon behaving decently to women and children, and it wasn't fair that by her own ignorance a woman should confer humiliation on a man. He didn't hold with girls knowing too much – or knowing anything too soon – but he did think that Jessie's sharp-tempered, over-worked mother (their one ally and confidante) might have told her a bit about marriage, at any rate on the day before the wedding. What, after all, were mothers for?

He never learned that Mrs Penryder's conception of her maternal function had caused her to avoid the embarrassments of sex instruction in the interests of teaching her young daughter how to hold the wealthy prize which she had so amazingly won.

'Never refuse a man anything, my dear – and above all, never answer him back. He won't like you any the better for it – and he'll only go on thinking he's right even if you do!'

So Jessie had never refused him anything; but her acceptances, he sometimes thought ruefully, inflicted a sorer blow upon his pride than she could have conveyed by her refusals. In those first few days of marriage, her tacit resentment against him, against nature, against life, for shattering her vague but respectably romantic dream of wedded superiority, made even harder to bear than he had expected the enraged communications which descended upon him from his affronted family. He had looked forward to his honeymoon with a voracity of expectation which was none the less exciting for being half ashamed; but the immediate sense that Jessie – for all her delight in the new clothes which he lavished upon her and the early morning parades on the sea-front – gave him of being a cad, a bounder, the inconsiderate violator of an unprepared and innocent virgin, made him thankful when they could escape from the strain of one another's exclusive company into the normal routine of housekeeping and business.

Digging his long polished cane into the mossy root of a stalwart oak, Stephen recalled how he had returned to the bosom of his frigid and critical family feeling anything but the beguiled, headstrong and obstinate lover that he was evidently considered. Nevertheless, his urbane freedom from subtlety saved him from completely realising that in her heart Jessie had never forgiven him the initial shock to her respectability.

'Men are all alike!' she told herself, repeating a cliché of her mother's with a sense of new and bitter understanding, and a consciousness that the one satisfactory aspect of her marriage lay in her victory – now only partial, but destined one day to be complete – over the hated Alleyndenes. Facing her future with the same resigned and disillusioned composure that she had brought to her task as governess, she taught herself to pay the price of that victory, adapted her habits to Stephen's robust demands, and prepared even before her first pregnancy for the coming of children. But her aversion to the sexual undercurrent of life was reflected, only half-consciously, in the early training of her sons and daughter. To her the men who indulged their passions were all 'immoral,' the women who met them half-way unanimously 'fast,' and love, in so far as it involved anything more than romantic day-dreams or the convenient social arrangements to which marriage represented an uncomfortable but necessary preliminary, was classified for her children in one of these two categories.

As Stephen left the wood he met young Arthur Wardle, the third gardener, coming through the door which led into the walled orchard where trees and bushes were now heavy with their autumn load of fruit. Although it was Sunday, the young man had been strolling observantly about the grounds to discover whether last night's brief storm of thunder and buffeting wind had harmed trees or flowers. He was more insistent, as Stephen had often noticed, upon his rights in relation to hours and wages than any other Dene Hall employee, yet he frequently showed unusual initiative by undertaking, without waiting for orders, additional duties which did not fall strictly within the terms of his employment.

'Any damage done, Wardle?' Stephen inquired.

'Nowt to speak on,' came the reply in surly tones. 'Ramblers is a bit wanky, but they'll pick up in sunshine.'

And without the word or gesture of subservient respect which Stephen was accustomed to receive from the household servants, Wardle disappeared into the wood, his slouching gait giving a curious impression of detached independence.

'That's an ill-mannered lout of a fellow!' commented Stephen. 'If it weren't for his grandfather he'd soon get the boot from me!' But even as he recalled the fact that old Tom Wardle had worked for the guv'nor and the grand-guv'nor for fifty years until he retired on a pension, he was also obliged to admit that no gardener in the district had the same skill as young Arthur with roses and fruit trees.

In the well-stocked orchard the sun-warmed apples were turning gold and vermilion, and the squat bushes beneath the trees hung heavy with mellow currants and goose-berries.

'Must ask the missis to let the kids come in and make an afternoon of it,' Stephen resolved. The ripening plums with their delicate purplish bloom made him think, irrelevantly enough, of the new heliotrope frieze costume which Jessie had worn in church that morning. He'd noticed how Mrs Rutherston, the Rector's wife, stared enviously at it as they walked up the churchyard.

The passing of years, which had turned his disappointment into a companion still inexplicable yet so familiar that he almost ceased to observe it, had never diminished his admiration for Jessie and her dainty elegance, her tiny hands and feet, her pretty London-made frocks. At thirty-six she retained all her grace and much of her beauty, though she was now, of course, a bit on the scraggy side compared with the rounded softness of her early twenties.

Never, at any time, had she rivalled in physique the garden statue upon which Stephen's eyes rested approvingly – the nude effigy of a voluptuous pseudo-Grecian female which Joseph, whose preferences in all things were less extravagant than his father's, had removed from the front drive to the more discreet seclusion of the orchard. Before Stephen fell in love with Jessie he had always been attracted by women with ample outlines and well-developed busts, and beneath his devotion to the individual, the more primitive fascination remained. He was accustomed to derive a secret pleasure from contemplating the sculptured solidity of the figure which represented his grandfather's taste. Not only did he find it, as Enoch had found it, gratifying in itself; it was also associated in his mind with an agreeable recollection.

'Now that's a fine figure of a woman!' he mused appreciatively, his thoughts transferring themselves from the opulent statue to Bertha Brewer, the tobacconist's daughter at the Hanley shop where he constantly renewed his deliberately limited supply of costly cigars. A pleased smile came over his face as he pictured Bertha's broad shoulders and ample, seductive bosom.

If pressed by a trustworthy and sympathetic inquirer, Jessie would probably have intimated, with a characteristic little shrug of resignation, that she 'knew all about' Bertha Brewer. Her genuine conviction that men were all alike embraced their standards of conduct outside matrimony as well as within, and though she would never have imperilled her secure position as Stephen's wife by openly accusing him of keeping a mistress, the disillusioned cynicism of her sore and secret heart assured her that he was consistently unfaithful to her with the substantial but comely Bertha.

There, however, she misjudged him. Stephen was no ascetic advocate of unrelieved monogamy – except, of course, for all decent women – but in practice his behaviour was usually orthodox. Wild oats, in his view, were one thing – though the proper place for them was Paris, or at any rate Brighton – but overt marital infidelity, in your own district and under the puritanical nose of the missis, was quite another, and one not readily hazarded by a man of responsibility and discretion. So his admiration for Bertha remained surprisingly but genuinely confined to a periodic contemplation of her curves, platonic in fact if not in spirit.

'After all, I haven't been such a bad husband,' he reflected, vaguely endeavouring as usual to explain to himself the uncomfortable sense of something elusive and uncaptured beneath the pleasant surface of his daily life. As he closed the orchard door firmly upon recollection and temptation, he mentally apologised to Jessie for his straying thoughts. Even if considerations of social prudence had not restrained his normally polygynous instincts, the humiliations inflicted by his ruthless brothers and sisters upon his lovely little wife would have prevented him from giving her further cause for distress. Almost as much as she, he looked forward to the day when she would reign as mistress of Dene Hall and have the laugh on the lot of them.

'Who'll know, or care, then, that I married beneath me?' he speculated aloud, well pleased as always with his one dramatic departure from Alleyndene tradition. Opening the elaborate ironwork gate which led into the ancestral rose-garden, he noticed that the shadow on the grey granite sundial had almost reached the hour beyond noon. Round the brass figures on the sun-clock ran its engraved inscription: 'So teach us to number our days: that we may apply our hearts unto wisdom.' Even time, he thought, the enemy which had carried away his forbears and must one day gather him to his fathers, would not easily

destroy the new vitality – unexpectedly fine and strong for all
its plebeian origin – which his initiative had infused into the
under-adulterated blood of the Alleyndenes.

How much wiser he had been to look for a wife outside his
family and even his class, instead of intermarrying with a relative
as most of his ancestors had done for nearly two centuries,
growing poorer in brains and narrower in experience until their
creative energy gave out altogether in the unfortunate Hetty!
What did it matter that Jessie came from a household of Cornish
nobodies, when there wasn't a woman in all Staffordshire who
could have borne him three better-looking or brighter children
than the youngest generation of Alleyndenes!

5

Plucking a tiny golden bud from the bush of curled tea-roses
beside the sundial, Stephen inserted it carefully into the lapel of
his frock-coat.

It was so fresh and sweet, yet so hardy and vital – as Norman
and Ruth and Richard had been in their attractive childhood.
They were growing a bit leggy now – more like the young
rambler assiduously climbing, in spite of the storm, the newly
erected trellis in the corner. Whatever private misgivings might
once have assailed him over his marriage with Jessie, the youngsters alone had made that daring experiment worth while.

Norman, the eldest – a tall boy now, and a real Alleyndene
with his dark implacable brows and morose brown eyes – had
been born at Dene Lodge the year after their marriage, and
Richard, the youngest, in the late autumn of 1895. But in
Stephen's heart Ruth was his favourite – Ruth, the daughter
so welcomed and treasured, who had arrived when the roses
were at their loveliest in the brilliant June of 1894. She had
come as if to compensate them for the girl-baby prematurely
still-born fifteen months earlier because a drunken stable-boy
had frightened Jessie – always a little timid after dark – on a
moonlight night of waving trees and strange black shadows.
The lad had got the sack, of course, but that didn't give them

back their lost baby, and when Ruth was born, Stephen lavished upon her all the pitiful compunction, the thwarted love, that he had felt for the little cold body of her elder sister, so perfect and so still.

In deference to the wishes of Granny Alleyndene they had christened her Ruth Veronica – the second name being that of the beautiful Huguenot ancestress from whom, judging by the dark, reserved, delicately moulded face among the family portraits, she had inherited so many of her characteristics.

'I'm Ruth Veronica Ralleyndene,' she used to say impressively to visitors, 'but Daddy calls me Jill.'

In Stephen's vocabulary, Ruth and Richard, so close together in age, were always Jill and Jack; he preferred these nursery names to the greater formality of his mother's choice, about which poor Jessie had been so cursorily consulted. He had used them ever since the two children began, almost as soon as they could walk, to act the familiar rhyme up and down the double bank of rough grass below the iron balustrade in front of Dene Hall. Even the pail of water had been perilously manipulated by chubby, unreliable fingers until its too realistic effect upon shoes and petticoats had caused Jessie and Nanna to unite in forbidding it. He could not guess that in later years, when his daughter's generation had been crucified upon the peculiar cross reserved for it by history, the hymn *There is a green hill far away* would always remind Ruth of this grassy bank, down which she and Richard used to roll like a couple of puppies except during the brief, breezy weeks when the yellow daffodils bloomed there in the spring, or the lavender harebells quivered in the autumn.

Norman was fifteen now, and Ruth twelve and Richard eleven, but Stephen still liked to remember them in their nursery days, with the toy bull-dog snorting in front of the guarded fire and Richard sitting beside it on the floor. Propped against the broken chair with its humped cane seat known to the family as 'Mount Vesuvius,' he was drawing, drawing, always drawing, the spit and image of his grandfather Penryder. Ruth's eyes were grey – the Alleyndene brown delicately fused with Jessie's blue – but Richard had the gentian-coloured eyes of

his mother's family, and their slight, shortish figure, and their
auburn-tinted hair.

On Sunday evenings after tea, when Stephen settled down in
his own drawing-room and thankfully exchanged *The Times* for
the *Weekly Sentinel*, Jessie and the children had sacred music.
Sometimes she played them 'Come everyone that thirsteth' out
of Mendelssohn's *Elijah*, or 'He shall feed His flock' from
Handel's *Messiah*, but more often they sang hymns – 'Jesus,
Gentle Shepherd' and 'We are but little children weak' – or
songs from the old cabinet, such as 'Jerusalem the Golden,'
'Angels ever bright and fair' and 'The Better Land.' If he closed
his eyes and shut out the ardent wealth of autumn roses, he
could see the three children standing beside their mother – Ruth
and Richard together as usual, Norman set a little apart by his
superior height and his three years' seniority – singing with shrill
gusto the familiar lines which held, for them, no implication of
sadness:

> 'Dreams can-not picture . . . a world . . . so fair;
> Sorrow and death,
> Sor-*row and death*
> Cannot en-ter there!'

When the singing was over, their mother used to read to them
out of *The Garden of Time*, a Christmas present from their first
governess, Miss Pratt. Inside it was inscribed: 'To dear Ruth and
little Richard, with love from Ellen Pratt. Christmas, 1902,' and
it told the story of David, Daffodil and Koko the black poodle,
after whom they had christened their own black-nosed bull-dog.
Ruth adored the dog only second to Richard, and once, when
Stephen had threatened to send him away for committing what
he called 'a depredation' upon the drawing-room carpet, she had
cried so long and so bitterly that for the sake of her health and
his anxious wife's peace of mind he had been obliged to relent.

Pity, he thought, that the child took things so much to heart;
it might make her a bit difficult to get on with when she grew up.
The real trouble with Jessie was that she'd always been too easily
hurt by things he only meant as a joke, and he didn't want to

see Ruth handicapped by the same tendency to exaggerate trifles. He'd noticed her eyes become suspiciously wet when Jessie read from their story-book at the chapter in which Father Time showed Daffodil the vanishing Seconds, Minutes and Hours, and told her that, once gone, they would never return.

'They will never come back for all the longing in the world; they will have vanished down the long Vista of Years, and you will only be able to see them through the misty Veil of Memory.'

Was the kid perhaps wondering what it was like to grow up, to shoulder responsibility, to have everything exciting behind you instead of before you?

'There are people,' Father Time had told Daffodil in the story, 'who find themselves barred from the past by nettles and thorns, dead flowers and withered leaves, which prevent them even wishing to look back, for the nettles are sins, and the thorns are remorse; the dead flowers are sorrows, and the withered leaves, blighted hopes.'

The immature, groping mind into which Stephen, for all his affection, could not penetrate, had indeed fastened with alarm upon those melancholy phrases. Would she ever be one of the unhappy people who found themselves barred from the past by nettles and thorns? Ruth was wondering with a little shudder. Surely, surely not! It couldn't be possible that she would ever know sin, and sorrow, and remorse, when she wanted so badly to be good. Vainly trying to picture the unimaginable adult future, she asked herself with fear and misgiving whether it would at all resemble the end of the story which her mother was now reading.

'Still the golden Seconds followed each other, and still the relentless scythe of Father Time cut them down. Then Days passed, large as hornets, and Weeks as large as bats; but she saw none of them. And though at length some Years crept slowly in front of her – like great white birds – and drew lines upon her forehead, and planted white hairs among her golden ones, and in Koko's coat, she still dreamt on till the wind, sighing mournfully through the garden, aroused her suddenly. Starting to her feet, she found everything had changed; the grass had grown rank;

weeds had taken the place of the flowers and the sky was covered with dark clouds.

'"Koko," she called, and her voice sounded strange and weak, "we must go – we have been here too long"; but Koko took no notice, for he was dead, and the falling leaves were gradually covering him.

'Father Time looked at her rather sadly, and she cried, "How long have I been here; it hasn't seemed so very long, yet everything has changed. Koko is dead and my hair has turned white," and she looked with dismay at a lock that the wind had blown over her shoulder.

'"It is a long time all the same," he answered; "this is Time's Garden, where nothing ever stands still," and then Daff knew that she was old.

'"I'm very tired," she said, "I think I will go home," and she moved slowly away from the old garden. Only once did she look back, and she noticed that the one thing that was unchanged was the stone figure of Father Time. The petals from the cherry blossom were still falling, but they had turned to snowflakes.'

As Jessie finished reading, Stephen had observed Ruth with some perturbation.

'Why, Jill, whatever's the matter?' he exclaimed, putting aside the *Sentinel*, for two large tears were rolling down the sides of his daughter's nose.

'It's so sad!' sobbed Ruth. 'Oh, Daddy, will everything really be sad like that when I get old and grow up?'

'Well—' Stephen temporised, somewhat baffled by this sudden call upon his limited stores of philosophy.

'I'm afraid, dear, life often *is* rather sad for grown-up people,' Jessie had interposed. 'But yours may be happy – we can't tell. It's all in the hands of Fate.'

Two more tears followed the first, and Stephen continued hastily.

'Now, come, Jill, dry your eyes! I shouldn't cross your bridges before you get to them if I were you! After all, you've got a good home, and good parents to take care of you and make everything so right for you. There's many a little girl in Staffordshire will give a deal to be in your shoes when you're grown up!'

But the following Sunday he removed *The Garden of Time* from the drawing-room bookcase before the reading began. Instead Jessie chose some of the *Parables from Nature* – 'Lesson of Faith,' 'Knowledge Not the Limit of Belief,' 'The Circle of Blessing' and 'Not Lost but Gone Before,' that tale of a Frog and a Dragon-fly Grub which seemed as reassuring about the future as *The Garden of Time* had been discouraging.

Well, he reflected, his eyes again on the shadow creeping round the sundial, the youngsters were growing out of childhood now, and it was no use regretting the march of years which sooner or later, for all his care, would draw the lines of life's experience upon their fresh young faces. This summer, by his own wish, Ruth had even helped her grandmother and Jessie to entertain the guests at the annual garden party held for the employees and tenants every July, just before the family went to Barmouth or Colwyn Bay or Llanfairfechan for their August holiday.

'Oh, Daddy, must I come? I did so want to finish *Mary Barton*!' she had protested, stretched over her book on the lawn at the back of Dene Lodge, with the molten gold of the sunshine overhead and the smoke-cloud of the Potteries in the distance.

In spite of his tendency to indulge her, he had insisted.

'I'm afraid you'll have to turn up this time, Jill. You're getting a big girl, and our people expect it. Besides, the new Rector says he's bringing his lad, and who's to look after the boy if you don't? Norman won't be back from Ludborough till next week, and you can't expect the little chap to stay tied to his elders the whole afternoon. Seems to me he gets too much of that as it is!'

And sure enough the Rector had come with his son, a lonely-looking only child for whom Stephen, with his handsome, vigorous progeny, felt sorry and a little contemptuous. Secretly he sympathised with the sulky, disdainful expression which his pouting daughter wore as she trailed the lad round the grounds, and was conscious of an amused response to her bored expostulation, 'Oh, Daddy, I'm so *tired* of Denis!' when he suggested that she should take her visitor to see the rabbits in the kitchen garden and give him a strawberry ice.

As Jessie had remarked afterwards, it wasn't fair of the boy's

parents to let his hair grow so long, and it was absurd, when
he'd become so tall, that he should still be wearing a large
turned-down Eton collar. Clearly his mother hadn't a notion
how to dress him – and in any case she never put in an
appearance at the garden party at all. Well, that wasn't much
loss, nor would the Rector himself have been! A common little
man, Stephen considered him, and much too pretentious with
his florid sermons right above the folk's heads, full of Greek and
Hebrew allusions that no one could make head nor tail of!

As Stephen emerged from the rose-garden on to the front
drive once more, the gong in the hall rang ponderously for
dinner. Before going in to join his mother, he took one final
glance over the placid vista of his future estate, and this time
the significance of the congested workmen's cottages below the
rim of the horizon did not escape him.

'Can't have subversive doctrines talked here!' he said to
himself. 'It won't do, with all our work-people at the back of
the church every Sunday. If that chap preaches another sermon
of the same sort, his cloth won't shield him. Parson or no parson,
he'll get a piece of my mind!'

CHAPTER V

WIFE

'Nothing . . . is more common, than to call our own
condition the condition of life.'
SAMUEL JOHNSON, *History of Rasselas,
Prince of Abyssinia.*

I

WHEN OLD MRS ALLEYNDENE died in the spring of 1907,
Jessie breathed a secret sigh of intense relief. At last she, and
not her mother-in-law, would be mistress of Dene Hall; at last
that large, quarrelsome, domineering family, with their unveiled
insults to herself, her people, her former subordinate position in
the household, would finally disperse and vanish.

Sometimes the family seemed to her to be like a gigantic octopus, imprisoning and crushing all whom its numerous tentacles
drew in from outside. Harsh and intolerant towards one another,
the Alleyndenes nevertheless combined like a defence battery
against external criticism, and treated as intruders and aliens
those unsuspecting outsiders who merely came into their circle
through marriage. How Jessie detested their ostentatious prosperity, and the utter dependence upon it of herself, her mother
and her sisters! They were more at the mercy of the family than
ever since the death, three years ago, of her beloved father, and
the breakup of his penurious, happy-go-lucky Bohemian home.
Dear to her though he had been, she realised that he had not, on
the whole, made a success of life; he tottered perpetually on the
verge of financial catastrophe and was not even a very efficient
drawing-master. Those Alleyndenes, she knew, had thought him
well out of the world, but in an outburst of unwonted toleration
they had allowed her to bestow his Christian name upon her

younger son because it happened also to have been given to one
of their own over-rated ancestors!

And now, except for Stephen – Stephen from whom she would
never be released while life endured – they would all go away.

'Good riddance to bad rubbish!' her thoughts cried vindictively.
'They haven't only been cruel to me. They treat the servants
abominably with their rough ways and senseless practical jokes!'

Sitting at her mahogany writing-table in the pleasant morning-
room of Dene Lodge, discreetly answering letters of condol-
ence on thick white note-paper with wide black edges, Jessie
contemptuously recalled examples of the Alleyndene sense of
humour. She remembered the 'ghost,' made out of a broom-
handle and a melon-rind smeared with phosphorus, which had
nearly frightened poor cook out of her senses one stormy night
in the maids' corridor at Dene Hall; the hassocks, balanced over
half-opened doors, which descended destructively on loaded
tea-trays; the poisonous concoctions, made from mustard, pep-
per and vinegar, surreptitiously inserted into half-finished beer
bottles.

'As for the children,' she concluded, 'the example they set
them is atrocious! They've never done them anything but harm
– especially Ruth. Once Granny's buried I won't have anything
more to do with that Emily. I'll see she doesn't come back here
even on a visit!'

She recalled how every year, during the first decade of her
marriage, she had taken the children to Dene Hall to stay with
their grandparents in order that Dene Lodge might be turned
out for its annual spring-cleaning. Stephen usually contrived on
these occasions to find some excuse for visiting customers or
staying peacefully at the North Stafford Hotel, but in spite of
the purgatory which her fortnight with his family represented for
Jessie, she would no more have thought of modifying or omit-
ting the customary domestic upheaval at Dene Lodge than of
flying to Timbuctoo. But after 1900, when Joseph Alleyndene's
restraining influence had been removed by death, Jessie refused
to endure any longer the turbulent weeks with Granny and
Emily and the younger members of the family at Dene Hall.
The spring-cleanings continued, but were celebrated instead by

short visits to Robert and Dorothy in Manchester, and later to Elizabeth and Hermann at Highgate.

Jessie still went hot with indignation at the memory of that breakfast-table scene which put an end to the Dene Hall fortnights. It had been a beautiful April morning, with the valiant daffodils in bloom on the bank below the carriage drive, and Ruth, then nearly six, had jumped vigorously up and down the lawns with her skipping-rope as soon as she was dressed. Coming in to breakfast hungry and sparkling as a woodland elf, she gobbled up her moderate helping of bacon, threw down her knife and fork with a clatter and turned to Emily, who presided sourly over the breakfast dishes while Granny Alleyndene sat behind the coffee-tray.

'Please, Auntie Emily, I want some more bacon!'

Emily, bored and dissatisfied with her monotonous life which the presence of her nephews and niece rendered even more tedious, turned distastefully upon the noisy child.

'You *want* some more bacon, do you, Ruth? And who's been taught to say what they want, eh, without asking whether they may have it? Who's a greedy little grub who gulps down her breakfast before her elders and betters have a chance to begin?'

Jessie, nervous as ever with Stephen's relatives but flushed and affronted, had interrupted angrily.

'Really, Emily, the children's manners are my business, not yours!'

Emily looked over Ruth's head at Jessie with scornful dislike.

'Why don't you make a better job of it, then? Didn't you have practice enough with Philip and Hetty?'

She turned to Ruth.

'If your mother can't improve your manners I shall try myself! A day in the attic with bread and water for dinner would soon teach you brats to behave at table!'

Ruth, who had been growing steadily paler during the altercation, burst into violent crying, while Richard, round-eyed and startled, gazed wonderingly at her with his spoon in the air.

Trembling all over, Jessie averted her head from Emily and held out her arms to Ruth.

'Come here, darling – it's for Mother to say what shall happen to you, not your Aunt Emily!'

Ruth, now scarlet with tears and humiliation, rushed sobbing to Jessie while her grandmother repeated helplessly: 'Emily, Emily, can't you stop scolding the child! Really, there's nothing but trouble whenever Jessie and the children come here! ... You'd better take her upstairs, Jessie, and let her finish her breakfast afterwards. What's to be done with you all I simply don't know!'

It had been Richard, aged four and a half, who had answered that rhetorical inquiry. Laying down his porridge spoon, he remarked solemnly, 'What we like is being by ourselves!'

Later that morning, Jessie with the children had descended upon the embarrassed Stephen at the North Stafford Hotel. The quarrel had been patched up superficially, of course, but after that spring they never stayed at Dene Hall again except for Elizabeth's wedding, which took place in the summer holidays when Dene Lodge was closed and the maids away.

All the same, it hadn't been possible completely to rescue Ruth from Emily's pursuing antipathy. She and Daniel were always sending for the children to 'field' the balls at the Dene Hall tennis parties, and more than once when the game was over, Jessie had found Ruth with tear-stained face crouching miserably behind the bushes. Emily seemed to take a special delight in tormenting and deriding her, making ridiculous promises in order to enjoy the child's blank dismay when she announced before all the others that they couldn't be kept, and only a daft little grub like Ruth would have taken them seriously. Granny's helpless remonstrances seemed to have absolutely no effect, and it was Jessie who had to contend with the bedtime storms of tears, the midnight nightmares, the shrill 'Mummy, Mummy! Auntie Emily's after me!', the swollen eyes and bad headaches of the early morning.

Why couldn't Emily leave poor Ruth alone, she demanded furiously of the empty air? Why couldn't she exercise her malice on impervious, unimaginative Norman, or even on Richard, who – for all that he was younger than Ruth, and Jessie's favourite – had a sure defence in the dreamy, half-amused detachment which his perpetual absorption in his drawing gave him? Why must it always be Ruth, who wanted so badly to be thought well of, who was much too sensitive to snubs and scoldings and brooded over them continually?

Indignantly she recalled Emily's contemptuous excuses:

'Ruth's far too self-conscious. A bit of healthy teasing will knock the nonsense out of her!'

Healthy indeed! mused Jessie. Were those midnight tears healthy? As for knocking the nonsense out of Ruth, a good many other things seemed to get knocked out as well – the child's sense of fun, for instance, and her confidence that grown-up people would be kind to her. Jessie had never heard of sadism, but she couldn't help wondering whether Emily's despised and resented spinsterhood had anything to do with her dislike of children and her treatment of Ruth.

Evidently marriage *was* better for you than being an old maid, calculated Jessie with a sigh. It was better although it brought you no joy and very little sympathy, and insults to endure that your own mother and sisters would never believe even if you could bring yourself to tell them!

2

Quite what Jessie wanted from life she did not know; she only knew that she had never liked what it brought her. Because her marriage had disappointed her, she made a philosophy of disappointment. Because the Alleyndenes disparaged her, she turned disparagement into an art. The only one of Stephen's brothers and sisters who had never offended her was Elizabeth, and Elizabeth was, in consequence, the sole member of the family towards whom she felt that negative toleration which passed with her for liking.

They had a bond of sympathy, too, in the opposition which, for three years, Granny Alleyndene had consistently maintained to Elizabeth's marriage with the clever German medical student whom she had met in London while staying with a schoolfriend. Only when Hermann Finckel was appointed to a post at

St Matthew's Hospital which carried a salary that even in
Alleyndene eyes seemed munificent, did old Mrs Alleyndene at
last relent.

Jessie jerked her mind back from the past and began her
sixty-fifth letter of acknowledgment.

'Dear Mrs Bullock,' she wrote mechanically in her small
precise script, 'My husband and I thank you very much for
your kind letter of sympathy on our sad loss. I am glad to
be able to tell you that the end came peacefully and without
pain, but it has, of course, been a great shock to us. Although
we had known for some time that Mrs Alleyndene's health was
failing, we hoped she would be spared to us for many years to
come . . .'

Elizabeth had been married at the end of August in 1902, and
Jessie brought the children from Llanfairfechan to Dene Hall for
the wedding. While Miss Pratt, the governess, helped Elizabeth
with her gown before getting Ruth into her bridesmaid's frock,
and Norman went down to the church with Uncle Robert to
make sure that everything was ready for the ceremony, Jessie as
she dressed kept an eye upon the two younger children playing
in the garden. On the bed lay her wedding apparel chosen with
her usual unerring taste – a dress of cream silk voile over cream
taffeta, with elbow sleeves and a godet skirt eight or nine yards
wide round the feet, trimmed with tiny accordion-pleated taffeta
frills. Beside it were ranged her black patent leather shoes, black
silk stockings, long white kid gloves, and the cream straw hat
turned up at the back with clusters of white daisies which
Stephen had bought her on his last visit to London. She felt
thankful that he admired the frock she had chosen to wear with
it when she tried it on the evening before.

'That's a fine rig-out you've got, Jess,' he observed approvingly.
'What did they rush you for it?'

'Seven guineas. It's from Baker Street – one of Madame
Geraldine's own designs,' she told him. Struggling with its
hooks and complicated frills, she lost sight for a moment of
the children in the garden.

Lying on their stomachs at the foot of the grassy bank with
a piece of cardboard and a box of chalks, Ruth and Richard

were busy with a wedding message for Aunt Elizabeth which they intended as a 'surprise.' Richard drew and coloured the design round the edge of the card, while Ruth, pencil in hand, laboriously composed a large printed couplet:

'LONG LIFE AND HAPINESS TO THEM
AUNTIE LIZZIE AND UNCLE HEMAN.'

They were busy putting the card in the porch when Emily Alleyndene, already dressed and deliberately avoiding the excited crowd in Elizabeth's bedroom, came sullenly down the drive. Ruth called to her excitedly:

'Auntie Emily, Auntie Emily, do tell us what a wedding's like! Will Auntie Lizzie be all dressed up? Will she have a long train like the Queen at the coronation?'

'You kids talk a great deal of bosh,' said Emily sourly. 'What's more, we can't have this rubbish outside the front door. Give that scribble to me!'

As the children hesitated she seized their card, tore it in half and threw the pieces behind a laurel bush growing against the porch.

'Now make yourselves scarce,' she added petulantly. 'We're all too busy to-day to have you children cluttering up the place with your mess.'

Immediately Emily's back was turned on them, Ruth, who was always proud of her handiwork, began to whimper. Richard, more of an artist than she but less histrionically dependent upon applause, endeavoured to comfort her.

'Never mind, Ruthie. We'll do another now she's gone away.'

But somehow the creative impulse had vanished. Hand in hand, the two children wandered disconsolately round the garden until Miss Pratt came to fetch them to be dressed for the wedding.

The traces of tears still reddened Ruth's cheeks when she was taken to Jessie's room in her muslin frock and blue ribbons to be inspected by her parents.

Stephen, faultlessly attired as usual in frock coat and pin-striped trousers, had emerged from his dressing-room in an irritable mood. It was due, Jessie gathered, to the persistence of a discharged workman who had inappropriately selected that morning to pester him with his claims.

'It's another case of potter's asthma,' he told her. 'The chap's demanding compensation and he's not entitled to it. I've told him again and again it's not like lead-poisoning. It isn't a disease compensation can be claimed for. But most of these fellows are so ignorant the law means nothing to them, so they come here and take it out of me!'

Jessie knew that Stephen, like his father before him, regarded himself as an enlightened employer. His workers had, indeed, more consideration and better conditions than the employees in many other potteries, but, as he never tired of saying at home, you'd no call to shoulder burdens which the Government itself didn't see fit to lay on you. If this inquiry into industrial diseases which was always being talked about came off within the next few years, why, then he and other master potters might have to assume new responsibilities. But he wasn't going to anticipate the findings of any such investigation. Not he! With all this German competition in the business, even the most considerate employer couldn't incur new expenses due to special cases of individual hardship.

That morning, with her mind on the wedding, Jessie hardly listened. Ever since her first acquaintance with the Pottery, dust and lead had been the causes of innumerable casualties among the workers. The victims had always bothered Stephen, and she supposed that they always would. It was very sad for them, of course, but that kind of thing happened to the poor wherever they were, and she didn't see how Stephen could help it.

A discreet knock sounded on the door, and Miss Pratt came in with Ruth, followed by Richard in white satin knickers and a white silk shirt with a big frilled collar.

'What's this, Jill,' exclaimed Stephen testily, observing the fading evidences of weeping on Ruth's pale face. 'In tears again! I never knew anything like you children – the moment you get into your grandmother's house every blessed thing seems to go wrong! What on earth's the matter now?'

As Ruth remained inarticulate and the corners of her mouth

again began to tremble, Richard, in his placid, reasonable tones, assumed the task of explanation.

'It's Auntie Emily, Daddy. She's always horrid to us and 'specially to Ruth, but this time she was horrider than usual. She tore up our card what we'd drawn for Auntie Lizzie and threw it behind the bushes.'

Somewhat mollified by this accusation of Emily – with whom, as he was always the first to admit, he'd never been able to hit it off – Stephen patted Ruth's head sympathetically.

'Don't let your Aunt Emily upset you, Jill. It's a bit of the green-eyed monster that's wrong with her!'

Ruth looked puzzled.

'What do you mean, Daddy – the green-eyed monster?'

Stephen chuckled. To him as to all his male contemporaries, the bitterness of untrained and unemployed spinsterhood, with its hours of ennui and its thwarted desires, was a standard joke of which the humour – so flattering to masculine freedom and superiority – could always put him into an amiable temper.

'Why,' he explained, 'your Aunt Lizzie's got off first – that's what it means. Your Aunt Emily's nose has been put out of joint. She's on the shelf and she knows it, so she takes it out of you children to get a bit of her own back.'

Jessie, carefully pulling on her white kid gloves one finger at a time, ventured upon a protest.

'I'd rather you didn't talk to Ruth like that, Stephen. However Emily treats her she can't possibly understand what you mean, and it wouldn't do her any good if she did!'

But something deep down in Ruth had intuitively understood a good deal. Long afterwards, during the Great War – when Dr Finckel, fired with Teutonic patriotism, hurried back to Germany to serve in the *Sanitätschor*, leaving his English wife, under suspicion as an alien, to die of pernicious anæmia and a broken heart, and his little half-German Wilfred to be reluctantly brought up by the childless Henry and Beatrice Alleyndene – Ruth was to compare the fate of her two aunts, and to wonder whether Emily, repressed and unloved, felt herself compensated by her sister's tragedy for the fact that she had been left within

the prison walls of her dominating home while Elizabeth had
escaped.

It had been such a pretty country wedding, with nothing in
the warm rich morning or the serene well-organised service to
suggest the opposition which had preceded it or the grief that
was to come. Sitting behind Granny Alleyndene with Norman
and Richard, Jessie watched Elizabeth – not so tall as most of
the Alleyndenes and more softly rounded – come up the church
on Stephen's arm and stand at the altar beside the fair, spectacled
young man with the closely-cropped head. She saw Ruth, who
walked with Robert's little daughter Joan in front of the six
grown-up bridesmaids, carefully holding her aunt's bouquet of
lilies and orange-blossom, and listening with wide-open dark
eyes to Mr Skerrett, the old Rector, gravely reading the opening
sentences of the Marriage Service.

'*Dearly beloved, we are gathered together here in the sight of
God, and in the face of this congregation, to join together this
Man and this Woman in holy Matrimony; which is an honourable estate . . . and therefore is not by any to be enterprised,
nor taken in hand, unadvisedly, lightly, or wantonly, to satisfy
men's carnal lusts and appetites, like brute beasts that have no
understanding . . .*'

In front of her Jessie saw old Mrs Alleyndene's erect back
stiffen as the Canon Law indictment of normal human impulses
fell harshly upon the listening ears of the elegant congregation.
They raised their modestly downcast eyes from their prayer
books when its uncompromising baldness relaxed into politer
exhortations.

'*. . . but reverently, discreetly, advisedly, soberly, and in the
fear of God; duly considering the causes for which Matrimony
was ordained.*

'*First, It was ordained for the procreation of children, to be
brought up in the fear and nurture of the Lord, and to the praise
of his holy Name.*'

But the rocks and shoals of human perversity were not yet
completely navigated. As the Rector hurried apologetically over
the second injunction, Ruth half turned and cast a puzzled,
questioning glance at her mother.

'*Secondly, It was ordained for a remedy against sin, and to avoid fornication; that such persons as have not the gift of continency might marry, and keep themselves undefiled members of Christ's body.*'

The clerical voice took grateful refuge in the social propriety of the third injunction and the congregation sighed with relief, conveniently forgetting how seldom that simply expressed ideal of human conduct was ever in practice accomplished.

'*Thirdly, It was ordained for the mutual society, help, and comfort, that the one ought to have of the other, both in prosperity and in adversity. Into which holy estate these two persons present come now to be joined . . .*'

As she stacked the answered letters carefully in a neat pile and pushed them to the far corner of her desk, Jessie's mind drifted from the wedding ceremony to the inappropriate and disconcerting conversation between Ruth and her grandmother which had followed immediately afterwards. Later that afternoon, when Elizabeth had driven away with Hermann, and the guests had all gone, and the gardeners were taking down the big marquee on the top lawn, and Stephen had carried Norman and Richard off to the second field to shoot rabbits, and she and Ruth were resting quietly in the cool, shaded morning-room, old Mrs Alleyndene came in on her way to the servants' hall to give the maids their final orders for the day.

'Well, Ruth,' she observed, 'you conducted yourself very creditably, my child. And what did you think of your aunt's wedding?'

'Oh, it was *lovely*, Granny! I loved Auntie Lizzie's dress, and the flowers and all the music. But I didn't understand everything Mr Skerrett said at the beginning, about marriage being an honourable 'state, and then those funny long words. Forni-something. What did it mean?'

Sitting silently in the window-seat embroidering a crimson satin piano-back with her pink silk-lined work-basket open beside her, Jessie saw Mrs Alleyndene's eyes narrow and her lips tighten. The opportunity for giving one of those moral homilies which all young people needed nowadays was too good to be missed. Ruth was only a child, of course. She couldn't be expected to understand the appalling mysteries of life or the mortal sins of which dissolute humanity was guilty, but the talk would come back to her when she was older and she would realise, then, what Granny had meant.

'Fornication is a very terrible word, my dear. It is not a word we use in ordinary conversation, because it describes a kind of wickedness which it is best not to mention or even to think about unless we must. But the Bible and the Prayer Book tell us how to avoid sin of every kind, and that is why they sometimes have to use these improper phrases.'

'But what does it *mean*, Granny?'

'It refers, Ruth, to those lost and evil men and women who live together without the blessing of marriage.'

'But, Granny, I thought that was what marriage meant. I thought it meant the husband and wife lived in the same house for ever and ever?'

As Jessie stirred uncomfortably in the window-seat, Mrs Alleyndene took Ruth's face between her hands and gazed down with grim intensity into the child's puzzled eyes.

'When you are older, my dear, you will know that there are some sins, especially for women, which God will only forgive after long repentance. The sin you asked me about just now is one of those. It is the worst that any woman can commit.'

'Then is it always wicked to have anything to do with a man unless you're married to him?'

'Nearly always, my child. Our human nature is sinful and weak, and unless a man seeks you in marriage you are in danger of falling into shame and temptation.'

Shame? Temptation? Ruth's smooth brow furrowed over the strange, menacing words.

'Oh, Granny, I do wish I knew how not to commit a sin when I don't know 'zackly what it is!'

Mrs Alleyndene released the troubled little face as she pronounced solemnly the final injunction.

'The rules of virtuous conduct are laid down for us once and for all, Ruth, in the Bible and the Ten Commandments. If you read your Bible regularly it will teach you how to avoid both sin and shame. Always be pure and good, my dear; be dutiful to your parents now, and later on to your husband and children. Never let your feet stray from the path of righteousness, and remember that nothing so terrible can happen to a woman as to lose her purity.'

Jessie put down her embroidery with an impatient gesture as Mrs Alleyndene closed the door. She had deeply resented the conversation between Granny and Ruth, but she knew that to say so would at once destroy the façade of respectful politeness which concealed the dislike and disapproval between herself and her mother-in-law. At Ruth's tender age, she considered, there was no need for such advice. It did nothing but put ideas into the child's head, and the only way to get them out was to change the conversation immediately.

'What about a little walk, dear?' she said. 'Wouldn't you like to come down to the farm and see the new chickens?'

So Ruth went upstairs to put on her hat, and Jessie never knew that she had been too much alarmed and bewildered to ask the final question for which she most anxiously desired an answer: 'Granny, what is purity, and how does one lose it?'

3

It was nearly five years, now, since Elizabeth's wedding, and Jessie felt sure that Ruth had long forgotten Granny's premature injunctions. More than twelve months ago the elderly Rector had retired and gone to live at Malvern, so it was not Mr Skerrett who had married Elizabeth, but Mr Rutherston whom Stephen so much disliked, whose duty it was to conduct the funeral of old Mrs Alleyndene.

In the small country churchyard on that early May morning, the birds sang as though their hearts were bursting with gladness at the beauty of the spring. Above the heads of the crowding mourners, the pointed tower of the red sandstone church soared like an aspiring pinnacle into the melting blue of the sky. Beyond the exquisite carven lychgate lay the industrial outcrop of Witnall cottages, separated from the churchyard only by a narrow belt of tussocky fields. Once country meadows, they

were now littered and grimy, as though the encroaching urban
sea had cast its squalor before it.

'*We brought nothing into this world*,' boomed the approaching diapason of Mr Rutherston's sonorous bass, '*and it is certain
we can carry nothing out. The Lord gave, and the Lord hath
taken away; blessed be the name of the Lord.*'

The Alleyndenes, as Jessie had learnt long ago, didn't really
believe that democratic exhortation. They came into the world
inheriting lands and dividends, and they went out leaving their
descendants to fight their way through a barbed-wire entangle-
ment of entails and trusts.

How they hate one another! she thought, when the first part
of the service was over and she stood with Ruth and Richard
beneath a scented bush of flowering lilac, watching the long
queue of Alleyndene relatives follow Stephen and Norman out of
the church behind Mr Rutherston and the leaden coffin. Robert
and Dorothy, Henry and Beatrice, Elizabeth and Hermann,
Daniel and Philip, Emily and Hetty, Alleyndene cousins from
Trentham and Stone, Deakin in-laws from Fordham and Cheet
– there they all were, pushing and jostling one another as usual
for precedence of position beside the grave. How I hate them all!
her unripened heart continued for her. How I wish that Norman,
now he's nearly sixteen, wasn't getting to be so completely one
of them! A hard, undemonstrative, quarrelsome family, united
only by weddings and funerals. No knowledge or love of one
another, but merely a feeling of obligation to honour convention
by appearing at the formal celebration of joys or tragedies.

Standing at a respectful distance from the Alleyndene phalanx,
groups of employees from the Pottery and tenants from the farm
and cottages on the estate crowded the small churchyard to
its low boundary wall. Some of them could remember, as
youngsters, seeing old Mrs Alleyndene drive up to Dene Lodge
– a comely bride, if a bit prim and formal – when Enoch's
tyrannical régime was at its zenith. Outside the lych-gate, lining
the steep lane that ran down into Witnall, stood the shabby wives
and mothers of the local cottagers, holding dirty open-mouthed
children by the hand or endeavouring to silence the wailing
babies in their arms.

'I wonder,' mused Jessie, moved by a sudden distasteful curiosity, 'what their lives are really like? Does a family death mean the same to them as to us? I suppose it must, or they wouldn't worry so much about not coming on the parish. It does seem strange that anyone should mind leaving such a miserable existence as that!'

Had the Pottery been five thousand miles from Dene Hall instead of five, Jessie could hardly have known less of its human material. Occasionally she drove down the sycamore-bordered road into Witnall to call for Stephen at his office, a dainty, incongruous little figure between the big bottle-shaped ovens and the smaller muffle kilns. She disliked soiling her pretty serge and cashmere frocks with the chalky dust which covered the paths and floors, so she avoided the men whose hands and overalls were caked with clay. Nor did she often visit the women working, for nine shillings a week, in the gloss and biscuit warehouses, or talk to the girls cutting out transfers and burnishing the gold on the china, or painting patterns with amazing mechanical accuracy on cups and plates. If Stephen was not waiting for her in his office she sometimes ventured forth to find him, stepping fastidiously over the piles of clay in the yard – the leaden-coloured ball clay, the yellowish buff clay and the blue-white china clay. But the lives of the men and women who worked in that thick, sticky commodity seemed as far removed from her experience as the lives of Greenland Esquimaux.

Industrial processes were also, for Jessie, as remote and incomprehensible as the economic confabulations of the politicians who regulated them. She knew even less of local industrial diseases, in which lead had killed its thousands, but dust its tens of thousands, or of the campaign being fought by Trade Union organisers and public-spirited humanitarians for improved working conditions in the various pot-factories. It never seemed to her unjust that she should benefit from the wretchedness, the suffering and the premature deaths of those men and women who had so long resigned themselves to intolerable conditions with the patient endurance of the British working class. The circumstances and psychology of her father's home, with its genteel but bitterly resented poverty, had been

quite different from the accepted privations which she regarded
as inevitable for the poor.

> *God made them, high or lowly,*
> *And ordered their estate,*

she had sung in her childhood. The lines still represented her
view of the relationship between her family and the working
potters – though not, of course, the relationship between her
family and the Alleyndenes.

That was another matter altogether. No one knew what she'd
had to put up with from the Alleyndene snobbery – not even
Millicent, who was next to her in age, and much less Nellie, or
Alice, or Ethel, or Susie. If only she'd had a brother, he might
have stood up to Stephen with his overbearing ways, or to Daniel
and Philip with their atrocious manners. But for women like
herself and her sisters, poor, untrained and dependent upon the
bounty of her husband and his arrogant brothers, there seemed
to be no choice but submission. At least, now, she'd be mistress
of Dene Hall, and that would offer some compensation for her
long servitude to the family even though it did involve a number
of new and exacting obligations.

'I must go and see Mrs Rutherston again,' she decided, as she
drove back to Dene Lodge with Stephen and the children. Not
that she liked the Rector's wife any better than the Rector, who
irritated her with his short legs, his episcopal voice and his fussy,
pompous manner. Mrs Rutherston's clothes were never right
for the particular occasion; they were either too shabby or too
elaborate, and she had a far-away look in those vague blue eyes
of hers which suggested that she wasn't really paying attention
to what you said. Judging by other people's accounts it seemed,
indeed, that she often wasn't, and that was unpardonable in a
clergyman's wife, whose chief duty was to take an interest in the
ladies of the parish. Jessie recalled the first time that she met Mrs
Rutherston, at the Mothers' Union tea a year ago.

'I expect you find living here much cheaper than Sterndale,'
she had said in gracious tones, conscientiously fulfilling her rôle
of prospective Squire's wife putting the new Rector's wife at her

ease. 'My husband always says they put up the prices at those watering places – even to residents.'

But Mrs Rutherston, instead of appearing at her ease, looked surprised and a little disconcerted by Jessie's inquiry.

'I don't really know,' she answered. 'I'm afraid I haven't compared the prices yet. In fact, I'm not even sure I've kept my old account books.'

Not compared the prices yet – and she's been here over three weeks! And thrown away her old account books! She certainly can't be a very practical woman.

'Well,' Jessie continued perseveringly, 'you'll find the shops here very reasonable, and they say it's going to be a good year for fruit and vegetables. I suppose you make your own jam?'

'I'm afraid I don't. I'm not very domesticated.'

'I could easily show you. We always make our own strawberry jam as soon as the season comes in. I've got an excellent recipe my mother always used. You put one and a half pounds of sugar to each pound of strawberries, and . . .'

But she saw to her chagrin that Mrs Rutherston was no longer listening. Her attention had apparently been diverted by an argument between the Rector and Mrs Wesley Bullock, the doctor's wife, at the other end of the parish room. With concealed indignation, Jessie asserted herself more emphatically.

'I am hoping to come and see you this week, Mrs Rutherston,' she said stiffly. 'I ought, of course, to have come before, but I've always been a very conscientious housekeeper. I have my two boys and my girl to look after, and, of course, I give my mother-in-law a good deal of help with her duties at the Hall. What with one thing and another, I haven't very much spare time.'

'I shall be delighted to see you, Mrs Alleyndene, but I wonder if you could give me some idea which day you're coming? I'm out a good deal in the afternoons, and I should hate to waste your valuable time with a fruitless journey.'

So she *does* mean to do her duty by the district, thought Jessie, a little mollified. She mayn't be very capable in the house, but at least she's going to be useful in the parish.

'Let me see – Thursday would be my most convenient day. What about Thursday?' she asked.

'Well – there's a lecture in Hanley that afternoon on "The Czar and the new Duma," by a Russian professor from Manchester, and I *had* thought of going, but of course . . .'

'Oh, I wouldn't dream of asking you to alter your plans for *me*, Mrs Rutherston! Friday will suit me almost as well. I will come on Friday, at four o'clock. Good afternoon.'

Driving soon after Granny Alleyndene's funeral for her second formal visit to the Rectory, Jessie reflected that the real reason for Mrs Rutherston's anxiety to be informed of a call beforehand was probably that she didn't want to be taken by surprise. Even on the last occasion, when Jessie was expected, the silver had not been properly polished and there was a big hole in the crochet tablecloth. Well, she meditated with satisfaction, buttoning her long black kid gloves as the victoria rolled elegantly down the sycamore-shaded hill, at least I shall know *this* time how the Rectory looks when people arrive unexpectedly!

She was not disappointed. Looking up at the square brick house with its walled garden, untilled vegetable plot and shabby outhouses showing several shattered panes, she noticed that the front lawn was rough and neglected, and the whole place badly needed a new coat of paint. So weather-beaten were the old wooden gate-posts that they had been replaced by stone, but in spite of this substitution the original posts still remained, lying beside the drive waiting to be chopped into firewood. In the large oblong windows the curtains, made of different materials for the various rooms, hung loose and uneven, giving the house a patchy, haphazard appearance from the bottom of the drive.

'She's obviously no housekeeper,' decided Jessie, as she walked up to the front door. 'She's no more idea of looking after things than a fly! They don't seem to take any pride in the place at all; even if they *are* poor, that's no reason why they shouldn't keep it clean and tidy. It's setting such a bad example to the whole parish!'

She rang the bell twice before the door was opened by Denis. Fancy, she thought, letting that lanky, delicate-looking boy answer the bell in the afternoon; it's altogether beneath the dignity of a Rector's wife. He looked so dreamy and uncared for, too, even though Mr Waggett at the Grammar School *had* said he didn't lack brains . . . In the early morning it was sometimes excusable for a servant to be invisible, but at four o'clock she certainly ought to be changed into her black dress, with clean cap and apron. But perhaps the Rector's wife hadn't *got* a servant? She was just the sort that couldn't get girls to stay.

'Is Mrs Rutherston at home, dear?' she inquired.

'I'm sorry,' he said, 'but I'm afraid Mother's out. She's gone to a suffrage meeting in Stoke.'

'Gone to a— Oh . . . ! Does your mother often go to suffrage meetings?'

'I don't know. She goes to a lot of political meetings. I think some of them have to do with suffrage.'

So that's the explanation, Jessie told herself irately, as she returned, tealess, down the dusty drive. That's why she behaves so oddly and sometimes looks so distraught! Hurrying back to Dene Lodge, where much of the furniture was already stacked for removal, she could hardly wait to give this information to Stephen, who was home early from the Pottery and had just finished his tea.

'What *do* you think!' she exclaimed, as she rang the bell for a fresh pot, 'Mrs Rutherston goes to suffrage meetings! I went to call on her, thinking we ought to take some notice of them after Granny's funeral, and there was the house looking as untidy and deserted as you please, with nobody about except the boy. He told me his mother had gone off to a suffrage meeting in Stoke!'

Stephen cut himself another slice of Madeira cake to keep her company.

'Just what I'd have expected! That chap's a downright Radical, but his wife's twenty times worse.'

'What on earth did they come here for, I wonder?'

'Bishop's appointment. Not much choice, I suspect. I've been making inquiries among the customers and it seems they were none too popular at Sterndale; some sort of rumpus blew up before they left. Bit of bad luck for us.'

'Well, there's nothing of what I call *breed* about them!'

'You're right there, Jess. They're not exactly out of the top drawer! Tradespeople who've gone into the Church to give themselves a leg-up socially – that's what I'd put them down as. If the grandguv'nor were alive to-day, he'd turf them out of the place!'

<h1 style="text-align:center">4</h1>

A fortnight after Stephen and Jessie had completed their move from Dene Lodge to Dene Hall, Mr Reginald Halkin of the Fordham Paper Works came over from Fordham to discuss business with Stephen.

For two generations the Alleyndenes had used Halkin's Pottery Transfers for the designs on their dinner-services and tea-sets, and it was only natural, when the business conversation was over, that Stephen should invite Mr Halkin to stay for luncheon. The afternoon was so fine and warm that when the meal was over, Stephen ordered coffee and liqueurs to be brought out of doors to the garden seat which stood on the narrow edge of lawn above the grassy bank in front of the house. Neither he nor Mr Halkin noticed Ruth, whose schoolroom luncheon had finished long ago, lying face downwards in her favourite hiding-place beneath the corner of the steep bank with the inevitable book in front of her.

Resting before the open window in the morning-room where Granny Alleyndene had once exhorted Ruth to be pure and virtuous, Jessie could hear occasional fragments of the two men's jovial conversation. They were talking – at first respectfully but before long with unfeigned irreverent enjoyment – of Stephen's deceased mother and the inconveniences which sometimes followed from the strict enforcement of her rigid moral principles. Jessie could reconstruct for herself the inaudible gaps in the final story, for it was one that she had heard Stephen, in genial after-dinner mood, relate more than once to his business acquaintances.

'Well, as I was saying,' Stephen observed, refilling Mr Halkin's liqueur glass with brandy, 'the missis had no mercy on the evil-doer, especially of the female variety. She wasn't going to have any goings-on in *her* establishment. Not,' he added with a reminiscent grin, 'that it didn't happen occasionally.'

'Indeed, and how was that?' inquired Mr Halkin, willingly taking his cue. As he never tired of telling his friends, he was 'one of the best,' who enjoyed a good joke about a seduction or a bastard as well as anyone.

'I remember once, back in the 'eighties, when I was first going to the Pottery,' related Stephen, now thoroughly in his element, 'we had a cook called Agnes, who got in the family way. The missis always swore afterwards it was Jim, the groom, but he was a first-class groom and you may bet your life she didn't inquire into the thing too closely from his end. The joke was she saw the woman every morning about the meals and didn't even notice anything wrong.'

'Honny soit qui mally ponce, eh?' commented Mr Halkin.

'Late one night the housemaid comes in as white as a ghost. "Oh, please, Mum, can you come at once – Agnes is very ill!" Up goes the missis, and finds the woman writhing and groaning, and she still hasn't an idea what it's all about, so she sends Jim for old Dr Bennett. He didn't waste much time with the woman – he didn't need to – and in a few minutes down he comes to the missis, grinning and rubbing his hands. "Not much of a job for diagnosis, Ma'am," he says. "There's a happy event about to occur up there!" Well, you should have heard the old girl carry on – and then didn't the malefactor get it in the neck!'

'By Jove! What did your mother do?'

'Well, to make a long story short, the missis sends for a cab to take Agnes straight to the Workhouse – bundled her out neck and crop, shrieking and groaning and begging for mercy. The old girl turned a deaf ear to it all; wasn't even going to have her own carriage used, so the woman had to wait in the kitchen till the cab arrived. The result was the brat was born in the cab as dead as a door-nail – we had some first-class language about it from the cabby next day; he wanted compensation – and the woman nearly followed suit when they got her to the Workhouse. The missis said it was a judgment on her for her wickedness.'

'Well, well! And what happened to your cook in the end?'

'The Lord knows. Turned herself into a whore, I should think, if she'd got any nous. No chance of getting any sort of character

out of the missis after *that* episode, though she'd been with us for
five years and was quite a decent cook. Soft as butter, the old girl
was with us kids – but hard as nails with the lower orders when
they went astray!'

Jessie sighed impatiently as Stephen's voice, growing more
resonant as his glee increased, drifted across the drive. Men
were all alike, she thought with wearisome reiteration. The more
they made women suffer, the better they enjoyed themselves. She
felt quite thankful when Mr Halkin left and Stephen drove off
to Witnall to call on the Rector. He'd done nothing but rave
ever since Mr Rutherston mentioned the present-day relations
between capital and labour in his sermon on Sunday morning.
He'd sworn, Stephen said, that if that chap talked politics in the
pulpit again he'd give him a piece of his mind – and by God, he
was going to!

As he had not returned when the time came for tea, Jessie
ordered it to be served in the rose-garden for herself and Ruth
and the new governess. Ruth, she noticed, looked pale and
ate practically nothing; probably it was the hot day coming
unexpectedly when most of the spring and early summer had
been so cold. Unless . . . She recalled the fact that Ruth would
be thirteen next week.

'You're looking rather poorly, dear,' she remarked discreetly
while the governess was helping Nancy to carry the tea-things
back to the house. 'I wonder if Miss Varcoe had better give
you a dose of Turkey Rhubarb to-night? Or is it, perhaps –
something else . . . ?'

But Ruth ignored her question completely.

'Mother,' she said desperately, 'I heard Daddy and Mr Halkin
talking after lunch this afternoon. They were just above me on
the top of the bank. I heard everything they said.'

'You heard . . . That was *very* wrong of you, Ruth! Haven't
I always told you listeners hear no good of themselves?'

'But they weren't talking about me. It was all about Granny
and a cook called Agnes. Mother, what does it mean to be a
whore?'

Jessie repressed an exclamation of horror. Really, it was too
bad of Stephen, telling these dreadful stories and using such

coarse language without first making sure that none of the children were about.

'Hush, Ruth! Never let me hear you say such a thing again! It's a word no little girl should remember, much less repeat.'

'But Daddy used it.'

'That's a different matter altogether. Grown-up men often use expressions, especially when they're talking to each other, that no lady would dream of uttering.'

Ruth understood her mother well enough by now to know that the particular explanation which she sought would not be furnished however much she persisted. Bewildered and distressed by the menacing mysteriousness of life as soon as you looked beneath its reassuring surface, she tried a different line of inquiry.

'Mother, what was the matter with Agnes, and why did Daddy think it was all so funny? What had she done wrong, and where did the poor little dead baby come from?'

Jessie, embarrassed and profoundly indignant with Stephen, looked unhappily at the bees, soft and furry, moving lazily in and out of the roses, as though their contented humming would provide her with inspiration. How could she be expected to teach Ruth, at thirteen years old, the ugly and unseemly facts of life? No one had taught them to her; she'd had to find out about marriage and babies by bitter experience. She didn't mean quite that to happen to Ruth, but surely the eve of marriage was the proper time for these disclosures? How much was one justified in telling a child of thirteen about sex at all? It had been difficult enough to prepare her for adolescence without provoking a whole series of awkward questions.

Hesitating and anxious, she plunged into a tentative, incomplete account of young girls ruined for ever by seduction, of illegitimacy and social ostracism. Not once did it occur to her that she was describing remediable injustices, or that the penalties laid upon women by society were open to challenge.

'So you see,' she concluded, 'how careful of herself a girl has to be. When men do wicked things like this, it's always the woman who pays the price.'

'But why should she?' asked Ruth.

'Well, dear, it's the law of Nature. It's women who have the little babies and have to bring them up. I suppose God meant them to suffer.'

'Well, I don't think it's right of God!' Ruth burst out passionately.

'Hush, dear. You mustn't say things like that. It's hard for us sometimes to understand God's ways, but He knows what is best for us.'

There was a pause while Ruth meditated, her essentially constructive mind unconsciously rebelling against her mother's attitude of resentful acquiescence.

'But why don't women stand up for themselves?' she inquired at length.

'It wouldn't do any good, darling. Men are the lords of creation; they've got nearly all the money in the world, and they learn all kinds of things women aren't clever enough to know about. It's just the way we're made. You'll understand it all when you're older.'

'But, Mother,' Ruth reiterated in despair, 'don't *any* women try to stand up for themselves?'

'No *nice* women do. There are some dreadful people called suffragettes, who talk a great deal of nonsense and do all kinds of wild things no lady would dream of. But men only laugh at them, and most of them would soon give it all up if they'd got husbands and children of their own.'

It only took Ruth an instant to decide what the future must hold for her.

'Well,' she announced resolutely, 'when *I'm* grown up I'm going to be very clever and make lots of money and be a suffragette myself!'

'My dear child!' exclaimed Jessie, affronted and perturbed. 'You don't know what you're talking about! If you're going to be so silly I shan't discuss the subject any more. Look, there's Daddy coming up the drive! You'd better run away now and help Miss Varcoe pick the flowers for to-morrow.'

As Stephen approached, she made up her mind to tackle him, then and there, about his carelessness in discussing improper subjects within earshot of the children, but when he came into the rose-garden she realised that the moment was not auspicious. Flinging himself into the deck-chair beside her, Stephen removed his 'boater,' mopped his brow with his large white silk handkerchief, and turned to her eagerly, overflowing with his news.

'What *do* you think, Jess? Rutherston's resigned!'

'Resigned?' repeated Jessie, 'The Rector *resigned*! Well, I never! Whatever made him do that?'

'The determination of yours truly to stand no nonsense. I didn't expect quite such a blow-up, I'll admit – but it'll be good riddance to bad rubbish and no mistake!'

After calling fruitlessly at the Rectory, he told her, he had found Mr Rutherston in the vestry of St Peter's, making copies of marriage and baptism certificates from the church register for one or two parishioners. Stephen, who had an unrivalled faculty for remembering the smallest detail of every scene in which he had played a conspicuous part, vividly re-created for Jessie the quarrel between himself and the Rector.

Waiting until the certificates were completed, he had tackled with characteristic directness the main object of his visit.

'I wanted to have a word with you about your sermon last Sunday, Mr Rutherston. It didn't strike me as quite appropriate to the folks in this congregation. At all events, I regard the pulpit as the wrong spot for politics. Talk like that only unsettles the lower orders and makes them forget their place.'

Immediately incensed, Thomas Rutherston drew himself up to his full height, which barely reached Stephen's shoulder.

'It is not for God's representative to choose between the members of his congregation, Mr Alleyndene,' he proclaimed with dignity. 'My text of last Sunday – '*I have given you an example, that ye should do as I have done to you*' – was uttered by our Lord to rich and poor alike. The message of the Gospel is for *all* the servants of Christ.'

'Quite so – oh, quite so!' said Stephen imperturbably. 'But politics are not its proper channel.'

Thomas became yet more dignified. Sterndale may have had its ups and downs, but there was none of this sickening business of kow-towing to the Squire. Not that Alleyndene was really a squire at all; he just thought that because he could buy up anybody in the parish, he could dictate to the minister of God at the Rectory. Well, Thomas would show him that he didn't propose to stand that sort of thing. A Rector of Witnall had put the Alleyndenes in their place once before, and another Rector could do it again.

'It is for me, sir, not for you, to decide how I am to give my sermons,' he announced haughtily.

'On the contrary,' said Stephen, 'I'm the People's Church-warden, and I'm not going to have our folks turned into Radicals by the parson or anybody else. There's enough revolutionary talk in the place as it is, with these so-called Labour politicians ruling the roost at Stoke and Hanley. If you've got ideas of that sort in your head, you must keep them to yourself, that's all!'

'Upon my word!' cried Thomas, suddenly losing control of himself. 'It's a fine thing when the laity start telling the clergy how to preach! A man with a reputation all over the Midlands, too! It's clearly thrown away in a place this like! Never in my life have I been so treated! At Sterndale I had some of the finest men in the land in my congregation – Lord Rosebery himself came to my church when I was many years younger than I am now – and never once did anyone presume to find fault with my sermons! I won't put up with it – I'll write to the Bishop . . .'

'I too can write to the Bishop, Mr Rutherston,' put in Stephen heatedly. 'I can tell him what's already obvious to me and my co-directors – that you've had a subversive influence in Witnall ever since you took over the living!'

'Very well!' shouted Thomas. 'I won't stay here to be insulted! This isn't the place, in any case, for a preacher and a scholar! You can look for some clerical ignoramus who'll rattle through the services and echo your hidebound, uneducated ideas from the pulpit like a parrot! I'll send in my resignation to the Bishop to-night!'

'So much the better as far as I'm concerned,' said Stephen, picking up his hat. 'Good afternoon, Mr Rutherston!'

There was silence for a moment in the rose-garden as Stephen finished his recital. Then Jessie inquired: 'Do you think he meant it, Stephen? Will they really go?'

In spite of the relish with which he had told his tale, Stephen's dark brows knit in a scowl of anger and determination.

'By Jove, they'd better! If Rutherston doesn't act on his word, I'll hound him out of the parish! To be talked to like that, in the church where my family's worshipped for three generations, after all the brass I've spent on the place, and the guv'nor before me – it isn't good enough!'

'Well, I hope when they've gone we shall get someone a bit better-class.'

'Tell you what, Jess, I'll drop a personal note to old Cheddle-field and ask him if he can't send us a different sort of chap. The Alleyndenes have never been the kind to put up with highflown tomfoolery in parsons, and our folks down in Witnall are the same way of thinking. If I were you,' he added, 'I'd keep away from the church till these Rutherstons are out of the road. I shouldn't like you to get mixed up with any sort of unpleasantness.'

'You may be sure I shan't. I've always disliked that loud-voiced, self-righteous little man. As for the wife with her wild ideas and slovenly ways, I never want to see her again, nor that lanky boy either!'

Jessie hummed lightly to herself as she went up the imposing staircase to her big first-floor bedroom. Her satisfaction at the ignominious downfall of the Rutherstons had diverted her mind from Stephen's delinquencies, and the recent perturbing talk with Ruth was completely forgotten.

5

But Ruth did not forget. Lonely and disconsolate, she wandered about the grounds of Dene Hall, brooding over the mysterious, upsetting story of her grandmother and Agnes, and missing her brothers more and more as the summer term went by.

Stephen and Jessie had decided, that Easter, to send Richard to the Lower School at Ludborough, the big public school in South Staffordshire where Norman had been a boarder for the past three years.

'He's always drawing and painting and getting so dreamy,' Jessie explained to her sisters, 'and of course we don't want him to grow up in any way *peculiar*. Now he's eleven and a half, he needs more boys of his own age than he gets at the little school in Witnall.'

So in May, just after Granny's funeral, Norman had escorted his small brother to Ludborough, and Ruth was left behind to make the best of her isolated days without them. As the type of school then considered suitable for girls of Ruth's class did not flourish in the Potteries, the amiable Miss Pratt was replaced by a somewhat better qualified Miss Varcoe, and Ruth was relegated to solitary lessons as the line of least resistance. Once or twice Jessie had caught her talking aloud in the oddest way – you might almost call it declaiming – to the shrubs round the tennis court, which had lost its terrors now that Emily and Hetty had gone away to live in Torquay.

The letters that came periodically from her brothers seemed to intensify rather than mitigate Ruth's loneliness. From Norman she heard only once in two or three weeks, but Richard, enthusiastically articulate and undaunted by the pitfalls of spelling and grammar, wrote to her every Sunday. One Monday morning in the middle of June, Jessie put letters from both of them on the breakfast table beside Ruth's plate. She saw her daughter's face light up, as usual, with pleasure at the sight of the untidier and bulkier envelope. Putting it aside to read more slowly, Ruth opened Norman's neat epistle first.

'Dear Ruth,' it ran,

'Thank you very much for your last letter. I hope you will forgive me for not writing last week, as I had rather a lot to do and there was really nothing much to say and I thought I would wait for the photos of the cricket eleven which were only just ready yesterday evening. I am sending the three in which I come out the best but they are not really satisfactory as the negative is too thin. Please let Father and Mother see them when you have finished with them.

'I was very glad to hear from Father this week that he has decided I am to go straight into the Pottery when I leave here. I think college is rather a waste of time when you are going into business, but of course the classes at the Technical School will be a great help. I am sure I shall be useful to Father and I shall be glad when the time comes although in many ways I shall be sorry to leave here. We are having the annual shooting competition from now until Friday and Webster says I have a good chance of winning though of course you can never be sure.

'I hope you are having a pleasant term with Miss Varcoe and getting on well with your lessons. Richard seems to be enjoying himself at the Lower School and has made friends with a little chap called Jesson whose elder brother is in the Upper School in my form.

'Now I think I must close as it will soon be time for chapel.

'Your affectionate brother,
'NORMAN ALLEYNDENE.'

Ruth picked up Richard's letter and opened it eagerly.

'My darling Jill,' she read in his flowing, generous handwriting, already decorative though still a little smudgy, 'You see I am writing to you again, because if I don't like writing to other people I like writing to you.

'This morning at chapel we had nice hymns for a wonder. I am painting such a nice thing, I started it in painting class this week. It is a little grey church & a house & a storm coming on. Mr Pemberton, our visiting master, told me this morning that we have our paintings sent somewhere & mounted & they are given to us at the end of the term. Won't that be nice? I am going to begin Oils next term, Mr Pemberton says, though most of the chaps who take speshial drawing don't begin Oils till the Upper School.

'There is an awfully nice chap here called Jesson Minor, his other name is Eric. His brother Valentine is in the Upper School in the same form as Norman though he is a year younger. Last term Jesson Major was second & Norman was only sixth. Yesterday after the match Jesson Major took Eric & I out to tea. He is very clever & hansome and is going to be a sculpter when he grows up, so he was rather intrested in my painting. His father is an arkitect & his people live in Chelsea which is a part of London. Eric wants me to go & stay with them in the hols sometime, do you think Daddy & Mother will let me?

'I was awfully sorry to hear poor old Koko has had to be distroyed but I suppose he was getting awfully old. I wish you were here & I could talk to you. It must be frightfully boring for you at home with only Mother & Daddy & Miss Varcoe. Never mind, it is ½ term on Tuesday & after that it won't seem so long till I come home. The wild roses are beginning to come out in the lanes. This morning Eric & I found two bushes quite out. We are going to look at the petals under my microscobe this afternoon.

'We had two cricket matches yesterday. I played in the 2nd XI & caught one chap out & made 1 run.

'I think that is all the news. With love to Mother, Daddy, Miss Varcoe, Wardle & you,

'Your ever loving
'JACK.'

'Any news from the boys, dear?' asked Jessie, who had received the usual dutiful note from Norman but nothing from her adored and cherished Richard. As she stretched out her hand automatically for the letters Ruth passed over the one from Norman, but considerations of tact no less than a sense of outraged privacy induced her to withhold Richard's.

'You see,' she explained apologetically, 'bits of it are rather *private*.'

'Oh, then I won't read it, of course,' said Jessie, affronted. 'I'm sure I don't *wish* to interfere if you and Richard prefer to keep secrets away from your mother!'

A difficult, unresponsive child, she thought, as Ruth wandered off to walk about the garden until Miss Varcoe was ready for her lessons. She and Norman are both Alleyndenes – proud, self-contained and undemonstrative; so different from dear Richard, with his artistic, affectionate nature. If it had been Richard he'd have shown me that letter at once. He's a Penryder through and through. The trouble about Ruth is that under her pride she's sensitive to a degree, which Norman isn't. She gets that from Stephen's side too. My own family have always been practical and made the best of things. Even poor Father never fussed about what couldn't be helped.

Looking out of the dining-room window, she saw Arthur Wardle, the third gardener, greet Ruth with a smile and a touch of the cap that he never condescended to give to the rest of the family. I wonder, she asked herself, what makes a daughter of mine so fond of talking to gardeners and grooms and pottery employees, instead of making friends with the nice little girls of her own age in the district? It doesn't seem natural, and that young Wardle's rough ways certainly won't improve her manners, especially as the servants say he's mixed up with some of those dreadful Socialists in Stoke and Hanley. If he weren't such a good gardener I'd persuade Stephen to get rid of him.

Jessie recalled how one morning, last autumn, Ruth had even prevailed upon Briggs, the groom, to drive her down by herself to the Pottery, where Stephen had found her deep in conversation with Jim Hardiman, the young hollow-ware presser, whose pale face was so curiously lit up by his deep-set, contemplative blue eyes. He was an intelligent man, Stephen had told her, and was studying chemistry at the Technical School in the hope of qualifying to become a manager – but whatever could a child of Ruth's age have to say to an ordinary working potter? Jessie had wanted to punish Ruth for that unconventional expedition, but Stephen had only laughed and said that it showed initiative and refused to scold her.

Jessie would have been still more disturbed if she could have seen inside Ruth's mind as she disappeared into the fir plantation. By means of the judicious indirect questioning in which parental concealments were making her an adept, she had learnt from her friend Arthur Wardle far more than she was ever likely to hear from Jessie about the sufferings of working women at the hands of her father's class, and the cruelty of a still Victorian society towards unmarried mothers and unwanted babies. Gradually her shocked, struggling thoughts had come symbolically to identify the penalised and ejected Agnes with the hunted fox that she had seen vainly trying to escape from the pitiless hounds near Rough Close early in the year. Even Jessie, who was with her at the time, had never guessed how long that accidental encounter with the North Staffordshire Hunt had haunted and distressed her.

It had been a bright, frosty morning, and Ruth and her mother, warmly wrapped up in furs and rugs, had gone for a long drive in the wagonette by Rough Close and Barlaston Common. They had just turned homewards and were rattling briskly along the road high above the ditch behind the trotting chestnut mare, when suddenly Jessie seized Ruth by the arm.

'Look, dear!' she cried, 'the North Staffordshire Hounds – and I do believe that's the fox, just in front of them! Why, if we're lucky we may see the kill!'

Ruth did not know that the same society which made a ceremony of the slaughter of a fox was later to make a sacrament of the slaughter of its sons. She only wished that her mother had not stopped the wagonette and obliged her to witness the scene of socially canonised carnage which remained vividly in her memory until it was obliterated by the wholesale physical and spiritual havoc of the Great War.

One by one, she watched first the hounds and then the huntsmen in their bright pink coats come leaping over the brow of the low hill, like little painted mechanical figures wound up to jump the obstacles in a toy steeplechase. Down the field towards the road they came, trampling into mud the blades of frosted grass which shone in the melting sunshine like emeralds encrusted with miniature diamonds. Suddenly, only a few yards in front of them, she saw the terrified, exhausted fox, panting and limping, its bushy red-brown tail betraying its presence to the merciless advancing death which it could no longer evade. Fascinated with dread, she watched the hounds surround the fox just in front of the ditch, yelping and struggling. For a second a red shutter seemed to descend upon her eyes; then she saw the leading huntsman ride up, plunge his hand amid the waving tails, raise the dead fox aloft from the writhing mass of brown and white bodies, cut off its brush and fling back the limp carcass to be torn asunder by the slobbering ravenous mouths.

As they drove home Ruth had felt too ill to speak, keeping her white face averted from her mother and surreptitiously pinching her cheeks until their deceptive pink left no hint of her inward horror. Immediately after lunch she was violently sick, but during the meal itself she had eaten enough to maintain her pretence of normality while she listened to Stephen's eager congratulations.

'So you actually saw the kill? By Jove, Jill, that was a bit of luck! The other little girls in Witnall won't half envy you when they get to know!'

A bit of luck, she repeated to herself now as she walked in the blessed privacy of the cool plantation. She and Richard and Norman and Father and Mother were the lucky ones of this world, though they hadn't done anything special to deserve it. Wardle had said so. But what about all the others? Was it lucky, he'd asked her, to be the poor fox, at the mercy of huntsmen and hounds in overwhelming numbers? Was it lucky, she asked herself, to be Agnes, turned out of the house by Granny and made to lose her little baby, because she had no money and no one to defend her?

'Oh, when I grow up I'm going to change it all!' she cried passionately to the swaying resinous firs, her mind leaping over the years which were to teach her that not in one lifetime, nor one century, nor one epoch, would the campaign of the few for justice and mercy be won.

Two days afterwards, as Jessie passed the schoolroom just before tea-time, she heard Ruth's voice loudly raised within. Whoever could be there with the child? she asked herself, perplexed, knowing that Miss Varcoe had gone to Stoke for her afternoon off, and that she had not given Ruth permission to invite anyone to tea. Surely she had not dared, on her own account, to ask Briggs or Wardle into the house? Determined to put a stop immediately to any such breach of propriety, Jesse turned the door-handle softly and looked in.

But Ruth was alone, dramatically perched upon a high wooden chair. On the table behind her lay the schoolroom Bible, open at the twenty-third chapter of St Matthew's Gospel which she and Miss Varcoe had been reading aloud in her Scripture lesson that morning.

'*Neither be ye called masters: for one is your Master, even Christ.*

'*But he that is greatest among you shall be your servant.*

'*And whosoever shall exalt himself shall be abased: and he that shall humble himself shall be exalted.*

'*But woe unto you, scribes and Pharisees, hypocrites! for ye shut up the kingdom of heaven against men; for ye neither go in yourselves, neither suffer ye them that are entering to go in.*

'*Woe unto you, scribes and Pharisees, hypocrites! for ye devour widows' houses, and for a pretence make long prayer: therefore ye shall receive the greater damnation.*'

Ruth recited the verses aloud from memory and then continued feverishly in her own vehement words:

'Woe unto you, sinners and murderers, that deprive all innocent animals of their lovely life! Woe unto you that spoil the happiness and freedom of the world by doing cruel things! Woe unto you, Pharisees and hypocrites, that condemn the poor, unhappy woman and destroy her little child!'

As she spoke her imaginary audience began to change its character; from a shadowy gathering of vague Israelites with white robes and large noses, it gradually turned into the brushed, washed, respectable Staffordshire congregation to whom her father read the Lessons every Sunday morning.

'Cruelty is the worst of sins!' she declaimed with suffused, flashing eyes, her gesticulations a faithful reproduction of the histrionic gestures habitually indulged in by the recently-departed Reverend Thomas Rutherston. 'Woe unto you, parishioners of Witnall, Pharisees, hypocrites, for practising cruelty, the sin against the Holy Ghost . . . !'

Unable to endure this exhibition any longer, Jessie pushed the door open and went in.

'What on earth are you doing, Ruth?' she inquired sharply. 'Get down off your chair and stop that nonsense at once!'

But Ruth, too much startled by the interruption to adjust herself immediately to her familiar surroundings, was able neither to move nor speak. She only turned very pale, and as usual when her overmastering emotions proved too much for her control, burst violently into tears.

It certainly wasn't normal behaviour for a child of her age, agreed Stephen when Ruth had been scolded, comforted, and banished to her bedroom to lie down. So after tea they sent for Dr Wesley Bullock, who had conducted Ruth into the world which she found so bewildering, and left him upstairs with her in the hope that he would succeed in winning her confidence.

'Nothing serious,' he assured them when he had talked to Ruth for about half an hour, until her tears dried and a watery smile began to lift the corners of her lovely but dejected little mouth. 'She's a bit anæmic, but that's not unusual in girls of her age. The real trouble is, she's inclined to be fanciful and a deal too introspective – and there's no doubt she misses her brothers. Companionship is what she needs, and a change of air. Have you thought at all about sending her away to school?'

'To tell you the truth,' Stephen replied, 'I can't say I have. The lads have gone, of course – but I don't much care for the notion of little girls leaving a good home. None of my sisters went – but if you say that's what the child wants, I won't stand in her way.'

'Well, that *is* what I should advise. Sea air if possible, and a complete change of surroundings – south coast for choice.'

A promising idea leapt into Jessie's mind.

'Why, Stephen, what about Playden Manor, that school near Rye? It's very healthy, so Nellie tells me, right on the top of a hill looking towards the sea – and she says the headmistress is an Oxford woman and quite a scholar. You know,' she reminded him in a discreet aside. 'It's the place where Nellie teaches piano and singing. She goes there twice a week and she could easily keep an eye on Ruth . . .'

'The very place!' said Dr Bullock, sedulously maintaining his official unawareness of Jessie's addendum. 'Fine air, nice girls, pleasant country – oh, yes, and good teaching; no doubt, no doubt! Mustn't forget the young lady's got to learn something, must we? Why not take a trip down south and have a look at it?'

'Right you are!' assented Stephen. 'There's no time like the present, eh, Jess? We'll run down next week and size it up.'

So in September 1907, Ruth became a pupil at Playden Manor School, near Rye, in the country of Sussex.

6

To Jessie's surprise – for everything that went well surprised her – the Playden Manor experiment proved an unqualified success. From Ruth's point of view it was entirely justified, while even Jessie enjoyed her visits to Rye with its cobbled medieval streets and ancient walls crowned by the round Ypres Tower. Once she walked with Ruth to the pocket harbour, where shabby tar-smeared boats with tattered tawny sails crossed the bar to take refuge in the sheltered zigzags of the tranquil Rother.

From Playden, the hamlet on the hill beyond Rye along the road to Tenterden, Jessie could look from the windows of Ruth's dormitory across the vivid wind-swept level of Romney Marsh to the dazzling emptiness of Camber Sands, and the dark-blue white-frilled breakers of the English Channel two miles from the school. The fresh racing air smelt so different from the smoke-laden breezes which blew northward over the Potteries, ruining Jessie's clean lace curtains when they'd been up less than a month. The black tide of industrialism had overflowed into Witnall now; it threatened, before many years had gone by, to penetrate even the country meadows surrounding Dene Hall.

'I'm beginning to feel quite literary!' Jessie remarked once to Stephen after spending a night at the Mermaid Inn. Ruth had already described to them the narrow street in which it stood, climbing steeply uphill between heavily-timbered old houses with red irregular roofs towards the conspicuous church tower, pressed down like a candle extinguisher upon the summit of the little town.

'It's a place writing folks take to, then?' queried Stephen proudly.

'To be sure they do! Would you believe it, there was an American author called Henry James – very famous, so they tell me – living in a big house at the top of Mermaid Street quite close to the inn!'

In the intervals between Jessie's visits, Ruth wrote her mother long appreciative letters about examinations, school reports, winter lacrosse matches, and summer picnics on Camber Sands.

She also mentioned her friendship with Madeleine Gibson, whose father was second master at Ufferton, the famous public school in Kent. Madeleine, she said, was so good at lessons that when she was old enough she was going to try for a scholarship at Oxford.

'I don't know whether I told you before,' Ruth wrote at the end of her first term, 'but the girls here are all divided into the Smart Set and the Swotters. The Smart Set explains itself, and the Swotters are all the people who have got to work for their livings afterwards whether they have got brains or not. When I first came I was put into the Swotters as a matter of course because of Auntie Nellie teaching music here. Of course I didn't say anything but this term one of the Smart Set in the Sixth discovered I was one of the Alleyndenes of Dene Hall and wasn't there a rush to make me one of them! But by that time of course I was friends with Madeleine who's got to earn her living because her father says he can't afford to keep her at home when she's grown up, so I decided to stay a Swotter like her. Wasn't it a sell for the snobs who tried to get me into their silly Set!'

Jessie made a wry face over her daughter's letter, uncertain whether she felt the more disconcerted by the implicit slight on poor Nellie or by Ruth's democratic preference for Swotters. She would have frowned even more had she been favoured with details of the Camber picnics, in which Ruth held forth eloquently to an audience of sea-birds and sandhills on the malevolence of snobs and the wrongs of repressed and bullied under-mistresses. Quite obviously those hard-working and con-scientious women, instead of being the dictatorial Olympians whom Ruth had expected, were despised by the parents and tormented by the girls just because they were obliged – as dear Madeleine would be obliged one day – to work for their livings.

'Unfairness and injustice rage like prowling lions about this earth, seeking whom they may devour!' proclaimed Ruth to the tufts of prickly grass stretching their sharp green spikes along the sand. 'The man who works is honoured and respected, but the woman who does the same is rejected and despised. Behold, I show you a mystery; the time is at hand when women will all work and all be changed! When that which is perfect is come, that which is unfair and unequal shall be done away!'

'What *do* you think you're doing, Ruth?' inquired Madeleine herself, a thin gentle girl with pale brown hair and brilliant hazel eyes.

'I'm only practising my speeches,' Ruth explained. 'When I'm grown up I'm going to lead the people. I'm going to be a great speaker like Mrs Pankhurst.'

In the summer term of 1910, Jessie went down to Rye for a long week-end to celebrate Ruth's sixteenth birthday. She found Witnall quiet and a little dull after the death of Edward the Seventh, and Stephen had bored her more than usual with his incessant discussion of the new regulations for pottery employers which were likely to follow the 1908 Inquiry into Industrial Diseases.

On Sunday morning, calling at the school to take Ruth to church, she found her deeply involved in conversation with Madeleine over a poem which the Upper Fifth had been set to write for Composition in honour of the tenth anniversary of Miss Hilton's headship. Flushed and exasperated, Ruth had been wrestling with refractory dactyls and elusive spondees when the prospective English scholar of Drayton College, Oxford, came into the form-room to fetch a prayer-book. Leaning over Ruth's shoulder, Madeleine read the four blotted lines of persevering eulogy:

> 'Cheering us forever onward,
> She, a leader of mankind,
> Fires the skilful, nerves the backward,
> Raises those who droop behind.

'Sounds like a skirt,' observed Madeleine dispassionately.

Ruth threw down her pen in profound dejection.

'Oh, Madeleine, it's not a bit of good my writing poetry! I can't do it however I try.'

Madeleine was too honest to disagree.

'I can't think why you bother about it,' she said. 'You're so good at nearly everything else – specially History and Elocution.

At least you're marvellous at remembering poetry even if you can't write it – and then look at you in school debates! Why, if I could speak like you can, without turning a hair, I don't believe I'd ever try to write again!'

'But you see,' objected Ruth, 'if I can't write and be a journalist or something, I don't quite know what I *am* going to do when I grow up. I don't want to be a teacher, I should hate it, and I'd simply loathe being a private secretary, always at the beck and call of somebody rich and bad-tempered. What I'd *really* like is to be a great preacher or a Member of Parliament or a barrister or an ambassador, but what's the good of that, when women can't go in for the Church or politics or the Bar or the Diplomatic Service? Anyway, even if they could I don't suppose Mother and Father would ever let me.'

As the door opened and Jessie came in she bowed her head assiduously over her exercise book, and Jessie wondered, as she had so often wondered lately, why, now that her children were growing up, silence was apt to fall suddenly when she entered a room.

'Good morning, dears!' she said cheerfully, refraining with an effort from commenting upon the obvious hiatus in the conversation. 'Are you nearly ready, Ruth? The bell's been ringing about ten minutes.'

Ruth had been excused from the usual village service at Playden in order to take her mother to the old parish church in Rye. As the bell continued its insistent summons she walked thoughtfully beside Jessie down Rye Hill, and through the ancient Landgate to the heights of the town. From the steep narrow street in the shade of the church tower she showed her mother the famous gold-figured clock-face upon the lofty grey stone, and above it the two carven figures which mechanically recorded the vanishing hours on either side of the gilded inscription:

'For our time is a very shadow that passeth away.'

'Yes; time passes,' thought Jessie, standing beside her dark, grave-eyed daughter, already nearly a head taller than herself, as the music of the Psalms reverberated grandly from the vaulted roof. She watched the long sweeping pendulum beneath the clock with reluctant fascination, as though its slow, sinister swing were the creeping scythe of Father Time whose legend had distressed Ruth in her childhood. How dilatory seemed the moments here, and yet how rapidly they mounted into days, months and years! 'Why,' she recalled, 'I was only two years older than Ruth when I went to take care of Philip and Hetty! And now I'm forty, though I don't look it. Oh, no, I don't look it! When Ruth's a year or two older, people would take us for sisters if only we weren't so unlike in appearance. I wonder what life's going to bring her? She'll have to learn from experience, of course, just as I did, but I hope it won't mean a loveless marriage and a constant pretence, as it's meant for me. At least she'll have money of her own one day, and people always treat you better when they know that.'

Strangely enough, at school prayers that evening Miss Hilton chose for her weekly address the subject 'From Girlhood to Womanhood.' A number of the seniors were leaving that term, Ruth explained, and Miss Hilton was talking especially to them. For some reason that she could not elucidate, Jessie had never felt quite at her ease with the small, plain, ardent headmistress. Inspired by a genuine respect for intellectual integrity and a passionate zeal for social righteousness, Miss Hilton had intended to become a college tutor, but chance and a persuasive Board of Governors had turned her into the Principal of a fashionable private school. With awe tempered by criticism, Jessie listened to her vehement words:

'Many of you will soon be leaving Playden Manor, and going out into that wider world where you will not find life as simple, perhaps, nor as straightforward, as it has been for most of you here at school. When you first grow up there will come a time of adjustment which you may find difficult and exacting, but remember in the midst of its stress that yours is no new or unique experience. Each generation as it passes from tutelage into the life of its day has to go through a period of transition, and in our own age, with its strong movements for women's independence, for democratic freedom and for social reform, the rate at which change occurs has become swifter, the problems it presents more difficult to solve.

'For this reason it is, perhaps, harder for you to adjust successfully your relationship to the older generations, than it was for your mothers and fathers twenty or thirty years ago. But wherever life takes you, you cannot do better than remember the principles laid down in 1864 by Ruskin in his Preface to *Sesame and Lilies*. They apply just as much to you to-day as they did to the girls of that time. "Whatever else you may be, you must not be useless, and you must not be cruel. If there is any one point, which, in six thousand years of thinking about right and wrong, wise and good men have agreed upon, or successively by experience discovered, it is that God dislikes idle and cruel people more than any others – that His first order is, 'Work while you have light'; and His second, 'Be merciful while you have mercy.'"

'Begin, then, to prepare yourselves now for the dangers and problems of adult life. Think on these things constantly, and always remember the high ideals you have learnt at school. Choose your friends carefully and never, in the hope of seeming "smart" or worldly-wise, let your standards of conduct sink lower than those we have tried to teach you here. Never listen to immodest jests and stories on topics which should not be discussed by women who hope to lead noble lives. Try always to preserve that purity of heart through which, we are told, we may learn to see God. Beware of getting drawn into the so-called Bohemian sets in London and other large cities, where only too often, I regret to say, loose talk is apt to lead to looser morals.'

Like that Valentine Jesson, thought Jessie, her mind straying for a moment as her eyes feasted themselves upon the azure splendour of lupins and delphiniums in the herbaceous borders of the school drive outside the windows of the Assembly Hall. How tiresome he shouldn't be quite moral, when Eric seems such a nice boy and the Jessons are so useful for Richard to know!

Her memory went back to an April morning last holidays, when they had sat longer than usual over the breakfast table discussing the recently completed Federation of the six pottery

towns – Stoke, Burslem, Hanley, Longton, Fenton and Tunstall
– which the Staffordshire author, Arnold Bennett, persisted in
calling five. Not until Stephen had finished expounding for the
twentieth time his reasons for opposing the Federation and had
departed with Norman to the Pottery, did Richard venture to
open the letter lying beside his plate. Immediately he had read
it he went white, and pushed the thick embellished note-paper
back into the envelope.

'What's the matter, Richard?' inquired Jessie, who had recognised Eric Jesson's round, sprawling hand. 'Has something gone
wrong with Eric?'

'No – o, it isn't Eric, it's Val,' he said awkwardly, and Jessie
recalled his admiration for Eric's handsome elder brother. She
looked her inquiry, and Richard went on mumbling.

'His father's been asked to remove him from Ludborough . . .
It doesn't make much difference *really*, because he was leaving
next term anyhow – but it's a bit rotten for Eric, though of course
Val's in a different house from us and the chaps'll only think he's
gone to Paris a term earlier . . .'

'Oh, Richard, how terrible! How dreadful for his parents,
poor things! Whatever's he done?'

Richard was silent, but his pale face flushed crimson.

'Was it—?' Jessie glanced across the table at Ruth, sitting
opposite Richard, distressed for his distress though the thought
passed through her mind: I wouldn't have told Mother that
about Valentine. I'd have kept it to myself.

Instinctively Jessie dropped her voice.

'Was it – immorality?'

Richard nodded. He kicked the table-leg savagely, and Jessie
did not reprove him. For a moment nobody uttered a word, and
then Richard began, brokenly, to defend Valentine Jesson.

'I can't believe it was all his fault – he's such a decent chap,
and so awfully good at designing and modelling . . .'

Jessie leaned towards him, her back to Ruth, and spoke to
him earnestly in an undertone.

'But you do realise, dear, don't you, that nothing, *nothing*
can make up for that particular offence – not talents, nor good
looks, nor success in after-life? Your father and I would rather

see you dead at our feet than have you guilty of anything so dreadful! We should feel it just as much a shame and a disgrace as if your sister became a wicked, fast woman and had a baby without being married!'

She did not know that when they had all finished their breakfast, Ruth followed her dejected brother into the bicycle shed, where he was blowing up his tyres in preparation for a solitary ride.

'Jack, I don't understand what Valentine Jesson *did*, exactly.'

For once he turned his back miserably upon her.

'You heard what mother said – immorality.'

'But how could he be immoral at a public school? There aren't any women there, are there?'

'Lord, you don't need women, to be immoral.'

'I don't understand.'

'Oh, hell, Jill!' he cried, at the end of his endurance, 'why can't you let things *alone*!'

'I don't see why I should. You're younger than me and yet you know something I don't. Is it a thing I *ought* to know?'

'Well,' he admitted grudgingly, 'if you get married when you're grown up, and have a kid – a son ... Yes, I suppose you ought, in a way.'

'Then don't be mean. You know Mother never tells me anything. If it's something I ought to know I want to know it even if it's awful.'

So Richard, unhappy, embarrassed, wishing himself a thousand miles away, embarked upon a halting and reluctant explanation. Ruth listened silently, realising as he proceeded his wretchedness in fulfilling her demands, and restraining for his sake her sense of shock and disgust. But as soon as he had ridden away down the drive she rushed into the fir plantation and flung herself face downwards, unconscious for once of the peeping creamy primroses, the delicately veined petals of the paper-white anemones, the upturned golden cups of the dew-filled aconites.

'Oh, how horrible!' she sobbed. 'Why must life be like this, so ugly, so sordid, when it could be so beautiful? Oh! I hate it, I hate it!'

Still unaware of this sequel to her admonition to Richard,

Jessie at Playden Manor observed only that Ruth's face, which had been flushed and animated when Miss Hilton's address began, became pale and solemn as the talk continued.

'Sometimes,' Miss Hilton proceeded passionately, 'not even years of repentance and remorse can compensate a girl for taking a disastrous step at the very time when her pure youth, her fresh beauty, should be an inspiration to all who surround her. Do not forget that Ruskin also said: "Let heart-sickness pass beyond a certain bitter point, and the heart loses its life for ever." Remember, girls, that whether you are going in for careers, or whether, as in the case of most of you here, you intend to adopt that noblest of all vocations, marriage and motherhood, it is part of your high responsibility to set an example to the men with whom you associate – your husbands, your brothers, your sons, your colleagues. It may well be that, through you, some young man who has stumbled and strayed may be brought back to the path of righteousness. The happiness and nobility of a Christian home are invariably the creation of the woman at its centre, so do not fail to set always before you the ideal of shining in this dark world like pure lamps of inspiration.

'Some of you, some day, will have sons of your own. Their education will demand from you much thought, much prayer and infinite sacrifice. But one thing I hope from all of you who have been trained here. I hope you will demand from your sons the same standard of moral conduct as you expect from your daughters. Discipline and purity and restraint are not ideals for women only, though there are still, I fear, too many husbands and fathers who think so. Without these spiritual gifts of self-control, of the power, when God demands it of us, to resist temptation and curb the overmastering impulses of our frail human flesh, we cannot attain to that noblest ideal of citizenship, the measure of the stature of the fullness of Christ!'

Jessie did not notice the curious confusion, in Miss Hilton's address, of modern values with ancient standards. Nor did she realise how characteristic was this confusion of the teachers belonging to Miss Hilton's era – the era that was so soon to plunge its bewildered societies into the catastrophe by which their old conventions and continuities would be broken for ever. But she did wonder, as so often in the past, whether all this talk about morality had any other effect than to make a young girl's mind dwell unnecessarily upon subjects which were best ignored until life brought her up against them and she found her feet – as of course she would do, like others before her.

Ruth had ceased, now, to ask awkward questions – at any rate of her mother – but how could Jessie know what unsuitable lines of inquiry she might not be pursuing through all those heavy-looking volumes which she had brought home for the last two holidays? There were books on history, and economics, and a new subject which Ruth called 'sociology' – something, Jessie thought, that sounded more suitable for learned men than for a girl whose chief duty in life, after all, was to get suitably married. No doubt Miss Hilton was an excellent scholar and that sort of thing, but Jessie couldn't see how all this book-reading was going to help Ruth to find a husband. It seemed likely, indeed, to prove a hindrance rather than a help, especially as Ruth was inclined to take everything too seriously already.

A chord sounded on the piano, and she stood up with the girls to sing the last hymn, Rudyard Kipling's 'The Children's Song.' Their shrill young voices echoed through the open windows into the cool garden where the long evening shadows were softly stealing the vivid colours from the summer flowers:

> 'Teach us to bear the yoke in youth,
> With steadfastness and careful truth;
> That, in our time, Thy Grace may give
> The Truth whereby the Nations live.
>
> 'Teach us to rule ourselves alway,
> Controlled and cleanly night and day;
> That we may bring, if need arise,
> No maimed or worthless sacrifice . . .'

7

In the last week of February 1911, Jessie received an unusually
long letter from Ruth for her own birthday.

'MY DEAREST MOTHER,

'I am writing to wish you many many happy returns of the
day and I do hope you will enjoy it. I expect you will, as you
are going to Ludborough to see Richard. Has his voice quite
broken now? I suppose there will be no solos in the school
concerts for him any more, but of course it will mean more
time for his painting so I daresay he won't really mind. I am
so glad Norman likes his new work at the Pottery, please
give him my love and say I will write next week if I have a
moment.

'I hope you will like the d'oyleys I have done for you. I
meant to do six but I have only had time to do five so far,
as I am not much good at the fringing part and I have not
been able to sit at them at all. You know what it is at school.
Yesterday we had our first Lacrosse match as we haven't
dared to play anyone before through the weather being so
bad. I played centre and we won 5–2. The field was just like
a sponge, however we managed to keep our feet pretty well.

'We had half-term report this morning. I had a very good
one. Among other things I had 92 for Elocution, 89 for
History, 88 for Singing, 83 for Scripture, 82 for Geography
and 80 for French. I was top in Elocution, History, Singing
and Scripture, and Madeleine was top in English, French,
German and Geography. We were bracketed top in everything
else except Geometry and Sewing, and Madeleine was made
a prefect. Miss Hilton said she was very pleased with me and
that I shall be a prefect next term too.

'I hope you will enjoy the Repertory Company when it
comes to Witnall next week. I shall be so anxious to hear all
about it as you know how fond I am of plays. We are doing
Highland Saturday, by Ellison Campbell, for the Féte next
term. I am going to be the hero, Angus Maxwell, because I am

so tall, and Madeleine is going to be Mary Ann McCrae. There is a book of Ellison Campbell's plays in the school library; I have read them all and I think they are lovely.

'I must really stop as I want to finish your last d'oyley. I wish I weren't so clumsy at this kind of thing but I have tried my hardest to make them neat. Ever so many wishes for a very happy birthday.

'Your loving
'RUTH.'

Jessie passed the closely-written sheet across to Stephen.

'Ruth seems to have done pretty well this term, so far,' she observed. 'Why, isn't that a letter from Miss Hilton you've got there?'

'Ay. She's writing about Jill's report; it's a bit out of the ordinary, so I gather. And she says she'd like a talk with me next time we're down south.'

'Well, that shouldn't be difficult. We always meant to fit in our week-end with Elizabeth and Hermann before Easter, and now Norman's at the Pottery you could stay over an extra day, couldn't you?'

'It might be as well. But what beats me, Jess, is why the old girl wants to see me because Jill's had a *good* report. I could understand it if she'd got complaints to make and didn't want to commit them to paper, but what in the name of fortune . . . ? I hope it doesn't mean Jill's been over-working and gone a bit queer again, like that time when old Bullock made us send her to school.'

But when they saw Miss Hilton he was soon enlightened, for after a brief word of greeting she went straight to the point.

'You've heard from me, Mr Alleyndene, and no doubt something from Ruth herself, about her really excellent half-term report. I wonder . . . have you begun to think about her future at all?'

Stephen meditated. Well, no; he couldn't exactly say that he had. She'd a good home, and there were plenty of decent young chaps of her own class in the district. What more did a girl in Ruth's position want?

Privately Miss Hilton thought that Ruth already showed signs of wanting a great deal more. Though undeniably good-looking and likely to become even beautiful, her next prefect-to-be was perhaps a little too disdainful and independent to attract the average young middle-class male, however decent. That aloof reserve, that barrier of self-contained haughtiness might well fascinate, with its problematical challenge, a man of unusual personality or gifts, but it didn't seem probable that the scions of conventional Staffordshire families whom Stephen Alleyndene approved were likely to be in any way extraordinary. Nor would they be the type, decided Miss Hilton, to understand that unexpected quality of strong humanitarianism in Ruth which she had always done her best to foster. Her fighting spirit already aroused on her pupil's behalf, she again tackled Stephen.

'I don't know if you realise that we regard Ruth as one of the most promising girls at Playden Manor. She has done exceedingly well ever since she came to us.'

There was something, Jessie felt, a little – well, almost menacing – in this insistence upon Ruth's superfluous cleverness, but Stephen's dark countenance relaxed in a smile of gratification.

'Jill always did have plenty of nous,' he remarked proudly. 'She takes after her father, Miss Hilton – far more than either of the lads, as I've always said, though my wife can't see it.'

Miss Hilton looked him straight in the eyes with challenging directness.

'Well,' she inquired, 'do you consider it quite fair to a girl of so much ability to let her simply live at home and do nothing in particular after leaving school?'

He couldn't say, responded Stephen, surprised, that the matter had ever occurred to him in that light. 'Of course we're not anxious to lose our daughter, but we scarcely expect her to be at home very long. I don't doubt she'll marry early.'

'I'm not so sure of that, Mr Alleyndene. A girl of Ruth's critical type isn't easily satisfied. And even if she were, marriage alone, with the smaller families of the present day, is not necessarily a full-time occupation.'

But here Jessie interrupted indignantly. It was just like one of these unpractical, scholastic spinsters to lay down the law about matters of which she understood nothing whatever.

'I don't know how you can say that, I'm sure!' she exclaimed. 'Speaking from personal experience, Miss Hilton, and with the servant problem what it is to-day, I've always found the care of my home and family more than enough to fill my time. And any woman who managed her house *capably* would say the same.'

But for once Stephen completely ignored her.

'I'd like you to speak frankly, Miss Hilton,' he said. 'You've got something on your mind with regard to my daughter. If you were in my shoes, what would be your own notion about Ruth?'

'I should give her three years at a good university – Oxford for choice,' replied Miss Hilton promptly. 'She'd be qualified, then, to have a career if she chose to adopt one.'

There was a silence for a moment in the headmistress's study as the unaccustomed minds of Stephen and Jessie absorbed the revolutionary suggestion. As soon as Jessie had grasped its implications, she waited for the expression of Stephen's resolute opposition, but to her astonishment it did not come.

'Well,' he admitted reluctantly, 'it seems an outlandish notion to me, and since there's no question of Ruth having to earn her living, I don't see much point in it. We've never been a family to spend overmuch time on book-learning, Miss Hilton. Sharp's the word and get on with the job – that's been the motto for us, and I can't say we've done badly on it. Still,' he added reflectively, 'times change, and there seems a deal more to be said for education now than there was in my young days.'

'Then you're prepared to think over the idea?'

'Ay. I'll think it over. I didn't stand in Jill's light when the doctor advised me to send her to school, and if there's anything in this college notion I'll take time to consider it.'

'I'm *very* glad to find your mind so responsive to modern tendencies, Mr Alleyndene,' said Miss Hilton judiciously. 'Now, let me see, Ruth will be seventeen in June, I think? Assuming, just for the moment, that you *did* consent to her going to Oxford, she could take Responsions – the University entrance examination – next December, and the examination for Drayton – my own

college, and the one I should recommend as by far the most
suitable – in the following March. Suppose she succeeds in
getting a place, as I fully anticipate she will, that means she
would go up to Oxford in 1912, the October following her
eighteenth birthday – a most appropriate time. I take it you
did intend her to stay at school for another year?'

'Well,' commented Stephen, forestalling a further protest from
Jessie, 'we *had* discussed bringing her home in the summer, but
if this Oxford business comes to anything I realise she'll have
to stay on. It's lucky I'm not a poor man, Miss Hilton!'

'I was about to touch on that point,' tentatively began the
headmistress. Her knowledge of the Alleyndene finances had
been increased, only a few evenings ago, by a dinner-hour
description of Dene Hall from Madeleine Gibson, who had
spent ten days of the Christmas holidays with Ruth.

'I daresay you don't know,' she continued, 'that there are two
different examinations at the Oxford women's colleges, one for
entrance only, and another for those who seek scholarships.
About a scholarship for Ruth, I'm not so sure. She'd get one
if she worked for it, I'm fairly certain, but the women's colleges
are poorly endowed, and I don't altogether feel Ruth ought to
take a scholarship even if she won it. Now with Madeleine
Gibson, my other star pupil, it's a different matter. Her father's
a schoolmaster, soon to retire, and I gather the scholarship is
necessary.'

But again Stephen, in whose experience scholarships were
rewards reserved for 'the tradespeople' and sometimes for the
exceptionally meritorious children of grooms and gardeners,
proved unexpectedly co-operative, even if his point of view was
one to which Miss Hilton was hardly accustomed.

'Thank you, we don't need anything like that in *our* family,'
he announced with dignity. 'I hope I can send my daughter to
the university without making her work herself into a nervous
breakdown or dipping my hand in the college's pocket. The
Alleyndenes have always paid their way, Miss Hilton, and they
always will!'

Well, thought the headmistress, it's at least a solution to find
a father who regards a scholarship as ignominious! 'I'll certainly

see that Ruth gets well coached for the entrance examination,' she observed aloud. 'I haven't the slightest doubt she'll get in easily enough through that. *If* you consent, of course.'

As their homeward train slid smoothly through Leicestershire into Staffordshire, Jessie, alarmed beyond expression by this unexpected consequence of Stephen's pride in his beloved daughter, turned anxiously for at least the tenth time to her husband.

'Oh, Stephen, do you think it's wise? Ruth's got quite enough idea of herself already, and I don't want her to turn into one of those strong-minded women . . .'

But Stephen, to whom the vision of Ruth as a college student became more attractive the longer he thought about it, refused to be perturbed. It would make his brothers sit up, he reflected, when they knew he'd got a daughter with nous enough to go to Oxford!

'It'll do the lass no harm to think well of herself,' he said. 'All the Alleyndenes have done that. Trouble is, they haven't always had enough learning to back up their notions. In the old guv'nor's time it didn't matter, but you can't get far nowadays without education. It won't hurt Jill to have a bit extra spent on hers.'

'But what's the use? As you told Miss Hilton, Ruth won't have to earn her living, and you surely want her to marry early, as any normal girl should? If a woman's too intellectual, it's liable to put people off.'

'Of course Jill'll marry! Don't you fret yourself, Jess! I never knew a chap yet that was put off by brains when there was plenty of brass about. Money'll do owt, as they say in these parts.'

But he had to confess to Jessie afterwards that he'd never expected his final decision to send Ruth to Oxford would start young Richard off on another tack as soon as he came home for the summer holidays.

'If Jill's going to college and having a career,' persisted Richard with unwonted obstinacy, 'I don't see why you shouldn't let me learn to be an artist, instead of just going into the Pottery like Norman. It's no use my stopping on at Ludborough, when they've already taught me all they know about drawing and painting themselves. Why can't I leave next summer, and go and study in Paris?' The same as Valentine Jesson, his mind continued, but he knew better than to repeat the words aloud.

This time, however, Stephen proved adamant.

'Look here, my lad, do you think I'm going to send you next year, before you've even turned seventeen, out of your own country to that hot-bed of vice and iniquity – to be ruined for life, may be, like your friend Eric's brother? No, my boy! You'll stay at Ludborough like other lads till you're over eighteen, and then, perhaps, if you show the same intelligence as Jill, you'll go to Oxford like your sister, where there'll be professors and other responsible people to look after you. They're a cold-blooded lot, I daresay, but that's all to the good. If you're of the same mind about art and so forth when you're twenty-one, maybe we'll think about it again – but there's no brass in painting pictures.'

'There's plenty of vice and iniquity outside Paris,' muttered Richard rebelliously, but he knew that, for the moment, he must accept defeat. I'll talk to him again, he decided, until he sees that Oxford's no use to a chap who's going to be an artist. I'll get Jill to help me. If he really means to keep me at school till the summer of 1914, I've got three years to make him change his mind.

But when the time came for Richard to leave Ludborough, he did not go to Paris, nor even to Oxford.

CHAPTER VI

DAUGHTER

'Lady, will you go with me
　　over the dark, the wave-demented sea?
Lady, I must tell you
　　how frail love's boat is,
I must bring to your notice
　　the skulls on the beach,
　　　　the spars, foam-flecked, of ships wrecked.

'Lady, are you brave enough
　　to go on such a journey?
You will be safe enough,
　　your hand in mine, till you know
　　that passion's star is a falling star,
　　and passion's voice a lost voice calling far
　　into the dark, and getting no reply.'
　　　　A. C. BOYD, *Maritime Invocation*.

I

THE TENNIS BALLS skimmed like swallows, just clearing the net and bouncing vigorously on the level green lawn in front of Drayton College. It was Saturday at Oxford, a warm, scented evening in a lovely June; the last Saturday of the summer term, 1914.

A long rally kept the four young girls on the tennis court energetically occupied until at last the German student, Frieda Königsberger, powerful, muscular, fair-haired and freckled, slammed the ball into the net.

'Forty-fifteen!' called Madeleine Gibson.

'Ball, please,' demanded Ruth Alleyndene, and picked up the ball on her racquet as Madeleine threw it to her from the net.

Stretching her long slim body to its full height, she banged her swift overhand service down on to the opposite court. It came back feebly; Madeleine returned it with a clean backhand stroke, and Barbara Lambert, Frieda's partner, sent it violently rocketing into the air.

'Let it go! It's out!' yelled Madeleine. 'That's game and set!'

Running quickly backwards and ducking on to the path outside the court to avoid the spinning ball, Ruth barely avoided a forceful collision with the commanding figure of Miss Penelope Lawson-Scott, Principal of Drayton College, Oxford, since 1902.

'Please don't apologise, Miss Alleyndene. I quite realise you could not avoid it,' said the Principal as Ruth picked herself up with embarrassed excuses. Through her rimless pince-nez she beamed upon the tall girl's flushed, lovely face, and her thin lips curved in the large crooked smile which only appeared the more menacing the more benevolent she intended to make it.

'I came,' she continued, 'to convey some agreeable news to you. It will, no doubt, gratify you to learn that by the unanimous vote of the Senior Common Room you have been awarded the Ellison Campbell prize – that is to say, the prize annually presented by Miss Campbell for the best work done by a Second-Year student in English or History in alternate years.'

'Oh, Ruth, how *splendid*!' exclaimed Madeleine Gibson, as incredulous surprise deepened the colour on Ruth's warm brown cheeks and rendered her for once inarticulate.

Miss Lawson-Scott turned to Madeleine with appreciation.

'I can only regret, Miss Gibson, as I am sure Miss Alleyndene does, that there are not two prizes instead of one. Had this been the year for the English school to receive the award, you would undoubtedly have been at the head of the list.'

'Honestly, I'd rather Ruth had it,' replied Madeleine without hypocrisy. 'After all, I've got scholarships and things, and it's time Ruth had something to show for her work.'

'Your generosity does you credit, Miss Gibson. The prize will be presented in Hall by Miss Ellison Campbell at three o'clock on Tuesday afternoon, and the whole of College will attend as usual.'

When Miss Lawson-Scott had left them, the two girls walked

slowly, arm in arm, along the iris-bordered garden path, discussing the Ellison Campbell prize and wondering if it would interest the famous dramatist to learn that Ruth had once played the part of the hero in *Highland Saturday*. From the term in which the senior girls at Playden Manor had performed that distinguished comedy, Ruth's admiration for Ellison Campbell's plays had remained undimished, and she remembered very clearly Miss Campbell's visit to Drayton the previous summer to present the English prize to Enid Barker. It was fixed in her mind by the fact that it had followed so soon after the spectacular funeral of Emily Wilding Davison, the daring suffragette who had given her life for a cause with which Ruth secretly intended to identify herself as soon as she went down from Oxford.

Ever since the Derby episode which the newspapers described as a 'suffragette outrage,' but which Ruth regarded as an act of superb self-sacrifice, she had heard the Drayton dons – most of whom were earnest if discreet supporters of the Women's University Suffrage Society – debating whether such melodramatic martyrdoms advanced or retarded votes for women. One or two of the more judicial were inclined to adopt the opinion expressed by *The Times* 'leader,' which Ruth had read with passionate indignation because it excluded the dying suffragette from the sympathy extended to Herbert Jones, the King's jockey, who had been slightly injured in the horse's fall.

'The case will, of course, become the subject of investigation by the police, and we may possibly learn from the offender herself what exactly she intended to do and how she fancied that it could assist the suffrage cause. A deed of the kind, we need hardly say, is not likely to increase the popularity of any cause with the ordinary public. Reckless fanaticism is not regarded by them as a qualification for the franchise. They are disposed to look upon manifestations of that temper with contempt and with disgust. When these manifestations are attended with indifference to human life, they begin to suspect that they are not altogether sane. They say that the persons who wantonly destroy property and endanger innocent lives must be either desperately wicked or entirely unbalanced. Where women are concerned, the natural gallantry of the public always inclines them to take a favourable view, and accordingly they are gradually coming to the conclusion that many of the militant suffragists are not altogether responsible for their acts. The growth of that belief will not improve the prospects of woman suffrage. The bulk of the suffragist party, and the abler of its leaders, are doubtless conscious of this truth. They seem, however, to be quite unable to lay the spirit which some of them have helped to raise, and to prevent the perpetuation of crimes, the utter insanity of which as a means of political propaganda is even more striking than their wickedness. We are much mistaken if yesterday's exhibition does not do more hurt to the cause of woman suffrage than years of agitation can undo.'

'"A favourable view!"' repeated Ruth angrily. 'We're so irresponsible that even when we risk our lives we don't understand why we do it. That's what men call a favourable view of women!'

Long before she left Playden, Ruth had been emotionally stirred by the acts and speeches of the militant suffragettes – the eloquence of Mrs Pankhurst, the dramatic escapes of Christabel, the courageous defiance of Mr and Mrs Pethick Lawrence. Surely in such a movement there was a career for a girl whose ideas so insistently surged into eloquence against her lips that again and again she must address chairs and tables, sand-dunes and sea-birds, for want of a more responsive audience? It chanced that last vacation she had been invited to take part in two public debates organised by the masters of Witnall Grammar School to raise funds for a new gymnasium. Both the motions – 'That Ireland is ready for Home Rule,' and 'That women should be admitted to a limited franchise' – were lost, as was only to be expected at Witnall, by overwhelming majorities, but at each debate Ruth had spoken with such forensic vehemence on the proposer's side that her astonished parents were seriously alarmed.

'That kid's got your grandfather's gift of the gab and no mistake! Much good it'll do her!' she overheard her father exclaim afterwards to her mother.

'Well, what did I tell you?' Jessie had responded, with the wry satisfaction of a prophet whose anticipation of evil is being all too rapidly fulfilled. 'That's what comes of sending her to Oxford!'

But Stephen, who had taken Ruth's part as long as she could remember, even when – as so often recently – she had begun to express her fervent disapproval of his ideas and traditions, had refused to believe that any symptom of revolution could seriously threaten the firmly established foundations of his family.

'Well,' he observed, 'I've heard folks say Oxford's the home of lost causes. I don't doubt when Jill's finished espousing the lot of 'em, she'll settle down and begin to talk a bit of common sense. You mark my words, she'll turn out a chip of the old block in the end!'

Perhaps she would, thought Ruth rebelliously, but not exactly in the way that Father meant. For the first time, after that conversation, she began to meditate upon the mysteries of heredity. Did she really owe the torrent of irrepressible words that so often tormented her to old Willy Penryder, the Cornish Methodist preacher whose visionary mind had welcomed the unprofitable career of art-teacher for his eldest son, and whose Liberal propensities were so sedulously unmentioned by the Alleyndenes and by Jessie herself? Or did she perhaps derive her inappropriate eloquence from the more romantic ancestor whose supposed portrait hung in the billiard-room beside that of his beautiful French wife – the half-legendary Hugh Alleyndene who had publicly exhorted his fellow gentry in Staffordshire to protect a fugitive group of Huguenot craftsmen from intolerance and persecution, and before he died had seen that little band of refugees well on the way to prosperity in their adopted country?

'After all, strange as it seems now, Father's family did once stand for liberty of opinion and action! Why shouldn't I be a throw-back; a reminder of the time when they thought for themselves?' she reflected with self-satisfaction.

It was at Playden that Ruth first became aware of political movements which, like woman suffrage, were unexplored topics at Dene Hall. Politics at home meant the unquestioning acceptance of assumptions which were never discussed; any view that might appear to challenge them was dismissed with scorn or disapproval and remained undebated. But at Playden, through classes which Miss Hilton, educationally in advance of her time, held on Current History and Sociology and Economics, Ruth had grasped the existence not only of Liberalism but of a struggling Labour party, derided by the rich but regarded as their only hope of a distant millennium by many of the poor. Gradually the animated yet distressing conversations which she had held with her friends Jim Hardiman and Arthur Wardle began to acquire more meaning for her; fragmentary remarks of theirs drifted back into her mind and became invested with significance.

Though much that she learned bewildered and oppressed her, Drayton College had triumphantly developed her ambition, first consciously expressed at Playden, to play a vital part in some revolutionary movement.

'Let *me* be alive, even if living means pain!' she would pray with the sacrificial fervour of one to whom real suffering had always been a stranger. 'Let me lead the people even though I may have to suffer deeply to do it!'

How rich the world was, how absorbing, how infinitely varied! she thought, leaning out of her study window with her arm round Madeleine's waist. She didn't really care how often Madeleine, loyally affectionate but relentlessly honest, chose to call her a prig. Never had she realised until she left the imprisoning security of Dene Hall that happiness did not lie in comfort or possessions, but in work, in ideas, in freedom.

Some of the students at Drayton argued, of course, that Oxford didn't really give you freedom – by which they merely meant freedom to see as much as they wanted of the undergraduates at the men's colleges. That kind of freedom, certainly, was non-existent. Why, even when Richard came up last term to take his entrance examination for Wolsey College, they couldn't have Madeleine, who had stayed so often at Dene Hall, to tea without a chaperon! But it wasn't a freedom that Ruth consciously missed. The hesitating, embarrassed conversation of the Staffordshire youths whom she met during vacation at dances in the North Stafford Hotel or the Witnall Assembly Rooms left her with no overwhelming desire for the society of her masculine contemporaries. They all asked her politely for one or two dances, and she never had to sit out, but she wasn't the sort whose programmes were snatched by uproarious young men and instantly filled with one set of initials.

No doubt, she decided disdainfully, she was too intellectual for the average male – and she did not regret it. She'd rather live with the authors whose works she had recently added to her long list of 'Books Read' – Meredith's poems, Hardy's novels, Ellison Campbell's plays, Dostoievsky's *Crime and Punishment*, William Morris's poems and *News from Nowhere*, H. G. Wells's *Modern Utopia*, the feminist philosophies of Mary Wollstonecraft and Olive Schreiner – than talk to any young man whom her father regarded as matrimonially eligible. Not even to her dear Richard could she describe the satisfaction given her by a passage from Meredith's *The Egoist*, which seemed to explain much that had puzzled her in Stephen's unforgotten conversation with Mr Halkin.

'The capaciously strong in soul among women will ultimately detect an infinite grossness in the demand for purity . . . Earlier or later they see they have been the victims of the singular egoist, have worn a mask of ignorance to be named innocent . . . have suffered themselves to be dragged ages back in playing upon the fleshly innocence of happy accident to gratify his jealous greed of possession, when it should have been their task to set the soul above the fairest fortune, and the gift of strength in women beyond ornamental whiteness.'

From that time onwards she had demanded more and more news from Miss Hilton about the militant suffrage campaign until her headmistress, a natural feminist but a firm believer in those virtues of temperance, balance and discretion which her own vehement disposition made it difficult for her to acquire, protested against this monomania.

'What will your parents say, Ruth, if Playden turns you into a suffragette? I sympathise with the ideals of the militants, of course, but I can't say I approve of their methods. I don't believe in illegal expedients so long as legitimate ones remain. There *are* other people working for the franchise, you know, my dear, besides the militants. Women who have watched the movement grow in patience, using reason and argument instead of violence, and refusing to abandon constitutional channels however great the provocation.'

But Ruth was not persuaded. Why keep the laws if you could get what you wanted by breaking them – especially when they were bad, unjust laws to begin with?

'But the constitutional movement's so slow, Miss Hilton! It's so dull, so middle-aged, just to wait for things to happen instead of *making* them change!'

'Some day, Ruth,' said Miss Hilton, 'you'll realise that history has its own cycles. When the times are ripe, change comes – sometimes through the long slow building of individuals, sometimes through catastrophes like the Black Death, sometimes through shocks and cataclysms, such as wars and revolutions.'

'But revolutions have to be *made*. Surely the militant movement's a kind of social revolution?'

'Even revolutions have their times and seasons, my dear. Why, wasn't I telling your form only the other day that the French Revolution didn't come till the people had grown sufficiently prosperous and educated to carry it through, though the reasons for making it had been there for years? Just in the same way, votes for women will come when women are ready to use them.'

But she protested no further. So long as Ruth remained at school she passed on to her, critically but without omission, the news of the suffragette burnings, smashings, imprisonments and hunger-strikes, in all their martyristic crudity and their obstinate, uncompromising endurance.

'There's only one thing that worries me about Ellison Campbell,' remarked Ruth to Madeleine as they went down to dinner in Drayton hall. 'It's her being a vice-president of that ridiculous National League for Opposing Women's Suffrage.'

'I'd no idea of that,' said Madeleine. 'Nobody told us about it when she came here last summer.'

'She didn't belong to it then. Miss Lawson-Scott says she's been working with them for about nine months. It does seem queer, a famous woman like that, who's an example of what women can do at their best, trying to prevent other women from getting what they want instead of helping them. I suppose there's some deep explanation, if one only knew it!'

2

She had certainly changed since the previous June. Observing Ellison Campbell from the row of Second-Year chairs in the middle of the student audience, Ruth wondered what private catastrophe, what inward psychological conflict, could so alter a human being in a mere twelve months.

It had now become customary for Miss Campbell, before presenting the prize student with her cheque for twenty guineas of which half was to be spent on books, to deliver a short address upon tendencies in English literature or current history. Never an accomplished or confident speaker, she found the ordeal disturbing, but Miss Lawson-Scott had so forcibly emphasised the stimulating effect of her words upon the ambitions of the students that Gertrude felt reluctant to put a drastic termination to this part of the ceremony. In her literary talks she always returned by swift stages to the drama, a point at which her self-consciousness disappeared, but the historical surveys had become a species of minor purgatory. Again and again she wished that she had not originally been persuaded by the for-midable Principal to include the History School within the scope of her gift.

As she stood now upon the raised dais of the great hall, deploring in halting phrases the prevalence of violence in the present-day world – Balkan battles, suffragette outrages, the threat of civil war in suspense-ridden Ireland – the intense light from the tall oblong windows made her clothes and features unusually conspicuous to the interested, critical gathering of observant young women.

In 1913, Ruth remembered, when Miss Campbell presented the English prize to Enid Barker, many of the students had been impressed with some quality of ruthlessness which rendered almost statuesque her gaunt frame and large pale features.

'It's almost as if the success of *Hour of Destiny* had made her cold and determined and even cruel, instead of warm and jubilant as you'd expect,' Madeleine had whispered to Ruth, for they had all read the dramatic criticisms of Miss Campbell's triumphant first night on the previous Saturday. At any rate, cruel or kind, ruthless or generous, she had been an impressive personality. Her very colouring, seen for the first time, had appeared striking and unusual. She had worn a large, tulle-trimmed straw hat of a peculiar shade of turquoise blue, which had thrown into vivid contrast the dull yet rich colour of her hair.

'Like wet sand which the tide's just washed over,' romantically decided Ruth.

But now she was quite different. No longer grim or determined, she looked instead worn and sad – and somehow lost, Ruth thought. The life had been quenched in her plain but memorable face; it resembled a large, careful yet expressionless mask of someone who had died unhappy. Even her clothes, of a cheerless indeterminate grey, contributed to that impression of stark disillusion, and though her hair was still sandy in hue, its richness had faded to a sad neutrality.

'It can't be just time, after only twelve months, and she's too old to have had a love-affair,' meditated Ruth, with the remorseless age-perspectives of one whose twentieth birthday occurred the following week. 'And obviously it isn't failure; everyone says she's about the most successful woman in England. She must have a secret sorrow. Except that she isn't second-rate, she looks just like Tennyson's "Sensitive Soul at Variance with Itself."'

So deeply immersed was Ruth in these intriguing speculations that the abrupt ending of Ellison Campbell's speech and Miss Lawson-Scott's summons to her to appear on the dais took her almost by surprise. But she betrayed no sign of her unpreparedness as she walked up the room with her grave, arrogant air and mounted the half-dozen steps to the platform.

It had been, as a rule, the English prize student whose career and potential future had aroused Ellison Campbell's interest, but in 1913 she had not been able to summon up much enthusiasm for the little spectacled girl with the mouse-coloured hair who flushed and stammered as she received her cheque. This slim, graceful History student in the blue linen frock, who carried her dark head so proudly and moved up the platform as though she had mounted platforms for years, was quite another species, who would remain in her memory. It had not surprised her to learn that the elegant, self-possessed young woman was President of the Drayton Debating Society and almost certain of First Class Honours. If only she did not fall into the usual snare of marriage with a man who was attracted by her appearance but cared nothing for her brains, she might even have a career worth watching.

A bit too tall and thin, perhaps, Gertrude's thoughts continued, as Ruth stood before her. It was a type that would easily grow frail and haggard under the stress of life; but now the child was perfect with her deep-set grey eyes, her pale clear skin with its delicate tinge of sunburn, her red lips curving into a wide Cupid's bow over her small even teeth. Gertrude regarded that unimpaired youth and freshness with reluctant envy, knowing only too well that even at twenty such lovely grace had never been hers.

What did it remind her of, this girl's quality of young vital determination which challenged the haughty reticence of her dark eyes and brows? . . . Why, in spite of the complete dissimilarity of external appearance, it was just the quality that Janet had possessed when they first met all those years ago at Sterndale. It brought Janet back to her – Janet to whom she hadn't written or spoken now for nearly twelve months – with a vividness that made her hands quiver and her knees tremble, though Ruth Alleyndene was undoubtedly beautiful, while Janet had been no more than comely and full of life. All the same, she'd had a kind of beauty with those ardent blue eyes and that warm wavy fair hair . . . 'But I mustn't think of Janet; it's no use. She let me down unforgivably at a critical moment, and one can't ever undo the past.'

Resolutely Ellison Campbell closed her well-disciplined mind upon those aching memories, and turned to Ruth.

'I have pleasure,' she said in the deep, musical Scottish voice which invested the wintry stiffness of her demeanour with a

summer touch of human warmth and rendered even her worst
speeches tolerable, 'in presenting you with this prize for the best
progress made by a Second-Year student of history. I understand
that your work is most promising and sometimes, already, even
distinguished. I hope that the prize will help you, if only as a
token of encouragement, to do even better, and get whatever you
want in the way of a career when you leave the university.'

'Thank you, Miss Campbell,' said Ruth with dignity. 'I shall
do my utmost to deserve it.'

'Where does she get it from, that poise, that balance?' wondered Gertrude, as Ruth went down from the dais carrying the
insignificant envelope as though she were a queen bearing her
crown. 'Fortunate young woman, to be born with such a gift;
to have no conflict with shyness, no struggle for self-possession!
O God,' her suffering heart cried unsubdued to her dominant
mind, 'how long shall I have to go on performing these public
functions for the sake of duty – and without Janet's interest and
sympathy; without the unfailing encouragement that used to be
mine before those suffragettes got hold of her and took her away
from me! O God, how long?'

After tea, Ruth sat alone on the library steps with the cheque
in her hand, looking absently at the Fellows' Garden in its June
dress of larkspur and roses, and wondering upon what books to
spend the first money that she had ever earned. Her mind roamed
with pleasant indecision over numerous titles relating to the rise
of democracy, socialism, the women's movement, international
politics. She certainly ought to possess Arnold Toynbee's *Lectures on the Industrial Revolution*, and *The Emancipation of
English Women* by W. Lyon Blease; and then, of course, there
was Norman Angell's *The Great Illusion*, and the Webbs' big
book on *Industrial Democracy*.

As she stared meditatively at the path, the fleeting irrelevant
recollection came back to her of the young man whom she
had encountered there last Sunday, trying to get through from
Walton Street to Woodstock Road as though the college garden
were a public thoroughfare. For some reason his face had been
vaguely familiar, but whatever chord of recollection it struck
was not sufficiently interesting to justify the tantalising pursuit

of identification. Almost as soon as she recalled him, she forgot
him again in the silent construction of her list of books –
books which would give her something really important to
say when she stood on the public platforms of her daring
imagination; books which would teach her still more about
political parties, suffrage, Fabianism, the Labour movement,
and the many other enthralling topics which were taboo among
her elders at Dene Hall.

Dearly as she loved Richard, her boon-companion since babyhood, she knew that it was useless trying to interest him in
politics. He was leaving Ludborough at the end of the term
and at present could talk of nothing but his determination to
persuade Father to let him study art in Paris, even though all
the arrangements had been made for him to go to Oxford. She'd
like to have him there with her for her last year, of course, but,
as Arthur Wardle had said to her, 'It bain't no use meytherin',
Miss Ruth. You can't turn painter into politician. Now if only
you was t'other way round, t'would be better. We might get Mr
Richard elected as Member for Witnall one day instead of Major
Magnus, all Army and Dreadnoughts and British Empire. But it
bain't no use!'

At least, thought Ruth, she had Wardle and Jim Hardiman to
talk to at Witnall about her visions of revolution and reform.
They smiled, as she knew well enough, when she spoke proudly
of a political renaissance with herself as its leader and inspiration, but they didn't smile, as all Father's friends did, at the idea
of women having votes. It seemed as natural to them that women
should want votes as that the workers should want power. No
use, they'd say, talking about fairer laws for women, or a better
chance for children, until women got the political weapon which
would enable them to achieve these reforms for themselves. No
use hoping for an eight-hour day and decent conditions in
coal-mines and steel-works and pot-factories until, at some
far-distant date, England had a Socialist Government with the
workers in office.

Women and workers – their cause was bound up together,
as Hardiman had insisted. You couldn't really work for one
without working for the other. When she left college she'd

have to be a Socialist as well as a suffragette. Perhaps father and mother would turn her out – and Norman, who'd already been five years at the Pottery and was becoming a solemn, astute, reliable young business man, would agree with them, of course. Well, she didn't care. As soon as she finished at Drayton she'd be independent of them, equipped to earn her own living and think as she chose. She'd get an organising or secretarial job – perhaps with the suffragettes, if she was lucky – where there would be a chance of making speeches as well.

She looked reflectively across the tennis courts and the games in progress there beneath the brilliant slanting light of the western sun. Beyond those green lawns and that tranquil garden the world was drifting rapidly towards Armageddon, but Ruth, for all her study of history, was no more conscious of the intrigues maturing in chancelleries and embassies than of the tennis balls thudding continuously on the soft grass-covered mould. Indifferent alike to the marching doom of Europe and the rhythmic regularity of vollies and rallies, she sat clasping her prize on the library steps in the evening sunshine, dreaming of freedom, democracy and achievement.

3

Another summer term – but how bitter a contrast to those days of vanishing glory which had made up its two predecessors!

Oxford was not itself in war-time; it had become a mournful, alien city of half-empty colleges, marching cadets and departing undergraduates. At Drayton, the previous Michaelmas term, Frieda Königsberger had not come back. Yet it was still impossible to think of handsome, vivacious Frieda as an enemy, a Boche, a Hun – Frieda, who had so often spent long discursive evenings on the river with herself and Madeleine, talking of politics, and the future of women, and God, and immortality. That automatic transmogrification of a friend into a foe seemed as incredible as the monstrous fact of the War itself, which made one's head throb unceasingly from the constant effort of thought and adaptation.

Ruth would be glad, now, when her last year was over and she could get some work better suited to the crushing realities of the present than the sheltered pre-occupations of a college student. She hadn't so long to wait, she reflected with relief, as she walked up the High Street from her last lecture in the warm consoling sunlight which yet seemed to mock the bleak obsessions of her aching heart. Next week she would begin her Finals; after that there was only the Viva Voce in July and then she would be free. It didn't seem fair to be still enjoying Oxford – in so far as one could enjoy anything – when Richard had not been able to go to Paris or even to come up to college.

Nothing, she sometimes thought now, would ever be itself again. There would be no celebrations at Dene Hall for her twenty-first birthday such as Norman had been given three years ago, though the birthday itself occurred conveniently enough at the end of the week that she returned home after taking Schools. The familiar, engrossing world had never been the same since that 4th of August on which they had intended to break, for the first time, their family rule of a summer holiday in Lancashire or Wales, and go for a month to St Anthony-in-Roseland, the Cornish village near the small fishing-town of St Mawes where Jessie's father had been born.

St Anthony, which Ruth had never seen, had now come to symbolise for her all the lovely, romantic, unattainable things of which Europe's cataclysm was depriving her generation, for the War had upset her parents' unusually enterprising scheme and that summer none of them had left Staffordshire. From August onwards the most unbelievable events had occurred in rapid succession. Even Father, that lifelong devotee of unswerving routine, had become a 'Colonel' in the local detachment of the semi-military North Staffordshire Volunteers, and led their parades on the Witnall Grammar School cricket field.

'Bit of luck your father's kept his figure, eh, Jill?' he had remarked to her the previous vacation when he appeared before her for the first time in his Volunteer's uniform. 'I'll bet there's many a man of fifty would give a deal to set off this get-up as well as yours truly!'

'You look splendid, Father,' she had told him truthfully, for the unfamiliar khaki gave his handsome, burly stature a dominating impressiveness unattainable by most of his contemporaries. But secretly she was appalled by the fact that the shattering War had been able, in a few months, to invest Stephen himself, the embodiment of local order and tradition, with the external symbols of militarism. They had turned him into a stranger who accepted without criticism the ugly standards of a barbarous society.

Not that it was likely that her father would ever be seriously involved in the more grotesque occupations of wartime. The Volunteer detachments, after all, consisted only of glorified special constables whose scenes of action centred upon local bridges and pit-heads and gas-works, where Stephen could fulfil, in fancy dress, his customary congenial rôle of employer and squire. It was in terms not of Stephen but of Norman that the world had changed – Norman whom the German invasion of Belgium had lifted out of that niche in the Alleyndene Pottery Company which he had seemed destined from birth to fill so capably and so appropriately, asking nothing different until he joined his ancestors in the family vault. So completely had the war uprooted him that he was now in India with the Royal Garrison Artillery, which he had joined, after prolonged and weighty deliberation, in September 1914.

'I had no choice,' he told Ruth with his characteristic air of making an unanswerable pronouncement. 'It was my duty to set an example to the neighbourhood.'

But Richard's fate seemed the strangest of all, for Richard was an artist without one quality that suggested his adaptation to soldiering. His talent had developed so rapidly and so remarkably that Father, although adamant on the subject of Paris, had actually had a studio built for him in the grounds of Dene Hall during his last term at Ludborough, and presented it to him as a surprise when he came home in the closing days of July. But, after all, the studio had hardly been used, for a week later the newspapers were filled with nightmare stories of mobilisations and invasions and ultimatums, and Richard, always impulsive and sensitive to atmosphere, had rushed up to London in response to an excited invitation from Eric Jesson.

It wasn't until he came back that he told Stephen and Jessie that he and Eric and Valentine had all volunteered for commissions in the newly formed Chelsea Rifles.

'Well,' he explained, when his appalled parents protested that he was only a schoolboy and still under age, 'you wouldn't let me go to Paris, and I didn't see myself putting in time at Oxford with all this call for men going on!'

But it soon became clear that Paris itself would not remain a place where art could be tranquilly studied while civilisation floundered into chaos. When Richard's commission materialised a few weeks afterwards, he assured Ruth that he didn't really regret the decision that the three of them had made. Although they had been carried away at the time by the mounting emotions of the hour, the cheering and shouting London crowds, the universal demand for recruits, he agreed with Valentine that one couldn't just go selfishly on with an art student's life when all Europe was in turmoil. And, after all, it wasn't likely to mean a very long interruption. England would smash the Germans in six months – everyone said so – and a short experience of active, practical life wasn't such a bad preliminary to creative art. The plunge into adventure, the contrast with Ludborough and Dene Hall, would give his work just the emotional basis that it needed after a boyhood so uneventful and serene.

'I do wish Richard and Eric hadn't gone into the same regiment as that immoral Valentine,' Jessie confided to Ruth when her first anguish of distress was subsiding into pessimistic resignation. But even this disconcerting association was soon overshadowed by the sheer enormity of the danger into which Richard had precipitated himself. The question whether England would survive the War was not to arise for nearly four years, and, in any case, did not interest Jessie, but the question whether Richard would survive it soon dominated her entire conversation. Similarly but silently obsessed by the same terrible doubt, Ruth endeavoured to escape the perpetual discussions in which her mother involved her. But their insistent horror was not to be evaded, and during the Easter vacation it had become acute.

It had become acute because Richard was now in Gallipoli.

Exactly why the Chelsea Rifles, that heterogeneous and temperamental collection of embryo artists, amateur politicians,
medical students and stalwart employees from Battersea brick-
yards, should have been sent to participate in the War's most
spectacular failure is still a matter for conjecture by historians;
but no doubt the authorities responsible for their departure
believed – as the rest of England believed before April 25th,
1915 – that the Dardanelles campaign was an enviable species
of Mediterranean picnic.

At first Richard seemed to have no foreboding of what was to
come. When his regiment was ordered to sail from Southampton
for an unknown destination, he wrote to tell Ruth how thankful
he was that they weren't going to that hideous inferno in France.
His early letters had been warm with pleasure in the sights and
sounds of their outdoor life, the larks twittering above the ripe
cornfields, the flaming reds and russet browns of the autumn
woods and heaths in the open country round Aldershot. He was
lucky, he said, to belong to a crowd which enjoyed these things
too; such a different crowd from the sort that you'd find in an
ordinary infantry battalion.

From his first term in the little boys' school at Witnall,
Richard, unlike the more typical Alleyndenes, had displayed
an unusual gift for friendship. Once the friends were established in his life, his generous and romantic devotion to them
tended to make the relationship permanent. No amount of
parental disapproval, Ruth knew, had ever shaken his loyalty
to Valentine Jesson. As soon as he joined the Army, his capacity
for affectionate admiration rapidly spread from the officers' mess
to everybody else in his platoon. He sent Ruth eager descriptions
of the non-commissioned officers and privates who served under
him, commenting appreciatively upon the contrast in idiosyncra-
sies between Chelsea art students and Battersea builders, and
enumerating the various personal and even national exceptions
from the typical British Tommy.

'Some of the chaps are pretty tough, of course. There's a
regular contingent of old Cockneys from the south side of the
river, but we've got a good sprinkling of clerks and students,
as you might expect. In my own platoon there's actually an

American, a frightfully decent chap who has been to Harvard. I couldn't think what he was doing in the battalion at all, but he said he joined up to see a bit of life. Of course he can't be an officer because he's an American citizen and they're neutral, but he's so awfully quick and efficient that he's certain to get promotion, and it'll be a great joy to have someone like that as an N.C.O.'

At the beginning of March, Miss Lawson Scott gave Ruth permission to go down to Southampton and see Richard off. Afterwards Ruth wished that she hadn't gone, for when she said good-bye to him, his face puckered and the corners of his lips trembled in just the way that she remembered after he had been punished for some childish misdemeanour. She realised in her black desolation that it was not a man, armoured with the shield and buckler of judgment and experience, but a gifted, generous, malleable boy who was going out to face the portentous unknown. They'd been ordered, he whispered just before going on board, to the Eastern Mediterranean, and there were rumours of a great surprise attack on the Gallipoli Peninsula later in the spring . . .

It had been a grey, un-March-like day, windless and heavy with fog; a thick mist lay upon Southampton Water, and the transport, with Richard waving forlornly from its upper deck, seemed no sooner to have got under way than it disappeared. Long after the mist had swallowed it, a thin twist of smoke from its funnel was visible in the clearer air above the harbour. Motionless with grief and a sense of catastrophic foreboding, Ruth watched the smoke until it, too, became part of the formless indeterminate pallor which obscured the horizon. In the train going back to Oxford she shed the first bitter, difficult tears of the War, for she had long overcome, by a proud adamant control, her childhood's tendency to easy weeping.

'Thank heaven Father and Mother said good-bye to him at Witnall!' she thought as she dried, humiliated, her swollen eyes. 'I couldn't have endured having them here this afternoon. It's bad enough when one's all alone.'

After that the silence had seemed interminable until in April his letters began to come from Mudros, describing the port with its small half-civilised Levantine houses, and the savage crater-like harbour flooded with the unearthly light which illumined every crevice of the barren island and the naked hills. He wrote of the flowers which starred so briefly the short dry grass in the swift Mediterranean spring, the black transports towering above the picturesque sailing vessels of the Greek fishermen, the violent-hued sunsets which turned the Asian peaks into fiery volcanoes, the deep indigo of the night sky with the great pale stars like giant lamps reflected in the jet-black water. He had pictures of them all, he said, for he had added a small stock of colours and canvases to the less personal equipment of active service.

She did not know when he left Mudros. He never described the departure of the transports moving towards Gallipoli to the strange sound of humanity cheering its own mad immolation, which echoed across the world from coast to coast, from capital to capital, in that first delirious, unforeseeing year of the Great War. But two days after she returned to Oxford for her final term, the news of the terrible landings on Cape Helles began to come through, and her own overwhelming dread was reinforced as usual by her mother's letters, which killed and buried Richard or Norman by every other post.

'How thankful I shall be when you have finished with Oxford,' wrote Jessie, to whom Ruth had not, as yet, confided her private plans. 'We want you at home so badly, in case anything happens to our darling boys.'

'If I do go home it won't be for long,' decided Ruth, reflecting that even in those days, when death had become a haunting and familiar shadow, so few of the individuals whose lives it threatened vicariously could look the stark fact of it courageously in the face, or refrain from sheltering behind the indirect phrases which minimised its horror. Although the piled-up corpses of each day's slaughter rotted obscenely in the sun on every battlefield from east to west, the original owners of those corpses had not died; 'something had happened to them' (as it certainly had), or they had 'fallen,' or 'gone west.'

For the first fortnight of that summer term, Ruth found herself quite unable to concentrate on her last period of revision before

Schools. She became almost as incapable as Madeleine, whose work had fallen completely below standard since Easter because Jerry Pomeroy, the headmaster of Ufferton's youngest son, who had gone down from Oxford last year, was involved in the relentlessly developing Second Battle of Ypres. Madeleine wasn't exactly engaged to Jerry – it was just an 'understanding'; but that 'understanding' was steadily destroying her chances, once thought impregnable, of a First in English.

'I mustn't fail too,' Ruth told herself repeatedly. 'Richard would hate me to do that, and it wouldn't be fair to Father when he's spent so much money on me. I *must* try to concentrate. After all, it's worse for Madeleine than it is for me. Although I've always adored Richard, although every threat of danger to him feels like a spear twisting in my inside, it can't be quite so bad as being in love. I've never been in love yet . . . I suppose I'm too inhuman, as Madeleine says. The other day, when I tried to comfort her because Jerry's letter hadn't come, she told me I was too conceited and priggish to understand. Perhaps I am . . . perhaps that's why no one has fallen in love with me yet, in spite of the War . . . All the same, I don't think I want them to – not until it's quite over. I believe I could fall terribly in love if I once started . . . and it would be too awful if he were at the front like Jerry. It's bad enough having Richard there. I couldn't bear more than that.'

She found the demands of Schools a little easier to fulfil when the news of the landing casualties, gradually filtering through official *communiqués* and telegrams in all their grim disproportion to the ends achieved, contained no mention of Richard and very little of the Chelsea Rifles. Long afterwards she learnt that they had been attached to the Royal Fusiliers for the landing on X beach, a narrow strip of sand on the north side of Cape Tekke where that day's monstrous losses were smallest.

By half-term, Richard's letters had begun to arrive from the Peninsula itself; they were infrequent and much less communicative than before, but that was only to be expected. Slowly there developed within her mind a vivid picture of the alien country where the schoolboy of a year ago went in daily peril of his life and in daily responsibility for the lives of others. She

saw the rough, broken ground partially covered with gorse and
scrub; the dark clumps of pines growing from bleak crests in the
drenching sunlight; the sandy slopes which suddenly vanished
into spreading infernal fans of black and yellow smoke; the
tawny rocks reflected in the deep clear water; the lovely terrible
hills clad in the sapphire haze of swiftly approaching summer.
Whenever she slept, that nightmare beauty enveloped her. She
dreamt of gleaming fortresses jewelled with artillery trained
upon a golden sea, of deep shadowed ravines up which she
climbed after Richard, hopelessly and perpetually, while bullets
hailed down upon her from machine guns concealed by giant
clumps of exquisite lilies and daffodils.

'Oh, God!' she prayed as she woke each morning to wipe the
sweat from her forehead in her safe, familiar college room, 'Oh,
God, let this term go quickly! Let me do as well as everyone hopes
while Norman and Richard are still alive, and then give me work
which will end these nightmares by bringing me within range of
their experience!'

4

The examiners released Ruth after a forty-five minutes Viva Voce
on a sultry afternoon of mid-July.

'It's over at last!' she thought, as she sat exhausted in her
favourite corner on the top of the library steps and gazed at
the serene, familiar garden which after to-morrow she might
not revisit for years. The shining green lawns were already
beginning to turn brown and dry, and a regiment of brilliant
antirrhinums, crimson and saffron and scarlet, had replaced the
blue June irises beside the garden path.

Although she now knew Madeleine's fate – for the English
Viva Voce was held a fortnight earlier and Madeleine had
only been awarded a Second – her mind was still more deeply
relieved by the end of her long purgatory of postponement
than apprehensive of the results to be announced next day. As
soon as they were put up she and Madeleine – who in spite of
her disappointment had gallantly come to Oxford to see Ruth

through her own ordeal – were going for a quiet week in Burford, on the edge of the Cotswolds, to recover their equilibrium and decide what form of war-work to do.

Madeleine, who was obliged to support herself and help with the education of two small brothers, had already been appointed English mistress at the Holborn Girls' High School, but she didn't mean to be out of it altogether; she would work, she told Ruth, at one of the Red Cross supply depôts, or perhaps learn to drive an ambulance between the London railway stations and the military hospitals. Ruth, whose plans for a career were quite indefinite now that the suffragettes had abandoned their campaign and political organising no longer mattered, was determined to devote the whole of her time to the War while it lasted. But she had not yet decided whether a clerkship at the War Office or canteen work abroad or some kind of active service with a Red Cross Voluntary Aid Detachment would bring her nearer in spirit to Richard and make her days of suspense more tolerable.

It seemed irrational, perhaps, to go in for nursing or motor-driving immediately after taking a degree, but the headlong drift of possessed humanity was no longer guided by reason. Even in the more impervious strongholds of tradition, the familiar face of normal life had become blurred and unrecognisable. Commemoration, for instance, had been but a dim and sorry shadow of itself; she wondered afterwards why she had stayed in Oxford to witness a ceremony which involved no colourful conferring of honorary degrees, no gathering of boys and girls or of doctors and dons, no dances in the colleges whose empty quadrangles were peopled only by ghosts and memories. The Sheldonian Theatre remained closed and silent while a small, sad body – the official university and a thin sprinkling of students and residents – fulfilled their shorn and truncated rites in the Divinity School. The mournful words of the Professor of Poetry delivering the Creweian Oration still rang in Ruth's ears as he lamented that the late academic year had been without parallel, since war was everywhere: '*Nec in terra solum vel in summis fluctibus, sed et in aere et in ponto profundo dimicantur.*'

Just after she went home to spend the fortnight that must still

be passed before her Viva Voce, the papers had published news
of a great battle in Gallipoli on June 28th.

'BRITISH ADVANCE IN GALLIPOLI
1,000 YARDS GAINED
THE SPLENDID 29th DIVISION,'

The Times announced hopefully, and followed its headings by a
column describing a half-mile advance near Krithia, the capture
of two lines of Turkish trenches 'east of the Saghir Dere and
five lines of trenches west of it,' and the taking of the Turkish
Boomerang Redoubt 'most brilliantly' by the Border Regiment.
But beneath the optimistic despatch had appeared, in small print,
a fragment of news derived from enemy sources:

'TURKISH CLAIM TO SUCCESS

'Berlin, *June 30th*.

'Constantinople. On the Dardanelles front three attacks which
took place on our left wing near Ariburno on the 28th inst.
and which had been prepared by enemy artillery fire, failed,
with extraordinarily heavy loss to the enemy. An attack near
Seddei-Bahr was beaten off by a counter-attack. We took three
enemy trenches. Our Anatolian batteries inflicted heavy loss on
the retreating enemy, and reduced the enemy battery on the
summit of the Tekeh to silence.'

After reading this paragraph, Ruth took her bicycle from
its shed and pedalled violently across the remaining miles of
Staffordshire to the Derbyshire moorlands beyond Cheet, hoping
that her mother and father would have finished discussing the
news from Gallipoli before she returned. The warm air above
the dry, scented heather pulsated gently in the summer sun; the
larks sang enraptured, almost invisible against the rich blue; the
bees hummed drowsily in and out of the motionless harebells,
soothing her in spite of herself as she lay there mutely enduring
her trance of despair.

'I mustn't imagine Richard in every battle,' she had told
herself, struggling against the same submerging terror as she

had felt when she read of the landings, and later of the first British action against the Turks on June 4th. And only yesterday, just before she left Staffordshire to attend the Viva Voce, a long letter had come from Richard as if to reassure her, although it was dated ten days before the attack.

'It is getting terrifically hot here now,' he wrote, 'and instead of daffodils there are acres upon acres of moon daisies and scarlet poppies, but you can't stand about admiring them, or the snipers hidden among them will pot you at once. This rather spoils the landscape, and so do the ruined farms and the dead Turks lying about all over the place. We get out at night and bury them when we can.

'We're not always fighting by any means, so you needn't picture me playing the hero all the time, though I'm glad to say my platoon has already distinguished itself once or twice. Meury, the American lance-corporal, did an awfully fine thing the other day; he saved about fifty men from being blown to bits by picking up a live bomb and throwing it back over the parapet before it exploded. He's sure to get the D.C.M. for it, and I only wish it could be the V.C., because he's one of the finest soldiers we have here and doesn't know what fear is. He says he's got a charmed life because he's a Yank. I wrote a letter about him to his father who runs a newspaper in New York; apparently his people were frightfully upset when he joined up and he didn't hear from them afterwards for about 4 months.

'We live absolutely underground here and when we've done our turn in the fire trenches we spend the rest of the time digging and making roads, though when it comes to spade-work our clerks and students aren't in it compared with the Wigan miners in a regiment close by. If we want any other sort of exercise we have to get it by walking down to the shore and looking at the ships. The shells are always coming over like great screaming birds, and when they do you have to run for cover, but there's usually plenty of time. I often think that anybody looking from the sea at night at our dug-outs in the cliffs might imagine we were some lamplit mediæval town on a steep sea-coast. Sometimes the men sing songs after dark while they're carting the stores.

'In the day time, now it's getting so hot, everything is illumined by the same strange light that I wrote about from Mudros. It gives a curious impression of colour where no colour is – nothing but grey rocks and stones and pale dusty sand, and khaki uniforms which have faded in the sun till, from a distance, a man standing still is barely visible against his background. It seems queer in this wild desolate country so close to Troy to hear typewriters tapping on the beaches and telephones ringing and bullets popping everywhere. Valentine says we're cave-dwellers with a difference, because the real cave-dwellers were so busy learning to live that they never dreamed men would ever compete in discovering more and more terrible ways to die. He and I have often discussed since we came out here whether it was really worth while the human race getting itself out of those caves if their descendants were only going to return to them under far worse conditions. It makes me feel absolutely sick sometimes to think of the millions of men all over the world who are living in ditches and shell-holes and dug-outs just because a handful of politicians in a few countries can't make sensible treaties or keep them when they do.'

All through the Viva Voce, sentences and pictures from Richard's letter had haunted Ruth's brain. She could not give the examiners her full attention even though she knew, from the number and weight of their questions, that she must be on the border-line between two Classes, and was perhaps being viva-ed for a First.

'Now, Miss Alleyndene,' they had asked her, 'can you tell us in what ways political thought since the French Revolution has repudiated the basic theories of Aristotle's *Politics*? . . . Which of the great nineteenth-century treaties offers us, do you consider, the best example for a peace to terminate the present European War?'

In spite of her pre-occupation she had answered graphically, filling in the interstices of her written papers, giving life and meaning to abrupt, unvarnished statements of fact. Her style, though fluent enough, was a commonplace, pedestrian vehicle compared with the clear melodious speaking voice which her singing and elocution lessons at Playden Manor had forged into an instrument of power and beauty, evoking vivid and colourful images never attainable by her slower, less gifted pen. Had that eloquence perhaps redeemed her competent, accurate performance from mere efficiency? she wondered, as she got up stiffly from the library steps and went to her room to select the books she was taking to Burford.

The next afternoon, walking down with Madeleine to the Sheldonian Theatre, where the results were to be posted because the Examination Schools had already been converted into a military hospital, she found to her surprise that the old surge of ambition was temporarily obliterating both her fears and her plans. That she should have done well, should have justified herself and Miss Hilton and her father, suddenly seemed as important as though the War had never happened. When the lists went up after they had waited for ten minutes, she found herself incapable of reading them.

'You look, Madeleine.'

She had hardly spoken before Madeleine was impulsively thumping her back, for the alphabetical precedence of her name made its distinguished position unusually conspicuous.

'You've done it! You've got a First! Oh, Ruth, I wonder if it *was* the Viva? Won't Miss Lawson-Scott be pleased!'

Hand in hand they raced back to Drayton to tell the Principal. As they turned into the college gates they passed Jean Raynor, the Drayton librarian, and rapturously stopped to announce their news.

'I'm delighted, Miss Alleyndene! I do congratulate you,' the librarian responded. 'I think Miss Lawson-Scott must know already, as she was looking for you only five minutes ago. She asked me to send you straight up to her room if I saw you when you came in.'

'I'll go up at once!' cried Ruth, all fear of the intimidating Principal now scattered to the four corners of the university. She ran up Miss Lawson-Scott's private staircase on jubilant feet and knocked excitedly at her door.

But Miss Lawson-Scott's face looked grave and austere, and Ruth's eager announcement: 'I've got a First – I came to tell you at once!' did not alter its expression.

'I congratulate you indeed,' she said with an effort. 'I – I only

wish I had not such distressing news to give you just when your
excellent work has received its reward.'

'Tell me,' urged Ruth. Her vitality fled from her with the suddenness of sunshine chased by a thunder-cloud, and all excellent
work, whether her own or other people's, vanished instantaneously into a past remoter than the Wars of the Roses.

Resolutely Miss Lawson-Scott climbed out of her abyss of
reluctance.

'A long telegram has just come from your father. I regret to
have to tell you that your brother has been killed in action.'

'It's Norman,' said Ruth. The words broke from her involuntarily, as though she were talking in her sleep.

Miss Lawson-Scott turned over the telegram on her desk.

'Your father telegraphs as follows: "Kindly break to my
daughter that her brother Richard was killed in Gallipoli June
28th, and ask her to return home immediately."'

'*Oh!*' cried Ruth, and closed her eyes as the fire-flecked
darkness from her evil dreams blotted out Miss Lawson-Scott
and the tall open windows which framed the untroubled green
corridor of the college garden.

Miss Lawson-Scott rose from her chair and held Ruth firmly
by the arm.

'Sit down a moment, my dear . . . This is a terrible shock
for you.'

But Ruth remained standing.

'I must go,' she said mechanically. The black mist cleared and
left her starkly face to face with a visible world now drained
of its colours because the eyes which had seen colour in all
things would never behold them again. 'I must go and pack,'
she repeated. 'Thank you for telling me.'

Later, in the passage outside her room, a group of Third-Year
students – up, like herself, for the Viva Voce – hung round
her door, distressed, anxious, proffering help; but they seemed
relieved, she noticed, when she refused it, and they could go away
and leave her to Madeleine. It was her first acute realisation of
the fact that human beings, unless themselves experienced in
suffering, shrink defensively from the man or woman who is
newly acquainted with grief.

As she packed her books and clothes automatically, barely conscious of Madeleine's stricken presence, some bars of music attached to a fragmentary sequence of remembered words tortured her mind with their maddening elusiveness:

> *Dreams can-not picture . . . a world . . . so fair;*
> *Sorrow and death,*
> *Sor-row and death*
> *Cannot en-ter there!*

In what unknown dominion of time or eternity was that improbable world to be found? From what regions of her vanished childhood, never again to be recalled without poignant grief, did the mocking words arise?

She could not remember.

5

At Wimereux the high March winds blew riotously from the sea, turning the hospital tents into icy ballons, buffeting the huts along the cliff-edge until they creaked and shuddered as though animate with pain.

Hurrying between the flapping tents on an all too familiar occupation, Ruth wondered why the physical requirements of her patients were always the most persistent in the worst possible weather. When at last the evening's duty was over and she walked with slow fatigue across the open stretch of damp, rough grass to the Sisters' Quarters in the green-shuttered stone building which had once been a summer villa, the hostile wind seized the flowing white cambric of her nurse's cap and tore it roughly from her head. As she clutched at the loosened strands of her long hair in the tossing darkness, she recalled the rueful complaint of a new medical officer just over from England: 'I don't know why they called this damned place "52 Stationary Hospital." I can't find anything stationary about it except its name!'

At the foot of the cliffs far below their sheer margin, the boiling waves thundered and broke with reverberant monotony. Although she knew that summer weather meant a speeding-up of the War, and the premature death of innumerable young men for whom women would mourn as she had mourned for Richard, Ruth's shivering flesh cried out for the return of the gentler days which had gilded and burnished the French countryside six months ago when she first came to the hospital.

The ribbon-line of huts and tents between Wimereux and Boulogne had shimmered then in the rich Indian summer which mocked the pitiless catastrophe of Loos. On clear days the chalk cliffs of the English coast loomed white across the Channel, ghostly sentinels guarding that detached and unimpaired island whose immunity her uncalculating sons had come in their millions to defend. At night the dividing waters moved gently in unillumined darkness; the British lighthouses no longer flung their vanishing golden arcs with intermittent regularity over the black expanse of sea. How simple, thought Ruth, would be the problem of the soul's reconciliation to the body's mortality if only some such brief intimation of survival could flash now and again across the fathomless unknown!

Inland behind the small town spread the gentle undulating fields, benign in the golden aftermath of harvest reaping. Villages and hamlets, such as Ambleteuse and Wimille with their dominant churches, still lay withdrawn from the military area of hospitals and camps into a secret serenity as old as the traditions of the French peasant, who lived only for his plot of intensively cultivated land. Elms and willows, the glint of midday sunshine and the dramatic fires of the evening sky, were alike gathered into the placid reflections on the mirrored surface of a farmyard duck-pond or an old mill-stream. Sometimes the sunset stillness was so profound that Ruth's ear could catch the plaintive cheeping of a late swallow as it darted down upon a richly harvested field in its homeward flight. But more often the distant sullen murmur of artillery, and the faint vibrating shudder which ran like a subterranean earthquake beneath her feet, after each outburst of firing, absorbed her senses to the complete exclusion of every nearer sound.

Through these spreading fields, as autumn passed into rainy winter and the casualty lists grew smaller, Ruth had frequently walked during her off-duty hours. Sometimes another V.A.D. nurse from 52 Stationary Hospital accompanied her, but more often she went alone, thinking interminably of Richard, and seeking to reconcile her continued existence with the fact of his intolerable death. She knew now that her unfulfilled need of him would travel beside her always. She herself might still experience life, naked, poignant, intense, but Richard had stood for all that made life endurable.

It still surprised her that Stephen and Jessie had not opposed her decision, reached even before she returned home from Oxford, to volunteer for foreign service as a Red Cross nurse. Sometimes she wondered whether she had taken undue advantage of the stricken numbness that descended upon Dene Hall after Richard's death. For several days her parents did not remember to ask her nor she to tell them about her First in History. It had ceased to be relevant in a world where women apparently no longer counted unless they could fill subordinate rôles in the Army auxiliary services, or hurriedly raise sons to young husbands whose drastically shortened expectation of life left little opportunity for begetting children.

After a fortnight of mutual inanimate grief in which none of them could communicate comfort to the others, Stephen and Jessie had passively acquiesced in Ruth's arrangements for her few weeks of training at the Red Cross Hospital in Stafford. Neither they nor she recognised this unopposed exercise of initiative as the typical first stage of a transition period which would change the women of Ruth's generation more rapidly and profoundly than they could ever have been changed by the mere use of the vote. Shocked by twelve months of calamity into accepting situations which would once have seemed to them unthinkable, Ruth's parents did not ask themselves whether the sheltered, supervised and highly specialised life which their daughter had led represented an adequate preparation for the crude rigours of active service.

'Best let Jill go, since she seems so set on it,' Stephen had said. 'She's but young, but I'm told they keep a careful eye on them

in these Army hospitals, and it'll be better for her than sticking
about the place fretting over the poor lad.'

And Jessie had actually agreed without altercation. This
change in her mother surprised Ruth even more than the
acquiescence of Stephen, for she was beginning to perceive
her father as one of those reactionaries who sustain their
adamant principles by making deliberate exceptions to their
own rules on behalf of individuals who arouse their emotions.
In his indulgence of Ruth as in his marriage to Jessie, Stephen only
proved himself the more completely an Alleyndene by stepping
outside the Alleyndene tradition.

Jessie, as usual, was less explicable to the girl who owed so
little of her own nature to her mother's flesh and blood. Ruth did
not understand that comparative reticence had taken the place of
Jessie's pessimistic discursiveness because she had at last an evil
to face which was more than the mere negation of good. The
same melancholy stoicism which had enabled her in extreme
youth to endure humiliation from the Alleyndenes and cling
tenaciously to her unenviable post as governess, now impelled
her to rally her stricken resources by a secret canonisation of
Richard's memory. Never to her life's end did she realise that
she had perhaps precipitated the death of the one human being
whom she deeply loved by words spoken long ago at the dictates
of her upbringing and standards. Even her latest letter to Ruth,
though descriptive of family problems and characteristically
apprehensive of her daughter's moral security, revealed that
in the endeavour to endure her grief 'as Richard would have
wished,' she had discovered for the first time a method of using
to the utmost her genuine practical gifts.

'As if,' she wrote, 'it was not bad enough our dear boy having
gone and Norman being in India and you in France, there seems
to be nothing but trouble with the relations. Aunt Emily writes
that Aunt Hetty is so much worse she thinks she ought to be
put under restraint, so your father, much as he dislikes Aunt
Emily, will have to go down to Torquay next week and take the
matter in hand. Uncle Hermann has entirely ceased to write to
Aunt Elizabeth. There seems no prospect of his making a home
for her in Germany, and he cannot of course come back to this

country now he has joined the German medical service. Poor Elizabeth is absolutely broken-hearted and even Wilfred seems to bring her no comfort. Too cruel the War should have broken up the one happy home in your father's family.

'I do hope you are not having too bad a time in this bitter weather, my dearest, and that you have one or two nice girls to go about with. I hate to think you may come into contact with some of those dreadful women we read so much about in the papers who get themselves into trouble with soldiers. It is terrible to think of the immoral lives some girls are leading nowadays because of this awful War.

'You will, I am sure, be surprised to hear that your father and I have decided to make a great innovation. We are going to turn part of Dene Hall into a convalescent home for officers! I do wonder what you will think of our plan. Your room and Norman's will not of course be touched, and Richard's room and garden studio will always remain *exactly* as they are, but we can easily manage without the guest rooms now nobody pays visits, and also two of the maids' rooms are vacant since we cut down the staff. We are having them properly done up and your father has told the War Office we can take six officers. I am going to look after them myself with the help of one or two girls from the Witnall Red Cross. We have been very lonely at home now you are all gone away, and ever since our darling Richard laid down his life so bravely I have wanted to do something worthy of his memory. If only I could have been a V.A.D. nurse and come out to you in France I should have been thankful, but as the age-limit is thirty-eight I am of course beyond it. If you come on leave next month as you expect, you will find the house just about ready for our patients.'

'Mother will manage them well and it ought to do her good,' decided Ruth, for she knew that only through the anodyne drug of ceaseless hard work had she learnt to endure her own restless and agonising thoughts of Richard. It hadn't been easy at first, when she was obliged to listen to the relentless conversation of the wounded men from Loos, on whose account she had been rushed with a large contingent of briefly trained amateur nurses across the Channel. She still could not forget what

the sergeant from the Leicester Light Infantry had told the
Derbyshire lance-corporal in the bed beside him.

'He hadn't a scratch, but he was fair concussed by the explosion. I bet you my life he couldn't have moved a yard. So I left
him well covered by the ditch and went for the stretcher-bearers
– carefully markin' the spot, of course. It weren't difficult as there
was a pile of stones not ten yards away, where there'd been a
ruined farm.'

'An' 'e copped it in the meantime, eh?'

'That's what I'm goin' to tell you. When I'd got the stretcher-
bearers and come back we looked for the spot for half an hour
and never found it. Then somethin' struck me about the lie of
the land and I realised we was *on* the spot, only the spot weren't
there. No ditch, no pile of stones, no officer – only a new crater
the size of a young quarry.'

'Did you never find anythink of 'im?'

'Not so much as a button or a bootlace. But it was a dry day
and one corner of the crater was dampish.'

'Shell got 'im, I s'pose – or maybe buried?'

'Shell's my theory. Minnie. Bust up to smithereens!' And the
sergeant made a significant gesture expressive of complete and
instantaneous disintegration.

The lance-corporal turned to Ruth.

'Nurse, did you read that newspaper man's description of the
chap 'e saw blown up t'other day at Lens – "a red mist with a
bit o' rag in it"? 'E said . . .'

'Oh, *please*, Bailey, don't tell me now! I've got Tasker's
dressing to do in a minute and I mustn't lose my nerve, you
know . . . Who did you say the officer was, sergeant – the one
you never found?'

'Cosway, his name was, nurse. Not a young chap but keen as
mustard, and well up in politics and suchlike.'

At least, thought Ruth, fighting with the same invading sickness that had seized her years ago when she saw the fox torn to
pieces, at least they knew how Richard had been killed – though
no one, apparently, had seen it happen. Brief and obviously
hurried letters from senior officers described how he had been
found shot through the neck with his jugular vein severed.

'Death must have been practically instantaneous and he can hardly have suffered. Please accept my sincerest sympathy. Your son was a very popular young officer and will be greatly missed.'

Long before the Gallipoli letters arrived, they heard from the Jessons that Valentine had been killed in the same action as Richard, also instantaneously, by a shell. Blown up perhaps, Ruth speculated shuddering, like that poor Lieutenant Cosway of the Leicester Light Infantry. Later a sorrowful note from Eric had confirmed the earlier information, and later still Richard's few possessions had been returned to them, including a number of small oil-painted canvases and water-colour sketches. Smitten beyond tears by their gay promise, their vivid exuberance of light and shade, Ruth looked upon the menacing loveliness of the tawny and sapphire Peninsula, and marvelled that in her nightmares she had known the accursed land so well.

Although they had told her that Richard hadn't suffered, her imagination, too capable as always of graphic visualisations, dwelt insistently upon the processes of decay through which his dear and comely young body must have passed when the stained sand had been flung with the unceremonious haste of war-time burials over that small copper-tinged head, those gentian-blue eyes, that boyish mouth with its full, soft lips, kindly and immature. The grotesque mutilations that she saw among the wounded added their horror to the obscene images in her mind, and she struggled to save herself from the desperate verge of complete obsession as she listened impatiently to the ceaseless lamentations of Susan Shepherd, her uncongenial room-mate in their sleeping-hut on the edge of the cliff, about her 'boy' who was now in the line near the River Somme.

Before joining the Red Cross, Shepherd had been a waitress in a Brixton café, but her 'boy,' it appeared, occupied a superior position.

'He's in electrical,' she explained to Ruth. 'We were syvin' up, and if it hadn't been for this 'ere bloody war, we'd 'a' bin married in two year or less. Sometimes I don't know 'ow to bear it, I don't!'

'Perhaps you'll be able to get married just the same. Anyhow, do try to be brave about it! He wants you to be brave, I'm sure,'

Ruth urged conventionally, fighting to curb her irritation. After all, who am I to criticise her? I haven't had a 'boy' at all, and probably never shall have. Still too priggish, Madeleine would say. She did mean it; it wasn't just because she was upset over Jerry. She'd say the same if I told her about Shepherd, though she's got nothing to worry her any more.

Just after Christmas she had received a long letter and a poem from Madeleine, now remorsefully conscious of her immunity from the universal tension since Jerry Pomeroy, who emerged unscratched from the Second Battle of Ypres, had had his knee smashed by a chance shell-splinter in Ploegsteert Wood. As soon as he recovered he would be invalided out of the Army with a permanently stiff leg, and his wound was so complicated that it might be a year or two before he could leave hospital, but Madeleine didn't care now that bombs and bullets no longer had power to shatter her future. The poem was not one of her own careful verses which were beginning to appear in the *Bookman* and the *Westminster Gazette* and *Oxford Poetry*; it was by a writer called Norman Hugh Romanes, and she had chanced to see it in the *Windsor Magazine*.

AVE ATQUE VALE. E.G.R.R. (Dardanelles, 1915)

Less than those long leagues divided
Does Death divide us now in twain;
Our spirits are one again,
And fare together, as you and I did,
But for your showing the way more plain.

You seem all about me, and nearer
Than in old days could ever be;
Doubt and finality
Themselves have died in making dearer
By death thy presence here with me.

Did Death think then that by losing
What all must lose, we should give o'er?
Lo, he has given us more
Than ever we from our own choosing
Could count on in the days before.

Bravest and best beloved, defeated
With the shafts of thy keen aim,
The destroyers are put to shame,
And they, not we, are to be pitied
For one who so marvellously overcame.

Though her own poems were modern and experimental, Madeleine perhaps guessed the comfort that these simple, direct verses would bring to Ruth in her forlorn desolation. Ruth repeated them to herself again and again, gradually realising how much of Richard's generous devotion survived, through her memory of him, the sad remnants of his body. At least, she reflected, as the wintry gusts blew her like a reed against the door of the Sisters' Quarters, there was nothing left of him now but a few bones in the dry sand; and bones were clean, impersonal, anonymous, the mere anatomical framework of that flesh and blood which embodied the brief and vulnerable beauty of man.

Somehow the final mingling with the dust of Richard's corruptible body seemed to set his incorruptible spirit free. As the summer returned Ruth flung herself with less effort and more energy into the harsh duties of nursing, recognising with melancholy gratitude that she had been saved by them from the bottomless abyss of neurosis in which his death had all but engulfed her.

6

Yet after the War she remembered nothing of Wiméreux but the sudden descending horror which caused her to leave it. For Ruth the gigantic catastrophe of the Somme battle was always eclipsed by this grim, insignificant tragedy.

When rumours that the offensive was imminent began to come down the line towards the end of June and rows upon rows of clean empty beds, like white placards heralding destruction, silently awaited the rush of casualties, Susan Shepherd's persistent complaints wearied her more than ever. Years later, she could still picture Shepherd in their bare wooden hut, with her turned-up nose, her large flexible mouth, her limp brown hair drawn into a wispy bun, her untidy profile and the curious appeal made by its helpless, yielding charm. But at the time she felt only less exasperated by Shepherd's habitual slovenliness and the shrill whine of her thin Cockney voice, than by her incurable habit of drawing the curtains between their cubicles at the least appropriate moment in order to resume her endless jeremiad.

''E'll never come back now, with this here battle rygin'! I sort o' know it, it's a feelin' I got inside all the time, somethin' crool. Ow, Alleyndene, if only I'd had 'im! If I'd had 'im just the once, I wouldn't tyke on so, I swear!'

Although her months of contact with savage pain and primitive grief had deepened Ruth's normal reaction against the harsh moral judgments of Alleyndene tradition, she was still sufficiently the product of her education and her era to feel shocked by this unqualified assertion of physical desire.

'But, Shepherd,' she protested as her voluble half-dressed companion began to sniff, 'you wouldn't want to abandon everything you believe in – all your ideals of decent behaviour, I mean – just because Ronnie's in danger, would you? If he were to come here and see you this very evening, I don't believe you'd *really* do anything wrong!'

Shepherd regarded her with a strangely mature expression of pitying contempt.

'Wrong, d'you call it? Wrong! What if it is, anywye? Ain't everything gawn wrong jus' now! What abaht this 'ere bleedin' war – not exactly a bit o' Gawd Almighty, eh? All this 'ere talk about waitin' for marriage, with these bloody battles goin' on and yer boy at the front – it's all my eye! The old 'uns have 'ad their bit o' fun and no interference, but they'd rather see the lot of us bleedin' corpses than let us 'ave ours if it means breakin' their blarsted rules and regerlytions!'

She stopped for breath, sniffing and pushing the wisps of brown hair out of her light, suffused eyes.

'Why shouldn't Ronnie have 'ad 'is bit o' love before goin' into the line? Maybe now he'll get popped off, and never ha' known it! With things as they be, I wouldn't 'a worritted myself about bein' a bad girl an' that, if only I'd given Ron his bit o' joy before he went. I ain't got no "ideels of decent be'yviour" or whatever bloody nyme you called 'em – not in these dyes, no, thank you! If Ronnie comes back and wants me I'll tyke 'im, married or unmarried, so 'elp me Gawd!'

The chaos of unceasing convoys which followed the Somme slaughter had continued for perhaps ten days when Ruth came off duty one evening to find Shepherd sitting alone in their hut, motionless as a carven image of grief. The vacant pallor of her face and the numb silence which replaced her usual volubility told Ruth at once what had happened.

''E's dead, Alleyndene,' said Shepherd at last in a dull, flat tone not remotely recognisable as her customary whine. ''E's dead an' gawn. I got a letter from my dad this afternoon.'

Ruth sought vainly for words of understanding, knowing that even after her own acquaintance with disaster, the gulf of temperament and experience between herself and Shepherd was too deep to be spanned by sympathy.

'Oh, Shepherd,' she began helplessly, 'I'm sorry ... I'm so terribly sorry ... What *can* I say?'

Shepherd stood up suddenly, cold and abrupt.

'You don't need to sye nothin'. I always knew 'e was for it. Oh, my Gawd!' she moaned under her breath, and turning her back on Ruth she walked over to the window and gazed, rigid and speechless, at the summer sea with its tiny curled waves washing gently against the deep cliffs immediately below.

In the middle of that night, Ruth woke suddenly from the feverish confusion of a shapeless nightmare. When she returned to their hut after supper she had found Shepherd in bed, and thinking that she was perhaps sleeping from the exhaustion of shock, had crept on tiptoe while she undressed. No word had come from beneath the tumbled blanket, and unexpectedly Ruth fell asleep at once, worn out by the anguish and turmoil of the long unbroken day in the crowded hospital. Startled now by some unusual sound or movement, she wondered for a moment whether the white calico-clad figure stealthily climbing over the low window-sill was part of reality or some figment of her tortuous dream. Then the truth flashed upon her, and because her instinct to save life was stronger than the instinct of self-preservation, she flung herself upon the frantic, fighting maniac who had ceased to be Shepherd.

It was all over in a second, but to Ruth the mortal struggle against the shallow open casement seemed to last for centuries. She did not feel the pain of her scratched and bitten hands as she tried vainly to get Shepherd into her arms, but she heard the creaking and cracking of the thin match-boarding which alone divided them both from death. Even as she cried aloud for help she staggered under the sudden blows that descended upon her face and head with the abnormal strength of the suicide's desperation, and felt rather than saw the wild body wrench itself from her weakened grasp and disappear.

Sharply striking the slate-grey cliff in its descent, Shepherd's half-naked figure bounced off the steep rock and fell heavily on to the green seaweed-slimed stones which covered the beach at low tide. Clinging with her torn hands to the broken window, Ruth peered over the edge to see a dim shapeless heap, like a pierced sack of flour, just visible in the ominous darkness at the foot of the cliff. Barely conscious of who or where she was, she reeled backwards on to the floor of the hut as the door opened, and began to vomit as though her body were rejecting the very life within it.

7

When the lovely May of 1917 awakened the pine-woods and sand-dunes at Hardelot to new birth after the longest and coldest winter of the War, Ruth could at last recall without flinching the haunting horror of the previous July and bless the hospital authorities for the consideration that they had shown her.

She had explained until she was weary of explanation that the supposed courage for which they commended her was merely the instinctive reaction to a crisis never clearly distinguished from her intermittent nightmares. She had protested against her three weeks' banishment to the Sick Sisters' Hospital in the woods near Le Touquet and the fortnight of sick leave which followed it. Her protests were useless, for long after the cuts and bruises had healed on her face and hands she felt limp and listless, and was still, they said, unfit for duty.

'It's the shock,' they told her. 'You'll get over it all in good time.'

And when she returned from leave for the usual interview with the Transport Sister at Boulogne she did feel quite strong again, though the prospect of walking between huts and tents on the cliff edge in the strong sea-wind filled her with sick apprehension.

But that trouble too had been foreseen and met.

'Nurse Alleyndene?' repeated the Transport Sister as she drew the folder containing Ruth's record from the pile before her. 'Ah, of course – you're the V.A.D. who was involved in that tragic suicide case at Wimereux. I congratulate you on your courage, Nurse . . . Now what would you say to a change of scene?'

'Thank you, Sister. I'd be glad to leave 52 Stationary and start again somewhere else. But please,' she added, 'don't send me away from the sea. It's the greatest consolation I have.'

'That's strange,' said the Sister, momentarily personal. 'I've always thought the sea so sad – it separates one from home and one's people and makes one feel solitary.'

'It doesn't seem much of a separation compared with death . . . Anyway, I was at school by the sea and I got to love it then. If you *could* send me where I can still walk by it when I'm off duty . . . ?'

The Transport Sister consulted a list on the table in front of her.

'Well, I had been thinking of Rouen for you – it's a beautiful old town and there's plenty of life there – but if you prefer the coast there's a vacancy for a V.A.D. at 73 General. It's a big hospital on the sea-shore at Hardelot-Plage – used to be a hotel before the War. But I must warn you Hardelot's only a small country village and rather isolated; there isn't even a big army camp.'

'I don't mind so long as it hasn't any cliffs.'

'Oh, no; it's quite flat, with very fine sands. The hospital's among the dunes and there's pretty country behind – pine-woods and meadows.'

Ruth had first seen Hardelot at the end of August, when the sweet pungent scent from the hot pine-needles drifted with every land breeze across the sand-hills, and the lush marshy meadows beyond the forest were luxuriant with golden rod and purple loosestrife. Close to the sea among the tumbled dunes she found the converted hotel with its annexe of huts, a solid white-painted structure which stood four-square against the wildest winter gales. Immediately she entered it she had the sense of coming home, for she recognised the view from its windows as the twin seascape to that of her enchanted schooldays, though the great flat expanse of sand was deeper in colour than the sands at Camber, and the dune-bordered country surrounding Rye had possessed no counterpart to the resinous pine-woods with their rich hinterland of verdure and corn.

From the doorway of her hut behind the Sisters' Quarters, she could look westward across the smooth misty sea towards the Sussex coast beyond the horizon, where on late afternoons the sun dipped superbly into the water. To the north, on the further side of a slanting purple hill, Boulogne received its daily ship-loads of men and women in military uniform. To the south, where the dunes faded into the blue-grey haze of a sunlit summer, Le Touquet awaited its convoys of patients and its overseas officers on local leave. Through the exquisite miles of pine-wood spreading eastward from the Plage ran the fragrant, needle-carpeted path to the undulating meadows beyond which lay the base-camps of Étaples.

This time Ruth's room-mate was carefully chosen by the unconventional Regular Army Matron, whose intelligent re-interpretations had modified so many of the more archaic hospital rules. She shared her hut with a cheerful north-country spinster well-established in her capable thirties, who seemed to have no friends at the front. There would be no risk here of tragedy, no subjection to volubility and inquisitiveness; no impact of fear or violent emotion.

That year's paralysing cold had frozen the armies to immobility and the winter had been quieter than the one succeeding

Loos. The April clamour of offensives round Arras had lately brought heavy convoys to Hardelot, but Norman was still safe in Quetta and the convalescent officers now replaced one another in animated succession at Dene Hall. Ruth's immediate world, though darkened by her enduring grief for Richard, seemed to have attained the peace of neutral stability. Hardelot offered its consoling beauty, the hospital its placid unexacting friendships; at the moment her negative serenity of soul seemed a fair substitute for those vague ambitions which the War had postponed to an unimaginable future.

'I can bear it indefinitely if it goes on like this,' she thought as she returned from luncheon to her ward of Vimy Ridge convalescents, and began the two-o'clock round of temperatures and pulses. She sat down at the table to enter them in the Day Report book, and had almost finished writing when a shadow fell across the paper from the doorway, and a step beside her chair made her start and look up.

She saw a very tall, black-haired young man in a khaki uniform of a cut so fastidious that she took him for an officer until she perceived the double stripe of a corporal across his sleeve and the dark-blue and red ribbon of the Distinguished Conduct Medal upon his chest. In spite of the British uniform his thin bronzed face with its strong features and dominant chin struck her as un-English, and immediately he spoke she understood why.

'Pardon me, Sister, is this Ward 11? I'm told Nurse Alleyndene's in this outfit.'

'I am Ruth Alleyndene,' she said; and because she had never seen an American soldier before she inspected him with critical interest, observing the thick blue-black crest of straight silky hair which fell, apache-like, over his forehead, the large dark eyes of a luminous southern brown which smiled upon her from beneath their extravagant length of curling eyelashes. The outward tilt of his long straight nose combined with the high arch of his narrow black eyebrows and the upward-curving corners of his firm, full lips to give his face a permanent expression of adventurous inquiry. His unusual height, his brilliant smiling eyes and this questing vivacity of countenance would have made him, she thought, conspicuous and distinguished in any assemblage of soldiers.

'I am Ruth Alleyndene,' she repeated; and her eyes inquired, 'But who are you?'

'My name's Meury,' the young man replied. 'Eugene C. Meury of the Chelsea Rifles. I knew your brother in Gallipoli.'

'You knew Richard!' she cried, and felt herself turning pale. Why, she thought, for she had re-read those letters from Gallipoli until she knew them by heart, this must be Richard's American N.C.O., who threw a bomb back over the parapet and got awarded the D.C.M. ... Perhaps he knows something more about Richard? Perhaps he was near him when he died? To give herself time before putting those urgent, painful questions, she asked him one or two others.

'Then the Chelsea Rifles are in France – and you're still with them?'

'Yes. They're in France right now. They've been around Arras ever since we came over from Salonika last fall, but I left the regiment after the show at Monchy. Now the United States are in the War I'm attached to a Base Depôt at Étaples till our people come over, and I can apply for a commission in one of our own divisions.'

'I suppose there aren't many of you serving with the Allies?'

'Only a few. Your Army boys weren't too keen on having us, but I got around them somehow in '14. Luckily I was just through Harvard and I'd had my twenty-first birthday that spring, so they couldn't turn me down on the score of age.'

'But whatever made you do it?'

'Well, I'd come over on a trip to England with some particular friends from Boston, and I thought it'd be a fine way of seeing life. When my friends found they couldn't hold me they begged me to join the Chelsea Rifles as having a better class of private than most – more like our boys from home.'

'And you don't regret it?'

'I wouldn't say that altogether – but now our boys are coming over I'm mighty glad I can tell them a few things. Of course, when I joined up I never guessed the darn thing would last more than a few weeks. I hadn't exactly reckoned on Gallipoli – but once I got there I made up my mind to stick it.'

There was a short pause while Ruth nerved herself to ask what she wanted to know.

'Corporal Meury, you've come to tell me something about my brother?'

'Right, Miss Alleyndene – or rather, to give you something. Your brother left a letter for you in case he got knocked out in the attack. He said he couldn't mail it because it would never pass the Censor. I promised I'd keep it if I didn't get hit myself, and give it to you whenever I came to England.'

'I wonder why he didn't leave it with Eric Jesson?' she reflected aloud. 'Eric had been his friend for years.'

'I couldn't say for sure. Maybe young Jesson got tight too often and wasn't to be relied on . . . and then I was nearly three years older, and that's a lot when you're in the Army. Anyway, I've got the letter, and the other day when they sent me on leave to London I rang up your home.'

'You rang up Dene Hall – all the way from London!'

'Sure. It's no distance, though the guys at your exchange took a whale of a time locating it. They told me at the Hall you'd gone to France, but I'd some job finding out just where you were.'

I'm certain you had, thought Ruth, remembering the excitement and consternation still caused not only in Dene Hall but at the Alleyndene Pottery Company by long-distance trunk calls.

'Who answered the telephone?' she inquired.

'It was a man's voice – deep and rather slow. I guess it must have been your dad.'

'Well, it was just like Father not to tell you where I was. He's always been terribly cautious, and he still hasn't grasped that France is a bit different from Staffordshire. How did you get round him in the end?'

'I simply told him I'd served under your brother, and had a drawing of his to give you.'

'And . . . have you?'

'Yes. He gave me about half a dozen he wouldn't put with the rest.'

'And you've got them here with you now – and the letter?'

This time it was the American who paused.

'I figured,' he said at last, 'that when you'd seen the paintings and read the letter, there might be a question or two you'd want to ask me. I thought maybe you'd let me take you out somewhere and give you the things right away from your patients.'

'But I can't possibly! It's against the rules – and anyhow I'm on duty this afternoon.'

'We're all set on that. I knew a bit about your crazy regulations, so I called on your Matron before seeing you and fixed it up. She says you can have the afternoon off, and she's sending an orderly to take care of this show. You've only got to see her a second before we start, and she said I could take you any place I liked so long as we didn't talk just around your hospital. I've got my automobile outside and we'll run over to Paris-Plage. It's all fixed.'

Ruth felt quite sure that it was. In spite of the fear that had gripped her from the first mention of Richard, she was shaken with inward amusement at the young American's invading efficiency, his capture of those whose business it was to tighten the red tape of sex-segregation, his indifference to obstacles which swept all the regulations, conventions and inhibitions of a British Army Hospital into negligible oblivion.

'Well,' she said, smiling, 'as you've arranged everything so thoroughly I suppose I'd better come ... Shall I join you at your car when I've seen Matron?'

'Right. It's parked over there by the Quartermaster's Stores. It's only a hired car, but it's got lots of pep.'

It certainly had, as it raced exuberantly through Neufchâtel and Stella-Plage and Camiers between meadows chrome-yellow with buttercups and ditches rose-red with ragged robin. In the strong May sunshine the open countryside, brilliant with the pink and white of apple-blossom, the gold of laburnum, the emerald of young beech, took on the vivid, unnatural clarity of a picture postcard. At Étaples the miniature harbour with its ranked masts of fishing smacks wore an air of afternoon somnolence, as though taking a rest from the War.

When they sped like a spinning-top between the hospitals, shaving off the sharp edges of the corner beneath the railway line and jumping the pot-holes in the heavily-travelled highway between the camp and the village, Ruth tentatively warned him of the sharp turn where the road to Paris-Plage left the harbour for the bridge over the Canche. But he only laughed, showing a perfect row of white teeth, strong and even.

'Just quit worrying,' he said cheerfully. 'I don't have accidents.'

Their dazzling speed and the inner surge of her apprehensions reduced conversation to a minimum.

'If they go in for winning the War like this it'll soon be over,' she thought, intrigued in spite of her dread by the suddenness and strangeness of her unusual situation.

Only a fortnight earlier, the day before she left London on her last leave, she had helped Madeleine to take some of the girls from the Holborn High School to the Thanksgiving Service at St Paul's Cathedral which celebrated America's entry into the war. It had been a gentle spring morning, pearly-grey with soft subduing mist. From hotels and offices and government buildings and even, for the first time in history, from the Victoria Tower of the Palace of Westminster, the Stars and Stripes were flying beside the Union Jack, and the streets had been full of spectators wearing tiny American flags in their button-holes.

Inside the Cathedral they stood up to sing the hymn, 'O God, our help in ages past,' with a new sense of humility, grateful to whatever Providence had persuaded a vigorous, inexhaustible young nation to help England to bear her burden of annihilating war. But Ruth's emotions were most poignantly stirred when the organ thundered into the famous 'Battle Hymn of the Republic,' which she heard then for the first time, though she was to know it by heart before many months were past. She realised at that moment how it might happen that one gripping, compelling song, in despite of reason, of civilisation, of true religion, could carry a whole people into war.

Mine eyes have seen the glory of the coming of the Lord;
He is trampling out the vintage where the grapes of wrath
*   are stored;*

> *He hath loosed the fateful lightning of His terrible, swift*
>   *sword:*
> *His truth is marching on!*

Glancing down at the printed leaflet which announced, 'A solemn service to Almighty God on the occasion of the entry of the United States of America into the Great War for Freedom,' Ruth noticed to her surprise that the author of the Battle Hymn was named Julia Ward Howe. It seemed significant that this youngest of the world's Great Powers should have had their most challenging war song written by a woman. Evidently, she reflected, women matter more in the United States than they do in England; there aren't the same obstacles and traditions to be overcome in a new civilisation.

The excited children whom Madeleine had brought, hardly knowing what they sang, joined in the last two verses with an enthusiasm only surpassed by the many Americans thronging the Cathedral.

> *He hath sounded forth the trumpet that shall never call*
>   *retreat:*
> *He is sifting out the hearts of men before His judgment-*
>   *seat:*
> *Oh, be swift, my soul, to answer Him! be jubilant, my*
>   *feet;*
> *Our God is marching on!*
>
> *In the beauty of the lilies Christ was born across the sea,*
> *With a glory in His bosom that transfigures you and me;*
> *As He died to make men holy, let us die to make men*
>   *free,*
> *While God is marching on!*

The words still rang in Ruth's head as the car lurched through Le Touquet woods into Paris-Plage, and she glanced at Eugene Meury's intent, eager profile.

'In a few months' time,' she thought, 'France will be full of young men like this, with lean, clean-shaven faces and tall athletic bodies, and the strong chins and arrogant lips of their pioneer stock. What a contrast they'll be to our under-sized, decimated armies – and yet how I wish they hadn't to come! Their God is marching on – is He? If so, where's He hidden Himself?'

An unspoken prayer took shape in her mind as Corporal Meury stopped the car and stretched out a long brown hand to help her alight.

'Oh, God, if you're really there, come from behind your clouds and show yourself! Come before the best of America's life, like ours, disappears into the ground or under the sea!'

8

At Paris-Plage they walked along the empty esplanade and sat down on a low seat in front of the long row of once fashionable hotels.

Silently Ruth examined, one by one, the savage, brilliant canvases which Eugene Meury had taken from the car – sketches so different from the glowing impersonal landscapes that came from Gallipoli with Richard's possessions. She turned white at the ruthless rendering of a dead Turk's blackened putrescent body lying beside a shallow open grave, but a cry burst from her as she saw in another painting a field of tall pale daisies and scarlet sinister poppies, and between them a dark evil face peeping above a half-concealed gun.

'It's just like my dreams! It's exactly the same, except that for me it was always lilies and daffodils which hid the sniper!'

She shuddered, wondering whether some strange telepathy had actually existed between herself and this embittered unfamiliar Richard. Would his last letter explain the disquieting contrast between these private sketches and the others? She turned to Corporal Meury, her breath caught by her inward agitation.

'You've got the letter with you?'

'It's here.' He opened his pocket-book and took out a sealed envelope, tattered at the corners and addressed in the generous, flourishing hand which brought a choking lump to Ruth's throat. He did not look at her as he passed it over, remembering how tears had stood in the despairing blue eyes of the boy who gave it to him.

'I guess you and your brother were real friends,' he said, feeling her hand tremble as she took it.

'Yes. I loved him better than anyone I've ever known,' she admitted, a little surprised because it seemed so easy to talk to this young American of those intimate emotions which she had always concealed from everyone but Richard and Madeleine. 'I've another brother in India and I'm fond of him up to a point, but he's never been necessary to me as Richard was. Norman and I resemble each other so much in some ways, it makes our differences quite exasperating.'

'Looks as if it might be long,' said Meury, watching her examine the bulky envelope. 'Maybe I'll take a walk and admire the view while you read it.'

Left alone on the seat with only the calm sea before her and the American's tall thin figure a discreet distance away, Ruth forced herself to open Richard's farewell message.

'MY DEAREST JILL,

'To-night I am writing you a long letter because there is a stunt on to-morrow and I don't expect to come out of it alive. In fact I may as well be honest with you and tell you that I don't mean to come out of it. You were always the one person in the family with whom I could be quite honest, and that is why I'm going to tell you one or two things about this War that I would like you to remember. I have kept it all out of my letters before, but this is the last I shall ever write you, and I want you to know.

'As I couldn't get a letter like this past the Censor I am giving it to Meury, the American lance-corporal I told you about who got the D.C.M., to put into your hands if ever he goes to England. You may think it queer my not giving it to an officer, but Val and Eric are the only officers I know really intimately now. When you have read this you will understand why it is no use for Val to have it, and Eric is so often tight nowadays that if I gave it to him the chances are you would never get it at all. Meury is not only the pluckiest chap in the platoon but awfully efficient as well, so I feel this letter is more likely to reach you through him than anyone else out here.

'When we first joined up I probably gave you the impression that everything was splendid. The battalion was encamped in lovely country, and I got quite fond of a lot of the chaps who seemed so different from the ordinary Tommy. We were all going to be fine fellows and heroes, and see the world and have a glorious time.

'Well, the real thing isn't like that at all. If you had seen men with their faces blown in or their bowels running out and kids of seventeen gone stark staring mad and gibbering for their mothers, you would know it isn't. I wonder how much you are told about the true facts of the fighting here? We never have any real rest from it, as the so-called rest camps get shelled almost as much as the fire-trenches. There's not a spot on the bloody Peninsula where there's no risk of getting shot. Do people at home realise from the colossal casualty lists anything of what this hell is, or don't they get published? Anyhow you can take it from me there is no marching and singing patriotic songs and cheering our brave boys out here. It's all blood and bones and decaying bodies and chaps turned to skeletons with dysentery and one long eternal insufferable stink. The whole place reeks of defunct Turks and Australians, especially when they swell up and burst in the sun. These rotting corpses simply breed flies and so do the filthy Turk trenches, whatever we do to scavenge ours. I can't believe we have only been here two months for it feels like two years. All this foul bayonet fighting makes me sick. I can't stick ripping out another man's guts and I can stick even less the people who say they like it. Besides, whatever we do in that way is no good anyhow as there never seem to be any reinforcements to follow up our attacks.

'But I'm not only trying to tell you what war does to people's bodies, even though it does tear their insides out and emasculate them and mutilate the most intimate parts of their persons for the public gaze. What's even worse is what it does to your mind. At first there's the appalling monotony and the hideous obscene language and the everlasting drills and parades, and thick-headed old sergeants without a scrap of education or humanity teaching you to shove your bayonets into men's stomachs by working you into a hysterical frenzy over sacks of straw. After a few weeks nobody seems to care 2*d*. about pictures or decent books; it's all cards and girls and whisky and what sort of harlot you're going to pick up when you next get a pass. By the time you get to the front you've got nothing left in the way of philosophy or religion to help you face death or stick the sights or bear up under the smells. There's no way of forgetting what you can't prevent and can't avoid, except through the whisky bottle, and whatever you do the only rule is expediency and not getting found out.

'When we were first in camp old Eric, who is not much of a fighter anyhow, soon fell for the girls and the whisky, but Val and I thought we might have some use for our intellects when the War was over and we didn't want the rot to get us if we could help it. We have never cared for getting drunk and going with prostitutes, so when life got really intolerable we decided that the only thing to do was to be everything we possibly could to one another. You will know what I mean if you remember a conversation we had in the bicycle shed years ago about Val having to leave Ludborough. I don't know how much you know nowadays and I shall never know what you think of this letter, but I tell you that if it hadn't been for Val I should never have stuck this damned War as long as I have.

'There was no trouble at all to begin with, but soon after we got here and were always crowded together some swinish fellows began to talk. A few days ago the C.O. sent for me and told me that next time we are out of the line there will probably be an inquiry – which of course might mean a court-martial and expulsion from the Army. Well, I don't intend to let it come to that and nor does Valentine. We don't feel we have done anything wrong or harmed anyone, but after the hell I have been through already I can't face the hullaballoo and the public disgrace and the scenes there would be at home, especially as our beautiful respectable family would take good care I didn't live it down and forget it, or make a success of any career even if I had the chance. Knowing so well what the Alleyndenes are I can't confront Father and Mother with the fact that their son is what they would call vicious and immoral instead of a virtuous patriotic hero. So we have decided to quit. Please try to forgive me and not think too badly of me. Life has been so ghastly at times that it is difficult to explain everything properly.

'I think that's all I have to say, except just this – that if ever you get married and have a son, don't, whatever you do, let them make him fight in a war. Don't let them cheat him into thinking it's all fine and glorious, but tell him the truth as I have tried to tell you.

'And now, Jill darling, I'm afraid it will have to be goodbye. I wish I could have talked to you once more but it was not to be. I got out your photograph just now and looked at it, because I shan't ever see you again. But if there is anything after death and I can find a way, I promise I will try to come back and watch over you.

'In life and in death, dearest Jill,

'Your ever loving
'JACK.'

9

Ruth lifted her stricken face from Richard's letter with a feeling that centuries had passed – centuries in which the entire structure of courage and reconciliation that she had built for herself since July 1915 had been relentlessly shattered.

Returning like some startled Rip van Winkle to 1917 and Paris-Plage, she saw that the American was now standing quite close to her, though his eyes were still tactfully fixed upon the horizon. She called to him in a strained, unfamiliar voice.

'Corporal Meury!'

He came to her at once and she questioned him abruptly.

'Corporal Meury, do you think Richard was really killed in action? I mean – could he possibly have killed himself?'

The second's pause, the young man's instant start of apprehension, told her immediately that he knew, or suspected, all
the facts of which Richard's letter had made her aware.

'My God, Miss Alleyndene!' he exclaimed. 'Whatever put such
a notion into your head? Your brother was honourably killed on
the field of battle.'

Ruth glanced down at the sheets of writing in her hands.
Richard's writing – the decorative capitals, the broad graceful
downward strokes as though he were using a brush instead
of a pen.

'Corporal Meury, do you know what's in this letter?'

'Not a darn thing. It was sealed up when your brother
gave it me.'

'Then, if you will, I'd like you to read it . . . Yes, I really mean
that. I believe you're the only person living who can tell me
the truth.'

She watched his face, as he read the letter, grow pale and
concerned, and did not speak until he had finished.

'Look here,' she said then, 'you're a very brave man. I should
have known that even if I hadn't seen your ribbon and read
Richard's letters. You must realise courage isn't possible at all
unless one knows the whole truth about things, and makes one's
self face the worst that could happen.'

'Yes,' he answered humbly. 'Maybe I do know that.'

'Then can't you give me credit for wanting to know the truth
and face it too? Now please tell me – did you ever hear anything
of what Richard writes about? I mean – between himself and
Captain Jesson?'

'Well . . . there were rumours in the Company . . . but that
didn't mean they were true.'

'But do you think they were true? If he and Valentine Jesson
hadn't been killed in the battle, would there have been an inquiry,
and perhaps a court-martial?'

'Yes . . . maybe something of the sort might have happened.'

'Then do you believe Richard killed himself to escape the
disgrace that might have come to him?'

'I guess that's a thing we'll never know. Your brother was
found dead after the action, shot through the neck. The bullet

went through his jugular vein and he can't have lived more than a few seconds after . . . If you're really set on the truth, I found him myself. I was one of the few guys who came through the show without a scratch, and when they told me he hadn't come in I went out and looked around for him.'

If he had been alive you might have got the V.C. for that, thought Ruth; and in spite of her anguish a thrill ran through her. But it died as she braced herself for another question.

'Had he – did he look as though he'd suffered much?'

'No. His face was as peaceful as it could be – just as if death had been a relief. I noticed that specially, because it was so different from some of the dead Turks we found over the hill, all twisted and distorted.'

'Then it was the kind of attack he might easily have been killed in – if he didn't kill himself?'

'Lord, yes! There were bombs and bullets flying about all over the place . . . Now you take Jesson. One shell got six of them – four men and a corporal and Jesson himself. There wasn't enough of them left to bury, but we found Jesson's hand in the scrub afterwards; we knew it was his by a scarab ring his mother had given him to wear for luck. Now whatever Jesson intended about getting hit, he just couldn't have fixed that shell the way it came.'

There was silence for a moment while Ruth gazed blankly at the pearl and turquoise sea, trying to assimilate what he had told her. Then Meury spoke very gently.

'Don't be too rough on your brother, Miss Alleyndene, whatever he may have done. The Peninsula was hell enough for tough guys like me who enjoy a scrap now and again, but it must have been a picnic to us compared with boys like your brother and Jesson – artists and such, who just couldn't stick the racket of the guns and the ghastly sights when men got smashed up or disfigured. I guess it was more that than the danger which upset him, and you can't wonder. I don't say I've ever been tempted just his way myself, but the Lord knows what I mightn't do if this darn War goes on much longer!'

'I wasn't thinking of being rough on him,' said Ruth shakily. A memory came back to her of Playden Manor on a Sunday evening and Miss Hilton in her address quoting from Ruskin: 'Be merciful while you have mercy.' It was about morals too, that talk of hers; about avoiding moral offences ... Richard, since his death, had been a hero at home, but suppose instead of the telegram announcing that he had been killed in action there had come another: 'Regret to inform you Lieutenant Richard Alleyndene expelled from the Army for a moral offence' ...? What *was* a moral offence? she asked herself for the first time. Cruelty? Treachery? Exploitation? Oh, no; it was giving expression to your love for a person whom the law didn't permit you to feel about in that way. To love the wrong person too well, without calculation – that's the only 'moral offence' our society calls by that name.

She went on communicating her thoughts aloud to Meury.

'If I'm rough on anyone it's likely to be my family, for teaching us, as they always did, that so-called immorality was worse than death or any other horror. I'm beginning to think there are plenty of things far, far more deserving of punishment. Surely it's a worse crime to be a statesman and involve a whole nation in war, than just to go in for some sort of unorthodox relationship which however wrong it may be in itself doesn't hurt anyone else!'

Her emotions became intolerable and she covered her face.

'Oh, Richard, my darling, my little brother whom I always played with – so kind, so dear, so gifted, so comforting! Who'd have thought this War would come and ruin the world for you, and force you into a position where you had to seek death when you'd everything to live for!'

As though she were back in her childhood she sobbed uncontrollably, groping blindly for her handkerchief, completely indifferent to Eugene Meury's reassuring presence. Conscious that his own simple, direct emotions were being uncomfortably stirred by her desolate grief and her unfamiliar beauty, he laid his hand tentatively on her shoulder.

'Don't cry, dear ... Take my handkerchief. Maybe it's rather rough – it's only from the canteen – but it was clean this noon.'

He handed her his khaki handkerchief and she dried her eyes, struggling for control as he continued:

'I guess this feels like an awful blow, but if I were you I'd try and remember your brother was a fine officer in every way but just that we've been talking of, and he never let up on a tough job for all he loathed and detested fighting. He just got in a jam and took the way out he thought most honourable, for the sake of your family and his own good name. In a sense it was a mighty fine thing to do, and anyhow I know he wouldn't want you to go on grieving and breaking your heart for him when it's all over and he's been at peace these eighteen months . . . I'm going to take you along right now and give you a cup of tea. I guess you're a tea-drinker like all your people and you'll feel a lot better when you've had a cup. If it's against the rules for you and me to be seen together in a café, why, this is where we give the rules the go-by!'

Late that afternoon, when he had driven her back to the hospital, Ruth walked up and down the hard brown sand by the water's edge, trying to adjust her memories and her hard-won philosophy of reconciliation to the true facts of Richard's death. As the sun went down in sanguine splendour the scent of pines drifted seawards on the evening breeze, and she saw without consciously observing the myriads of tiny shells – mauve and rose-pink and saffron-yellow – which covered the shore like a speckled carpet.

'For the sake of your family and his own good name.' So Corporal Meury had put it. And what, indeed, would the Alleyndenes have said? Shame? Disgrace? Never be able to lift up our heads again? Well, would it have mattered if they hadn't? Richard was very young, and the scandal wouldn't have stopped him from becoming a first-class painter. Family discredit would not have been the end; only death was the end, because it prevented anything from happening to you any more. Oh, to think that they'd got even Richard, and driven him to desperation as Granny had once driven Agnes with her baby – Richard who might have been a great artist!

No shadow, at any rate, would lie on his name now. No fame, but no reproach either. He'd achieved that by dying – dying to save the Alleyndenes from a shock to their moral standards! Oh, God, was there nothing left but suicide and despair? – first poor inefficient Shepherd whose 'boy' had gone west, and now Richard, so generous, so talented, so beloved!

Yes, there was something . . . something that hadn't been there this morning. There was her acquaintance with the young American, Richard's corporal, so soon to be an officer in one of the rescuing divisions from the unknown West. She repeated his name to herself – 'Eugene Meury' – and suddenly realised his existence as stimulating and consoling when more than anything in life she needed stimulus and consolation. A brave young man with an inexhaustible fund of strength and kindness; the only source of comfort in a world which had once more been taken up and smashed to pieces when it was just beginning to acquire cohesion.

He did ask me when he put me down at the camp if we could go out together some other time. Shall I see him again, I wonder? Shall I see him soon?

10

Ruth had not long to wait for an answer to her question.

Afterwards, looking back upon that strange transfigured summer, she could not recall the various excuses for writing to her that he had made when he could no longer pretend that he was still comforting her on account of Richard, nor remember by what imperceptible stages they had passed from journeys to Boulogne or Le Touquet formally undertaken with the Matron's permission, to meetings which were necessarily clandestine because they had become so frequent.

Although 73 General had been filled with patients from the Messines offensive after the first week in June, the rush was not sufficient to cause those cancellations of off-duty time which had followed the Somme and the battles round Arras, while Meury, as he assured her, hadn't a darn thing to do. It was no one's particular job to keep an eye on a detached American, so leave from the Étaples camp was easy to obtain. Now that she found herself for the first time in conflict with them, Ruth wondered why she had attached so sacred an importance to keeping those rules which had denied her, at Oxford, the society of undergraduates and forbade her, in the Army, the companionship of soldiers. They seemed to her now absurd and unnatural – besides being ludicrously easy to circumvent if reasonable precautions were taken. She was obliged, when first they began to meet privately, to restrain Meury's vivacious anxiety to run her openly round in his hired two-seater in order to defy the British Army's practice of sex-segregation – which, as he said, 'no American woman would stand for.'

'The Queen Alexandra's Imperial Military Nursing Service isn't likely to change its rules for me,' Ruth told him, amused as ever by his easy sweeping aside of difficulties which he saw no obligation to confront. 'Look at its name, to begin with! I don't want to be sent home after nearly two years' service.'

Their companionship involved fewer risks when for her sake he 'wangled' permission to discard his British corporal's uniform for that of an American cadet, and surprised her by appearing in an officer's peaked cap and an immaculate tunic of the finest khaki. Since segregation rules did not operate in the United States Army, the sight of an American officer with a nurse would not provoke curiosity, and if she conveniently forgot to attach the brass letters of her Staffordshire Voluntary Aid Detachment to the shoulder-straps of her navy-blue coat, she might easily be taken for some advance species of American volunteer nurse.

'I've just put in for my transfer,' he told her at one of their earliest meetings in the middle of June. 'Our First Division won't get over here till the end of this month, but Pershing fixed his headquarters in Paris on June 13th, so I'm right on that. There's a rumour I'm getting a commission as a junior officer in the Operations Department. I guess someone's been pulling strings at home – maybe my dad. He owns a newspaper and knows all the big shots in New York and Washington.'

'What exactly does it mean, a commission in the Operations Department?'

'Well, it signifies a rest from the line to begin with. I'll be studying the British and French methods of deploying troops so as to help instruct our rookies when they get over. It means I'll go most anywhere I like in England or France – musketry

schools, grenade schools and such – observing how you people
train for war.'

'I should have thought you knew all there was to be known
about that already!'

'I guess I do. You can't help learning a thing or two about
fighting if you've been through Gallipoli without a scratch –
not mentioning some mighty big shows in France, and all the
plagues of Salonika without a mosquito bite. But it's a fine
way of putting in time till some of our divisions are ready for
a personally conducted trip round the trenches.'

The places chosen for their rendezvous during that summer
were elaborately varied. Sometimes Ruth met him on the narrow
path, half concealed by willows and hazels, which led from the
Chemin du Pont Saint-Augustin over a rustic bridge into the
pine-woods, where cloud and sunshine dappled the ground with
its warm brown carpet of needles and cones. Sometimes she
waited for him far from the hospital in the meadowside lane
which wound gently towards the old Château d'Hardelot past
a chain of shallow reed-crowded meres, like mirrors reflecting
the azure sky and cotton-wool puffs of cloud. She dared not
go too near the Château, for it was now an Army Instruction
School, but in the days of its ancient dignity its decorous garden
had been proudly kept, its guardian sentinels of ilex and poplar
carefully trimmed, its portals inscribed with the gallant boast
'*Gaudeam adferro.*'

In retrospect the country surrounding it wore so divine a summer radiance that she sometimes wondered whether the unfamiliar excitement of her meetings with Meury, which obliterated
even the dark undercurrent of her remorseful disillusioned grief,
had not also heightened the colours of the flowers, the melting
richness of the afternoon sky, the gay splendour of the butterflies
flitting from purple willow-herb to white sea-campion, from
pink bush-vetch to yellow toadflax. On the hottest days the
reeded meres shimmered violently blue, as though they had
absorbed into their still depths the passion and intensity of relentless war, and the butterflies – red admirals, orange fritillaries,
madder-brown heaths, powder-blue chalks – sprang in a cloud
from the clumps of golden ragwort at the lightest touch of a

finger. She could listen as she waited to the thin sweet piping of invisible larks or hear the cuckoo bursting its throat with energy in the pine-woods surrounding the Château.

Her letters to Madeleine – though not her letters to Jessie and Stephen – were vital with descriptions of this new, unusual acquaintance. His companionship held for her the attraction that so often draws the analytical introvert to the dynamic extrovert, for whom problems exist only to be solved. At the end of June she wrote of a half-day which they had spent together at a blue-painted farm near Camiers, known to the Army as 'the Manor House.' Here Meury described to her the landing on June 25th of the First Division of United States troops, for which he had been given a pass to Cherbourg. He was already wearing the badges of an American lieutenant, and had arranged to leave Étaples next day for a gunnery school at Le Touquet.

'Lord, Miss Alleyndene, it certainly gave me a thrill to see our doughboys getting out of those transports and hear the commands given in our own lingo! I didn't know how homesick I'd been till I heard that.'

'I wonder,' mused Ruth, whose once insistent political pre-occupations had been revived by a bundle of newspapers from home, 'how much difference America being in will make to the peace terms – if peace ever comes? You seem to be the only people who have brought ideas into the War as well as guns – that's if President Wilson really means what he says about no compensation and no conquest and no humiliation of the enemy. What do you think of his suggestion of a League for Peace – or a League of Nations, as he's begun to call it?'

Meury looked meditatively at the ducks quacking and quarrelling on the edge of the broad quivering pond in front of them.

'Can't say I've given much thought to it at all. My family are Republicans and we've no great opinion of Wilson – though I guess my dad's paper'll back him now he's taken us into the War. In a way my country's a kind of religion to me – I wept like a kid when I saw those boys land – but all this idealism the President talks, well, I just don't know.'

'But you'd like to see America take the lead in promoting world peace after the War, wouldn't you?'

'Sure, I'd be glad of anything to put an end to war. I've seen too much of it to want another generation to go through what I have. There's not a word about it in the letter your brother sent you I don't endorse. I'm all for my country helping to root it out of the world if it can be done – by a League of Nations or any other darn thing – but I figure it's going to take centuries to put over a new notion of that kind.'

'It isn't so new as all that. People have had the same idea in other ages; I used to write about it in my Oxford essays. You must have come across Grotius and Sully in your lectures at Harvard – to say nothing of William Penn.'

'Well,' he admitted, 'I did get credits for History, certainly, but I'm blest if I remember a thing about it now. I'm not like you; I'm no sort of a highbrow. At Harvard I got through school without flunking, but polo and baseball and skiing were more in my line. I never gave a damn for politics.'

'And yet your father runs a newspaper and mine makes pots!'

'Your brother did tell me. It's funny the way heredity works out. I guess I've never thought about things just the way you do, analysing people's motives and tracing the effect of their actions and all that. Maybe I feel more than I think, and it's all such a confusion sometimes, the mixture of Europe and America in me, it just gets me down. I'd say' – he struggled valiantly for words in which to make articulate his dawning thought – 'I'd say I'm just like hundreds of American boys of my own class, with all the coming and going and pioneering of our forbears moulding us and making us do things for reasons we don't really understand.'

'Can you explain at all why you went into our Army when you did? That interests me a good deal.'

'I didn't stand for any of this hero business; I can promise you that. I've a lot of Europe in me, and being over there at the time the adventure of it just got me. I wanted to be in it before any of our boys at home, but now America's coming over I feel all thrilled and wrought up. I don't know just how it is or why, but something in the idea of the United States makes me get emotional. Now and again, when I picture those huge prairies back home and the mixture of peoples in the cities and the rush of the traffic in New York – why, I find the tears running down my cheeks the way they did at Cherbourg!'

It had seemed important to her at the time, that discussion, evoking national issues and the conflicting standards of old and new civilisations. But it was eclipsed in her mind, because of the aftermath, by another conversation over an omelette and coffee a week or so later. Safely concealed from inquisitive observers in the small back garden of the *estaminet* at Condette, they had talked for the first time about his family in America.

'You see,' he explained to her that evening, 'my people were French, way back. I guess that's one reason I took to the War.'

'Why,' she exclaimed, 'so were some of mine! One of my Alleyndene ancestors married a Huguenot woman from a family called Fourdrinier. They were silk-workers who settled in Staffordshire after the Revocation of the Edict of Nantes.'

'Well, that's something to live up to!' cried Meury with admiring envy. 'I can't match that; I was only talking about my grandfather, Christopher Meury. He came over from Paris in the eighteen-fifties with his Italian wife to be the Washington correspondent of *L'Avenir*. A friend put him wise to a deal in real estate, and he bought our paper, *The Atlantic Daily Ledger*, with the profits. It was just on the edge of folding up, but he pulled it together and it's going strong now, with offices in Boston and Washington and Atlanta, besides New York. The idea is I'll go on it in some capacity and take over from my dad one day, but the Lord knows what I'll be fit for after this little old War!'

'Then you don't know where your father's people came from originally?'

'Not before my great-grandfather. He spelt his name with an "i" instead of a "y" and lived in Marseilles. Gosh, wouldn't it be queer if your people used to know mine, ages back?'

'I wonder if they did!' she cried, smiling as a sudden feeling of enchantment swept over her. Somehow this coincidence of nationality seemed to forge a new link between them. When you came to think of it there was a remote resemblance in their height and colouring and the oval thinness of their faces, though her peat-coloured hair was crisp and springy where his had the blue-black smoothness of heavy floss silk, and her eyes were grey and deep-set while his sparkled beneath their thick curling lashes with the golden-brown gaiety of southern lands. His full lips, kindly and firm, were southern too, with their suggestion of latent passion; but only a young, striving people could have moulded the strong profile and dominant chin.

'I suppose,' she added, 'you're American both sides?'

'Sure – but like most Americans I'm a pretty good mixture of half Europe. My mother was a Vandermeer – one of our old Dutch-American families; it's from them I get my maypole stature. And then, of course, there's the bit of Italian in me from my grandmother, though we didn't talk too much about that till the Italians became our gallant allies.'

'You seem to be everything but English,' she remarked, fascinated by the conglomeration of races out of which, in only three generations, the United States had welded him into the definite, unmistakable type which the world recognised as American.

'That's a fact, Miss Alleyndene, and I certainly regret it. I've been crazy about your country ever since my dad took me over there for a vacation when I was a kid of twelve. Still,' he added resolutely, as though he were reciting a set piece which he was determined to get through, 'I'll have remedied that in the next generation. The girl I'm engaged to comes of real old English stock. She's from Boston and her father was a professor at Harvard.'

Ruth looked up involuntarily at the western sky, for it seemed to her that a cloud must have drifted over the face of the sinking sun. But it still glowed with undiminished benevolence upon the vivid contours of the summer land.

'What's her name?' she asked, after a barely perceptible pause.

'She's called Dallas Lowell, and she's as cute as she can be – very small, with blue eyes and real flaxen hair. Of course, it was partly because of her my dad got so mad with me for joining up; he wanted to see us get married soon and start a new generation to carry on the paper. I'm the only son, you see; the others are all girls. But he's forgiven me now; I guess Dallas made him. She's been just fine; she's waited for me three years and she still writes me by every mail.'

'Have you a photograph of her?'

'Yes. I've carried it through every show I've been in.'

He took his note-case from his pocket and handed Ruth a small tinted photograph. She looked down at the delicate, exquisite features of a very young girl with clear china-blue eyes like a Dresden shepherdess and hair the pale sunlit yellow of a woodland primrose.

'How pretty she is!' said Ruth with sincere admiration, though the words seemed to emphasise the curious blankness which had fallen upon the day.

'You're right there, Ruth,' he responded. 'Of course, she's only a kid. She wasn't nineteen when we got engaged, my last term at Harvard. That only makes her twenty-two in another month's time.'

'Life does seem to age one out here,' Ruth observed slowly. 'I've just had my own twenty-third birthday – it was a fortnight ago – but I expect I'd seem like a hundred, compared with her.'

'You're only a year older than Dallas, then, and a year and a bit younger than me, but if she could see us I guess we'd both look like war-worn veterans. She's been to college since I came over here, but her home life's pretty slow; there's nothing to change her. Look here,' he added irrelevantly, 'I'm about through with this Miss Alleyndene business. Why don't I call you Ruth all the time?'

'Why not? You can if you like.'

'And you'll call me Eugene?'

'No!' she cried, with a laugh that touched some hitherto unsuspected chord of pain, 'I won't call you Eugeen! You come of French stock and you've got a beautiful French name, and I refuse to murder it. I'll call you Eugène, or nothing.'

'I guess you're right about that,' he said. 'We don't give our foreign names a chance. Anyway, call me what you darn well choose . . . Why, you're not going, are you?'

'I oughtn't to be too late to-night,' she said. 'I'd better get back before it's dark. Fortunately Parker – the woman who shares my hut – thinks I'm a model of good behaviour, but even she may get suspicious if I always rush in exactly at ten.'

'But it's not eight o'clock yet! Do stay a while longer, Ruth,' he urged.

'I think I mustn't – Eugene. And perhaps it'll be a good idea if I walk back. You really oughtn't to run me so near the hospital every time,' she added, impelled by an urgent desire to be alone and confront – well, what? What was it that she had to think out? She wasn't quite sure, but it was something imperative.

'You're sure it's not too far?'

'Oh, no; it's only two or three miles. It'll do me good.'

'Well – if that's the way you feel about it . . .'

He took her hand and led her through the *estaminet* in the brotherly, informal fashion to which she was growing accustomed. It could only be her imagination which tricked her into thinking that he looked at her with a new haunting intentness as she waved her hand to him and walked on alone.

After all, she was a bit tired that evening. It must be due to the heavy morning of abdominal dressings, she decided, as she moved slowly between the holm-oaks and hazels to the corner by the Pré Catelan restaurant, where the dusty white road with its narrow accompanying tram-route turned downhill between the pine-woods to the dune-encircled coast of Hardelot-Plage. There were clumps of anchusa, she noticed, growing between the tram-lines – blue and violet-shaded anchusa with turquoise-tipped magenta stamens and tight pink buds sheathed in green cases . . .

In that far-off Renaissance country which she could barely imagine, Eugene Meury had fondled and caressed the blue-eyed, flaxen-haired girl whose portrait he carried. Dallas Lowell had the right to feel his touch, to receive his kisses, to experience that further knowledge of him which would one day make her his wife. With the direct reaction to primitive situations which the crudities of war had so quickly made habitual even to young women brought up amidst the prim circumlocutions of pre-war provincial society, Ruth's mind dwelt resolutely upon the future relationship of Dallas and Eugene.

'She will lie in his arms,' she thought. 'She will have his child.'

And suddenly, as that vividly pictured embrace possessed her imagination, something which had long lain dormant sprang within her to violent life. A strange sensation, as recognisable and compelling as it was unfamiliar, tore sharply through the deepest recesses of her being; her breasts tingled and her blood, turned to fever-heat by desire, flooded her face with burning colour.

'Oh, God!' she cried aloud, still thinking of Dallas. 'Oh, God, I can't bear it!'

Exhausted by the automatic and overwhelming responses of her body to the acute images called up by her mind, she turned aside from the road into the forest and sank limply on the carpet of pine needles beneath the tall, gently swaying trees. It was no longer in her power to decide whether she would confront her predicament; the predicament itself confronted her. It had seized her with both hands and shaken her out of the dreamy half-knowledge in which her sexual emotions had dwelt undisturbed.

'I love him! I'm in love with Eugene Meury! . . . Oh, why didn't I know that love meant what's just happened to me? Why didn't I know!' she repeated aghast, realising with a self-contempt that relegated her naïve ignorance to a part already archaic, that hitherto she had imagined love to be no more than a romantic inclination of the mind. 'So that's why I made Madeleine angry! That's why Susan Shepherd despised me!'

Like one awakened from a trance she looked with the heightened perceptiveness of anguish at the scene before her. Already intensified by the stimulus of life lived under the shadow of death, its outlines and colours had now acquired a sharpness unknown to the landscapes of normal experience; the rose-tinged whiteness of the sandhills seen through the dark tree-trunks against the vehement blue of the sunset sea would remain in her memory for ever. Trembling beneath the indifferent feathery pines, bereft of strength to a degree commensurate with the poignant keenness of her vision, Ruth knew herself to have passed from the chrysalis stage of immaturity into the bitter, incomparable awareness which constitutes the final essence of adulthood.

11

'DEAR RUTH,' wrote Eugene from the Officers' Training School at Camberley in the middle of September, 'Thanks a lot for your last note. It is fine to hear that you expect to come over on ten days' leave at the end of next week; also that you plan to spend your second weekend in London. You must be needing a rest badly after the terrible rush of wounded that has been coming to you from the Ypres sector during the last month or so.

'I want you to know that I am counting on you to take dinner with me at the Savoy on one of your days in town. We might go to a show afterwards if you would care for that. It is perhaps a bit too soon at this writing to ask you to fix an evening? If you could make it Saturday I could get away earlier than the other days, but please do not put yourself out one bit on my account. Should some other time suit you better, you can be sure I shall be there whenever you say.

'You don't know how delighted I am at the thought of meeting you again.

'With all kind regards,
'Cordially yours,
'EUGENE C. MEURY.'

'DEAR EUGENE,' Ruth replied.

'Very many thanks for your letter and kind invitation. It will give me a great deal of pleasure to have dinner with you and go to the theatre afterwards. I have promised to go straight to Dene Hall from Folkestone, but I shall return to town on the Friday evening, September 28th, and stay until Tuesday with my friend Madeleine Gibson at her flat in Lincoln's Inn Fields. Saturday evening will therefore suit me very well indeed.

'The battle for Passchendaele Ridge seems no nearer an end than it did three weeks ago. [Recalling the Censor, she crossed out the words 'Passchendaele Ridge' and substituted "the battle you mention."] The convoys are coming down as fast as ever and we get practically no off-duty time, but

Matron says we must have our leave just the same or we shall never get through the autumn. Everyone seems to think the fighting in that particular sector may go on till Christmas unless the weather makes it impossible. I do not know if any of your people are up there with our troops, but I am glad that your course will keep you in England till the end of October.

'Looking forward to seeing you on Saturday September 29th.

'Yours sincerely,
'RUTH ALLEYNDENE.'

Ruth read her letter over three times before she decided to send it. She posted it with the feeling that she had lost a battle which she did not particularly want to win. I shall see him again, her heart sang ecstatically; and she handled her suffering patients with the remorseful tenderness of one who sees life beckoning to her at the very moment that she is conducting others through the gate of death. I shall see him again. I know I oughtn't to, but I daresay I shall manage not to give myself away. After all, I've had a good deal of practice in hiding my feelings.

Was it, she still wondered, just a coincidence – his transfer to England almost immediately after that evening at Condette? It could not have been more than ten days later that she received his first letter from Camberley, telling her that he was attached to the Officers' Training School there for three months.

'It's a way of letting me know I shan't hear any more of him,' she thought, but she could not resist sending a friendly though brief reply. Precisely six days afterwards another letter, characteristically brisk and executive with its trenchant American phrases, awaited her in the rack. Since then they had arrived at the rate of one or two a week, provoking her to recurrent speculations and violent outbursts of perverse happiness, followed by equally desperate renunciations.

She arrived at Dene Hall, still tired and footsore after the uncounted days on her feet, to find the convalescent officers now completely in possession. Cues, playing cards and ping-pong balls littered the billiard-room; gramophone records resounded from the drawing-room, the morning-room, the garden. Strongly as she approved of their presence, the officers' conversation and demands seemed to turn Dene Hall into a pale replica of 73 General, and the disappearance of her friends Arthur Wardle and Jim Hardiman added to her vague sense of fatigued disappointment. Wardle, her father told her, was in prison as a conscientious objector; Hardiman had been called up under the Derby scheme and was serving in Palestine. Their absence, it seemed, and that of many others like them, had now diverted Stephen's attention from the Volunteers.

'Your father's got something else to do but form fours on the cricket field. What with these new taxes and all our skilled workmen being called up, I don't know how we're going to carry on. The girls do their best, but they can't replace a man who's been throwing or mould-making for a dozen years or more.'

Jessie was now absorbed in her patients' welfare to the complete exclusion of every other interest. On the rare occasions that Ruth saw her mother, her conversation was confined to meat-cards, bread-rations and the complications caused in a household by different categories of food-tickets. Neither Jessie nor Stephen asked Ruth for any details of her life in France; to them it was an alien, irrelevant country about which they did not want to hear. It was not until the day before she left for London that Ruth had any talk with her mother which approached the tentative frontiers of intimacy.

'Couldn't you possibly stay until Saturday evening, dear?' urged Jessie, becoming conscious of Ruth's presence just as she was about to be deprived of it. 'Madeleine would still have you for Sunday and Monday. When you do see her, by the way, I hope you'll persuade her to take things more quietly. She was here for a week at the beginning of the holidays and I didn't think she was looking well at all. She's got a morbid idea she ought to work specially hard because she has nobody at the front now, but I tell her at that rate she won't be fit to marry Jerry when he *is* invalided out of the Army. Now what about stopping till Saturday?'

'I'm afraid I really can't, Mother. It isn't so much Madeleine, but I promised an officer I know that I'd dine with him and go to the theatre on Saturday evening.'

She saw Jessie's interest quicken, as though all her senses had suddenly stood to attention.

'An officer, dear? Somebody from Witnall? One of the Heathcotes or the Tallinors?'

'No, nobody from Witnall. An American officer I met in France.' She saw no reason to add that he had also been Richard's corporal who had once telephoned to her at Dene Hall.

'Oh, an *American*! . . . You know, Ruth, I've always so hoped that when you stopped going backwards and forwards to France and really settled down, it would be with an Englishman – not with a foreigner who'd take you right away from home!'

'Oh, Mother, there's nothing like *that* about it!' exclaimed Ruth, laughing at the dismay in Jessie's face because she wanted so much to cry. 'He's only a friend; he's been engaged to a girl in America since before the War.'

'Well,' said Jessie, looking intensely relieved, 'I'm thankful to hear it. But you'll be careful with him, won't you, dear? Some of these Colonials are very wild.'

'Really, Mother, I do know how to take care of myself by this time!' Ruth assured her. Anyhow Eugene isn't a Colonial, she added under her breath, but she knew that Australians, South Africans, Canadians and Americans were all one to Jessie.

At Madeleine's pretty three-roomed flat in Lincoln's Inn Fields she felt for the first time that she was really on leave. They went together that evening to the Connoisseur's Theatre to see the thousandth performance of Ellison Campbell's famous war play, *Great Possessions*. The distinguished dramatist was there herself in a box, but Ruth and Madeleine were too far away in the dress circle to see her clearly.

'Her hair looks as if it's gone quite grey,' Madeleine observed.

Ruth bent forward, but still could not get a distinct view of the stiff angular figure.

'I'm not sure. It may be only the light.'

Madeleine certainly did appear fragile and tired, she thought when they returned home. The extra teaching at Holborn

High School required by wartime economy and the evening ambulance-driving on depleted rations were obviously taxing her frail constitution severely. But when she left for the High School early next morning, Ruth forgot her at once. Looking out of the window at the plane-trees turning brown and yellow in the pleasant square, she decided to spend the savings of many months from her meagre salary upon a new evening dress and cloak in which to meet Eugene. After a prolonged search through Regent Street she chose a silk taffeta of the deep sapphire blue that suited her so well, with shaded flowers at the waist – the blue and violet shades of the anchusa which grew beside the road from the pine-woods to Hardelot-Plage. To wear over it she bought a sapphire-blue cloak of thin soft velvet, with a tiny turned-back collar of grey chinchilla framing her face.

When she swung through the doorway of the Savoy restaurant early that evening, her composed dignity of bearing gave no indication of the restless pounding of her heart. Eugene was already waiting in the lounge. For a second he looked at her half startled, barely recognising her; then he hurried eagerly to the doorway and seized both her hands.

'Gosh, you look lovely in that blue get-up! Do you realise I've never seen you in mufti before?'

He led her through the still half-empty restaurant to their table, and they sat down and looked at each other for several moments without speaking. She's just like a beautiful Madonna, he thought, examining intently the pale serious face, the delicate aquiline nose, the level dark brows over inscrutable, deep-set eyes.

'Do you know,' he said aloud, 'I've been wondering all afternoon if you'd be changed? Crazy of me, isn't it, when it's not three months since I saw you last?'

'Well, I must be crazy too, because I've been wondering about you in just the same way.'

'You have, Ruth! . . . I'm not sure now that you *aren't* a bit different! Your face seems as if it were thinner somehow. I guess you had a frightful time with all those wounded guys coming down from Ypres.'

'Yes,' she said, crumbling her roll. 'It's been a pretty ghastly six weeks altogether – but I'm going to forget about it all, just for to-night.'

Forget? Forget? I can forget the wounded perhaps, but how can I forget, with him beside me, what I thought about all the time I was nursing them? Looking up at his vivacious brown eyes, his lean smiling face, his long capable hands thinly covered with fine dark hair, she hardly noticed the swift unobtrusive changing of the courses nor realised what variety of skilfully camouflaged ration the dishes contained. They discussed idly what show they would see, but by eight o'clock they still had not decided between *Round the Map* at the Alhambra, *The Maid of the Mountains* at Daly's, and *Chu Chin Chow*, to which Eugene, with increasing enthusiasm, had already been three times.

The restaurant was crowded now with officers in diversities of uniform accompanied by beautiful women in evening dress, struggling with gay lips and haunted eyes to capture for a companion whose life might end to-morrow the lovely transitoriness of the fleeting moment. Through the desperately bright, scintillating atmosphere throbbed the light sad notes of the orchestra playing *Un Peu d' Amour*. Was it Ruth's fancy that Eugene's mobile features suddenly hardened into sharp lines of pain? She herself could have howled like a baby with frustration and longing as she listened to George du Maurier's tender, poignant words:

> '*La vie est vaine—*
> *Un peu d'amour,*
> *Un peu de haine*
> *Et puis – bonjour!*
>
> '*La vie est brève—*
> *Un peu d'espoir,*
> *Un peu de rêve,*
> *Et puis – bonsoir!*'

'My check, please,' said Eugene abruptly to the waiter. He turned to Ruth.

'Are you really set on a show? Doesn't it seem kind of stuffy

in town to-night? It's a grand evening – why don't we run out
a little way in my car and get some air?'

'I'd like that much better,' Ruth said honestly. Nothing mattered if she could be alone with Eugene for a while longer – near
to him and alone.

'You won't be cold in that thin wrap?'

'Oh, no, I'm sure I shan't. It's as warm as a summer evening.'

12

She got into his car and they turned south-westward, driving
through Westminster and Chelsea to Putney Bridge. He crossed
the bridge and, climbing Putney Hill, took the road which forked
right between Putney Heath and Wimbledon Common.

Beyond the London streets the September night seemed incomparable in its tranquil beauty. Translucent fleeces of diaphanous
cloud floated in the deep brilliant sky, where the brightness of
the stars was dimmed by a vivid giant moon. The shadows of
occasional pedestrians walked with their owners, sharp-edged
and long, doubled and sometimes trebled by the slanting rays
of moonlight. At the edge of the heath the silver birches,
standing in erect martial ranks, cast their impalpable images
across the grass like elongated spectres, black and grotesque.
As the country opened out the birches glimmered grey and
ghostly against the darker clumps of hazel and oak, twisting
in strange umbrella-shaped curves above the thick undergrowth
of bracken and gorse. Here and there soft drifts of thin fog
lay in the hollows beneath the trees. The fragrant smell of
the damp autumn earth rose richly into the mild evening air.
Shining patches of moonlight showed the ground starred with
white clover and pale clusters of yarrow.

Eugene stopped his car at a clearing just beyond King's Mere.
From the unruffled mirror of the jet-black water the moon shone
huge and incandescent. Leaving the car on the grass near the
main road to Roehampton Vale, he took Ruth's arm to save
her from stumbling and turned down a path which curved
across the heath towards Wimbledon. Beside it ran a dry,

shallow ditch filled with thistles and sorrel, and fringed with clumps of brown feathery grass. In front of them the windmill on Wimbledon Common, turned to a brilliant whiteness by the moon, appeared a colossal phantom with arms extended for a spectral embrace.

After a few moments of walking Eugene stopped, drawing Ruth's hand into his.

'Look here,' he said in a voice that shook, 'I shouldn't have brought you out to this dark lane on such a gorgeous night. You're too darned attractive!'

She seemed to have waited so long to hear those words that for a moment the earth stood still, and the moon, the trees, the grotesque shadows across the heath, became in that instant transfixed in her memory. How shall I bear this exquisite happiness? It is too much; it will destroy me.

She answered quietly, 'That's what I feel about you, Eugene.'

With the lightning urgency of released passion he folded her in his arms; his kisses pressed so hard upon her lips that she swayed backwards, half faint from the surging conflict of joy and pain. Clasping him convulsively she hid her burning face against his shoulder, and felt his hands groping importunately about her neck, her breasts, her hair. She seemed to have passed through æons of acute experience before his grip relaxed and he stood looking down at her, his body tense, his eyes dark with anguish.

'Oh, Eugene!' she cried, half laughing, half weeping, 'I've been fighting against this ever since that evening you told me about . . . her.'

His grasp tightened again; she felt the soft remorseful pressure of his fingers against her breast.

'Darling,' he said anxiously, 'I could have kicked myself that night for not telling you before – I felt no end of a damn swine . . . You see, it had been just grand taking you out and talking to you after all those years in the ranks and never meeting a decent girl of my own sort. I knew right away it was dangerous for me, because you're so beautiful, and when I wasn't with you I couldn't get your face out of my head. I've watched it in my tent, growing out of the darkness like a flower, and yet when I saw you again it was always better than my dream. But I thought I could hold myself in and not let you know.'

She listened with a catch in her breath. His eager words seemed to enrich her personality like water flooding a parched land, bringing fruitfulness to the stony valleys, life and colour to the barren hills.

'You see,' he continued, 'I never guessed you'd give a damn for a guy like me, after what you'd told me about going to Oxford and getting First Class Honours and all that. I'm not intellectual, and I don't go thinking things upside down and inside out the way you do.'

'Why did you imagine I was so ready to meet you and take the risk of getting found out?'

'Oh, I figured you were feeling bad about your brother and a bit lonesome . . . Then when I talked about our people having maybe known each other way back in France and you seemed so taken by the idea, well, it struck me you just might be feeling one ten-thousandth part of what I was, and I thought I ought to tell you about Dallas before it went any further . . . And when I'd told you and you cut off home a good two hours before you had to – why, then I began to catch on, and I just cursed myself no end. I knew I oughtn't to see you any more, and that's why I got myself transferred to England.'

'You can't imagine how I watched every post, wondering whether I should hear from you again!'

'Well, maybe you shouldn't have – but when I got to Camberley it was just hell not meeting you and seeing your face and hearing your lovely English voice. It got me down and I *had* to write – but I know I shouldn't have done it, any more than I ought to be out here with you now . . . because, you see, I can't throw Dallas over after she's waited three years.'

'No, you can't give her up . . . I do realise that, my dear.'

'Anyhow, not while the War's on,' he said, struggling like a captive to find the weak spot in his prison wall. 'Not till I've seen her again. But, darling – it's just hell to have to say it but I guess I've got to – I'll have to go through with it then if she still wants me. You see, her family and mine have been friends since before I was born. It was because of her father I went to

Harvard instead of Princeton, and since we've been engaged my
dad's made her eldest brother our representative at the Boston
office. God, once this War's over the whole lot of them'll be
sitting around waiting to kill the fatted calf for our wedding!'

He covered his face in despair and groaned.

Ruth laid her hand tenderly on his bent head with its thick
ruffled hair gleaming black in the moonlight.

'Never mind, my love. Let's make the most of each other while
we can.'

The most? What was the most? They stood looking mournfully at one another, their young flesh aflame and quivering,
but between them stood more than the fair fragile wraith of
Dallas Lowell. Torn by a contest between his upbringing and
his desires which all but annihilated his slender philosophical
resources, Eugene gathered her into his arms once more.

'Kiss us again, darling!'

He had hardly spoken when the dull thud of a distant gun
reverberated through the night, carrying to London the sinister
warning of an air-raid. The moon now rode triumphantly in the
bright iridescent sky; above the patches of low mist the air was
still and very clear. As they listened, grown suddenly taut in each
other's arms, a far-away dog barked and whined. Immediately
the sound had died away, a brilliant fountain of star-shells
from the batteries on the outskirts of London announced the
approach of the raiders. The white calcium lights seemed to
soar slowly upward and drift away on the gentle wind. They
had not disappeared when the roar of falling bombs began to
mingle hideously with the clamour and clatter of the anti-aircraft
bombardment.

When the first explosion echoed violently across the common,
rocking the ground beneath their feet with the nightmare oscil-
lations of an earthquake, Ruth felt a convulsive shudder pass
through the man beside her. As a second reverberation sounded
nearer, the hand that held hers became damp and cold, but
not a tremor shook the cheerful voice in which, immediately,
he spoke.

'I guess that's Jerry dropping his pills again – and not so darned
far away from us either!'

She knew, then, the cost of his heroism; she realised, from the quiver of his flesh communicated to hers, the long story of raids and attacks and bombardments in which his indomitable spirit had conquered the shrinking panic of his body until Richard had been able to write, believing it, 'He doesn't know what fear is.' This is superb courage that I am witnessing, she thought; the conquest over nerves tortured by a thousand indescribable experiences that I can't even imagine. Dear, dear Eugene, I haven't a shred of your reason for being shocked and shaken. I mustn't lose my nerve; I must help you all I can.

'It did sound quite near,' she said aloud. 'I expect the bombs are falling somewhere by the river. The guns will probably follow its track; they nearly always do.'

The reverberations seemed closer now. Puffs of smoke from the bursting shells floated across the face of the moon; two long luminous pencils of searchlight made a white pointed roof over the heath. Suddenly, almost above their heads, droned the intermittent hum of a Gotha engine. The searchlight seemed to locate it, for at once the shrapnel from the anti-aircraft guns began to beat like hail upon the thicket of silver birches across the main road.

At the first sound of it Eugene encircled Ruth with his arms and drew her down with him into the deep ditch beside the path. They were barely concealed there when a terrific explosion, nearer than any which had yet occurred, rocked the earth where they lay, and a roar followed as though the ground itself had burst asunder. To Ruth's amazement her hands were still warm and dry; she held Eugene's tightly in hers as she lay clasped in his protective embrace. Even in that moment of mortal terror, his nearness and the compelling power of his physical virility entered her blood and turned it to flame. At least, she thought, if we die, we die together. God, give me strength; help me to help him and be calm myself! Don't let me show my fear or do anything to make him ashamed of me!

But that shattering roar was the last. Whether or not the aeroplane had escaped it dropped no more bombs, and a sudden palpitating silence, audible and almost tangible, followed its departure.

When the silence had lasted for five minutes Eugene helped Ruth to stand up, and they climbed out of the ditch to see, not far away, a flickering redness of fire against the sky. In its sinister light the black silhouette of Richmond Park appeared sharply outlined, as though carved from tin.

'Gosh, you've got some courage!' he exclaimed, wiping his forehead. 'If it hadn't been for you, darling, I'd have lost my nerve. That's the worst of being out of the line for a bit; your clockwork runs down.'

'It doesn't cost me anything to have courage, as you call it,' Ruth responded gaily. She felt half-drunk with exhilaration – the matchless exhilaration of danger survived, of fear overcome, of love found equal to a sudden demand. 'I've only been in danger once before in my life,' she continued, 'and that was when my room-mate at Wimereux threw herself out of the window and nearly dragged me with her! But you . . . I think you're the bravest man I've ever known.'

'I guess not just now, darling. Maybe I'll remember how to act like a hero when I'm out there again . . . Look here, Ruth, I think I ought to start driving you home. I bet you're pretty well shaken up, though you certainly don't show it, and if the bombs have fallen around this heath it may take us hours to get back. Your friend Madeleine will be throwing fits thinking you're dead!'

She took his arm and they walked slowly, reluctantly, across the heath back to the car. A big dent, they found, decorated its bonnet, and several fragments of shrapnel lay on the driver's seat. As he started the engine Ruth turned and looked at the moonlit lane where he had first pressed his urgent kisses upon her mouth. Those moments, at least, were hers until death eclipsed her power to recall them. With tense eagerness she sought to memorise every incident, to keep her recollections intact lest one day they should become all that she had left.

She never forgot the crowds that night on Putney Bridge, the clanging bells of struggling fire-engines, the arrested traffic, the rumours, the noise, the confusion. Two persons, they learnt, had been killed close to the river, on Putney Common; two lovers sitting under a tree clasped in each other's arms . . . Nearly three hours went by before Eugene could penetrate the thronged humanity packing the streets between Putney and Holborn, and put Ruth down in Lincoln's Inn Fields.

Beneath the shaded light in the tiny dark hall he held her close and sought her lips once more.

'It isn't good-bye, is it, Eugene? I shall see you again before I go back?'

'You can bet your life on that. Whatever happens I'll come up and see you off at Victoria . . . darling, my darling . . .'

In the flat Madeleine, pallid and shaken, rushed to the door at the first rattle of Ruth's key in the lock.

'Oh, Ruth! Thank God you're safe! It's so late I thought you must be hurt; the noise here has been simply terrific. Why, what ever *has* happened to your lovely cloak? I thought you'd been to the theatre?'

Glancing down, Ruth saw the deep creases in the blue velvet, the fragments of grass and straw which clung, hitherto unnoticed, to the delicate pile and soft fluffy fur.

'I never went. We drove out to Wimbledon Common instead. A bomb dropped quite near us and we had to take cover in a ditch . . . Oh, what *does* it matter! I've never been so happy in my life before! Eugene's in love with me, Madeleine. He told me he loved me to-night.'

Madeleine looked keenly at her, troubled and bewildered.

'But I thought you told me he was engaged to a girl in America?'

'So he is – but what do I care!' she cried deliriously. '*I'm* the person he loves – I, you understand, not Dallas! When it's all over he can go back to America and marry her if he must, but he's mine for the duration of the War!'

'Oh, Ruth!' began Madeleine, but the expression on Ruth's face checked her words of protest, of warning.

'Dear Ruth,' she said gently, and took her into her arms.

13

Ruth was barely conscious of her return journey to Hardelot, so deeply was she immersed in re-living her last moments with Eugene before the leave train left Victoria. At Boulogne she was still feeling the vehemence of his kisses which had bruised her lips, the clinging vitality of his ardent embrace. She roused herself from her waking dream sufficiently to be thankful that movement orders were not – as so often in the nursing services – the consequence of her leave. A Red Cross transport ambulance took her back to the lovely village where the sand-dunes, the pines, the deep flower-filled meadows were now hallowed for her and glorified, because she had shared them with Eugene.

At 73 General the Matron, Miss Eveleigh, greeted Ruth with as much enthusiasm as a Regular Army Sister ever permitted herself to show to a V.A.D. She regarded Nurse Alleyndene as one of her best workers; a studious, reserved type of girl, but thoroughly conscientious and capable. In her experience these intellectual types were usually the most trustworthy, though she could never get her Ward-Sisters to believe it. The red efficiency stripe on Ruth's sleeve, testifying to twelve continuous months of good service in Army hospitals, reminded Miss Eveleigh that she was about due for a second. She deserves it, she thought; she's worked hard. I must remember to put in for it.

'And how is Mr Meury?' she asked unexpectedly.

Ruth started, taken completely by surprise. What does she know? How much has she guessed? Not all her long practice of self-control could prevent her from blushing as she replied, 'Oh, he's quite safe at the moment, thank you. I saw him once or twice in England; he's over there at a Training School for officers.'

'A very fine type of young American,' commented Miss Eveleigh graciously. She judged Ruth to be a girl who would not love lightly – unlike some of her nurses, who seemed discontented unless they picked up a new young man every week – and like all normal, unembittered persons, she took pleasure in a developing romance.

Her own emotional experience with a naval commander in Malta – husband of a pretty young wife and father of two attractive children – had not embittered her even though she herself had dissuaded him from deserting his family and ruining his career on her account. She did not regret her resolution. If she had decided otherwise the commander would not now be an Admiral nor she a Matron, but she often wished that their standards and traditions had not prevented them from making a fuller use of the many opportunities which they had conscientiously repudiated. The whole episode was responsible for her critical attitude towards the sex-segregation policy of British Army hospitals, which never, she considered, succeeded in separating those who deeply desired to be together. She was even capable of discreet blindness to breaches of discipline when she felt that the interests of the parties demanded it.

Though breaches of discipline had temporarily lost their allurement, Ruth spent that autumn in a deep glowing preoccupation which, despite the prodigal tragedy of Passchendaele, renewed for her the compelling magic of the spring.

'Whatever's the matter with you, Alleyndene?' protested Parker, her neglected room-mate. 'You're never what I'd call garrulous at the best of times, but since you went on leave you've been as mum as an oyster. If I'd ever seen you look at a man I should think you were in love!'

But Ruth only smiled. Keep it to yourself, her instinct said. This incomparable thing is my very own. Even sharing it with Madeleine made it a little less mine. Again and again in her scanty hours off duty she crossed the wooden bridge leading to the pine-woods from the Chemin du Pont Saint-Augustin, or lingered in the marshy meadows near the old Château d'Hardelot, reconstructing those walks and talks with Eugene of which the significance was now so radiantly clear.

Every three or four mornings came his short, incisive notes, couched in that mingling of sixteenth-century speech forms with New World vernacular which makes American a language quite other than English. Every three or four evenings went back her longer replies – 'highbrow letters,' she told herself, 'and much duller than his, but I don't care so long as he goes on wanting

them.' In November she learnt that he was returning to France
to be attached as regimental observer to a British regiment,
'which I'm told is near Cambrai.' After nearly a week of waiting,
restlessly expectant, in the hospital camp lest he should come to
see her on his way up the line, a letter arrived marked with the
familiar triangle of the active service censor. He and a British
officer, he told her, had crossed the Channel in charge of
a draft which they had been obliged to take straight on to
Armentières.

'I daresay you'll figure how I cursed and swore at your Old
Contemptibles in the Transport Office when I found I couldn't
get two hours to run over and see you. If the entire British Army
had been held up going over the top till our draft came along, you
may bet your bottom dollar we would have been kept cooling our
heels in Boulogne for four whole days. But just because nobody
had been busy scheming a big jamboree, the darn train was there
waiting for us in the siding!'

He was at the front again. True, he was only a regimental
observer, but she knew Eugene by now. He wasn't one to keep
to a passive rôle in the danger zone when others were active.
She covered her eyes as though she could shield them from the
shadowy fires of imagined shell-explosions which had beset her
vision all the time that Richard was in Gallipoli.

At the end of November she went on night duty in a medical
ward supervised by Sister Plummer, a little round robin of
a Lancashire woman belonging to a batch of trained nurses
recently recruited from civilian life, who had come to Hardelot
after a few months at Abbeville. Hospital rumour credited her
with a past, and she was apparently engaged, astonishing as it
seemed, in periodically maintaining a present. Ruth found her
avid descriptions of her adventures irksome and nauseating,
though she could not help but respect her standard of devotion
to her patients. Their thirty beds were divided between lightly-
gassed cases progressing wheezily towards recovery, malarias
whose paroxysms of shivering fever would recur throughout
their lives, and nephritics with puffed cheeks and swollen eye-
lids slipping somnolently to death. In the middle of December
they took in a number of mustard-gas cases from Cambrai,

their twisted lips discoloured, their blinded eyes blistered and suppurating. From Cambrai. From Cambrai.

The hut stood close to the sea on the edge of the dunes. Against the sloping sand-hills the waves pounded heavily, instead of crashing as they had crashed upon the cliffs at Wimereux. Why then was Ruth haunted for the first time since she had come to Hardelot by the whimpering ghost of Susan Shepherd? Why did she hear, in the dead hours of the winter nights, the thin whine of her plaintive cry?

'Ow, Alleyndene, if only I'd had 'im! If I'd had 'im just the once, I wouldn't tyke on so, I swear!'

'Oh, leave me in peace!' she would cry desperately to that pathetic wraith, but its visitations left her with a heritage of disquieting questions. Had it been fair, she asked herself as she read Eugene's brief, ardent letters, to rouse his emotions in the way that she had – emotions which the cruelty of circumstance forbade her ever fully to satisfy? Her knowledge of masculine needs and impulses was vague and incomplete, but the conversation of the Army nurses, appended to her mother's half-veiled hints throughout her girlhood, had left her with the impression that the desires of men were persistent and formidable. Suppose, she reflected, Eugene was driven by prolonged frustration into Richard's expedient and thence into Richard's way of escape? Again and again, terror seized her.

By Christmas, with its accumulated burden of memory from other wartime Christmases, the worst mustard-gas cases were dead; the malarias shivered less and slept more; the nephritics lay comatose and undemanding. On Christmas Eve, when Sister Plummer had gone to second supper and she had finished decorating the ward with its brave, sad adornments of scarlet holly and silver cardboard, Ruth sat down before the stove to write to Eugene. ('Oh, where is he now? What is he doing? Let me see him again, O God! Let us make love to each other just once more . . . I'm not sure I really ought to send him this letter. Perhaps I shan't in the end, but I've got to write it.')

She addressed the envelope first, slowly and carefully, pouring her adoration into each syllable of the name that seemed to her so beautiful.

'Lieutenant Eugene Christopher Meury, D.C.M.,
  'American Expeditionary Force,
    'Attached 4th Dorsetshire Yeomanry,
      'B.E.F.,
        'France.'

'MY DEAREST LOVE,' she began,

'It is Christmas Eve and all through my waking hours and even in my dreams I have been thinking of you to-day. This evening before coming on duty I re-read all your letters. I have wanted to do so for so long, yet put it off because I knew the effect they would have on me.

'There are times when I have wished I had gone all through the War without ever meeting you. One was when those mustard-gas cases came down from Cambrai and I realised what you might be facing. But they do not last long, because I cannot imagine life without you now. I cannot even remember what it was like before I knew you. I love you so much that it is no use pretending any longer that I am content just to love you for the duration of the War. When you first told me about Dallas I felt as though something had broken inside me. I accept her prior claim, of course. I always have. If you were disloyal to her you would not be the person I love. But it is no use thinking it will not be harder than death to give you up when the time comes.

'Do not be sorry, though, or feel that you ought not to have spoken as you did on the night of the air-raid. I can bear it; I am glad to bear it for the privilege of knowing you and loving you. I have been through so much since the War began; this is only one thing more, even though it is greater than all the rest put together. I would rather suffer and be alive, than be immune to love and dead, as I was before I met you.

'When I had read your letters you possessed my mind so completely that I wondered if by any chance you had been reading mine and were thinking of me as I was of you. The consciousness of your presence became so strong that, cold and dark as it was, I went for a walk along the frozen road through the pine-woods, and stood under the tree where I first

realised I loved you, that evening after we had supper together
at Condette. I shall never forget the mingled pain and ecstasy
of that sudden knowledge. It was like being born again. I
stayed there afterwards for about half an hour, watching the
sun set over the sea.'

'Writing to your sweetheart, eh?'

Ruth started violently as she looked up to see the round
cheerful face of Sister Plummer, her weather-beaten cheeks red
from the wind, her white cap frosted with feathery unmelted
snowflakes like tiny Christmas birds.

'That's all right, my dear; I'm not prying. Only when a lovely
girl of your age takes to writing letters as long as that, it's
generally her sweetheart who gets them!'

She knelt down in front of the stove, spreading out her hands
to catch its warmth. The red glow turned her short, capable
fingers to rose-pink translucent candles.

'Now what about a nice cup of tea, love? My, it's a cold
night and no mistake! If we don't get six inches of snow by the
morning, my name's not Maggie Plummer!'

When the tea was made Ruth sat dreamily with her cup in
her hand, mentally composing the rest of her letter to Eugene
while Sister Plummer, who never required undue encouragement, relaxed into a series of whispered confidences. Ruth's
silence was mistaken for quiet attention, and before she realised
what its consequence might be she found herself listening to the
tale of Sister Plummer's latest amatory adventure.

'Well, when we got back to Abbeville I said to him, "Cheerio,
Tom, I suppose it's good-bye?" and he picked up my hand – like
that, you know.' She took Ruth's hand firmly in hers and tickled
the inside of her palm. 'And he said, "No, it needn't be unless you
want. There's an *estaminet* I know down Huchenneville way; it's
got a good room over the bar." So that was that, and on my next
half day . . .'

When the story was concluded Ruth's attention had become
quite genuine, for she perceived the opportunity of asking a
question the answer to which she dreaded yet suddenly felt
impelled to know. She put her inquiry as casually as she could.

'But Sister – didn't it involve taking an awful risk? I mean . . . think how terrible it would have been if you'd found you were going to have a baby. Was it just luck or . . . what?'

'Not up to snuff about that, my dear – a pretty girl like you! Well, I never! It's often enough I've said, What are the mothers of England doing, letting their girls go off to France and elsewhere knowing no more how to take care of themselves than a babe unborn!'

'But what could they tell us? Is it something *you* know?'

A complacent smirk came over the nurse's face.

'I wasn't born yesterday, my dear! There's no need to get caught if you know how to avoid it. I don't say the ways are all fool-proof, but you can guard yourself pretty well if you're careful and take trouble.'

Ruth nerved herself to continue the conversation. There was nothing that she felt less inclined to hear than the details of Sister Plummer's promiscuities, but this astounding, unsuspected information was something of which she had to know more.

'I've never heard about this idea of preventing babies. We didn't talk about things like that at school or college. It – it seems as if it might mean quite a revolution in the position of women if they needn't have children unless they want them. Won't you – could you – tell me just a little about how it's done?'

Sister Plummer told her. Her details were thorough, her enjoyment of their effect upon an uninformed young girl complete. Once or twice, feeling alarmed and strangely isolated in this alien territory, Ruth clenched her hands to the point of torture in the belief that she was concealing the shock and aversion which the unrestrained recital inflicted upon her carefully-nurtured ignorance of anatomy.

'And so,' concluded Sister Plummer with relish, 'there's no need to worry at all. All you've got to do is to stock up when you go on leave.'

'I see,' said Ruth slowly. 'I quite see it's all right if you go on leave . . . But suppose you don't? I mean, suppose it all happens before you get the chance? Is there nothing you can do then?'

'Why, yes,' said Sister Plummer. 'Where there's a will there's a way, as I've always said. It's perhaps not so safe but I've known it work often enough.' She waved her hand towards the half-dozen beds at the far end of the ward. 'Look at those malarias, all sleeping so peacefully because they've had their treatment! That gives you the tip you want.'

'The malarias? Whatever has it to do with them?'

'Why, what are you always dosing them with? What's the only thing that does them any good, poor dears?'

'Really I don't understand.'

'Don't you, now? Well, it's like this . . .'

Ruth listened attentively while Sister Plummer explained that quinine tablets, admittedly essential in cases of malaria, possessed other properties not contemplated by the hospital dispensary.

14

The great German offensive of 1918 seemed to have lasted from the beginning of time. March, April, May. Like the other nurses, Ruth had foregone her spring leave; like them, she worked fourteen hours a day and was called up on five nights out of seven to help with convoys.

'If I have to cut another dead man off a stretcher I shall have a nervous breakdown,' she told Parker at the beginning of April, wiping tears of fatigue from her reddened eyes. Yet dead men with contorted mouths and cold yellow faces continued to arrive upon stretchers day after day, and she seemed as far from a nervous breakdown as ever.

'If only I could get an hour off duty I could manage for another week,' she told herself at the beginning of May, stiffly rubbing her swollen feet with methylated spirit. She did not get the off-duty time; yet she managed for another month.

She managed, perhaps, because all through the tumult of that titanic offensive Eugene remained unhurt and had even, for a month, been out of the line. American contingents were now being rushed across the Atlantic as fast as the crowded transports could bring them, and amongst the new troops came two advance units of the volunteer 45th Division – the 'Sunrise

Division' from the Eastern seaboard. As soon as these advance units – picked men who had received some military training in civilian life – arrived at St Nazaire in the last week of March, Eugene wrote to tell Ruth that he had left the Dorsetshire Yeomanry to become one of their officers. They were to receive, he said, a month of intensive preparation before going to the front, and she gathered that this training was to be given a long way south of Hardelot. But even if he had been near her she knew that in those extreme days she would have had no chance of seeing him.

At the end of April she learnt that he was again in the war zone with the advance units, which were now attached as reinforcements to the First American Division. She did not know that this Division was at Montdidier, nor realise that by the first week in June a number of counter-attacks at several points of the line – Château-Thierry, Cantigny, Villers-Bretonneux – had begun to replace the continuous Allied retreat.

On June 5th, when Ruth was on evening duty in her surgical ward, the post-orderly brought her letters from Jessie and Stephen. When she had finished the dressings and six-o'clock temperatures, she directed her ward-orderly – now at last released from convoy duty – to begin the evening washing and bed-making while she sat down for ten minutes to read them. Since the beginning of the offensive posts had been erratic, and because Stephen's letter was dated four days earlier than Jessie's she opened it first.

'MY DEAR JILL,

'Thank you for your interesting letter of May 23rd which arrived here on the 27th inst. I am very interested in the details, but I do hope things are letting up somewhat at your end and that you will soon get a bit of rest from your heavy work. Pray take care of yourself. Your father may not say much, but he is very proud of the way you have stuck to your guns during these recent exceedingly trying months. Reggie Halkin from the Paper Works informs me that the Tallinor girls got themselves sent back from France, as they told Sir Harrison the strain was too much for them.

'We have felt something of it even in our backwater here, for three weeks ago the War Office wrote to me asking if we could find some extra accommodation for convalescent officers. Well, yours truly felt it was up to him to do his bit, so I set to work to persuade your mother to use Jack's room and studio for the purpose. She was rather unwilling at first as you can imagine, but I pointed out it was the right way to honour the lad's memory, and in any case, a many things will have to be changed after this War, and at last I got her to agree. Two of the new officers came in yesterday, and one is a most interesting fellow by the name of Mansfield, an army chaplain, who in civilian life was Vicar of an East End parish in Bethnal Green. It seems that when the push began our chaps at the front had not much time for parsons, so Captain Mansfield turned stretcher-bearer instead and got buried by a shell while working between the lines. The result was some injury to the base of the spine; it will mend in time, but meanwhile he has to lie up for a few weeks prior to taking another medical board.

'Oddly enough this Mansfield knows a deal about the parson called Rutherston and his family who used to be at Witnall round 1906. I daresay you will not remember them as you were still quite a little girl when they left, but he was a ranting, pretentious sort of chap with a suffragette wife and a lad of twelve or thirteen, and I got rid of him after a row about his sermons, which were most unsuitable for our congregation. It appears the wife ran away from him just before the War and took a job of sorts under Mansfield in Bethnal Green. He seems to have a better opinion of her than your mother and I formed at the time, and thinks the parson did not treat her properly. Of course there was a regular scandal in Rutherston's parish, and the upshot was he went off his head and is now in a mental home, all of which goes to prove that your father is not far wrong in his judgments. Mansfield tells me the wife died last Christmas and the lad is now in the Army somewhere serving in the ranks, which I don't doubt is good enough for him.

'A letter arrived yesterday from Norman saying that his

battery is being moved to Mesopotamia at last, but things there seem to have quietened down a bit and we must hope for the best. Hardiman writes from Egypt that he has been promoted to sergeant. He always was a capable chap.

'I think that is all the news so I will now close, wishing you the best of luck.

'Your affectionate Father,
'STEPHEN ALLEYNDENE.'

'PS. – You will be sorry to hear that your friend Madeleine Gibson is now on the sick list suffering from pneumonia. Your mother had a line from her father to-night.'

Madeleine ill – and perhaps seriously! Ruth seized Jessie's later letter and opened it in haste.

'MY DEAREST RUTH,

'I am grieved indeed, my darling, to have some extremely sad news to give you. Our dear Madeleine passed away yesterday in the Kingsway Hospital from double pneumonia after only five days' illness. Her father writes that last week she got soaking wet while driving her ambulance and caught a bad chill, but carried on at school and said nothing about it. On Monday evening one of the other mistresses, not liking the look of her, went round to her flat and found her all alone, quite delirious and with a temperature of 104 degrees. They got her into hospital at once, but apparently there was not much hope from the start. As you know, she has never been robust.

'It is a terrible tragedy, for I expect she told you that Jerry was invalided out of the Army a fortnight ago and they were to have been married in the summer holidays. Poor Jerry is almost off his head, and is saying that somehow or other he will make the authorities send him back to the front. Mr Gibson asked me to break the news to you, knowing what a blow it will be.'

A blow! But it just isn't true! It *can't* be true! Why, I write to

Madeleine every week, and I stayed with her only last September, that time when . . .

A voice uttered her name, breaking into her black bewilderment, and she looked up to find Mungavin, the V.A.D. nurse from the Sisters' Quarters, standing beside the table holding out a letter. Ruth trembled and turned pale; even the news of Madeleine's death vanished from her mind when she saw Eugene's handwriting on the crumpled envelope.

'A young American officer brought it to the Mess,' explained Mungavin. 'He says it's urgent and he wants an answer. If you're on duty and can't let him know, he'll wait till you go off.'

A young American officer . . . Oh, he's here! He's only across the road! He's waiting in the Mess to see me . . .

'Is he very tall?' she asked breathlessly. 'Much taller than me, and thin and dark?'

'Oh, no. He's not like that at all. Shortish and rather fair.'

Then that must mean something has happened to Eugene. . . . But how? Where? It can't be so terribly serious or he wouldn't have written himself, unless . . . She suddenly remembered Richard's letter, and time seemed to stop. Unless he's been killed and this is his last letter.

The thudding of her heart almost suffocated her as she tore open the thin envelope with cold, shaking fingers.

'DARLING,' she read in the bold, schoolboyish handwriting which appeared less vigorous than usual, 'This is to tell you I was hit in the action up at Cantigny on May 28th, but there is nothing to go off the deep end about. It is just a blighty, a clean bullet wound through the left shoulder. What counts far more is the great piece of luck I have had getting straight through to Le Touquet.

'I think I told you when I was at the Gunnery School here I got to know a grand old girl from Philadelphia who was just starting a little show for wounded American officers. Well, as soon as I was round from the dope they gave me at the Clearing Station to extract the bullet, I put in an application to be sent to this place and got around the M.O. to pull a few wires for me. I never expected to bring it off, but here I am!

'I just can't tell you how I am counting the hours till you can come over and see me. Winthrop Sherman, the boy from my room who is bringing you this note, says he will be delighted to run you over any time you can make it. He is only nineteen, convalescing after a septic appendix and bored stiff because he can't find a thing to do. He will wait at Hardelot till you have asked your Matron. Please darling, go down on your bended knees and beg her to let you come. I don't know how to make you understand what seeing you will mean to me after eight months away from you and mostly in the line. I am hungry and thirsty for your beautiful face, especially after thinking a week ago I might not see it any more.

'Your devoted and adoring
'EUGENE.'

After weeks of overwork and the previous shock of the afternoon, the reaction was overwhelming. To the horrified concern of Mungavin, Ruth put down the letter and burst into tears.

'I say, Alleyndene, what is it? I do hope nothing frightful's happened?'

'Oh, no – not frightful at all,' Ruth explained with the sudden volubility of relief. 'It's only that my best friend's been wounded; he's in hospital at Le Touquet; he wants me to go over and see him. I must ask Matron. I must find Sister – she's in the next ward.'

Noticing that some of the patients were watching her, Ruth dabbed her eyes in sudden embarrassment. Mungavin touched her shoulder sympathetically.

'Look here, I'll find Sister if you like. I'll ask her if I can watch the ward while you go to Matron.'

Five minutes later Ruth was in Miss Eveleigh's office, asking for permission to drive to Le Touquet and see Eugene. She was quite unconscious of the picture that she made as she stood there, her slim body tall and erect in the blue dress and starched white apron, her pale cheeks flushed, her grey eyes still shining wet from her recent tears. But the Matron saw it. She had seen so many similar pictures since the War began, and each time she had prayed that the boy might be spared, the story end happily . . .

'Well, nurse,' she said, 'the work is not so heavy as it was. You could take a half-day and see him to-morrow.'

'Oh, Matron! May I really . . . !' Ruth's uplifted face glowed like a young rose uncurling its petals in the light of the sun.

Miss Eveleigh blew her nose vigorously as the door closed.

'I really mustn't let these things affect me so much,' she told herself, taking the top letter from a pile marked 'Unanswered Correspondence.'

15

'Why, I do believe you're shy of me after all this time!' cried Eugene, his laughing face vividly bronze above his white silk pyjamas, his gay excited eyes sparkling with delight. But Ruth noticed that under those luminous eyes were dark lines of fatigue, that beneath the surface sunburn his cheeks were drawn and pale.

She stood at the foot of the bed and gazed at him, visibly shaking from the conflict of her emotions and quite unable to speak. The tears which had lately seemed so near the surface suddenly started to her eyes as she saw his bandaged shoulder and the wide sling that held his left arm. She was obliged to take out her handkerchief and wipe them away.

At once Eugene became as concerned and observant as she.

'Look here, darling,' he said gently, 'I guess you've been handed out as rough a deal as I have. You're thinner than ever and your gorgeous eyes look all sunken and tired. Now you just sit down in that lounge-chair and rest yourself till we get properly acquainted again.'

'Not till I've kissed you,' said Ruth brokenly. She went up to him and their lips clung together, shyly at first, then passionately, desperately. She had to dry her eyes once more before she went back to her chair.

'I do want to hear what happened at Cantigny – unless you feel you can't talk about it yet.'

'Oh, yes, I can talk about it to you. I guess you're the only person whom I'll ever be able to tell just all that happens to me.'

His young face hardened suddenly; the look of strain deepened beneath his eyes. 'When I get back to the States there's nobody who'll want to hear a darn thing about this War – or understand what I'm getting at if I try to tell them!'

'Then tell me about Cantigny now, my love.'

He looked at her intently and she saw that this time it was his eyes which were bright with tears.

'Darling, you made a coward of me. I thought about you all night before the attack on the Heights. Your face came to me like a flower against the darkness, the way it always does, till I just about went crazy thinking maybe I'd never see it any more. I didn't know how to get myself over the top . . . and then, after all, the whole thing was through for me in less than five minutes. I hadn't gone twenty yards when the bullet got me – it must have been from pretty close range because the terrific impact knocked me flat. I guess I was a bit stunned by the fall, for the next thing I knew I was back in the trench I'd just quitted. When I came to I thought my arm was off – it was as numb as could be and I didn't get any feeling back in it for over two days.'

A young American nurse in a finely laundered frilled cap and high-heeled white suède shoes came in with an elegant tea-tray, which she put down on the polished locker beside Eugene's bed. As she left the room she cast a glance of curiosity discreetly tempered with commiseration at Ruth's Red Cross uniform.

Her visit had broken the tension between them. They looked at each other and laughed.

'She doesn't like my hat and coat, and I don't blame her,' said Ruth. 'There's something terribly British about our uniform!'

'Never mind, darling; you look lovelier in it than she does with all her heels and frills. Anyway, you could take your hat off now, couldn't you? I do like your hair better.'

She took off her hat and poured out his tea, holding the saucer for him while he drank. Her own remained completely forgotten until he reminded her gaily that she had had none. When they had both finished she spoke again of the battle at Cantigny.

'Thank God it was over for you so quickly . . . Tell me, Eugene, do these actions ever haunt you afterwards?'

'Sometimes they do, and there's nothing so sure as an air-raid for bringing them back. But the show at Cantigny didn't get me down like a job I tackled a day or two before.'

'Was it a trench raid? They always seem about the worst things to me.'

'No, it wasn't a raid. In fact it wasn't a dangerous job at all – just clearing out a church in a village called Fenelles. When our unit occupied the place it'd been fought over for three weeks by Germans and Americans, each taking it from the other in turn. And as neither side could clear out their seriously wounded, they'd dumped them in the village church to get on as best they could without a doctor or ambulance man in miles.'

Although Eugene was not articulate in any literary sense, his descriptions conveyed vividly to Ruth the atmosphere and scene of his activities. While she listened, her mind formed a graphic picture of the white wayside church with its red gabled roof and tiny pointed turret as it had appeared to Eugene and his men when they marched up the littered remnant of the village street. She could see the white-washed wall, still almost intact, separating the churchyard from the road, and the tombstones and wire wreaths which carried the *immortelles* smashed into a debris of twisted wire and splintered stone. She knew that each diamond of stained glass had gone from the windows except for the miniature rose-window of deep cerise which the golden light of the sunset turned blood-red, until the blood of the wounded within seemed to rise into the air and fill the whole church with the sinister colour of war and pain.

'The first man to go in was my Company Commander, Russell Chase . . . I'd like you to meet Russell one day, Ruth; he's a great guy, only a year or so older than me, and a first-rate officer. I knew him a bit before the War; our families have done business together for years. His father owns the biggest chain of book-stores in the States, and Russell had just gone into the firm when the War began . . . Well, as I said, he was the first one to go into that place, and he came out looking as white as he did the day a gas-shell burst in his dug-out and all but choked him. "Lord," he said, "it's a bloody inferno in there! There's three Germans and two Americans still alive and we've got to get them out. The rest are all dead and rotten, and I'd bet they've been there a month judging by the stink of the show; it reeks like hell. We've got to clean it up, Meury, and get those poor devils down to the Base. Do you think your boys can tackle a job like that?"

'Well, I took it on, darling, and my outfit cleaned up that place – but Lord! Chase hadn't exaggerated! The stench and the sights in the church were just beyond words. We found about thirty or forty dead in there; some of them must have been finished for two or three weeks, because the bodies had swollen up and burst. They'd used the altar as an operating table, and a man whose leg they'd tried to amputate lay across it. He must have died just as it was done and been left there to rot.'

'Oh *God*!' whispered Ruth.

There was dead silence for a moment.

'Well, thank the Lord I've got *that* off my chest,' Eugene said cheerfully. 'Let's talk about something else now. We'll talk about you. How often do you figure your Matron's going to let you come over and see me?'

'She's really very decent about it, Eugene. I'm going to ask her if I may come every half-day. I can but try!'

'Well, in two or three weeks I ought to be able to come and get you myself, and then you won't have to ask!'

'Oh, not so soon as that!' she cried anxiously. But she knew all too well from her surgical experience among men with first-class constitutions how quickly that firm brown flesh would heal, that virile body recover resilience.

'Well, you're not going yet, anyway . . . and you don't have to go on sitting so far away from me. I've got one good arm still and I guess it can hold you!'

She drew her chair close to the side of the bed, trembling as she always trembled when in close contact with his strong physical vitality. His uninjured arm crept round her shoulders; his fingers touched the studs which fastened her collar.

'All armoured up as usual, aren't you, darling? I can't get at you the way I could that night you were in mufti.'

Blushing from a strong sense of guilt, Ruth unfastened the studs and slipped undone the buttons beneath them.

'I'm getting quite an abandoned woman!' she murmured jerkily, but she did not shrink from him when she felt his hand gently caressing the soft curves of her neck, the deep hollow between her breasts.

Later that evening, as she waited outside the little hospital for young Winthrop Sherman to run her back to Hardelot, she knew that she had never been so vehemently alive.

'I must write and tell Madeleine all about Eugene,' she thought.

It was only then she began to realise that Madeleine was dead.

16

August 4th, 1918, was not only the fourth anniversary of the outbreak of war; it was the last day but one of Eugene Meury's convalescence. To-morrow he had to take the midnight train from Étaples to Paris, and report at American headquarters before rejoining the 45th Division.

By Miss Eveleigh's permission Ruth was spending the afternoon with him at Le Touquet – to say good-bye, so the Matron understood. Sometimes – though less often now than formerly – Ruth's conscience still troubled her. It didn't seem quite fair to Matron, who trusted her and was always so humane and generous, to steal so many hours with Eugene in addition to those that she was allowed. But her intermittent remorse soon perished. Their meetings in the lanes, the woods, the meadows, had renewed the incomparable enchantment which last year's spring and summer had laid upon Hardelot. Renewed and intensified it, for now certainty had replaced speculation; their love for one another had cast out fear. It had cast out all fear but the fear of death, which alone could end it.

When he called for her at the hospital he seemed, she thought, to walk with a gay, arrogant self-confidence which could not be fully explained by the new vigour that his weeks of rest had given him. As soon as they were in the car together, he told her with shy pride that he was now Captain Meury.

'I only got word of my promotion this morning. Oh, darling, when I get back to the 45th I'll be commanding a company! I guess even my old dad'll be pleased about that!'

'Do you know where it is, your Division?' she asked, after she had made him stop the car so that she could congratulate him in the way she thought suitable.

'Somewhere down in the Vosges direction, I'm told, though I shan't know just where till I see our brass hats in Paris. But I've heard a rumour some of our Divisions are going to be sent to clear the Argonne Forest, and it seems the 45th is likely to be one.'

'The Argonne!' she cried, and something went cold within her. 'But, Eugene, that's supposed to be impregnable! Why, the Germans have been fortifying it for nearly four years.'

'Well, our boys'll do it if it can be done – and if it can't, they'll still do it! When the 45th gets there, there'll be lots of fun. We've got plenty of tough guys who'll go all out on a job like that.'

Sitting in the empty hotel café at the far end of the esplanade, they looked at the sapphire sea drowsing in the languor of a prolonged midsummer heat-wave. Now that the intimate companionship of the past few weeks was almost over, its approaching end deprived them of speech.

The Argonne, thought Ruth. That may mean he won't come back this time. Oh, but it isn't possible! Everyone who has really counted in my life is dead already . . . Richard . . . Madeleine . . . everyone except Eugene. One doesn't lose *everybody* one cares for, even in wartime. In a way, the fact that I've lost so much makes Eugene quite safe . . .

She looked up to see that he had suddenly covered his face.

'Eugene! What is it?' she cried, touching the brown barrier of his hands.

He burst out then into passionate speech.

'Darling, it's no use – I can't keep it under any more! This whole business gets me down. It's just hell, not being able to ask you to marry me before I go back! If only Dallas'd get tired of this waiting game! If only I'd a notion she'd taken up with some other fellow, but she's waited now four years and she writes just as often as ever.' He rubbed his eyes furiously with his handkerchief and she knew why he had covered them. 'I may be all wrong about it, darling, but it still seems as if I can't let her down.'

'His honour rooted in dishonour stood.' Who had written that familiar line? Whoever it was, it must not be true of Eugene.

'No; you can't,' she said, but she felt as though she were signing the order for her own execution.

'I'll have to go through with it, Ruth – but God! I just can't figure what sort of life we'll have together. I don't even remember her clearly – what she looks like and the sound of her voice – but I might get myself accustomed to that again. What I'll never settle down to, after you, is having to live with someone who knows just nothing about this wartime life we've been through over here. How can I ever really *talk* to her, darling, when since I went she's just gone on living the way we lived over there before 1914? She's only a kid still – in experience anyway – and I've had four years of war. These things that have happened to me – in Gallipoli, in the Balkans, most of all here in France – why, they'll stand out as the vividest things I've ever done, the things that'll matter most till I finish! And not a hint of them shall I ever be able to give her!'

'Surely she'll understand a little, if she really loves you?' ventured Ruth, forlornly seeking comfort for him because she could find none for herself.

'She may try but she never will. Not really, I mean. I can't put the inside significance of things into words like you can. I can describe them, in a sort of a way, but I've a notion Dallas won't want to hear my descriptions. She won't be upset so much as bored; she'll want me to forget it all because it doesn't fit on at any point to the life she knows.' He gazed disconsolately westward over the sea, as though his tortured speculations could cross the Atlantic beyond England and penetrate the half-comprehending psychology of America at war.

'Darling, you just can't imagine how far off and unreal that life of mine in the United States seems over here! That world and this really don't intersect anywhere. In England it's different – you've people on leave, and the wounded, and the air-raids always on top of you like the one we got into. They know *something* there, even if it's mostly second-hand and watered down. But our people in America don't realise a thing; every mail I get from home tells me that. If I come through this War and go back there I'll be a stranger living among strangers to my life's end – except just now and again, perhaps, when I get talking with one of the boys, or maybe someone comes over from Europe who knows and remembers too . . . Oh God! How'll I bear it!'

'You know I'd gladly come over and face it with you, my dearest, and be an alien as well – if it weren't for Dallas.'

'My God, if only it weren't!' He clasped his hands over his forehead and groaned, overwhelmed by the complications of his dilemma. 'But even if I got her to give me up, I'm not sure it would be any kind of life for you, darling. My family are such dyed-in-the-wool Yankees, without ever having really let go the social viewpoint of Europe. I guess there'd be no scope for your brains, or your education, or your interest in politics – and they'd never forgive me, let alone you, for letting Dallas down. If only I weren't the only son I'd chuck the whole business and clear out, but I figure I've no right to let the pioneer work of my father and grandfather go for nothing. I can't explain just how it is, Ruth, but our job's a kind of religion with us in the United States, and if you're disloyal to your business, why, you somehow feel you've been disloyal to your God.'

'Dear Eugene, don't worry about it any more,' said Ruth gently. 'After all, the War's not over yet; we can't tell what may happen to either of us. When it's over we can face the problem again and give each other up if we must, but meanwhile . . .'

She looked out at the calm misty waters of the English Channel. No time. No future. Our moment must be now, or it may be never. She knew then what the resolution was which had been growing within her for weeks, the resolution that involved throwing down for ever from their sacred pinnacle the standards and conventions of her post-Victorian girlhood.

'Eugene, you do really love me? You'd *like* us to have belonged to each other . . . ?'

He drew his chair closer to hers, and took her hands and held them against his breast.

'Darling, I guess you don't need to have me tell you that any more.'

'Then, my dearest,' she said, and her voice sounded strange to her, 'there's one thing I can be to you, one thing I can do for you now, that Dallas can't and in a way never will be able to. Never, because . . . because I don't believe the physical side of love can ever bring quite the same comfort as it does when one's body suffers and goes in danger of death. Won't you let me give you that comfort, Eugene – let me be your lover before you go back? We shall have created something between us like that – a relationship, a belonging to each other – and nothing that happens afterwards will ever be able to take it quite away.'

He started, pushing her further from him, his dark eyes, smouldering with desire, intently searching and scrutinising her face.

'You can't know just what you're saying, Ruth. You don't mean you're willing to take me without marriage, without security?'

'But that's what I do mean.'

His thin young face turned scarlet; beads of perspiration stood on his forehead.

'Look here, darling, you're tempting me more than I can bear . . . You see, I love you so terribly, and I couldn't go treating you, of all people, in a way that wouldn't be ethical. I've wanted you so often, I've about gotten accustomed to fighting the idea.'

'Well, I don't want you to fight it any more.'

'But I can, darling. I'm not the sort that finds it too difficult . . . You see, I've not had a woman up to date. I didn't just feel it would be right to go to a decent girl after trying things out the way some of the boys do here.'

'Oh, Eugene! I never thought it was possible!' cried Ruth, intensely relieved. (You're just being too nineteenth century for words, she told herself severely, but that did not alter her profound feeling of thankfulness.) 'Why, I thought in four years of war you'd have been with all sorts of women – prostitutes in Greece, and here at the Base, and so on,' she added vaguely.

'Nothing doing in *that* direction!' Eugene protested vigorously. 'Gosh, did you really think I'd be carrying on that way when I was going about all the time with you? No, thank you! None of your Mademoiselles from Armenteers for me. I'd rather go homo than that!'

'Oh, dearest, don't – you mustn't!' she exclaimed in alarm, her night-duty terrors again present with her. And suddenly, as so often, the past came back to her, a remembered orchestration, sometimes clear, sometimes dim, accompanying the varied theme of her life. This time it took the form of two intermingled voices; one, Eugene's own deep incisive accents saying – was it really only fifteen months ago? – 'The Lord knows what I mightn't do if this darn War goes on much longer!' the other Susan Shepherd's reed-like whimper: 'Why shouldn't Ronnie have 'ad 'is bit o' love before goin' into the line? Maybe now he'll get popped off and never ha' known it! I wouldn't 'a worritted myself about bein' a bad girl an' that, if only I'd given Ron his bit o' joy before he went!'

Standing up, she put her hands on his shoulders and looked down into his face.

'I want you to take me,' she said resolutely. 'I want us to have belonged to each other before you go.'

She saw that his flesh, eager and vital, had already responded to that challenge; she knew that his scruples were weakening. Rigid with longing, he returned her look desperately, ashamed of his thoughts no less than of his feelings. His conscience spurred him to one final endeavour.

'Look here, Ruth . . . of course I'd do my best to take care of you and all – but just figure if things went wrong and you got a child . . . and suppose I'd gone west and wasn't here to help you . . . why, it's more than I can bear to think of!'

Oh, I want to have his child! I want it! her primitive heart cried wildly. But her social prudence, intimidated by every influence that had moulded her youth, responded instead:

'That's all right. I know how to take care of myself.'

'*You* know, darling? . . . Are you quite sure?'

'Yes. One of the Sisters told me. She'd had experience enough, so . . .' She checked herself in her implicit condemnation. By

to-morrow night she would have become just such another as
Sister Plummer. One of those dreadful women, her mother had
called them, who lead such immoral lives because of this War.
The Prayer Book described them even more frankly. 'To satisfy
men's carnal lusts and appetites, like brute beasts that have no
understanding.' She had heard the Church's judgment on them
long ago, at poor Aunt Elizabeth's marriage service. Well, what
did she care for the Church – or society either?

'You know I'm off in the evening to-morrow, don't you,
Eugene?'

'You did tell me. I guessed you'd find some way of saying
good-bye to me.'

'I know it won't be changed, because Sister wants to do some
shopping in Boulogne, and there's an afternoon ambulance going
in to fetch a new V.A.D. and bring her back. I could meet you at
six in the usual place near the old Château.'

'I'll be there,' he said. 'We could have supper at Condette, if
you'd like that. It's . . . it's near the pine-woods.'

'Quite near enough. Nobody will suspect anything if I'm in
by ten, and it's dark now at eight.'

'And you'll come into the woods with me after supper,
darling? You really will . . . ?'

'Yes, my love. I'll come.'

17

'*Comment!*' exclaimed Madame at the Condette *estaminet*, seriously perturbed. '*Monsieur et Mademoiselle n'ont rien mangé!*'

Ruth endeavoured to propitiate her.

'*Il fail si chaud ce soir,*' she explained.

'And you see,' Eugene added soothingly, 'I've got to go back
to the line to-night, and when I get there I shan't have a darn
thing to do but eat my head off!'

'*Tiens, vous retournez? Ah, que c'est dommage! . . . Au
revoir, Mademoiselle! Au revoir et bonne chance, Monsieur le
capitaine!*'

'*Au revoir, Madame*, and thanks a lot!'

'*Au revoir, Madame. Merci beaucoup.*'

They left the *estaminet* and drove slowly along the road to the pine-woods, keeping close within the deep shade cast by the hazels. Already the moon was up, an orange Chinese lantern of a moon, throwing dark interlacing patterns upon the road from the overhanging branches.

'You haven't to go back to Le Touquet?' she asked him.

'No; my traps are all dumped at Étaples. I've nothing to do there but park my car and get them.'

Her thoughts raced as they left the car concealed in the bushes beside the road where it forked towards Étaples, and entered the beaten path through the woods. Will he think me abandoned, disreputable, unworthy of his respect, because I offered myself to him in that way? Does he understand what I really meant – that I wished him, before he goes back to face death, to have the whole and not just an incomplete knowledge of love? Does he realise how much I wanted to abandon, for him, all the cautions and calculations with which my life has been hedged, to give all I had to give and hold back nothing for lack of gallantry and generosity? ... Suppose his love for me turns to contempt, because I let him take me so easily? Well, let him despise and humiliate me afterwards if he must! I'll accept even humiliation at his hands, rather than let him risk going to his death without all the experience of love that I can give him.

Leaving the path, they plunged deeper into the thick, untrodden forest. The hot evening air was heavy with the rich resinous perfume of the pines. Beneath their feet scarlet pimpernel and blush-pink sea-vetch clung to the dusty soil; clumps of blue and purple anchusa sprang opulently from the mushroom-tinted sand. At last they emerged from the undergrowth into a natural clearing among the tall trees. It was a place where they had already spent many undisturbed hours, talking lazily in the dappled sunshine and shadow on Ruth's half-days.

'Here?' he suggested.

She nodded.

They stood still and looked at each other without speaking, excited, expectant, afraid.

'Look here, Ruth,' he said abruptly, 'I'm not going to take you in my clothes.'

'Very well, my dear.'

She turned away from him into the dark shelter of the thicket. Her fingers trembled so much that she could hardly manipulate the complicated hooks and studs of her uniform. A long time seemed to pass before she laid the collection of demure garments upon the carpet of pine-needles and stepped shyly into the moonlit clearing. The soft air caressed her slender white body, the sand was warm against her bare feet.

He was there already waiting for her, very tall and thin and brown – like a young god from a nobler age, she thought, as she saw him naked against the trees. Then the terrifying strangeness of her breach with the safe familiar conduct of her world took possession of her and she faltered, hiding her face and fearing to look upon him. But she heard his voice . . . nearer to her . . . coming nearer, a voice that shook.

'Darling, how beautiful you are! Oh, darling, darling, you're so beautiful!'

She felt his hand strong and warm upon her arm, leading her across the clearing. At the farther end of it he flung his trench coat in the dark space between two giant pines, and took her hands from her face and pressed his lips upon hers.

'Let's lie down here in the shadow.'

Still with the sense of playing a critical rôle in some alien drama of which she was also a detached spectator, she stretched herself shivering on her back beneath the trees and looked up through the thin trunks at the fathomless darkness. For a moment she saw between the feathery branches the deep velvet blue of the sky and the winking silver eyes of the stars; then Eugene was down upon her, kissing her breasts, her lips, her eyes, blotting out the serene indifferent night. Gravely and tenderly, conscious that what was about to happen might indeed prove to be the sacrament of farewell, he folded her into his long thin arms. Her shivering ceased and wild excitement surged through her veins as his heart beat faster against her, his body quivered and grew tense.

And suddenly, as he felt her exquisite nakedness against his own, the violent emotions which he had so long repressed swept over him like a tornado, galloping away with scruples, memories, inhibitions, making deliriously simple the ultimate expression of his love. A swift frenzy of abandonment, unlike anything he had known before, overwhelmed him as he heard her sharp intake of breath and felt her sudden tension of endurance. Never had he dreamed that so fierce an enchantment of sensation could lie in inflicting the first incomparable agony of passion upon the lovely young body which had turned his own to one burning impulse of desire, nor she that in all human experience so intimate an alliance could exist between ecstasy and anguish. The pines swayed and murmured above their heads as they lay there together, locked in the closest and most desperate embrace attainable by mortal flesh confronted with the imminence of separation and the death of time.

18

At the gate of the tall villa which looked down from a thicket of firs upon the main square of Hardelot-Plage, the French Red Cross had put up a little shrine of the Madonna as an appeal for alms to help the wounded. Below the shrine was a ledge which held a vase now filled with tawny French marigolds, and a wooden box for contributions inscribed with the words: '*Pour les blessés de la guerre qui souffrent pour la patrie.*'

'*Les blessés de la guerre.*' There was more than one way of being wounded by this War, thought Ruth, as she stopped to look into the serene wooden face of the Mother of Sorrows. It had been so strange, after last night, to spend the morning and afternoon on duty in the customary fashion; to listen, apparently as usual, to the men's cheerful confidences with the feeling that life had ceased to be itself, that in one half-hour the personality of twenty-four years had been changed. Throughout the waking dream of those hours she could not believe that she had behaved normally, when instead of the familiar faces of her patients against the pillows, she had seen only his face; instead of her Ward-Sister's brisk instructions she had heard only his voice, saying, 'Darling, how beautiful you are! Oh, darling, darling, you're so beautiful!' Too dazed as yet to realise the full implications of her uncertainty, she found herself constantly wondering whether, in spite of the precautions that she had taken, she would bear Eugene's child – in shame, in glory. Could those simple untested measures really have withstood the ruthless urgency of Nature seeking to perpetuate its kind?

From the heart of the forest she and Eugene had walked hand in hand, without speaking, to the Étaples road curving white beneath the moon. When he took her in his arms to say good-bye her eyes had been dry and tearless, but the lips that sought hers had trembled, the face against hers had been wet . . . She stood beside the road until his tears had dried upon her cheek, and the distant throb of his engine had merged into the low sighing of the pines.

'When the world ends for me,' she thought, 'that's the last sound I shall hear . . .'

Now that it was evening again she felt very tired, for all day long her body had ached from the passion of which it had been the instrument. But she accepted its discomfort with gratitude and an unaccustomed masochistic exultation. Those moments in the pine-forest were Eugene's for ever; no other man would give her the sharp, desired pain of that first act of union. Because of it, she felt more than ever a part of the beauty which had emerged from the creative anguish of primitive life – the sandhills and the lovely sea, the evening sun which still shone golden from the dissolving crests of the gentle waves stealing over the shore. What was there about War that made the world so unbearably radiant, like the blurred brilliance of a vivid landscape seen through a mist of tears?

Immersed in the deep religious ecstasy which for the introspective is so often the consequence of passionate sex-experience, she silently addressed the tranquil Madonna.

'You too knew grief and loss and pain; did you know sin as well? Were you the mother of an illegitimate child, as I may be – I who understood so imperfectly how to avoid having a baby, and wasn't quite sure that I wanted to anyway . . . And if you were, was it sin to create the Son of Man who sought to become the

Saviour of the world by sharing humanity's martyrdom – such martyrdom as it is going through now? Have I sinned, I who in a short time shall be counting the days in fear and in hope – in fear of being entrapped by the creative urge of physical passion, in hope that the love between Eugene and myself may spring to life in my body? Surely to put into this tortured world something more of his vitality, his affirmative courage, his adorable gaiety – that couldn't really be a sin?'

A sudden apprehension of the terrifying weeks immediately before her darkened her mind, and she shuddered.

'Yes, I shall count the days – like any little maid-servant seduced by her master, like my grandmother's Agnes when she conceived the child for which she was punished and condemned. I shall watch them with growing dread, waiting to know whether I am to be confronted with one of the commonest but least remediable of human predicaments . . . O God, I am stripped bare of all pride, all self-righteousness! I can never again take refuge in the security of the chill, austere virtues – purity, chastity, abnegation! To me my love is enriched, augmented, but in the world's eyes it carries a stain upon its brightness, and because of that the complacency which wrapped me round like a protective garment is gone for ever. Oh, blind, self-satisfied fool that I have been – never to realise until the past few months how easily the compelling desire of the flesh can fly away with the halting, fastidious judgments of the conscious intelligence! I am vulnerable now and defenceless, awakened like the rest of suffering humanity to the fullest knowledge of grief and fear. May God forgive me for my intellectual arrogance, my sense of triumphant superiority to the passionate sorrows of tormented mankind!'

She looked round and saw that she was quite alone in that quiet corner of the village square. In the fading light she clasped her hands, closed her eyes, and bowed her head before the shrine. The old eloquence for which her war-time life had provided no outlet surged against her lips into prayer.

'Oh, Mother of Jesus, who suffered as we suffer and loved as we love, don't let my courage fail me whatever happens! Don't let me be afraid, even if what Eugene and I have felt for one another

manifests itself through me as a new life! Help me to overcome
everything in my heart that is base and unworthy, and grant that
the love between an American man and an English woman may
somehow help to bring closer together our two countries now
united in this War! For Christ's sake. Amen.'

19

The night-train from Paris swayed eastward with drawn blinds,
carrying Eugene to the Vosges. North of those low hills, menacing and grim, lay the sinister shadow of the Argonne.

Alone in his carriage Eugene sat sleepless, journeying through
the black silence of that ghost-ridden land. He had said good-bye
to Ruth, his adored, his darling; he had said good-bye and might
never see her again. Had he really wronged her when he loved
her so dearly, when he would die to save her a single moment
of anxiety or pain? Oh, it was cruel, intolerable, this knowing
nothing, this being young and alone and bewildered, face to
face at the same moment with the overwhelming mysteries of
love and death!

Eugene crushed his face into his thin brown hands, and
the tears, forcing their way through his fingers, fell in swift,
protesting drops to the carriage floor.

20

'Well, nurse, it looks as if the bloody little War's just about over!
We've got the Turks and Austrians properly on the run!'

'Yes, and they're saying we've driven the old Bosche back over
the Sambre canal!'

'And the Yanks have captured St Juvin and Grand-Pré. That
means they're through the Argonne!'

'I did hear tell the Huns had started negotiations for peace.'

'Go ahn, Ginger, yer can't 'ave peace till yer've 'ad a bloomin'
Harmistice! Can yer, nurse? You tell 'im!'

Although that chill afternoon of late October was sere and

blustery, there seemed to be a feeling of spring in the air. It was impossible to avoid catching the infection of the men's excited voices, the shrill babble in the Sisters' Mess at lunch-time about the nearness of peace. And the Americans were through the Argonne. They had been able, most of them, to come from the United States and go straight into that forward-moving type of warfare which stiffens the nerves and uplifts the spirit, instead of enduring the long costly stalemate which had robbed England of a generation of men . . . But *he* shared the four years with us.

They are through the Argonne. That means I shall soon be hearing from him again.

It seemed a long time since Ruth had received one of Eugene's brief, vivacious letters with the new note of passion which had stirred in them since August, but he had warned her when the 45th Division went to the Argonne at the end of September that it would probably be impossible to write during such a campaign. Though his last letter had made light, as always, of the dangers and discomforts before them, she had formed from the guarded accounts of newspaper correspondents a picture of the dense, tangled forest country where he had been fighting in the wild winds and drenching rains which had descended upon France during the past four weeks.

At night she awoke once more in terror from dreams of black, forbidding miles of thickly wooded hills and deep swampy ravines, of smashed firs and silver birches lying amidst clinging vines and trailing brambles twisted with broken lengths of barbed wire, of desolate valleys and muddy morasses flooded by perpetual rain. Her phantom machine guns were not concealed now by lilies and daffodils, but by gashed timber and fragments of shattered concrete, by dripping trackless under-brush and damp brown foliage from the splintered autumn trees.

At least, before that grim campaign began, she had been able to give rest to Eugene's mind by assuring him that she was not going to have a child. She said nothing of the violent choking panic, unlike any fear that she had ever known, which had mounted as the days went by until she felt that she could no longer keep silence, no longer carry out her daily duties, no longer maintain even the appearance of sanity. She did not mention the paroxysm of helpless weeping into which she had fallen when, upon the verge of time, had come the knowledge of reprieve. She only described how she had walked back that evening to the clearing in the woods where she and Eugene had lain together, and sat there exhausted with her head in her hands, knowing herself not pregnant, until the clutching terror of the past three days had become a vanished nightmare.

It was a nightmare, she told herself, that she must never forget, since it had taught her the kinship that she shared with the poor and the base and the humble, whose lives she had desired from her childhood to alleviate, yet had only known indirectly through Wardle and Hardiman. Never before had she realised how deeply rooted within her were the traditions against which she rebelled yet which still held her captive, nor what disintegrating anguish the prospect of joining society's outcasts would cause her. She had shared those dreadful hours with every girl-child seduced and destroyed, with every prostitute for whom pregnancy meant the loss of a livelihood, with every over-burdened mother condemned by a new life to semi-starvation. She understood at last why Richard's courage had failed before the prospect of disgrace, why he had preferred death to being arraigned at the bar of family values and repudiated by the Alleyndenes.

'But for a mere physical expedient,' she reflected, 'I should be the same as Agnes. I *am* the same as Agnes; an object, in their eyes, for social ostracism and degradation.'

She was reprieved; yet it had been then, walking back to the hospital, that she had recalled these lines from William Morris's *Mother and Son* which she had read at Playden. She had never seen them since her school-days, but now they came back to her with the force of a bitter reproach, their insistent rhythm accompanying her footsteps along the road.

> *Many a child of woman*
> *   to-night is born in the town;*
> *The desert of folly and wrong;*
> *   and of what and whence are they grown?*

Many and many an one
of wont and use is born;
For a husband is taken to bed
as a hat or a ribbon is worn.

But thou, O son, O son,
of very love wert born,
When our hope fulfilled bred hope
and fear was a folly outworn.

On the eve of the toil and the battle
all sorrows and grief we weighed,
We hoped and we were not ashamed,
We knew and we were not afraid.

'And fear was a folly outworn.' Oh, I was afraid, she admitted; afraid, afraid! It was fear that made me guard against motherhood. Not of society but of my family. Oh, how glad I should have been to have Eugene's child, if only I'd been alone! How I should have loved it! How proud I should have felt to tell him, when he went in daily peril of death through life's worst experiences, that whatever happened, a part of him would go on! His people need never have known, nor Dallas either. He could just have seen it sometimes – and me – when he came to England.

Eugene, it seemed, had shared that feeling himself, or at least, with the peculiar telepathy of lovers, had understood the remorseful compunction in her mind. She knew by heart the last sentence of the letter in which he had replied to hers.

'I guess you won't hate me too much if I tell you that, relieved beyond words as I am, there is something way down inside me not altogether and entirely glad. And that is because, if ever I did have a child, I should want it terribly to be your child too.'

And now the War itself was almost over. She couldn't help sharing in the general gladness, even though the end would raise a whole series of personal problems which had never really been faced. At least it would leave in the world those people to whom the problems belonged, and she was ready to endure whatever complications and dilemmas might confront her, provided only that he who caused them would still be there. Life, now, was the only thing that mattered; the consideration of ways of living could be left until later. Perhaps, when he explained to Dallas Lowell that he loved someone else, she would forgive and release him; perhaps, if he told her that he had taken another woman before herself, she would hate him and let him go. So long as life remained, endless possibilities of fulfilment remained also, to be dreamed of and prayed for. Even if the worst happened and they were obliged to part, at least they would keep the consciousness of one another, the shared memory of their wartime experience. What was it Olive Schreiner had written? 'Sometimes such a sudden gladness seizes me when I remember that somewhere in the world you are living and working.'

She had just finished the afternoon round of medicines and was beginning the temperatures when she saw Tweedale, the V.A.D. successor to Mungavin in the Sisters' Quarters, coming down the sandy path to her ward at the far end of the compound. The heavy wind had blown her cap crooked, and she straightened it in the doorway as she called to Ruth.

'You'd better leave the temperatures, Alleyndene! You're wanted at once in Matron's office.'

Something in Ruth seemed to stop and grow silent, like a clock which has suddenly run down.

'Oh, what for?' she asked in a voice that she hardly recognised as her own.

'I don't know. She didn't say. She only told me to fetch you.'

Ruth called the afternoon orderly and gave him the thermometers; then she followed Tweedale across the compound on legs which had lost their normal power to carry her body. It seemed more like an hour than five minutes before she stood outside the Matron's door and knocked.

Miss Eveleigh sat at her table with the letter from Captain Russell Chase of the 45th Division of American Infantry before her, and read it again as though she hoped that she had only dreamed its contents on the first occasion.

'DEAR MADAM,

'I trust you will forgive me for troubling you, but I am

enclosing a letter which my friend Captain E. C. Meury of the 45th asked me to write to one of your nurses, Miss Ruth Alleyndene, in the event of his death. Captain Meury was killed in action on October 7th in the Argonne battle, but I am only able to write to-day as I was severely wounded on the same occasion. I fear my letter will be a great blow to Miss Alleyndene, and I would take it very kindly if you would give it to her yourself and perhaps warn her of what it contains. I should not like to think she would get it when she is on duty or in the middle of a crowd.

'Thanking you for your kindness, and hoping you will pardon me for laying this difficult task upon you,

'Faithfully yours,

'RUSSELL D. CHASE.'

When she heard Ruth knock, Miss Eveleigh braced herself to that task with a laden heart. These bitter obligations did not become any easier from repetition. Better get it over as quickly as possible.

'Come in, nurse,' she said. 'I am afraid I have something to tell you which will demand all your courage.'

Ruth stood motionless in front of the table. This has all happened before, she thought; where was it? But this time she did not even ask if the news was about Norman, for every instinct of fear within her cried out that it was not. She stiffened herself to meet the blow which she knew was coming.

'Your American friend, Captain Meury, has been killed in action.'

Still Ruth said nothing, but a change came over her face as though someone had suddenly put out a light within her and turned it into the face of a corpse. As much to break that spiritual catalepsy as for any other reason, Miss Eveleigh spoke again.

'I take it, nurse, that you and Captain Meury were engaged to be married?'

'No, Matron; we couldn't be,' Ruth answered dully. 'He was engaged to a girl in America. She'd waited for him for four years, so we couldn't let her down.'

'I see,' said the Matron gravely. The situation whose development she had not retarded presented itself to her with all its implications, but there was no purpose to be served, now, by rebuking the young woman who had allowed her to go on acting upon a false assumption. Poor children; oh, poor, poor children! What had happened between them? she wondered. Contrary to every army regulation and all the tenets of hospital service, she hoped that everything had happened which could happen. But there was nothing to be gathered from the set, colourless face of the girl before her, and it was unmitigated cruelty to keep her standing there when quite obviously nothing in heaven or earth could bring her any comfort.

'I am very, very sorry, nurse,' she said at last. 'Captain Meury was a splendid young man. Here is a letter which the officer who wrote from his Division asked me to give you. You need not go back on duty until to-morrow morning.'

Sitting rigid in her cubicle – as Susan Shepherd, whom she had forgotten, had once sat long ago at Wimereux – Ruth opened the letter from Captain Chase. A ring, wrapped in tissue paper, fell out of it on to her knee – Eugene's signet ring, which he had worn that night in the woods near Condette. Clutching it tightly against her breast, she read mechanically through the long letter.

'MY DEAR MISS ALLEYNDENE,

'It is my sad duty to report to you the gallant death of your good friend and mine, Eugene C. Meury, on October 7th in the Argonne Forest. I must beg you to forgive me the delay in conveying the news to you, but I am in hospital myself with a smashed thigh. For some days I was not allowed to write letters at all, and I did not want you to know until I was able to tell you everything that happened.

'On October 2nd, D and E companies, commanded by Eugene and myself, were ordered to advance through a section of the Argonne Forest up a thickly-wooded ravine, deep and narrow, and take the hill at the head of it. By the night of the 3rd we had reached the head of the ravine, but owing to the nature of the country and the rainy weather it had taken longer than we expected, and we were preparing to attack the hill in the morning when we were discovered by a German patrol. We endeavoured to attack the patrol, but the position was heavily guarded by numerous machine-guns concealed in the undergrowth, and meanwhile the enemy had thickly wired the ravine in our rear to cut off our retreat.

'Next day a series of attacks we made on the hill were met by German counter-attacks, and more enemy machine-guns and reinforcements were brought into position. Several of our best officers were killed or wounded in these all but hopeless attacks, and on the morning of the 5th we realised we were cut off from the rest of the battalion, with our supplies all but exhausted. I sent out details to try to get rations and convey the news of our situation to headquarters, but they never returned. By midday on the 7th most of our officers were disabled and our men starving after three days without rations. Casualties due to repeated enemy attempts to dislodge us from the ravine amounted to nearly half the companies, and we were practically surrounded by German machine-gun posts.

'We had decided that the only thing before us was death by starvation or from a final German attack, when a short distance to the south, in the big valley just beyond the ravine, we heard the Chauchat firing of our own troops and realised that some units of the 45th were looking for us to relieve us. The forest was too thick for us to indicate our position to aeroplanes even if this would not have meant immediate retaliation by the Germans, and after an hour or two you can imagine how our spirits sank to zero when the Chauchat firing grew fainter and we knew that the relieving troops had failed to locate us.

'It was then Eugene offered to lead a squad of men to attack the German machine-gun post on the extreme south which cut us off from our troops, in the hope of a few getting through to report our position and save the two companies. It meant pretty certain death for the officer leading the party, since he would have to take it up the south bank of the ravine, and as Eugene had already got one of his fingers smashed and a nasty head wound I told him to stop with the companies and I would go myself. He only said, 'No, you're the senior officer, Russell, and it's your job to stay with the outfit. Besides, you've got a wife and child in New York, and I'm not married. You've every reason for wanting to return to the United States and I've none; truly, I'd as soon die as go back. Get me the volunteers and I'm off.'

'There was no question of waiting until dark, you understand, because our relieving forces were already moving away in the wrong direction. I got a dozen of the boys to volunteer, and just before he started off with them he took the enclosed signet ring from his finger and asked me to send it you if any of the squad got through and we were relieved. I said, "Do you want me to give her any message with it?" and he replied, "Tell her I love her. Just that. She knows it already, but tell her again." Then he shook hands with me and was gone in a second. He and the squad crept through the undergrowth to the south point of the hill where the machine-gun nest was guarding a dip in the side of the ravine, and then he crawled up the slope and literally hurled himself on the post and its officer. I saw him go down twice and get up again before he finally fell. By that time part of the gun crew had been driven off by our boys and the rest killed.

'As soon as the gun was captured two or three of the squad disappeared south. They must have got in touch with the relieving forces in about twenty minutes, because two or three companies came up in under an hour and helped us to clear the enemy from the sides of the ravine. I got my thigh smashed and was pushed through into hospital that night, but before I was taken away some of the boys rescued Eugene's body. It was riddled with bullets, so he must have died pretty instantaneously and he can't have suffered long. I daresay it will not comfort you much to hear that he has been cited for the Distinguished Service Cross by the Battalion Commander, but at least this shows you our Army realises how fine his sacrifice was in saving the 'missing companies,' and will not allow his courage to go unrewarded.

'I know this letter has made hard reading, but do try to buck up all you can. That sounds just words to you now, I daresay, but it is what Eugene would ask me to tell you if he were here. When you have recovered from the shock a little, I know you will want to do your job in life, whatever it may be. I know you will want to make it just as fine a job as you would have made it if Eugene had not been killed.

'With respect and real sympathy,
'Sincerely yours,
'Russell D. Chase.'

21

Towards evening Ruth found herself on the sandhills far away from the hospital. She had no idea where she had been during the intervening hours, nor could she recall a single thought that had passed through her mind. But now, looking at the tide going out and leaving behind it shallow pools which caught on their surface the transitory fires of the western sun, she knew with the blinding force of full understanding that in all the gigantic desolation of earth and sky there remained no breath of his life – not even in her body, where alone it might have achieved continuation.

Lying with her arms outstretched on the sand-dunes in the bitter October wind, she cried aloud.

'Oh, why was I so afraid of consequences – such a coward, such a coward! Why did I fear my family, my upbringing, my traditions! Thanks to the Alleyndenes and their standards Richard threw his life away, and I've been no better, no braver! Because their hold on me was so strong in spite of everything, I sacrificed the existence of Eugene's child. Whatever they did and said I could have faced it, lived it down, and at the end of it all something of him would have been left. Now there's nothing – nothing – nothing!'

She pressed her face against the sand, clutching with her cold fingers at the prickly grass.

'Oh, my love, my love! I did so want to give you a child!'

Far away out to sea, the fishing boats drew slowly homeward.

Above her head the autumn wind moaned and the sea-birds cried and the night descended, drawing down its dark curtain over the ragged red banners of the sunset. But Ruth still lay on her face in the wet sand, weeping away her youth for the life that had been, and for that other life which would now never be.

PART III

(1921–1930)

CHAPTER VII

SON AND DAUGHTER

'Let heart-sickness pass beyond a certain bitter point,
and the heart loses its life for ever.'
              JOHN RUSKIN, Preface to *Sesame and Lilies*.

'The many problems and difficulties which marriage
with her would raise seemed trivial ... He braced
himself to the exquisite burden of life.'
              ARNOLD BENNETT, *Clayhanger*.

I

OUTSIDE the frost-diamonded windows of the Warsaw–
Moscow train, the marshes of devastated Poland stretched
away to infinity, flat, snow-shrouded, silent. Sometimes a broken
bridge or a cluster of wooden crosses interrupted the monotony
of the vast desolate plain; sometimes a clump of evergreen
firs or the skeleton silhouette of a ruined house stood with
dreary emphasis against the level horizon. Peering between the
grotesque frost-patterns which covered the landscape side of the
misty pane, Denis Rutherston looked out upon the grim wintry
face of December 1921.

Lying across the shabby seats of the over-heated second-class
carriage, Denis's five companions sprawled half-asleep among
the wicker baskets which contained their three weeks' rations.
Young dons from Oxford, Cambridge, Liverpool, Manchester
and Birmingham, they were members, like himself, of a voluntary university committee appointed to investigate the Russian
famine. But in Denis even the heavy afternoon somnolence
produced no desire for sleep. His mind was too deeply preoccupied with the conversations, dwelling exclusively upon hunger,

typhus and refugees, which he had heard during their twenty-four hours' wait in Warsaw.

'A vast stupidity,' he murmured to himself as he gazed, for the fourth day in succession, upon the immense areas of national misery created in Central Europe by the blasting trail of the Great War. Already, in this strip of territory ravaged by the Czarist armies retreating before von Mackensen in 1915, he had caught glimpses of men and women living like rats in old German dug-outs, of beggars dying from starvation and exposure in the grimy corners of ramshackle railway stations. Would he ever be able to convey to his London University students at Prince's College, Hampstead, the remotest impression of the bleak wilderness, stretching across the entire length of a continent, left in its wake by modern warfare? Only four days out from England – and there might well be fifteen or twenty more before they reached the doomed Volga Valley and their destination, the headquarters of the Friends' Famine Mission at Buzuluk, in the province of Samara.

Tremendous though the real contrasts were, the desolation of Poland carried his mind back to the desolation of Belgium after the Armistice three years ago. In a village near Mons, where the winter rain dripped incessantly upon the grey marshy fields, he had first awakened with a shock of agonising realisation to the fact that this war-scarred country was now a land of comparative security, in which the death that he had prayed for was no longer to be had for the taking. With the force of revelation had come the further knowledge that if his unexpected and undesired survival was to be of value to himself or anyone else, he must evolve some new creed, some philosophy of life, which looked forward and not back. He must substitute the process of constructive thought for the old stoicisms of resignation and endurance.

'I suppose we shall have to cool our heels here for about a week!' grumbled Denis's Birmingham colleague as the train dragged itself lethargically into Stolpce on the Russian frontier. But they had only to wait until the next day for the ancient log-stoked engine to join the standing train. The enthusiasm of the Soviet authorities had so vigorously disinfected coaches and corridors with sulphur that the six young men sneezed and coughed with their eyes streaming until they had opened the windows for a few seconds, and allowed the chilling, perilous air to blow through the carriages. Beside the snowy line where they tramped, clearing their lungs, thin leafless birch trees made a fine intricate pattern against the leaden sky. Like a narrow black caterpillar, a convoy of sledges crawled across the grey verge of the horizon.

As the train crept from Minsk to Smolensk – an old red-walled town with its domed snow-crowned churches and circular towers built majestically along a line of low hills – Denis's thoughts again dwelt upon his post-war search for a vital philosophy. Immersed in his memories, he hardly noticed the battle of would-be passengers at Smolensk to join the long-awaited train, nor the speed with which the Soviet couriers who had joined them at Stolpce sprang from their carriage to assist the armed guards in repelling unauthorised travellers. He looked up only for a second when his companions pointed out a long refugee train standing in the station, its ragged hungry passengers crowded together in luggage waggons with only a stove for comfort. Poles and Jews transplanted from the Polish war area to the Volga Valley in 1915, they now fled from the famine region where doom had been foreseen from the time that the great drought of 1921 followed the failure of the winter snows and the spring rains. Doom hardly less inevitable awaited them amid the ruined, typhus-infested sites of their old homes in Eastern Poland.

'I mustn't dwell in the past,' he had told himself repeatedly during those weeks of military stagnation in Belgium. 'That long-drawn tragedy of family hatred and frustration has no message for the future ... unless it compels me to evolve some principle of thought and action which may serve as a guide for those who are struggling to prevent a repetition of the past four years. My early life was a chaos created by conflict, a miniature reproduction of the world at war. If this experience of futile tragedy can urge me to work for peace and order as the only lasting bases of civilisation, then perhaps it was worth enduring.'

Because he had been an undergraduate whose Degree course was still unfinished, Denis was demobilised five months after the Armistice. He had no home now, no relative but Thomas, nor had he, it seemed, any friends. The constant tension between his parents had always prevented the formation of local friendships, and most of his school and college contemporaries were buried in France or Flanders or Gallipoli. Like a ghost compelled to revisit the habitations of a former existence, he returned to a modest Turl Street lodging in the feverish, discursive, revolutionary Oxford of 1919.

Throughout that uneasy summer term, the Senior and Junior Common Rooms of the University were agitated by acrimonious controversies on the obstinacy of France, the ambitions of Italy, the importunities of Jugo-Slavia, the uncompromising ruthlessness of Bolshevik Russia, the baffled idealism of disgusted America. Denis could not afford to join the Oxford Union, for Thomas's expenses still absorbed his meagre private income, and only his scholarships enabled him to return to his college to take the shortened course in Greats. But he listened from the gallery to debates in which the speakers compared the tolerant provisions of the Congress of Vienna with the savage revengefulness of the Treaty of Versailles, or maintained that the League of Nations, like the Holy Alliance, was doomed from the start by the cynical inability of statesmen to accept any international system which presupposed the fundamental benevolence of human nature.

He never imagined that these debates, metallic with youthful aggressiveness and persevering wit, would assist his psychological recovery; yet when he went down he found that they had left him with an ambition to base his philosophy of peace and order upon a direct knowledge of the countries involved in the downfall of both. In the summer of 1920, he was appointed to a junior lectureship in Social Philosophy at Prince's College, Hampstead. Three months afterwards his father's sudden death left him free, for the first time in his life, to spend his money upon his own pursuits.

Early in 1921, he accepted an invitation from America to lecture at the Summer School held by the University of Wisconsin.

Towards the end of that year he volunteered to join, as London's representative, an informal university committee appointed to visit the Russian famine area, and report on the rumour that the Soviet was diverting supplies intended for the victims to maintain the Red Army. The risk of cholera, typhus and dysentery alarmed him no more than the fantastic proportion of accidents on the ancient and disintegrating Russian railways. He was beginning to believe that life held greater possibilities for him than he had ever imagined, but there was still nobody on earth whom his death would leave desolate.

'Here's Moscow!' enthusiastically announced the Communist committee member from Cambridge when the old engine panted into a great urban station on the third morning after leaving Stolpce. His five companions stretched themselves sleepily and reluctantly, for on the previous night a couriers' concert of revolutionary songs and folk-tunes, held in the corridor and accompanied by the drinking of ferocious vodka, had kept them awake till the early hours of the morning. From the station they drove in a lorry through the trodden snow to the Friends' Flat in the Goroscherskaya, where they were to wait for two days until the Trans-Caspian express from Moscow to Tashkent was ready to carry them on to Buzuluk. Denis's drowsy mind registered a confused impression of shouting crowds and clanging electric trams, of pedestrians scattering wildly in front of charging opulent motor-cars, and sleighs dodging skilfully through the feverish traffic.

In spite of the grimy grey snow and the crisp winter air, he had never seen, even in mid-summer, so exuberant a riot of vivid colours. Against the turquoise pavilion of the sky, domes and minarets as numerous as the precious stones of the New Jerusalem gleamed sapphire and emerald, jasper and gold. Bells rang vigorously, summoning throngs of devout worshippers whose numbers made Denis speculate upon the rumours of religious persecution which gratified England's anxiety to believe the worst. Crowds streamed unmolested into the white Church of our Saviour on the far side of the Kremlin. At the entrance to the Red Square a long queue of devotees waited before the shrine of the Iberian Virgin, sublimely unimpressed by the gigantic inscription on the blank wall above their heads:

RELIGION IS THE OPIUM OF THE PEOPLE

All through the day and for the greater part of the night, relief-workers circulated in and out of the Friends' headquarters. Their practical preoccupations contrasted strangely with the other-worldliness of ardent Tolstoyan visitors, who called to discuss the abstract mysteries of the universe with anyone who had time to spare from its immediate problems. Their discursive investigation of the topics which had perturbed his Putney grandfather impressed Denis even more than the Tchaikowsky Ballet at the Grand Theatre, where the six of them paid five million roubles for a box and discovered that it amounted to no more than two pounds in English currency. Though the lives of millions in revolutionary Russia depended upon the speed with which reconstruction could be accomplished, time, it seemed, was still regarded as subordinate to the eternal values. The famine was strangling the education budget; Lunacharsky was striving to combat illiteracy by building eleven thousand new schools; but the Union of Socialist Soviet Republics continued to nurture its children of light for whom discussions with no practical ending and no logical conclusion eclipsed in importance these material dilemmas.

When the overloaded Trans-Caspian express began its lethargic journey to Tashkent, Denis had as much time as he required to meditate upon the incongruities of Moscow. Again and again the train lurched into a snow-drift, and the engine-driver abandoned his losing battle with the Russian winter. After three hundred miles of adventurous travel, an antiquated wood-burning engine replaced the coal-burner, and the pace of the express became even tardier. Sometimes, when the temperature rose, the passengers waited for several hours while the wood-stacks beside the line dried slowly after saturation by melting snow. Sometimes the salvage engines themselves proved magnificently ineffective. One of these, decorated with portraits of Lenin and Trotsky, and resplendently painted in red and blue, carried the slogan 'Workers of the World, Unite!' in several languages, but it failed to move the train until a plebeian assistant in plain iron and steel was sent to its rescue.

'All the same,' thought Denis, as they rattled day after day over the monotonous miles of uninhabited steppe where the snow lay spread like a cotton-wool quilt, 'all the same, the colossal haphazard inconveniences of this fantastic country are one way of measuring the completeness of the Revolution. They're the grotesque, exasperating consequences of the process of birth. In Moscow, for all its welter of faiths and values, its wild disorganisation of currency and transport, I did have the sense of new life striving to penetrate the shattered surface of a world in which no temple of tradition has been left unshaken.'

Next term, he reflected, when he returned to Hampstead to lecture to his students upon the influences which were transforming twentieth-century thought, he would try to show them how the years 1914 to 1918, with their acceleration of revolutions not merely political, but social and moral, already represented the Great Divide in theories of human conduct. Here in Russia, where the crude machinery of material and spiritual change was so painfully apparent, he could see how decisively the present was breaking with the past, how sharply the new values were repudiating the old.

A gulf not of seven years but of seven decades seemed to stretch, for instance, between the militant suffrage movement with its narrow political preoccupations, and this huge experimental country where the theoretical sex equality now being sceptically vaunted by the statesmen of the older nations was in process of practical realisation. How archaic to-day appeared his father's opposition to woman suffrage, how inconsistent the relationship between his parents with the spirit of the new epoch! His mother, he knew, would have welcomed it; it was one of life's cruel ironies that she, with her essentially modern outlook, should not have survived to see it. But he felt thankful that Thomas was dead. The pre-war years had sufficiently startled and distressed his father; he would have been lost, forlorn and utterly misplaced in the nineteen-twenties.

When the train at last approached Samara and the famine

area, it seemed to move yet more slowly, as though weighed down by a sense of coming calamity. At every station after passing the frontier, Denis had seen the stark, primitive posters with their rough cartoons of distorted famine victims, their ill-proportioned khaki figures representing the classes upon which famine taxation was imposed. With the courier's help he translated and copied the black and red appeals for help in heavy Russian characters, and the rough verses attached to unflattering caricatures of the grudging giver.

COMRADES!   CITIZENS!

THE NINTH SOVIET CONFERENCE ADVISES EVERYONE TO FIGHT THE FAMINE!

Read, Mark and Fulfil!

> The general public helps thus
> Gives five kopeks
> And is happy
> Thinking he has done his duty!
> The five kopeks reaches the famine area,
> The peasant gets a mouthful of bread
> And again is hungry.
> There is no use in haphazard help.

'No use at all,' the young men agreed, as they listened unhappily to the thin wailing of lost hungry children at Samara station in the deep trough of the pitiless night. That forsaken cry still echoed in their ears as the express, now drawn by an up-to-date oil-burning engine fed from the oil-wells of Baku, hastened through the heavy atmosphere of tragedy towards the great famine-stricken valley.

The morning light of Christmas Eve, 1921, shone bleakly upon the green roofs of a riverside town. Above the water, the battered framework of a wooden bridge destroyed by the Czechs in their homeward post-war journey from Siberia loomed in the distance like the skeleton of a prehistoric monster. The green and silver domes of churches stood silhouetted in tawdry magnificence against the clear winter sky. Ten days after leaving Moscow and nineteen from the homely, remote security of England, Denis Rutherston reached Buzuluk.

2

In the bare, well-warmed living-room of the Friends' Mission headquarters, Ruth Alleyndene raised her head from the household accounts as the low, poignant sobbing which had sounded from the Mission doorstep throughout the night and early morning suddenly died away.

After listening for a moment in the heavy, portentous silence, she tried again to occupy herself with the weekly housekeeping. As one of the only two English women then attached to the Buzuluk headquarters, she was obliged to take her turn in organising the meals for that miscellaneous assembly of relief-workers, chauffeurs, sleigh-drivers and warehousemen. But she could not give her mind to the task of providing, with no help from circumstances, some alternative to bully beef and tinned apricots for to-morrow's Christmas dinner. Household management was not an occupation in which, under any conditions, her interest would have been excessive, but at Buzuluk it was complicated to the limits of distraction by the haphazard arrival of supplies from Moscow and the violent inflation of the currency. So rapidly was the value of the rouble descending, that whenever the Moscow train was late the bundles of paper currency which it carried had become completely worthless.

The door opened and a tall, powerful Scotsman came in. Without a word he seized a red record book from Ruth's table and made a short entry.

'That woman who's been crying all night seems to have stopped,' she observed.

'Yes. Just gone west,' the Scot responded laconically.

'Thank God!' she said, but when he had gone she closed the ledger and sat staring at the ruthless winter sunlight pouring through the high wooden-framed windows. Her thoughts gathered round the dead woman whose stiff emaciated body – one of the hundred corpses daily contributed by the stricken town to the pile of frozen bodies in Buzuluk cemetery – would eventually be gathered like refuse from the snow by the municipal sleigh. Sometimes she felt that death was the only reality left in the world. It still seemed to be winning in its race with the resources and invigorations of life, though instead of using blood and mutilation it now found its weapons in starvation and typhus. Already the fever had smitten two or three of the Mission workers, though not herself. Oh, never herself, however deeply she might desire the fate against which others fought with fear and desperation!

In the searching light of that December morning her thin face, pale even in early youth, was now almost colourless. Above the worn hollows of its contours, her grey eyes appeared unnaturally large and dark; her crisp hair was combed smoothly from her forehead under the white nun-like cap worn as a protection against dirt and the typhus-carrying lice. Though her beauty had not vanished, three years of suffering and experience had given it a stern, ascetic quality which was essentially mature; already it verged upon the haggard frailty which Ellison Campbell had foreseen long ago at Drayton. When she looked into the square of unframed glass on the wall of her cubicle, she could not believe that she was still no more than twenty-seven. She might well have been ten years older than the lovely, glowing girl who had lain with Eugene Meury in the pine-forest at Hardelot.

It was useless, she decided, to celebrate Christmas when there was no life, no hope, no laughter and play of children; useless to try to forget the present when it died daily on your doorstep. Like the rest of the Mission, which was still able to feed only a carefully chosen proportion of the famine population, she now felt nothing but thankfulness when another starving human creature stumbled from racking agony into somnolence and death. But the rule which forbade relief-workers to prolong the sufferings of those already doomed did not make their pitiful, bewildered appeals any easier to withstand. In this stark terrible Russia of 1921, even the sorrowful past seemed less painful to contemplate than the present in which thousands of unoffending men and women fought a lost battle for life and died in anguish.

She looked back, now, upon her two years in Cologne which followed the War with no real consciousness that they had ever been. Even the chance meeting on the Domplatz one bitter afternoon with Frieda Königsberger – a worn, silent Frieda, her muscular vitality drained by the blockade, her gay responsive cordiality vanished beyond retrieval – seemed less a fact of authentic life than the inexplicable encounter of a dream. Ruth had not realised that the troubled twilight of her mind during those mechanical months of light, uneventful nursing reflected only too accurately the world-psychology of that grey period between war and peace, for the swift grotesque events of 1919 held even less meaning for her than for most of the stunned millions who were slowly emerging from their four years nightmare.

Throughout that spring she remained unaware that the liberal, republican Germany to which she had migrated in order to nurse the local sick from the British Army of Occupation, was discussing at Weimar a new constitution embodying political equality for women. In the blank darkness which eclipsed the end of 1918, she had been equally indifferent to the fact that, in England, women candidates were standing for Parliament during a General Election which ended in powerless ignominy for rejected Labour. Cut off from the general diffused excitement over the number of activities that newly enfranchised women were undertaking for the first time, she did not know that Lord Curzon, Mrs Humphry Ward and Ellison Campbell – who had ceased to be prominent in the opposition movement since 1917 – were the only famous anti-suffragists left at home after the War.

No Madeleine existed now to tell her that a woman had been elected Member of Parliament in November 1919, or that a Sex Disqualification Removal Act received the Royal Assent a month later. Even the news that women at Oxford had Degrees conferred upon them in October 1920 completely failed to arouse her enthusiasm. She had never discussed either

Socialism or feminism with Eugene, yet because he was dead she had ceased to be moved by either. As for the League of Nations, the controversies eddying round it at the Paris Peace Conference only recalled an afternoon which they had spent together at Camiers. The subject aroused a faint emotional interest in her because she had once talked it over with him. That was all.

Throughout 1919, Jessie wrote plaintively to her of the blank futility which seemed to envelop Dene Hall now that the convalescent officers were gone.

'I started the work because I felt I must do something after our dear boy's death, but now it is over I am lost without it. My life with your father has never given me enough occupation for my energy, and I shall have to find some kind of social work to fill my time. The housing shortage in the Potteries is bringing still more working-class people into Witnall, and though it does not really appeal to me, I shall probably take a district and help the Rector with the poor families in the parish.'

Stephen's letters, though less frequent, were equally glum; he wrote of taxation, of labour troubles, of the rise of retail prices by November 1919 to one hundred and twenty-five per cent above their pre-war figure. In 1920 his predictions became even more pessimistic.

'What with these strikes and unemployment riots, I don't know how Norman and I are going to carry on. If ever you do decide to come home, which your mother and I are beginning to give up hope of, you will probably find your father on the verge of bankruptcy.'

Ruth replied with automatic conscientiousness to her parents' lamentations, but the social and economic changes indicated by their letters left no impression upon her mind. Because her sense of awareness had failed, those two years in Cologne made her understand, long after they were over, the meaning of the phrase 'like a watch in the night.' The familiar dark silhouette of the gigantic twin-spired Cathedral, the Rhine flowing serenely magnificent before her hospital in the Kaiser-Friedrich-Ufer, seemed only to emphasise with their dominant immutability the monotonous swiftness of her days.

Throughout those vanishing shadowy months her mind dwelt

not in Cologne but in Hardelot. Over and over again, she returned in memory to her meetings with Eugene there and elsewhere – the Savoy dinner, the air-raid on Wimbledon Common, the evenings at Condette, the night in the forest. A day spent in Coblenz during the late spring, when the Rhineland hillsides were mauve with blossom, and dwarf cherries bloomed pink and white in every German orchard, sent her back to Cologne with a pain at her heart which almost awakened her from the long dull numbness. She had not realised that Coblenz would be full of American officers, and the sound of their cheerful incisive speech, the sight of their peaked caps and fastidious uniforms, brought back the old sequence of tormenting questions which had come with the end of the War.

Had Eugene really loved her? Had he really wanted her in the way he had taken her? Had he died thinking more of her, or less, because she had given her body to him so urgently? That last communication through Captain Russell Chase – was it a full endorsement of their relationship, or merely a hurried message sent in the ultimate emotion of desperate battle? She would never know now; this silence would never lift. Oh, worse than death was the grave's repudiation of one's most passionate, imperative questioning!

Whatever answers Eugene might have given her, she asked, now, no more of fate than permission to join him in the oblivion which she believed was the end of life as it had been the end of love; that oblivion in which also dwelt Richard and Madeleine. What was the use of going on living when everyone who mattered was dead? She remembered a sentence from the *Pilgrim's Progress* which her mother had read aloud in their childhood: 'How welcome death is to them that have nothing to do but to die.'

It wasn't fair, she thought, to commit suicide like Susan Shepherd, for that meant distress and humiliation for your family. But surely, when life had nothing left to hold you, and you were no longer necessary to anyone's happiness, you were entitled to put yourself – as Richard perhaps had done – in the way of an honourable end? It wouldn't be difficult to die, however horribly, when Eugene had already trodden that bitter road before her. The first time she took up her pen after knowing that it would be useless ever to write to him again, she had added to her quotation book some lines from Mark Rutherford's *Catherine Furze*:

'When we come near death or near something which may be worse, all exhortation, theory, promise, advice, dogma, fail. The one staff which, perhaps, may not break under us is the victory achieved in the like situation by one who has preceded us.'

In France, during the terrible influenza epidemic which followed the Armistice and forced her again to wear the mask of efficiency, she volunteered constantly for double duty when half the staff went sick. Many of the nurses died, but the germ eluded her. Throughout her two winters in Germany she avoided no risks, took no care of herself when in contact with infectious disease, went deliberately underclad in snow and rain. Nothing touched her; no ill results followed. Here in Russia typhus stalked rampant, but she remained immune. Sometimes she thought that grief must have inoculated her against every form of physical affliction. She seemed to have spent centuries living, herself unimpaired, under war conditions in the company of the sick and suffering; yet she could not imagine what she would do in other surroundings. She dreaded the normal; she could hardly remember what it had been before the War, and felt nothing but fear of what it must be now.

That morning at Buzuluk, she shuddered to recall her brief endeavour, after the Cologne hospital had closed in the early spring of 1921, to re-adapt herself to Dene Hall while she considered how to use the unwanted existence of which she was still left in possession. Her father appeared perpetually harassed, her mother discontented unless she was out of the house on some local mission, while she found Norman, whom she now saw for the first time since his return from the East as a major in the summer of 1920, even less congenial than before the War. He had become so mature in his appearance, so censorious in his judgments and so rigid in his outlook, that he seemed to belong more appropriately to Stephen's generation than his own. His war-time life in the East remained a closed book which he never opened.

Even the old friends of her childhood had passed beyond the range of immediate contact. Arthur Wardle no longer worked as gardener at Dene Hall: he had taken over the considerable task of reorganising the moribund Labour Party in Witnall with the intermittent help of Jim Hardiman, who had never settled contentedly into his former niche at the Pottery after his war service in Palestine. They persuaded Ruth to join the Party, but the organisation was still too embryonic to offer satisfying occupation to an intelligent volunteer.

One afternoon towards the end of the summer, a tennis tournament held on the Dene Hall courts by a dozen boys and girls of the post-war generation, light-hearted and free from the torture of memory, made her conscious to the point of hysteria of her irremediable maladjustment. There might after all, she was thinking, be no solution but self-destruction, when she saw in that evening's Manchester newspaper an appeal for volunteers to help the Friends in their work for the victims of typhus in Poland. They also proposed, the paragraph stated, to set up a relief organisation in the Volga Valley, where the threatened famine was now inevitable. When she read that America was co-operating in both campaigns, her decision to offer her nursing experience to the Quakers took less than five minutes. Here, in the contact with a deadly epidemic, in the care of diseased and starving refugees, was a final chance to rid herself of her superfluous existence.

Her parents, who had adapted themselves to her presence more easily than she had adjusted herself to theirs, received with dismay this proposal to renew, without any obligation of honour, the risks and anxieties of the war-time years.

'I can't think,' she overheard Jessie complain to Norman, 'why she wants to go on running into danger like this, just as if the War were still on, when it's all been over for ages!'

'Can't settle down, I suppose,' commented Norman. 'But after all, that's nothing new, is it? She never could.'

'No. She's always been terribly restless. At one time I was quite afraid she'd go and get engaged to that young American she used to meet in France. He was supposed to have a fiancée in America, but you never know where you are with these foreigners. Of course, I was sorry when he was killed, poor young man, but I didn't want Ruth to go away and live in New York.'

'I'm not sure you were right, Mother. Surely even New York would have been better than getting mixed up with refugees and epidemics in a barbarous country like Russia?'

Stephen's response to the situation was less critical and more practical. All this new taxation, he confided to Ruth, was creating great difficulties for him – to say nothing of the high cost of living and the money lost to trade generally through national strikes like the recent coal dispute. If he didn't look out he'd simply be crushed by the burden of super-tax, and it would help rather than inconvenience him to transfer to her a small part of his excess capital.

'I don't want to make you live at home, Jill, if you'd rather have a little place of your own and take up some hobby or other. Things are very different from what they were in my young days; you're of age now, and entitled to please yourself. Witnall's a one-eyed spot for young people, and I don't blame you if you can't settle down here.'

'It's very good of you, Father, but it isn't really Witnall that's wrong,' she explained, touched as always by his simple, valiant efforts to understand and comfort a nature so different from his own. 'There just doesn't seem to be any particular place for me in the world since the War. At least it gives me some object in life to go and help where people are needed.'

By the end of August she had left the dry brilliance of the 1921 summer in England for the dry desolation of the 1921 drought in Poland. Here she saw, for the first time, the eastern face of the Great War which hitherto she had only known in the West. Travelling among the ruined villages of Volhynia, working for the ragged, starving, fever-stricken refugees who were returning in desperation from the Volga Valley at a time when most European governments were obstructing the Soviet experiment and finding the loftiest reasons for doing so, she achieved once more that measure of resignation which seemed the only attainable substitute for peace.

Day by day, as the tragic year moved to its fall, the rolling plain destroyed by the War turned a deeper brown, a warmer gold. Across the flat miles of monotonous marsh stretched the interminable lines of fallen trenches and the black zigzags of barbed-wire entanglements. To the north of the Stochod river the trenches were dotted with white concrete emplacements, the wire sunk in brown rushes where the bright lingering butterflies recalled to Ruth the red admirals and orange fritillaries which had hovered at the edge of the reed-covered meres near the Château d'Hardelot. In fallen hovels and old German dug-outs the refugees clung to their wretched existence, living miserably upon roots and bark and fungus in the desolate region where corn-fields had turned to waste grass, village churches to heaps of stones, beautiful villas to blackened walls, gardens to rank weeds and tangled thistles. When the raw evening mists arose from the lonely swamps, the ghosts of the thousands of dead Cossacks who lay there seemed to stalk the land, carrying horror and corruption for hundreds of miles from north to south. In the persons of the refugees came the new encroaching wilderness of the Russian famine, threatening to destroy yet again a country already twice destroyed by war.

One afternoon when the autumn air was restless with falling leaves, and drifts of amber and vermilion covered the damp earth in the sombre woods of holm-oak and birch, she found a path half obscured by thick undergrowth which led to a war-time German cemetery. As she tried to decipher the names on the rough unpainted crosses above the graves of Landstürmers who had fallen in 1916, she realised that no Graves Commission operated in Poland. Some of the crosses were crooked and others lay on their side, sinking more deeply year after year into the welter of coarse, spreading nettles which covered the cemetery and the deep leaf-mould beneath the trees. This desolation of men and leaves and crosses rotting together in silence amid the overgrown nettles recalled the macabre images which had possessed her mind after Richard's death, and had haunted her again, more vividly, more terribly, in the months that followed October 1918.

'These men are lost, forgotten, abandoned,' she thought shivering, 'and yet women once loved them as I loved Eugene! If the Americans hadn't cared for their dead, his grave in

the Argonne would have become just as these – a strip of
untended, nettle-covered earth marked by a fallen cross in a
golden forest.'

When the autumn leaves had scattered until only the copper-
red birch-shoots were left on the bare dry branches, there came a
sudden change of wind. Dark battalions of heavy cloud gathered
upon the horizon; the yellow marshes turned to sodden grey
beneath driving gusts of rain. When the rain hardened to snow,
the relief-workers began to prepare for the defence of the refugees against encroaching winter by repairing boots, sorting out
mittens, sewing fur on coats and experimenting with makeshift
stoves. But Ruth, because of her war-time experience, was sent as
a temporary supply nurse to the over-crowded League of Nations
hospital at Baranowicze on the Russian frontier.

Baranowicze was the centre of the sanitary cordon placed by
the League across the Russo-Polish frontier, with the intention
of saving Europe from the typhus now carried from Turkistan to
the Volga and from the Volga to the Vistula. In the grey isolation
of that cheerless outpost, the tragedy of Poland and the tragedy
of Russia – two aspects only of the world-tragedy which began
in August 1914 – met one another face to face. Long lines of army
huts formed the hospital and refugee camps, stretching drearily
across the wintry plain where it had been possible to walk for
miles without seeing house or smoke or furrow since the devas-
tation of Eastern Poland by the Russian retreat in 1915. Here for
a few days' quarantine waited the starving, verminous, diseased
men and women who were fleeing in their thousands from the
death-in-life of the Russian famine to the death-in-life of their
charred and ruined Polish homes two thousand miles away.

Every day Ruth looked out upon the same bleak, monotonous
prospect – the changing but indistinguishable groups of pallid
refugees crowded before the wooden huts in the dirty trampled
snow; the long avenue of tall, tapering firs cutting across the
camp; the illimitable greyish-white plain interrupted only by
dark solitary fir trees standing like finger-posts against the laden
sky. But there was little time to watch the landscape even if its
aspect had been enchanting, for the League of Nations hospital, which possessed only three hundred beds, contained over

six hundred patients. Sometimes three or four dying children, wrapped only in blankets because the sheets were exhausted, lay whimpering in each bed.

During November, when Ruth was sent to Baranowicze, the death-roll from typhus amounted to nearly fifteen hundred. Burials were as wholesale and automatic as in a mediæval plague-stricken city, and the staff – itself permanently diminished by disease – concentrated on saving the hopeful cases. Broken in by the great German offensive of 1918 to days and nights passed almost without sleep, Ruth sometimes worked for eighteen hours out of the twenty-four. The flesh seemed to vanish visibly from her frame; beneath the dark rings under her eyes, the moulding of her cheek-bones showed clearly through her pale delicate skin. But still the typhus evaded her; still she remained immune. In the midst of this mortality and despair she felt that she had reached the bedrock of human experience, the ultimate end of that migration from Dene Hall standards of comfort and prosperity which had begun for her in 1915.

Because of the fear that, escaping fever, she would collapse from over-exhaustion, she was transferred early in December to the Mission at Buzuluk, where the surroundings were no less grim but the work was lighter. In the quiet occupations of relief distribution and housekeeping after her fourteen days' journey, her aching feet began to lose their fatigue, her brain to recover its capacity for sleep. Drowsy from her accumulated burden of work and memory that Christmas Eve, she struggled to concentrate on the Mission account-books. She had just started to check over the list of stores, when a tentative knock sounded on the door.

'Come in!' she called, looking up.

The door opened, and a tall young man walked across the room to her table.

3

As soon as Ruth saw him, she remembered with a smitten heart the last occasion on which a tall stranger had suddenly appeared before her. But except for the fact that both of them had materialised, as it seemed, from nowhere, there was nothing in common between the two young men. This one, instead of being dark and brown-skinned and vivacious, was pale and blue-eyed and serious, with a high forehead crowned by a waving crest of light-brown hair. Moreover, he was not much taller than herself, whereas Eugene had looked down upon her five-foot-ten from the loftiness of six-foot-three.

'I beg your pardon,' said Denis Rutherston, 'but I belong to a committee of investigation from the English universities. I understand arrangements have been made to put us up at the Mission.'

'Yes, we were expecting you,' she answered, 'but of course we'd no idea when you'd arrive. Nobody ever does know in this place.'

'I can well imagine that, if all the trains are like ours. My colleagues stayed to watch the stores unloaded at the station, so I walked on to make sure about our rooms.'

'It's rather a depressing two miles, isn't it?'

'It is. I must confess I didn't expect to see corpses lying about in the streets, as if it were still the War . . . Are they famine victims from Buzuluk itself?'

'No, none of them,' she said. 'Buzuluk's been a dead town for ages, without inhabitants. They come in from the surrounding villages as a last hope of getting something to eat. But there's no last hope in this part of Russia. There's no hope at all.'

'Isn't there – not even at the Mission?'

'Not for everyone. We can't feed them unless they're on our list – not even when they die on our doorstep, as one did this morning. Our supplies would give out in no time if we didn't limit the relief to certain categories. Most of the villagers who come from outside are past saving anyway . . . If you'll excuse me a moment, I'll go and see about your accommodation.'

While she went out to interview the Russian cook and house-maid he sat gazing at the chair which she had occupied, his mind puzzled, his interest aroused. That blue nurse's uniform she was wearing . . . it reminded him of a blue dress that he had once seen on a girl who might have been the younger sister of this grave, tired-looking young woman. Where was it, and when? . . . As she came in again, his recollection cleared with a suddenness which left him with a slight sense of shock. Intently he examined her eyes and mouth – still lovely in its fine curves, though harder at the corners than it had been seven years ago – and smiled ruefully as he spoke.

'I believe I've met you before. Aren't you Miss Alleyndene?'

'Yes,' she said, and surprise made her voice a little cold. 'Yes, I am – but how did you know? I've no idea who you are.'

'No,' he admitted, 'you wouldn't remember me, but I remember you. I've seen you twice. The first time was at a garden party at your house in Staffordshire, when we were both children. My father was Rector of Witnall for a short time, but he . . . well, he didn't exactly hit it off with your father, and in the end we left in rather a hurry.'

She knit her dark brows, faintly interested by this unexpected reminiscence of the days before chaos had come.

'I recollect my parents talking about it – and you too, as a kind of prehistoric legend. You were wearing a large Eton collar, and my mother said it looked absurd and at your age you ought to be in stick-ups.'

He flushed a little, but ignored the humiliating implications of her remark as deliberately as if he had known that it sprang from her aching comparison between himself and that other stranger.

'Your mother was right, I'm sure. Neither of my parents had the slightest idea how to dress me. I detested your garden party, but my mother was indulging in one of her periodic absences from home, and my father insisted on my going with him to give us an air of family respectability. You were told off to show me round, and you looked just about as bored as I felt. I remember you had on a white frock and your hair was tied up with a big white ribbon.'

'I was a horrid little girl, I'm sure.'

'Oh, no, not horrid – only rather frightening to a small boy on his best behaviour. You were even more alarming on the second occasion.'

'Was I?' In spite of her resentment against him for reawakening the pain of her memories, she wanted to hear more. A faint smile curved the sad contours of her face as she asked him: 'And when was that?'

'It was at Oxford, in the summer of 1914 – the end of my Second Year.'

'Mine too. Isn't it queer to think what a lot happened before the Flood!'

'I thought you must be about my contemporary. I was twenty-seven last March.'

'And I last June. How did we meet at Oxford?'

'Well, I'd been for a long walk one Sunday and I was late, so I decided to take a short cut through Drayton College to the Woodstock Road. I was feeling rather nervous, because I'd never been inside a women's college before, and when I was about half-way across the garden you came down some steps and met me right in the path. I asked you if I could get through that way, and you said, "Certainly – if you don't object to using us as a short cut."'

Ruth laughed – and started as she did so, for laughter felt as strange in that dead Russia as in her dead life.

'Was I really as rude as that?'

'Quite as rude. I said to myself, "She looked at me as if I'd come to pay a surreptitious visit to one of the college scouts.' And so you did.'

'And you recognised me again?'

'Almost at once. You haven't the sort of face one forgets, you know – especially as you were looking almost as contemptuous this time as you did the last.'

'I'm sorry . . . You see, when you came in suddenly like that, you reminded me of the only occasion something rather similar happened to me before. It's the real reason why I came out here. I mean . . . he was.'

'I see,' he said gravely, understanding at once that those two words had told him the essential fact of her story. He had noticed when he first saw her that she wore a man's signet-ring on the middle finger of her left hand. 'I was just going to ask you what you were doing in Russia.'

She looked up at the window, through which the winter sunshine now gleamed brilliantly from a flawless midday sky. She did not remember that only once before in her life had come the spontaneous impulse to confide; she merely knew that a sense of consolation filled her at the prospect of talking to this stranger who was not entirely a stranger after all.

'Look here,' she suggested, 'we may be interrupted by any number of people at any moment, and I can't have you catechising me in front of your committee. Would you care to go for a short walk and look at the town before your friends see it? It isn't exactly a cheering spectacle, but we could talk at the same time.'

'Certainly; let's go. I shall be glad to stretch my legs a bit more after ten days in the train from Moscow.'

'Wait a moment, then, while I put on my coat.'

She rejoined him in a few minutes wearing tall snow-shoes, a heavy leather coat and a close-fitting helmet decorated with the red and black Quaker star. They went out from the warm security of the Mission into the naked winter street, hard, sparkling and comfortless in the iron grip of sixty degrees of frost. On either side of the frozen road the low two-storied wooden houses were falling into decay. Once they had been gaily painted each year, pink or blue or green, but now it was over seven years since the paint had been renewed. Dingy and dilapidated, they were also mute and empty, monuments of despair in the lost, deserted town.

A hundred yards from the Mission, Ruth and Denis passed the gaunt body of a tall peasant lying face downwards in the snow. Close beside him the open glazed eyes of a dead child stared up at the sun. He was evidently the victim of dysentery or typhus, for his small round face, though distorted with suffering, was not wasted like that of the man.

'You'd better see the worst first,' said Ruth. 'I'll take you to the cemetery. When you've been there, nothing on earth will ever shock you again.'

The midday sun had now deepened to a blueness so intense that it recalled to her mind, with its single preoccupation, the vehement summer skies of war-time France. Beyond the cemetery, the grey foothills of the Ural mountains loomed like distant shadows above the snow. Close to the ordered rows of crosses stood a grey and white church, its green dome and silver cross gleaming in the sunshine.

As they moved nearer to the graves, Denis noticed upon the flat snow-field between the crosses a shapeless indistinguishable heap which he took at first for a rubbish-dump of faggots and rags. He stopped transfixed, defeated by the stupendous effort of realisation, when he recognised the sinister mass as a pile of four hundred half-naked bodies, frozen stiff and shrivelled to skin and bone. Distorted caricatures of humanity, they lay awaiting burial in the communal pit which could not be hacked from the iron earth fast enough to keep pace with the daily mortality. Here and there, from that tumbled medley of death, a rigid arm was raised as though beckoning, a fleshless foot pointed outwards as if engaged in some grim corpses' dance. Only the pale defenceless faces turned up to the sky retained the pathetic semblance of human dignity.

In silence Denis and Ruth walked from the cemetery to a small raised mount outside the town, where they could see the Cossack country across fifty miles of level snow, unbroken except for the occasional dark patches which marked woods or villages.

'I brought you here so that you could look into Asia,' she said. 'Have I answered your question yet about what I'm doing in Russia? Do you understand how desperately people are needed here to fight death as we fought it during the War? I'd far rather be still doing that than living at home, comfortable and secure and utterly useless.'

'But nobody need be useless in England to-day. There's a new order struggling to be born there just as much as here – only in Russia it's come, however painfully, whereas at home we're moving towards it very slowly.'

'I can't believe it's even on the way. I've never pretended to like the world that's come out of the War. It seems to me a greedy, revengeful, throat-cutting world – not at all the sort of place my brother and . . . other people gave up their lives to make. That's why I'm keeping out of it and hoping I shall have the luck to follow them.'

'What makes you think,' asked Denis slowly, 'that people with constructive ideas ever get the kind of society they'd like to live in? Even in Russia that hasn't happened, and probably never will. Some of us just have to carry on knowing our best work doesn't march with history. We have to face the fact that there'll be long periods, perhaps corresponding with the greater part of our lives, when it'll make no headway at all. *Must* you have quick returns? Isn't our contribution to the time Cicero called "that long age in which we shall not be" the only immortality that matters, and the only kind we can be sure of?'

'It may be for some people. But I haven't found any contribution I can make.'

'So you're running away from life instead?'

She waved her hand towards the graveyard with its gruesome burden of starved and frozen dead.

'You call *this* running away!'

'It isn't running away from death. After all, it's death you've tried to catch up with, isn't it? – the same as I once did. But it *is* running away from life. The War's over now. It's left wrack and ruin behind it, it's true, but that's all the more reason why builders are wanted instead of healers. Pestilence and famine ought to be left to professional menders like doctors and nurses, not to people with minds trained to think politically. They're thrown away on work like this, because they're needed so badly for social reconstruction.'

'You're very sure you know all about what's wanted, aren't you?'

'Please forgive me. I do apologise for laying down the law. What I really meant was, I can't bear to see someone with your personality and education burying herself in the wastes of Russia, tidying up after death and hoping to find it herself, when the countries that fought in the War, and ours not least of them, are beginning to find their way back to life.'

'Why should I live if I don't want to?'

'Oh, I don't know! There's no intrinsic reason – but it's a kind of obligation, isn't it, so long as one has any usefulness left? Don't think I'm talking from the top of my head. All you're going through now I went through myself just after the War.'

'*You* went through it! How?'

'Well, in 1918 I decided, like you, that I'd finished with life. When the War first broke out it seemed to me radically unimportant because it was so utterly stupid and irrational, but in the end I joined up as soon as I could get a medical board to pass me, meaning to go to France and get killed at the first opportunity. I *was* sent to France – but the Armistice was signed an hour after I landed. I'd so completely made up my mind to die, it took me weeks to accommodate myself to the idea that my number wasn't up after all.'

'But why did you wish for death?'

'For much the same reason as yourself – that is, if I've understood you correctly. You see, I'd lost everyone and everything I cared about and all my confidence in life was gone, because the War and family troubles together had smashed up my work at Oxford just after I'd got a First in Honour Mods. By 1918 my mother, whom I loved dearly, was dead, and my father had gone out of his mind from worry and anxiety. I only had one great friend at school and college, and he crashed in flames over the German lines during the battle of Cambrai. So my reasons for remaining alive weren't exactly compelling.'

'I see,' she said, looking from her past into his as he spoke. In imagination she reconstructed his experiences from her own, so dissimilar in their circumstances yet so like in their effects. How strange, she thought, that we should meet as we have in this tragic remote region – two individuals who have both been deprived of everything that made life worth having, and yet when it's all over find themselves still alive, still young, still called reluctantly back by the claims and obligations of a world that insists upon continuing and demanding after the people who matter are dead.

'What did you do when you found the War was over?' she inquired.

'Went through hell in Belgium. I shall never forget the outlines of the buildings in Mons and the flat marshy country outside it as long as I live.'

'And after that?'

'Returned to Oxford and endured hell there too. Everyone was suffering from reaction and a kind of impatient ferocity, as though they were still sitting on a crater that was going to blow up at any moment. I got out of it as soon as I could – did a Shortened Course and took my Greats Degree in one year instead of two. Then a cleric who used to be a friend of my mother's discovered there was a lectureship in Social Philosophy going at London University. I put in for it and got it, much to my astonishment. It was the first piece of real luck I'd ever had. I've been lecturing there for four terms.'

'Perhaps your luck will continue now,' she said, and turned from the distant Ural mountains to the sad snow-capped town. 'We'd better be starting back; it's nearly lunch-time. Was it for your Social Philosophy lectures you came out here?'

'Partly. I don't see how anyone can attempt to prophesy about future social tendencies without knowing something of Russia. Though my work's in England and I wouldn't wish it elsewhere, I often think Russia and America will divide the future between them.'

'America!' she cried. 'You know America?'

'Not well, but I've been there,' he answered, wondering why the faint flush of colour brought into her cheeks by the crisp air had suddenly faded. 'I gave some lectures in Madison this summer, at the University of Wisconsin. You know it yourself?'

'No. But *he* was an American – the one who wasn't my brother.'

'I see . . . He was in the War?'

'Yes. He was killed in the Argonne.'

There was a long pause as they walked down the empty street, their footsteps almost noiseless in the thick powdered snow. At last Denis continued.

'I never felt I did quite a man's job in the War. I didn't believe in a thing we said we were fighting for, but it seemed contemptible not to be in danger when everyone else had to be.

I think that's really why I came to Russia – and I'm glad I did. What I've seen this morning makes me want to go back at once and try to work up some interest at home.'

'I don't suppose you'll succeed. Even Nansen couldn't do much. The Americans roused themselves to some effect, but England has an infinite capacity for remaining unmoved by the troubles of foreigners.'

'Our post-war Britain hasn't engaged your affections, I can see.'

'I can't pretend to know much about it really, because for two years after the Armistice I was nursing in Cologne. But I went back to Witnall for a few months when the hospital closed, and everyone was still talking about Huns and Boches and Bolsheviks. I suppose if you go on calling your enemies names, it saves you from feeling responsible for their problems.'

'I know. "Typhus in Poland" – nobody's business in particular, but a nice safe humanitarian job to put on to the new League of Nations.'

'Do you think it's going to do any good?' she asked. 'The League, I mean?'

'It might,' commented Denis reflectively. 'I think it would, if we could only obliterate the diplomats and politicians who were in charge of things before the War. Their minds are hard set in the old ways, and scepticism isn't a helpful attitude towards a new order.'

'But we haven't got rid of them. They're still in control of almost everything.'

'I know. People of that sort have a habit of clinging on – especially as most of the men who ought to take their places have been safely killed off. I wouldn't mind betting you that ten or fifteen years hence, the pre-war statesmen will still be running our foreign affairs. By that time, if the League exists at all, they'll have turned it into a convenient instrument of the old diplomacy, doing their work for them all the more effectively under a safe camouflage of altruistic benevolence.'

'But they mustn't be allowed to! It's the one chance of preventing the whole thing from starting all over again . . . Oh, God!' she cried, her interest at last awakened as they arrived back at the Mission, 'if only women could do something to shape the course of politics!'

Standing on the doorstep, Denis looked eagerly down at her.

'I do believe,' he said slowly, 'you still haven't realised that now they can . . .'

4

At nine o'clock on New Year's Day, 1922, the sleighs with their drivers stood ready waiting outside the Mission. The first contained two sacks filled with dried camel-grass, which provided seats for the prospective travellers; the second, a freight-sleigh made of rough logs nailed to wooden runners, was packed with stores. On the top of them sat the Soviet interpreter who was to assist Ruth in her fortnight's work of store distribution at the village of Shimovka, thirty versts from Buzuluk.

When she came out into the pale early sunshine, wrapped in a heavy sheepskin *shuba*, with fur gloves and boots covering her hands and feet, Denis Rutherston followed and sat down beside her in the travellers' sleigh. The other members of the universities' committee had already left to inspect the American headquarters at Sarochinskoie in the east of the province, but Denis had persuaded them that his task of investigation required this visit to an outlying village before he rejoined them.

'At least you get plenty of sun in this place,' he remarked, lifting his face to the clear cascade of light as the sleighs moved down the frozen road and their journey began.

'Yes. If it stays like this we ought to be in Shimovka before dark.'

The rough-haired, flat-footed Bactrian camels which drew the sleighs lumbered slowly out of Buzuluk, murmuring raucously. In less than half an hour Ruth and Denis were on the steppe, swaying from side to side along a track identifiable only by birch-twigs stuck in the snow. Before them stretched an immense undulating plain, its whiteness rarely broken by trees and houses. Armies had swept backwards and forwards here, leaving ruin behind them, and now the famine had come to create a wild horror of desolation which in itself confronted Russia with problems surpassing those of any other post-war country.

At long intervals they passed through tiny hamlets, assembled round one primitive street, where nothing living now remained. From the dismantled houses half hidden by snow-drifts the wooden walls had been stolen for fuel, the thatched roofs ravaged to provide ingredients for the 'bread' made of bark and grass and clay upon which the starving peasants struggled to exist. As the camels padded in sinister silence through the untrodden snow of the deserted streets, it seemed to Denis as though the little group of human creatures in the moving sleighs had died and come to life again in some lost region of purgatory without colour or sound. Inside those ruins he could picture the unburied dead slowly disintegrating into skeletons, mute obscene witnesses to the decay and corruption which nearly eight years of chaos had spread over five continents and seven seas.

He and Ruth spoke very little. After two or three hours of travel, the swinging motion of the sleigh and the numbing effect of the extreme cold gave their journey the unreality of a continuous mirage. Too drowsy for conversation, they huddled together under their heavy rugs as the camels moved on beneath the blue ocean of sky. Through his dreaming mind as he sat so close to her, strangely contented and at peace, a familiar sequence of verses echoed with the reiterated force of a message. How often, he wondered, had he heard his father read them, at Sterndale, at Witnall, at Carrisvale Gardens?

'He was despised and rejected of men; a man of sorrows, and acquainted with grief: and we hid as it were our faces from him; he was despised and we esteemed him not.

'Surely he hath borne our griefs, and carried our sorrows: yet we did esteem him stricken, smitten of God and afflicted . . .

'Yet it pleased the Lord to bruise him; he hath put him to grief: when thou shalt make his soul an offering for sin, he shall see his seed, he shall prolong his days, and the pleasure of the Lord shall prosper in his hand.

'He shall see of the travail of his soul, and shall be satisfied.'

In spite of their familiarity, he had never before realised how completely those words embodied the supreme ideal of consolation – consolation not only for the person whose burden was carried, but even more for the one who carried it. Seeing Ruth Alleyndene daily during that week at Buzuluk – a week which might have been a year in its intense personal experiences, its contact with horror and death, courage and sacrifice – he had come to believe that he would find compensation for the heartbreak and humiliation of his own past if only, somehow, he could lift from her shoulders the dead-weight of her sorrow.

Since their visit to the dead in Buzuluk cemetery she had never again referred to the aching memories which had sent her to Cologne and brought her to Russia, for throughout that week they had seldom been alone together. But her undying grief was visible to him in every gesture that she made; in the mechanical efficiency, conscientious but unillumined, with which she carried out her daily tasks; in the sadness of her eyes and the rarity of her smile. It was true that every Mission worker looked oppressed and sorrowful, hag-ridden by the twin spectres of pestilence and famine which stalked the smitten land, but Ruth was pursued by other ghosts than the crowding phantoms of the Russian dead. How was it, when she and his mother resembled one another in no single feature, that her tired conscientiousness brought back to him the memory of Janet's resigned competence at Bethnal Green, her haunted eyes reminded him of Janet's sad defencelessness as she lay dying in the Mary Magdalene Hospital?

Could one atone to the dead by seeking to mitigate the suffering of the living, or did one only comfort oneself for previous sins of omission? However that might be – and he was beginning to understand that the attainment of reconciliation was a duty that a man owed to himself, since it increased his usefulness in a society which had never stood so acutely in need of strength and rescue – he felt that he would mortgage every hopeful prospect upon which he had calculated, if only he could sometimes make her laugh as she had laughed, unexpectedly, during their first meeting at his accurate evocation of the past.

That distant past seemed to him to raise no barrier against the friendship and the service which he hoped to offer her. The humiliating dispute between his father and hers had played,

he supposed, a determinant part in the wreck of Thomas's
ill-starred career. It had never ceased to rouse his father's
unforgiving resentment to the end of his clouded days, but
it belonged to an epoch so remote that it seemed as absurd to
allow that old quarrel to influence his conduct as it would have
been to refuse work in the United States because America had
once fought a War of Independence against Great Britain. Brief
though the chronological tale of years might be, a gulf wider than
a century and deeper than the bitterest personal hatreds divided
1906 from 1922. If the understanding born of those half-buried
griefs could teach him how to comfoɪt Ruth, then, after all, they
were not utterly futile. 'He shall see of the travail of his soul and
shall be satisfied.'

Towards evening, when the sleighs had only a few more versts
to travel, the sky darkened and a sudden blizzard gathered,
flinging the sharp snow into their faces as they approached
the dilapidated outskirts of another village. Their sleigh-driver
beckoned to the interpreter seated among the stores. He spoke
first to the driver and then to Ruth.

'Apparently it's dangerous to go on and we shall have to stop
here for the night,' she explained to Denis. 'He says he knows a
place where we can sleep.'

Five minutes later they stood before the broken untidy palings
dividing a squalid row of wooden cottages with sloping thatched
roofs from the deep trampled slush which served as a street.
The drivers left the sleighs covered by a waterproof rug in the
littered yard behind the cottages, and led Ruth and Denis into
one which could only be entered from the back through a reeking
cow-shed where a thin solitary cow nosed and shuffled amid the
accumulated filth of the winter months. As they crossed the yard
a violent gust of wind tore asunder the dripping veils of snow and
showed in the west a sudden blaze of gold and scarlet, as though
the gates of heaven had opened to reveal their treasures.

They needed this glimpse of beauty to invest them with
courage, for nothing could have been further from heaven than
the dark sordid room into which they were conducted. At first
they seemed to step into thick opaque blackness, for the thatch
hung low over the narrow sealed window, and the falling curtain

of snow obscured the remaining glimmer of light. Then someone lit a candle-end which he stuck in the neck of a bottle, and they saw that one-third of the room was filled by an enormous lighted stove, upon the top of which two half-dressed men lay in a tangle of dirty bed-clothes. On a bench in the corner an old sick woman groaned and mumbled; in front of the stove sat a middle-aged man, a young woman and a little girl of eight or nine. Ruth and Denis, with their interpreter and the two drivers, brought the numbers in the one-roomed cottage up to eleven. It was now barely five o'clock and the darkness would not lift before seven next morning.

'Fourteen hours!' whispered Ruth to Denis. 'We've got to endure it somehow and feed these people as well!'

She sent one of the drivers to bring from the freight-sleigh a sack of rice, a tin of salt beef and a packet of tea. The young woman boiled the tea in the samovar while Ruth took from the sack sufficient rice to provide supper and breakfast for them all. Late in the evening when the rice was cooked, the woman piled it on the newspaper which had covered the sack and Denis emptied the beef out of the tin. Crouching over the paper on the floor, the eleven strangely assorted human beings ate the meat and rice in their fingers. Another flickering candle-end cast their bowed, grotesque shadows upon the bare grimy wall. They might have been a group of prehistoric men and women taking part in some ancient pagan rite.

When the meal was over, Ruth and Denis stretched themselves at the opposite ends of a long bench pulled away from the wall, and vainly tried to sleep. Even if their stiff limbs and aching heads had not caused them increasing discomfort as the endless night dragged on, the chorus of snores and groans and the heavy foul atmosphere would have made rest impossible. Hour after hour, the risk of typhus involved less for herself than for Denis from the fœtid air and the crawling, inevitable lice weighed Ruth down with a dull sense of oppression. After her long contact with the disease she was probably immune, but the possibility that he might take and succumb to it became at last intolerable. For the first time since the War, too, she was conscious that for some inexplicable reason she no longer wanted to die herself.

At one o'clock she slid from her end of the bench and crept over to his.

'Are you asleep?'

'Not yet. It's a bit thick in here, isn't it?'

'It's quite intolerable. I can't stand it any more. I'm going to wrap myself in the rugs and sit in the sleigh. Dare you come too?'

'I'm willing to chance anything you are.'

They put on the sheepskin coats which had covered their feet and stole through the shed where the famished cow slept restlessly upon the piled dung and rotting straw. The storm had ceased, leaving behind it a temperature which had leapt up by thirty degrees.

Outside the cottage the fresh air poured over them like cool water; the frosty stars shone clear and friendly from the deep quiet night. They found the snow powdered thickly over the waterproof rug which covered the sleighs, but beneath it the empty travellers' sleigh was clean and dry.

When Denis had tucked the heavy rugs over their feet he drew her closer against him for warmth, putting his arms round her with a shy tenderness which brought a sting of tears to her eyes. Though the tentative gentleness of his embrace so little resembled the passionate urgency of Eugene's, it recalled another night of peril when her companion had sheltered her with his own body from the threat of death. But this time she felt no surge of unjust antagonism because Denis was not Eugene. Closing her eyes, she laid her head on the curved pillow of his arm.

Too deeply absorbed by the lovely strangeness of his situation to desire sleep, Denis looked down at her pale, still profile – the sensitive curves of forehead and nose, the dark lashes shading her eyes, the firm, grave outline of mouth and chin. There was strength in that face, and loyalty and valour; not much sense of humour, perhaps, but her experience had hardly been conducive to its development. In any case humour was seldom an attribute of the brave and resolute; it made for charming companionship, but too often acted as a brake upon achievement. Ruth Alleyndene was intelligent and courageous and capable of great intensity of purpose, and those were the qualities needed by the political England of the nineteen-twenties.

Conscious of his eyes upon her, she opened hers and smiled at him. Suddenly moved by a bewildering conflict of emotions, he fled in self-defence to a topic which appeared more impersonal than it was.

'Did you ever read *Clayhanger*?'

'I must have, when it was first published. Arnold Bennett's our local author, you know. Why do you ask?'

'It did sound irrelevant, didn't it? – but it joins on to our conversation the day we met. I wondered if you remembered a sentence at the end of the book where he speaks of "the exquisite burden of life." It's a phrase I've often found encouraging in the past two or three years.'

'"The exquisite burden of life,"' she repeated. 'That's what you think I've shirked, don't you?'

He was silent for a moment.

'Nobody could say that after the risks you've run and the hardships you've faced,' he answered at length. 'All the same, I do think your real burden's an intellectual burden and not the mere dead-weight of endurance. You've got a mind and a trained one, whereas work of the practical, exhausting kind you're doing here kills thought in the end if you go on with it long enough.'

'I know. That's why I did it.'

'You had to for a time – I realise that, because my need was the same. I destroyed my own desire for suicide by doing "fatigues" on Salisbury Plain, though I didn't know it was gone till after the War . . . Couldn't you bring yourself now to take up the burden of thought again? I'm sure your job in life is to examine and interpret and persuade. You've spent long enough in mending people's bodies; what matters now is to try to change their minds.'

Why, she reflected, that's almost what Captain Russell Chase wrote to me after he'd seen Eugene die! 'When you have recovered from the shock a little, I know you will want to do your job in life, whatever it may be. I know you will want to make it just as fine a job as you would have made it if Eugene had not been killed.' Perhaps, after all, I haven't really justified his confidence.

'But what am I to interpret and examine?' she asked. 'And whom shall I persuade?'

'There seem to me,' said Denis slowly, 'to be two things now especially worth doing and unquestionably urgent. One is to get people to accept a new economic system as a basis for peace, and the other to make them acknowledge peace as the essential factor in a new economic system. I'm sure the struggle for peace through rationality is going to be the great crusade of the future. Certainly the survival of civilisation will depend on its success.'

'But this is still a man-dominated world. Who's going to listen to a woman talking about anything but women's rights?'

'That's where you're out of date. What you say was true of my mother's time, but it's no longer true in ours. I don't believe there'll ever be a lasting peace until politically-minded women give their minds to getting it in the same way as they gave them to the suffrage movement. For one thing, they're more biologically interested than men in eliminating war – and then, like the suffragettes, they've often got a capacity for dramatising things that men can't equal.'

'I should have thought the first people to go into the question ought to be philosophers like yourself, and psychologists – specialists who can discover what's wrong with the human mind and human ideas. There must be something wrong somewhere. Sane and normal persons wouldn't deliberately work for their own destruction, as the statesmen of so many nations have done in the past.'

'I agree, but typical theorists like myself can only influence the few – and very slowly at that. The book I'm working on now may take ten years to write. What's needed to speed things up are men and women who'll make these issues dynamic and urgent from public platforms the world over. It's the man in the street we want to get at. In spite of all the politicians who suffer from stupidity or vanity or megalomania, war doesn't happen nowadays through the mysterious influence of omnipotent "authorities." No authority on earth could force war on a democratic people unless their inextinguishable aptitude for cherishing wrong-headed notions made them ready and even anxious to accept it. It's true this wrong-headedness ought to be investigated and explained, but if in the meantime we could find one or two public speakers with the eloquence of Isaiah and the technique of Sarah Bernhardt, the future might be saved. Look what Demosthenes did to lift the spirit of Athens! Look at the effect of Fichte's lectures on the revival of Prussia after her defeat by Napoleon!'

He went on eagerly expounding his thesis, but Ruth no longer listened. His last few remarks had carried for her the significance of an exhortation. She recalled the opening words of Milton's Sonnet on his Blindness.

> *When I consider how my light is spent,*
> *Ere half my days, in this dark world and wide,*
> *And that one Talent which is death to hide,*
> *Lodg'd with me useless . . .'*

That young eloquence which for years she had repressed and despised – might it have some value after all? The earth, so long static, dead, uninhabited, suddenly became peopled with anxious, watching eyes and blank bewildered faces, waiting for ideas, interpretations, guidance. As clearly as though a messenger had come down from heaven with an injunction specially addressed to herself, she knew now what she wanted to do.

Why had she never realised it before? Why had she permitted herself to live in exile among these Kedar's tents, performing mechanical tasks with a mind anæsthetised by memory, when throughout the world were puzzled pathetic peoples listening in vain for voices crying resurrection? She had told Denis that she chose her banishment because of Eugene, but she knew now – as in her heart she had always known – that Eugene, with his strong impulse towards action, would never have wished her to become immobilised through sorrow. He himself had insisted, when he brought her Richard's letter, that Richard would not want her to go on grieving when it was all over and he had long been at peace . . .

'You're right, of course,' she said suddenly. 'I ought to go back.'

A glow ran through him as though a fire had been kindled in his soul; he had not known such a glad sense of achievement since the tranquil freedom of his early days at Oxford.

'You really mean that? You'll leave this death and come back to life?'

'I think so. I mustn't go till after the thaw, because there'll be a great deal of extra work in March getting out the seed-corn before the floods hold up all the transport. But I could go home when it's over, if only I'd some idea how to begin work of the kind we've been talking about. I daresay you'll remember enough of Witnall to know it's hardly the sort of place where one starts crusades.'

He looked meditatively at the huge indigo vault of the star-studded sky.

'Well, things do sometimes begin from the most unexpected places, but it'll probably be a few years before anything revolutionary comes out of Witnall. I might just possibly find you some kind of job with the Labour Party. I know several people at their headquarters in Eccleston Square. I'm afraid there wouldn't be much money in it, but perhaps,' he added, dimly recalling the opulent green lawns at Dene Hall and its eccentric outline of turrets and pinnacles, 'you wouldn't expect too much in the way of a salary?'

'I don't think I should need to. Last time I was at home my father said he'd finance me in anything I cared to do if only I wouldn't go abroad again. He's a real old Tory and I don't suppose he ever imagined my working for Socialism, but I think I could talk him round. It's the work itself that worries me far more. I shan't know how to tackle anything intellectual after all these years of nursing and travelling. It'll take me about six months to learn to concentrate.'

'But is it the kind of work you'd like?'

'I always meant to do something of the sort,' she said. 'I used to think I'd join the militant suffragettes when I went down from college, and organise for them, and speak.'

'How my mother would have appreciated you! But you're too

late now, both for them and for her. What centuries ago it all seems, doesn't it? I can hardly believe it isn't eight years since she wrecked her personal life and broke up our home, because of the suffrage movement. It might have happened in the Dark Ages, and yet she only died in 1917, just when the vote was won ... *Can* you speak, by the way?'

'I once thought I could. When I was a child I used to make long speeches to chairs and tables, and dream of being a great leader like Mrs Pankhurst. It may have been just youthful arrogance, but I'd like to try again.'

'You must certainly try again. If you've any gift that way they'll soon find it out ... but we really oughtn't to talk any more. Since you're determined to stay here another three months you mustn't run risks by getting over-tired. Are you warmer now? Do you think you can sleep?'

'You've warmed me in more ways than one,' she said, smiling drowsily up at him.

'Then put your head on my arm again, and close your eyes.'

Five minutes afterwards, alone in the silence of Russia's vast desolation beneath the cold January stars, Denis Rutherston and Ruth Alleyndene lay fast asleep on the sleigh in each other's arms.

5

'You know, Jill,' said Stephen, 'it isn't that I mind your going off to London, but I'd rather you'd chosen to do almost anything than mix yourself up with that Socialist crowd. What with one thing and another, these labour troubles are just about ruining the Potteries. I don't suppose you realised it at the time, but the coal strike last year brought the whole industry of this district to a standstill, and it's those folks down south who start all the mischief.'

'I'm very sorry, Father,' she responded, 'but I wanted to do political work when I was still at Oxford. If it hadn't been for the War I should have joined the suffragettes, and you wouldn't have liked that any better.'

'Ay, it would have upset your mother a good bit, I don't doubt. But I must say votes for women don't seem to have done much damage so far, whereas if these revolutionaries get into power they'll turn everything upside down, and the whole country'll go to the dogs!'

Ruth smiled – the composed, resolute smile which had always baffled, moved and defeated him.

'People say that about every new movement,' she observed equably.

'Well, the old ones are good enough for me; you know where you are with them ... What really beats me, Jill, after all the trouble I had years ago, getting that common chap Rutherston out of the parish because he talked Radical rubbish to our congregation, is your letting his son, of all folks on earth, put you up to joining the Reds.'

'But it wasn't Denis Rutherston who did that. I think I've always been a Socialist at heart, and Wardle persuaded me to join the Witnall Labour Party last summer.'

'So that's who it was! It's enough to make the old guv'nor turn in his grave – and the missis too!'

'I daresay I've done a good many things Granny wouldn't approve of ... Look here, Father, don't make the money over to me if you'd rather not. If they keep me on at Eccleston Square they'll pay me a small salary, and I can manage on that.'

'I don't grudge you the cash, Jill. I'm not going to have my daughter living like a pauper. Whatever you choose to do with it, I'd rather you had it than waste any more of your best years in outlandish places like Germany and Russia. I only wish you hadn't turned Socialist, that's all.'

'You know, Father,' she said slowly, 'in a way my political beliefs are the result of everything I've seen and done these last seven years. I couldn't change them – not even to please you.'

'Ay, I know. I can see it's no use talking to you. Just sign your name at the bottom of the page, my dear, and the money's yours. By the way,' he added, as she sat down in front of his desk, 'how's this young Rutherston turned out?'

'Oh, he's a perfect darling! It's ludicrous to think how he bored me when I was a little girl. I don't suppose he'd appeal to you,

Father, because he's the typical scholar – thin and pale, with rather a precise, academic way of talking. But he's tremendously kind and he understands everything. He's the sort of person who knows what you're going to say before you've said it.'

'Well, it's to the lad's credit if he's got on in the world. I always said he hadn't half a chance with those second-rate parents.'

When she had signed her name on the deed of transfer, Ruth went out into the wide empty garden, fragrant with the smell of sweet-briar and wet grass after a brief shower of summer rain. Though she had now become a capitalist to the satisfactory extent of five thousand pounds as a preliminary to joining the fight against capital, her mind dwelt less upon her illogical position than upon Denis Rutherston, whose persistence had prevailed upon his Labour friends to offer her work in the research department at Eccleston Square. She still recalled with gratitude the night that they had spent together on the Russian steppe, and their short ride next morning towards the domes and windmills of Shimovka stretching across the horizon. He had left her so reluctantly, alone in that small town with the bearded interpreter, when the sleighs returned to the Mission. She recognised his fear that she might be smitten with typhus or attacked by the peasants so far from the aids of civilisation.

'I'm not likely to get fever after all this time,' she had assured him. 'As for the peasants, they're dependent on us for the means of life. They'd no more touch a relief-worker than violate an angel from heaven!'

On his return journey he had written her a long letter from Moscow, describing the American centre which she had never seen. Two months later, just before she left Buzuluk after the thaw, another came relating his endeavours to interest his friends and students in the task before the Soviet.

'My weeks in Russia still seem like a dream, but it is a dream which gives a new perspective to my vision of life. Throughout my time there I had the sense of something gigantic and significant struggling to be born; of the famine and typhus and great treks of the refugees as part of its birth-pangs. As you anticipated, however, I have not succeeded in finding many people who share my interest in the present empirical stage of

the Soviet experiment. I am still greeted with sceptical smiles
when I assert that the Mission stores, far from being diverted to
the Red Armies, are not even touched by the starving men who
unload them. I cannot convince the average newspaper-reader
that the famine victims would rather die than steal the seed-corn
provided by the Americans for this year's planting. My students
have collected a small fund for the Mission work, but I am afraid
it will be a mere drop in the limitless ocean of your requirements.
I trust that you are still well and still of the same mind as when I
left you at Shimovka, for there seems to be a real possibility that
the work I mentioned will materialise.'

'I only hope, now it has, that I shan't be too rusty for it,' she
thought, as she walked to the last of the three terraces where the
nearest hayfield stood ready for cutting. The long thick grass was
luxuriant with marguerites and cow-parsley and feathery tufts of
meadow-sweet, which flung its honeyed perfume into the warm
damp air. What a curious, indescribable change seemed to have
come over Dene Hall now that she had returned to it, not as
a reluctant indefinite sojourner, but as a worker taking a brief
holiday between two significant undertakings! When she first
saw her home after the grey half-drowned wastes of Russia amid
the spring floods, she thought that the house must have been
decorated and the garden re-planted, so beautiful appeared the
reddish-grey turrets and gables, so rich the scarlet tulip-beds and
the pink-and-white lustre of the rhododendrons. Like a captive
reprieved from death, she walked wonder-stricken among the
flowers and blossoming shrubs, touching the glowing petals and
delicate branches to assure herself of their reality.

Actually, from the critical standpoint of those who knew no
ravaged Russia with which to compare its agreeable security,
Dene Hall had definitely 'gone down' since the days of its aristo-
cratic isolation before the War. Because of the acute housing
shortage in Stoke and Hanley, the plebeian outcrop of cottages
had now begun to climb the hill where it rose towards the Hall
from Witnall in the valley. Along the once secluded country road
outside the lodge gates, local motor-buses rattled on their way
from Hanley to Cheet. From the carriage drive in front of the
house the smoke-cloud of the Potteries seemed to have rolled

nearer – or was it only that, even in England, the dirt and dilapidations of eight years still remained unrepaired?

It was altogether a different Staffordshire from the county which Ruth had left for France in 1915. Even the Alleyndene Pottery Company, influenced by the National Society of Pottery Workers formed just after the War, had completely changed in spirit from the individualistic business of seven years ago. The district itself suffered from widespread economic depression; credit was restricted and effective demand reduced to a minimum, while the high post-war prices defeated the capacity of buyers whose own prosperity had been impaired by the colossal errors of the Peace. Rates and taxes had risen so high and domestic labour had become so difficult to obtain, that more than once Ruth heard Stephen and Jessie discuss the possibility of selling Dene Hall.

Already the plantation at the southern corner of the estate was gone; the land had been sold to a building society, and bungalows called 'Little Cot' or 'Mon Repos' were in process of erection where the haughty firs planted by Enoch Alleyndene had stood for eighty years. The old order was threatened from its very foundations. Soon, Ruth thought, when she turned her back upon Witnall as she believed for ever, she would be free from the obligation to maintain even a semblance of loyalty to its external splendours and its proud tradition.

6

Early in September, Ruth moved into a flat at the top of Albany Mansions, looking eastwards over Battersea Park on the south side of the Thames. In these economical, unpretentious surroundings she thankfully cherished the freedom and privacy that even at twenty-eight would not have been accessible to a young unmarried woman of her type and background before the War.

She unpacked the books and pictures which had remained unread and unhung since her Oxford days, with a sense of relief at having escaped, not so much from her parents or even Dene Hall itself, as from her brother Norman. It was Norman, her contemporary, and not Stephen, her father, who had been the most adamant opponent of her political plans; Norman to whom she had worse than nothing to say, because he had survived into the post-war world when Richard, her dear companion, was dead. His very censorious existence seemed to emphasise the departure of Richard and Eugene and Madeleine from the depleted youth of their generation.

'He must be a throw-back,' she thought, trying to be charitable now that his critical presence no longer oppressed her. 'He certainly doesn't resemble our grandfather if he was as genial and tolerant as father says, and he's not even like our great-grandfather, because in his way old Enoch was a glorious exhibitionist. It must be William, who helped to suppress the Radicals after the Napoleonic Wars, who's the ancestor responsible for Norman. After all, William invented our Blue Under-Glaze Ware as well, and Norman really does care for the Pottery.'

In London, even more clearly than in Staffordshire, she soon realised that she was living in an England where the changes brought by the past eight years exceeded in many ways those of the previous eighty. For women especially, the world had moved swiftly after half a century of defeated endeavour. No longer voteless and politically powerless, they were already at Westminster, pushing measures through the House of Commons which would have provoked mirth and derision in pre-war Parliaments. No longer content with automatic exclusion from historic institutions and masculine professions, they were knocking at the gates of the House of Lords and the doors of the Diplomatic Service. They had conquered the barricaded citadel of the Law and were accepted as inevitable by the medical profession; at Oxford they had prevailed upon the University to grant them equal standing with men. As Olive Schreiner had once prophesied, there was no closed door which they did not intend to force open, and no fruit in the garden of knowledge which it was not their determination to eat.

At late-night gatherings of the 1917 Club or the informal discursive parties to which she was taken by fellow-workers from Eccleston Square, Ruth listened to ardent controversialists debating whether these spectacular changes had been due to the War or the suffrage movement.

'The suffragists were too narrow – especially the militants. They only saw the women's movement as a political revolution, whereas it was even more social and moral – to say nothing of economic, which it's hardly become even yet. The War showed what women could do and it also set them free. They had to stop being protected, because sensitive plants were no use to a country in war-time.'

'Yes, I acknowledge all that. I know the War hastened things; these changes might have taken another twenty or thirty years without it. But you must admit that the War wouldn't have caused them by itself if the suffrage movement hadn't prepared the ground first.'

There was much talk, too, about the 'superfluity' of women, though the subject was associated with other topics, discussed in frank phrases that would once have been discreetly camouflaged, which were even less familiar to Ruth – birth-control, 'the right to motherhood,' the recognition of sex-experience as a private responsibility with which neither the State nor society was entitled to interfere. Whatever might be true of Witnall and similar provincial towns throughout the country, the old codes and cautions were being abandoned by those who ultimately created opinion. The rigid structures of pre-war morality had been undermined, though exactly what was taking their place had not yet become quite clear. Feeling herself far from the shore, Ruth sat silent and listened. The barriers seemed to be down everywhere, broken in pieces for that still young generation which had been so fast bound by authority. She was part of an age of transition to which her own most poignant experiences had unconsciously contributed.

Soon after she was settled in the Battersea flat and had begun to enjoy her work of supplying information acquired from the Party library to Labour Candidates and Members of Parliament, the General Election of 1922 swept the Coalition into history. An open-air meeting in the Earl's Court Road had already demonstrated that Ruth still possessed the speaking powers once displayed in Oxford debates. Because she knew the district so well, she was sent to the Potteries to help Harper Parker, and old Jos Davenport of the National Society of Pottery Workers, with their campaigns at Hanley and Witnall. Before the election ended her speeches created a mild local sensation, for an enterprising Staffordshire reporter succeeded in interviewing both Robert and Daniel Alleyndene on their attitude towards their young Socialist relative, and had inserted several pungent paragraphs before either of Ruth's uncles awoke to the fact that they were supplying material to that octopus the Press.

'I never thought to see a daughter of mine helping those revolutionaries!' mourned Jessie to her sister Millicent. But Stephen only looked grim and said little – perhaps because Norman saved him the trouble of putting his sentiments into words.

'It's a good job your grandfather's under the daisies,' he contented himself with remarking one evening, after he and his disgruntled son had privately attended a meeting in a crowded schoolroom on the boundaries of Hanley and Witnall. 'I grant you, though, Jill knows how to speak,' he added with rueful pride, after listening for ten minutes to Ruth's endeavours to convert some of his oldest employees to views which he abominated.

'So much the worse!' grumbled Norman. 'Thank the Lord she's at least had the decency to keep away from home for this particular jaunt!'

When the election was over, Ruth was offered as much speaking by the Party as she wanted, for the newly elected Member for Hanley wrote to headquarters to commend her, and Arthur Wardle, with whose wife she had lodged during the campaign, sent a long letter to Eccleston Square describing how intelligently she had used her knowledge of Staffordshire. Although, he explained, Witnall was still a Tory division and they had expected Sir Harrison Tallinor's big majority, Jos Davenport had put up an excellent fight in reducing it from the overwhelming 1918 figure, and nobody had helped him more than Ruth Alleyndene.

The changing psychology of the British electorate had now made Labour – no longer a pariah group, condemned and derided – the second largest party in the State, and the work of converting the country to Socialism went forward with a new impetus. Throughout the first half of 1923, Ruth spent many cold, grimy hours travelling to meetings in the industrial Midlands and the North. She was sent to Manchester, where the January fogs caused the taxicabs to crawl like cautious snails between London Road and Exchange Stations; to Halifax, where the blackened houses on the hillsides looked down upon the smoking chimneys and chattering streams in the valley; to Leeds and Bradford, where the dripping veils of February rain gave a damp identity to the dark winter landscape. Whenever hospitality was not forthcoming from members of the local party, she stayed in hotels with red-carpeted corridors between shiny chocolate-brown dadoes, where even the best bedrooms contained marble-topped washstands, plush curtains with sooty surfaces, and wall-papers of which the heavy floral designs barely concealed the perpetual onslaught of dirt and damp. Sometimes in these chilly provincial mausoleums where central heating was apparently regarded as a menacing token of sybaritic decadence, the only source of warmth at Ruth's command seemed to be the rediscovered fires of her glowing oratory.

Early in the year she went north to take a series of meetings in Glasgow, and made the closing speech at a large peace demonstration organised by the combined left-wing parties. It was only after she left the meeting that she recalled how keenly a gaunt elderly woman, dressed in dark grey tweeds and seated amongst the local dignitaries on the platform, had observed her while she was speaking. She realised with reminiscent surprise that she had been once again in the presence of Ellison Campbell, whose *Scottish Chronicles* were nightly crowding the Rendezvous Theatre and raising her now international prestige to heights seldom reached by a woman in any profession. Only one or two perspicacious critics understood why Miss Campbell had turned from her former preoccupation with contemporary problems to these Chronicles of her nation's past. They realised that she found herself defeated by the endeavour to interpret the fitful, headlong post-war world in which she towered so incongruously, an historic figure-head raised upon the time-honoured foundations of nineteenth-century creeds and precedents.

'Whatever can have brought her to a peace meeting?' speculated Ruth, not realising that no important Glasgow function was now complete without that austere, dominating presence. As Arnold Bennett to Staffordshire and Thomas Hardy to Dorset, so Ellison Campbell had become to the Lanarkshire district in which she lived and wrote.

Ruth went back to London by the night train in order to be in time for her usual Saturday afternoon with Denis Rutherston. Whenever she was not away speaking for the Party, or for peace organisations, or for the women's societies which were now agitating for an Equal Franchise Bill to give votes to women between twenty-one and thirty, he came to tea at her flat and they sat together afterwards, smoking and talking before the open fire. Sometimes they touched tentatively upon the relationship of the serene, strenuous present to the clouded past, but more often they discussed the advance of Socialism in English politics, or the progress of Denis's attempt to work out a philosophical basis for the post-war impulse towards peace and reconstruction. On Sundays the two of them made joint expeditions into the country with Denis's colleagues from Hampstead or Ruth's fellow-workers from Eccleston Square. Clad in the open-necked sweater and ascending skirts of the period, she often tramped bare-headed all day through the Kentish lanes or over the Sussex Downs, accompanied by three or four long-legged young men.

What would her parents think, she sometimes wondered, of those pleasant uninterrupted Saturdays, that unorthodox Sunday attire, those easy uncalculating friendships with a sex which was now at a premium? Despite the political anxieties of a Europe distraught by the fall of the German mark and the invading presence of the French in the Ruhr, she looked back upon that year of work and companionship as a tranquil period of rest and healing with which her shattered, disintegrated life had nothing to compare. She did not know until long afterwards how much of that peace she owed to Denis Rutherston's restraint and understanding.

Denis knew, now, what he wanted of Ruth. Though his

emotional reactions were slow and his habitual distrust of his instincts was profound, he believed that he had known from the time of their first meeting in the Mission room at Buzuluk. Already he found it difficult to remember anything that happened on the days when he did not see her. But it was not because of the inauspicious family prelude to their story that he curbed so relentlessly all expression of his absorbing love for her; in 1923 the desire of the Rutherstons' son for the Alleyndenes' daughter was not the incredible aspiration that it would have appeared in 1913. He realised that his moment had not yet come; he knew that her psychological convalescence, if it was really to restore her balance and vitality, should suffer no strain.

'I mustn't say anything for a long time,' he told himself firmly. 'She must get back her foothold in life before she's confronted by any new problem.'

The wisdom of his judgment was proved when she showed him at Easter a letter that she had just received from America through the British Red Cross. The envelope carried the Chicago postmark, and the notepaper was headed 'Chase Book Stores Incorporated. Vice-President's Office.'

'MY DEAR MISS ALLEYNDENE,' read Denis,

'I hope you will pardon me for venturing to reopen a former correspondence, but I have some information to give you which is not, I think, likely to reach you from your side of the Atlantic. It will probably interest you to know that under the auspices of the American Battle Monuments Commission, a great military cemetery containing many thousands of graves has been constructed at Romagne-sous-Montfaucon in the Department of the Meuse, about twenty miles from Verdun. I am told that it is to be known as the Meuse-Argonne Cemetery, and upon its completion last year the dead from the Argonne Forest were reinterred there. It is here that the body of our good friend Eugene Meury has now been laid to rest.

'I understand that, in order to perpetuate the memory of the dead belonging to the armed forces of the United States, an agency entitled the American Graves Registration Service was established just after the War to take care of the American military cemeteries in Europe, and to furnish information and assistance to relatives and friends visiting those cemeteries. Should you wish to visit our friend's grave at any time, I am sure this organisation will give you any help you may require.

'I have often wondered what happened to you when we all returned to our homes after the war. I hope you have found a job in life which has brought you satisfaction.

'Sincerely yours,

'RUSSELL D. CHASE.'

'I can't go yet,' she said, and Denis saw that even now, though she had read the letter several times, her hands trembled and the colour had fled from her face. 'I can't go and see the place where he lies dead, when the last time I saw him he was so tremendously alive.' (Oh, so vehemently, so desperately alive, that night in the pine-forest – my love, my lost love, my darling! . . .)

'Sometimes, my dear,' said Denis gently, 'it's best to face up to the thing one dreads and get it over. To have a place one can't visit or a person one daren't see – surely that's a limitation of experience and a source of weakness to one's whole self?'

'Oh, I know, Denis! Some day I shall have to go to Romagne; I shan't feel I've really said good-bye to Eugene till I've been there. But it's too soon at present. I'm still not a whole person, and I can't go yet.'

7

On a mild Saturday afternoon in mid-September, Denis took Ruth for a walk in Richmond Park.

She had just come back from the 1923 League of Nations Assembly at Geneva – a gathering both mournful and ferocious after the colossal catastrophe of the Japanese earthquake and the Greco-Italian dispute which had followed Mussolini's bombardment of Corfu. The face of England wore that placid autumnal serenity which tends to enhance the agreeable British belief that world-crises and other disturbances are caused exclusively by foreigners.

Although it was Saturday the Park was almost empty, for the afternoon had turned damp and grey. Thin tatters of mist like transparent muslin trailed across the chestnut-brown of the changing bracken and turned the trees outlined against the horizon to blue-grey shadows. Beneath the spreading fans of the elms and the huddled grotesque branches of the oaks, patches of grass showed brilliantly green and soft as shaded velvet.

'Let's sit here for a few minutes,' said Denis, stopping beside the flat grey stump of a giant tree-trunk near a group of hawthorns.

Ruth sat down beside him with a feeling of bewildered apprehension which seemed inexplicable. In the wood behind them blackbirds piped and pigeons cooed lazily; occasionally the grating squawk of a pheasant interrupted their soft orchestration. Before them lay the Pen Ponds, a silver sheen of smooth water divided by a tall clump of beeches and chestnuts. Their sombre leaves were reflected as they fell like leaves falling upon the surface of a mirror. An aeroplane droned sleepily overhead, invisible amid the drifting canopy of cloud.

'Tell me, Denis,' asked Ruth, lifting her eyes from the gentle melancholy scene to look at him inquiringly, 'why did you want to bring me here instead of coming to the flat as usual?'

For a moment he did not reply; then he pointed towards the valley beyond the Park where Putney Vale lay hidden amid the vague phantoms of trees.

'Over there,' he said slowly, 'my mother lies buried. She was a suffragette, as I've often told you. All her mind and heart was in politics. She ought to have been a political organiser or a Member of Parliament, instead of being tied to a child and a household. She'd have given her soul for the kind of work you're doing now.'

'Is that why you helped me to get it, Denis?'

'Partly. You see, two days after she died I read her diaries. Before that I'd often blamed her in my heart – a very young and priggish heart, I'm afraid. But when I'd read those diaries I felt

I understood her, too late, as I'd never understood any soul on earth. I realised then that all our misery at home – hers and my father's and mine – had come about because her intellect never had sufficient outlet. Her desire to use it had been thwarted by my father in the name of duty and morality.'

'What a cruel, unnecessary tragedy it sounds!' said Ruth, her eyes fixed upon the dim outline of the distant woods. He went on still more deliberately.

'It was – only I didn't know it in time. But the next day, at her burial service down in that valley, I vowed I'd never bring any woman unhappiness in marriage. I prayed that my own desires might be denied and my own powers frustrated, rather than I should be the means of causing anyone such misery as my mother had suffered. I didn't mean, then, to survive the War, but the War refused to accept my life just as it refused yours. Since it ended, I've renewed that vow whenever I've stood by her grave.'

She said nothing, and he laid his hand upon hers, clasped lightly in her lap.

'To-day, my dear, as it were in her presence, I renew it again with all my heart. You've got courage and great ability and work that's worth while. If you'll consent to marry me, I promise I'll do everything in my power to further whatever part in life you choose to play.'

She drew her hands out of his and hid her face with a sudden gesture of despair. She had depended upon him so confidently, taken him so completely for granted, that his words came to her with a shock of genuine surprise. Oh, why need he have spoiled everything, forcing her to decide between keeping him in her life as her husband, or sending him away when he had become so necessary to her happiness! Did she want to marry him or not? She did not know; but she knew that she could not allow him to go on trusting her, believing in her integrity, basing his proposal to her upon a false assumption. When he had heard all the truth, he would not want her any more.

Turning away from him, she answered abruptly, 'I'm not a virgin.'

There was barely an instant's pause.

'I was asking you to be my wife,' said Denis's gentle, precise voice. 'I'm not exclusively interested in one part of your anatomy.'

Her colourless face flushed crimson.

'Oh, Denis, I'm sorry! Forgive me. I thought it would make all the difference to you, as it does to most men. You see, I felt I'd been deceiving you, because it's the one important thing about Eugene and myself I've never told you.'

'Why should you? It wasn't my business.'

'But it *is* your business now, isn't it?'

'I'm not so sure. Because I ask you for access to your body in marriage, that doesn't mean I'm entitled to insist on being the only person who's ever had it.'

'But supposing I'd had a child,' she pursued. 'You wouldn't have wanted to marry me then, would you?'

Denis looked at her downcast eyes with sudden sorrowful intuition. Oh, my poor love! She wanted a child by him so badly that if I tell her what is true – that I wouldn't have cared, that I'd have admired her for her courage – it will hurt her more than anything I could say.

'Dear heart,' he urged, 'why do we discuss hypotheses? You only torment yourself for nothing; the past is gone and we can't change it. But whatever it was or might have been, I've no inclination to set myself up as a censor of morals. My father's moral judgments and the ruin they caused cured me of that.'

'You must be very exceptional,' she said. 'I've always taken for granted no one would want to marry me when they knew about Eugene.'

'Well, that ancient scruple doesn't trouble me at all. I want someone who'll do more than just go to bed with me. I don't pretend to be less sensual than most men, but I do want a companion as well, and I don't think I'm exceptional in that or anything else. I'm quite sure my generation of men doesn't make the same fearsome shibboleth of rigid chastity in women as the one before it. After all, why should we? Chastity's only a virtue in the sense of being a voluntary self-discipline, and that's not a matter of technical virginity. It's an attitude of mind.'

She wrung her hands in her bewilderment, her anguish of
indecision.

'Denis, I don't want you to think we were just promiscuous
and undisciplined. Eugene wasn't that sort at all. It only happened once.'

'Don't tell me about it, my dear, if you'd rather not.'

'But I want to tell you. It's been on my mind for five years
– not because I regret what I did, but because everything that
happened still seems as vivid as if it were yesterday, and I keep
going over it again and again . . . You see, although I knew we
couldn't marry because of Dallas Lowell, I don't believe we'd
actually have been lovers if a whole series of different things
hadn't led me that way.'

'Different things? Coincidences, you mean?'

'Not exactly coincidences, but a succession of events which all
seemed to point in the same direction. First of all, my room-mate
at Wimereux committed suicide because she'd never given herself
to the boy she was engaged to, and when he was killed she
felt she'd deprived him of the most important experience in
life. Then, when I met Eugene and he gave me Richard's last
letter, I discovered something else I've never told you. I found
out from the letter that Richard was homosexual, and perhaps
wasn't killed in the ordinary way, but got himself shot to escape
a court-martial. When Eugene tried to comfort me and persuade
me not to judge Richard harshly – though I shouldn't have
anyhow – he used some words I've never forgotten. He said,
"I don't say I've ever been tempted just his way myself, but the
Lord knows what I mightn't do if this darn War goes on much
longer!"'

'Did he really say that? Nothing you've told me about him
suggests he was anything but completely normal.'

'I'm certain that's true. I think now he only said what he did
to defend Richard. But at the time my fears for him got so
mixed up with Shepherd's suicide, I began to think I'd no right
to let him make love to me and expect him to stop half way.
And then, just as it happened, a Sister at my hospital told me
about birth-control and I realised I could take him without the
full risk of having a child. It wasn't that I didn't want one, but I

was afraid. I wanted one so desperately that when he was killed I minded not having his child almost as much as losing him.'

'I can understand his making you feel like that. It's largely a question of vitality.'

'Well, in the end I offered myself to him without his asking me, just before he went back to the front for the last time. He never would have asked me, and we had quite a long argument before he realised I meant what I said. But I went on till I'd persuaded him. I wanted our relationship to be complete. I was afraid that if it wasn't, after he'd made love to me for so long, he might go the same way as Richard. It all seemed so natural and right at the time, and yet I've never got over it since – wondering whether he really wanted me, and whether, even if he did, he thought less of me for going so far.'

There was a long silence before Denis spoke again.

'Do you really think that anything you've told me makes you less desirable as a wife than you were before?'

'Oh, Denis, I don't know! All my values are in such a state of chaos, I'm not sure what I do believe! I certainly don't accept the rigid standards I was brought up by. I repudiated those once and for all when I let Eugene be my lover. But really I'd rejected them long before, because of something that happened when I was quite a child.'

'And what was that, dear?'

She stared at a duck with her cheeping family of five baby ducklings swimming across the gleaming surface of the Pen Ponds, but she actually saw the grassy bank below the carriage drive at Dene Hall on a summer afternoon of 1907.

'I was reading in the garden at home one day when I overheard my father talking to a friend of his. He was telling him a story about my grandmother – how she turned one of the servants out of the house in the middle of the night because she was going to have an illegitimate baby. The child was born in the cab on the way to the Workhouse and its mother nearly died as well, but no one seemed to think Granny anything but a paragon of righteousness. What I couldn't get over was not only her cruelty, but the way my father enjoyed the story. I daresay you haven't a very flattering idea of him, but in some ways he's immensely kind and generous. It was the first time I realised that people like Father didn't apply their standards of decent behaviour to their treatment of the poor.'

'Was that what made you a Socialist?'

'Quite definitely it was. That and a queer feeling of identity with my grandmother's Agnes that I've had ever since Eugene and I were lovers. I can't see any difference between Agnes and myself except that I was luckier – if it *was* luckier not to have his child.'

She clasped her hands and looked away from him towards the grey horizon. The expression of pain on her face told Denis, clearly and finally, that no love she might come to feel for him would ever rival her love for Eugene, no maternal tenderness to which a child of his own might one day move her would eradicate her regret for that former denial of life. After a moment's pause she sighed and went on.

'I can't have been more than twelve or thirteen, that day I heard Father talking, and I lay face downwards on the grass all the afternoon wondering what Agnes had done and why she'd been treated so cruelly. At tea-time I tried to make my mother explain it, but I got nothing out of her except the idea that all men were hopelessly wicked and all women their victims unless they were carefully protected. My mind refused to accept that idea, even then. I was in such a state of desperation that finally I went to one of our gardeners – Arthur Wardle, the one who's now secretary to the Witnall Labour Party – and asked him to tell me what it all meant. His explanation wasn't exactly unprejudiced, as you can imagine, but at least his prejudices erred on the side of humanity, whereas my grandmother's . . .'

She stopped suddenly, arrested by a still earlier memory. The morning-room at Dene Hall . . . Jessie sitting in the window-seat over some crimson embroidery . . . her grandmother gazing down into her face with a narrow sadistic intentness, pronouncing the verdict of her era upon fornication. The words which had mystified her at the time echoed back through the years . . . 'Remember that nothing so terrible can happen to a woman as to lose her purity.'

Well, she thought, I have lost mine. How much the worse am I for that? Perhaps I shall never be able to decide, and Denis refuses to pass judgment. The Alleyndenes, if they only knew it, passed judgment on me long ago. And of this, at least, I am certain: I'd rather be the prisoner at the bar of that family tribunal, than the judge imposing the sentence.

'Ever since then,' she went on, 'I've believed that cruelty is the greatest of all immoralities. It may be I'm only trying to excuse myself, but the way my grandmother treated Agnes seems to me a far greater sin than any unorthodox relationship between men and women – or for that matter between women and women or men and men. I can't help feeling that the really immoral people are the ones who punish and ostracise without understanding a thing about the persons they condemn.'

'I agree with you entirely,' said Denis. 'To my mind the pitiless condemnation of sex-offences illustrates exactly that self-indulgent evasion of fundamentals which society's capable of at its worst. If people want something to detest and spit on, why don't they go for modern war and those who make it? A war such as the last is infinitely more destructive of biological progress than the sex-aberrations of a few persons whose psychological make-up isn't quite that of the herd.'

The aeroplane, like a giant dragon-fly, hummed again overhead, a timely reminder of the race already begun between the inexorable advance of science and the tardy growth of human wisdom. Life or death is the issue, civilisation itself the stake – and yet how little we can do as individuals, she and I! We shall work more effectively if we work together; surely, even if she can't love me, that will persuade her?

The torment of suspense suddenly gripped him; even his capacity for patience and endurance could bear it no longer.

'Oh, my dear!' he exclaimed, 'one could debate these moral problems for ever – and meanwhile you haven't answered my question. Can you consider being my wife . . . or am I asking too much?'

Impulsively, penitently, she seized his hand.

'Denis, dear Denis, I can't answer you! It's just that I've never thought of you as a husband. You're necessary to me – you've brought me back to life; but somehow I still can't connect that other relationship with anyone but Eugene.'

'Perhaps that's because of all your misgivings,' he urged, fighting the cold fear brought by her words that his quest was hopeless, that he was going to fail.

'Perhaps it is. I don't know. Could you give me a little time to think it over?'

'All the time you want, dear. I've always realised I mustn't hurry you. If I'd followed my impulses I should have asked you a year ago . . . but I waited and brought you out here instead.'

'It's strange you should have brought me here, Denis, and in September . . . because, you see, this place has memories for me too. It was over there, on Wimbledon Common, that Eugene first told me he loved me . . . one September evening in 1917. The sound of that aeroplane above us just now brought it all back to me, because we were still on the heath when we were caught in an air-raid. There were one or two fires afterwards, and I remember how the outline of Richmond Park stood out against the redness in the sky.'

'Have you ever been back there since?'

'No, never again. Somehow I never felt I could.'

He got up from the tree-stump and looked down at her, hesitating, reluctant to cause her avoidable pain.

'Then perhaps you won't want to do what I was just going to ask you?'

She smiled at him remorsefully.

'I'll gladly do anything that'll make you feel any happier, or myself less unkind. What is it?'

'I wondered whether you'd walk across the Park with me to my mother's grave? You see, even if you never marry me, I feel it's right for you to go there. In some ways you're so like her – and then your work and everything you stand for are precisely what she herself wanted to do and be. I daresay you won't realise why, but your very existence in relation to hers gives me a new sense of hope. It's made me believe that people's ideals are sometimes fulfilled in the end, only not necessarily in one life or one generation.'

She stood up and linked her arm through his. As she looked

across the Park to the mist-enshrouded Vale, a sullen gleam of sunshine penetrated the heavy clouds, turning to golden-brown the pale sandy paths which intersected the wide deserted stretch of grass and bracken. Denis was right in what he said to me about Romagne, she thought. One mustn't be afraid of places, or people, or even of memories. Freedom from fear can only come when one has faced what remains, in all its sad incompleteness, its bitter inadequacy, its forlorn imperfection.

'I'll come, Denis,' she told him. 'I think I can face it, with you.'

8

Half an hour later they stood beside Janet's grave under the closed feather fans of five tall elms. Against the miscellaneous tombstones in the public cemetery – marble cenotaphs, solid square vaults, beckoning angels with outspread wings, scrolls and crosses in brown, grey or white – the autumn leaves piled softly in the windless air. An unobtrusive army of gardeners worked incessantly, brushing the leaves into heaps and carting them away.

When they left Richmond Park by the Robin Hood gate, Ruth looked uneasily up the long ascent from Roehampton to Putney Heath. The silver birches, no longer a ranked army of spectres, gathered themselves into a friendly suburban wood; the windmill on Wimbledon Common diminished from a giant phantom to the proportions of daily life. The glamour of an earlier September had departed from the quiet pleasant landscape; no element of other-worldliness remained to challenge comparison with the vanished setting of that vivid lovely dream. Henceforth, she thought, life at its best will be like these tranquil woods and this brown autumn heath – pleasant, friendly, reassuring. The enchantment has gone – gone with Eugene. I must learn to live without looking for it; it will never come back.

She turned from the confused throng of incompatible memorials to the humbler graves close to the wood, where the long grass grew rough and damp. No vermilion dahlias nor bronze chrysanthemums decorated these quiet plots of earth; they stretched beneath emerald moss starred with tiny white flowers. Ruth bent over Janet's grave to read the inscription upon the small granite cross.

In loving memory of
JANET HARDING RUTHERSTON
Died December 18th, 1917.
Aged 43.
'Do men gather grapes of thorns or figs of thistles?'

'You know, Denis,' said Ruth after a long pause, 'I always thought she was older than that.'

'She seemed much older. You see, everything came upon her too soon, including myself. She was only nineteen when I was born.'

'And you left her memorial without any message of hope? They certainly wore their crowns of thorns, those women who faced hostility and died before it was over. But don't you think some of the grapes are being gathered now?'

'I'm afraid it was rather an egotistical inscription. I didn't mean it for her struggle and its impersonal aspect, so much as for myself. It represented my mood when the stone was put up, just before I went to France.'

'But you don't feel like that any more, do you?'

'Perhaps, Ruth, it depends on you.'

She flushed and was silent. He went on.

'I didn't leave her entirely without a message of hope, all the same. If you look on the other side of the cross you'll see one.'

Moving round the grave, she read the two words on the back of the stone.

'"Jerusalem captured." Whatever does it mean?'

'It was the last entry in her diary, on December 9th, 1917. "Victory of General Allenby in Palestine. Jerusalem captured." She was taken ill a week later. I always thought that sentence symbolic. I don't know quite what her personal Jerusalem was; it was bound up with the friendship between herself and Ellison Campbell, and at some stage or other Miss Campbell failed her.

But politically her Jerusalem was woman suffrage, and that became part of the Constitution five weeks after she died.'

'Yes,' mused Ruth. 'In that sense Jerusalem *was* captured – by her generation of women for ours and our successors. I wonder what she'd have thought of the world we're making – the world she worked for and never saw?'

'She'd have been glad of it, I think, for all its violence and disillusion. At any rate *you'd* have satisfied her, as I told you just now. You're the woman she wanted to be and never was, because circumstances in those days were too strong.'

'I suppose that's true. Even now, I'm not entitled to vote – I shan't be thirty till next year – but I suppose I've really got the freedom and independence she sought for.'

'Yes, and the dignity that independence brings. You see,' he said, as they walked slowly out of the cemetery, 'I believe there's an inherent dignity in all human life – a dignity that every human being is entitled to, whether man or woman, white or coloured, rich or poor. I think one of the worst crimes anyone can commit is to deprive another person of this dignity. That was my father's real offence against my mother.'

'He must have been terribly cruel to her, Denis.'

'Not according to his own lights – that was the tragedy. He wasn't wicked or ruthless in the deliberate way she thought him. He was simply one of those people who never become adult and learn to face life as it is. Because his universe wasn't the well-ordered fairy-tale he expected, he was perpetually filled with moral indignation. Nobody ever more earnestly desired what he regarded as righteous conduct to be universal – and the result was that he thrashed about his world like an irresponsible child in a nursery full of brittle toys.'

'Ellison Campbell doesn't seem to have behaved very responsibly either. Didn't she realise how much she must have meant in a disappointing life like your mother's?'

'I don't know. Mother never talked about her to me. I only know they disagreed about woman suffrage, and their final separation was somehow due to that.'

'It's the one thing about Miss Campbell I can't understand, when she's really such a product of the women's movement

herself . . . I've had one or two contacts with her in my own
life, you know. Oh, nothing personal, but at school I played
the part of the hero in one of her plays, and at college I won an
annual prize she gave there. She came to Drayton and presented
it to me, in 1914. And only last spring, when I spoke in Glasgow,
she was sitting on the platform.'

'It was just before the War that she quarrelled with my mother.
I know I was up at Oxford at the time.'

'Was it? I remember thinking how ill and unhappy she looked
when she gave me my prize. Could it have had anything to do
with the quarrel, I wonder?'

'I don't know,' he repeated. The falling yellow leaves in the
chestnut avenue between the chapel and the gate renewed for him
the melancholy of those old far-away sorrows which so long had
baffled him. 'There's a great deal about the past that still seems
inexplicable. My mother never gave me her confidence.'

'All the same, I'm glad you showed me her grave, Denis. It's
made me want more than ever to go on with the work she
began.'

'And I to fulfil the vow I made at her burial,' he said, taking
Ruth's hand as they turned into the stretch of road where she had
walked with Eugene Meury three months before Janet's death –
was it six years ago or six hundred? 'I don't ask you to give me
the answer I want until you feel that by doing so you'll be more
yourself, not less. Don't give it at all unless you're sure you can
still become the kind of person you want to be – not in spite of
marriage, but because of it.'

She took him at his word. Throughout October when her
office hours were over and her speeches finished, she walked
up and down Battersea Park beside the wide grey sweep of the
Thames, meditating upon this latest of life's dilemmas. Would
she betray her passion for Eugene by giving herself to Denis?
Would marriage make her unfaithful to that beloved ghost
whose outstanding gift had been his vitality?

'Everything he said and did,' she thought, 'was an affirmation
of life. He, of all others, would recognise that though he is dead
I still have to live; that life to be effective must contain a measure
of happiness . . . But is it fair to Denis himself, when I can never

banish Eugene's image nor cease to give it precedence? Should I take him at his word when he says he will be content with what is left and ask no more? Is it right to accept what he offers and give so little in return?'

She leaned over the railings, looking down at the reflected sunshine scintillating from the tiny wavelets which ruffled the river surface in the full flood of the autumn tide.

'Life will never sparkle again, but perhaps it will glow – like a fire on a frosty evening when the embers are burning red and bright . . . I have known love and it isn't love that I feel for Denis, but he understands my thoughts and shares my values in a way that Eugene never could have. I shouldn't have cared whether he did or not, but if I marry Denis it will be because he does.'

In November came the General Election, which for the first time in England's history put a Labour Government into office, but this time, because of her mother's entreaties, Ruth did not work or speak in Staffordshire.

'I can't stand the way your father and Norman go on about it,' Jessie explained.

So Ruth persuaded the national organisers to send her instead to another industrial area, the chain of ship-building towns and colliery villages in Northumberland and Durham. When she returned to London from a vigorous campaign which had left no opportunity for private meditations, her personal problem seemed in some mysterious fashion to have solved itself.

Just before she went to Dene Hall for the Christmas holiday, she told Denis that she would marry him.

9

'So you've decided to get spliced in April, eh, Jill?' Stephen repeated, as though by constant reiteration he could the better realise, not only the fact of Ruth's impending marriage, but the incredible identity of her future husband.

'Yes, Father. That gives us a chance to get two or three weeks' honeymoon in Denis's vacation. The office will let me have the time off if they know long enough beforehand.'

'You don't mean to say you're going on working for the Reds after you're married!'

'Of course. I wouldn't dream of giving it up.'

Father and daughter faced one another across the dining-room table. Dinner was over, and Jessie had gone to the drawing-room with Norman. It was an unpretentious meal and soon finished now that the numerous courses and elaborate service of pre-war days had long been abandoned, but the family tension produced just before they sat down by Ruth's announcement of her engagement to Denis had made it seem interminable. Beneath the flickering light of the shaded candles, Stephen Alleyndene saw not only his consistently incorrigible daughter, but a world which was passing with dizzy speed beyond his comprehension. He felt baffled and bewildered by an epoch in which a Labour Government sat at Westminster, and young women, even of his own flesh and blood, spoke on Socialist platforms and married their inferiors.

'You know, Jill,' he remarked for the tenth time, 'it's more than I can fathom, your picking on that young Rutherston of all folks on earth. I might just as well have saved myself that first-class row with his father and let things be . . . I take it your mind's really made up?'

He's getting old, thought Ruth, looking at Stephen's broad shoulders bent over the table, his still abundant hair gleaming silver in the candle-light. It's aged him having to run the Pottery in a post-war Staffordshire so different from anything he or his ancestors imagined – and now I suppose I've disappointed the one personal hope that he still had left.

'I'm sorry you're upset about it, Father,' she said with compunction, 'but I *have* decided to marry Denis. I didn't make up my mind in a hurry. I've been thinking it over since September.'

'Nice thing for me,' he burst out explosively, 'if you turn up here with progeny the spit and image of the Reverend Thomas Rutherston!'

Ruth flushed and, to her mortification, tears filled her eyes.

'I don't remember Denis's father. Was he really as awful as all that?'

'Ay, he'd a devil of a temper, and he wasn't exactly one of the aristocracy. Still,' he added, touched by her distress as he always had been and always would be, however vehemently she defied his beliefs and opposed his prejudices, 'I daresay I was a bit hard on the chap. Times change, and notions with them. Denis as I recall was a clever lad, if a bit on the dreamy side, and I don't doubt he's turned out well enough.'

'He certainly has! He got a First in Honour Mods at Oxford, and then a Distinction in Greats in spite of the War. And people who ought to know say he's one of the best Philosophy lecturers London University's ever had.'

'Well, you've been of age a good long time now, Jill, and it's your own life you've got to lead. If you choose to marry beneath you, I suppose it's no affair of mine. After all,' he concluded with reminiscent magnanimity, 'I did the same myself, and there's a deal to be said for it. You and the lads always had more *nous* than the rest of the family put together.'

'That's not saying a great deal, is it? Denis's brains will add something substantial to our limited stores of intelligence.'

'Ay, he's evidently a learned sort of chap. He's bound to make his mark, and I daresay he'll be good to you. If you're satisfied, Jill, your father's content.'

'Then you'll welcome Denis properly when I ask him here?'

'You can take it from me, my dear, that I'll do my best to make him feel at home. Dene Hall's had a fine tradition of hospitality in the past, and I don't mean to forget it just because the place is breaking up all round me. You've made young Rutherston your future husband, and that's enough for Stephen Alleyndene.'

He kept his promise. When he received Denis at Dene Hall for Christmas, two days afterwards, only his nearest intimates would have known that his greeting expressed the conscientious cordiality of the squire and the employer, rather than the genial informality of an equal. With unconcealed curiosity he appraised the unknown young man who had replaced the pale dreamy boy of his recollection. Privately wondering why his headstrong, adventurous daughter should have chosen a husband so much less vivid and positive than he would have expected, he examined critically the contemplative blue-grey eyes, the thick plume of light-brown hair, the long fine hands, the deep cleft between the sensitive nostrils and the full, curving upper lip. Denis, conscious of an inward amusement that must soon betray itself in his own expression, cast down his eyes before the big grey-haired man with the lined handsome face, whom he had vaguely recalled as glossy and black and exuberant.

'I don't suppose you remember me, sir?'

'Ay, I remember you. But I must admit I never guessed you'd come here one day asking to marry my daughter!'

'You think me unworthy, then?'

'Oh, I don't say that! You're not a bit like your father, my boy, and from my point of view that's all to the good. Besides, times have changed. You've only got to look at this place to see the way they're going!'

Taking Denis over to the drawing-room window, he waved his hand towards his hereditary acres spreading beneath the grey December sky. The lowest of the three terraces had now been eclipsed by the rough grass of the hayfield; beneath the doomed trunks of the few surviving firs showed the bricks and planks of the encroaching builders. No stretch of magpie-haunted meadowland now intervened between Dene Hall and the outskirts of Witnall; the sea of urban dwellings had risen and broken on the very edge of the Alleyndene estate.

'I daresay you won't recall it as it was,' said Stephen sadly, 'but just cast your eye over what you can see. Jerry-built low-class bungalows in the plantation my old grand-guv'nor set such store by! Workmen's cottages almost at our doors, and the price of labour risen till I can't afford sufficient gardeners to keep up the grounds! It's enough to make my ancestors rise from their graves and haunt me!'

Into Denis's mind came the melancholy words of G. K. Chesterton:

'We only know that the last sad squires ride slowly to the sea,
And a new people takes the land.'

Well, he and Ruth had identified themselves with the newest – or was it the oldest? – people of all. He wanted to see those who had possessed nothing inherit their share of England's green dominion, but because he had never been wealthy or endowed, he understood better than she the bitterness of those to whom the land had belonged.

'We live in a revolutionary age, sir,' he said gently. 'Even in my own day, comparatively short as it has been, I've seen changes happen too swiftly for some individuals to adjust themselves at all.' (My poor father, whom you despised, he thought – those changes killed him. Ruth's parents have suffered, but they're tougher than mine; they're less highly-strung and more adaptable, for all their conservatism.)

Stephen turned from the window.

'The times are too much for me, my boy, but you and Jill belong to them and you'll have to work out your salvation in your own fashion. Mental equipment's a grand thing nowadays – I took good care my own kids didn't want for it. I don't doubt you've enough in your head to compensate for what you lack in your pocket. If you make my daughter a good husband, I've no more to say.'

When Ruth and Denis had gone back to London, the family verdict endorsed the wisdom of Stephen's capitulation to the inexorable tide of circumstance.

'You know, Father,' Norman admitted grudgingly, 'with her views she might have done worse. It wouldn't have surprised me if she'd turned up here married to one of those wild unemployed Communists without a farthing to his name!'

'He really isn't such a bad young man, Stephen. Much more *personable* than I'd expected, if you know what I mean.'

'Ay, I grant you that, Jess. The lad's turned out a gentleman. It's more than anyone could say for his father.'

The occasion seemed to Jessie auspicious for asserting her determination to have Ruth 'properly' married. For more than ten years she had visualised this family function, and she did not intend to be deprived of her hour because her daughter had inconveniently chosen the son of Thomas Rutherston.

'We can't have Ruth getting married in London, Stephen. If we don't have the wedding here she'll go off to a registry office, and people will think there's something wrong. After all, she's nearly thirty, and it's better for her to marry Denis Rutherston than no one.'

'Well,' Stephen acknowledged with his slow, recurrent bewilderment, 'things aren't what they were. It seems a bit of a come-down for me after turfing out young Denis's father, but I doubt if there are many folks left in Witnall who remember old Rutherston.'

The opposition which Jessie had expected from Ruth herself did not arise.

'I always meant to be married at Witnall unless you and father objected,' she wrote. 'I have a theory that the ghosts of sad and bitter things are somehow laid if a pleasant thing occurs where they happened. I like to feel that my marriage to Denis will exorcise from St Peter's not only the memory of Aunt Elizabeth's unhappiness, but also Father's quarrel with Mr Rutherston. We are asking the Vicar of St Etheldreda's to marry us. He seems the ideal person when Denis has known him for so long, and you had him as a convalescent officer at Dene Hall. The one thing I do draw the line at is a wreath and veil. I have got beyond the absurdity of those medieval trappings.'

Her adamant attitude on the subject drove Jessie to exasperation.

'I can't imagine why she won't have a proper wedding-dress. Anybody would think she'd been married before! She might be a widow of fifty instead of a young woman of twenty-nine!'

In the end it was Denis who achieved a compromise on this apparently trivial dispute over sartorial etiquette.

'You could wear a white dress and hat, couldn't you, darling?' he suggested, understanding that for her the traditional symbols of virginity would represent a dishonest betrayal of the past. 'I'd like you to wear white myself. You see, you had on a white dress the first time I saw you, at the Dene Hall garden party.'

So it was in the customary apparel of a widow about to re-marry that Ruth appeared as a bride at St Peter's, Witnall, on an April day of soft intermittent sunshine and gentle fleeting showers. She had insisted that she and Denis preferred a quiet wedding, but when she arrived at the lych-gate with Stephen, she saw that the inhabitants of Witnall and the employees from the Alleyndene Pottery had descended upon the churchyard like a swarm of zealous bees.

Beneath the pointed tower of the red sandstone church, they eddied round the budding lilac-bushes where the blackbirds sang vigorously, or stood upon the low boundary wall above the old sloping tombstones. But now they were no longer, as at Aunt Elizabeth's wedding and Granny Alleyndene's funeral, the humble despised strangers who witnessed an exclusive pageant from a respectful distance; they were her friends, her fellow-workers, her comrades in the Witnall Labour Party and the influential supporters of England's government. Tears of genuine astonishment sprang to her eyes when she saw the crowds awaiting her, and realised from their affectionate, enthusiastic cheering that she who had once been aloof and arrogant was now popular, cherished, beloved.

They followed her into the church, occupying every available seat, filling the side-aisles and the curtained space which concealed the font where she had been baptised. Upon the altar stood two silver vases of Madonna lilies, as they had stood one Easter-tide long ago when Denis knelt before the tablet commemorating Enoch Alleyndene's three lost children, and meditated upon the resurrection of the dead. Again the lectern and choir-stalls were massed with daffodils and scarlet anemones. Brilliant multi-coloured tulips adorned the narrow sills beneath the stained-glass windows; the Witnall boys and girls who came with their parents carried bunches of creamy primroses or frilled yellow aconites. From the darkest corners of the old country church shone the pale gold and flawless white of early spring flowers.

As Ruth walked slowly up the central aisle on Stephen's arm, she saw, not the elegant groups of Heathcotes and Deakins and Tallinors who had received Jessie's formal invitation, but the dear friendly faces of those guests whom she herself had invited – the blue smiling eyes of Jim Hardiman, the red benign countenance of old Jos Davenport, the reassuring appreciative gaze of Arthur Wardle and his young wife and three little children. She thought, 'We're celebrating more than my wedding to-day, they and I.'

In front of the altar Denis joined her; the gentle welcoming strains of the organ ceased. Frederick Mansfield, his war-time lameness overcome, his strong lean face and iron-grey head impressive in their benevolent dignity, began to repeat the marriage service. The sentences to which, as bridesmaid to Aunt Elizabeth, she had once listened in troubled bewilderment again smote insistently upon her ears.

'Dearly beloved, we are gathered together here in the sight of God, and in the face of this congregation, to join together this Man and this Woman in holy Matrimony; which is an honourable estate . . . and therefore is not by any to be enterprised, nor taken in hand, unadvisedly, lightly or wantonly, to satisfy men's carnal lusts and appetites, like brute beasts that have no understanding . . .'

When she heard the accusing words she shivered, as though the lovely, bitter past had risen from its grave to condemn her, but Denis took her hand in his and raised it to his lips.

Twenty minutes later, standing in the vestry on the very spot where Stephen Alleyndene had quarrelled with Thomas Rutherston nearly seventeen years before, Ruth Alleyndene signed the register and completed the ceremony which made her Denis Rutherston's wife.

10

Towards the end of their honeymoon at Portofino on the Gulf of Genoa, Denis and Ruth sat together below the Castello on the Capo di Madonna and gazed across the deep turquoise water at Rapallo on the other side of the bay. In front of the opposite shore the water faded to a milder, opaquer blue, as though its colour had been mixed with Chinese white.

'It looks an innocent sort of place for a treaty between Germany and Soviet Russia,' she remarked.

'That was before the march on Rome,' he said. 'There's nothing innocent about Mussolini's Italy. Even the British Navy takes care to keep an eye on it.' And he pointed to the slim milk-blue outlines of four British gun-boats lying quiescent in the distant harbour.

The third week in April was almost over. The end of the month would see the London term begin and Ruth back at her place in Eccleston Square. Five days hence they were due to return to the green and white-painted cottage in Campion Place, St John's Wood, which Stephen and Jessie had furnished as their wedding present. In a week's time their life together would begin in earnest, with all its problems, its complexities, its adaptations.

Behind their grey wooden seat in the cool shadow of the old castle wall, freesias and stocks and orange wall-flowers flung their warm scent into the air. In the deep fresh grass which covered the surface of the rocky peninsula, wild white hyacinths and periwinkles and buttercups sprang from the ground as profusely as weeds, and lords-and-ladies thrust up their petals like curled tongues with dark brown stripes on a background of dull red. Against the wall of the castle, branches of pink and purple blossom drooped heavily from the taller shrubs of prunus and lilac, and the lavender-blue of wistaria climbed the lofty impervious stone. Little bronze lizards, lightning streaks of animation in the hot sunshine, darted across the dry wooden railings which marked the edge of the cliff.

Below those railings a series of rocky terraces, crowned with the snow-white of cherry blossom, the silver-green of olives and the bright yellow-green of young fig-leaves, descended sharply to the sea. Across the clear transparent water above the reddish-grey volcanic rocks, green motor-boats trailing volumes of spray dashed into the narrow horseshoe-shaped harbour. On the cobbled stones of the small quay, loquacious groups of bead and lace-sellers mingled with strolling players, itinerant tourists, and fishermen mending their nets in rowing boats painted blue, jade, yellow or scarlet. The grey-green hills above Rapallo, striped darkly with ravines and dotted with clumps of fir and pine, broke near the water's edge into pale cliffs of the same creamy yellow as the turrets and villas which speckled the lower slopes. In the high far distance, the peaks of snow-mountains glimmered faintly from the mild blue sky. Above them floated tiny transparent drifts of cirrus cloud, tinted the saffron-pink of tea-rose petals. It seemed incredible that within this benevolent land of colour and sunshine the dark menace of Fascism was steadily growing, an embryo monster so soon to cast its evil shadow over the tortured civilisations struggling towards peace and re-birth.

Amid the gentle tumult of sound – the lazy humming of the bees, the sweet chirping of innumerable contented birds, the far-off grinding of the motor-boats like persistent corn-crakes – Ruth and Denis sat in silence each thinking of the other, critically yet with kindness. Only after their wedding had she fully realised the contrast which would confront her between that earlier union springing spontaneously from passion, and a marriage based upon tender affection and mutual respect. Her memory of desperate love made adjustment more difficult, she knew. Passion had been, for its brief duration, violent and abandoned, while affection was considerate and infinitely patient; yet the rapture in that passion had made everything easy and unpremeditated, whereas the relationship between herself and Denis involved a conscious co-operation which demanded as much from intelligence as from instinct.

Undoubtedly more difficult, but perhaps, in the long run, better worth while? In mind as well as in flesh she was one with Denis; how far had that fierce mutual yearning of two young enraptured bodies, two contrasting temperaments and nationalities, meant that she was really one with Eugene? It was a question to which neither past nor future could reply; and yet, throughout their fortnight at Portofino, her restless analytical mind never ceased to ask it.

'Supposing I had married Eugene, should I have missed the sympathetic insight, the sensitive perception of *nuances* and distinctions, that I get from Denis? He understands everything, while Eugene would neither have understood nor cared for the subtleties in which the shadow-world of the intellect abounds. Why is there this strange divorce between the flesh and the spirit? Why does one's body refuse to respond rapturously and completely where one's mind loves and admires, yet is kindled to flame by the very vitality which excludes that divine intricacy of spiritual comprehension? Or is this a biological fact? Must passion so profoundly involve antagonism that where there is no antagonism there can be no ardent response of the flesh? "Behold, I show you a mystery" – that seems to be the only adequate comment on the relationships between men and women.'

'She's thinking about him again,' surmised Denis sadly, looking at her grave, preoccupied expression, but his memory of Thomas's insistent catechising had taught him not to harass her with questions. Though his four weeks' experience of American students enabled him to picture the gay vivacity of spirit which had captured and still possessed her, he felt no jealousy of the dead man whose strong arms had held her, whose virile young body had known hers. Not resentment but pity seized him for the domination of her memory by that vivid ghost. He envied him only his stern knowledge of war, his constantly-tested personal courage which had been so vital an ingredient of his physical capacity for love.

A tiny breeze stirred the long grass and the smooth pointed leaves of the olives. Lifting his eyes to the edges of the lower peaks softened by their fringe of dark firs, Denis came as near as his rational detachment permitted to a prayer that he might prove equal to the obligations which he had undertaken. In those paths of life where his own aspirations lay, he realised that Ruth's personality would overshadow his, her beauty which the past two years had restored make him insignificant. He knew that her uncompromising decisiveness would throw too vivid a light upon his philosophical hesitations, her impatience spur him to action before he had sufficiently considered its remotest possibilities. She was gifted and ambitious, and because of her past she would never be wholly his in mind or body.

But she had suffered, she was acquainted with grief, and fundamentally her values were the same as his own; they were rooted in those qualities of compassion without which civilisation had no enduring substance, no capacity for growth. And he loved her. He loved her, in the last resort, beyond calculation – as she had loved Eugene, as she would never love him. She had provided him with that object of worship in the search for which he had been defeated throughout his childhood and youth, and his gratitude to her for inspiring this conscious devotion would be everlasting. In the long run, he told himself, it is not the love one gets, but the love one gives, which is the constructive element in human experience. I shall grow in grace because I love her; it is not necessary that she should love me.

A beautiful two-year-old Italian boy, dark-eyed and brown-skinned, ran in front of them with his nurse, chasing a sulphur-hued butterfly. Her meditations broken, Ruth followed the baby with her eyes.

'Look, Denis! Isn't he lovely? It would be worth while, wouldn't it, having one like that!'

'It's entirely for you to decide, darling. I'd never condemn any woman to that ordeal against her will – or any child to be the intolerable burden I was to my mother.'

'I don't pretend to have a strong maternal instinct,' she said. 'I'm too much interested in other things for that – and yet ever since I grew up, I've felt that without children my life wouldn't be complete. You know what I'd have given to have Eugene's child, whether he could have married me or not. Now I'd like one of yours – but not just yet. I want a year first of work and marriage combined. After that I shall probably be ready. But even before I go back to England . . .'

She hesitated, reluctant to hurt him, yet anxious to obey while it lasted the urgent impulse which had seized her to face and overcome her most poignant dread. Denis encouraged her.

'Before you go back, darling – what?'

'You remember, yesterday when you were writing letters, I went and sat in the olive groves on the way to Portofino Vetta? Well, I was half asleep, gazing at the grape-hyacinths and butterfly-orchids in the grass up there, when a warm breeze suddenly brought down the smell of pines from the woods higher up the mountain. I thought for a moment I was in Hardelot again. I came back to the present knowing as clearly as if a voice had told me that before I start my work again, I must go to Romagne.'

She stood up and looked down at him, her grey eyes alight, her cheeks faintly flushed. The midday sun found golden threads in her dark uncovered hair.

'Denis, I may be all wrong – just haunted by memories even more than usual because of our marriage. But it doesn't seem to me quite fair to you to begin our life together until I've said good-bye to Eugene – once and for all. I've known so long that I ought to – and now, for some reason, I feel I can. Would you think it very strange if I went to Verdun on our way home?'

'I want you, dear, to do anything that will give you peace of mind.'

'But do you quite understand? ... I should have to go alone.'

'I imagined that. I could wait for you in Paris.'

She looked towards the gate which led into the castle garden from the public pathway across the peninsula. Except for the bees and butterflies, they were alone together. She put her hands on his shoulders and pressed her lips gently against his in a poignant surge of gratitude and tenderness.

'Dear Denis, I love you! You're very good to me.'

II

Four mornings afterwards, Ruth walked alone through the half-rebuilt streets of Verdun, where the twin towers of the grey Cathedral stand high above the olive-green waters of the Meuse.

The marks of shells, deliberately unrepaired, still scarred the Cathedral's stone face and the great walls of the fortifications. Steep and grim, the huge disfigured barricade commanded the open rolling country to the south-east from the highest point of the city above the plain. Along the streets where rebuilding was everywhere in progress, piles of stones from the ruined houses left only a narrow passage for pedestrians and traffic.

'He knew these streets; he must often have crossed this bridge,' she thought, standing on the narrow Pont des Augustins where the Meuse branches into a broad canal curving past the Citadelle in the direction of St Mihiel. A sense of dreamlike incredulity, familiar to those who visit after many years some place of which they have constantly thought and read, possessed her as she looked across the river to the new houses with cream walls and vermilion roofs being erected along the Quai de

Londres. The buildings which they replaced, ancient, dilapidated and picturesque, had risen sheer from the banks of the deep green water flowing beneath their windows, but now their post-bombardment successors, practical, modern and provincial, gave space for an elegant embankment named in honour of London, which had adopted the shattered city after the War.

Early that afternoon, Ruth left Verdun in a hired car which carried her towards the Argonne Forest. All over the spacious, undulating country on that April day of sun and wind, the blossom of blackthorn and cherry gleamed like snow against the pale clear sky. Already, amid the debris of villages razed to the ground, little white houses with red roofs and green shutters appeared like new toys left intact in the midst of a child's fallen castle of bricks.

Once again, beyond the ruins, the emerald fields were chequered with brown squares of fertile ploughland. Black and white cows fed peacefully in deep meadows golden with cowslips. Round the fallen roofs of half-buried dug-outs flitted saffron-yellow butterflies; hawks hovered almost motionless over the ghosts of pill-boxes outlined against the horizon. Above banks mauve and blue with mayflowers and violets, invisible larks piped sweetly as they had piped near the Château d'Hardelot seven years ago. It seemed a fantastic legend that within this lovely spring earth lay scattered the bones of four hundred thousand Frenchmen, many still undiscovered beneath the tumbled, pock-marked hills where brambles and thistles and fragments of rusted wire hid the humped outlines of old trenches round the Forts of Vaux and Donaumont and the battered crest of Mort-Homme.

Towards the car came a marching line of young blue-clad soldiers, wearing dark blue steel helmets. The tramp of their feet rang evenly from the straight road of blue-grey asphalt.

'Nous traversons la Voie Sacrée,' announced the chauffeur. He explained to Ruth that along this road throughout the War, when every other line of communication was smashed by shells or controlled by shell-fire, a continuous convoy of lorries had brought supplies for the entire Army of Verdun. When they left the Voie Sacrée where it branched off to Bar-le-Duc, and drove along the main St Menehould road through Dombasle-en-Argonne and Recicourt, she knew from the apprehensive thumping of her heart that the forest was near.

At Parois the chauffeur turned off into a narrow shell-torn track, which led through the village of Neuvilly into the southern section of the Argonne. Here, not yet six years before, the American infantry had begun their eighteen-days' 'Wilderness Campaign' through twenty-two kilometres of tangled trees and clinging vines and thick trailing brush. Between Parois and Neuvilly Ruth clasped her hands tightly together as they approached the forest, an immense black shadow looming across the horizon like a barrier cutting off the lanes and fields of commonplace experience from some lost, unknown world.

'Wait a minute!' she cried breathlessly as the car passed cautiously between the half-reconstructed cottages of Neuvilly. She could see now the new emerald tufts of the silver birches against the deep brown trunks of the taller trees, the jade-blue clumps of dark firs above the fresh green of birch and beech. At the edge of the forest the white shimmer of cherry and blackthorn lighted up the sombre grey-green of willows and the shiny peacock-green of ivy clinging to aged moss-covered bark. Beneath the dense undergrowth of broom and hawthorn the ground was carpeted with mauve and white anemones, the rich marshy earth brown with dead bracken and fallen leaves.

'*Voici, Madame!*' said the chauffeur, producing from his pocket a crumpled notebook which he opened at a page of laborious hieroglyphics. It was a paragraph, he explained, written by 'Le Général Pershing,' which would one day adorn the great American monument to be erected beside the ruined twelfth-century church on the heights of Montfaucon. She cast her eyes – at first hurriedly and then with slow attention – over the sentences conscientiously copied for the benefit of visitors from the United States.

'The Meuse-Argonne battle presented numerous difficulties, seemingly insurmountable. The success stands out as one of the great achievements in the history of American arms. Suddenly conceived and hurried in plan and operation; complicated by close association with a preceding major operation; directed against stubborn defence of the vital point of the Western Front; and attended by cold and inclement weather; this battle was prosecuted with an unselfish and heroic spirit of courage and fortitude which demanded eventual victory. Physically strong, virile and aggressive, the morale of the American soldier during this most trying period was superb.'

A lump rose into her throat and choked her.

'Thank you,' she whispered, handing back the notebook to the chauffeur, and they drove slowly on into the Argonne.

The narrow track from Neuvilly cut direct between the massed trunks of firs and beeches, until it joined the main road which skirted the deep ravine known as the Four de Paris, and ran through the breadth of the forest to Varennes on the way to Romagne. Getting out of the car Ruth looked down into the dark rectangular ravine, enclosed on both sides by steep wooded slopes. Through the morass at the bottom, marshy and soft with the leaf-mould of years, a thin brook ran from east to west. So deep was the valley that the tops of the tall trees growing from the bottom stood level with the main road. Far below their branches, many still splintered and leafless, a thick tangle of vines and brambles covered the slopes.

'It might be here that he died,' she thought, suddenly cold. But the chauffeur told her that the story, now legendary in Verdun, of the 'missing companies' was associated with a similar ravine, 'L'Abri du Crochet,' deep in the heart of the forest where the road did not penetrate. But of course one could not be sure. Madame would realise that even after a few years the famous legends of war-time attached themselves to half-a-dozen places.

For over an hour Ruth stayed in the forest, sometimes riding slowly in the car, sometimes pushing her way through stiff broom and tangled willow down the rough woodland paths which led on either side of the road into the sinister depths of the thick, ravaged trees. Beside these paths, broken boughs and dead brown bushes lay in heaps amid the bright incongruous patches of anemones and violets; others, still standing, waved shattered grotesque arms, or leaned, gashed and withered, against the moss-grown trunks of their neighbours. Everywhere amid the thicket lay the rusting, rotting remains of the war-time occupation – tin cans, tangles of barbed wire, chimney pots from disintegrating dug-outs, decaying duck-boards thrust across old communication trenches. Through the thick interlacing branches the sun filtered dimly; high in their midst the blackbirds chirped and the pigeons cooed, serenely indifferent to the ruin wrought by human folly. Now and again the staccato call of the cuckoo sounded clearly above the rustle of leaves and the snapping of twigs as Ruth struggled through the lonely tracks.

The farther she went, the more amazed she became that the vulnerable bodies of mortal men had ever succeeded in penetrating those shadowed impervious miles when barbed wire had twisted its merciless trails through briar and brush, and every dense jungle of shrubs had concealed a machine-gun. At La Harazée the grim clearings between the trees seemed haunted by the ghosts of men who had fought their way to death in the pathless undergrowth, for she knew from her weeks in the devastated areas of Poland that humped irregular mounds covered with rank tussocky grass and coarse thistles concealed the bodies of the shattered, unidentifiable dead. Behind these wide treeless patches where the shrouding underbrush had once obscured the corrupt burden of the stained and poisoned earth, a huge mine-crater, bare and gaping, yawned beneath the overhanging willows. Brambles trailed over it, and round its edge piles of chopped tree-trunks lay amid the brown mouldering bracken.

'Go slowly!' she urged, when the chauffeur suggested that they ought to leave for Romagne-sous-Montfaucon while the sun was still high. As she looked back at the woodland trails branching off on either side of the shell-pitted roadway through the forest, the throbbing of the car seemed to translate itself into reminiscent words.

Know this is your War; in this loneliest hour you ride
Down the roads he knew . . .

'But they're not quite true for me,' she thought. 'I'm not lonely now, because I've got Denis. I shall never be alone again . . . And yet they *are* true, for there's no one left with whom I shared the War – that period of my life which, as Eugene once said of himself, will always remain the most poignant, the most intense. Denis never knew it even as I did, and certainly not in the same way as Eugene – Eugene who saw it through from beginning to end: who shared both England's war and America's. Denis suffered because of it, but it meant nothing to him but the possibility of a death which he desired but was not granted. It was all that really mattered of Eugene's life, and it ended by taking his life away from him. It left nothing but that which now lies in darkness beneath a plot of earth at Romagne.'

12

The sun was dipping towards the low line of wooded hills to the north-west, when the car ran through a marble gateway crowned with sculptured eagles into the broad valley which enclosed the spreading acres of the American dead.

Leaving the car in the pale circular sweep of drive beneath the green hill of climbing crosses, Ruth walked up to the custodian's office on the nearer slope to find the number and position of Eugene's grave. When she knew it she returned to the hillside, and gazed across the wide shallow cup of the valley at the thousands upon thousands of white-painted wooden crosses marshalled like marching soldiers in their ordered ranks. In the mellow golden light of the descending sun, the closely cut sward shone so vividly green that a blue tinge crept over the painted wood, and the cemetery appeared as a gigantic field of bluebells planted in rows.

Half fascinated and half appalled by that macabre illusion, she remembered how Denis had spoken, a few days earlier at Portofino, of America's part in the War.

'People are so ignorant of economics, they think the War's over, but if I know anything of economic laws its real aftermath hasn't even begun. Take America. She seems to have escaped all the War's worst consequences – to be safe and prosperous when other nations are ruined and insecure. But that can't go on for ever. In the long run even America won't escape the effects of universal dislocation.'

Contemplating the great bluebell field of the dead, she found herself endorsing his judgment.

'They didn't lose half their generation's life, as we did, but God in Heaven, they lost enough! How can even a great country like the United States be deprived two hundred thousand times over of such gaiety and vitality as Eugene's, and not have to pay for it in the end? Perhaps, as Denis said, the day will come when America will realise more clearly than to-day what the War took from her life and her future.'

And all at once, as she stood above that valley of death, her memories of the War and its aftermath came back to her in a torrent of recollection. She pictured again the dead buried in the sands of Gallipoli; she recalled her dying patients in France after Loos and the Somme and Passchendaele; she remembered the devastated villages of Volhynia, the forgotten German cemetery in a Polish wood, the stiff frozen bodies in Buzuluk churchyard; she now saw before her the fifteen thousand graves of American soldiers gathered together at Romagne from the trackless undergrowth and dark ravines of the Argonne Forest. How vast, illimitable and incalculable was the desolation which the War had brought! Stretching across the earth from America to Russia, from Flanders to Gallipoli, were the hidden whitening bones of a generation of men. Civilisation had barely survived their loss; if another such doom were to come upon the world, mankind would live no more. Surely, then, we cannot permit it; surely the instinct of self-preservation must override humanity's diabolical capacity for self-destruction!

'The light is fading,' she said to herself. 'I must face it now.'

Descending into the valley, she mounted the marble steps and moved slowly up the wide grassy path which divided the graves on the opposite hill. One day at the head of that path, a memorial chapel would be built, but now only a tall flagpost stood against the azure vault of cloudless sky, the Stars and Stripes waving from its summit above the quiet battalions of the dead. Below the gentle outline of the distant hills, the spire of the village church of Romagne rose from the placid homeliness of red-roofed cottages, blossoming fruit-trees and rich furrows of brown ploughland. No sound could be heard but the soft reassuring sounds of the countryside – the lowing of cows, the tapping of woodpeckers, the throb of a distant lawn-mower, the lazy hum of awakening bees.

The graves, Ruth noticed, had no gardens round them as in the English military cemeteries. White and slender with black stencilled inscriptions, the crosses rose straight from the clipped acres of meadow, their unadorned lines adding to her oppressive sense of an incalculable multitude. Swallows darted over them; tiny bronze beetles with a burnishing of iridescent green crept along the warm dry ground between little gay clumps of cowslips and violets. The mild air, vibrant in its promise of approaching summer, was sweet with the friendly smell of newly-mown grass.

'Oh, God! This is one lovely prodigious falsehood!' she cried, as she looked for Eugene's grave at the south-western corner of the cemetery close to a thin copse of cherry-trees in bloom. 'There is no terror or agony here of war and death as I have known them – only a noble misleading endeavour to beautify and conceal their gruesome realities, to mitigate the intolerable rawness of memory! France, England, America, Germany – you who perpetuate as nations this colossal machinery of consolation – how can you help but increase the illusion born afresh with each generation that war is an instrument of honour, a road to glory!'

At the far end of the last row of crosses where officers and privates lay side by side, the black letters of his name smote suddenly upon her shrinking consciousness.

EUGENE C. MEURY
CAPT. 271ST INF. 45TH DIVISION.
NEW YORK. OCT. 7TH, 1918.
D.S.C.
D.C.M.

Rigid and cold, she gazed upon the inexorable words with dry, burning eyes. Beneath that cross nothing remained of the beautiful young body with which hers had once been so passionately united but the sorry fleshless structure of a man, its horror and pathos decently hidden beneath the external dignity of spring flowers and Christian symbols.

Disillusion and bitterness swept down upon her as she realised, in a moment of acute vision, the unconquerable magnitude of that task of peace and reconciliation to which her loss of him had given so poignant a relevance.

'Perhaps death wasn't the cruellest fate after all, Eugene! At least you died before you shared America's grim disappointment with the Europe that she came over to succour! You laid down your life believing that we appreciated your sacrifice. You didn't know we were going to hoodwink your President, make a diplomatic tool of his League of Nations, call your great and generous country contemptuous names, deny you the credit of your victories. You couldn't guess that immediately the War ended the peoples you saved from defeat would turn wild with hatred, go brawling and stampeding about Europe demanding blood, money, land from the conquered, crying havoc, humiliation, revenge, evoking in a new guise the spirit of militarism. You never suspected that within a year or two of peace we should be terrorising, thieving, persecuting as pitilessly as ever – and finding, as usual, the most holy and high-sounding names for our conduct! Dear Eugene, I'm glad you didn't realise that in spite of your sacrifice, those of us who were left would have to begin the struggle for justice and mercy all over again! You were so magnanimous, so confident of our worth-whileness, so single-hearted in your courage and devotion. You might have done worse than die while your faith in us was still entire!'

She looked up and saw that in the calm sky, now faintly tinged with vermilion, the sun in its glowing descent was almost touching the soft edge of the wooded hills. Throughout the cemetery each cross, facing east, was now confronted with its own slanting shadow. As the shadows lengthened, the long lines of phantom crosses made strange patterns across the grass. Her farewell was almost over; the time had come to depart.

Kneeling before Eugene's grave in the shadow of his cross, she summoned his beloved spirit for the last time.

'Good-bye, Eugene! Henceforth I mustn't think of you as the centre of my life and the only source of all that is dear to me. I

have made someone else the axis round which everything I am
and do will revolve, and though nobody can ever be quite what
you've been to me, I must never again let you hold me back
from life and experience. I have to go away from you now, to
work and marriage and Denis, and leave you lying here until this
earth burns up in its final flame of annihilation, or crumbles into
such dust and ashes as you, yourself, now are. Good-bye, my
love! Rest here in this quiet grave so inappropriate to your gay
vitality; sleep in the peace you never sought and never desired.
Oh, my love, my dear, dear love – good-bye!'

13

That night, alone in the little reconstructed hotel at Verdun, Ruth
dreamed for the hundredth time of Eugene – the old dream so
familiar to many women of her generation who had lost their
lovers in battle.

The dream took at first its usual shape, in which he returned
to her when the War was over to explain that he had never really
been dead, but only missing. He was a prisoner of war, mutilated,
ashamed of his wounds, and afraid to meet her who had known
him in the full vigour of his young, virile manhood.   .

But suddenly, in the middle, the dream changed its course, and
instead of Eugene being shabby, nerve-racked and disfigured, he
became all at once the handsome, vital young man who had
come to Hardelot to tell her that he was now Captain Meury.
Then, in a moment, the scene was no longer Hardelot, but a
railway terminus, and he was seeing her off by train on a long
journey. For a second, when the carriages began to move, a
shadow dimmed the gay vivacity of his thin brown face. But
almost immediately the swift sadness was gone again, and as he
watched the train leave the station, he saluted her and smiled.

CHAPTER VIII

HUSBAND AND WIFE

'Nothing but the Infinite pity is sufficient for the infinite pathos of human life.'

J. H. SHORTHOUSE, *John Inglesant.*

'So long as one bears one's life in one's own hands, the burden is intolerable. It is only by seeing that life as part of a universal life that peace is found.'

LOUISA CREIGHTON, *Life and Letters of Mandall Creighton.*

I

EVER SINCE SHE left Eccleston Square at midnight, when the General Strike orders of the Trade Union Council came into force, the pains had been growing more definite. At first nagging and shallow, they had now become grinding and deep, and the intervals between them were shorter. When the clock struck six Ruth got out of bed and opened Denis's door.

'Are you awake, Denis? . . . Look here, I think the twins are coming. I've been having pains on and off all night.'

He was sitting up in an instant, his blue eyes startled and concerned beneath his unruly mop of hair.

'You're quite sure? Why, it's a whole month before the time!'

'I know, but I suppose they're premature. Twins often are, aren't they – and anyhow, the last week's been enough to make anything happen.'

It had indeed, he thought perturbedly, flinging on his dressing-gown and searching for his slippers. Why hadn't she listened when he tried to persuade her to knock off work in spite of the preparations for the strike?

After Dr Geraldine Vane, suspecting the truth, had sent her to be X-rayed and discovered that she was pregnant with two children, Ruth had arranged to leave Eccleston Square temporarily at the end of April. When the doctor warned her that the birth of twins was often complicated and their rearing difficult, the office promised her three months full-time leave, and a further six months of half-time work if she needed it. But instead of a peaceful, friendly farewell on Friday evening, April 30th, her work had increased and her responsibilities had been doubled from the time that the lock-out notices, due to expire a fortnight later, had been posted at every pit-head thorughout the country on April 16th.

During that final week of April 1926, a position of deadlock existed, not only between the miners and the Government, but between the General Council of the Trade Union Congress and the miners, whose Federation had rejected the proposed termination of the National Wages Agreement and refused to accept the Coal Commission's Report. On the Friday evening, when the lock-out notices expired and the coal strike began, Ruth reported to Denis the announcement of Arthur Pugh, the T.U.C. Chairman, to the Special Conference of Trade Union Executives.

'While we are hoping and striving for an honourable peace, it may be that the General Council will require to call upon our affiliated bodies throughout the country to take part in a struggle which will test the resources, the Trade Union loyalty, and the spirit of working class unity and sacrifice of our people.'

On the Friday and Saturday, cursing herself for being so heavily handicapped at a time of national emergency, Ruth enveloped her ungainly proportions in a voluminous cloak and remained in attendance on the Special Conference at the Memorial Hall, taking down orders and telephoning instructions. For three hours that Saturday evening Denis waited for her in the Hall, until at last the Conference sang 'The Red Flag' and broke up. As they walked through the calm waiting spring night from Farringdon Street into Fleet Street, she told him that the negotiations had failed and on Tuesday the General Strike would begin. Noticing how pale she looked from fatigue and the prolonged tension of those critical days, he implored her to regard that exhausting Saturday at the Memorial Hall as the end of her service.

'But I can't desert in a crisis like this!' she insisted. 'After all, the twins aren't due for another four weeks.'

So she spent Sunday and Monday at the office, immersed in the preparations which followed the Council's issue of strike orders to the Transport Workers, the Printing and Building Trades and a number of other Unions. Excitement and confusion descended upon Eccleston Square. The staff and a group of volunteers remained there day and night interpreting orders, distributing instructions, and drafting communications to the strikers in the provinces. Ruth would not have left even at midnight if her colleagues had not put her into one of the last available taxis and sent her back to St John's Wood.

'I suppose I'd better ring up the nursing home and get myself there as soon as I can,' she said, her executive mind at once beginning to take charge of the situation.

'I should think so,' agreed Denis, struggling hastily into his clothes. 'Can you dress yourself, darling? It'll save time if I telephone the home and get a taxi.'

'Oh, I can dress all right. I'm not so far gone as all that!'

But the effort seemed immense, the pressure of her clothes intolerable, when every few moments came those harsh torturing pangs, grinding round inside her like a blunt circular saw. Her grotesque body doubled over the window-sill, she looked down with twisted brows into the small paved garden in front of their little detached house. A few short daffodils gleamed golden at the foot of the stone birdbath; clusters of ranunculi and dwarf irises which she and Denis had planted the previous autumn pushed themselves between the crazy-paving. Outside their green wooden gate, the pale yellow light of an early spring morning washed blandly over the quiet emptiness of Campion Place.

She was struggling to brush her short dark hair, its crispness turned limp by fatigue and pain, when Denis came in with an anxious expression.

'I've been trying to telephone for a quarter-of-an-hour, and there's no answer,' he said. 'I can't get on to the nursing home, and there isn't a single taxi on the rank by the station . . . Did you say the Transport Workers came out at midnight?'

'Yes. The orders must have taken effect just after I left the office.'

'Well, I suppose the people on the telephone shifts haven't been able to get to their work . . . and every available form of transport's been booked up. There probably isn't a taxi for miles.'

They looked blankly at one another, suddenly realising what a General Strike meant in terms of personal inconvenience . . . of personal peril. Ruth felt herself threatened by rising hysteria at the thought that she, who had played so assiduous a part in precipitating this first instalment of revolution, had become one of its earliest victims. Then, for several seconds, another bout of gnawing and grinding demanded all her powers of endurance. With the coming of temporary relief, she realised that Denis had been seized by one of those moods of hesitation which were apt to possess him in moments of crisis. When he's faced with an emergency which demands immediate action, she reflected, he investigates the pros and cons of alternative possibilities as deliberately as if he were confronted with a philosophical dilemma.

'I've got Miriam up,' said Denis, as though repudiating her implicit criticism. 'She could run to the nursing home with a note warning them you're coming.'

'That's a good idea, and she could go on from there to Dr Vane. It's not much further.'

'The point is, how are you to get there yourself?'

'I'd better walk. I think I can do it if we start at once.'

'But, darling, it's more than a mile to Palmerston Square. Perhaps the Matron at the home can find someone with a car.'

'What, at six-thirty in the morning, with the telephone service all disorganised, and every car in London commandeered by people going to work from a distance! I don't think I dare risk waiting on the chance. I've an idea I haven't very long.'

'Oh, darling, I *am* sorry!' he exclaimed, half paralysed with misery. From the time that Janet had once described to him his own precipitate and ill-organised arrival, he had resolved that the mother of his children should bear them in dignity and decency, with every alleviation that science could provide. And now this unforeseen political crisis, this unique experiment of a movement with which they were both associated, had descended upon them and made Ruth's predicament even worse than Janet's!

'Never mind, my love, it isn't your fault. I've only myself to blame for overworking.' She jerked out the words resolutely as the clawing iron fingers began at her again. 'You write the note and get Miriam to hurry off with it, and I'll put a few things into my dressing-case. Someone can bring the children's outfit later.'

She moved laboriously about her bedroom, collecting night-gowns and sponges, leaving half open as a guide to Denis the drawers filled with the double sets of diminutive garments which Jessie had stitched with a renewed sense of appropriate vocation. Five minutes seemed to pass before she succeeded in lifting the light suitcase on to a chair. Crouching over it with the feeling that the relentless burden of the children must weigh her to the ground, she discovered that she was muttering incessantly under her breath.

'Oh, my God, my God! Oh, my God, my God, my God!'

In a few minutes Denis came in and finished her packing. He helped her on with her cloak and, clinging to his arm, she began to walk. Overwhelmingly conscious that her hour of peril was upon her and she might never see her home again, she looked back at the small green and white house which during the past two years had witnessed so many conflicts and adjustments, so much loving co-operation. Would she ever return to welcome the friends who had often gathered there, arguing with ferocious good-humour over glasses of sherry or cups of coffee, prophesying national policies, discussing the state of the world?

The chill, deserted streets along which they crept so slowly seemed devoid of human life. No sound of stirring traffic echoed on the light spring breeze. Close as they were to the great road-centres of London, the silence was so complete that the shrill piping of the birds in the budding plane-trees beside the pavement made a clamour that penetrated Ruth's ears like a persistent tin whistle.

They were not yet half way to Palmerston Square, and her pains seemed now to be coming very fast – so fast that her body felt as though it were being pulled in half. How much longer could it carry the weight of the tearing, struggling lives within it? The sweat poured down her forehead into her eyes; blindly she put up the hand with which she was supporting herself against the railings to wipe it away. Her thoughts, escaping from her control, ran on with the vague inconsequence of semi-delirium.

'How much longer can I bear this? . . . and how is it that nothing I've read, nobody I've talked to, ever made me understand what it's really like? . . . This is how Agnes must have felt when Granny turned her out of the house that night . . . I wonder if there really is a God, with queer primitive ideas of justice like a tribal deity, and He's paying me out for what my grandmother did all those years ago? . . . Why is it that Agnes, a woman I never knew who's probably been dead for ages, always comes into my mind at every crisis of my life? . . . What an object I must look to Denis, with my face all wet and streaked with soot from the railings, and my feet and ankles swollen double their size . . . I wonder if they'll go slim again when this hell is over . . . if it ever is. Oh, my comrades in the movement, why did you have to go and strike this week? But then, from your point of view, I've failed you in an emergency . . . and anyway it's good for me to know what life's like without any conveniences . . . damned good for a lady Socialist, a Staffordshire bourgeoise . . . Oh, God, it's coming again! This time I *can't* bear it without screaming – I know I can't . . . That window over there hasn't any curtains. I wonder if the room's empty and I could lie down on the floor and have my babies without going any further . . . I can't, anyhow. Oh, damn! Oh, hell! . . .'

'Denis,' she said aloud, 'if something doesn't happen soon, I'm afraid your children will arrive in the street.'

'Darling,' he urged her, 'do put your arms round my neck and let me try to carry you. I can manage it, I know, if you'll only let me.'

Looking at his pale face, his slender unsubstantial frame, she began to laugh. Once it had begun, her laughter, like her thoughts, went out of her control. She felt it shaking her, doubling her up, tearing through her, until it and the agony of her labour pains became one. The beads of perspiration from her forehead mingled with the tears that streamed down her face.

'Oh, darling – you might manage me but you couldn't carry *all* of us – and the suitcase, too! We'd just bowl you over, and anyhow I couldn't bear anyone to touch me. Don't worry . . . I daresay the gutter's not a bad place for a Socialist family to arrive . . . Oh, *my God!*'

As she clung, writhing and straining, to the gatepost of the house that they were passing, she did not hear him call and signal to the little private car which turned the corner. She only knew that someone picked her up and bundled her on to a tiny back seat which seemed barely large enough for her stretched, heavy body; that a sudden tumult of wind and speed added its stabbing intensity to that which was already unendurable . . .

A violent opening and shutting of doors followed . . . a rush upstairs in somebody's arms . . . the smooth softness of the bed receiving her breaking back, and a voice above her saying, 'You're only just in time!' Firm hands laid hold of her struggling knees and ankles; something hard and sweet-smelling pressed down upon her face just as a red-hot sword seared the lower half of her body, and tore it apart until, losing every remnant of control, she shrieked aloud. A second too late for that final excruciating pang of birth, suffocating oblivion spread over her, and as she went down into darkness one last thought registered its impression upon her brain: 'Now I do almost know what it's like to have a baby born in a cab!'

2

When Ruth learned, a fortnight afterwards, how nearly death had come to her, she received the news with surprise rather than perturbation.

Once unconsciousness had closed over that last overwhelming agony, she had never felt really ill – only interminably tired, possessed by a limitless desire to sleep and sleep, without waking to take the food which well-intentioned but exasperating persons forced upon her, or opening her eyes to look at Jessie and Stephen who had hurried so urgently from Dene Hall by car.

Even now she could feel no more than a tepid interest in the fact that Jill had weighed five and a half pounds but Jack only four. The repeated effort and strain of endeavouring, as everyone urged her, to nurse these red whimpering atoms of humanity seemed unendurable when effort and strain were the last experiences that she desired. She wished, as she repeatedly asserted, to do nothing but lie in peace amid the flowers sent, in spite of strike overtime, by her friends from Eccleston Square, and watch the shadows of the trees in the garden move backwards and forwards across the ceiling.

So that was what it meant, this submerging lethargy, this all-conquering fatigue! That was why Denis's face, glimpsed vaguely like a face in a mist-clouded mirror, had looked so anxious and pale! What a strange irony – to have sought, year upon year, release in death from the burden of memory, and then to have death pursue and almost capture her when at last she desired to live for the sake of her work and Denis and their children!

'You really do look a little better, darling,' he said, intensely relieved, when he came to see her that evening.

'I feel awake for the first time since I came here. I believe it's because they told me this morning how nearly I was done for! It made me realise there's plenty of fight left in me still. And then Jack's actually put on a few ounces, and that cheers me a good deal.'

'Me too. How's the stalwart Jill?'

'Oh, as obstreperous as ever – very definitely the stronger sex.'

He sat down beside her bed.

'I had a letter from your father this morning. Has he written to you himself?'

'Not since he came here. I believe he's got an idea that reading letters would retard my recovery. Poor Father – he was terribly worried about the Strike, wasn't he?'

'More than worried. In fact he asked me to tell you he's

decided to retire from business and leave your brother in charge of the Pottery. He say's the Strike's finished him off and he's done with Staffordshire. He wants to come to London to be near you and the children.'

'Then is Norman going to live at Dene Hall?'

'Well . . . apparently your father's decided to sell it. He's negotiating with a syndicate which thinks of buying it for a girls' private school. I gather Norman says the place is much too big for him under present-day conditions and he'd rather live at Dene Lodge. I haven't upset you by telling you, have I, darling? After all, your people have been thinking about this move for some time.'

'Yes, it's been coming . . . The Dene Halls of England belong to the past now,' she said, but she wondered if Denis realised how deeply her roots were thrust into that past, even though her own work heralded its eclipse. How queer to think that she would never stay at Dene Hall again! She had so often pictured herself taking Jack and Jill there, and watching them tumble up and down the grassy bank where she and Richard had played with the pail of water . . . and now, because the old things were vanishing so quickly, it would not happen. Into her mind came incongruously the hymn which had always brought back to her, after Gallipoli, the memory of those childish games up and down the bank.

> *There is a green hill far away*
> *Without a city wall . . .*

She felt the ready tears of weakness pricking her eyes, and abruptly changed the subject.

'What about the Strike? I ought to have been doing overtime at the office these past two weeks, and instead I've hardly thought about it. Tell me what's happening.'

'Well, as a matter of fact the Strike's practically over. The transport workers have gone back; so have the dockers and the printers. They say Hyde Park's going to be opened again to-morrow.'

'I see . . . That means defeat?'

'Only of the General Council. The workers themselves wanted to carry on.'

She raised herself on her elbow against the pillows.

'I *must* get better quickly! I want to go back to the office as soon as I can – there's so much to be done.'

'You'll have to be patient for a little while longer, darling. Matron says you won't be ready to leave for another two or three weeks – nor the children either. They're going to be rather a job for you, I'm afraid. They're both so tiny.'

'I know that. You needn't think I mean to neglect them. But the world won't stand still while the twins grow up.'

'She's like my mother,' he thought yet again, as he walked back to his solitary supper in the small silent home. 'She has the same impatience, the same intolerance towards everything that stands in her way. In one sense it's a good quality; it makes for getting things done quickly, but it doesn't make for thinking them through and looking at them from every angle before one acts . . . She's right about her work, though. Whatever else we have to give up, we must have someone really competent to look after the twins so that she can go back to the office as soon as the nursing stage is over. She's always happiest when she's working hardest, and the most ideal companion when she's had some kind of success. Whoever was first responsible for the fallacy that a woman's desire for power is less than a man's? Why are women expected to be content with personal interests when men need impersonal achievement for fulfilment and satisfaction?'

'He's completely mature,' thought Ruth, as she lay on her back engaged in her favourite occupation of watching the shadows on the ceiling until they merged into the soft May dusk. 'He's mature in a way that his father never was, nor my father either; that perhaps Richard never would have been, nor even Eugene. But his mind is too complicated. Eugene saw only one way of doing a thing and did it at once, but Denis sees so many ways that he doesn't know which to choose . . . Oh, but it's not fair to be always comparing the living with the dead! The living exasperate one continually – the very fact of being constantly in a relationship with a person makes that inevitable. By contrast the dead are flawless; we forget their faults and remember only their virtues; they're immune for ever from disillusion and decay . . .'

The door opened, and a benevolent elderly face peered into the room.

'Why, Mrs Rutherston, you're all in the dark! Wouldn't you like your light on?'

'No, thank you, Nurse. I don't want to read. I was thinking.'

'You are a caution, aren't you? – lying on your back and staring at the ceiling all day long, when you might be reading those nice cheerful magazines! Well, I'll leave you for a bit, but your tray'll be up in half an hour.'

'I can't imagine Eugene old or even middle-aged,' meditated Ruth, hardly conscious of the interruption. 'I can't picture him as a ruthless business man, a newspaper proprietor in his fifties, calculating and uncompromising – and yet I suppose that's what he might have become if he'd lived. Oh, it's time, change, continuation, that destroys and betrays! It's what the church clock at Rye called it – "a very shadow that passeth away" . . . and yet not altogether, because time means fulfilment too. One day, just by going on living and thinking and working, Denis and I may create something more lasting than children between us. I believe in Denis. I'm glad I married him. I don't feel passion for him; I never have and never shall. But "the mutual society, help and comfort that the one ought to have of the other" – this does exist between us, and I think it always will.'

As she grew stronger and overcame the fretful impatience of convalescence, the more impersonal aspects of her recent ordeal eclipsed her narrower preoccupation with herself and Denis. Suppose, she reflected after dizzily getting up for the first time, suppose I'd been a working man's wife, with no salary to help me pay my doctor's bills, and no private income to meet the expense of staying in this nursing-home till the twins are safely over their first weeks and I've had all the rest I need? What if I'd been pushed out of hospital after ten days or a fortnight, hardly able to stand, with two delicate babies to care for and the housework to do and perhaps other young children to look after as well?

Her appalled mind and tired body shrank from the prospect.

'Denis,' she said, when he came that afternoon, 'I can't get over thinking how much pain there is in the normal world, even when there's no war or plague or famine to add to it. Before I had the twins I always thought of suffering in terms of these exceptional disasters. It just shows I'm nothing but a spoiled bourgeoise still.'

He too had faced reality during those days of suspense.

'Certainly,' he admitted, 'there's a vast disproportion between what women have suffered all through the ages and the amount of interest men have taken in it. I can't help feeling that if *we* produced the children, the medical profession would have found some way of making the whole thing easier generations ago.'

She remembered as he spoke how she had once heard Dame Millicent Fawcett tell a political meeting that in the nineteenth-century House of Commons, the mere mention of women or of childbirth provoked the honourable and gallant Members to 'roars of laughter.' Such, she thought, was the reception given to the merciful minority who were trying to alleviate the kind of experience I've just been through! At any rate we've changed all that by getting votes and putting a few women into the House . . . Some day I'd like to stand for Parliament myself, if anyone will have me, and do what I can for the women in small homes for whom the process of birth has no mitigations of comfort or decency. I know now that it isn't only the pain that's intolerable, but the sense of humiliation which goes with it – the feeling of helplessness, of being completely under Nature's control. How much of this suffering we could afford to relieve, if only we denied ourselves the luxury of war!

'Oh, Denis,' she exclaimed, 'I'm so thankful I didn't die! Aren't you glad we've got a few more years to try to get things done?'

'Then you have found it worth while, darling – our life together?'

'Yes, my dear. Infinitely worth while.'

3

In the late autumn of 1927, Denis was invited to give a course of six lectures in Social Philosophy at the Sorbonne. He accepted the invitation, polished up his French which had grown rusty since his years in the Censorship office, and went to Paris for a fortnight.

Walking alone beside the Seine one windy November afternoon, he looked back upon the three years of his marriage to Ruth with mingled emotions which left a balance of glad contentment. In the clearer proportions lent by distance, he perceived not only the courage but the significance of her refusal to be defeated by circumstances in her attempt to combine a political career with marriage and children. She had set herself to solve one of the most urgent of modern problems – how were women to maintain and improve the position they had won without sacrificing the biological fulfilment which public obligations had never denied to men?

Realising how much more than a personal conflict her struggle involved, he wrote her a long letter repeating the promise of co-operation that he had made her at Richmond.

'When people are married,' he concluded, 'I am afraid they often allow their appreciation to be taken for granted instead of expressing it. I do want you to know how much I love and admire you for the way that you have cared for our children, in spite of your inclinations being political, like my mother's, and not domestic. I used to think that because you are so much better qualified intellectually than she was, and because your political prospects are so much more promising than hers could ever have been, you would resent the claims of the twins on your time even more than she resented mine on hers. But instead you seem to have given them more thought and care than they would have had from the usual domesticated mother with only her household and children to consider.'

'Dear Denis,' thought Ruth, reading his letter in Regent's Park on a Saturday afternoon, with the eighteen-months-old twins asleep in their perambulator beside her, and the saffron and scarlet dahlias still blooming in their circular beds. 'It's worth all the nightmare of those early months to have him realise what they cost me, and why I went through them with such obstinate determination.'

She recalled, with a sense of deep thankfulness that they belonged to the past, the weeks of fatigue and monotony after she left the nursing-home, the interminable series of nursing periods and interrupted nights, the constantly renewed endeavour to bring her premature babies to their normal weight and development without relaxing her grasp of political events or losing her contact with party organisation. For nearly nine months now, she had been back at the office; for over six she had given two evenings a week to public meetings. Yet the children were healthy and from the age of a year could have challenged comparison with any baby who was neither premature nor a twin. Jill, a vigorous, placid child who smiled with pellucid blue eyes inherited from Janet, turned the scales now at a solid twenty-five pounds. Jack, dark-browed and curly-haired, with the sulky brown eyes of the Alleyndenes, had always been more delicate and temperamental. Once, for several days, Ruth had despaired of rearing him at all, but now his weight was nearly normal. He had talked earlier than Jill, though he was two months later than she in walking.

Every week, after Dr Vane's visits had ceased, Ruth and Betty Perrin, the twenty-two-year-old nurse from the Wellgarth Nursery Training School, took it in turns to push the twins to the Paddington Infant Welfare Centre. Every Saturday, when Betty had her half day, Denis helped Ruth in the tasks of feeding and bathing and dressing. She pictured him now, with a book in his hand, conscientiously watching Jack and Jill scramble over one another like kittens in their play-pen on the lozenge of lawn behind the little house, or holding one small slippery body on his knee and drying it with awkward tenderness while she bathed the other.

Taking her writing pad and fountain pen from the side of the perambulator, she began a long reply to Denis's letter.

'You know how bad I always am at expressing myself on paper, but I do want to try and explain why I think it is that

I have treated the twins differently from the way your mother treated you. I don't want you to begin sitting in judgment on her after all these years, for I believe it is not so much my conscience as my circumstances that are different – to say nothing of the contrast between you and your father.

'To begin with, I wanted the twins and we agreed about having them, whereas your mother was not only unready for a child and quite ignorant, but apparently was never consulted. She was also expected to know how to manage you without any instruction, as though the knowledge of a baby's needs could be acquired by instinct. I prefer to trust the specialist at the Welfare Centre rather than my own inexperienced judgment! After all, the more anxious and incompetent one is over one's children, the more trouble they are and the more time they take.

'Don't you see that it is just because I *am* better qualified than your mother and still able to go on with my work, that I care for the twins so much? Naturally a woman with strong political interests resented a child when public opinion insisted that he ought to monopolise her whole time to the exclusion of everything else! I really think the cruellest thing society can do to children is to insist on their mothers sacrificing everything for them. An intelligent and talented person simply gets to dislike the creature for whom she is expected to do that! Once it is possible both to marry and to keep the work you love, I think that work makes you care for your children more, not less. It helps you to understand better what part they are likely to play in the future, and to show them their way about the world when they grow up.

'No wonder there is such a barrier between the women of this generation and their mothers from the last! How *can* a mother be interesting to her grown-up children if ever since they were born she has struggled along in the kitchen and the nursery, knowing nothing about economics or politics or the social changes going on in the outside world? The older generation apparently forgot that children don't remain babies all their lives. In your mother's day, especially to convention-alists like your father, motherhood was just another name for domesticity, so naturally, hating domesticity, she hated you!

It was an inevitable reaction against assumptions which are passing away.

'I can't see how any intelligent mother nowadays dare refuse to be interested in politics, since politics are shaping our children's lives whether we like it or not. If our own mothers had been encouraged to learn what was going on in the world, instead of being told that their place was the home, the War might never have happened and they could have kept their sons, instead of passively 'giving' them to die before their time like Richard and Eugene. They were not allowed the knowledge or the chance to influence international relations, but I believe that *we* could prevent another war if we really put our backs into it. What's the use of having ideal children and a perfect nursery, if you do nothing to stop them from being blown to bits within the next twenty years!

'Please forgive all this theorising, but it has been on my mind for ages and I wanted to get it down.'

When Denis came back he urged her to incorporate the substance of her letter in some of her speeches.

'I hope you'll repeat all this at the next General Election. It might help to clear up the confusion in the minds of women with lives like my mother's. There still seem to be a good many who are told one thing by their families and their carefully-trained consciences, and quite another by their intelligence.'

'I did try to say something like it to the women's meetings in the 1924 Election,' she told him, 'but of course the tide was running so strongly against us then. Besides, I do know much better what I'm talking about since I've had the children. That's another reason for being glad of them!'

Less than a month afterwards, they realised that Ruth's opportunity for expressing her views at a General Election was likely to be even better than either of them had imagined.

4

'DEAR MRS RUTHERSTON,' ran the letter from Witnall,

'We are writing to put before you a request which we hope you will consider. You will be sorry to hear that poor old Jos Davenport had a stroke last month and is no longer able to carry on as our candidate. This letter goes at the unanimous request of the Executive Committee to ask if you would be willing to stand as Parliamentary Labour Candidate for the Witnall Division of Staffordshire at the next election.

'Since you know Witnall as well as we do, there is no need for us to tell you that it has always been a Tory seat which has not yet responded to progressive influences in the same way as Burslem and Hanley. But since the War the Party membership has increased every year. We added considerably to our vote in 1922, when you gave us such valuable help, and again in 1923, though of course we dropped a good bit at the Red Letter election of 1924. You may not, however, be aware that a large part of the area has changed its character in our favour since the Witnall and District Housing Scheme came into operation early last year.

'During the past eighteen months we reckon that a sufficient number of Stoke and Hanley workers have been housed in the new estates to raise our vote by 25 per cent. There are a good many young married women living in the reconstructed areas and if, as seems probable, an Equal Franchise Bill goes through under the present Government, our women voters will be in the majority. This makes it especially appropriate for us to have a woman candidate. Given an election under circumstances at all favourable to the Party, we feel that Labour has a better chance than ever before of coming out at the top of the poll.

'If you feel able to consider our proposition, we wonder whether you would be prepared to fight the campaign under your maiden name? Though your folks are Tories they have always had the reputation of being good employers, and the name Alleyndene will be worth hundreds of votes from

the neutrals and the doubtfuls. We know you have now a
fine reputation as a worker and speaker for the National
Party. You made yourself very popular when you worked
here during the 1922 election, and if you will accept our
invitation to attend the Selection Conference at the beginning
of January, we can guarantee there will be no opposition.

                              'Your old comrades,

'ARTHUR WARDLE, Secretary and Agent   ⎫   Witnall
                                          ⎪   Labour
'JAMES HARDIMAN, Hon. Treasurer   ⎭   Party.'

She passed the letter over to Denis with flushed cheeks and
brilliant, excited eyes. A multitude of emotions – affection,
gratitude, eager anticipation – kindled so bright a flame of
vitality in her face that the tiny lines seemed to vanish which
had appeared on her forehead since the birth of the twins.
She, Ruth Alleyndene – daughter of Stephen who had ejected
Thomas Rutherston the Radical parson, great-granddaughter of
Enoch who had opposed the democratic claims of the parish and
showed no mercy to his employees in the earthenware workers'
strike of 1881, great-great-granddaughter of William who had
helped to suppress the Political Reformers between 1817 and
1820 – she to be Labour Candidate for Witnall, and perhaps in
some far distant future its first Labour Member of Parliament!
The drama of the situation – its poetic justice, as she herself
phrased it – appealed irresistibly to the strong histrionic element
in her nature.

'You'll consider it, of course?' queried Denis, half proud of her
reputation among her own people, half envious of the politician's
direct influence compared with the indirect, profounder methods
of the teacher-philosopher.

'I couldn't have if father had still been at the Pottery – and
father and mother living at Dene Hall. But it's quite different now
the Hall's a girls' school and they're both settled in London, and
father only goes to Staffordshire once a month. I shan't worry
myself about Norman's feelings. It'll be fun to make him angry,
the old Die-hard!'

That evening she wrote to tell Wardle and Hardiman that

she would attend the Selection Conference. She also informed them that – 'not wishing to involve my husband in my political escapades' – she had used her maiden name for her professional work ever since her marriage.

In January, two days before the Conference met, she went up to the district which she had left, the sheltered child of a wealthy bourgeois family, in 1915, and to which, after a life-time of experience – war and love, loss and despair, pestilence and famine, work and recovery, marriage and a national crisis, childbirth and the shadow of death – she was returning, the chosen candidate of the Witnall Labour Party, in 1928.

When the train entered Staffordshire she looked through the carriage window at the familiar landscape as though she had never perceived it before. She saw the cows feeding in wide marshy fields the vivid artless shade of the green bice in a child's paint-box; she observed the long intersecting lines of bare black hedgerows, the narrow geometrical ditches turning right and left at inexplicable angles spanned by small stone bridges. Slowly across the pale cobalt sky drifted feathery ranges of white or dun cloud; against the wan misty horizon, sentinel rows of leafless poplars cast their thin shadows over brown tufts of prickly grass.

Sometimes a copse of dark evergreens enclosed a group of old shabby cottages; sometimes a delicate plume of blue smoke ascended between grey church towers or spires crowned with iron weather-cocks. Cabbage fields and damp haystacks with pigs rooting beside them surrounded farms where grain was stacked beneath red metal roofs; in the distance, low wood-crowned hills curved above terra-cotta ploughlands. When a dark blot of cloud hid the sun and dissolved into a sudden momentary shower, the panorama of soft blues and greens and sepias deepened in colour. Five minutes later, the sun, penetrating the iridescent haze, drew sparkling beams of light from the watery surface of the winter swamps. Outside Stafford, a field-labourer's horse and cart splashed serenely among the brown manure-heaps on cultivated land. Between Stone and Moddershall, a farmer tramped with his dog across the wet empty meadows.

'No one from abroad visits or talks about the Midlands,' thought Ruth. 'They're hardly known by American travellers, and yet they're the very heart and spirit of England!'

At Stoke she carried her suitcase across the damp cobbled square, dominated by the bewigged statue of Josiah Wedgwood the First holding the Barberini Vase in his outstretched hand, and took a room at the North Stafford Hotel. Until the Selection Conference was over she did not want her presence in the Potteries to be known to Norman, who was now married, with apparent if incredible satisfaction, to Jennifer Irwin, a well-to-do Lancashire girl sixteen years his junior, who sat on his knee, pulled his hair, called him 'old thing,' and repeatedly told him that he was 'just too, too pre-war!' Responding after some initial grumbles to her reiterated persuasions, he had 'modernised' Dene Lodge, putting in a second bath-room, replacing the stables by a compact red-brick garage, and installing in the large old-fashioned kitchen a number of labour-saving devices which the local cook and housemaid examined with suspicion, reluctantly used for a few days, and then abandoned.

From Stoke to Hanley, from Hanley to Witnall, Ruth wandered up and down observing what changes had occurred since her wedding. She even took a 'bus, one afternoon, to the black and gold gates of Dene Hall, and walked slowly up the drive where her father had first met her mother between the lighted lanterns of the rhododendrons. But the neglected shrubs, and the prim white curtains which concealed the tall mullioned windows, so depressed her spirit that after a brief inspection she hurried down the road to Witnall as though the great house had become a ghost.

'Syndicate's no call to brag,' Jim Hardiman told her. 'It's a lat job in these parts, is boarding-school. I doubt but folks'll flit before year's out.'

Hardiman's hair was grey now and his pale face was lined; his deep-set blue eyes looked keenly at his world through gold-rimmed spectacles. In spite of his official position in the Witnall Labour Party, Norman, with morose justice, had made him a manager at the Alleyndene Pottery.

Ruth understood, after talking to him for an hour, how the

Staffordshire Radical movement of the nineteenth and early twentieth centuries – the movement which had been first nonsense and then anathema to her father – had now grown into a Labour movement conducted inside the Pottery industry by the workers themselves. The industry, he told her, had been scheduled that year under the Workmen's Compensation Acts – a fact which she had never learnt from Norman. Although the provisions of the Acts would not come into force until 1929, the ravages of silicosis – now the official name for potter's asthma – had been reduced through medical inspection and a process of dust extraction by electric fans. One of the first needs of the whole district, said Hardiman, was new housing of the kind now in progress under the Witnall scheme. In the Five Towns slum clearance had hardly begun, for the sites were uneconomical and more than three-quarters of the old houses were undermined. Even the Witnall building estates only touched the fringe of the problem, since the workers – still wedded to habits already traditional in the time of Ruth's great-grandfather – were accustomed to live close to their employment and looked with critical disfavour upon any new system.

Standing on the top of the steep hill where the motor-buses began their journey from Hanley to Cheet, Ruth contemplated the area which a native of Staffordshire had once described as 'separated from civilisation by the North Staffordshire Railway till communications were established by Mr Arnold Bennett.' She learned anew the landmarks familiar to her childhood; the rubbish tips, covered with scrap iron and potsherds and coarse persevering grass, which were used to fill in subsiding land; the small inconvenient cottages built during the Industrial Revolution; the narrow haphazard streets in which, whatever the weather, the ground was always wet.

'Even now,' she thought, 'this part of the country is still isolated, skirted as it is by the chief roads and railways of England. It's still a nineteenth-century area in which, for generations, working women have been subsidiary creatures, underpaid and discouraged from organisation; and it's nineteenth-century not least in its sombre grimy face. If ever a district needed a beauty specialist, this is it – and yet how I love its smoky skies, its squat sloping potbanks, its sullen red flares lighting up the darkness, its decorative bowls, its translucent porcelain vases, its cream earthenware vessels treasured by kings and queens! Who would believe that this grim region could produce so much loveliness? It is part of everything I am, and always will be.'

In the second week of January 1928, Ruth Alleyndene was formally adopted as prospective Parliamentary Labour candidate for the Witnall Division of Staffordshire.

5

At the United Franchise Demonstration in the Queen's Hall the excited audience was on its feet, singing loudly in unison to the swelling triumphant pæan of the organ.

> 'Bring me my bow of burning gold!
>   Bring me my arrows of desire!
> Bring me my spear! O clouds, unfold!
>   Bring me my chariot of fire!
> I will not cease from mental fight,
>   Nor shall my sword sleep in my hand,
> Till we have built Jerusalem
>   In England's green and pleasant land.'

In the chair on the platform, white-haired and impressive, sat Eleanor Rathbone, destined fifteen months hence to be elected Member of Parliament by the Combined Universities. Sir Oliver Lodge, bearded and benevolent, and Margaret Ashton, the veteran suffrage campaigner from Manchester, had already spoken; young Nancy Stewart Parnell, and Rebecca West who had battled for the franchise in her early incisive writings published in her 'teens, were still to speak. But the clamorous ranks of men and women, crowding the gangways to the doors and overflowing into the Mortimer Hall, were waiting for Stanley Baldwin, Prime Minister of Great Britain since 1924.

It was March 8th, 1928. A month earlier, exactly ten years

and a day since the first instalment of woman suffrage had become part of the Constitution on February 6th, 1918, the King's speech had promised that 'proposals will be brought before you for amending the law relating to the Parliamentary and local government franchise.' This evening Mr Baldwin was coming to the Queen's Hall to repeat his announcement, made that day in the House of Commons, that the Bill enfranchising women between twenty-one and thirty would be presented in Parliament the following Monday. Sitting beside Denis in the arena, Ruth guessed his thoughts though she could not share his memories. If only the dead could return to witness this logical conclusion of their endeavours! Janet's spirit would be here then, with those of other men and women who had worked or written in faith, ridiculed and unrewarded – Mary Wollstonecraft, John Stuart Mill, George Meredith, Sir Albert Rollitt, Mr Faithfull Begg, Lady Constance Lytton, Olive Schreiner, Emily Wilding Davison . . .

Above the crowded platform hung the flags and banners of the modern women's organisations which had inherited the struggle for equal rights from the departed pioneers – the Women's Freedom League, the Six Point Group, St John's Social and Political Alliance, the National Union of Societies for Equal Citizenship. Beneath the gently stirring kaleidoscope of colour – green, white and gold, purple, white and green, red, green and white – sat representatives from the executive committees of these societies. Ruth was whispering their names to Denis when the audience rose to its feet with a roar, and Mr Baldwin, solid, square-headed and affable, came in with his wife.

A few minutes later, they were listening to the speech in which the Prime Minister recorded the historic ending of a campaign that had lasted for over half a century.

'This wonderful meeting represents the greatest common measure of agreement on one great political issue amongst women who, on every other subject, probably hold diverse views. It is representative of the united democracy of all franchise societies who support equal citizenship . . . There are no grounds, no logic and no expediency, for withholding the franchise to-day from one sex more than from another.

In a few weeks you will have a legal recognition of that equality . . .

'It is sixty years ago this year since John Stuart Mill moved a Franchise Bill in the House of Commons to omit the word "men" and insert the word "person." . . . There was no extension of the franchise from 1832 to 1918, or, if you like, 1928, but there were men who prophesied disaster and woe. But circumstances changed. It was two hundred years ago when arguments, convincing in themselves, were used by Condorcet, and a hundred years ago when Mary Wollstonecraft used the same arguments. It was sixty years ago when Mill used them, and history and the logic of events has now brought us to the day when those dreams are going to be realised.'

Through Denis's mind, as he listened to the Prime Minister who had once been a convinced anti-suffragist, drifted sentences from John Stuart Mill's speech of May, 1867, which he and Ruth had re-read only that morning.

'. . . Sir, before it is affirmed that women do not suffer in their interests, as women, by the denial of a vote, it should be considered whether women have no grievances . . . Are there many fathers who care as much or are willing to expend as much, for the education of their daughters as of their sons? Where are the Universities, where the High Schools, or the schools of any high description, for them? . . . Hardly any decent educated occupation, save one, is open to them. They are either governesses or nothing . . . No sooner do women show themselves capable of competing with men in any career, than that career, if it be lucrative or honourable, is closed to them . . . This is the sort of care taken of women's interests by the men who so faithfully represent them. This is the way we treat unmarried women. And how is it with the married? . . . Now, by the Common Law of England, all that a wife has, belongs absolutely to the husband; he may tear it all from her, squander every penny of it in debauchery, leave her to support by her labour herself and her children, and if by heroic exertion and self-sacrifice she is able to put by something for their future wants, unless she is judicially separated from him he can pounce down upon her savings and leave her penniless. And such cases are of quite common occurrence. Sir, if we were besotted enough to think these things right there would be more excuse for it; but we know better . . . Sir, grievances of less magnitude than the law of the property of married women, when suffered by parties less inured to passive submission, have provoked revolutions . . .'

But Mr Baldwin was continuing, rousing cheers of appreciation which drowned the echo of that early voice crying in the wilderness.

'In the interval, women have made good in every department of public life. There are those who think that women – that women's work – has always to be confined to the home. This is not historical. Woman has laboured with man on the land from the days of Eden, and your opportunities, your responsibilities, during the last half-century have multiplied beyond all belief, and I think England will never forget what the Great War meant to you and to us. So it is that by a mere procession of time, ideas, customs, conditions perfectly natural to our great-grandfathers become perfectly absurd to us.

'Women have, in fact, always had as great a stake in the welfare of the country as men, but it has not been in fact admitted. It is to-day. Nobody challenges your position – at any rate not enough nobodies to make any opposition. At the next election neither man's will nor woman's is going to prevail, but it is for both of us, men and women, to exercise the best influence we can for the sake of the country. Whatever the result, the whole nation, men and women alike, will express themselves effectively in the ballot-box without any qualification or disqualification of sex. That prospect does not alarm me in the least. I would rather trust a woman's instinct than a man's reason . . .'

A tiny shiver passed over the female half of the audience, like a sudden breeze rustling through a field of wheat. The prospective Parliamentary Labour candidate for the Witnall Division of Staffordshire leaned over to Denis, her grey eyes sparkling with amusement.

'He couldn't have dropped a bigger brick than that, could he?'

'Don't be too hard on him, poor man; he's doing his best. It's really an excellent speech – it ties the whole thing so well together.'

They listened in silence as Mr Baldwin concluded.

'Many of you who have not been long in this movement look for a new heaven and a new earth. I have been too long in politics to take the Apocalyptic view. But . . . I have faith in a free democracy. I rejoice in its advent, and I believe that the public life of this country will be enriched by the step which we are taking. But it is for you to justify my faith, and much more than my faith. You have to justify the faith of those women whose names, if not on your tongues, are all in your hearts to-night – those who saw this goal from afar, but to whom it has not been permitted to reach it themselves . . .

'To-night I think we may all feel that the time of agitation has passed. You are on the threshold. You have but to pass it, but what are you going to make of the Promised Land? It is yours to plough and to sow and to reap. Yet I do not think that we would say that the sixty years of agitation have been wasted. They have had their educational and disciplinary value . . . The tale of that struggle will be told for many generations to come, and the protagonists will be remembered for their indomitable courage in a cause they believed in and for which they were prepared to suffer . . .'

Denis missed the last few sentences of the Prime Minister's speech, for his eyes were suddenly caught by a face among the multitude of distinguished faces on the platform – an ageing, wistful face which still bore the faded remnants of a fragile beauty. Though he had never seen it before, it was familiar to him – familiar from the photographs of a woman twenty years younger, pinned on his mother's bedroom wall at Carrisvale Gardens. He knew it for the face of Mrs Pankhurst, no longer a revolutionary fugitive under the Cat and Mouse Act, but the respected and highly respectable Conservative candidate for Whitechapel.

She had not been asked to speak, for the organisers of the meeting belonged to the 'constitutional' suffragists who had opposed the militants, but she was there, a silent witness to the tumult and conflicts of the past, a symbolic link between that past and a future in which English women would experience political equality with men. Were those tired, reminiscent eyes seeing the vision of another evening nearly twenty-three years before, when two young girls mounted chairs in a crowded Manchester hall and cried to another famous statesman: 'The question! Answer the question!'

But it was Mr Baldwin, and not Sir Edward Grey, who replied to that challenge. It was not Janet, who had heard the challenge given, but her son and his wife, her political successor, who listened to the reply.

Before the Prime Minister left the meeting, he announced that the Second Reading of the Franchise Bill would be taken before Easter, and the measure carried through afterwards with all speed. He added: 'We are making a provision that, unless some cataclysm causes an election in the next few months, the register will be so arranged that the new voters will be able to vote at the General Election . . . I wish you in the use of your franchise – it may be your work in Parliament – to whatever party you belong, the best of luck.'

'Well,' remarked Denis, 'at any rate that's a magnanimous gesture from our chief political opponent!'

'Oh, it is!' admitted Ruth. 'But I do wish our party could have brought in the Bill, after the years they supported woman suffrage when it was derided or ignored. I suppose Mr Baldwin thinks the young women will all vote Conservative.'

'I wonder,' thought Denis, 'what they'll do at Witnall? It's odd that the Potteries, where working women have always been auxiliaries, should now have two women Labour candidates. But Lady Cynthia Mosley has an easy job at Stoke, compared with Ruth . . .'

Three weeks after the Equal Franchise Bill passed the House of Lords on May 23rd, Mrs Pankhurst died and was buried in Brompton Cemetery. She had lived just long enough to see the end of the movement to which she had given her health, her maturity, and, in the last resort, her name. A long procession of men and women, many bringing flowers, followed the coffin to its grave. Among them walked the jockey, Herbert Jones, who had been injured when Emily Wilding Davison brought down the King's horse at the Derby in 1913. He carried a wreath inscribed with the words: 'To do honour to the memory of Mrs Pankhurst and Miss Emily Davison.'

6

'I've got a nice job here for someone!' announced the organiser of the public meetings department at Transport House, where the Labour Party headquarters was now established after its move four months earlier from Eccleston Square. He came over to Ruth's desk with a letter in his hand.

'Care to take it on?' he inquired.

'What is it?' she asked. Her heart missed a beat when she saw the New York postmark on the envelope. 'Surely,' she thought, 'I ought to be able, after ten years, to see an American letter without jumping out of my skin – especially as he never wrote to me from America . . .'

Unfolding the thick typewritten sheet, she saw that the letter came from an address in Fifth Avenue. It was headed 'National Peace-Lovers' Association.'

'DEAR SIR,' she read,

'As secretary of the American Peace-Lovers' Association, I write to inform you that we are planning a great peace drive to take place this fall in connection with the forthcoming signature of the Kellogg Pact in Paris.

'The first part of this drive, which will be conducted for two weeks in one hundred cities of the Eastern States and New England, will be timed to coincide with the Presidential Election campaign, when political enthusiasms are at their height. We are anxious to get a series of resolutions on peace, endorsed by great meetings, to send to our new President, whether he be Governor Smith or Mr Hoover. The high spot of our program will be a mass demonstration at the Metropolitan Community Hall, New York, on the morning of November 11th. This will be followed by a solemn celebration, in which a number of ex-service organisations will collaborate, at St Andrews' Church, Fifth Avenue, to commemorate the tenth anniversary of Armistice Day.

'We are a body with a progressive viewpoint, and our intention is to make a special appeal to the younger men and women, many of whom have only dim recollections of the Great War. We would like you to suggest to us a speaker, preferably a young woman as so far the majority of our speakers are men, who could come over for this campaign and represent your country from the radical angle. We are not so much interested in a name which carries great publicity, as in getting someone who knows how to put her message across. We would like her, however, to be not more than thirty-five years of age and to have had, if possible, some experience of war at first-hand. Our organisation will pay hotel costs and travelling expenses, and would much appreciate the courtesy of an early reply.

> 'Faithfully yours,
> 'LINCOLN T. BRANDT.'

'Well,' her colleague repeated, 'would you care to take it on?'

'But why me?' she asked, immediate objections occurring to her which applied to the twins, to Denis, to the possibility of a General Election in the autumn – to anything, in fact, but the dread of reopening that old aching wound which a visit to America would revive in all its poignant acuteness. 'Why not Ellen Wilkinson – or Lady Cynthia?'

'Well, Ellen's in Parliament and could hardly take a month off at the beginning of the session – and then they ask for direct war experience. You've had far more of that than most of our women.'

'I know. But suppose the General Election comes this autumn?'

'You can take it from me there'll be no General Election till the spring. All the parties are agreed on that. Think it over and let me know to-morrow morning.'

When Ruth got back to St John's Wood that evening, the twins, with shrieks of delight, were chasing a toy balloon round the bird-bath in the small paved garden. Their little plump bodies, dressed in green sun-suits, had turned brown in the sunny warmth of July; their bright eyes sparkled; their hair fell in chestnut curls or soft flaxen strands over their flushed, excited faces. The vivid balloon bounded along the crazy-paving; suddenly a puff of wind blew it against a prickly bush of sweet-briar and its scarlet gaiety dissolved into the air with a loud explosion.

Jack's laughing face puckered. He was about to burst into tears when he changed his mind.

'Bang!' he exclaimed, disdainfully brave.

'All gone!' asserted Jill, with confident finality.

Oh, I *can't* leave them! thought Ruth forlornly. She pictured herself three thousand miles across the dividing Atlantic, and each child died a hundred deaths in her mind.

'Betty,' she said uncertainly to the young nurse, 'I've had an invitation to go on a short speaking tour in America. Do you think you could be responsible for the children for a month?'

'Why, of course, Mrs Rutherston! I had Jeremy all the time Mrs Mowbray was in India.'

I don't see why she shouldn't take charge, argued Ruth. I had a ward full of dying men to look after when I was younger than she.

Over the supper-table that night she discussed the proposition with Denis.

'You go!' he urged her. 'These opportunities don't recur – and they'll think all the more of you at Witnall for having had the experience.'

'I'm not thinking about Witnall so much; they'd understand. It's the twins.'

'Well, they're hale and hearty enough now, aren't they? Surely Betty and Miriam and I can look after them between us – and now your mother's in London I could always get her in an emergency. You know, darling, you really want a change. For the last two years you've been absolutely tied to your work and the children, while I've been to Paris and Geneva and Vienna. Look how you travelled before they were born! If you don't go abroad again soon, you'll be getting restive and wanting to leave me.'

'I shall never want to leave you, Denis. Four and a half years is a pretty good test, isn't it ... The real truth is, I can't face America – because of him.'

He looked at her gravely. Nearly ten years now – and still that bright seductive ghost had not ceased to walk through the dark paths of her soul. She had tried to exorcise it, to bid it a final farewell; yet it continued to rise again, alluring, irresistible.

'Darling,' he urged, 'you've always told me he was a brave man, and positive, affirmative, in everything he did. He wouldn't want his death to close a whole continent to you – to limit your experience and your opportunities. If you feel like that, it's a reason for going. After all, it won't be so hard as seeing Romagne.'

'I suppose I must accept,' she said apprehensively.

From August to October, she wondered perpetually what could have induced her to take so rash a decision. But for Denis's persuasions, she would have reversed it a dozen times. It was not until she found herself, equipped with a new wardrobe trunk and a folder full of notes for speeches, waving to Denis from the promenade deck as the liner left Southampton, that she really believed she was going to America.

Seven days afterwards, she leaned over the rail gazing bewitched at the enlarging horizon of New York as the boat steamed up the Hudson from Quarantine in the early morning sunlight of the rich Indian summer. She had read and seen pictures of that celebrated skyline; yet dizzy incredulity seized her as she looked upon the climbing towers of a new age untrammelled in its experimental audacity. Beneath blue skies unobscured by the grime and smoke of resigned industrial England, those soaring temples were dedicated by a young people to the pagan deities of speed and efficiency which had ousted the old conventional gods of the chapels and churches. No whisper of the economic doom which 1929 was to bring upon the last illusory stronghold of prosperity trembled in the radiant air; the shadow of the disaster lying just ahead had not yet quenched the confidence of New York's aspiring pinnacles nor dimmed the brightness of her sparkling streets. She danced and scintillated in the brilliant autumn sunshine, a brave city symbolic of undaunted humanity's progress in a world ravaged and wrecked by passionate humanity's folly.

'Oh, Eugene, this *is* your country!' breathed Ruth, her eyes half blinded with its poignant enchantment. But she had no time now to dwell upon her heart's unsleeping allegiance, for she was unexpectedly surrounded by a number of questioning reporters. Immediately afterwards a group of organisers from the Peace-Lovers' Association greeted her, shaking her hand, commenting with appreciative un-English frankness upon her height, her beauty, her elegance, her air of distinction. At the gangway a messenger boy stopped her, carrying a sheaf of deep red roses. Reminiscent emotion overwhelmed her as she read the card attached: 'To welcome you to New York. We wish you were coming to Chicago. Edna and Russell D. Chase.'

Later that morning she called at the office of the Peace-Lovers' Association to receive her instructions and the itinerary of her tour from the cordial, spectacled secretary, Lincoln Brandt. Like a large-scale map laid out beneath the startling eminence of the twenty-first floor, she could see the spreading autumn gold of Central Park.

'Our publicity's going fine!' the chief stenographer told her. 'Of course, it helps us no end having the *Atlantic Daily Ledger* behind us.'

'The *Atlantic Daily Ledger*?'

'Yes; it's one of our biggest newspapers. Christopher Meury, the old man who owns it, used to be as hard-boiled as he could be, but since he lost his son in the War he's been crazy about peace. The *Ledger*'s had columns on the Kellogg Pact.'

'His son was killed in the War,' she repeated stupidly.

'Yes. He's got four lovely daughters, but the son was the only boy. Look, here's the paragraph they gave us yesterday!'

Ruth bent over the newspaper-cutting handed to her from a folder on the desk. In large black letters startling to her English eyes, the headings splashed across two columns of print.

'GREAT PEACE DRIVE BEGINS MONDAY IN 100 CITIES

'International Speakers Support Pact with Messages of Goodwill

'A great campaign for peace, described by its sponsors, the Executive Committee of the National Peace-Lovers' Association, as "the most comprehensive peace effort yet made in the Eastern States," will be inaugurated here Monday, October 29th. Meetings and demonstrations will follow in the main cities of New England and the East, including Boston, Philadelphia, Baltimore and Washington. Resolutions passed at the meetings will be submitted to the newly elected President after November 11th. On this day the campaign will end with a mass demonstration at the Metropolitan Community Hall, when the speeches will be broadcast throughout the East and Middle West. Speakers and audience will afterwards attend a solemn Armistice Day celebration in St Andrew's Church, for which numerous ex-service organisations have promised their support. International speakers announced by Lincoln T. Brandt, secretary of the Association, include Ruth Alleyndene, young British Laborite, Paul Petit-Jean, junior lecturer in Foreign Affairs at the University of Grenoble, and Gustav Winkelmann, president of the Frankfort Students' Peace Union. Chinese and Japanese students from Columbia University will also take part in the drive.'

That evening Lincoln Brandt and the chairman of the Association entertained Ruth to dinner at the Waldorf-Astoria. As they drove through Broadway afterwards to see *Gentlemen of the Press* at the 48th Street Theatre, she noticed above another playhouse a colossal scintillating sky-sign announcing one of Ellison Campbell's Scottish Chronicles, *Night at Glencoe*. How incongruous the name of that dour, imposing woman appeared, she thought, flashing in red and gold letters across the blazing, brilliant street! Miss Campbell's plays must have made a fortune for her by now, and every year her unique reputation seemed to grow more impressive in its isolated austerity.

'You've got to-morrow to look round in,' Lincoln Brandt said when he left her after the theatre at her small hotel in Washington Square. 'But if I were you I'd rest all you can. The fun begins properly on Monday!'

7

He prophesied truthfully. With her train journey to Philadelphia on Monday morning, Ruth entered upon the breathless, exacting, agitating, exhausting and stimulating experience which is the fate of every foreigner who ventures to lecture in America.

From the time that the organisers of her meeting met her at Philadelphia with flowers and banners ('We only want a brass band to accompany us along the streets, and the spectacle would be complete,' she decided), her anxieties about the twins, Denis, Witnall, the General Election, were pushed out of her mind by the unremitting pressure of consecutive engagements. Her days became a brilliantly lit succession of public luncheons, teas and dinners, at which every conversation led by devious and tactful routes to the chief questions at issue between England and America – the freedom of the seas, the problem of the Debt. When she had followed discussions or conducted arguments on these topics until her throat ached and her voice threatened to disappear, she had still to face the speech for which she had come. Welcoming enthusiastic audiences greeted her from enormous auditoriums like civic cathedrals; often, when the meeting was over, they kept her there for another hour, autographing albums and answering questions.

During the nights she travelled from city to city, stretched aching and restless along the lower berths of dark stuffy sleeping-cars in which sleep seemed the least attainable objective. Throughout the semi-consciousness of those strange, interminable hours, the war-scenes which she described from so many platforms came back to her like a series of cinematograph pictures. Against the thick heavy curtain which enclosed her berth, she watched appear and disappear the cliffs of Wimereux, the pine-forests of Hardelot, the twin-spired shadow of Cologne Cathedral, the winter clouds massing on the horizon over the marshes of Poland, the stark dead awaiting the municipal sleigh in the frozen streets of Buzuluk. And always, at the last, came the dark ravines and splintered birches of the Argonne Forest, and the white crosses climbing like bluebells up the green hill at Romagne.

The itinerary arranged by Lincoln Brandt took her as far north as Portland, Maine, and as far south as Richmond, Virginia. She carried away fleeting, indefinite memories of the chief towns and cities in which she spoke – the red sun-washed roofs of Boston, with its sedate streets and English-fronted houses; the Chesnut Street skyscrapers of Philadelphia, towering above the little Congress Hall which saw the Declaration of Independence; the low-spreading city of Baltimore, which merged on the horizon into the rose-pink earth of Maryland; the classic avenues of Washington, where all roads led to the White House beneath the august shadow of the domed Capitol; the Jefferson Memorial at Richmond, like a giant sentinel on guard between the brisk commercial North and the old somnolent South.

In New England the towns, large and small, clustered so closely together that she passed in and out of them with a speed which left no impression beyond the English quality of their names – Worcester, Springfield, Taunton, Hartford, Newhaven, Bridgeport, New Britain. The maples had turned scarlet in the woods of Massachusetts when she reached Cambridge and saw the lecture halls and fraternity houses of Harvard. Within the quadrangles the autumn creeper trailed orange and crimson over terra-cotta walls; the brown and yellow leaves dropped lightly from the trees beside the Charles River where Eugene had once walked with Dallas Lowell . . .

From city to city she was followed by a correspondence which became so exacting that her communications to Denis degenerated into cables. Only once, on a journey from Albany to Providence, did she find time to send him her impressions of this swift, spirited, vehement, hospitable, emphatic, impatient America.

'Somehow or other it reminds me of all the books I have read about fifteenth-century Italy – George Eliot's *Romola* and Merejkowski's *Forerunner* and, oddly enough, Pater's *Renaissance*. There seem to be the same Renaissance types here – vital, gay, adventurous, courageous. Many of the younger men and women are amoral according to English standards; at least you get that impression if you read Judge Lindsey's *Revolt of Modern Youth*, which everybody here is discussing. But they have a very definite moral code of the American variety – especially in anything to do with business, which seems to be their God. Luckily for them they are a pioneer people still living in a pioneer country, alive with just that pagan aliveness which stirred Europe to flame in the fifteenth century. To-day by contrast we seem so old, so dead, the best of such life as we had gone down in the War. Although I am tired beyond words, how can I help kindling to a kind of ecstasy when I am called on to share – even if only temporarily – in this enormous vitality?'

Physically exhausted but mentally enriched by cumulative experience, she returned to New York by the night train from Boston in time to make one of the chief Armistice Day speeches at the Mass Demonstration in the Metropolitan Community Hall. She was acclimatised now to perpetual adaptation, and it did not seem strange to her to speak, after a sleepless night, to an enthusiastic interrogative concourse of young men and women at ten o'clock on a Sunday morning. Fatigue made her vulnerable to emotion; the reminiscent vivacity of the youthful faces before her stirred a poignant response to their eager idealism, their valiant bewildered generosity. The prayer which she had once uttered before the shrine of the Madonna at Hardelot shaped the closing words of her speech.

'We can't expect nations to overcome the passions and hatreds which lead to war unless we're prepared, as individuals, to wrestle with them first in our own hearts. When we're old these resentments and prejudices begin to wear the faces of cherished beliefs, but it's easier when we're young to recognise them for the fetters of the spirit that they are. The idea that you can do nothing finer for your country than lay down your life is one of these beguiling prejudices. The possibilities of life are infinite, but death in war, however noble, is no more than a confession of defeat by the resources of the human mind.

'Nearly two thousand years ago, a Jewish community was told that it was expedient for one man to die for the people. Perhaps, as part of that inscrutable design which according to our beliefs we call the logic of history or the dispensation of Providence, it was expedient that one generation should die for the people in order to demonstrate, once and for all, the waste and futility of war. Through the loss of them to-day the world is bankrupt and shattered, the lives of many of us are shadowed for ever by the memory of what might have been. But if the courage which the youth of America and England once gave to war can be used by their successors on behalf of peace, if we who are still young have learnt that to live for one's country is a finer type of patriotism than to die for it, then the martyrdom of the nations ten years ago may lead at last to their redemption. The Kellogg Pact, like this peace campaign now ending, is a gesture of faith by the American people in the fundamental rationality of man. I believe it is destined to draw still closer together our two countries, united long ago in the anguish and grief of war!'

When she left the meeting with the French and German speakers to walk up Fifth Avenue for the service in St Andrew's Church, she was startled to find herself surrounded by the peaked caps and khaki uniforms of war-time France. Some of the uniforms were growing tight now, the heads above them turning grey, but the old martial vigour stiffened the arms which carried the Stars and Stripes or the regimental flag. Between the tall buildings in the clear November sunshine stretched a long line of pennons and banners, motionless as a summer forest of thin trees when the last note of a bugle sounding 'Taps' gave the signal for the Two Minutes' Silence. In the deep hush which enveloped the city, she thought as she had thought at Romagne more than four years ago:

'But this has nothing to do with war as I have known it! The pomp and pageantry of this procession is no more like a modern campaign than Fifth Avenue resembles the smashed trees and fallen dug-outs in the Argonne Forest!'

The service which followed the march was a strange mingling of war and peace. Looking down from the gallery of the church upon the assembled flags and standards, she felt the old pain prick her eyeballs, the old ineradicable glamour of war-time memory capture her senses, when the organ surged into the familiar victorious threnody of 'The Supreme Sacrifice':

Oh, valiant Hearts, who to your glory came
Through dust of conflict and through battle-flame;
Tranquil you lie, your knightly valour proved,
Your memory hallowed in the Land you loved.

Proudly you gathered, rank on rank to war,
As who had heard God's message from afar;
All you had hoped for, all you had, you gave
To save mankind – yourselves you scorned to save.

Was it only her imagination, or did she really see among those uniformed ranks the slim erect figure of a very tall young soldier; the figure that had once cast its shadow across the table in her ward at Hardelot? 'No, no,' she told herself, 'it's an illusion! I'm so tired; I've slept so little for nights. I must be having hallucinations.'

But she leaned farther over the edge of the gallery as the singing rolled on.

Splendid you passed, the great surrender made,
Into the light that nevermore shall fade;
Deep your contentment in that blest abode,
Who wait the last clear trumpet-call of God.

Long years ago, as earth lay dark and still,
Rose a loud cry upon a lonely hill,
While in the frailty of our human clay,
Christ, our Redeemer, passed the self-same way.

'That can't be an illusion!' she thought. 'It's so clear to me now – the silken gloss of jet-black hair, the faint outline of a strong arrogant profile in the dimness. In all the dreams of those night-journeys I saw the places where we walked together – the pine-woods, the sand-dunes, the road to the old Château – but he was never there. Could he have come back to me now, in this church where his comrades are singing on the tenth anniversary of Armistice Day?'

Tense and transfigured, she stared into the dark corner where she thought that he stood while the hymn thundered to its conclusion.

> Still stands His Cross from that dread hour to this,
> Like some bright star above the dark abyss;
> Still, through the veil, the Victor's pitying eyes
> Look down to bless our lesser Calvaries.
>
> These were His servants, in His steps they trod
> Following through death the martyr'd Son of God;
> Victor He rose; victorious too shall rise
> They who have drunk His cup of sacrifice.
>
> O risen Lord, O Shepherd of our Dead,
> Whose Cross has bought them and whose Staff has led—
> In glorious hope their proud and sorrowing Land
> Commits her Children to Thy gracious hand!

Prayers, psalms, the Lesson followed, but she was only half aware of them as her eyes watched the shadow which had taken to itself the semblance of a man. The words of the prophet Micah penetrated her consciousness like the distant echo of bells ringing in some utopian future:

> 'But in the last days it shall come to pass, that the mountain of the house of the Lord shall be established in the top of the mountains, and it shall be exalted above the hills; and people shall flow unto it.
>
> 'And many nations shall come, and say, Come, and let us go up to the mountain of the Lord, and to the house of the God of Jacob; and he will teach us of his ways, and we will walk in his paths: for the law shall go forth of Zion, and the word of the Lord from Jerusalem.
>
> 'And he shall judge among many people, and rebuke strong nations afar off; and they shall beat their swords into plowshares, and their spears into pruning-hooks: nation shall not lift up a sword against nation, neither shall they learn war any more.

'But they shall sit every man under his vine and under his
fig tree; and none shall make them afraid: for the mouth of
the Lord of hosts hath spoken it.

'For all people will walk every one in the name of his god,
and we will walk in the name of the Lord our God for ever
and ever.'

The movement of feet sounded through the church; the blue
and white and red standards were raised aloft; their bearers
stood to attention and the shadow rose with them. Like balm
upon the congregation poured the sweet triumphant harmonies
of Ireland's Offertory Anthem:

'Many waters cannot quench Love, neither can the floods
drown it. Love is strong as death . . .'

In the crowded gallery Ruth fell on her knees, unable to watch
or listen any longer. 'Oh, it's true!' her heart cried passionately.
'Not all the waters through which I have passed have ever
quenched my love for you! Eugene, my darling, I have tried
to banish you; I have said farewell to your spirit, but you won't
be banished; your spirit won't be denied! Love is stronger than
death, my beloved; it is stronger than life or resolution. I cannot
bid you farewell, for you will live in my heart till my world
passes away!'

She did not hear the rest of the anthem nor the conclusion of
the service. When at last she uncovered her face and rose stiffly
from her knees, the congregation was leaving the gallery, the
procession of uniformed men and women moving along the
aisles below. The shadow had vanished. No tall young soldier
with jet-black hair and a lean bronzed face marched beneath the
massed colours through the open door.

Dazed with memory and half blinded with tears, Ruth stumbled from the darkness of the church into the white midday
brilliance of Fifth Avenue.

8

She was walking mechanically southwards, her imagination still possessed by Eugene's zealous ghost, when she heard a voice calling her.

'Miss Alleyndene!'

She turned to see a young woman of about her own age, small and slight and flaxen-haired, with pale cheeks and delicately reddened lips.

'Forgive me for using the name you speak under,' said the young woman. 'I'm told you're married, but it's the only one I know.'

'It doesn't matter,' said Ruth. 'Everybody here calls me Ruth Alleyndene.'

She had met so many strangers now, been addressed by such numbers of unknown men and women who had crowded round her after her meetings, yet for some inexplicable reason a faint stir of interest lifted her from her deep preoccupation. Her attention passed from the trimly cut black frock with its white frills to the delicate face and limpid china-blue eyes, which belied the years revealed by the lines round the firm, composed lips.

'I've just come from the service at St Andrew's,' said the stranger, 'and before that I heard you speak at the Community Hall. I thought your speech was grand, especially when you talked about your experiences in the War. You almost made me feel I'd been there myself, and I've always wanted to know exactly what it was like – because, you see, my fiancé was killed in France.'

'I'm sorry,' murmured Ruth. The air seemed suddenly tense with significance. Her companion went on.

'I guess you knew him out there. His name was Eugene Meury – Captain Meury of the 45th Division. I wonder if you remember him?'

'Yes,' said Ruth, 'I remember him very well.'

Had she gone as pale as she felt? It was fortunate that they were walking now in the shadow of giant sky-scrapers, chill and dark on that glittering morning as the bottom of a canyon. Inexorably, the gentle voice beside her continued.

'I don't know whether you've heard my name, but I'm called Dallas Lowell. Maybe he never spoke of me to you?'

'Oh, but he did! I knew you were engaged to him.'

'Did you? You know, I'd just love to talk to you if you could spare the time. Won't you come along right now and have lunch with me? My club's only two blocks away, at the top of the Coolidge Building.'

I can't, thought Ruth. I'm too tired, too shattered by the meeting and that service, and I haven't slept properly for nights. If I go I shall give myself away . . .

'I'm so sorry,' she said, 'but I really ought to get back to my hotel. I'm sailing to-morrow. I've all my packing to do and a terrible accumulation of letters.'

'But you must lunch somewhere, surely? I've wanted to know you for so long. When I realised you were the Labour speaker taking part in our peace campaign, I was too thrilled for words. I'd consider it a great favour if you'd come.'

Ruth's resolution wavered. Oh, I can't fight her. I've no strength left. I mustn't be rude to her, of all people in this country . . .

'You're very kind . . . if you'll really forgive me for hurrying away afterwards.'

Her head seemed to spin when the elevator had rushed them to the thirty-seventh floor of a titanic new building, where the narrowing tiers of cream-tinted stone culminated in a triangular penthouse enclosing a glass observation tower high above the city. Beyond The Battery she could see the wide sapphire sweep of the Upper Bay below the East River, and a black, red-funnelled liner like a ladybird with folded wings crawling past the Statue of Liberty. With her mind half dreaming but her senses sharply alert, she stared at the sunshine washing the walls of the lower sky-scrapers to whiteness while Dallas Lowell ordered luncheon.

'It must seem queer to you,' said Dallas when the waiter had gone, 'the way we over here still know so little about the War. At the time it didn't mean a thing to me – not even in 1917 when we went in ourselves, and Eugene wrote me he'd met you, after your brother had been killed. It was just an enormous cruel insanity that took Eugene away from me when we were first engaged.'

'What happened to you afterwards?' asked Ruth, trying to eat the iced grape-fruit in front of her. 'Are you married?'

'Oh, no! I haven't thought of it since. You see, I'd looked on Eugene as my future husband from the time we were children. Somehow it's never been possible to switch over to someone else. Till I was twenty-three and he was killed, I'd had no personal life apart from him.'

Ruth laid down her spoon feeling as though the sweet juice would choke her. She's lost more than I have, she thought, with a sense of deep humiliation. I've got Denis and the children – and I had Eugene as well. Why have I been so arrogant as to think myself specially afflicted by fate? I had him, and she never did. I took him from her – that sweet tired-looking woman. She must never know – never, never, never! I must carry my burden of memory without revealing its weight.

'For months after he died, everything just went blank for me,' Dallas continued. 'You over there at least understood something about the War, but most of us were as ignorant as we could be. Eugene's life seemed to me utterly wasted, thrown away. I guess most of us in the peace movement think it was now, but for a different reason. I thought what he'd died for was your quarrel and France's and Germany's, but not ours, and it made me mad. For years I detested England and France for taking him. I wouldn't even go to Europe for a vacation until I made a trip in 1924 to see his grave at Romagne-sous-Montfaucon.'

'In 1924!' Ruth stifled an exclamation and spoke quite evenly. 'You visited his grave in 1924? France is so lovely in the summer and autumn, isn't it? – with the roses in bloom in all the cemeteries. When did you go?'

'I went over in April. His birthday was that month, and they gave me special leave from the office.'

'You've got a job, then?' asked Ruth, thinking how easily they might have met beside that wooden cross. 'I hope it's something you like?'

'Yes. I adore my work, because I'm doing some of the things Eugene would have done if he'd lived. You see, Mr Meury,

Eugene's father, was awfully good to me after he died. He was just about broken himself – Eugene was his only son – but he never took an hour off from his job. He said if he did he'd give way himself, and what I needed to help me overcome it was occupation. I was quite inexperienced at newspaper work, but, of course, I'd been to college, and he gave me a little job in the advertising department of the New York office. I found I'd a flair for handling copy and planning out space, and after a time I got interested and worked my way up. Now I'm manager of all the *Ledger's* advertising. It's a big job to hold down, but I'm thrilled with it.'

'I'm so glad . . . You've been very brave,' said Ruth inarticulately, giving up the attempt to eat her fried chicken. We've both rebuilt our lives on the same basis, she thought. A hundred years ago, Dallas Lowell and I would have been among those lost war-victims, neglected and unrecorded, whose mainspring of life was permanently broken when the men for whom they were destined died. At least the twentieth century, if it did smash the world for thousands of women, has given them the compensation of work. And that's so much less at the mercy of chance than personal relationships.

When the ice-cream had come and gone, they lit their cigarettes and smoked for a few minutes in silence. Ruth felt calmer now, though her fatigue still enveloped her like a stifling cloak. Throughout the meal, though she had hardly touched it, her sense of shock had gradually diminished. How could I ever have felt so bitter and resentful against her, she wondered, when she's so dignified and mature and reassuring? The image I've had of her all these years has been so different from the truth. Neither Eugene nor I was fair to her. I suppose our love made us both unjust.

When coffee was served they followed the waiter to a small lounge where Ruth saw that they were quite alone.

'It's generally crowded,' explained Dallas, handing Ruth her cup, 'but there's never a soul about on Sundays. You can't imagine,' she added, 'how glad I am you came here. Ever since the War I've wanted to meet someone who knew Eugene when he was over there, and could tell me about it – and him. You see, so many of his friends were killed in the Argonne too. Those who came home wouldn't say much – or they couldn't find words even when they wanted to be kind, and tried. Sometimes I've wondered whether he'd have been able to talk to me himself if he'd come back – or whether he'd have thought I shouldn't understand. I must have seemed so far away, and completely out of it.'

'He often talked about you,' said Ruth. (That's true, at least – how cruelly true!)

'Did he really?' cried Dallas. 'It's fine to hear you say it!' A faint note of urgency crept into her quiet, controlled voice. 'You know, I often used to wonder if he'd forgotten what I was like. He was never much of a letter-writer, though he did write regularly. Sometimes I feared he'd find me quite inadequate after all he'd been through . . . I was even afraid he mightn't *want* to marry me when he got back home.'

Ruth clenched her hands tightly in her lap.

'Oh, he would have wanted to – I'm sure he would.'

'*You* say that!'

Startled as though a bomb had exploded in the air, Ruth knew that her face had turned quite colourless. The gentle, decisive words had splintered into fragments their polite affectation of impersonal formality. She said nothing, waiting for Dallas Lowell to go on.

'He was in love with you, wasn't he?'

She looked up at last. The grey and the blue eyes faced one another steadily, without pretence.

'Yes.'

'And you with him?'

'And I with him.'

The silence which followed was so deep that each could hear the other breathing – jerkily, unevenly, like runners at the end of a race. It was Dallas who broke it.

'Thank you for telling me, Ruth Alleyndene. I've waited ten years to learn the truth.'

'How did you know?' Ruth whispered.

'I didn't. I only guessed. You see, at first – after he'd told me about going to see you in France because he'd promised your poor brother – he wrote about you a good deal. He told me what a relief it was to talk to an English girl of his own sort after being a private soldier for so long. I understood that, and I tried not to mind. And then, quite suddenly – it was after he'd gone to the Training School at Camberley – he never mentioned you any more. I guessed why. I didn't think you'd quarrelled – I knew better than that. I guessed he'd fallen in love with you, and I was desperately jealous. I'd always been crazy about him. He was my hero when we were still babies . . .'

She looked at Ruth. Ruth returned the look in silence. Dallas continued.

'I didn't know what I ought to do. You see, I knew *him*. I knew he was loyal and considerate, and I was pretty sure he'd never let me down . . . but the longer the War went on, the more positive I became he'd stopped loving me. It was his letters . . . I wrote every mail and he always wrote back, as kindly as could be. But he didn't answer any of the questions I asked about him, or the War, as he'd done at first, and I guessed he hadn't read a thing I'd written. I just didn't know how to act. If he'd asked me to release him I would have, of course. I loved him too much to hold him to a promise he didn't want to keep. But he never suggested anything of the sort, and I didn't see how I could begin when I'd nothing to go on but my own intuition. I thought nobody had ever suffered quite as I did – the way you do think when you're very young. And I hated you as I'd never dreamed I could hate a living soul.'

The chromium clock on the wall struck two, but Ruth had lost all sense of time. With tightly clasped fingers, she sat motionless and waited.

'I was still wondering what to do when we realised the War was ending . . . and then the cable came saying he was killed. For a long time I just lived in darkness, hardly knowing I lived at all. I couldn't think of anything except that I should never see him again . . . because, of course, I'd really hoped all the time that when everything was over I could win him back . . . Months later, when I remembered you, I found I felt quite different about you. I guessed you must have suffered too, because I knew, if he loved you, you couldn't help loving him – he was so handsome and brave and full of life.'

She closed her eyes for a second, as though recalling his image, before she continued:

'I knew you were probably the one person who'd made that hell of war bearable to him . . . and I wondered whether you'd perhaps done something else for him, something beyond my power. I thought, maybe, even if you loved him, you might be too English and conventional for that . . . You see, long before the War ended I'd begun to grow up and realise things. By the time he went to the Argonne and the papers here carried stories of that awful campaign, I knew that if I could have given him all of myself, body and soul, to do what he liked with, I'd have done it without conditions. I loved him so, I just couldn't bear to think of him dying without knowing love from beginning to end. But *I* couldn't be any use to him that way . . . there was the Atlantic between us!'

She looked at Ruth again, a searching look of infinite tenderness, but this time Ruth did not see it, for her face was hidden in her hands. Dallas went on, slowly and deliberately:

'When he was killed, I hoped perhaps he *had* known it after all, and through somebody worth while – somebody who was his equal. I thought maybe he'd known it through you. Don't tell me unless you want to.'

Ruth nodded her head convulsively. Her throat felt paralysed; speech would have choked her. The cool, quiet voice continued:

'I'm ever so glad – so glad you did what I'd have given my life to do for him myself, if I only could have. Don't cry,' she added, for the tears were now running down Ruth's cheeks and she made no effort to hide them. 'Don't cry unless it helps. I *am* glad – I really mean it. So often, you know, since the War, I've suffered agonies, wondering whether perhaps after all it wasn't you, and he'd gone after experience in ways he'd have regretted later. Now I don't have to wonder and grieve any more. When I heard you speak this morning, I realised you were everything I'd hoped to find you. You're noble and courageous, and you want the same things for the world as I do – the things Mr Meury goes out for in the *Ledger* whatever it costs him. I'm glad it was you who knew Eugene . . .'

Her own voice shook. Ruth gathered herself together and spoke.

'I don't suppose I can ever make you understand what a relief it's been to meet you and tell you . . . to find you the sort of person I *could* tell. I realise now that all these years I've felt I wronged you, injured you – though God knows I tried hard enough not to, at the time. You were right about him too, if that comforts you – I mean about the kind of person he was. Just before the only time we were lovers, he told me he'd stayed virgin for your sake. I believe he'd have died so, if it hadn't been for me.' Tears blinded her again. 'Do you still forgive me for taking him?'

Dallas Lowell stood up and put out both her hands.

'You needn't feel that way about me any more. If we never meet again, Ruth Alleyndene, you can be sure I'll always remember you with gratitude for giving him what I couldn't give. I'll feel less lonely because there's someone in the world who loved him just the same as I did.'

The afternoon sunlight poured over them as they stood with clasped hands above New York city, each silently vowing herself to a future whose obligations were shaped by the unforgettable past.

9

As Ruth turned out of the Coolidge Building and continued her journey down Fifth Avenue, one or two passers-by stared curiously at her reddened eyes and pale tear-marked face. But she did not notice them. She noticed nothing – neither the Sunday emptiness of the pavements, nor the stream of holiday traffic, nor the opulent displays of jewellery and furs and gossamer undergarments in the closed plate-glass windows of the fashionable stores. Her preoccupation was so deep that she never thought of taking a 'bus or a taxi back to her hotel. Her tired feet moved forward with the slow regularity of an outworn machine, while chaotic emotions whirled through her mind with undirected intensity.

'What a queer state I must have been in!' she thought afterwards, when two days of rest on the boat had restored her balance. 'I'd had no sleep in the train from Boston, and not much the night before when that discussion at Concord lasted into the small hours. And as soon as I got to New York there was my speech at the Community Hall demonstration, and then the parade and the service, and then that talk with Dallas Lowell. Why, Sunday had lasted a week already by the time I got to Madison Square and had that strange experience before the Eternal Light!'

But at the time she saw the day neither in sequence nor in proportion. The past two hours possessed her with their unexpected, overwhelming conclusion.

'So that's the woman for whom I lost my virginity! What a curiously inappropriate person to have made it happen! She's so loyal, so generous, so devoted, so full of a quiet tenacity which is both strong and compassionate. Did I really think Eugene's vitality had been utterly thrown away? Because he lived and died, a great newspaper is working for peace, and the two women who loved him have joined the fight for reason and justice between the nations.'

She stopped mechanically as the lights changed and the cross-town street-cars clanged up and down 42nd Street.

'How odd it is that the fact of losing my virginity still dominates me after all these years – and in modern America too, where everyone is reading Judge Lindsey's book and discussing companionate marriage! How ludicrously old-fashioned I should seem to these present-day boys and girls, who regard sleeping with different people as just part of life's normal experimentation! In theory I think I agree with them. I believe that what matters most is to have life and have it more abundantly, and in so far as unorthodox sex experience is a source of greater vitality, it seems to me fully justified. And yet in my heart I shall never feel about it as casually as they do. My values have changed, but my conscience is pre-war; it was formed by the precepts and traditions of my Staffordshire ancestors. I rebelled against them and always shall, but they moulded me just the same. I can't believe that the giving away of one's utmost physical self to somebody is a light matter, however it happens. It still seems to me such a profound experience that one can't over-estimate it. I know that having Eugene as my lover changed me for ever – far more than if I'd cared for him, even as deeply as I did, without that physical knowledge.'

At 34th Street the signals held her up again. She waited, hardly aware of them.

'I wonder if that evening in the forest meant as much to him as it did to me? That's one of the things I shall never know, but I suspect it didn't. It's part of the sheer cruelty of nature that sex experience means more to women than to men. After all, every occasion of physical intercourse carries with it for a woman the risk of death, and though birth-control has lessened that risk, it hasn't done away with it altogether and perhaps never will. Women need all that the twentieth century can give them to compensate for this fundamental fact of biology . . . and yet how I ache sometimes to recapture that stranger who knew passion and who once was I . . . that stranger who walks to-day like a ghost in the dim ranks of old recollections. Oh, Eugene, Eugene!'

She awakened again to perceptiveness as the long straight highway broadened into the imposing width of Madison Square. Though bars of gold still lay slanting across the street, the sun was already withdrawing behind the high office buildings. In the middle of the Square, raised far above her head at the top of a slender white column, she saw the illumined star of the Eternal Light where the procession had assembled that morning. She stopped to read the carved inscriptions on the stone base of the column:

Erected to commemorate the first home-coming of the victorious American Army and Navy of these United States officially received by the City of New York on this site, Anno Domini, MCMXVIII. This star was lighted November xi, MCMXXIII.

It's been burning now for exactly five years, she thought. It will still be burning when all of us who remember the war are dust and ashes.

Stooping, she read the names inscribed on the front of the square solid stone.

MONTDIDIER – NOYON – MEUSE-ARGONNE – AISNE – LYS

On the second side she found a line from the 'Star-Spangled Banner'; on the third, facing north, more names and another inscription.

In Memory of those who have made the Supreme Sacrifice for the Triumph of the Free Peoples of the World

YPRES – LYS – SOMME OFFENSIVE – VITTORIO-VENETO – CHAMPAGNE – MARNE

The fourth side of the stone tersely conveyed the idea which had given shape to the memorial:

An Eternal Light
An Inspiration
AND A PROMISE OF
ENDURING PEACE

After all, she concluded, the very fact that democracies throughout the world are making the same effort for the same end unites us whether we know one another or not. Oh, beautiful city where Eugene once lived! Although I have so little knowledge of this country, I feel that, because I once loved an American, I understand something of where it is going and what it is trying to do!

Between the sky-scrapers a long shaft of sunshine shimmered into the square. For a second it blinded her eyes, and when she looked up, the outlines of the tall buildings were gone. The consciousness of time vanished from her mind and the sense of space: instead of the New York traffic passing through Fifth Avenue on the tenth anniversary of Armistice Day, she thought that she saw the swift pageant of America's past moving down the long corridors of history.

Where Madison Square had been, spread the huge silent continent in which the only paths were the trails of Indians, and the Mississippi flowed southward through forests untrodden by the feet of strangers. To this empty land came the reckless sailing ships from Europe, urged westward by the wild lust for adventure or the stern claims of an implacable God; the men and women whom they carried fought for life against the harsh earth, the pitiless cold, the scorching inexorable sun. She saw America emerge at last from the years of conflict between men of the same blood, the same speech and the same heritage; a century later the North struggled with the South for the sake of that unity which still defeated the restless warring nations of the international world. She watched the hazardous treks of the pioneers, pushing in faith with their covered waggons through the windy interminable miles of Mid-Western prairie to the desert sands where many left their bones to rot in the sullen blood-red glare of the sunset, until at last they reached the mountains looking across the sun-baked earth of California to the Golden Gate of the uncharted Pacific. From east to west rose the cities, clamorous Towers of Babel pushing nearer to heaven in an age of steel and concrete, until the harmonising process of time and the dwindling current of immigration merged a dozen languages into one vigorous tongue.

The pioneers and the builders vanished; instead of the sailing ships toiling westward, transport after transport hurried to the east. Upon the foreign shores of the fighting nations they landed their powerful, confident soldiers, proud and unimpaired beside the pale depleted manhood of England and France and Germany. She saw them face the enemy at Château-Thierry, at Cantigny, at St Mihiel; they carried their war to the blue slopes of the Vosges and the dark tree-shadowed ravines of the Argonne, where the young Eugene Meury whom she loved had fought and died. Then it seemed as though a shadow passed through the ray of light which had illumined the long procession, and she felt that if she turned her head she would see standing beside her the phantom which had risen amongst the pennons and banners in St Andrew's Church. Was it only in her thoughts that she spoke to him, or did she utter the words aloud?

'Eugene – you who shared our War – tell me how to bring our countries together in these uneasy twilight years of peace!'

Was it only in a dream that he answered her?

'Look, darling, and I'll show you something more about our country!'

She remembered afterwards how she had seen a cloud descend upon the lovely city, heard frantic, bewildered voices crying fear, confusion, unemployment, starvation, watched men and women struggling through the panic night of insecurity – until after a long eclipse the darkness lifted, and the light showed her a great coming and going of ships and aeroplanes across the Atlantic.

Again the voice that she knew seemed to speak.

'We shall pass through chaos and sorrow and loss; confidence and hope will disappear; our commercial enterprises will go down, our proud strength be impaired. But when it is over we shall understand better what England endured because of the War. We shall know what poverty means, and despair, and the collapse of wealth and prestige, and through this knowledge your country and mine which fought the War together will develop a greater kindness and tolerance for one another. We who speak the same language and share the same inheritance will stand united against the powers of reaction on the side of those forces that make for life!'

With the shock of a somnambulist awaking, she came suddenly to herself. The shaft of sunshine had disappeared and with it the spectral figures which had walked in its brightness; she saw only the high buildings, the traffic in Fifth Avenue, the white column which carried the star of the Eternal Light. But she felt deeply exhausted; her forehead was damp and she shivered as she returned to the sights and sounds of daily existence from that curious waking dream.

'How extraordinary that was! Have I been asleep? What happened to me? How long have I been here? Did I really see some kind of vision, or did my imagination invent it? Was

Eugene actually with me, or was that just another hallucination of an exhausted brain? He didn't talk the language I remember; the words he used were not words he would ever have chosen – and yet it was his voice I heard, speaking of America and his passion for her as he spoke that time at Camiers just after she had come into the War. How strange that a man with whom I was physically in love, whom I desired with my whole body, should have come to represent for me so spiritual a concept as the relationship between England and America!'

A remembered fragment of poetry stirred in the depths of her memory.

> They say that the Dead die not, but remain
> Near to the rich heirs of their grief and mirth . . .

'You were wrong, Rupert Brooke,' she thought. 'The dead do die, and vanish from us for ever – and yet they live on, not only in our memory of them, but in the things we do that we should never have done if they had not lived. The very fact that I am here in America is part of your immortality, Eugene. It's a continuation of the prayer that I prayed before the Hardelot Madonna, and in a way the answer to it too. That wasn't your spirit which I saw and heard just now; it was my own dreams, my own hopes, speaking, but they embodied themselves in your image because you have always been the vividest part of the world's whole life to me. When I said good-bye to you at Romagne I meant it to be for always; but now I know that I cannot say good-bye to you, that I was wrong to try, for without you my life would be incomplete. My task is to reconcile with all that I am and do, the fact that you lived and died. As Dallas has realised, it is not enough to try to forget or ignore the past. One can't see life as a whole, and accept what one sees, until one has accepted the fact of death. Once I have done that, I can never really lose you again.'

Between the tall cliffs of the sky-scrapers the crimson sunset deepened amid indigo clouds, but across Madison Square their shadows had lengthened and it was already twilight. As Ruth turned down Fifth Avenue she looked back, and saw that within the star on the top of its slender pillar the Eternal Light had begun to shine white and clear through the November dusk, 'an Inspiration, and a Promise of Enduring Peace.'

10

Six months after Ruth returned from America, the General Election of 1929 descended upon an expectant and now complete democracy. Throughout that winter and spring she had spent her week-ends in Witnall, released at last by her visit to the United States from the fear that, as soon as she turned her back on her home, some disaster would happen to the children.

Never, she thought, as she travelled with Denis from Southampton, had the misty atmosphere and soft outlines of the English landscape appeared so beautiful. The vivid lights and sharp-edged shadows of New York were more definite, more stimulating, but they did not offer the same comfortable reassurance as this shabby, rainy island. And, incredible as it seemed, no catastrophe had occurred in her absence. Stephen and Jessie were contentedly engrossed in the re-decoration of their new house in Victoria Road, Kensington; Miriam and Betty had carried on her household with exemplary competence; the twins, absorbed in the emotionless preoccupations of very young children, had not even missed her. Only Denis, it seemed, had done that.

'Another rebuke for my pride!' she told herself. 'Even to Jack and Jill I'm not indispensable.'

But the realisation that her family could manage without her left more freedom in her mind for the topics that her masculine constituents were eager to discuss. Saturday evenings and Sunday afternoons were spent upon investigating such questions as trade recovery and unemployment, Mr Lloyd George's new scheme for providing half a million unemployed with work, the international tangle of disarmament, reparations and war-debts, slum clearance and the raising of the school-leaving age. Sometimes disgruntled 'doubtfuls' were present who attacked Labour's promise to re-establish diplomatic relations with Russia, or criticised its policy of meeting the increased cost of social services by a raised income-tax and higher death-duties.

The women came to her meetings too – tired women with kind, sallow faces, perpetually engaged in a losing battle against eternal grime – but they left to their husbands and fathers the task of putting questions or opening discussions.

'I wish I could rouse them,' she said to Denis. 'Their long tradition of working under men has made them so subservient and repressed. Even now their jobs are mostly dull and mechanical, and it's not easy to become politically-minded when you've never had to use your initiative.'

Sometimes, when canvassing the north-eastern end of her constituency, she passed the Dene Hall gates – their black turning rusty now, their gold growing tarnished – but she had never prevailed upon herself to walk up the drive since the cheerless January afternoon just before her adoption. She knew only that the girls' school had failed last year, as Hardiman had prophesied; that the once suave and prosperous acres had been sold to the same building society which five years ago, to Stephen's exasperated reluctance, had 'developed' the fir plantation. The property, Arthur Wardle told her, was to be converted into a middle-class housing estate, but she did not realise until a month before the election that the first stages of transformation had already begun. A flat-presser from the Alleyndene Pottery, who occasionally appeared as a voluntary worker at Ruth's committee-rooms in the Burslem Road, was the first to give her the news.

'Dost know they're pullin' down th'owd Hall?'

'What!' she cried, with a sense of shock. 'You don't mean to say Dene Hall's being demolished already?'

'Ay. I heared tell it's twothree week sin folks began on it.'

I must see it again before it's gone, she thought. But after she had taken the 'bus up the country road which 'ribbon development' was rapidly changing into a suburban thoroughfare, and had walked for the last time along the quarter-mile of carriage drive to the dominating mansion whose history had made full circle in less than a hundred years, she knew that memory would have been kinder to her than that last impression.

It was Sunday in April. The sweet, fresh morning brightened benevolently over the wide Staffordshire landscape. One by one, the distant summoning church-bells died away upon the clear spring air. By noon the sun rode high in the serene blue, turning to an opaque brownish-grey the smoke-cloud which had steadily moved nearer from the Potteries. But the turrets and pinnacles of Dene Hall were no longer there. The roof had already fallen beneath the tools of the house-breaker; piles of crumbling brick showed where the stables had been destroyed.

Between the small rectangular leads of the mullioned windows, the fine panes were smashed and splintered. The ceilings of the upper rooms had tumbled in; plaster and broken glass covered the floor; bats darted in and out of the dusty gloom. Beneath the budding giant beeches the long drive was rough with weeds. The stone fountain had disappeared, and a scattering of rooks' feathers drifted among the spreading crowfoot on the circular sweep of rust-red gravel. Brambles and thistles, shrivelled brown after the winter snow, smothered the trunks of the old trees growing from the sloping wilderness which had once been a terraced lawn. The grassy knoll where Ruth and Richard had played was rank with sorrel and dock and nettle. A few brave daffodils still pushed their yellow heads between the coarse spreading roots.

It seemed to Ruth that a chapter had come true from *The Garden of Time* which Jessie had read aloud to three children long ago.

'There are people who find themselves barred from the past by nettles and thorns, dead flowers and withered leaves, which prevent them even wishing to look back, for the nettles are sins, and the thorns are remorse; the dead flowers are sorrows, and the withered leaves, blighted hopes.'

Sorrows? Blighted hopes? Yes, the past had held those. But sins? She was still uncertain. Remorse? Oh, no; not remorse. Never, never again!

In the deep haunted silence, so incongruous on that spring morning where in every other garden the birds were singing, she walked slowly through the tangle of bricks and weeds to the rose-garden and the walled orchard. The fruit trees, struggling into blossom, were twined with tall brambles; tiny brown wrens squeezed themselves in and out of holes in the mouldering wall. Among the plantains and bindweed which choked the roots of the rose-bushes, the grey granite sundial lay fallen on its side. She stopped to read the familiar inscription: '*So teach us to number our days: that we may apply our hearts unto wisdom.*'

Tears rushed to her eyes.

'I'll buy it from them,' she resolved. 'I'll put it up at home instead of the bird-bath.'

She did not close the ironwork gate when she left the rose-garden, for the rusty lock was broken, and the roses – her father's pride, her great-grandfather's treasure – would never bloom again. Already they confronted the fate which time with its briars and thistles had held in store for them; they had nothing more to fear from the opprobrious ravages of change and decay.

As she turned at last up the drive towards the tarnished gates, elaborate symbols of a bygone magnificence, she looked back at the doomed house which no longer challenged the Staffordshire countryside with its eccentric, flamboyant silhouette. The swift transitions of a violent age had written 'Finis' against those claims to power that once embodied themselves in her old sad home, and she was herself part of the new forces which had overthrown their dominion. Like Enoch who designed it, like Joseph whose sojourn there had been so brief, like Richard who had died before he could fulfil his inheritance of gifts and endowments, that ambitious habitation was crumbling into dust. Mournful words seemed to drift down the wind sighing amid the boughs of the swaying beeches.

And the place thereof shall know it no more.

11

By the second week in May, columns of speculation about the election campaign filled the London and local newspapers. A weekly review published cartoon portraits of Stanley Baldwin,

Ramsay MacDonald and David Lloyd George, labelled 'Resignation,' 'Anticipation,' 'Imagination.' In Witnall the hoardings were plastered with blue and white posters, showing the suave, distinguished features of Sir Harrison Tallinor – smilingly confident in the imperviousness of his nine thousand majority which he hoped that the new voters would substantially increase – side by side with the stolid countenance of 'Honest John' Baldwin over the slogan 'Safety First.' Occasionally his supporters pasted these placards over the orange and scarlet appeal which Arthur Wardle had judiciously composed:

Voters of Witnall!
Stand by Your Own Finest Traditions
and send an
ALLEYNDENE
to Westminster!

'I'm na meythered by tranquillity talk,' Wardle told Ruth. 'War's bin ower ten year an' more, an' folks bain't so frittened as they was. It's a nesh notion, is "Safety First"; there's naught about it. Any road, it'll take more nor that to fetch out Witnall!'

Sometimes, as Bill Alcock from the Burslem Road garage drove her up and down the constituency in Wardle's dilapidated Ford – a 1923 model which announced its appearance by a screeching of brakes and a rattling of mudguards – she passed Sir Harrison's blue and silver limousine speeding smoothly back to Tallinor Park three miles from Cheet. He always raised his hat and bowed to her with a sweeping courtesy which disguised, skilfully, but sometimes not quite completely, the gentle smile of pity and patronage to which her appearance invariably moved him.

'It's a walk-over this time, old chap,' he assured his friends. 'It just shows you what the Reds have come to, adopting that wild girl of Alleyndene's!'

When Ruth came finally to Witnall to fight the election, she brought Jack and Jill with her, in charge of Betty, for the rest of the campaign. Though the Dene Hall property was sold, the farm on its outskirts had escaped submersion in the housing estate; it had recently changed hands, and was now owned by a Labour supporter. Here, for the rest of May, the twins remained, valuable if unconscious assets to the Party. The meeting at which they stood on the table and shrieked in unison 'Vote for Mummy!' was one of the most successful events of the whole election.

'I can help you at week-ends,' Denis told her, 'and of course I'll come up for polling day. I don't know why the powers that choose election dates always seem to select the very middle of the university term.'

But she doesn't really need me there, he thought. She's quite different since she came back from America. Something has quietened in her, after all these years. Whatever it was that happened over there, I'm glad I made her go.

Once again life for Ruth became a series of meetings, though except for the weather they had nothing in common with her autumn speeches in the United States. Day after day, from north to south, from east to west, the sun shone from clear blue skies upon seventeen hundred and thirty-two striving politicians. In city streets and country lanes the young trees and blossoming shrubs gleamed white and gold, lilac and green. The light winds and soft air seemed a pleasant augury for the new women voters in contrast to the dismal skies and wet pavements of every previous General Election since the War. Even in the Potteries the streets were clean, the cobbles dry. The vehement terra-cotta roof of the new Witnall Town Hall, where the results were to be announced from the balcony, gleamed cheerfully in the benign warmth of perpetual sunlight.

Instead of the brilliant auditoriums of New York and New England, Ruth spoke in small crowded schoolrooms where the absence of adequate ventilation transformed the grimy atmosphere into a thick smoke-laden haze. She addressed her supporters in the Miners' Hall at the end of the narrow alley behind the gas-works; she held open-air meetings in the littered market-place, on the pit-banks, in the club-rooms of iron and steel factories, and even, one lunch-time when Norman was absent, at the gates of the Alleyndene Pottery.

Once, during the last week of her campaign, she waited up

until midnight to speak to the Witnall municipal workers when their evening duty was over. She remembered for a long time the canteen-room above the Corporation Yard where the men gathered to hear her; the low green shades, lined with dingy white, above the billiard-tables; the buff walls with their high olive dado; the crooked framed photographs of football teams, showing dimly complacent through the tobacco smoke; the canteen serving soft drinks at one end while she spoke at the other. In front of her sat the rows of gas-workers and scavengers – critical, intelligent, full of relentless questions. Behind them, glimpsed beneath half-drawn blinds through the open windows, lay the silent, moonlit town.

But the meeting which remained most clearly in her memory was the mass demonstration of women in the Witnall Assembly Rooms two days before the poll, for it was there that she tried to fulfil Denís's injunction to tell the women voters at the next election some of the conclusions to which her own marriage had brought her. The audience, too, found that after-noon memorable, for it was new to many of them to learn from a woman politician that their personal problems had a political aspect. They talked long afterwards of her tall figure, her grave dark-browed beauty, the passion of her gestures, the lovely varied notes of her rich melodious voice.

Standing above the chairs placed in rows along the polished floor where her young intimidated male contemporaries had once asked her nervously for single dances, she began by speak-ing of the Potteries themselves. Parts of the district typified, she said, that desecration of England's pleasant face which was among the worst crimes of the Industrial Revolution. In Staffordshire, as in Lancashire and Yorkshire, the profiteers of a callous age had basely exploited both man and nature for purely commercial ends. One of the first tasks of a Socialist government would be to erase that hideous handiwork of the nineteenth century, to substitute for it the cleaner, lovelier products of a new Industrial Revolution which would take the squalor out of industry, and bring to it that bright efficiency, that higher standard of comfort and achievement, which had impressed her so much in America.

America, she told them, had its black spots too – its grim Passaic, its Southern plantations cultivated by a race which, though freed from slavery, had never acquired freedom of spirit; its strangely named Bethlehem on the Susquehannah, dedicated to purposes so different from those of the Sermon on the Mount. But all that was best in America's life deplored these things too, believing them to be incompatible with the honour of a free people. The United States, at any rate, refused to resign themselves to adverse physical conditions. They were permanently in process of overcoming those enemies of humanity – cold and darkness, smoke and fog, mud and dirt, snow and ice, rain and floods – which in the North and Midlands of England made life a misery to all but the very rich for three-quarters of the year.

'When we're in power,' she continued, 'we want to transform the factories and eradicate the slums. We'd like to bring warmth and cleanliness and the conveniences of life to all those women who spend their youth and beauty and intelligence in overcoming obstacles that no well-planned civilisation would tolerate. But we can't do these things unless you – the majority, now, of this country's voters – insist that we must. In this area especially, you've learnt too long the lesson of subservience. If women hadn't been consistently taught that meekness and patience and endurance are always virtues, many of our worst evils would have been done away with long ago. It's time we learnt to be aggressive in our own interest and our children's. We ought to be impatient and indignant about atrocious living conditions, about the indifference of public authorities to our health and comfort, about the perpetual, unnecessary waste of our time on ill-planned houses and fourth-rate domestic tools. And above all, we ought to refuse to tolerate war.'

She moved forward to the edge of the platform. A faint stir of interest illumined the patient, phlegmatic faces before her. Though their foreheads were lined with anxiety and disappointment, their tired eyes looked up at her with appreciation and kindness.

'Do you realise,' she said, 'that if only we could get rid of war, we should have all the money we need to transform the lives of women throughout this country? Some of you here remember the suffrage movement – a great movement for which my husband's mother, like many others, sacrificed her life and her happiness. In that movement it was always said that war went on because men were in power; they cared more for military glory than for the true dignity of human life. A great South African author, Olive Schreiner, once wrote that because women bore children in anguish, they would never allow them to be sacrificed to the passions and hatreds of war if once they had political power. To-day women have that power, for the vote is the greatest of political weapons. Yet we still bear children not only in anguish but in avoidable peril; and the world is still an armed camp.

'It wouldn't take a century to rebuild the devastations of a century, if we had some of those millions which we now spend on weapons that would destroy civilisation if once they were used. Only eleven years ago, we were still blowing away our national resources on bombardments whose total effect was to increase a hundredfold the misery and tragedy of human life. Do you know that Field-Marshal Sir William Robertson, who was Chief of Staff during the War, once estimated that the three preliminary bombardments of Arras, Messines and Passchendaele cost this country fifty-two million pounds? Do you realise that for this sum we could have had a National Maternity Service, with all that it would have meant in the reduction of maternal mortality, for nearly twenty years? Isn't it time that we saved ourselves from the stranglehold of these suicidal values? Hasn't the day come when we are entitled to ask what the achievement we call our civilisation is really *for* – to insist that the function of progress is to save life and not to kill?

'Remember,' she concluded, 'the movement against war and the movement for better human conditions are bound up together, and the modern women's movement is concerned with both. If only the women who now have votes on the same terms as men could realise what the abolition of war would mean to the wives and mothers still enslaved by intolerable living conditions, the end of poverty and injustice would be in sight. If only they would work for peace as their predecessors worked for their own liberation, we should have no more of the monstrous folly which throws away a nation's resources on the destruction of mankind!'

When May 30th brought polling day, the fine weather still held. Throughout Witnall, discussions centred upon those unknown factors, the young women and the Liberal vote. In the morning, Ruth and Arthur Wardle drove round the constituency, visiting the twelve committee-rooms and the seventy-five polling stations. Denis, with Jim Hardiman, followed them in another car. From the crowds moving in and out of the polling booths quite early in the day, he realised that the voting was going to be heavy. No traditional excuse of wind or weather could be used by any lethargic elector; even the invalids who would not have faced bleak winds or soaking rain drove dutifully to the poll. In a narrow street at the Hanley end of the division, he saw a group of small boys dancing ghoulishly round a bonfire fed with Conservative posters. Charred fragments of blue and white paper spun through the air; the flames swallowed enormous slogans printed in thick blue letters:

TALLINOR AND PROSPERITY
TALLINOR FOR TRANQUILLITY
VOTE FOR TALLINOR AND THE BRITISH EMPIRE

A dozen battered Fords and Baby Austins, lent by schoolmasters, commercial travellers and pottery managers, scuttled up and down the constituency like shabby black insects. From the majestic gates of Tallinor Park to the Alleyndene Pottery on the boundaries of Hanley, they dodged impudently between the dignified wheels of Conservative limousines collected from Labour's opponents all over the county. Amongst them, Ruth noticed with amusement, was the new Bentley belonging to her brother Norman. Late in the afternoon, when a grinning youthful countenance appeared at the window of a Rolls Royce and greeted her with a blatant wink, she realised that her supporters, with unscrupulous glee, were going to the poll by the dozen in Sir Harrison's cars.

'Dinna get skeered by Tory motors,' Hardiman reassured Denis. 'There's naught to motors in Witnall. Our folks'll foot it in sunshine except at north-east, and that's his any road. It's a grand day, is to-day.'

At nine o'clock the poll closed and the two candidates with their agents and chief supporters went to the Town Hall for the count. Though the English county divisions could never challenge the boroughs in their competition to announce the first result, there was considerable rivalry amongst the counties themselves. Witnall, a compact division except for the north-eastern section sprawling towards Cheet over scattered farms and country mansions, had once been the winner in the tellers' race. By nine-thirty, the sealed boxes containing the ballot papers were already deposited at intervals along the rows of trestle tables in the counting room. Long before the hour struck, the tellers set vigorously to work.

Beneath the hanging chandelier in the centre of the long narrow chamber, Sir Harrison Tallinor, grey-haired and smiling, stood imperturbably between his two pretty daughters. Amused as he still was by the negligible femininity of his opponent, he felt profoundly sorry for his old acquaintance, Stephen Alleyndene. Whoever would have expected that sound, cautious business man to produce such a disconcerting daughter! He watched Ruth with the veteran's tolerant pity for the newcomer as she walked round the tables, and felt thankful that no such uncomfortable predicament had ever occurred in his own united family.

Too tired at last to move from box to box any longer, Ruth stood beside a group of tellers looking down at the growing pile of ballot papers until the names 'Alleyndene' and 'Tallinor' seemed to change places and the crosses beside them to run into one another. Was it only her imagination, or did the faces of Sir Harrison and his agent begin to reflect a faint incredulous dismay? An exclamation from an Alleyndene Pottery mould-maker reinforced her astonishing impression.

'Eh, look at Sir 'Arrison! 'E bain't so peart as was! They sen if it's near thing, 'e'll be down on tellers like ton o' clay, demandin' recount.'

Ten minutes afterwards only a few boxes remained unfastened. Denis went up to Arthur Wardle, who had just finished a tour of the tables.

'How are we getting on?'

Wardle's narrowed eyes, his tightened lips, betrayed his excitement.

'There bain't no tellin' yet, Mr Rutherston. It's so near there's nowt to it. But even if your wife's not beat him, she done a champion job. She's made skittles of Tory majority!'

From the other side of the room, Ruth saw Denis watch the last tumbling papers, his face pale and anxious, his sensitive hands thrust deep into his pockets.

'I believe,' she thought, 'he wants me to win almost more than I do! He's never once suggested that he'd like to be the candidate himself – or the Member, if I ever am. Dear, dear Denis!'

And suddenly, in one kaleidoscopic flash, she remembered all that she owed him. He had restored her to life after seven years of war and desolation; through him she had found the work which had brought her within sight of a coveted position of service to the State. He was the father of her beloved children; he had given her a home in which, because he had never known peace in his own childhood, her son and daughter were growing up in an atmosphere of loving serenity. Hardest of all, he had recognised the claims of a dead man upon her unresting spirit; he had done what he could to help her to accept that living sorrow. He had urged her, even at the risk of weakening his own hold upon her affections, to visit Romagne and to go to America; and in America, through a series of strange, unexpected events, she had achieved, after ten years, reconciliation with the past. She was free, now, to await the future; that future which lay in the balance to-night and which Denis would share.

At that moment, looking up, he caught her eyes fixed on him with the deep absorbed tenderness of her gratitude and love. Overjoyed at surprising in her, at this time of all others, an emotion which he had often feared that he could not inspire, his blue eyes opened wide and he smiled at her, radiantly and brilliantly, across the tellers' tables.

The count was nearly over.

12

An hour later, Jessie Alleyndene leaned across to her son from her plush chair in the front row of the balcony at the Queen's Hall, where they both occupied, self-consciously and uncomfortably, the seats for which Ruth had sent them the tickets. On the platform below, a stentorian voice announced the election results as they came in to the packed excited meeting organised by the Independent Labour Party.

'Whatever can have happened?' she speculated uneasily. 'Witnall's usually one of the first results to come through.'

'You forget there's a new crowd of women voting this time,' said Norman. 'It's bound to make the whole thing take longer.'

'Yes, I know. But the other early results have all been announced – Cheltenham, and Barnsley, and Ashton-under-Lyne.'

'Why, Mother, you're quite an election fan! You know far more about it than I do.'

'Well, you see, dear,' Jessie explained apologetically, 'I've had to take an interest since Ruth started doing this work. She's always been speaking for somebody or other, and I've tried to feel I wanted them to get in.'

It was after half-past eleven. Jessie had hardly spoken when the chairman was on his feet again, announcing a Labour victory at Wakefield and, immediately afterwards, the defeat of Harold Macmillan by Labour at Stockton-on-Tees. By midnight, Labour had a clean sweep in the three divisions of Salford, and Labour gains had been reported at Warrington, Reading and Sheffield. Cheers like the sound of a giant waterfall roared through the building when the voice from the platform recorded that the Party, having won twenty-one seats as against eighteen for the Conservatives, was now leading in the race for power. But of Staffordshire, and of the Witnall Division, no mention was made. As the cheers died away, Jessie fidgeted restlessly in her chair.

'Do you think they can have forgotten to announce it?' she suggested. 'It's never been later than nineteenth.'

'Oh, they wouldn't do that! Some complication must have delayed things.'

Between midnight and one o'clock the hour seemed to Jessie to pass more slowly than any hour she had ever known, though Labour victories now followed one another with the disconcerting swiftness of raindrops in a thunder shower. Ellen Wilkinson, the first woman Member of the new House, was returned for East Middlesbrough. Labour gains were reported at Eccles, Central Hackney, Rossendale and West Swansea. The Attorney-General lost his seat to Labour at Central Bristol. At 1 a.m. the Party's lead was definite and increasing.

'Labour 59, Tories 35!'

The shouted figures rang through the hall.

And then, just after the elated yells had died away, the announcement for which Jessie was listening came through. Though the air was vibrant with noise, the words seemed to fall like exploding bullets into a waiting stillness.

'Staffordshire. Witnall Division!'

The chairman made a histrionic pause.

'Oh, Norman!' whispered Jessie. 'I can't stand it . . .'

The jubilant voice from the platform bawled excitedly:

'Ruth Alleyndene, Labour, 19,223; Tallinor, Tory, 19,186. Majority after two recounts, 37. LABOUR GAIN!'

This time the shrieks and yells seemed to last interminably. In a row of seats to Jessie's left a group of young men and women broke into frantic stamping and cheering. They were workers, though she did not know it, from Transport House, and the girls seemed as unconscious as Jessie herself that both they and she were assiduously mopping their eyes.

When the chorus had died down and a short series of Conservative victories brought temporary quiescence to the rising spirits of triumphant Labour, Jessie got up with relief from the warm crimson cushion of her chair.

'Let's go, Norman,' she said. 'There's nothing else to wait for, and these people make me nervous. I feel as if I were in the middle of the French Revolution.'

Promptly Norman took her arm and escorted her to the door.

'Taxi, Mother?' he inquired at the entrance.

'We might walk a little first, dear. It was very hot in there and I'd like to get some air.'

He took her arm again and they turned into Langham Place. Amid the surging, resentful chaos of Norman Alleyndene's thoughts, a feeling of inarticulate tenderness for his mother saved his mind from turning completely sour. For nobody else would he have attended a riotous Socialist meeting when his father decided that, after all, he couldn't face a mob of rowdies.

At fifty-nine, Jessie's figure still possessed the slim daintiness of her early twenties. Her delicate face, now slightly flushed from the turbulent, overheated hall, had retained its soft prettiness and was almost unlined. Beneath the trim cloche hat which fitted closely, in the fashion of the moment, over her neatly waved and shingled grey head, the short curls in front of her tiny ears wore a faintly coquettish air though they were now turning white.

'So she's done it – and what a near thing too!' she remarked, after they had walked for a few moments in silence. 'You know, I never really thought she could, with that big majority against her.'

'Yes. She's done it all right,' commented Norman bitterly, reflecting how wise he had been to keep out of the Potteries during election week. 'I bet you anything she's been in and out of the Pottery all day and every day, pumping her Moscow theories into the girls and the men. Not that they needed her theories,' he added morosely. 'They were Red enough before she got there, all the lot of 'em, God knows!'

To-morrow, he meditated cynically, I shall go back to find them all talking about her. 'Ruth Alleyndene. *Our* Member! *Our* Ruth!' (Our Ruth, indeed! Damn their impertinence!) I shall go back and be nothing but that negligible person her brother, who refuses to lend a hand with the revolution, which they all say they want and would simply loathe if they got! It counts for nothing with them that I've modernised the Pottery and brought back some of its old prosperity, and given jobs to crowds of 'em who'd otherwise be on the dole. Oh, no, that's nothing! I'm simply their employer and therefore their enemy!

Even his parents, he concluded in a final spasm of self-pitying resentment, didn't realise half of what he'd done for the business in the past three years. Hadn't he foreseen demands and started new branches of work to supply them? He'd been one of the first among the younger potters to anticipate the fashion for luxurious fittings in bedrooms and bathrooms. No doubt those tinted wash-basins and translucent porcelain baths, elegant though they were in themselves, would have been rejected as sacrilegious by his fierce but romantic great-great-grandfather, who thought in terms of gilt-embellished dinner services and blue under-glaze bowls. All the same, these new lines were bringing substantial dividends to the shareholders. They at least appreciated Norman Alleyndene if no one else did!

Absorbed in her own reminiscent thoughts, Jessie failed for once in her customary conscientious responsiveness to the mood of husband or son.

'I don't know what your father will say about it, I'm sure. He'll find it as hard to believe as I do. Why, when I first went to Dene Hall to teach your Uncle Philip and Aunt Hetty, there wasn't a trade-union man in the whole Alleyndene Pottery! The new Member for Witnall was Major Magnus Heathcote, who'd got some decoration or other in the Soudan. He represented the district right up to the War.'

'Those were good days for the Potteries. I often wish I'd been at the head of things then instead of now.'

'Well, I didn't take much interest in politics, not having a vote or dreaming women would ever be given one, but I seem to remember the Major got nothing serious in the way of opposition. We'd never heard of Socialists in those early days, of course. The people we were afraid of were the Radicals. That was really why your father made Denis's father leave the parish. He might have got over Mrs Rutherston being a suffragette, but Mr Rutherston would bring Radical theories into his sermons, although he was such a conservative sort of man ... And now to think Witnall's got a woman and a Socialist for its Member – and that of all people it should be Ruth!'

'*That* doesn't really surprise me. I've always thought she

might do anything, provided it were uncomfortable enough for everybody else!'

Jessie sighed.

'You two never did get on, even as children, and I don't really wonder. She was such a difficult, introspective child, always talking to herself or making speeches to trees and bushes. It used to worry me a good deal. I've never forgotten her telling me, when she was about twelve or thirteen, that when she grew up she was going to be very clever and make lots of money and become a suffragette.'

'Well, the War spared us that, at any rate,' interjected Norman.

'Yes,' agreed his mother, 'that's true. But all the same, she's become just the kind of person the suffragettes were. What I mean is, her idea of her future was nearer the truth than mine. Even in those days she'd a great sense of her own dignity and couldn't bear being scolded. She's never to this day forgiven your Aunt Emily for teasing her and making her look absurd before the others. I used to get furious with Emily for using her sharp tongue on the child – and Granny too, for never really trying to stop her ... As your father always says, if Granny knew Ruth was a Socialist, she'd turn in her grave.'

'And well she might!' murmured Norman grimly, as they stepped off the kerb to avoid a group of electioneering revellers, who were marching up Regent Street singing 'The Red Flag.' 'If the Socialists get power this time as well as office, the England our ancestors made won't last much longer.'

'Sometimes I think it's gone already,' said Jessie. Walking like this through excited crowds beneath the calm dark vault of the summer night made her feel better able to talk to Norman than ever before. In the chequered light of Piccadilly Circus with its garish glittering sky-signs, he ceased to be the grim, reticent man nearing forty of whom she had always been a little afraid. Instead he became an obscure but intimate personality with something in him akin to Richard – dear Richard to whom, even as a boy, she could talk so easily without any fear of being snubbed or misunderstood.

'You know, Norman,' she continued, 'I've seen some remarkable changes in my time. When I was a girl it would have been
thought quite wrong for a woman with a husband and a young
family to earn her living or do public work. She wasn't supposed
to have time for anything but her home – and yet I must admit
Ruth does far more for the twins than I ever did for you children.
I never pushed a pram, or bathed and dressed you as she does
Jack and Jill. Nurses didn't expect so much off-duty time in those
days. Old Nanna used to run out in the afternoon for about two
hours once a month.'

'Ruth would call that an argument for Socialism,' Norman
interposed.

'Well,' ruminated Jessie, 'perhaps it is . . . Anyhow, I never
realised how things were changing till Miss Hilton asked your
father about Ruth going to Oxford. That was a great shock
to me, and when he consented it was a greater shock still. I
knew then his daughter meant something to him that his wife
never had. In a way he'd always despised me, like the rest of
the Alleyndenes. When he was a boy, men from those wealthy
families *were* brought up to despise women . . . and yet he was
ready to treat Ruth quite differently. Your poor father – he little
thought he was turning her into a Socialist!'

Half-way down Piccadilly the crowds, denser than ever, surged
outside the Ritz Hotel. A soft warm breeze blew across the Green
Park, fanning their cheeks.

'And then, of course,' resumed Jessie, 'there was the War.'
(Ah, the War – the War that took Richard for ever! Poor Ruth,
it was the war that made her mature so early – and it made me
old in my heart even though I went on looking young long after
it was over. Why was it my face didn't turn haggard and my hair
white when Richard was killed? – because after that I never felt
young again.)

'When it was over,' she continued, 'women seemed to do more
or less what they liked – they went about and earned money
and had flats of their own, and now they've all got votes and
are Members of Parliament. I never thought I'd live to see such
things happen to my own daughter.'

She stopped. 'Let's get a taxi now, Norman. We're nearly

at Hyde Park Corner, and I must telephone a telegram to congratulate Ruth before I go to bed.'

Norman hailed a passing taxi and they got in.

'You know, Mother,' he said, glum yet half-amused as they drove through Knightsbridge, 'I believe, in your heart, you're really very pleased about Ruth.'

Jessie meditated for several moments, gazing at the dark mass of trees in Kensington Gardens.

'I don't know,' she said at last, 'whether I'm pleased about her or just so surprised I can't take it in. You see, Norman, everything's so different now from what it was in my young days, I sometimes think I've no right to have any opinions at all. I feel I oughtn't to do anything but just look on and watch what's happening, and remember all the extraordinary changes that have come in my lifetime. I've often thought, if only I could write them down, what a story they'd make!'

Norman did not reply, and they both sat silent as the taxi turned from Kensington High Street into the darkness of Victoria Road and drew up outside their gate.

'All the same,' Jessie concluded, when he had paid the driver and they were walking up the short garden path, 'I can't help envying Ruth. I'd give a good deal to be a young woman nowadays. They all have such interesting lives, and so many things to do that no one ever thought of when I was a girl . . . Here's my key. I expect your father's heard the result on the wireless, but he'll probably want to talk about it before we go to bed.'

As soon as the door opened Stephen himself, clad in Jaeger dressing-gown and carpet slippers, came into the hall.

'Well, Father, I take it you've heard the news?'

'Ay, I've heard it. I never left the instrument till it came through. There'll have been a fine to-do at the old place, with those two recounts!'

'You ought to have heard them cheering her at Queen's Hall, Stephen!'

'Well, it was high time they did, to be sure – but yours truly feels more at home with the wireless than the Reds. I'd like to have seen old Tallinor's face, though, when he knew he was licked!'

'It's all very well for you, Father. You're out of it now. You haven't got to live up there and watch your own flesh and blood hobnobbing with your employees.'

'Ay, I know, and I don't doubt it's going to make things a bit awkward for you at the Pottery, Norman. All the same, Jill's done well! She's got her head screwed on the right way. As I've always said, she takes after her father!'

13

Towards the end of 1929, the famous Merriam Society of novelists, poets and playwrights was due to celebrate both its fiftieth anniversary and the election of its new President. Immediately after the summer holidays, the secretary of the Society booked the Ballroom at Claridge's for an august and representative literary luncheon on the third Tuesday of November.

Founded in 1879 by the great satirical novelist, William Greycote Merriam, the Society's influence upon English letters already rivalled that of the Académie Française in France. Its membership was limited to fifty, but for its annual functions two hundred outside guests were invited. It was the custom to select these not only from literature, but from individuals with growing reputations in the political, academic and educational worlds. Since 1902, when Merriam died, the President had been elected for three-year periods which gave him, while they lasted, an unparalleled position in contemporary letters. From 1879 until 1929, the Society had never chosen a woman as President. It did so now only because, for the past ten years, Ellison Campbell had been the obvious candidate for that distinguished office.

But when she came to London for the anniversary luncheon which was also her official installation, it did not seem to Gertrude that she was the obvious candidate at all. Seating herself, as President-elect, beside Morgan Prestatyn Edwards, the famous Welsh poet and retiring President, she saw as in some dim dream of the past her own reflection in the long mirrors built into the pale green and yellow walls, and realised that she felt no older than she had felt when she came to London in 1900 to rehearse her first play. It was only that the years had caused a strange transference by which the strong feeling of inferiority that had once seized her when confronted by her seniors now afflicted her just the same in the presence of her juniors. She knew that they called her 'the Grand Old Maid of English drama,' and once, at a literary party where she had arrived very late, she had overheard a young man and woman who did not know her by sight discussing the recent revival of *Hour of Destiny*.

'I can't go to Ellison Campbell's plays,' the girl had said. 'Their whole atmosphere is too, too Edwardian!'

'Oh, rather!' the boy responded. 'They belong to the period when the naughtiest thing you could do on the stage was to lift up your skirts and show your ankles!'

Gertrude still thought of herself as plain, awkward and unimpressive; she was quite unaware that time had given her a distinction lacking to her gaunt, sandy-haired youth and early middle age. Her white hair and colourless face, her stiff upright carriage, her pale grey-green eyes whose keen vision required no spectacles, had become as familiar to literary London as the grey tweed suit and black slouch hat that she usually wore and the long polished rosewood cane which she always carried. Yet the ovation that she received when she entered the ballroom had, as usual, astonished her. Never could she conquer the feeling that enthusiasm shown for her plays or her presence was somehow due to a misunderstanding. Once she had had a dream in which she was tried and convicted for obtaining applause on false pretences.

As the luncheon continued through its series of luxurious courses, Edwards pointed out to her some of the younger guests who had come to see and hear her at this gathering which had so historic an importance in the story of English literature. Because a woman was being elected for the first time as President, the Society had invited a number of young women whose literary careers were only beginning. He called her attention to a table near by, where sat three who all came, he said, from Yorkshire. With the gentle reticent face and honey-fair hair of Storm Jameson, the author already of several novels, Gertrude was familiar. But she knew only by name the two others whose promise had been emphasised by trustworthy critics – Phyllis Bentley, slim, spectacled and serious, with the Lancashire intonations of the West Riding in her soft rich voice, and Winifred Holtby, whose golden hair and superb stature were inherited from Scandinavian ancestors settled in the East Riding centuries ago.

Gertrude looked with interest at the three young writers. She had hated the militant suffrage movement with its emphasis, which she thought blatant and extravagant, upon the claims of women as such, yet because she had touched in her plays upon so many aspects of social and economic conflict, it seemed to her important that women should be writing with expert knowledge about shipbuilding, and agriculture, and the industrial West Riding. Could these vital young novelists in their early thirties be trusted to uphold the standard of artistic integrity in English literature as she had tried to interpret it?

'You know Sherriff, of course?' said Edwards.

Gertrude replied that she did; but she avoided meeting the eye of the dark-haired young dramatist whose play *Journey's End* at the Savoy Theatre was creating such a sensation amongst playgoers from all over the world. Apart from the fact that he belonged to the experience-ridden younger generation whose presence always made her so nervous, she was not even sure that she admired *Journey's End*. She disapproved on principle of precise treatment in stage productions of reality, but she disliked it even more when the reality was that of the War. War literature, she thought, was already far too extensive. She had recently read *All Quiet on the Western Front* with scepticism and disgust, and could think of no reason why anyone should want to add a play to the multitudinous records of that frantic period which she could not now bear even to remember.

It was not that she had lost or even intimately known any man on active service, and during those years she had made large sums of money very quickly and easily. Several of her early plays, including *The Unconquered*, had been revived, and night after night were crowded with war-workers and men and women on leave. But the success even of these was eclipsed, early in 1915, by the production of *Great Possessions*, that drama now celebrated throughout the world, which had been inspired by her English mother's south-country traditions. It had run without a break for over four years, representing to many young men the prosperous, urbane, middle-class England for whose preservation they went out so readily to fight and to die. The War might well have remained in her memory as a period of hard relevant work and grateful rewarding publicity, had it not been for her brother Charles – and for Janet Rutherston . . .

She had never imagined that the burden of Charles could grow even heavier than she had always found it, until August, 1914. He began, with the outbreak of war, to complain that if only he had his health and strength he would go with the rest, although he was well over age. He complained, perpetually, raspingly, monotonously, for four interminable years. And then, in a sense, the War claimed him after all, for during the influenza epidemic he had vanished like a dry leaf on the swift surface of a stream, leaving her gasping and bewildered by her sudden freedom.

There would have been time enough, after that, to stay with Janet, or invite her to Clydevale House as she could never invite her while Charles was alive, or travel with her to those cities of Italy and Spain which they had talked about so often. But Janet too was dead; she had flung away her life on the home front as recklessly as any man in the trenches. Coming back alone from the funeral to see Charles's empty wheel chair still standing in the porch, Gertrude had broken down and wept as she had never wept after Janet's death. She knew then that she had lost the one individual who needed her; that she had joined those sad ranks of innumerable women who realise, with illogical grief, how precious was the burden which they had prayed for years to have lifted from their shoulders.

'You know they'll expect you to speak for half an hour, don't you?' Edwards reminded her.

'That's what I understood,' she said, but she could not immediately abandon her memories to concentrate on her speech.

After Charles died she had kept on the Glasgow house, for though its memories had always caused her pain, she could not abandon the place which had been their centre. But she spent most of her time in London now, in her small furnished suite at Tindall's with its big windows looking south-west over the Park. Sometimes, since Tindall's had been re-equipped with the chromium and leather furniture which made her feel that she was living in an operating theatre, she had talked vaguely of taking one of the new flats now being built in Baker Street and Portman Square. They were very convenient, her producer told her, and though they were expensive she knew that their upkeep came well within her means.

But somehow she could never bring herself to approach house-agents, or decide how to furnish a flat if she had one, or make all the other practical arrangements which purchasers of property have to face. Growing up in the house where she was born, she had never experienced this type of business, and though her circle of acquaintances was very large, not one had become familiar enough to be asked to share the responsibility. The isolation forced upon her by her youth's tragedy had now grown as high and impervious as a prison wall, shutting out the psychological encroachments of intimacy as jealously as a medieval battlement shut out intrusive strangers.

When coffee was served, she awakened to the necessity of giving her mind to both her speech and her audience. Looking casually round the room, her eyes were suddenly held by a pale, finely-moulded face, still young, yet mature in its dark meditative beauty.

'Who's that good-looking woman at the table in the corner?' she asked Edwards, her mind instinctively pursing some half-concealed memory.

'Don't you know? That's Ruth Alleyndene, one of the new women M.P.s. She won a Staffordshire seat for Labour by thirty-seven votes. I see her husband's with her – Denis Rutherston.'

'Oh, I know him!'

The words broke from her like a cry of anguish. She saw Denis now, tall and slender, looking across the room with Janet's vivid blue eyes from beneath Janet's wavy abundance of light brown hair. Ever since she had realised, from the Press reports of the Witnall election, that Ruth Alleyndene was married to Janet's son, she had known that sooner or later, at some public function, she was bound to meet them. To every large gathering she had carried, like a secret heavy burden, the dread of that moment, and at last it was here, facing her, accusing her, tracking her down from the past at the very time when she needed to be most confidently controlled. The room seemed to sway, to darken, just as Edwards rose to introduce her in his chairman's address.

'And now,' she heard him say as he bowed magnificently towards her, 'Wales must give way to Scotland . . .'

'I mustn't fail,' she told herself desperately. 'I must put them out of my mind. In another moment I shall have to speak.'

14

When the speeches were over, and the hand-shakings and congratulations were finished, and Morgan Prestatyn Edwards had conducted her ceremoniously out of Claridge's, Ellison Campbell walked slowly along Brook Street towards Grosvenor Square on her way back to Tindall's. It was a warm, bright afternoon for November, and the air, she thought, might do her good.

As soon as she saw them, she had known that she would not escape. Her dread of them had pushed itself with pitiless obtrusiveness into her analysis of English literary tendencies during the past three years. Surrounded by guests and members of the committee, she had found no opportunity to leave the speakers' table before Ruth Alleyndene came quietly up to her.

'I don't suppose you'll remember me, Miss Campbell. But you once presented me with your prize at Drayton – long ago, just before the War.'

Gertrude had struggled for composure, for the appropriate comment to make on that political career of which she had been the first to display prophetic recognition.

'I remember you very well. I thought at the time how different you looked from the other students. You haven't had long to wait for success.'

She wondered why Ruth smiled with that odd expression of bitterness. (Long? Not long? Oh, no! Only a century or two has gone by since that proud unimpaired youth of mine . . .)

'I've seen you once or twice since then, but always from a distance,' said Ruth.

'I believe I recall one occasion. Didn't you speak at a peace meeting in Glasgow some years ago? I didn't catch your name when the chairman announced it, but I thought I recognised you.'

'Yes, I was speaking. I realised you'd been on the platform directly I left the hall.' She turned and drew Denis forward. 'I think you once knew my husband.'

The moment had come. Automatically Gertrude put out her hand and felt it clasped by another – a slim shapely hand whose touch was familiar though she had never held it before. But the blue eyes that faced her contained a serenity which Janet's had not possessed, the fair even brows were smooth with benevolent composure.

'You were only a schoolboy when I last saw you – or was it an undergraduate?' she murmured mechanically. Then, obeying an overmastering impulse, she looked keenly into his face, examining every feature as though she could learn from it all that the years had left untold.

'You're very like your mother,' she whispered.

'So I'm told by everyone who knew her,' said Denis, pitying but only half comprehending her agitation.

It was over at last, that dreaded meeting, but the memory of it completely obliterated her presidential speech, her triumph, her occupation of a unique literary position which no woman had held before. She had walked no further than Grosvenor Square when a fatigue so stupendous came down upon her that she thought, as she had thought just before speaking, that she was going to faint. Signalling a taxi, she stumbled into it and fell panting on the hard leather seat.

'After all,' she told herself, gasping a little, 'I'm getting on. Over sixty, now. I can't stand strain and excitement as I could when it all began, thirty years ago.'

At Tindall's the hall porter, who had known her for years, noticed with concern her drawn face, her uncertain gait.

'Pardon me, Madam, but are you feeling unwell?'

'Oh, no, thank you, Simmons. I'm not ill – only very tired.

I've just had to make a speech at rather an alarming function. I think I'll lie down for an hour before I order tea.'

'Very well, Madam. I'll send the boy at once when you ring.'

Lying on her bed in the darkened room, Gertrude stared at the pattern made on the carpet by the long low rays of the afternoon sun, filtering through the south-west window beneath the half-drawn blinds. How tiring everything had seemed lately – those incessant demands of managers for yet another Chronicle, those requests from persistent editors for articles on modern playwrights, these interminable lectures and speeches for so many clubs and societies. Dr Tweedale, of course, had urged her to cut them down, but it seemed particularly important to give them just now, when no effort could be too great to keep respect for literature alive in the harsh minds of a sceptical generation through a sterile, depressed period of social history.

They puzzled her so much at times, these hard-headed younger men and women. Perhaps it was because they puzzled her that she found their society so exhausting. They seemed to have only material values and no ideals; yet they had no doubts either, and were ready to make experiments of a kind that she, at their age and earlier, had regarded as out of the question. Their attitude towards marriage, for instance, was even more revolutionary than Janet's had been. Quite a number of young women seemed to imagine that it was possible to marry and have children and bring them up decently, and yet occupy a leading position in some art or profession. The idea of dedicating yourself, body and soul, to a chosen vocation, and counting everything well lost that was sacrificed for its sake, seemed to have gone altogether. They would only stare blankly at her if she confided in them her belief that marriage and children would have vitiated her art, and respond with some modern jargon about the best of both worlds and getting rid of your inhibitions.

It was strange how completely out of touch with them she felt, for really they weren't so young after all. At their time of life she had thought herself quite middle-aged, but they were slim and muscular, looking like girls with their gay frocks, painted lips and smooth close-cropped heads. They were always smoking cigarettes, too, and talking with self-possessed equanimity in sharp, youthful voices, though some of them must be quite as old as Janet was when she died . . . But she never now thought of Janet as haggard and ill and stricken, but always as she had appeared the first time they met at the Sterndale Conversazione. Dear pretty fair-haired Janet, with her undisciplined enthusiasms . . . the only person, she sometimes felt, whom she had ever really loved . . .

Sixteen years, now, since she and Janet had parted for good. Never, since then, had she ventured to make another friend, to express her intimate thoughts and feelings to any human soul. It was a long time, sixteen years, to have lived on in the world and been quite alone . . . though occasionally she doubted whether those years would have been equally productive if she had gone on loving Janet and receiving her warm, vital affection. In her younger days, when life had been starved and empty as it could never be now in this period of her fame, she had thought that what her experience lacked was emotion. But when emotion came it proved too disturbing; it made her feel too much. This particular emotion, at any rate, had done so. There was always something strained and feverish about it that she could not explain, some abnormal quality which sought to dominate, to possess, to exclude all rival claims and competitive interests.

'My pride and fear and envy made me blind,' she thought. 'Otherwise I should have seen how near she was to breaking point. I didn't want to share her with her political loyalties, but I should never have left her if I had realised her mortal sickness of body and spirit. Time, I suppose, has justified those loyalties; all the same, it's what women actually achieve that counts to-day. The rights they've won can only be justified by their works. I don't think I was wrong about that, even though the suffrage movement did succeed as I never thought it could.'

Seeing Janet's son at the luncheon that afternoon had shaken her badly. It must have been the shock of meeting him, and the unforeseen necessity of calling upon all her powers of self-control, which had made her feel so old and so absurdly tired. Yet the odd thing was that the person who really reminded her of Janet was not Denis, but his wife. The likeness wasn't obvious, of course, though she remembered now that it had impressed her the first time she saw Ruth at Drayton. Ruth Alleyndene was tall and thin and dark, whereas Janet had been rounded and soft and fair; she was sophisticated and cultured, while Janet had been naïve and half-educated. But Gertrude thought that she detected in Ruth the same dynamic energy, the same impatient vitality, the same refusal to be chained by circumstance, the same swift intelligent responsiveness to unspoken suggestions and half-framed ideas.

If only she could get over the nervousness, the reminiscent tension, which Ruth and Denis had evoked, she might be able to speak the words that had choked her for years, and tell Ruth, as she couldn't tell Denis, that she had never really meant to quarrel with Janet or forsake her. Perhaps she could make Ruth understand that it wasn't anger or hatred which had kept her silent, but only the rigid pride which she couldn't afford to sacrifice because it had sustained her through so many ordeals. Could she tell Ruth, too, how often she had wished that there might be a resurrection of the dead for one reason only – that she could see Janet, and explain?

At that moment, without warning, a feeling of suffocation overwhelmed her. She sat up, gasping for breath, her hands clutching at her throat, her whole being concentrated upon enduring this unexpected discomfort until it passed. But it did not pass. Her lips, blue and stiff, framed the word 'Janet!' but no sound emerged, and then darkness, colder and more profound than winter midnight, eclipsed the long low rays of the afternoon sun.

15

As soon as the Merriam Society luncheon was over, Ruth went on to the House of Commons and Denis back to Prince's College. Later he dined with her at the House, for the Third Reading of the Widows' Pensions Bill brought in by the minority Labour Government was to be taken that evening, and he wanted to hear the debate. Since her election they had frequently had tea on the Terrace together beside the Thames under the shadow of

St Stephen's, or dinner in the Harcourt Room surrounded by men and women whose names were known wherever newspapers were read.

If only, he had often thought during that pleasant summer, Janet's ghost could walk down the stone corridors of Westminster to watch her daughter-in-law's progress in that House which had been called the finest political club in the world! She might have heard Ruth's maiden speech, on the unusual subject of Anglo-American relations, at the end of the previous session just before Ramsay MacDonald went to New York to discuss international co-operation with President Hoover. Several times, since then, Ruth had spoken. Without vanity, without aggressiveness, her political reputation was growing. Some day, perhaps, now that Margaret Bondfield had set a new precedent, she might even reach the Cabinet.

Once, he thought, he would have envied her, but now that his seven-years' study of the philosophical bases of war and peace was almost ready for publication, he realised where his own future lay. Next year, he had been privately informed, when one of the London Chairs of Philosophy became vacant, his name alone would be considered. Ruth did not know this yet; he would tell her at the beginning of 1930, when the resignation of the great philosopher, Thomson-Burford, would be officially announced.

'My career is one of those solid, cumulative affairs by which an academic reputation is built up,' he decided realistically. 'I'm not the kind of person to whom dramatic, unexpected things happen as they do to her. But perhaps in the long run our achievements, weighed in the balance of omnipotence, may turn an even scale.'

Late that evening in the Strangers' Gallery, he looked down upon her with love and pride as she sat at the back of the Government benches in the dim heavy atmosphere of Parliament on an autumn night, listening to conscientious speeches weighty with humane sentiments and statistical information. How beautiful she is now, he thought, contemplating the short peat-brown hair, the dark level brows above her deep-set eyes, the fine contours of her pale face with its curving red lips. She looks her age – she's been through too much not to do that –

but she has a graciousness and a distinction quite unlike the self-possessed arrogance of her lovely haughty youth. There's an understanding in her face, a kind of translucent compassion, which it never revealed in those early days.

When the debate was over and the division taken, he met her in the Lobby and they walked through the echoing vaulted darkness of Westminster Hall to get their underground train at Westminster Bridge. With the disconcerting instability of the English climate, the bright afternoon had changed to a sombre evening clammy with mist and impending rain. The sky was opaque and starless; the black outlines of the Thames were blurred with heavy drifting fog. At the entrance to the Underground station, a newspaper-seller exhibited a placard marked 'Late Night Special.' His raucous voice, too long habituated to the proclamation of wars, murders, fires, floods, earthquakes, accidents and assassinations, indistinctly announced some mournful occurrence to the murky night.

Accustomed though he was to the evening Press policy of conveying in heavy type just before bedtime some peculiarly disquieting item of intelligence which was not even mentioned next morning in the columns of *The Times*, Denis glanced automatically at the placard as he went to buy the tickets. Then he stopped, for the black letters declared:

DEATH OF FAMOUS WOMAN DRAMATIST

'Good God!' he exclaimed, looking at the heading across the piles of the *Evening Post* on the vendor's stall, 'Ellison Campbell's dead!'

'Dead! Ellison Campbell *dead*!' cried Ruth incredulously. 'Oh, Denis, she can't be! Why, she was talking to us only this afternoon!'

He bought a copy of the newspaper and quickly scanned its columns.

'She is, all the same. The *Post* says it was heart-failure. I suppose the speech or something was too much for her.'

Ruth looked over his shoulder at the heavily printed paragraph.

'We regret to announce the death of Miss Ellison Campbell, the world-famous dramatist. Miss Campbell died suddenly from heart-failure at her hotel this afternoon just after she had delivered the Presidential address at the Fiftieth Anniversary luncheon of the celebrated Merriam Society. The exact time of her death is uncertain, but it must have occurred between 3.30 and 5 o'clock, when a hotel servant went up to her suite to inquire if she wished to order tea and found the deceased lady lying on her bed. A specialist was summoned immediately, but he could do nothing except certify that death was due to a sudden heart-attack and must have been instantaneous.

'We understand that by Miss Campbell's own wish she is to be buried in Scotland beside other members of her family, but I gather from Mr Morgan Prestatyn Edwards, the Welsh poet and ex-president of the Merriam Society, that there is already talk of a memorial service in Westminster Abbey. Should the project materialise, Ellison Campbell will be the first woman writer to whom this signal honour had been accorded.

'A special memoir giving full details of the great dramatist's career appears on page 11.'

They walked through the barrier and down to the platform in silence.

'It's a long time since the War,' Ruth said at last. 'I'd forgotten the occasional suddenness of human mortality.'

Absorbed by their different memories of the baffling, dominant figure whose influence had so strangely touched both their lives, they hardly spoke again until they had let themselves quietly into their house beneath the open nursery window where the twins lay sleeping. Denis switched on the light in the small lounge, and Ruth turned to him with a puzzled inquiry.

'You know, Denis, it's always mystified me, that long friendship between Ellison Campbell and your mother, and the sudden way it broke off. Could you ever explain it at all?'

'Not really,' he said. 'As I've told you, I was never in Mother's confidence. I only know it had something to do with the suffrage movement.'

'That did break up homes and friendships, of course, but it

seems queer it broke this one. Miss Campbell must have known for ages that your mother was a militant, and your mother that she didn't agree with her.'

'Well, if you're interested you'll find any amount of material in the old bureau in my study. There are piles of Ellison Campbell's letters there, and all my mother's diaries. She kept them right up to her death.'

'And you've never been through them?'

'Not the letters. I looked at the diaries in Bethnal Green just after Mother died, but I only glanced at the parts about Ellison Campbell. I'm afraid the one thing that interested me then was the light thrown on my own sins of omission.'

'I'll go through those diaries to-morrow,' thought Ruth. But as she passed the door of Denis's study on her way to bed, a driving impulse of curiosity sent her instead into his room. She turned on the light and opened the bureau. Taking Janet's shiny black-bound diaries from their drawer, she laid them carefully on the floor beside her. In the pigeon-holes of the desk above them she found a dozen packets of letters, one for each year between 1901 and 1913, addressed to 'Mrs Thomas Rutherston' in Ellison Campbell's stiff, angular calligraphy. Each packet was carefully tied with rotting faded ribbon, once pink or blue. Among the letters lay occasional pencilled scraps of yellowing paper upon which Janet had hurriedly copied some of her own replies.

With practised eyes accustomed to the rapid scrutiny of official documents, Ruth examined first the diaries and then the letters, forgetting time as she became more deeply immersed in the past. She read with surprise of the affection which had compassed Janet's childhood, the little girl's successes at school, her interest in her extravagant clothes compared with the pathetic indifference to appearances of her later years. Her heart sank in pity at each revelation of that baffled questing spirit. She followed the troubled unavailing search for God, for a religious faith, for a political creed, for an honourable status as a citizen, for any hope, any anchor, in a bitter, turbulent, disappointing world.

'Should women only have influence – not power?' she read. 'Can the innocence which is only ignorance make a woman

good and pure and strong?' ... 'A motherhood which cannot
be voluntarily accepted as a sacred joy *must* be wrong.' ... 'If
only I had someone, something to help me, whom I could really
respect and worship!' ... 'It is no mere sentiment when I say
that my heart aches with thinking.' ... 'Last night I prayed to
God to let me die and then stopped in the middle of my prayer,
remembering that I had no God.'

In youth everything had promised so well. The girl had been
intelligent, affectionate, ambitious, even gay; yet all her hopes
were destroyed by the accident of making the wrong marriage.
Through the disappointment of that marriage she had become so
deeply involved in her friendship with Ellison Campbell that its
failure annihilated her. Ruth traced the growth of their strange,
unexpected relationship. Page by page, letter by letter, she
reconstructed the ironic tragedy of two gifted, well-intentioned
idealists, who because of the grief and frustration that warped
their personal lives, had sought comfort from one another with a
passionate intensity which proved its own undoing as soon as it
came into conflict with the strong impersonal interests of each.

At first, it had seemed, no shadow would ever descend upon
the absorbing glamour of that mutual emotion. 'If only I were
free, dearest, it would be different,' ran a letter in Gertrude's tall,
narrow handwriting. 'We could join each other and have great
happiness. But you know that as long as Charles lives I am tied to
him.' 'Gertrude's friendship, her brilliant intellect, the world of
literature and the theatre which knowing her has opened before
me, are all I want to make me happy, and far, far more than I
deserve' ... she read, in the pointed but less harsh calligraphy
of Janet's diary. 'Gertrude told me to-day that I made her realise
what Ruth meant when she said to Naomi, "The Lord do so to
me and more also, if aught but death part thee and me."'

But when Janet's share in the militant movement had passed
from theoretical sympathy to active participation, the first mur-
murs of storm began.

'I cannot feel anything but strong disapproval for this wanton
destruction of property,' Ellison Campbell had written at the
end of 1910. For over two years, it seemed, they had avoided
any direct discussion of Janet's political work in their letters.

Then, in Janet's diary for 1913, came the long record of Emily Davison's funeral, and a description of the attack of illness which had ruined the first night of *Hour of Destiny*. From these scrawled pencil entries which in places had become almost indecipherable, Ruth turned to Gertrude's letters containing her final ultimatum.

'I could not trust myself to come and see you after the way you deliberately failed me on the most critical occasion of my life so far . . . I cannot disguise from myself that you preferred to take part in that foolish procession rather than give me your full co-operation . . . The Janet I loved would never have failed me at a critical moment of my creative life.'

And Janet had been distressed, incredulous, bewildered, and at last despairing. The entries in her diary showed her utterly defeated in her search for some adequate explanation of Gertrude's cruelty. One paragraph was dated June 25th, 1913.

'The Earl's Court Road seemed quite dark, though really I suppose the sun was shining as usual. I felt exactly as if someone I loved very much had died. How could she want to end the friendship of years because of just one failure on my part? Why is it she does not realise that suffrage means as much to me as her plays mean to her? That is what I cannot understand.'

The references to Ellison Campbell, the lingering hopes which so soon departed, the grievous astonishment, the heavy disillusion, had finally ended, after the description of a dispute with Thomas, on a note of bitter resignation.

'It is quite hopeless for us to try to agree or work together, but now that Gertrude has given me up I do not care. Nothing matters to me any more at home since she refused to mend the breach between us or forgive me for what I wrote in anger, not meaning it.'

What was the true explanation of that quarrel which had been the final occasion of so much tragedy – Janet's abandonment of her home, Thomas's last and permanent breakdown, Denis's young forlorn struggle against poverty and disaster? Was it psychological or pathological? Janet, it seemed clear, was a normal woman whose talents had been thwarted, whose natural affections had been starved, whose maternal instinct had been assailed and vitiated before it reached maturity. She had accepted, humbly and gratefully, the friendship of a distinguished playwright, had turned to it for consolation and reassurance, had gained through it a vital contact with that world of literature and drama which Thomas had tried to forbid her. It was Ellison Campbell who had sought to possess, to exclude, to monopolise; who had resented Janet's alternative loyalties with a passionate jealousy which could not give itself a name nor recognise itself for what it was.

Enlightenment dawned slowly upon Ruth as she knelt before the revealing documents in Denis's bureau. How often had similar situations arisen throughout the ages which regarded the repressed, unfulfilled woman as an object of ridicule? How long will it be before we are all equipped with the charity and wisdom that knowledge brings?

The door opened and Denis's head appeared, his hair ruffled, his eyes dazed with sleep.

'My dear, what *are* you doing? Do you know it's after three o'clock?'

'I'm sorry, Denis. I'd no idea it was so late. I couldn't stop reading these letters and diaries once I'd begun.'

'Whatever made you start on them to-night? It was after twelve when we got home.'

She looked up at him from the fragments of the past, the fading records of heartache and failure and misunderstanding.

'I don't know. Something impelled me. It was just as if they'd both been waiting all these years for someone to discover the truth and give them peace.'

'The truth? What do you mean, darling?'

'You know, Denis,' she said, 'I believe Ellison Campbell had some kind of complex about your mother which made her jealous of the suffrage movement – just as if it had been another person who was stealing her away.'

'Some kind of complex? You mean . . . she was in love with my mother without realising it?'

'I may be quite wrong, but that's what I think. I'll tell you why in the morning.'

'It's just possible, I suppose,' he said meditatively. 'Of course nobody thought of such a thing in those days, least of all the people concerned. My poor mother! What a perturbation her life seems to have caused!'

'Yes – and partly because she believed in something very much. It's still our job to justify that faith and reconcile that conflict.'

'Haven't we done it already, darling – you and I?'

'I think we're doing it, Denis – and time is with us.'

She stood up and they kissed one another with tender familiarity, with confident affection. Then, falling on her knees again, she began to put the letters and diaries together.

'Go back to bed, my dear – you'll be getting cold. I'll come in a moment.'

Slowly she restored to their dusty pigeon-holes those evidences of a forgotten, unrecognised tragedy, a grief whose bitterness – like Richard's relationship with Valentine, like her own love for Eugene – had no place in the official categories of human sorrow. She arranged the envelopes in their careful chronological order, re-tied the faded ribbons, and closed the bureau upon all that remained of the passionate friendship between Janet Rutherston and Ellison Campbell.

But as she crept in the chill early morning darkness past the children's nursery to her bedroom, she found herself repeating a sentence from *John Inglesant* which Janet had quoted in her youthful diary: 'Nothing but the Infinite pity is sufficient for the infinite pathos of human life.'

16

In Westminster Abbey the wan autumn sunlight filtered obscurely through the high stained-glass windows, throwing reflected crimson and purple rainbows over the solemn effigies of dead statesmen and the beckoning images of bygone poets.

Beneath the grey vaulted roof, women of every rank and profession had gathered to do honour to Ellison Campbell, who had once been an arch-opponent of the women's movement. Because, by her life and work, she had indirectly conferred prestige upon them all, the women's organisations had sent their representatives; a number of dons and students were present from Drayton College; the women writers to whom she had been a symbol and a portent came one by one into the South Transept; the handful of women Members of Parliament sat side by side in the choir-stalls. Through every door crowded readers and theatre-goers by whom the austere, commanding personality of Ellison Campbell had been taken for granted as a national emblem for nearly thirty years.

As Denis and Ruth came into the Abbey, the cool sequence of Bach's *Chorale Preludes* poured from the organ like wind and sun playing over rippling water. Half way up the main aisle they parted; she went to the choir-stalls to join her fellow Members of Parliament, while he sat within near sight of her where the long transepts crossed.

It was for this, he reflected, looking at the small group of women Members, that his mother had fought, suffered, opposed his father. This day was an epitome of her fulfilled ideals. Homage was being paid by eminent women to the woman who, though she had failed Janet and denied her political claims, yet represented in her life and death that position of honour, irrespective of sex, for the right to which Janet had striven. And amongst those who rendered that homage was his own wife, whom Janet had not known but who embodied a political rôle for which she herself had prepared the way.

How high a price was still being secretly paid, in ruined health and shattered nerves, for that achievement! Denis had often heard wonder expressed because none of the suffrage leaders were now in Parliament, but it would be more surprising, he thought, if they had been. Their strength had gone in the pioneer battle; it was for their successors whose vitality was still unimpaired to march on through the pass that they had won.

The Preludes rippled into silence; the low emphatic dirge of Chopin's *Funeral March* swelled to its high clear notes of triumph as the choir moved slowly up the aisle. Their young emotionless voices sang the conquering words which began the Memorial Service.

'I am the resurrection and the life, saith the Lord: he that believeth in me, though he were dead, yet shall he live: and whosoever liveth and believeth in me shall never die.'

Denis saw handkerchiefs taken surreptitiously from pockets; eyes were discreetly wiped although nobody in the Cathedral that morning had known Ellison Campbell as a close personal friend. Even the distinguished members of the Merriam Society, mourning their President of a day amid the shadows of the Poets' Corner, had been aware of her only as a woman of genius, an illustrious presence dominating their councils. Of all that congregation, Denis's life alone had been touched intimately and tragically by the solitary tormented spirit which was now at peace. Yet their public grief, he knew, was a genuine emotion, arising from the remembered delight of evenings to which Ellison Campbell's name and work had lent their rich, dramatic entrancement. How many of those devoted readers and playgoers would feel a personal pity deepen their impersonal sorrow if they knew the story which gave a sombre relevance to the familiar words now being sung by the choir from the Ninetieth Psalm?

'Thou hast set our misdeeds before thee: and our secret sins in the light of thy countenance.

'For when thou art angry all our days are gone: we bring our years to an end, as it were a tale that is told ...

'Comfort us again now after the time that thou hast plagued us: and for the years wherein we have suffered adversity.'

The psalmist's lament died away; the congregation sat gravely listening to the lesson from Ecclesiasticus. Surely, thought Denis, the occasions on which those words had been read in memory of a woman could be counted on the fingers of one hand?

'Let us now praise famous men, and our fathers that begat us. The Lord hath wrought great glory by them through his power from the beginning. Such as did bear rule in their kingdoms ... leaders of the people by their counsels, and by their knowledge of learning meet for the people, wise and eloquent in their instructions: Such as found out

musical tunes, and recited verses in writing . . . All these were honoured in their generations and were the glory of their times . . .

'*And some there be, which have no memorial; who are perished as though they had never been; and are become as though they had never been born . . .*'

(Like Mother and Father, thought Denis. Like Richard, thought Ruth. Like Madeleine. Like Eugene . . .)

'*But these were merciful men, whose righteousness hath not been forgotten . . . Their bodies are buried in peace; but their name liveth for evermore. The people will tell of their wisdom, and the congregation will shew forth their praise.*'

That, meditated Ruth, was really how death was lost in victory. The noble, liturgical sorrows which carried honour and remembrance were never those that weighed the spirit down to the dust. The loss of husbands, the death of children, the sacrifices of war, the agony of women dying in childbirth, the stupendous dislocations of nature, earthquakes, hurricanes, famines – these were the epic tragedies, the sacred griefs of mankind, and because, for all their anguish, they had dignity, there was implicit in them a majestic consolation. The cruellest afflictions were those of humiliation, dishonour, frustration, defeat; the woes that must be concealed because they evoked not reverence but derision; the loves and losses that could not be acknowledged and were never pitied, because they did not fit into the stereotyped pattern which man had evolved for his social conduct.

'Denis's long struggle with poverty and degradation,' she thought, 'Ellison Campbell's passion for Janet which made her jealous and cruel when its monopoly was challenged – Richard's devotion to Valentine for which he sentenced himself to death – my love for Eugene which caused me to repudiate the conventions imposed upon itself by the society of my youth – different as these experiences were, we who suffered them have been misunderstood, condemned, denied the right even to grief. There has been no compensation for their pain, no comfort of reconciliation . . . except, perhaps, in so far as they bring us a new understanding . . .'

The choir were on their feet again, singing a famous anthem. The pure cascade of sound flowed through the Cathedral, carrying to many tired minds its message that life was not endless nor the weariness of living eternal, although achievement, laurel-crowned, bright with immortality, might march beyond the sovereignty of time.

'Blessed are the dead that die in the Lord, for they rest from their labours and their works follow them . . . their works . . . their works . . . do follow them.'

Beneath the lovely torrent of music, Ruth pursued her reflections.

'It may be that this deeper understanding does give the secret, intolerable griefs a nobility of their own. Perhaps, because Richard and Eugene and Ellison Campbell and I and thousands of individuals like us have suffered and believed that we sinned, men and women as a whole have grown more compassionate . . . and I suppose, if we took a long enough view, we should feel that any sorrow bears its own compensation which enlarges the scope of human mercy. Some of us, perhaps, can never reach our honourable estate – the state of maturity, of true understanding – until we have wrested strength and dignity out of humiliation and dishonour. That may be why Christ preferred the society of publicans and sinners; he knew that it's only through experience of sin that we acquire a real knowledge of the human heart, with all its woes and problems. Without that, our emotions would never grow up nor our judgment come of age.'

She stood with the congregation to sing the short minor verses, familiar to Denis and herself at college, which had been Gertrude's favourite amongst Oxford hymns.

> *God be in my head,*
> *And in my understanding;*
> *God be in mine eyes,*
> *And in my looking;*

God be in my mouth,
And in my speaking;
God be in my heart
And in my thinking;
God be at mine end,
And at my departing.

'After all,' she thought, 'let the cynics say what they will, we have gone forward. Human nature does change in the values to which it subscribes, the cruelties and wrongs it's prepared to tolerate. In my own time, short as it has been, this has happened. No age, I suppose, will ever see the whole of salvation, but every age sees a part of it – even this tragic and burdened age with its black night of calamity and its Lenten aftermath of sorrow and loss. To-day men and women, but especially women, live in a very different world from that of 1870, or 1900, or 1910. Even since 1914, we've passed through a whole series of social revolutions. There are others to come which I shall not see, for reason and mercy will have to fight their battle with passion and injustice for ever. Hatred and cruelty and perhaps even war will come again, in my children's time and the time of their children; they're the dark forces from our barbaric beginnings which are always being conquered and always rising again. But with every generation we know them better for what they are. We know more clearly what we should withstand and how we should build.'

In the silence which followed the end of the hymn came the grave voice of the Dean.

'We are here to give thanks to Almighty God for the life of Gertrude Ellison Campbell, and for her works which are now part of the treasure of posterity. "*The grass withereth, the flower fadeth: but the word of our God shall stand for ever*." Let us pray.'

Denis looked across at Ruth kneeling in the choir-stalls, her dark head bowed, her pale face with its preoccupied expression half hidden in her hands. Was she thinking, as he was, that the Word which translated itself through the works of great writers might also live, more humbly but with equal significance, in the painfully-wrought conclusions of his struggling philosophy and the vanishing eloquence of her spoken phrases? Perhaps from her vehement oratory no less than from his book produced by long, slow meditation, a few words would penetrate the minds of the men and women who listened or read, and remaining there to influence their thoughts and actions, become a permanent part of human inheritance.

Between Ruth and himself crept a slanting beam of light, the motes trembling in its soft translucence. Across that shadowy radiance her eyes met his as the final hymn thundered in processional majesty above their heads.

> *Time, like an ever-rolling stream,*
> *Bears all its sons away;*
> *They fly forgotten, as a dream*
> *Dies at the opening day.*

At that moment, he knew, they had shared the same memories, the same speculation, the same resolution. Janet – Thomas – Richard – Madeleine – Eugene – Ellison Campbell. How long before we too follow them into the darkness? At least we still have one another; let us work together while there is light.

The service was over. To the gentle strains of the *Nunc Dimittis*, the clergy and choir were passing out of sight. Ruth stepped from the choir-stalls to join Denis in the throng slowly moving down the central aisle. The doors of the Abbey stood open; a sharp breeze blew freshly over their heads. The last yellow leaves on the plane trees fluttered bravely against the pale wind-swept sky.

In the doorway Denis turned and inclined his head towards the altar.

'*Anima conturbata requiescat in pace,*' he murmured. But whether he spoke of his mother or of Ellison Campbell, Ruth could not decide.

She took his arm and they went out together into the clear wintry sunshine of a London November.